# WORLD'S GREATEST SHORT STORIES

# Contents

# A Christmas Tree and a Wedding

***Fyodor Dostoevsky***

The other day I saw a wedding . . . but no, I had better tell you about the Christmas tree. The wedding was nice, I liked it very much; but the other incident was better. I don't know how it was that, looking at that wedding, I thought of that Christmas tree. This was what happened. Just five years ago, on New Year's Eve, I was invited to a children's party. The giver of the party was a well-known and business-like personage, with connections, with a large circle of acquaintances, and a good many schemes on hand, so that it may be supposed that this party was an excuse for getting the parents together and discussing various interesting matters in an innocent, casual way. I was an outsider; I had no interesting matter to contribute, and so I spent the evening rather independently. There was another gentleman present who was, I fancied, of no special rank or family, and who, like me, had simply turned up at this family festivity. He was the first to catch my eye. He was a tall, lanky man, very grave and very correctly dressed. But one could see that he was in no mood for merrymaking and family festivity; whenever he withdrew into a corner he left off smiling and knitted his bushy black brows. He had not a single acquaintance in the party except his host. One could see that he was fearfully bored, but that he was valiantly keeping up the part of a man perfectly happy and enjoying himself. I learned afterwards that this was a gentleman from the provinces, who had a critical and perplexing piece of business in Petersburg, who had brought a letter of introduction to our host, for whom our host was, by no means con amore, using his interest, and whom he had invited, out of civility, to his children's party. He did not play cards, cigars were not offered him, every one avoided entering into conversation with him, most likely recognizing the bird from its feathers; and so my gentleman was forced to sit the whole evening stroking his whiskers simply to have something to do with his hands. His whiskers were certainly very fine. But he stroked them so zealously that, looking at him, one might have supposed that the whiskers were created first and the gentleman only attached to them in order to stroke them.

In addition to this individual who assisted in this way at our host's family festivity (he had five fat, well-fed boys), I was attracted, too, by another gentleman. But he was quite of a different sort. He was a personage. He was called Yulian Mastakovitch. From the first glance one could see that he was an honoured guest, and stood in the same relation to our host as our host stood in relation to the gentleman who was stroking his whiskers. Our host and hostess said no end of polite things to him, waited on him hand and foot, pressed him to drink, flattered him, brought their visitors up to be introduced to him, but did not take him to be introduced to any one else. I noticed that tears glistened in our host's eyes when he remarked about the party that he had rarely spent an evening so agreeably. I felt as it were frightened in the presence of such a personage, and so, after admiring the children, I went away into a little parlour, which was quite empty, and sat down in an arbour of flowers which filled up almost half the room.

The children were all incredibly sweet, and resolutely refused to model themselves on the "grown-ups," regardless of all the admonitions of their governesses and mammas. They stripped the Christmas tree to the last sweetmeat in the twinkling of an eye, and had succeeded in breaking half the playthings before they knew what was destined for which. Particularly charming was a black-eyed, curly-headed boy, who kept trying to shoot me with his wooden gun. But my attention was still more attracted by his sister, a girl of eleven, quiet, dreamy, pale, with big, prominent, dreamy eyes, exquisite as a little Cupid. The children hurt her feelings in some way, and so she came away from them to the same empty parlour in which I was sitting, and played with her doll in the corner. The visitors respectfully pointed out her father, a wealthy contractor, and some one whispered that three hundred thousand roubles were already set aside for her dowry. I turned round to glance at the group who were interested in such a circumstance, and my eye fell on Yulian Mastakovitch, who, with his hands behind his back and his head on one side, was listening with the greatest attention to these gentlemen's idle gossip. Afterwards I could not help admiring the discrimination of the host and hostess in the distribution of the children's presents. The little girl, who had already a portion of three hundred thousand roubles, received the costliest doll. Then followed presents diminishing in value in accordance with the rank of the parents of these happy children; finally, the child of lowest degree, a thin, freckled, red-haired little boy of ten, got nothing but a book of stories about the marvels of nature and tears of devotion, etc., without pictures or even woodcuts. He was the son of a poor widow, the governess of the children of the house, an oppressed and scared little boy. He was dressed in a short jacket of inferior nankin. After receiving his book he walked round the other toys for a long time; he longed to play with the other children, but did not dare; it was evident that he already felt and understood his position. I love watching children. Their first independent approaches to life are extremely interesting. I noticed that the red-haired boy was so fascinated by the costly toys of the other children, especially by a theatre in which he certainly longed to take some part, that he made up his mind to sacrifice his dignity. He smiled and began playing with the other children, he gave away his apple to a fat-faced little boy who had a mass of goodies tied up in a pocket-handkerchief already, and even brought himself to carry another boy on his back, simply not to be turned away from the theatre, but an insolent youth gave him a heavy thump a minute later. The child did not dare to cry. Then the governess, his mother, made her appearance, and told him not to interfere with the other children's playing. The boy went away to the same room in which was the little girl. She let him join her, and the two set to work very eagerly dressing the expensive doll.

I had been sitting more than half an hour in the ivy arbour, listening to the little prattle of the red-haired boy and the beauty with the dowry of three hundred thousand, who was nursing her doll, when Yulian Mastakovitch suddenly walked into the room.

He had taken advantage of the general commotion following a quarrel among the children to step out of the drawing-room. I had noticed him a moment before talking very cordially to the future heiress's papa, whose acquaintance he had just made, of the superiority of one branch of the service over another. Now he stood in hesitation and seemed to be reckoning something on his fingers.

"Three hundred . . . three hundred," he was whispering. "Eleven . . . twelve . . . thirteen," and so on. "Sixteen – five years! Supposing it is at four per cent. – five times twelve is sixty; yes, to that sixty . . . well, in five years we may assume it will be four hundred. Yes! . . . But he won't stick to four per cent., the rascal. He can get eight or ten. Well, five hundred, let us say, five hundred at least . . . that's certain; well, say a little more for frills. H'm! . . . "

His hesitation was at an end, he blew his nose and was on the point of going out of the room when he suddenly glanced at the little girl and stopped short. He did not see me behind the pots of greenery. It seemed to me that he was greatly excited. Either his calculations had affected his imagination or something else, for he rubbed his hands and could hardly stand still. This excitement reached its utmost limit when he stopped and bent another resolute glance at the future heiress. He was about to move forward, but first looked round, then moving on tiptoe, as though he felt guilty, he advanced towards the children. He approached with a little smile, bent down and kissed her on the head. The child, not expecting this attack, uttered a cry of alarm.

"What are you doing here, sweet child?" he asked in a whisper, looking round and patting the girl's cheek.

"We are playing."

"Ah! With him?" Yulian Mastakovitch looked askance at the boy. "You had better go into the drawing-room, my dear," he said to him.

The boy looked at him open-eyed and did not utter a word. Yulian Mastakovitch looked round him again, and again bent down to the little girl.

"And what is this you've got – a dolly, dear child?" he asked.

"Yes, a dolly," answered the child, frowning, and a little shy.

"A dolly . . . and do you know, dear child, what your dolly is made of?"

"I don't know . . . " the child answered in a whisper, hanging her head.

"It's made of rags, darling. You had better go into the drawing-room to your playmates, boy," said Yulian Mastakovitch, looking sternly at the boy. The boy and girl frowned and clutched at each other. They did not want to be separated.

"And do you know why they gave you that doll?" asked Yulian Mastakovitch, dropping his voice to a softer and softer tone.

"I don't know."

"Because you have been a sweet and well-behaved child all the week."

At this point Yulian Mastakovitch, more excited than ever, speaking in most dulcet tones, asked at last, in a hardly audible voice choked with emotion and impatience —

"And will you love me, dear little girl, when I come and see your papa and mamma?"

Saying this, Yulian Mastakovitch tried once more to kiss "the dear little girl," but the red-haired boy, seeing that the little girl was on the point of tears, clutched her hand and began whimpering from sympathy for her. Yulian Mastakovitch was angry in earnest.

"Go away, go away from here, go away!" he said to the boy. "Go into the drawing-room! Go in there to your playmates!"

"No, he needn't, he needn't! You go away," said the little girl. "Leave him alone, leave him alone," she said, almost crying.

Some one made a sound at the door. Yulian Mastakovitch instantly raised his majestic person and took alarm. But the red-haired boy was even more alarmed than Yulian Mastakovitch; he abandoned the little girl and, slinking along by the wall, stole out of the parlour into the dining-room. To avoid arousing suspicion, Yulian Mastakovitch, too, went into the dining-room. He was as red as a lobster, and, glancing into the looking-glass, seemed to be ashamed at himself. He was perhaps vexed with himself for his impetuosity and hastiness. Possibly, he was at first so much impressed by his calculations, so inspired and fascinated by them, that in spite of his seriousness and dignity he made up his mind to behave like a boy, and directly approach the object of his attentions, even though she could not be really the object of his attentions for another five years at least. I followed the estimable gentleman into the dining-room and there beheld a strange spectacle. Yulian Mastakovitch, flushed with vexation and anger, was frightening the red-haired boy, who, retreating from him, did not know where to run in his terror.

"Go away; what are you doing here? Go away, you scamp; are you after the fruit here, eh? Get along, you naughty boy! Get along, you sniveller, to your playmates!"

The panic-stricken boy in his desperation tried creeping under the table. Then his persecutor, in a fury, took out his large batiste handkerchief and began flicking it under the table at the child, who kept perfectly quiet. It must be observed that Yulian Mastakovitch was a little inclined to be fat. He was a sleek, red-faced, solidly built man, paunchy, with thick legs; what is called a fine figure of a man, round as a nut. He was perspiring, breathless, and fearfully flushed. At last he was almost rigid, so great was his indignation and perhaps — who knows? — his jealousy. I burst into loud laughter. Yulian Mastakovitch turned round and, in spite of all his consequence, was overcome with confusion. At that moment from the opposite door our host came in. The boy crept out from under the table and wiped his elbows and his knees. Yulian Mastakovitch hastened to put to his nose the handkerchief which he was holding in his hand by one end.

Our host looked at the three of us in some perplexity; but as a man who knew something of life, and looked at it from a serious point of view, he at once availed himself of the chance of catching his visitor by himself.

"Here, this is the boy," he said, pointing to the red-haired boy, "for whom I had the honour to solicit your influence."

"Ah!" said Yulian Mastakovitch, who had hardly quite recovered himself.

"The son of my children's governess," said our host, in a tone of a petitioner, "a poor woman, the widow of an honest civil servant; and therefore . . . and therefore, Yulian Mastakovitch, if it were possible . . . "

"Oh, no, no!" Yulian Mastakovitch made haste to answer;

"no, excuse me, Filip Alexyevitch, it's quite impossible. I've made inquiries; there's no vacancy, and if there were, there are twenty applicants who have far more claim than he. . . . I am very sorry, very sorry. . . . "

"What a pity," said our host. "He is a quiet, well-behaved boy."

"A great rascal, as I notice," answered Yulian Mastakovitch, with a nervous twist of his lip. "Get along, boy; why are you standing there? Go to your playmates," he said, addressing the child.

At that point he could not contain himself, and glanced at me out of one eye. I, too, could not contain myself, and laughed straight in his face. Yulian Mastakovitch turned away at once, and in a voice calculated to reach my ear, asked who was that strange young man? They whispered together and walked out of the room. I saw Yulian Mastakovitch afterwards shaking his head incredulously as our host talked to him.

After laughing to my heart's content I returned to the drawing-room. There the great man, surrounded by fathers and mothers of families, including the host and hostess, was saying something very warmly to a lady to whom he had just been introduced. The lady was holding by the hand the little girl with whom Yulian Mastakovitch had had the scene in the parlour a little while before. Now he was launching into praises and raptures over the beauty, the talents, the grace and the charming manners of the charming child. He was unmistakably making up to the mamma. The mother listened to him almost with tears of delight. The father's lips were smiling. Our host was delighted at the general satisfaction. All the guests, in fact, were sympathetically gratified; even the children's games were checked that they might not hinder the conversation: the whole atmosphere was saturated with reverence. I heard afterwards the mamma of the interesting child, deeply touched, beg Yulian Mastakovitch, in carefully chosen phrases, to do her the special honour of bestowing upon them the precious gift of his acquaintance, and heard with what unaffected delight Yulian Mastakovitch accepted the invitation, and how afterwards the guests, dispersing in different directions, moving away with the greatest propriety, poured out to one another the most touchingly flattering comments upon the contractor, his wife, his little girl, and, above all, upon Yulian Mastakovitch.

"Is that gentleman married?" I asked, almost aloud, of one of my acquaintances, who was standing nearest to Yulian Mastakovitch. Yulian Mastakovitch flung a searching and vindictive glance at me.

"No!" answered my acquaintance, chagrined to the bottom of his heart by the awkwardness of which I had intentionally been guilty. . . .

I passed lately by a certain church; I was struck by the crowd of people in carriages. I heard people talking of the wedding. It was a cloudy day, it was beginning to sleet. I made my way through the crowd at the door and saw the bridegroom. He was a sleek, well-fed, round, paunchy man, very gorgeously dressed up. He was running fussily about, giving orders. At last the news passed through the crowd that the bride was coming. I squeezed my way through the crowd and saw a marvellous beauty, who could scarcely have reached her first season. But the beauty was pale and melancholy. She looked preoccupied; I even fancied that her eyes were red with recent weeping. The classic severity of every feature of her face gave a certain dignity and seriousness to her beauty. But through that sternness and dignity, through that melancholy, could be seen the look of childish innocence; something indescribably naïve, fluid, youthful, which seemed mutely begging for mercy.

People were saying that she was only just sixteen. Glancing attentively at the bridegroom, I suddenly recognized him as Yulian Mastakovitch, whom I had not seen for five years. I looked at her. My God! I began to squeeze my way as quickly as I could out of the church. I heard people saying in the crowd that the bride was an heiress, that she had a dowry of five hundred thousand . . . and a trousseau worth ever so much.

"It was a good stroke of business, though!" I thought as I made my way into the street.

# A Little Cloud

## *James Joyce*

Eight years before he had seen his friend off at the North Wall and wished him God-speed. Gallaher had got on. You could tell that at once by his travelled air, his well-cut tweed suit, and fearless accent. Few fellows had talents like his, and fewer still could remain unspoiled by such success. Gallaher's heart was in the right place and he had deserved to win. It was something to have a friend like that.

Little Chandler's thoughts ever since lunch-time had been of his meeting with Gallaher, of Gallaher's invitation, and of the great city London where Gallaher lived. He was called Little Chandler because, though he was but slightly under the average stature, he gave one the idea of being a little man. His hands were white and small, his frame was fragile, his voice was quiet and his manners were refined. He took the greatest care of his fair silken hair and moustache, and used perfume discreetly on his handkerchief. The half-moons of his nails were perfect, and when he smiled you caught a glimpse of a row of childish white teeth.

As he sat at his desk in the King's Inns he thought what changes those eight years had brought. The friend whom he had known under a shabby and necessitous guise had become a brilliant figure on the London Press. He turned often from his tiresome writing to gaze out of the office window. The glow of a late autumn sunset covered the grass plots and walks. It cast a shower of kindly golden dust on the untidy nurses and decrepit old men who drowsed on the benches; it flickered upon all the moving figures – on the children who ran screaming along the gravel paths and on everyone who passed through the gardens. He watched the scene and thought of life; and (as always happened when he thought of life) he became sad. A gentle melancholy took possession of him. He felt how useless it was to struggle against fortune, this being the burden of wisdom which the ages had bequeathed to him.

He remembered the books of poetry upon his shelves at home. He had bought them in his bachelor days and many an evening, as he sat in the little room off the hall, he had been tempted to take one down from the bookshelf and read out something to his wife. But shyness had always held him back; and so the books had remained on their shelves. At times he repeated lines to himself and this consoled him.

When his hour had struck he stood up and took leave of his desk and of his fellow-clerks punctiliously. He emerged from under the feudal arch of the King's Inns, a neat modest figure, and walked swiftly down Henrietta Street. The golden sunset was waning and the air had grown sharp. A horde of grimy children populated the street. They stood or ran in the roadway, or crawled up the steps before the gaping doors, or squatted like mice upon the thresholds. Little Chandler gave them no thought. He picked his way deftly through all that minute vermin-like life and under the shadow of the gaunt spectral mansions in which the old nobility of Dublin had roistered. No memory of the past touched him, for his mind was full of a present joy.

He had never been in Corless's, but he knew the value of the name. He knew that people went there after the theatre to eat oysters and drink liqueurs; and he had heard that the waiters there spoke French and German. Walking swiftly by at night he had seen cabs drawn up before the door and richly-dressed ladies, escorted by cavaliers, alight and enter quickly. They wore noisy dresses and many wraps. Their faces were powdered and they caught up their dresses, when they touched earth, like alarmed Atalantas. He had always passed without turning his head to look. It was his habit to walk swiftly in the street even by day, and whenever he found himself in the city late at night he hurried on his way apprehensively and excitedly. Sometimes, however, he courted the causes of his fear. He chose the darkest and narrowest streets and, as he walked boldly forward, the silence that was spread about his footsteps troubled him; the wandering, silent figures troubled him; and at times a sound of low fugitive laughter made him tremble like a leaf.

He turned to the right towards Capel Street. Ignatius Gallaher on the London Press! Who would have thought it possible eight years before? Still, now that he reviewed the past, Little Chandler could remember many signs of future greatness in his friend. People used to say that Ignatius Gallaher was wild. Of course, he did mix with a rakish set of fellows at that time; drank freely and borrowed money on all sides. In the end he had got mixed up in some shady affair, some money transaction: at least, that was one version of his flight. But nobody denied him talent. There was always a certain... something in Ignatius Gallaher that impressed you in spite of yourself. Even when he was out at elbows and at his wits' end for money he kept up a bold face. Little Chandler remembered (and the remembrance brought a slight flush of pride to his cheek) one of Ignatius Gallaher's sayings when he was in a tight corner:

'Half-time now, boys,' he used to say light-heartedly. 'Where's my considering cap?'

That was Ignatius Gallaher all out; and, damn it, you couldn't help but admire him for it.

Little Chandler quickened his pace. For the first time in his life he felt himself superior to the people he passed. For the first time his soul revolted against the dull inelegance of Capel Street. There was no doubt about it: if you wanted to succeed you had to go away. You could do nothing in Dublin. As he crossed Grattan Bridge he looked down the river towards the lower quays and pitied the poor stunted houses. They seemed to him a band of tramps, huddled together along the river-banks, their old coats covered with dust and soot, stupefied by the panorama of sunset and waiting for the first chill of night to bid them arise, shake themselves and begone. He wondered whether he could write a poem to express his idea. Perhaps Gallaher might be able to get it into some London paper for him. Could he write something original? He was not sure what idea he wished to express, but the thought that a poetic moment had touched him took life within him like an infant hope. He stepped onward bravely.

Every step brought him nearer to London, farther from his own sober inartistic life. A light began to tremble on the horizon of his mind. He was not so old – thirty-two. His temperament might be said to be just at the point of maturity. There were so many different moods and impressions that he wished to express in verse. He felt them within him. He tried to weigh his soul to see if it was a poet's soul. Melancholy was the dominant note of his temperament, he thought, but it was a melancholy tempered by recurrences of faith and resignation and simple joy. If he could give expression to it in a book of poems perhaps men would listen. He would never be popular: he saw that. He could not sway the crowd, but he might appeal to a little circle of kindred minds. The English critics, perhaps, would recognize him as one of the Celtic school by reason of the melancholy tone of his poems; besides that, he would put in allusions. He began to invent sentences and phrases from the notice which his book would get. 'Mr Chandler has the gift of easy and graceful verse'... 'A wistful sadness pervades these poems'... 'The Celtic note'. It was a pity his name was not more Irish-looking. Perhaps it would be better to insert his mother's name before the surname: Thomas Malone Chandler; or better still: T. Malone Chandler. He would speak to Gallaher about it.

He pursued his reverie so ardently that he passed his street and had to turn back. As he came near Corless's his former agitation began to overmaster him and he halted before the door in indecision. Finally he opened the door and entered.

The light and noise of the bar held him at the doorway for a few moments. He looked about him, but his sight was confused by the shining of many red and green wine-glasses. The bar seemed to him to be full of people and he felt that the people were observing him curiously. He glanced quickly to right and left (frowning slightly to make his errand appear serious), but when his sight cleared a little he saw that nobody had turned to look at him: and there, Sure enough, was Ignatius Gallaher leaning with his back against the counter and his feet planted far apart.

'Hallo, Tommy, old hero, here you are! What is it to be? What will you have? I'm taking whisky: better stuff than we get across the water. Soda? Lithia? No mineral? I'm the same. Spoils the flavour... Here, gar on, bring us two halves of malt whisky, like a good fellow... Well, and how have you been pulling along since I saw you last? Dear God, how old we're getting! Do you see any signs of ageing in me – eh, what? A little grey and thin on the top – what?'

Ignatius Gallaher took off his hat and displayed a large closely-cropped head. His face was heavy, pale, and clean-shaven. His eyes, which were of bluish slate-colour, relieved his unhealthy pallor and shone out plainly above the vivid orange tie he wore. Between these rival features the lips appeared very long and shapeless and colourless. He bent his head and felt with two sympathetic fingers the thin hair at the crown. Little Chandler shook his head as a denial. Ignatius Gallaher put on his hat again.

'It pulls you down,' he said. 'Press life. Always hurry and scurry, looking for copy and sometimes not finding it: and then, always to have something new in your stuff. Damn proofs and printers, I say, for a few days. I'm deuced glad, I can tell you, to get back to the old country. Does a fellow good, a bit of a holiday. I feel a ton better since I landed again in dear, dirty Dublin... Here you are, Tommy. Water? Say when.'

Little Chandler allowed his whisky to be very much diluted.

'You don't know what's good for you, my boy,' said Ignatius Gallaher. 'I drink mine neat.'

'I drink very little as a rule,' said Little Chandler modestly. 'An odd half-one or so when I meet any of the old crowd: that's all.'

'Ah well,' said Ignatius Gallaher cheerfully, 'here's to us and to old times and old acquaintance.'

They clinked glasses and drank the toast.

'I met some of the old gang today,' said Ignatius Gallaher. 'O'Hara seems to be in a bad way. What's he doing?'

'Nothing,' said Little Chandler. 'He's gone to the dogs.'

'But Hogan has a good sit, hasn't he?'

'Yes, be's in the Land Commission.'

'I met him one night in London and he seemed to be very flush... Poor O'Hara! Booze, I suppose?'

'Other things, too,' said Little Chandler shortly.

Ignatius Gallaher laughed.

'Tommy,' he said, 'I see you haven't changed an atom. You're the very same serious person that used to lecture me on Sunday mornings when I had a sore head and a fur on my tongue. You'd want to knock about a bit in the world. Have you never been anywhere even for a trip?'

'I've been to the Isle of Man,' said Little Chandler.

Ignatius Gallaher laughed.

'The Isle of Man!' he said. 'Go to London or Paris: Paris, for choice. That'd do you good.'

'Have you seen Paris?'

'I should think I have! I've knocked about there a little.'

'And is it really so beautiful as they say?' asked Little Chandler.

He sipped a little of his drink while Ignatius Gallaher finished his boldly.

'Beautiful?' said Ignatius Gallaher, pausing on the word and on the flavour of his drink. 'It's not so beautiful, you know. Of course it is beautiful... But it's the life of Paris; that's the thing. Ah, there's no city like Paris for gaiety, movement, excitement...'

Little Chandler finished his whisky and, after some trouble, succeeded in catching the barman's eye. He ordered the same again.

'I've been to the Moulin Rouge,' Ignatius Gallaher continued when the barman had removed their glasses, 'and I've been to all the Bohemian cafs. Hot stuff! Not for a pious chap like you, Tommy.'

Little Chandler said nothing until the barman returned with two glasses: then he touched his friend's glass lightly and reciprocated the former toast. He was beginning to feel somewhat disillusioned. Gallaher's accent and way of expressing himself did not please him. There was something vulgar in his friend which lie had not observed before. But perhaps it was only the result of living in London amid the bustle and competition of the Press. The old personal charm was still there under this new gaudy manner. And, after all, Gallaher had lived, he had seen the world. Little Chandler looked at his friend enviously.

'Everything in Paris is gay,' said Ignatius Gallaher. 'They believe in enjoying life – and don't you think they're right? If you want to enjoy yourself properly you must go to Paris. And, mind you, they've a great feeling for the Irish there. When they heard I was from Ireland they were ready to eat me, man.'

Little Chandler took four or five sips from his glass.

'Tell me,' he said, 'is it true that Paris is so... immoral as they say?'

Ignatius Gallaher made a catholic gesture with his right arm.

'Every place is immoral,' he said. 'Of course you do find spicy bits in Paris. Go to one of the students' balls, for instance. That's lively, if you like, when the cocottes begin to let themselves loose. You know what they are, I suppose?'

'I've heard of them,' said Little Chandler.

Ignatius Gallaher drank off his whisky and shook his head.

'Ah,' he said, 'you may say what you like. There's no woman like the Parisienne – for style, for go.'

'Then it is an immoral city,' said Little Chandler, with timid insistence – 'I mean, compared with London or Dublin?'

'London!' said Ignatius Gallaher. 'It's six of one and half a dozen of the other. You ask Hogan, my boy. I showed him a bit about London when he was over there. He'd open your eye... I say, Tommy, don't make punch of that whisky: liquor up.'

'No, really.'

'O, come on, another one won't do you any harm. What is it? The same again, I suppose?'

'Well... all right.'

'Fran ois, the same again... Will you smoke, Tommy?'

Ignatius Gallaher produced his cigar-case. The two friends lit their cigars and puffed at them in silence until their drinks were served.

'I'll tell you my opinion,' said Ignatius Gallaher, emerging after some time from the clouds of smoke in which he had taken refuge, 'it's a rum world. Talk of immorality! I've heard of cases – what am I saying? – I've known them: cases of... immorality...'

Ignatius Gallaher puffed thoughtfully at his cigar and then, in a calm historian's tone, he proceeded to sketch for his friend some pictures of the corruption which was rife abroad. He summarized the vices of many capitals and seemed inclined to award the palm to Berlin. Some things he could not vouch for (his friends had told him), but of others he had had personal experience. He spared neither rank nor caste. He revealed many of the secrets of religious houses on the Continent and described some of the practices which were fashionable in high society, and ended by telling, with details, a story about an English duchess – a story which he knew to be true. Little Chandler was astonished.

'Ah, well,' said Ignatius Gallaher, 'here we are in old jog-along Dublin where nothing is known of such things.'

'How dull you must find it,' said Little Chandler, 'after all the other places you've seen!'

'Well,' said Ignatius Gallaher, 'it's a relaxation to come over here, you know. And, after all, it's the old country, as they say, isn't it? You can't help having a certain feeling for it. That's human nature... But tell me something about yourself. Hogan told me you had... tasted the joys of connubial bliss. Two years ago, wasn't it?'

Little Chandler blushed and smiled.

'Yes,' he said. 'I was married last May twelve months.'

'I hope it's not too late in the day to offer my best wishes,' said Ignatius Gallaher. 'I didn't know your address or I'd have done so at the time.'

He extended his hand, which Little Chandler took.

'Well, Tommy,' he said, 'I wish you and yours every joy in life, old chap, and tons of money, and may you never die till I shoot you. And that's the wish of a sincere friend, an old friend. You know that?'

'I know that,' said Little Chandler.

'Any youngsters?' said Ignatius Gallaher.

Little Chandler blushed again.

'We have one child,' he said.

'Son or daughter?'

'A little boy.'

Ignatius Gallaher slapped his friend sonorously on the back.

'Bravo,' he said, 'I wouldn't doubt you, Tommy.'

Little Chandler smiled, looked confusedly at his glass and bit his lower lip with three childishly white front teeth.

'I hope you'll spend an evening with us,' he said, 'before you go back. My wife will be delighted to meet you. We can have a little music and–'

'Thanks awfully, old chap,' said Ignatius Gallaher, 'I'm sorry we didn't meet earlier. But I must leave tomorrow night.'

'Tonight, perhaps... ?'

'I'm awfully sorry, old man. You see I'm over here with another fellow, clever young chap he is too, and we arranged to go to a little card-party. Only for that... '

'O, in that case...'

'But who knows?' said Ignatius Gallaher considerately. 'Next year I may take a little skip over here now that I've broken the ice. It's only a pleasure deferred.'

'Very well,' said Little Chandler, 'the next time you come we must have an evening together. That's agreed now, isn't it?'

'Yes, that's agreed,' said Ignatius Gallaher. 'Next year if I come, parole d'honneur.'

'And to clinch the bargain,' said Little Chandler, 'we'll just have one more now.'

Ignatius Gallaher took out a large gold watch and looked at it.

'Is it to be the last?' he Said. 'Because, you know, I have an a.p.'

'O, yes, positively,' said Little Chandler.

'Very well, then,' said Ignatius Gallaher, 'let us have another one as a deoc an doirus – that's good vernacular for a small whisky, I believe.'

Little Chandler ordered the drinks. The blush which had risen to his face a few moments before was establishing itself. A trifle made him blush at any time: and now he felt warm and excited. Three small whiskies had gone to his head and Gallaher's strong cigar had confused his mind, for he was a delicate and abstinent person. The adventure of meeting Gallaher after eight years, of finding himself with Gallaher in Corless's surrounded by lights and noise, of listening to Gallaher's stories and of sharing for a brief space Gallaher's vagrant and triumphant life, upset the equipoise of his sensitive nature. He felt acutely the contrast between his own life and his friend's, and it seemed to him unjust. Gallaher was his inferior in birth and education. He was sure that he could do something better than his friend had ever done, or could ever do, something higher than mere tawdry journalism if he only got the chance. What was it that stood in his way? His unfortunate timidity! He wished to vindicate himself in some way, to assert his manhood. He saw behind Gallaher's refusal of his invitation. Gallaher was only patronizing him by his friendliness just as he was patronizing Ireland by his visit.

The barman brought their drinks. Little Chandler pushed one glass towards his friend and took up the other boldly.

'Who knows?' he said, as they lifted their glasses. 'When you come next year I may have the pleasure of wishing long life and happiness to Mr and Mrs Ignatius Gallaher.'

Ignatius Gallaher in the act of drinking closed one eye expressively over the rim of his glass. When he had drunk he smacked his lips decisively, set down his glass and said:

'No blooming fear of that, my boy. I'm going to have my fling first and see a bit of life and the world before I put my head in the sack – if I ever do.'

'Some day you will,' said Little Chandler calmly.

Ignatius Gallaher turned his orange tie and slate-blue eyes full upon his friend.

'You think so?' he said.

'You'll put your head in the sack,' repeated Little Chandler stoutly, 'like everyone else if you can find the girl.'

He had slightly emphasized his tone, and he was aware that he had betrayed himself; but, though the colour had heightened in his cheek, he did not flinch from his friends' gaze. Ignatius Gallaher watched him for a few moments and then said:

'If ever it occurs, you may bet your bottom dollar there'll be no mooning and spooning about it. I mean to marry money. She'll have a good fat account at the bank or she won't do for me.'

Little Chandler shook his head.

'Why, man alive,' said Ignatius Gallaher, vehemently, 'do you know what it is? I've only to say the word and tomorrow I can have the woman and the cash. You don't believe it? Well, I know it. There are hundreds – what am I saying? – thousands of rich Germans and Jews, rotten with money, that'd only be too glad... You wait a while, my boy. See if I don't play my cards properly. When I go about a thing I mean business, I tell you. You just wait.'

He tossed his glass to his mouth, finished his drink and laughed loudly. Then he looked thoughtfully before him and said in a calmer tone:

'But I'm in no hurry. They can wait. I don't fancy tying myself up to one woman, you know.'

He imitated with his mouth the act of tasting and made a wry face.

'Must get a bit stale, I should think,' he said.

– – – – – – –

Little Chandler sat in the room off the hall, holding a child in his arms. To save money they kept no servant, but Annie's young sister Monica came for an hour or so in the morning and an hour or so in the evening to help. But Monica had gone home long ago. It was a quarter to nine. Little Chandler had come home late for tea and, moreover, he had forgotten to bring Annie home the parcel of coffee from Bewley's. Of course she was in a bad humour and gave him short answers. She said she would do without any tea, but when it came near he time at which the shop at the corner closed she decided to go out herself for a quarter of a pound of tea and two pounds of sugar. She put the sleeping child deftly in his arms and said:

'Here. Don't waken him.'

A little lamp with a white china shade stood upon the table and its light fell over a photograph which was enclosed in a frame of crumpled horn. It was Annie's photograph. Little Chandler looked at it, pausing at the thin tight lips. She wore the pale blue summer blouse which he had brought her home as a present one Saturday. It had cost him ten and elevenpence; but what an agony of nervousness it had cost him! How he had suffered that day, waiting at the shop door until the shop was empty, standing at the counter and trying to appear at his ease while the girl piled ladies' blouses before him, paying at the desk and forgetting to take up the odd penny of his change, being called back by the cashier, and finally, striving to hide his blushes as he left the shop by examining the parcel to see if it was securely tied. When he brought the blouse home Annie kissed him and said it was very pretty and stylish; but when she heard the price she threw the blouse on the table and said it was a regular swindle to charge ten and elevenpence for it. At first she wanted to take it back, but when she tried it on she was delighted with it, especially with the make of the sleeves, and kissed him and said he was very good to think of her.

Hm!...

He looked coldly into the eyes of the photograph and they answered coldly. Certainly they were pretty and the face itself was pretty. But he found something mean in it. Why was it so unconscious and ladylike? The composure of the eyes irritated him. They repelled him and defied him: there was no passion in them, no rapture. He thought of what Gallaher had said about rich Jewesses. Those dark Oriental eyes, he thought, how full they are of passion, of voluptuous longing!... Why had he married the eyes in the photograph?

He caught himself up at the question and glanced nervously round the room. He found something mean in the pretty furniture which he had bought for his house on the hire system. Annie had chosen it herself and it reminded him of her. It too was prim and pretty. A dull resentment against his life awoke within him. Could he not escape from his little house? Was it too late for him to try to live bravely like Gallaher? Could he go to London? There was the furniture still to be paid for. If he could only write a book and get it published, that might open the way for him.

A volume of Byron's poems lay before him on the table. He opened it cautiously with his left hand lest he should waken the child and began to read the first poem in the book:

Hushed are the winds and still the evening gloom,
Not e'en a Zephyr wander through the grove,
Whilst I return to view my Margaret's tomb
And scatter flowers on the dust I love.

He paused. He felt the rhythm of the verse about him in the room. How melancholy it was! Could he, too, write like that, express the melancholy of his soul in verse? There were so many things he wanted to describe: his sensation of a few hours before on Grattan Bridge, for example. If he could get back again into that mood...

The child awoke and began to cry. He turned from the page and tried to hush it: but it would not be hushed. He began to rock it to and fro in his arms, but its wailing cry grew keener. He rocked it faster while his eyes began to read the second stanza:

Within this narrow cell reclines her clay, that clay where once...

It was useless. He couldn't read. He couldn't do anything. The wailing of the child pierced the drum of his ear. It was useless, useless! He was a prisoner for life. His arms trembled with anger and suddenly bending to the child's face he shouted:

'Stop!'

The child stopped for an instant, had a spasm of fright and began to scream. He jumped up from his chair and walked hastily up and down the room with the child in his arms. it began to sob piteously, losing its breath for four or five seconds, and then bursting out anew. The thin walls of the room echoed the sound. He tried to soothe it, but it sobbed more convulsively. He looked at the contracted and quivering face of the child and began to be alarmed. He counted seven sobs without a break between them and caught the child to his breast in fright. If it died!...

The door was burst open and a young woman ran in, panting.

'What is it? What is it?' she cried.

The child, hearing its mother's voice, broke out into a paroxysm of sobbing.

'It's nothing, Annie... it's nothing... He began to cry... '

She flung her parcels on the floor and snatched the child from him.

'What have you done to him?' she cried, glaring into his face.

Little Chandler sustained for one moment the gaze of her eyes and his heart closed together as he met the hatred in them. He began to stammer:

'It's nothing... he... he... began to cry... I couldn't... I didn't do anything... What?'

Giving no heed to him she began to walk up and down the room, clasping the child tightly in her arms and murmuring:

'My little man! My little mannie! Was 'ou frightened, love?'... There now, love! There now!... Lambabaun! Mamma's little lamb of the world!... There now!'

Little Chandler felt his cheeks suffused with shame and he stood back out of the lamplight. He listened while the paroxysm of the child's sobbing grew less and less; and tears of remorse started to his eyes.

# A Mother

***James Joyce***

MR HOLOHAN, assistant secretary of the Eire Abu Society, had been walking up and down Dublin for nearly a month, with his hands and pockets full of dirty pieces of paper, arranging about the series of concerts. He had a game leg and for this his friends called him Hoppy Holohan. He walked up and down constantly, stood by the hour at street corners arguing the point and made notes; but in the end it was Mrs. Kearney who arranged everything.

Miss Devlin had become Mrs. Kearney out of spite. She had been educated in a high-class convent, where she had learned French and music. As she was naturally pale and unbending in manner she made few friends at school. When she came to the age of marriage she was sent out to many houses, where her playing and ivory manners were much admired. She sat amid the chilly circle of her accomplishments, waiting for some suitor to brave it and offer her a brilliant life. But the young men whom she met were ordinary and she gave them no encouragement, trying to console her romantic desires by eating a great deal of Turkish Delight in secret. However, when she drew near the limit and her friends began to loosen their tongues about her, she silenced them by marrying Mr. Kearney, who was a bootmaker on Ormond Quay.

He was much older than she. His conversation, which was serious, took place at intervals in his great brown beard. After the first year of married life, Mrs. Kearney perceived that such a man would wear better than a romantic person, but she never put her own romantic ideas away. He was sober, thrifty and pious; he went to the altar every first Friday, sometimes with her, oftener by himself. But she never weakened in her religion and was a good wife to him. At some party in a strange house when she lifted her eyebrow ever so slightly he stood up to take his leave and, when his cough troubled him, she put the eider-down quilt over his feet and made a strong rum punch. For his part, he was a model father. By paying a small sum every week into a society, he ensured for both his daughters a dowry of one hundred pounds each when they came to the age of twenty-four. He sent the older daughter, Kathleen, to a good convent, where she learned French and music, and afterward paid her fees at the Academy. Every year in the month of July Mrs. Kearney found occasion to say to some friend:

"My good man is packing us off to Skerries for a few weeks."

If it was not Skerries it was Howth or Greystones.

When the Irish Revival began to be appreciable Mrs. Kearney determined to take advantage of her daughter's name and brought an Irish teacher to the house. Kathleen and her sister sent Irish picture postcards to their friends and these friends sent back other Irish picture postcards. On special Sundays, when Mr. Kearney went with his family to the pro-cathedral, a little crowd of people would assemble after mass at the corner of Cathedral Street. They were all friends of the Kearneys — musical friends or Nationalist friends; and, when they had played every little counter of gossip, they shook hands with one another all together, laughing at the crossing of so man hands, and said good-bye to one another in Irish. Soon the name of Miss Kathleen Kearney began to be heard often on people's lips. People said that she was very clever at music and a very nice girl and, moreover, that she was a believer in the language movement. Mrs. Kearney was well content at this. Therefore she was not surprised when one day Mr. Holohan came to her and proposed that her daughter should be the accompanist at a series of four grand concerts which his Society was going to give in the Antient Concert Rooms. She brought him into the drawing-room, made him sit down and brought out the decanter and the silver biscuit-barrel. She entered heart and soul into the details of the enterprise, advised and dissuaded: and finally a contract was drawn up by which Kathleen was to receive eight guineas for her services as accompanist at the four grand concerts.

As Mr. Holohan was a novice in such delicate matters as the

wording of bills and the disposing of items for a programme, Mrs. Kearney helped him. She had tact. She knew what artistes should go into capitals and what artistes should go into small type. She knew that the first tenor would not like to come on after Mr. Meade's comic turn. To keep the audience continually diverted she slipped the doubtful items in between the old favourites. Mr. Holohan called to see her every day to have her advice on some point. She was invariably friendly and advising — homely, in fact. She pushed the decanter towards him, saying:

"Now, help yourself, Mr. Holohan!"

And while he was helping himself she said:

"Don't be afraid! Don t be afraid of it! "

Everything went on smoothly. Mrs. Kearney bought some lovely blush-pink charmeuse in Brown Thomas's to let into the front of Kathleen's dress. It cost a pretty penny; but there are occasions when a little expense is justifiable. She took a dozen of two-shilling tickets for the final concert and sent them to those friends who could not be trusted to come otherwise. She forgot nothing, and, thanks to her, everything that was to be done was done.

The concerts were to be on Wednesday, Thursday, Friday and Saturday. When Mrs. Kearney arrived with her daughter at the Antient Concert Rooms on Wednesday night she did not like the look of things. A few young men, wearing bright blue badges in their coats, stood idle in the vestibule; none of them wore evening dress. She passed by with her daughter and a quick glance through the open door of the hall showed her the cause of the stewards' idleness. At first she wondered had she mistaken the hour. No, it was twenty minutes to eight.

In the dressing-room behind the stage she was introduced to the secretary of the Society, Mr. Fitzpatrick. She smiled and shook his hand. He was a little man, with a white, vacant face. She noticed that he wore his soft brown hat carelessly on the side of his head and that his accent was flat. He held a programme in his hand, and, while he was talking to her, he chewed one end of it into a moist pulp. He seemed to bear disappointments lightly. Mr. Holohan came into the dressingroom every few minutes with reports from the box-office. The artistes talked among themselves nervously, glanced from time to time at the mirror and rolled and unrolled their music. When it was nearly half-past eight, the few people in the hall began to express their desire to be entertained. Mr. Fitzpatrick came in, smiled vacantly at the room, and said:

"Well now, ladies and gentlemen. I suppose we'd better open the ball."

Mrs. Kearney rewarded his very flat final syllable with a quick stare of contempt, and then said to her daughter encouragingly:

"Are you ready, dear?"

When she had an opportunity, she called Mr. Holohan aside and asked him to tell her what it meant. Mr. Holohan did not know what it meant. He said that the committee had made a mistake in arranging for four concerts: four was too many.

"And the artistes!" said Mrs. Kearney. "Of course they are doing their best, but really they are not good."

Mr. Holohan admitted that the artistes were no good but the committee, he said, had decided to let the first three concerts go as they pleased and reserve all the talent for Saturday night. Mrs. Kearney said nothing, but, as the mediocre items followed one another on the platform and the few people in the hall grew fewer and fewer, she began to regret that she had put herself to any expense for such a concert. There was something she didn't like in the look of things and Mr. Fitzpatrick's vacant smile irritated her very much. However, she said nothing and waited to see how it would end. The concert expired shortly before ten, and everyone went home quickly.

The concert on Thursday night was better attended, but Mrs. Kearney saw at once that the house was filled with paper. The audience behaved indecorously, as if the concert were an informal dress rehearsal. Mr. Fitzpatrick seemed to enjoy himself; he was quite unconscious that Mrs. Kearney was taking angry note of his conduct. He stood at the edge of the screen, from time to time jutting out his head and exchanging a laugh with two friends in the corner of the balcony. In the course of the evening, Mrs. Kearney learned that the Friday concert was to be abandoned and that the committee was going to move heaven and earth to secure a bumper house on Saturday night. When she heard this, she sought out Mr. Holohan. She buttonholed him as he was limping out quickly with a glass of lemonade for a young lady and asked him was it true. Yes. it was true.

"But, of course, that doesn't alter the contract," she said. "The contract was for four concerts."

Mr. Holohan seemed to be in a hurry; he advised her to speak to Mr. Fitzpatrick. Mrs. Kearney was now beginning to be alarmed. She called Mr. Fitzpatrick away from his screen and told him that her daughter had signed for four concerts and that, of course, according to the terms of the contract, she should receive the sum originally stipulated for, whether the society gave the four concerts or not. Mr. Fitzpatrick, who did not catch the point at issue very quickly, seemed unable to resolve the difficulty and said that he would bring the matter before the committee. Mrs. Kearney's anger began to flutter in her cheek and she had all she could do to keep from asking:

"And who is the Cometty pray?"

But she knew that it would not be ladylike to do that: so she was silent.

Little boys were sent out into the principal streets of Dublin early on Friday morning with bundles of handbills. Special puffs appeared in all the evening papers, reminding the music loving public of the treat which was in store for it on the following evening. Mrs. Kearney was somewhat reassured, but be thought well to tell her husband part of her suspicions. He listened carefully and said that perhaps it would be better if he went with her on Saturday night. She agreed. She respected her husband in the same way as she respected the General Post Office, as something large, secure and fixed; and though she knew the small number of his talents she appreciated his abstract value as a male. She was glad that he had suggested coming with her. She thought her plans over.

The night of the grand concert came. Mrs. Kearney, with her husband and daughter, arrived at the Antient Concert Rooms three-quarters of an hour before the time at which the concert was to begin. By ill luck it was a rainy evening. Mrs. Kearney placed her daughter's clothes and music in charge of her husband and went all over the building looking for Mr. Holohan or Mr.

Fitzpatrick. She could find neither. She asked the stewards was any member of the committee in the hall and, after a great deal of trouble, a steward brought out a little woman named Miss Beirne to whom Mrs. Kearney explained that she wanted to see one of the secretaries. Miss Beirne expected them any minute and asked could she do anything. Mrs. Kearney looked searchingly at the oldish face which was screwed into an expression of trustfulness and enthusiasm and answered:

"No, thank you!"

The little woman hoped they would have a good house. She looked out at the rain until the melancholy of the wet street effaced all the trustfulness and enthusiasm from her twisted features. Then she gave a little sigh and said:

"Ah, well! We did our best, the dear knows."

Mrs. Kearney had to go back to the dressing-room.

The artistes were arriving. The bass and the second tenor had already come. The bass, Mr. Duggan, was a slender young man with a scattered black moustache. He was the son of a hall porter in an office in the city and, as a boy, he had sung prolonged bass notes in the resounding hall. From this humble state he had raised himself until he had become a first-rate artiste. He had appeared in grand opera. One night, when an operatic artiste had fallen ill, he had undertaken the part of the king in the opera of Maritana at the Queen's Theatre. He sang his music with great feeling and volume and was warmly welcomed by the gallery; but, unfortunately, he marred the good impression by wiping his nose in his gloved hand once or twice out of thoughtlessness. He was unassuming and spoke little. He said yous so softly that it passed unnoticed and he never drank anything stronger than milk for his voice's sake. Mr. Bell, the second tenor, was a fair-haired little man who competed every year for prizes at the Feis Ceoil. On his fourth trial he had been awarded a bronze medal. He was extremely nervous and extremely jealous of other tenors and he covered his nervous jealousy with an ebullient friendliness. It was his humour to have people know what an ordeal a concert was to him. Therefore when he saw Mr. Duggan he went over to him and asked:

"Are you in it too? "

"Yes," said Mr. Duggan.

Mr. Bell laughed at his fellow-sufferer, held out his hand and said:

"Shake!"

Mrs. Kearney passed by these two young men and went to the edge of the screen to view the house. The seats were being filled up rapidly and a pleasant noise circulated in the auditorium. She came back and spoke to her husband privately. Their conversation was evidently about Kathleen for they both glanced at her often as she stood chatting to one of her Nationalist friends, Miss Healy, the contralto. An unknown solitary woman with a pale face walked through the room. The women followed with keen eyes the faded blue dress which was stretched upon a meagre body. Someone said that she was Madam Glynn, the soprano.

"I wonder where did they dig her up," said Kathleen to Miss Healy. "I'm sure I never heard of her."

Miss Healy had to smile. Mr. Holohan limped into the dressing-room at that moment and the two young ladies asked him who was the unknown woman. Mr. Holohan said that she was Madam Glynn from London. Madam Glynn took her stand in a corner of the room, holding a roll of music stiffly before her and from time to time changing the direction of her startled gaze. The shadow took her faded dress into shelter but fell revengefully into the little cup behind her collar-bone. The noise of the hall became more audible. The first tenor and the baritone arrived together. They were both well dressed, stout and complacent and they brought a breath of opulence among the company.

Mrs. Kearney brought her daughter over to them, and talked to them amiably. She wanted to be on good terms with them but, while she strove to be polite, her eyes followed Mr. Holohan in his limping and devious courses. As soon as she could she excused herself and went out after him.

"Mr. Holohan, I want to speak to you for a moment," she said.

They went down to a discreet part of the corridor. Mrs Kearney asked him when was her daughter going to be paid. Mr. Holohan said that Mr. Fitzpatrick had charge of that. Mrs. Kearney said that she didn't know anything about Mr. Fitzpatrick. Her daughter had signed a contract for eight guineas and she would have to be paid. Mr. Holohan said that it wasn't his business.

"Why isn't it your business?" asked Mrs. Kearney. "Didn't you yourself bring her the contract? Anyway, if it's not your business it's my business and I mean to see to it."

"You'd better speak to Mr. Fitzpatrick," said Mr. Holohan distantly.

"I don't know anything about Mr. Fitzpatrick," repeated Mrs. Kearney. "I have my contract, and I intend to see that it is carried out."

When she came back to the dressing-room her cheeks were slightly suffused. The room was lively. Two men in outdoor dress had taken possession of the fireplace and were chatting familiarly with Miss Healy and the baritone. They were the Freeman man and Mr. O'Madden Burke. The Freeman man had come in to say that he could not wait for the concert as he had to report the lecture which an American priest was giving in the Mansion House. He said they were to leave the report for him at the Freeman office and he would see that it went in. He was a grey-haired man, with a plausible voice and careful manners. He held an extinguished cigar in his hand and the aroma of cigar smoke floated near him. He had not intended to stay a moment because concerts and artistes bored him considerably but he remained leaning against the mantelpiece. Miss Healy stood in front of him, talking and laughing. He was old enough to suspect one reason for her politeness but young enough in spirit to turn the moment to account. The warmth, fragrance and colour of her body appealed to his senses. He was pleasantly conscious that the bosom which he saw rise and fall slowly beneath him rose and fell at that moment for him, that the laughter and fragrance and wilful glances were his tribute. When he could stay no longer he took leave of her regretfully.

"O'Madden Burke will write the notice," he explained to Mr. Holohan, "and I'll see it in."

"Thank you very much, Mr. Hendrick," said Mr. Holohan. you'll see it in, I know. Now, won't you have a little something before you go?"

"I don't mind," said Mr. Hendrick.

The two men went along some tortuous passages and up a dark staircase and came to a secluded room where one of the stewards was uncorking bottles for a few gentlemen. One of these gentlemen was Mr. O'Madden Burke, who had found out the room by instinct. He was a suave, elderly man who balanced his imposing body, when at rest, upon a large silk umbrella. His magniloquent western name was the moral umbrella upon which he balanced the fine problem of his finances. He was widely respected.

While Mr. Holohan was entertaining the Freeman man Mrs. Kearney was speaking so animatedly to her husband that he had to ask her to lower her voice. The conversation of the others in the dressing-room had become strained. Mr. Bell, the first item, stood ready with his music but the accompanist made no sign. Evidently something was wrong. Mr. Kearney looked straight before him, stroking his beard, while Mrs. Kearney spoke into Kathleen's ear with subdued emphasis. From the hall came sounds of encouragement, clapping and stamping of feet. The first tenor and the baritone and Miss Healy stood together, waiting tranquilly, but Mr. Bell's nerves were greatly agitated because he was afraid the audience would think that he had come late.

Mr. Holohan and Mr. O'Madden Burke came into the room In a moment Mr. Holohan perceived the hush. He went over to Mrs. Kearney and spoke with her earnestly. While they were speaking the noise in the hall grew louder. Mr. Holohan became very red and excited. He spoke volubly, but Mrs. Kearney said curtly at intervals:

"She won't go on. She must get her eight guineas."

Mr. Holohan pointed desperately towards the hall where the audience was clapping and stamping. He appealed to Mr Kearney and to Kathleen. But Mr. Kearney continued to stroke his beard and Kathleen looked down, moving the point of her new shoe: it was not her fault. Mrs. Kearney repeated:

"She won't go on without her money."

After a swift struggle of tongues Mr. Holohan hobbled out in haste. The room was silent. When the strain of the silence had become somewhat painful Miss Healy said to the baritone:

"Have you seen Mrs. Pat Campbell this week?"

The baritone had not seen her but he had been told that she was very fine. The conversation went no further. The first tenor bent his head and began to count the links of the gold chain which was extended across his waist, smiling and humming random notes to observe the effect on the frontal sinus. From time to time everyone glanced at Mrs. Kearney.

The noise in the auditorium had risen to a clamour when Mr. Fitzpatrick burst into the room, followed by Mr. Holohan who was panting. The clapping and stamping in the hall were punctuated by whistling. Mr. Fitzpatrick held a few banknotes in his hand. He counted out four into Mrs. Kearney's hand and said she would get the other half at the interval. Mrs. Kearney said:

"This is four shillings short."

But Kathleen gathered in her skirt and said: "Now. Mr. Bell," to the first item, who was shaking like an aspen. The singer and the accompanist went out together. The noise in hall died away. There was a pause of a few seconds: and then the piano was heard.

The first part of the concert was very successful except for Madam Glynn's item. The poor lady sang Killarney in a bodiless gasping voice, with all the old-fashioned mannerisms of intonation and pronunciation which she believed lent elegance to her singing. She looked as if she had been resurrected from an old stage-wardrobe and the cheaper parts of the hall made fun of her high wailing notes. The first tenor and the contralto, however, brought down the house. Kathleen played a selection of Irish airs which was generously applauded. The first part closed with a stirring patriotic recitation delivered by a young lady who arranged amateur theatricals. It was deservedly applauded; and, when it was ended, the men went out for the interval, content.

All this time the dressing-room was a hive of excitement. In one corner were Mr. Holohan, Mr. Fitzpatrick, Miss Beirne, two of the stewards, the baritone, the bass, and Mr. O'Madden Burke. Mr. O'Madden Burke said it was the most scandalous exhibition he had ever witnessed. Miss Kathleen Kearney's musical career was ended in Dublin after that, he said. The baritone was asked what did he think of Mrs. Kearney's conduct. He did not like to say anything. He had been paid his money and wished to be at peace with men. However, he said that Mrs. Kearney might have taken the artistes into consideration. The stewards and the secretaries debated hotly as to what should be done when the interval came.

"I agree with Miss Beirne," said Mr. O'Madden Burke. "Pay her nothing."

In another corner of the room were Mrs. Kearney and he: husband, Mr. Bell, Miss Healy and the young lady who had to recite the patriotic piece. Mrs. Kearney said that the Committee had treated her scandalously. She had spared neither trouble nor expense and this was how she was repaid.

They thought they had only a girl to deal with and that therefore, they could ride roughshod over her. But she would show them their mistake. They wouldn't have dared to have treated her like that if she had been a man. But she would see that her daughter got her rights: she wouldn't be fooled. If they didn't pay her to the last farthing she would make Dublin ring. Of course she was sorry for the sake of the artistes. But what else could she do? She appealed to the second tenor who said he thought she had not been well treated. Then she appealed to Miss Healy. Miss Healy wanted to join the other group but she did not like to do so because she was a great friend of Kathleen's and the Kearneys had often invited her to their house.

As soon as the first part was ended Mr. Fitzpatrick and Mr. Holohan went over to Mrs. Kearney and told her that the other four guineas would be paid after the committee meeting on the following Tuesday and that, in case her daughter did not play for the second part, the committee would consider the contract broken and would pay nothing.

"I haven't seen any committee," said Mrs. Kearney angrily. "My daughter has her contract. She will get four pounds eight into her hand or a foot she won't put on that platform."

"I'm surprised at you, Mrs. Kearney," said Mr. Holohan. "I never thought you would treat us this way."

"And what way did you treat me?" asked Mrs. Kearney.

Her face was inundated with an angry colour and she looked as if she would attack someone with her hands.

"I'm asking for my rights." she said.

You might have some sense of decency," said Mr. Holohan.

"Might I, indeed? . . . And when I ask when my daughter is going to be paid I can't get a civil answer."

She tossed her head and assumed a haughty voice:

"You must speak to the secretary. It's not my business. I'm a great fellow fol-the-diddle-I-do."

"I thought you were a lady," said Mr. Holohan, walking away from her abruptly.

After that Mrs. Kearney's conduct was condemned on all hands: everyone approved of what the committee had done. She stood at the door, haggard with rage, arguing with her husband and daughter, gesticulating with them. She waited until it was time for the second part to begin in the hope that the secretaries would approach her. But Miss Healy had kindly consented to play one or two accompaniments. Mrs. Kearney had to stand aside to allow the baritone and his accompanist to pass up to the platform. She stood still for an instant like an angry stone image and, when the first notes of the song struck her ear, she caught up her daughter's cloak and said to her husband:

"Get a cab!"

He went out at once. Mrs. Kearney wrapped the cloak round her daughter and followed him. As she passed through the doorway she stopped and glared into Mr. Holohan's face.

"I'm not done with you yet," she said.

"But I'm done with you," said Mr. Holohan.

Kathleen followed her mother meekly. Mr. Holohan began to pace up and down the room, in order to cool himself for he his skin on fire.

"That's a nice lady!" he said. "O, she's a nice lady!"

You did the proper thing, Holohan," said Mr. O'Madden Burke, poised upon his umbrella in approval.

# After the Race

***James Joyce***

THE cars came scudding in towards Dublin, running evenly like pellets in the groove of the Naas Road. At the crest of the hill at Inchicore sightseers had gathered in clumps to watch the cars careering homeward and through this channel of poverty and inaction the Continent sped its wealth and industry. Now and again the clumps of people raised the cheer of the gratefully oppressed. Their sympathy, however, was for the blue cars — the cars of their friends, the French.

The French, moreover, were virtual victors. Their team had finished solidly; they had been placed second and third and the driver of the winning German car was reported a Belgian. Each blue car, therefore, received a double measure of welcome as it topped the crest of the hill and each cheer of welcome was acknowledged with smiles and nods by those in the car. In one of these trimly built cars was a party of four young men whose spirits seemed to be at present well above the level of successful Gallicism: in fact, these four young men were almost hilarious. They were Charles Segouin, the owner of the car; Andre Riviere, a young electrician of Canadian birth; a huge Hungarian named Villona and a neatly groomed young man named Doyle. Segouin was in good humour because he had unexpectedly received some orders in advance (he was about to start a motor establishment in Paris) and Riviere was in good humour because he was to be appointed manager of the establishment; these two young men (who were cousins) were also in good humour because of the success of the French cars. Villona was in good humour because he had had a very satisfactory luncheon; and besides he was an optimist by nature. The fourth member of the party, however, was too excited to be genuinely happy.

He was about twenty-six years of age, with a soft, light brown moustache and rather innocent-looking grey eyes. His father, who had begun life as an advanced Nationalist, had modified his views early. He had made his money as a butcher in Kingstown and by opening shops in Dublin and in the suburbs he had made his money many times over. He had also been fortunate enough to secure some of the police contracts and in the end he had become rich enough to be alluded to in the Dublin newspapers as a merchant prince. He had sent his son to England to be educated in a big Catholic college and had afterwards sent him to Dublin University to study law. Jimmy did not study very earnestly and took to bad courses for a while. He had money and he was popular; and he divided his time curiously between musical and motoring circles. Then he had been sent for a term to Cambridge to see a little life. His father, remonstrative, but covertly proud of the excess, had paid his bills and brought him home. It was at Cambridge that he had met Segouin. They were not much more than acquaintances as yet but Jimmy found great pleasure in the society of one who had seen so much of the world and was reputed to own some of the biggest hotels in France. Such a person (as his father agreed) was well worth knowing, even if he had not been the charming companion he was. Villona was entertaining also — a brilliant pianist — but, unfortunately, very poor.

The car ran on merrily with its cargo of hilarious youth. The two cousins sat on the front seat; Jimmy and his Hungarian friend sat behind. Decidedly Villona was in excellent spirits; he kept up a deep bass hum of melody for miles of the road The Frenchmen flung their laughter and light words over their shoulders and often Jimmy had to strain forward to catch the quick phrase. This was not altogether pleasant for him, as he had nearly always to make a deft guess at the meaning and shout back a suitable answer in the face of a high wind. Besides Villona's humming would confuse anybody; the noise of the car, too.

Rapid motion through space elates one; so does notoriety; so does the possession of money. These were three good reasons for Jimmy's excitement. He had been seen by many of his friends that day in the company of these Continentals. At the control Segouin had presented him to one of the French competitors and, in answer to his confused murmur of compliment, the swarthy face of the driver had disclosed a line of shining white teeth. It was pleasant after that honour to return to the profane world of spectators amid nudges and significant looks. Then as to money – he really had a great sum under his control. Segouin, perhaps, would not think it a great sum but Jimmy who, in spite of temporary errors, was at heart the inheritor of solid instincts knew well with what difficulty it had been got together. This knowledge had previously kept his bills within the limits of reasonable recklessness, and if he had been so conscious of the labour latent in money when there had been question merely of some freak of the higher intelligence, how much more so now when he was about to stake the greater part of his substance! It was a serious thing for him.

Of course, the investment was a good one and Segouin had managed to give the impression that it was by a favour of friendship the mite of Irish money was to be included in the capital of the concern. Jimmy had a respect for his father's shrewdness in business matters and in this case it had been his father who had first suggested the investment; money to be made in the motor business, pots of money. Moreover Segouin had the unmistakable air of wealth. Jimmy set out to translate into days' work that lordly car in which he sat. How smoothly it ran. In what style they had come careering along the country roads! The journey laid a magical finger on the genuine pulse of life and gallantly the machinery of human nerves strove to answer the bounding courses of the swift blue animal.

They drove down Dame Street. The street was busy with unusual traffic, loud with the horns of motorists and the gongs of impatient tram-drivers. Near the Bank Segouin drew up and Jimmy and his friend alighted. A little knot of people collected on the footpath to pay homage to the snorting motor. The party was to dine together that evening in Segouin's hotel and, meanwhile, Jimmy and his friend, who was staying with him, were to go home to dress. The car steered out slowly for Grafton Street while the two young men pushed their way through the knot of gazers. They walked northward with a curious feeling of disappointment in the exercise, while the city hung its pale globes of light above them in a haze of summer evening.

In Jimmy's house this dinner had been pronounced an occasion. A certain pride mingled with his parents' trepidation, a certain eagerness, also, to play fast and loose for the names of great foreign cities have at least this virtue. Jimmy, too, looked very well when he was dressed and, as he stood in the hall giving a last equation to the bows of his dress tie, his father may have felt even commercially satisfied at having secured for his son qualities often unpurchaseable. His father, therefore, was unusually friendly with Villona and his manner expressed a real respect for foreign accomplishments; but this subtlety of his host was probably lost upon the Hungarian, who was beginning to have a sharp desire for his dinner.

The dinner was excellent, exquisite. Segouin, Jimmy decided, had a very refined taste. The party was increased by a young Englishman named Routh whom Jimmy had seen with Segouin at Cambridge. The young men supped in a snug room lit by electric candle lamps. They talked volubly and with little reserve. Jimmy, whose imagination was kindling, conceived the lively youth of the Frenchmen twined elegantly upon the firm framework of the Englishman's manner. A graceful image of his, he thought, and a just one. He admired the dexterity with which their host directed the conversation. The five young men had various tastes and their tongues had been loosened. Villona, with immense respect, began to discover to the mildly surprised Englishman the beauties of the English madrigal, deploring the loss of old instruments. Riviere, not wholly ingenuously, undertook to explain to Jimmy the triumph of the French mechanicians. The resonant voice of the Hungarian was about to prevail in ridicule of the spurious lutes of the romantic painters when Segouin shepherded his party into politics. Here was congenial ground for all. Jimmy, under generous influences, felt the buried zeal of his father wake to life within him: he aroused the torpid Routh at last. The room grew doubly hot and Segouin's task grew harder each moment: there was even danger of personal spite. The alert host at an opportunity lifted his glass to Humanity and, when the toast had been drunk, he threw open a window significantly.

That night the city wore the mask of a capital. The five

young men strolled along Stephen's Green in a faint cloud of aromatic smoke. They talked loudly and gaily and their cloaks dangled from their shoulders. The people made way for them. At the corner of Grafton Street a short fat man was putting two handsome ladies on a car in charge of another fat man. The car drove off and the short fat man caught sight of the party.

"Andre."

"It's Farley!"

A torrent of talk followed. Farley was an American. No one knew very well what the talk was about. Villona and Riviere were the noisiest, but all the men were excited. They got up on a car, squeezing themselves together amid much laughter. They drove by the crowd, blended now into soft colours, to a music of merry bells. They took the train at Westland Row and in a few seconds, as it seemed to Jimmy, they were walking out of Kingstown Station. The ticket-collector saluted Jimmy; he was an old man:

"Fine night, sir!"

It was a serene summer night; the harbour lay like a darkened mirror at their feet. They proceeded towards it with linked arms, singing Cadet Roussel in chorus, stamping their feet at every:

"Ho! Ho! Hohe, vraiment!"

They got into a rowboat at the slip and made out for the American's yacht. There was to be supper, music, cards. Villona said with conviction:

"It is delightful!"

There was a yacht piano in the cabin. Villona played a waltz for Farley and Riviere, Farley acting as cavalier and Riviere as lady. Then an impromptu square dance, the men devising original figures. What merriment! Jimmy took his part with a will; this was seeing life, at least. Then Farley got out of breath and cried "Stop!" A man brought in a light supper, and the young men sat down to it for form's sake. They drank, however: it was Bohemian. They drank Ireland, England, France, Hungary, the United States of America. Jimmy made a speech, a long speech, Villona saying: "Hear! hear!" whenever there was a pause. There was a great clapping of hands when he sat down. It must have been a good speech. Farley clapped him on the back and laughed loudly. What jovial fellows! What good company they were!

Cards! cards! The table was cleared. Villona returned quietly to his piano and played voluntaries for them. The other men played game after game, flinging themselves boldly into the adventure. They drank the health of the Queen of Hearts and of the Queen of Diamonds. Jimmy felt obscurely the lack of an audience: the wit was flashing. Play ran very high and paper began to pass. Jimmy did not know exactly who was winning but he knew that he was losing. But it was his own fault for he frequently mistook his cards and the other men had to calculate his I.O.U.'s for him. They were devils of fellows but he wished they would stop: it was getting late. Someone gave the toast of the yacht The Belle of Newport and then someone proposed one great game for a finish.

The piano had stopped; Villona must have gone up on deck. It was a terrible game. They stopped just before the end of it to drink for luck. Jimmy understood that the game lay between Routh and Segouin. What excitement! Jimmy was excited too; he would lose, of course. How much had he written away? The men rose to their feet to play the last tricks. talking and gesticulating. Routh won. The cabin shook with the young men's cheering and the cards were bundled together. They began then to gather in what they had won. Farley and Jimmy were the heaviest losers.

He knew that he would regret in the morning but at present he was glad of the rest, glad of the dark stupor that would cover up his folly. He leaned his elbows on the table and rested his head between his hands, counting the beats of his temples. The cabin door opened and he saw the Hungarian standing in a shaft of grey light:

"Daybreak, gentlemen!"

# Cousin Teresa

*Saki*

Basset Harrowcluff returned to the home of his fathers, after an absence of four years, distinctly well pleased with himself. He was only thirty-one, but he had put in some useful service in an out-of-the-way, though not unimportant, corner of the world. He had quieted a province, kept open a trade route, enforced the tradition of respect which is worth the ransom of many kings in out-of-the-way regions, and done the whole business on rather less expenditure than would be requisite for organising a charity in the home country. In Whitehall and places where they think, they doubtless thought well of him. It was not inconceivable, his father allowed himself to imagine, that Basset's name might figure in the next list of Honours.

Basset was inclined to be rather contemptuous of his half-brother, Lucas, whom he found feverishly engrossed in the same medley of elaborate futilities that had claimed his whole time and energies, such as they were, four years ago, and almost as far back before that as he could remember. It was the contempt of the man of action for the man of activities, and it was probably reciprocated. Lucas was an over-well nourished individual, some nine years Basset's senior, with a colouring that would have been accepted as a sign of intensive culture in an asparagus, but probably meant in this case mere abstention from exercise. His hair and forehead furnished a recessional note in a personality that was in all other respects obtrusive and assertive. There was certainly no Semitic blood in Lucas's parentage, but his appearance contrived to convey at least a suggestion of Jewish extraction. Clovis Sangrail, who knew most of his associates by sight, said it was undoubtedly a case of protective mimicry.

Two days after Basset's return, Lucas frisked in to lunch in a state of twittering excitement that could not be restrained even for the immediate consideration of soup, but had to be verbally discharged in spluttering competition with mouthfuls of vermicelli.

"I've got hold of an idea for something immense," he babbled, "something that is simply It."

Basset gave a short laugh that would have done equally well as a snort, if one had wanted to make the exchange. His half-brother was in the habit of discovering futilities that were "simply It" at frequently recurring intervals. The discovery generally meant that he flew up to town, preceded by glowingly-worded telegrams, to see some one connected with the stage or the publishing world, got together one or two momentous luncheon parties, flitted in and out of "Gambrinus" for one or two evenings, and returned home with an air of subdued importance and the asparagus tint slightly intensified. The great idea was generally forgotten a few weeks later in the excitement of some new discovery.

"The inspiration came to me whilst I was dressing," announced Lucas; "it will be the thing in the next music-hall revue. All London will go mad over it. It's just a couplet; of course there will be other words, but they won't matter. Listen:

Cousin Teresa takes out Caesar, Fido, Jock, and the big borzoi.

A lifting, catchy sort of refrain, you see, and big-drum business on the two syllables of bor-zoi. It's immense. And I've thought out all the business of it; the singer will sing the first verse alone, then during the second verse Cousin Teresa will walk through, followed by four wooden dogs on wheels; Caesar will be an Irish terrier, Fido a black poodle, Jock a fox-terrier, and the borzoi, of course, will be a borzoi. During the third verse Cousin Teresa will come on alone, and the dogs will be drawn across by themselves from the opposite wing; then Cousin Teresa will catch on to the singer and go off-stage in one direction, while the dogs' procession goes off in the other, crossing en route, which is always very effective. There'll be a lot of applause there, and for the fourth verse Cousin Teresa will come on in sables and the dogs will all have coats on. Then I've got a great idea for the fifth verse; each of the dogs will be led on by a Nut, and Cousin Teresa will come on from the opposite side, crossing en route, always effective, and then she turns round and leads the whole lot of them off on a string, and all the time every one singing like mad:

Cousin Teresa takes out Caesar Fido, Jock, and the big borzoi.

Tum–Tum! Drum business on the two last syllables. I'm so excited, I shan't sleep a wink to-night. I'm off tomorrow by the ten-fifteen. I've wired to Hermanova to lunch with me."

If any of the rest of the family felt any excitement over the creation of Cousin Teresa, they were signally successful in concealing the fact.

"Poor Lucas does take his silly little ideas seriously," said Colonel Harrowcluff afterwards in the smoking-room.

"Yes," said his younger son, in a slightly less tolerant tone, "in a day or two he'll come back and tell us that his sensational masterpiece is above the heads of the public, and in about three weeks' time he'll be wild with enthusiasm over a scheme to dramatise the poems of Herrick or something equally promising."

And then an extraordinary thing befell. In defiance of all precedent Lucas's glowing anticipations were justified and endorsed by the course of events. If Cousin Teresa was above the heads of the public, the public heroically adapted itself to her altitude. Introduced as an experiment at a dull moment in a new revue, the success of the item was unmistakable; the calls were so insistent and uproarious that even Lucas' ample devisings of additional "business" scarcely sufficed to keep pace with the demand. Packed houses on successive evenings confirmed the verdict of the first night audience, stalls and boxes filled significantly just before the turn came on, and emptied significantly after the last encore had been given. The manager tearfully acknowledged that Cousin Teresa was It. Stage hands and supers and programme sellers acknowledged it to one another without the least reservation. The name of the revue dwindled to secondary importance, and vast letters of electric blue blazoned the words "Cousin Teresa" from the front of the great palace of pleasure. And, of course, the magic of the famous refrain laid its spell all over the Metropolis. Restaurant proprietors were obliged to provide the members of their orchestras with painted wooden dogs on wheels, in order that the much-demanded and always conceded melody should be rendered with the necessary spectacular effects, and the crash of bottles and forks on the tables at the mention of the big borzoi usually drowned the sincerest efforts of drum or cymbals. Nowhere and at no time could one get away from the double thump that brought up the rear of the refrain; revellers reeling home at night banged it on doors and hoardings, milkmen clashed their cans to its cadence, messenger boys hit smaller messenger boys resounding double smacks on the same principle. And the more thoughtful circles of the great city were not deaf to the claims and significance of the popular melody. An enterprising and emancipated preacher discoursed from his pulpit on the inner meaning of "Cousin Teresa," and Lucas Harrowcluff was invited to lecture on the subject of his great achievement to members of the Young Mens' Endeavour League, the Nine Arts Club, and other learned and willing-to-learn bodies. In Society it seemed to be the one thing people really cared to talk about; men and women of middle age and average education might be seen together in corners earnestly discussing, not the question whether Servia should have an outlet on the Adriatic, or the possibilities of a British success in international polo contests, but the more absorbing topic of the problematic Aztec or Nilotic origin of the Teresa motiv.

"Politics and patriotism are so boring and so out of date," said a revered lady who had some pretensions to oracular utterance; "we are too cosmopolitan nowadays to be really moved by them. That is why one welcomes an intelligible production like 'Cousin Teresa,' that has a genuine message for one. One can't understand the message all at once, of course, but one felt from the very first that it was there. I've been to see it eighteen times and I'm going again tomorrow and on Thursday. One can't see it often enough."

* * * *

"It would be rather a popular move if we gave this Harrowcluff person a knighthood or something of the sort," said the Minister reflectively.

"Which Harrowcluff?" asked his secretary.

"Which? There is only one, isn't there?" said the Minister; "the 'Cousin Teresa' man, of course. I think every one would be pleased if we knighted him. Yes, you can put him down on the list of certainties — under the letter L."

"The letter L," said the secretary, who was new to his job; "does that stand for Liberalism or liberality?"

Most of the recipients of Ministerial favour were expected to qualify in both of those subjects.

"Literature," explained the Minister.

And thus, after a fashion, Colonel Harrowcluff's expectation of seeing his son's name in the list of Honours was gratified.

# Shock Tactics

*Saki*

On a late spring afternoon Ella McCarthy sat on a green-painted chair in Kensington Gardens, staring listlessly at an uninteresting stretch of park landscape, that blossomed suddenly into tropical radiance as an expected figure appeared in the middle distance.

"Hullo, Bertie!" she exclaimed sedately, when the figure arrived at the painted chair that was the nearest neighbour to her own, and dropped into it eagerly, yet with a certain due regard for the set of its trousers; "hasn't it been a perfect spring afternoon?"

The statement was a distinct untruth as far as Ella's own feelings were concerned; until the arrival of Bertie the afternoon had been anything but perfect.

Bertie made a suitable reply, in which a questioning note seemed to hover.

"Thank you ever so much for those lovely handkerchiefs," said Ella, answering the unspoken question; "they were just what I've been wanting. There's only one thing spoilt my pleasure in your gift," she added, with a pout.

"What was that?" asked Bertie anxiously, fearful that perhaps he had chosen a size of handkerchief that was not within the correct feminine limit.

"I should have liked to have written and thanked you for them as soon as I got them," said Ella, and Bertie's sky clouded at once.

"You know what mother is," he protested; "she opens all my letters, and if she found I'd been giving presents to any one there'd have been something to talk about for the next fortnight."

"Surely, at the age of twenty – " began Ella.

"I'm not twenty till September," interrupted Bertie.

"At the age of nineteen years and eight months," persisted

Ella, "you might be allowed to keep your correspondence private to yourself."

"I ought to be, but things aren't always what they ought to be. Mother opens every letter that comes into the house, whoever it's for. My sisters and I have made rows about it time and again, but she goes on doing it."

"I'd find some way to stop her if I were in your place," said Ella valiantly, and Bertie felt that the glamour of his anxiously deliberated present had faded away in the disagreeable restriction that hedged round its acknowledgment.

"Is anything the matter?" asked Bertie's friend Clovis when they met that evening at the swimming-bath.

"Why do you ask?" said Bertie.

"When you wear a look of tragic gloom in a swimming-bath," said Clovis, "it's especially noticeable from the fact that you're wearing very little else. Didn't she like the handkerchiefs?"

Bertie explained the situation.

"It is rather galling, you know," he added, "when a girl has a lot of things she wants to write to you and can't send a letter except by some roundabout, underhand way."

"One never realises one's blessings while one enjoys them," said Clovis; "now I have to spend a considerable amount of ingenuity inventing excuses for not having written to people."

"It's not a joking matter," said Bertie resentfully: "you wouldn't find it funny if your mother opened all your letters."

"The funny thing to me is that you should let her do it."

"I can't stop it. I've argued about it – "

"You haven't used the right kind of argument, I expect. Now, if every time one of your letters was opened you lay on your back on the dining-table during dinner and had a fit, or roused the entire family in the middle of the night to hear you recite one of Blake's 'Poems of Innocence,' you would get a far more respectful hearing for future protests. People yield more consideration to a mutilated mealtime or a broken night's rest, than ever they would to a broken heart."

"Oh, dry up," said Bertie crossly, inconsistently splashing Clovis from head to foot as he plunged into the water.

It was a day or two after the conversation in the swimming-bath that a letter addressed to Bertie Heasant slid into the letter-box at his home, and thence into the hands of his mother. Mrs. Heasant was one of those empty-minded individuals to whom other people's affairs are perpetually interesting. The more private they are intended to be the more acute is the interest they arouse. She would have opened this particular letter in any case; the fact that it was marked "private," and diffused a delicate but penetrating aroma merely caused her to open it with headlong haste rather than matter-of-course deliberation. The harvest of sensation that rewarded her was beyond all expectations.

"Bertie, carissimo," it began, "I wonder if you will have the nerve to do it: it will take some nerve, too. Don't forget the jewels. They are a detail, but details interest me.

"Yours as ever, "Clotilde.

"Your mother must not know of my existence. If questioned swear you never heard of me."

For years Mrs. Heasant had searched Bertie's correspondence diligently for traces of possible dissipation or youthful entanglements, and at last the suspicions that had stimulated her inquisitorial zeal were justified by this one splendid haul. That any one wearing the exotic name "Clotilde" should write to Bertie under the incriminating announcement "as ever" was sufficiently electrifying, without the astounding allusion to the jewels. Mrs. Heasant could recall novels and dramas wherein jewels played an exciting and commanding role, and here, under her own roof, before her very eyes as it were, her own son was carrying on an intrigue in which jewels were merely an interesting detail. Bertie was not due home for another hour, but his sisters were available for the immediate unburdening of a scandal-laden mind.

"Bertie is in the toils of an adventuress," she screamed; "her name is Clotilde," she added, as if she thought they had better know the worst at once. There are occasions when more harm than good is done by shielding young girls from a knowledge of the more deplorable realities of life.

By the time Bertie arrived his mother had discussed every possible and improbable conjecture as to his guilty secret; the girls limited themselves to the opinion that their brother had been weak rather than wicked.

"Who is Clotilde?" was the question that confronted Bertie almost before he had got into the hall. His denial of any knowledge of such a person was met with an outburst of bitter laughter.

"How well you have learned your lesson!" exclaimed Mrs. Heasant. But satire gave way to furious indignation when she realised that Bertie did not intend to throw any further light on her discovery.

"You shan't have any dinner till you've confessed everything," she stormed.

Bertie's reply took the form of hastily collecting material for an impromptu banquet from the larder and locking himself into his bedroom. His mother made frequent visits to the locked door and shouted a succession of interrogations with the persistence of one who thinks that if you ask a question often enough an answer will eventually result. Bertie did nothing to encourage the supposition. An hour had passed in fruitless one-sided palaver when another letter addressed to Bertie and marked "private" made its appearance in the letter-box. Mrs. Heasant pounced on it with the enthusiasm of a cat that has missed its mouse and to whom a second has been unexpectedly vouchsafed. If she hoped for further disclosures assuredly she was not disappointed.

"So you have really done it!" the letter abruptly commenced; "Poor Dagmar. Now she is done for I almost pity her. You did it very well, you wicked boy, the servants all think it was suicide, and there will be no fuss. Better not touch the jewels till after the inquest.

"Clotilde."

Anything that Mrs. Heasant had previously done in the way of outcry was easily surpassed as she raced upstairs and beat frantically at her son's door.

"Miserable boy, what have you done to Dagmar?"

"It's Dagmar now, is it?" he snapped; "it will be Geraldine next."

"That it should come to this, after all my efforts to keep you at home of an evening," sobbed Mrs. Heasant; "it's no use you trying to hide things from me; Clotilde's letter betrays everything."

"Does it betray who she is?" asked Bertie; "I've heard so much about her, I should like to know something about her home-life. Seriously, if you go on like this I shall fetch a doctor; I've often enough been preached at about nothing, but I've never had an imaginary harem dragged into the discussion."

"Are these letters imaginary?" screamed Mrs. Heasant; "what about the jewels, and Dagmar, and the theory of suicide?"

No solution of these problems was forthcoming through the bedroom door, but the last post of the evening produced another letter for Bertie, and its contents brought Mrs. Heasant that enlightenment which had already dawned on her son.

"Dear Bertie," it ran; "I hope I haven't distracted your brain with the spoof letters I've been sending in the name of a fictitious Clotilde. You told me the other day that the servants, or somebody at your home, tampered with your letters, so I thought I would give any one that opened them something exciting to read. The shock might do them good.

"Yours, "Clovis Sangrail."

Mrs. Heasant knew Clovis slightly, and was rather afraid of him. It was not difficult to read between the lines of his successful hoax. In a chastened mood she rapped once more at Bertie's door.

"A letter from Mr. Sangrail. It's all been a stupid hoax. He wrote those other letters. Why, where are you going?"

Bertie had opened the door; he had on his hat and overcoat.

"I'm going for a doctor to come and see if anything's the matter with you. Of course it was all a hoax, but no person in his right mind could have believed all that rubbish about murder and suicide and jewels. You've been making enough noise to bring the house down for the last hour or two."

"But what was I to think of those letters?" whimpered Mrs. Heasant.

"I should have known what to think of them," said Bertie; "if you choose to excite yourself over other people's correspondence it's your own fault. Anyhow, I'm going for a doctor."

It was Bertie's great opportunity, and he knew it. His mother was conscious of the fact that she would look rather ridiculous if the story got about. She was willing to pay hush-money.

"I'll never open your letters again," she promised. And Clovis has no more devoted slave than Bertie Heasant.

# The Open Window

***Saki***

"My aunt will be down presently, Mr. Nuttel," said a very self-possessed young lady of fifteen; "in the meantime you must try and put up with me."

Framton Nuttel endeavoured to say the correct something which should duly flatter the niece of the moment without unduly discounting the aunt that was to come. Privately he doubted more than ever whether these formal visits on a succession of total strangers would do much towards helping the nerve cure which he was supposed to be undergoing.

"I know how it will be," his sister had said when he was preparing to migrate to this rural retreat; "you will bury yourself down there and not speak to a living soul, and your nerves will be worse than ever from moping. I shall just give you letters of introduction to all the people I know there. Some of them, as far as I can remember, were quite nice."

Framton wondered whether Mrs. Sappleton, the lady to whom he was presenting one of the letters of introduction, came into the nice division.

"Do you know many of the people round here?" asked the niece, when she judged that they had had sufficient silent communion.

"Hardly a soul," said Framton. "My sister was staying here, at the rectory, you know, some four years ago, and she gave me letters of introduction to some of the people here."

He made the last statement in a tone of distinct regret.

"Then you know practically nothing about my aunt?" pursued the self-possessed young lady.

"Only her name and address," admitted the caller. He was wondering whether Mrs. Sappleton was in the married or widowed state. An undefinable something about the room seemed to suggest masculine habitation.

"Her great tragedy happened just three years ago," said the child; "that would be since your sister's time."

"Her tragedy?" asked Framton; somehow in this restful country spot tragedies seemed out of place.

"You may wonder why we keep that window wide open on an October afternoon," said the niece, indicating a large French window that opened on to a lawn.

"It is quite warm for the time of the year," said Framton; "but has that window got anything to do with the tragedy?"

"Out through that window, three years ago to a day, her husband and her two young brothers went off for their day's shooting. They never came back. In crossing the moor to their favourite snipe-shooting ground they were all three engulfed in a treacherous piece of bog. It had been that dreadful wet summer, you know, and places that were safe in other years gave way suddenly without warning. Their bodies were never recovered. That was the dreadful part of it." Here the child's voice lost its self-possessed note and became falteringly human. "Poor aunt always thinks that they will come back some day, they and the little brown spaniel that was lost with them, and walk in at that window just as they used to do. That is why the window is kept open every evening till it is quite dusk. Poor dear aunt, she has often told me how they went out, her husband with his white waterproof coat over his arm, and Ronnie, her youngest brother, singing 'Bertie, why do you bound?' as he always did to tease her, because she said it got on her nerves. Do you know, sometimes on still, quiet evenings like this, I almost get a creepy feeling that they will all walk in through that window – "

She broke off with a little shudder. It was a relief to Framton when the aunt bustled into the room with a whirl of apologies for being late in making her appearance.

"I hope Vera has been amusing you?" she said.

"She has been very interesting," said Framton.

"I hope you don't mind the open window," said Mrs. Sappleton briskly; "my husband and brothers will be home directly from shooting, and they always come in this way. They've been out for snipe in the marshes to-day, so they'll make a fine mess over my poor carpets. So like you men-folk, isn't it?"

She rattled on cheerfully about the shooting and the scarcity of birds, and the prospects for duck in the winter. To Framton it was all purely horrible. He made a desperate but only partially successful effort to turn the talk on to a less ghastly topic; he was conscious that his hostess was giving him only a fragment of her attention, and her eyes were constantly straying past him to the open window and the lawn beyond. It was certainly an unfortunate coincidence that he should have paid his visit on this tragic anniversary.

"The doctors agree in ordering me complete rest, an absence of mental excitement, and avoidance of anything in the nature of violent physical exercise," announced Framton, who laboured under the tolerably wide-spread delusion that total strangers and chance acquaintances are hungry for the least detail of one's ailments and infirmities, their cause and cure. "On the matter of diet they are not so much in agreement," he continued.

"No?" said Mrs. Sappleton, in a voice which only replaced a yawn at the last moment. Then she suddenly brightened into alert attention – but not to what Framton was saying.

"Here they are at last!" she cried. "Just in time for tea, and don't they look as if they were muddy up to the eyes!"

Framton shivered slightly and turned towards the niece with a look intended to convey sympathetic comprehension. The child was staring out through the open window with dazed horror in her eyes. In a chill shock of nameless fear Framton swung round in his seat and looked in the same direction.

In the deepening twilight three figures were walking across the lawn towards the window; they all carried guns under their arms, and one of them was additionally burdened with a white coat hung over his shoulders. A tired brown spaniel kept close at their heels. Noiselessly they neared the house, and then a hoarse young voice chanted out of the dusk: "I said, Bertie, why do you bound?"

Framton grabbed wildly at his stick and hat; the hall-door, the gravel-drive, and the front gate were dimly-noted stages in his headlong retreat. A cyclist coming along the road had to run into the hedge to avoid an imminent collision.

"Here we are, my dear," said the bearer of the white mackintosh, coming in through the window; "fairly muddy, but most of it's dry. Who was that who bolted out as we came up?"

"A most extraordinary man, a Mr. Nuttel," said Mrs. Sappleton; "could only talk about his illnesses, and dashed off without a word of good-bye or apology when you arrived. One would think he had seen a ghost."

"I expect it was the spaniel," said the niece calmly; "he told me he had a horror of dogs. He was once hunted into a cemetery somewhere on the banks of the Ganges by a pack of pariah dogs, and had to spend the night in a newly dug grave with the creatures snarling and grinning and foaming just above him. Enough to make anyone their nerve."

Romance at short notice was her speciality.

# Tobermory

*Saki*

It was a chill, rain-washed afternoon of a late August day, that indefinite season when partridges are still in security or cold storage, and there is nothing to hunt – unless one is bounded on the north by the Bristol Channel, in which case one may lawfully gallop after fat red stags. Lady Blemley's house- party was not bounded on the north by the Bristol Channel, hence there was a full gathering of her guests round the tea-table on this particular afternoon. And, in spite of the blankness of the season and the triteness of the occasion, there was no trace in the company of that fatigued restlessness which means a dread of the pianola and a subdued hankering for auction bridge. The undisguised open-mouthed attention of the entire party was fixed on the homely negative personality of Mr. Cornelius Appin. Of all her guests, he was the one who had come to Lady Blemley with the vaguest reputation. Some one had said he was "clever," and he had got his invitation in the moderate expectation, on the part of his hostess, that some portion at least of his cleverness would be contributed to the general entertainment. Until tea-time that day she had been unable to discover in what direction, if any, his cleverness lay. He was neither a wit nor a croquet champion, a hypnotic force nor a begetter of amateur theatricals. Neither did his exterior suggest the sort of man in whom women are willing to pardon a generous measure of mental deficiency. He had subsided into mere Mr. Appin, and the Cornelius seemed a piece of transparent baptismal bluff. And now he was claiming to have launched on the world a discovery beside which the invention of gunpowder, of the printing-press, and of steam locomotion were inconsiderable trifles. Science had made bewildering strides in many directions during recent decades, but this thing seemed to belong to the domain of miracle rather than to scientific achievement.

"And do you really ask us to believe," Sir Wilfrid was saying, "that you have discovered a means for instructing animals in the art of human speech, and that dear old Tobermory has proved your first successful pupil?"

"It is a problem at which I have worked for the last seventeen years," said Mr. Appin, "but only during the last eight or nine months have I been rewarded with glimmerings of success. Of course I have experimented with thousands of animals, but latterly only with cats, those wonderful creatures which have assimilated themselves so marvellously with our civilization while retaining all their highly developed feral instincts. Here and there among cats one comes across an outstanding superior intellect, just as one does among the ruck of human beings, and when I made the acquaintance of Tobermory a week ago I saw at once that I was in contact with a 'Beyond-cat' of extraordinary intelligence. I had gone far along the road to success in recent experiments; with Tobermory, as you call him, I have reached the goal."

Mr. Appin concluded his remarkable statement in a voice which he strove to divest of a triumphant inflection. No one said "Rats," though Clovis's lips moved in a monosyllabic contortion which probably invoked those rodents of disbelief.

"And do you mean to say," asked Miss Resker, after a slight pause, "that you have taught Tobermory to say and understand easy sentences of one syllable?"

"My dear Miss Resker," said the wonder-worker patiently, "one teaches little children and savages and backward adults in that piecemeal fashion; when one has once solved the problem of making a beginning with an animal of highly developed intelligence one has no need for those halting methods. Tobermory can speak our language with perfect correctness."

This time Clovis very distinctly said, "Beyond-rats!" Sir Wilfrid was more polite, but equally sceptical.

"Hadn't we better have the cat in and judge for ourselves?" suggested Lady Blemley.

Sir Wilfrid went in search of the animal, and the company settled themselves down to the languid expectation of witnessing some more or less adroit drawing- room ventriloquism.

In a minute Sir Wilfrid was back in the room, his face white beneath its tan and his eyes dilated with excitement. "By Gad, it's true!"

His agitation was unmistakably genuine, and his hearers started forward in a thrill of awakened interest.

Collapsing into an armchair he continued breathlessly: "I found him dozing in the smoking-room and called out to him to come for his tea. He blinked at me in his usual way, and I said, 'Come on, Toby; don't keep us waiting'; and, by Gad! He drawled out in a most horribly natural voice that he'd come when he dashed well pleased! I nearly jumped out of my skin!"

Appin had preached to absolutely incredulous hearers; Sir Wilfred's statement carried instant conviction. A Babel-like chorus of startled exclamation arose, amid which the scientist sat mutely enjoying the first fruit of his stupendous discovery.

In the midst of the clamour Tobermory entered the room and made his way with velvet tread and studied unconcern across to the group seated round the tea-time table.

A sudden hush of awkwardness and constraint fell on the company. Somehow there seemed an element of embarrassment in addressing on equal terms a domestic cat of acknowledged mental ability.

"Will you have some milk, Tobermory?" asked Lady Blemley in a rather strained voice.

"I don't mind if I do," was the response, couched in a tone of even indifference. A shiver of suppressed excitement went through the listeners, and Lady Blemley might be excused for pouring out the saucerful of milk rather unsteadily.

"I'm afraid I've spilt a good deal of it," she said apologetically.

"After all, it's not my Axminster," was Tobermory's rejoinder.

Another silence fell on the group, and then Miss Resker, in her best district- visitor manner, asked if the human language had been difficult to learn. Tobermory looked squarely at her for a moment and then fixed his gaze serenely on the middle distance. It was obvious that boring questions lay outside his scheme of life.

"What do you think of human intelligence?" asked Mavis Pellington lamely.

"Of whose intelligence in particular?" asked Tobermory coldly.

"Oh, well, mine for instance," said Mavis, with a feeble laugh.

"You put me in an embarrassing position," said Tobermory, whose tone and attitude certainly did not suggest a shred of embarrassment. "When your inclusion in this house-party was suggested, Sir Wilfrid protested that you were the most brainless woman of his acquaintance, and that there was a wide distinction between hospitality and the care of the feeble-minded. Lady Blemley replied that your lack of brain-power was the precise quality which had earned you your invitation, as you were the only person she could think of who might be idiotic enough to buy their old car. You know, the one they call 'The Envy of Sisyphus,' because it goes quite nicely up-hill if you push it."

Lady Blemley's protestations would have had greater effect if she had not casually suggested to Mavis only that morning that the car in question would be just the thing for her down at her Devonshire home.

Major Barfield plunged in heavily to effect a diversion.

"How about your carryings-on with the tortoise-shell puss up at the stables, eh?"

The moment he had said it every one realized the blunder.

"One does not usually discuss these matters in public," said Tobermory frigidly. "From a slight observation of your ways since you've been in this house I should imagine you'd find it inconvenient if I were to shift the conversation on to your own little affairs."

The panic which ensued was not confined to the Major.

"Would you like to go and see if cook has got your dinner ready?" suggested Lady Blemley hurriedly, affecting to ignore the fact that it wanted at least two hours to Tobermory's dinner-time.

"Thanks," said Tobermory, "not quite so soon after my tea. I don't want to die of indigestion."

"Cats have nine lives, you know," said Sir Wilfrid heartily.

"Possibly", answered Tobermory; "but only one liver."

"Adelaide!" said Mrs. Cornett, "do you mean to encourage that cat to go out and gossip about us in the servants' hall?"

The panic had indeed become general. A narrow ornamental balustrade ran in front of most of the bedroom windows at the

Towers, and it was recalled with dismay that this had formed a favourite promenade for Tobermory at all hours, whence he could watch the pigeons – and heaven knew what else besides. If he intended to become reminiscent in his present outspoken strain the effect would be something more than disconcerting. Mrs. Cornett, who spent much time at her toilet table, and whose complexion was reputed to be of a nomadic though punctual disposition, looked as ill at ease as the Major. Miss Scrawen, who wrote fiercely sensuous poetry and led a blameless life, merely displayed irritation; if you are methodical and virtuous in private you don't necessarily want every one to know it. Bertie van Tahn, who was so depraved at seventeen that he had long ago given up trying to be any worse, turned a dull shade of gardenia white, but he did not commit the error of dashing out of the room like Odo Finsberry, a young gentleman who was understood to be reading for the Church and who was possibly disturbed at the thought of scandals he might hear concerning other people. Clovis had the presence of mind to maintain a composed exterior; privately he was calculating how long it would take to procure a box of fancy mice through the agency of the Exchange and Mart as a species of hush- money.

Even in a delicate situation like the present, Agnes Resker could not endure to remain too long in the background.

"Why did I ever come down here?" she asked dramatically.

Tobermory immediately accepted the opening.

"Judging by what you said to Mrs. Cornett on the croquet-lawn yesterday, you were out for food. You described the Blemleys as the dullest people to stay with that you knew, but said they were clever enough to employ a first-rate cook; otherwise they'd find it difficult to get any one to come down a second time."

"There's not a word of truth in it! I appeal to Mrs. Cornett – " exclaimed the discomfited Agnes.

"Mrs. Cornett repeated your remark afterwards to Bertie van Tahn," continued Tobermory, "and said, 'That woman is a regular Hunger Marcher; she'd go anywhere for four square meals a day,' and Bertie van Tahn said – "

At this point the chronicle mercifully ceased. Tobermory had caught a glimpse of the big yellow Tom from the Rectory working his way through the shrubbery towards the stable wing. In a flash he had vanished through the open French window.

With the disappearance of his too brilliant pupil Cornelius Appin found himself beset by a hurricane of bitter upbraiding, anxious inquiry, and frightened entreaty. The responsibility for the situation lay with him, and he must prevent matters from becoming worse. Could Tobermory impart his dangerous gift to other cats? was the first question he had to answer. It was possible, he replied, that he might have initiated his intimate friend the stable puss into his new accomplishment, but it was unlikely that his teaching could have taken a wider range as yet.

"Then," said Mrs. Cornett, "Tobermory may be a valuable cat and a great pet; but I'm sure you'll agree, Adelaide, that both he and the stable cat must be done away with without delay."

"You don't suppose I've enjoyed the last quarter of an hour, do you?" said Lady Blemley bitterly. "My husband and I are very fond of Tobermory – at least, we were before this horrible accomplishment was infused into him; but now, of course, the only thing is to have him destroyed as soon as possible."

"We can put some strychnine in the scraps he always gets at dinner-time," said Sir Wilfrid, "and I will go and drown the stable cat myself. The coachman will be very sore at losing his pet, but I'll say a very catching form of mange has broken out in both cats and we're afraid of its spreading to the kennels."

"But my great discovery!" expostulated Mr. Appin; "after all my years of research and experiment – "

"You can go and experiment on the short-horns at the farm, who are under proper control," said Mrs. Cornett, "or the elephants at the Zoological Gardens. They're said to be highly intelligent, and they have this recommendation, that they don't come creeping about our bedrooms and under chairs, and so forth."

An archangel ecstatically proclaiming the Millennium, and then finding that it clashed unpardonably with Henley and would have to be indefinitely postponed, could hardly have felt more crestfallen than Cornelius Appin at the reception of his wonderful achievement. Public opinion, however, was against him – in fact, had the general voice been consulted on the subject it is probable that a strong minority vote would have been in favour of including him in the strychnine diet.

Defective train arrangements and a nervous desire to see matters brought to a finish prevented an immediate dispersal of the party, but dinner that evening was not a social success. Sir Wilfrid had had rather a trying time with the stable cat and subsequently with the coachman. Agnes Resker ostentatiously limited her repast to a morsel of dry toast, which she bit as though it were a personal enemy; while Mavis Pellington maintained a vindictive silence throughout the meal. Lady Blemley kept up a flow of what she hoped was conversation, but her attention was fixed on the doorway. A plateful of carefully dosed fish scraps was in readiness on the sideboard, but sweets and savoury and dessert went their way, and no Tobermory appeared either in the dining-room or kitchen.

The sepulchral dinner was cheerful compared with the subsequent vigil in the smoking-room. Eating and drinking had at least supplied a distraction and cloak to the prevailing embarrassment. Bridge was out of the question in the general tension of nerves and tempers, and after Odo Finsberry had given a lugubrious rendering of "Melisande in the Wood" to a frigid audience, music was tacitly avoided. At eleven the servants went to bed, announcing that the small window in the pantry had been left open as usual for Tobermory's private use. The guests read steadily through the current batch of magazines, and fell back gradually on the "Badminton Library" and bound volumes of Punch. Lady Blemley made periodic visits to the pantry, returning each time with an expression of listless depression which forestalled questioning.

At two o'clock Clovis broke the dominating silence.

"He won't turn up tonight. He's probably in the local newspaper office at the present moment, dictating the first instalment of his reminiscences. Lady What's-her-name's book won't be in it. It will be the event of the day."

Having made this contribution to the general cheerfulness, Clovis went to bed. At long intervals the various members of the house-party followed his example.

The servants taking round the early tea made a uniform announcement in reply to a uniform question. Tobermory had not returned.

Breakfast was, if anything, a more unpleasant function than dinner had been, but before its conclusion the situation was relieved. Tobermory's corpse was brought in from the shrubbery, where a gardener had just discovered it. From the bites on his throat and the yellow fur which coated his claws it was evident that he had fallen in unequal combat with the big Tom from the Rectory.

By midday most of the guests had quitted the Towers, and after lunch Lady Blemley had sufficiently recovered her spirits to write an extremely nasty letter to the Rectory about the loss of her valuable pet.

Tobermory had been Appin's one successful pupil, and he was destined to have no successor. A few weeks later an elephant in the Dresden Zoological Garden, which had shown no previous signs of irritability, broke loose and killed an Englishman who had apparently been teasing it. The victim's name was variously reported in the papers as Oppin and Eppelin, but his front name was faithfully rendered Cornelius.

"If he was trying German irregular verbs on the poor beast," said Clovis, "he deserved all he got."

# Down Pens

### *Saki*

"Have you written to thank the Froplinsons for what they sent us?" asked Egbert.

"No," said Janetta, with a note of tired defiance in her voice; "I've written eleven letters today expressing surprise and gratitude for sundry unmerited gifts, but I haven't written to the Froplinsons."

"Some one will have to write to them," said Egbert.

"I don't dispute the necessity, but I don't think the some one should be me," said Janetta. "I wouldn't mind writing a letter of angry recrimination or heartless satire to some suitable recipient; in fact, I should rather enjoy it, but I've come to the end of my capacity for expressing servile amiability. Eleven letters today and nine yesterday, all couched in the same strain of ecstatic thankfulness: really, you can't expect me to sit down to another. There is such a thing as writing oneself out."

"I've written nearly as many," said Egbert, "and I've had my usual business correspondence to get through, too. Besides, I don't know what it was that the Froplinsons sent us."

"A William the Conqueror calendar," said Janetta, "with a quotation of one of his great thoughts for every day in the year."

"Impossible," said Egbert; "he didn't have three hundred and sixty-five thoughts in the whole of his life, or, if he did, he kept them to himself. He was a man of action, not of introspection."

"Well, it was William Wordsworth, then," said Janetta; "I know William came into it somewhere."

"That sounds more probable," said Egbert; "well, let's collaborate on this letter of thanks and get it done. I'll dictate, and you can scribble it down. 'Dear Mrs. Froplinson — thank you and your husband so much for the very pretty calendar you sent us. It was very good of you to think of us.'"

"You can't possibly say that," said Janetta, laying down her pen.

"It's what I always do say, and what every one says to me," protested Egbert.

"We sent them something on the twenty-second," said Janetta, "so they simply had to think of us. There was no getting away from it."

"What did we send them?" asked Egbert gloomily.

"Bridge-markers," said Janetta, "in a cardboard case, with some inanity about 'digging for fortune with a royal spade' emblazoned on the cover. The moment I saw it in the shop I said to myself 'Froplinsons' and to the attendant 'How much?' When he said 'Ninepence,' I gave him their address, jabbed our card in, paid tenpence or elevenpence to cover the postage, and thanked heaven. With less sincerity and infinitely more trouble they eventually thanked me."

"The Froplinsons don't play bridge," said Egbert.

"One is not supposed to notice social deformities of that sort," said Janetta; "it wouldn't be polite. Besides, what trouble did they take to find out whether we read Wordsworth with gladness? For all they knew or cared we might be frantically embedded in the belief that all poetry begins and ends with John Masefield, and it might infuriate or depress us to have a daily sample of Wordsworthian products flung at us."

"Well, let's get on with the letter of thanks," said Egbert.

"Proceed," said Janetta.

"'How clever of you to guess that Wordsworth is our favourite poet,'" dictated Egbert.

Again Janetta laid down her pen.

"Do you realise what that means?" she asked; "a Wordsworth booklet next Christmas, and another calendar the Christmas after, with the same problem of having to write suitable letters of thankfulness. No, the best thing to do is to drop all further allusion to the calendar and switch off on to some other topic."

"But what other topic?"

"Oh, something like this: 'What do you think of the New Year Honours List? A friend of ours made such a clever remark when he read it.' Then you can stick in any remark that comes into your head; it needn't be clever. The Froplinsons won't know whether it is or isn't."

"We don't even know on which side they are in politics," objected Egbert; "and anyhow you can't suddenly dismiss the subject of the calendar. Surely there must be some intelligent remark that can be made about it."

"Well, we can't think of one," said Janetta wearily; "the fact is, we've both written ourselves out. Heavens! I've just remembered Mrs. Stephen Ludberry. I haven't thanked her for what she sent."

"What did she send?"

"I forget; I think it was a calendar."

There was a long silence, the forlorn silence of those who are bereft of hope and have almost ceased to care.

Presently Egbert started from his seat with an air of resolution. The light of battle was in his eyes.

"Let me come to the writing-table," he exclaimed.

"Gladly," said Janetta. "Are you going to write to Mrs. Ludberry or the Froplinsons?"

"To neither," said Egbert, drawing a stack of notepaper towards him; "I'm going to write to the editor of every enlightened and influential newspaper in the Kingdom, I'm going to suggest that there should be a sort of epistolary Truce of God during the festivities of Christmas and New Year. From the twenty-fourth of December to the third or fourth of January it shall be considered an offence against good sense and good feeling to write or expect any letter or communication that does not deal with the necessary events of the moment. Answers to invitations, arrangements about trains, renewal of club subscriptions, and, of course, all the ordinary everyday affairs of business, sickness, engaging new cooks, and so forth, these will be dealt with in the usual manner as something inevitable, a legitimate part of our daily life. But all the devastating accretions of correspondence, incident to the festive season, these should be swept away to give the season a chance of being really festive, a time of untroubled, unpunctuated peace and good will."

"But you would have to make some acknowledgment of presents received," objected Janetta; "otherwise people would never know whether they had arrived safely."

"Of course, I have thought of that," said Egbert; "every present that was sent off would be accompanied by a ticket bearing the date of dispatch and the signature of the sender, and some conventional hieroglyphic to show that it was intended to be a Christmas or New Year gift; there would be a counterfoil with space for the recipient's name and the date of arrival, and all you would have to do would be to sign and date the counterfoil, add a conventional hieroglyphic indicating heartfelt thanks and gratified surprise, put the thing into an envelope and post it."

"It sounds delightfully simple," said Janetta wistfully, "but people would consider it too cut-and-dried, too perfunctory."

"It is not a bit more perfunctory than the present system," said Egbert; "I have only the same conventional language of gratitude at my disposal with which to thank dear old Colonel Chuttle for his perfectly delicious Stilton, which we shall devour to the last morsel, and the Froplinsons for their calendar, which we shall never look at. Colonel Chuttle knows that we are grateful for the Stilton, without having to be told so, and the Froplinsons know that we are bored with their calendar, whatever we may say to the contrary, just as we know that they are bored with the bridge-markers in spite of their written assurance that they thanked us for our charming little gift. What is more, the Colonel knows that even if we had taken a sudden aversion to Stilton or been forbidden it by the doctor, we should still have written a letter of hearty thanks around it. So you see the present system of acknowledgment is just as perfunctory and conventional as the counterfoil business would be, only ten times more tiresome and brain-racking."

"Your plan would certainly bring the ideal of a Happy Christmas a step nearer realisation," said Janetta.

"There are exceptions, of course," said Egbert, "people who really try to infuse a breath of reality into their letters of acknowledgment. Aunt Susan, for instance, who writes: 'Thank you very much for the ham; not such a good flavour as the one you sent last year, which itself was not a particularly good one. Hams are not what they used to be.' It would be a pity to be deprived of her Christmas comments, but that loss would be swallowed up in the general gain."

"Meanwhile," said Janetta, "what am I to say to the Froplinsons?"

# The Way to the Dairy

***Saki***

The Baroness and Clovis sat in a much-frequented corner of the Park exchanging biographical confidences about the long succession of passers-by.

"Who are those depressed-looking young women who have just gone by?" asked the Baroness; "They have the air of people who have bowed to destiny and are not quite sure whether the salute will be returned."

"Those," said Clovis, "are the Brimley Bomefields. I dare say you would look depressed if you had been through their experiences."

"I'm always having depressing experiences;" said the Baroness, "but I never give them outward expression. It's as bad as looking one's age. Tell me about the Brimley Bomefields."

"Well," said Clovis, "the beginning of their tragedy was that they found an aunt. The aunt had been there all the time, but they had very nearly forgotten her existence until a distant relative refreshed their memory by remembering her very distinctly in his will; it is wonderful what the force of example will accomplish. The aunt, who had been unobtrusively poor, became quite pleasantly rich, and the Brimley Bomefields grew suddenly concerned at the loneliness of her life and took her under their collective wings. She had as many wings around her at this time as one of those beast-things in Revelation."

"So far I don't see any tragedy from the Brimley Bomefields' point of view," said the Baroness.

"We haven't got to it yet," said Clovis. "The aunt had been used to living very simply, and had seen next to nothing of what we should consider life, and her nieces didn't encourage her to do much in the way of making a splash with her money. Quite a good deal of it would come to them at her death, and she was a fairly old woman, but there was one circumstance which cast a shadow of gloom over the satisfaction they felt in the discovery and acquisition of this desirable aunt: she openly acknowledged that a comfortable slice of her little fortune would go to a nephew on the other side of her family. He was rather a deplorable thing in rotters, and quite hopelessly top-hole in the way of getting through money, but he had been more or less decent to the old lady in her unremembered days, and she wouldn't hear anything against him. At least, she wouldn't pay any attention to what she did hear, but her nieces took care that she should have to listen to a good deal in that line. It seemed such a pity, they said among themselves, that good money should fall into such worthless hands. They habitually spoke of their aunt's money as 'good money,' as though other people's aunts dabbled for the most part in spurious currency.

"Regularly after the Derby, St. Leger, and other notable racing events they indulged in audible speculations as to how much money Roger had squandered in unfortunate betting transactions.

"'His travelling expenses must come to a big sum,' said the eldest Brimley Bomefield one day; 'they say he attends every race-meeting in England, besides others abroad. I shouldn't wonder if he went all the way to India to see the race for the Calcutta Sweepstake that one hears so much about.'

"'Travel enlarges the mind, my dear Christine,' said her aunt.

"'Yes, dear aunt, travel undertaken in the right spirit,' agreed Christine; 'but travel pursued merely as a means towards gambling and extravagant living is more likely to contract the purse than to enlarge the mind. However, as long as Roger enjoys himself, I suppose he doesn't care how fast or unprofitably the money goes, or where he is to find more. It seems a pity, that's all.'

"The aunt by that time had begun to talk of something else, and it was doubtful if Christine's moralizing had been even accorded a hearing. It was her remark, however — the aunt's remark, I mean — about travel enlarging the mind, that gave the youngest Brimley Bomefield her great idea for the showing-up of Roger.

"'If aunt could only be taken somewhere to see him gambling and throwing away money,' she said, 'it would open her eyes to his character more effectually than anything we can say.'

"'My dear Veronique,' said her sisters, 'we can't go following him to race-meetings.'

"'Certainly not to race-meetings,' said Veronique, 'but we might go to some place where one can look on at gambling without taking part in it.'

"'Do you mean Monte Carlo?' they asked her, beginning to jump rather at the idea.

"'Monte Carlo is a long way off, and has a dreadful reputation,' said Veronique; 'I shouldn't like to tell our friends that we were going to Monte Carlo. But I believe Roger usually goes to Dieppe about this time of year, and some quite respectable English people go there, and the journey wouldn't be expensive. If aunt could stand the Channel crossing the change of scene might do her a lot of good.'

"And that was how the fateful idea came to the Brimley Bomefields.

"From the very first set-off disaster hung over the expedition, as they afterwards remembered. To begin with, all the Brimley Bomefields were extremely unwell during the crossing, while the aunt enjoyed the sea air and made friends with all manner of strange travelling companions. Then, although it was many years since she had been on the Continent, she had served a very practical apprenticeship there as a paid companion, and her knowledge of colloquial French beat theirs to a standstill. It became increasingly difficult to keep under their collective wings a person who knew what she wanted and was able to ask for it and to see that she got it. Also, as far as Roger was concerned, they drew Dieppe blank; it turned out that he was staying at Pourville, a little watering-place a mile or two further west. The Brimley Bomefields discovered that Dieppe was too crowded and frivolous, and persuaded the old lady to migrate to the comparative seclusion of Pourville.

"'You won't find it dull, you know,' they assured her; 'there is a little casino attached to the hotel, and you can watch the people dancing and throwing away their money at PETITS CHEVAUX.'

"It was just before PETITS CHEVAUX had been supplanted by BOULE.

"Roger was not staying in the same hotel, but they knew that the casino would be certain of his patronage on most afternoons and evenings.

"On the first evening of their visit they wandered into the casino after a fairly early dinner, and hovered near the tables. Bertie van Tahn was staying there at the time, and he described the whole incident to me. The Brimley Bomefields kept a furtive watch on the doors as though they were expecting some one to turn up, and the aunt got more and more amused and interested watching the little horses whirl round and round the board.

"'Do you know, poor little number eight hasn't won for the last thirty-two times,' she said to Christine; 'I've been keeping count. I shall really have to put five francs on him to encourage him.'

"'Come and watch the dancing, dear,' said Christine nervously. It was scarcely a part of their strategy that Roger should come in and find the old lady backing her fancy at the PETITS CHEVAUX table.

"'Just wait while I put five francs on number eight,' said the aunt, and in another moment her money was lying on the table. The horses commenced to move round, it was a slow race this time, and number eight crept up at the finish like some crafty demon and placed his nose just a fraction in front of number three, who had seemed to be winning easily. Recourse had to be had to measurement, and the number eight was proclaimed the winner. The aunt picked up thirty-five francs. After that the Brimley Bomefields would have had to have used concerted force to get her away from the tables. When Roger appeared on the scene she was fifty-two francs to the good; her nieces were hovering forlornly in the background, like chickens that have been hatched out by a duck and are despairingly watching their parent disporting herself in a dangerous and uncongenial element. The supper-party which Roger insisted on standing that night in honour of his aunt and the three Miss Brimley Bomefields was remarkable for the unrestrained gaiety of two of the participants and the funereal mirthlessness of the remaining guests.

"'I do not think,' Christine confided afterwards to a friend, who reconfided it to Bertie van Tahn, 'that I shall ever be able to touch PATÉ DE FOIE GRAS again. It would bring back memories of that awful evening.'

"For the next two or three days the nieces made plans for returning to England or moving on to some other resort where there was no casino. The aunt was busy making a system for winning at PETITS CHEVAUX. Number eight, her first love, had been running rather unkindly for her, and a series of plunges on number five had turned out even worse.

"'Do you know, I dropped over seven hundred francs at the tables this afternoon,' she announced cheerfully at dinner on the fourth evening of their visit.

"'Aunt! Twenty-eight pounds! And you were losing last night too.'

"'Oh, I shall get it all back,' she said optimistically; 'but not here. These silly little horses are no good. I shall go somewhere where one can play comfortably at roulette. You needn't look so shocked. I've always felt that, given the opportunity, I should be an inveterate gambler, and now you darlings have put the opportunity in my way. I must drink your very good healths. Waiter, a bottle of PONTET CANET. Ah, it's number seven on the wine list; I shall plunge on number seven to-night. It won four times running this afternoon when I was backing that silly number five.'

"Number seven was not in a winning mood that evening. The Brimley Bomefields, tired of watching disaster from a distance, drew near to the table where their aunt was now an honoured habituée, and gazed mournfully at the successive victories of one and five and eight and four, which swept 'good money' out of the purse of seven's obstinate backer. The day's losses totalled something very near two thousand francs.

"'You incorrigible gamblers,' said Roger chaffingly to them, when he found them at the tables.

"'We are not gambling,' said Christine freezingly; 'we are looking on.'

"'I DON'T think,' said Roger knowingly; 'of course you're a syndicate and aunt is putting the stakes on for all of you. Anyone can tell by your looks when the wrong horse wins that you've got a stake on.'

"Aunt and nephew had supper alone that night, or at least they would have if Bertie hadn't joined them; all the Brimley

Bomefields had headaches.

"The aunt carried them all off to Dieppe the next day and set cheerily about the task of winning back some of her losses. Her luck was variable; in fact, she had some fair streaks of good fortune, just enough to keep her thoroughly amused with her new distraction; but on the whole she was a loser. The Brimley Bomefields had a collective attack of nervous prostration on the day when she sold out a quantity of shares in Argentine rails. 'Nothing will ever bring that money back,' they remarked lugubriously to one another.

"'Veronique at last could bear it no longer, and went home; you see, it had been her idea to bring the aunt on this disastrous expedition, and though the others did not cast the fact verbally in her face, there was a certain lurking reproach in their eyes which was harder to meet than actual upbraidings. The other two remained behind, forlornly mounting guard over their aunt until such time as the waning of the Dieppe season should at last turn her in the direction of home and safety. They made anxious calculations as to how little 'good money' might, with reasonable luck, be squandered in the meantime. Here, however, their reckoning went far astray; the close of the Dieppe season merely turned their aunt's thoughts in search of some other convenient gambling resort. 'Show a cat the way to the dairy —' I forget how the proverb goes on, but it summed up the situation as far as the Brimley Bomefields' aunt was concerned. She had been introduced to unexplored pleasures, and found them greatly to her liking, and she was in no hurry to forgo the fruits of her newly acquired knowledge. You see, for the first time in her life the old thing was thoroughly enjoying herself; she was losing money, but she had plenty of fun and excitement over the process, and she had enough left to do very comfortably on. Indeed, she was only just learning to understand the art of doing oneself well. She was a popular hostess, and in return her fellow-gamblers were always ready to entertain her to dinners and suppers when their luck was in. Her nieces, who still remained in attendance on her, with the pathetic unwillingness of a crew to leave a foundering treasure ship which might yet be steered into port, found little pleasure in these Bohemian festivities; to see 'good money' lavished on good living for the entertainment of a nondescript circle of acquaintances who were not likely to be in any way socially useful to them, did not attune them to a spirit of revelry. They contrived, whenever possible, to excuse themselves from participation in their aunt's deplored gaieties; the Brimley Bomefield headaches became famous.

"And one day the nieces came to the conclusion that, as they would have expressed it, 'no useful purpose would be served' by their continued attendance on a relative who had so thoroughly emancipated herself from the sheltering protection of their wings. The aunt bore the announcement of their departure with a cheerfulness that was almost disconcerting.

"'It's time you went home and had those headaches seen to by a specialist,' was her comment on the situation.

"The homeward journey of the Brimley Bomefields was a veritable retreat from Moscow, and what made it the more bitter was the fact that the Moscow, in this case, was not overwhelmed with fire and ashes, but merely extravagantly over-illuminated.

"From mutual friends and acquaintances they sometimes get glimpses of their prodigal relative, who has settled down into a confirmed gambling maniac, living on such salvage of income as obliging moneylenders have left at her disposal.

"So you need not be surprised," concluded Clovis, "if they do wear a depressed look in public."

"Which is Veronique?" asked the Baroness.

"The most depressed-looking of the three," said Clovis.

# The Phantom Luncheon

***Saki***

"The Smithly-Dubbs are in Town," said Sir James. "I wish you would show them some attention. Ask them to lunch with you at the Ritz or somewhere."

"From the little I've seen of the Smithly-Dubbs I don't think I want to cultivate their acquaintance," said Lady Drakmanton.

"They always work for us at election times," said her husband; "I don't suppose they influence very many votes, but they have an uncle who is on one of my ward committees, and another uncle speaks sometimes at some of our less important meetings. Those sort of people expect some return in the shape of hospitality."

"Expect it!" exclaimed Lady Drakmanton; "the Misses Smithly-Dubb do more than that; they almost demand it. They belong to my club, and hang about the lobby just about lunch-time, all three of them, with their tongues hanging out of their mouths and the six-course look in their eyes. If I were to breathe the word 'lunch' they would hustle me into a taxi and scream 'Ritz' or 'Dieudonne's' to the driver before I knew what was happening."

"All the same, I think you ought to ask them to a meal of some sort," persisted Sir James.

"I consider that showing hospitality to the Smithly-Dubbs is carrying Free Food principles to a regrettable extreme," said Lady Drakmanton; "I've entertained the Joneses and the Browns and the Snapheimers and the Lubrikoffs, and heaps of others whose names I forget, but I don't see why I should inflict the society of the Misses Smithly-Dubb on myself for a solid hour. Imagine it, sixty minutes, more or less, of unrelenting gobble and gabble. Why can't you take them on, Milly?" she asked, turning hopefully to her sister.

"I don't know them," said Milly hastily.

"All the better; you can pass yourself off as me. People say that we are so alike that they can hardly tell us apart, and I've only spoken to these tiresome young women about twice in my life, at committee-rooms, and bowed to them in the club. Any of the club page-boys will point them out to you; they're always to be found lolling about the hall just before lunch-time."

"My dear Betty, don't be absurd," protested Milly; "I've got some people lunching with me at the Carlton to-morrow, and I'm leaving Town the day afterwards."

"What time is your lunch to-morrow?" asked Lady Drakmanton reflectively.

"Two o'clock," said Milly.

"Good," said her sister; "the Smithly-Dubbs shall lunch with me tomorrow. It shall be rather an amusing lunch-party. At least, I shall be amused."

The last two remarks she made to herself. Other people did not always appreciate her ideas of humour. Sir James never did.

The next day Lady Drakmanton made some marked variations in her usual toilet effects. She dressed her hair in an unaccustomed manner, and put on a hat that added to the transformation of her appearance. When she had made one or two minor alterations she was sufficiently unlike her usual smart self to produce some hesitation in the greeting which the Misses Smithly-Dubb bestowed on her in the club-lobby. She responded, however, with a readiness which set their doubts at rest.

"What is the Carlton like for lunching in?" she asked breezily.

The restaurant received an enthusiastic recommendation from the three sisters.

"Let's go and lunch there, shall we?" she suggested, and in a few minutes' time the Smithly-Dubb mind was contemplating at close quarters a happy vista of baked meats and approved vintage.

"Are you going to start with caviare? I am," confided Lady Drakmanton, and the Smithly-Dubbs started with caviare. The subsequent dishes were chosen in the same ambitious spirit, and by the time they had arrived at the wild duck course it was beginning to be a rather expensive lunch.

The conversation hardly kept pace with the brilliancy of the menu. Repeated references on the part of the guests to the local political conditions and prospects in Sir James's constituency were met with vague "ahs" and "indeeds" from Lady Drakmanton, who might have been expected to be specially interested.

"I think when the Insurance Act is a little better understood it will lose some of its present unpopularity," hazarded Cecilia Smithly-Dubb.

"Will it? I dare say. I'm afraid politics don't interest me very much," said Lady Drakmanton.

The three Miss Smithly-Dubbs put down their cups of Turkish coffee and stared. Then they broke into protesting giggles.

"Of course, you're joking," they said.

"Not me," was the disconcerting answer; "I can't make head or tail of these bothering old politics. Never could, and never want to. I've quite enough to do to manage my own affairs, and that's a fact."

"But," exclaimed Amanda Smithly-Dubb, with a squeal of bewilderment breaking into her voice, "I was told you spoke so informingly about the Insurance Act at one of our social evenings."

It was Lady Drakmanton who stared now. "Do you know," she said, with a scared look around her, "rather a dreadful thing is happening. I'm suffering from a complete loss of memory. I can't even think who I am. I remember meeting you somewhere, and I remember you asking me to come and lunch with you here, and that I accepted your kind invitation. Beyond that my mind is a positive blank."

The scared look was transferred with intensified poignancy to the faces of her companions.

"You asked us to lunch," they exclaimed hurriedly. That seemed a more immediately important point to clear up than the question of identity.

"Oh, no," said the vanishing hostess, "That I do remember about. You insisted on my coming here because the feeding was so good, and I must say it comes up to all you said about it. A very nice lunch it's been. What I'm worrying about is who on earth am I? I haven't the faintest notion?"

"You are Lady Drakmanton," exclaimed the three sisters in chorus.

"Now, don't make fun of me," she replied, crossly, "I happen to know her quite well by sight, and she isn't a bit like me. And it's an odd thing you should have mentioned her, for it so happens she's just come into the room. That lady in black, with the yellow plume in her hat, there over by the door."

The Smithly-Dubbs looked in the indicated direction, and the uneasiness in their eyes deepened into horror. In outward appearance the lady who had just entered the room certainly came rather nearer to their recollection of their Member's wife than the individual who was sitting at table with them.

"Who are you, then, if that is Lady Drakmanton?" they asked in panic-stricken bewilderment.

"That is just what I don't know," was the answer; "and you don't seem to know much better than I do."

"You came up to us in the club – "

"In what club?"

"The New Didactic, in Calais Street."

"The New Didactic!" exclaimed Lady Drakmanton with an air of returning illumination; "thank you so much. Of course, I remember now who I am. I'm Ellen Niggle, of the Ladies' Brasspolishing Guild. The Club employs me to come now and then and see to the polishing of the brass fittings. That's how I came to know Lady Drakmanton by sight; she's very often in the Club. And you are the ladies who so kindly asked me out to lunch. Funny how it should all have slipped my memory, all of a sudden. The unaccustomed good food and wine must have been too much for me; for the moment I really couldn't call to mind who I was. Good gracious," she broke off suddenly, "it's ten past two; I should be at a polishing job in Whitehall. I must scuttle off like a giddy rabbit. Thanking you ever so."

She left the room with a scuttle sufficiently suggestive of the animal she had mentioned, but the giddiness was all on the side of her involuntary hostesses. The restaurant seemed to be spinning round them; and the bill when it appeared did nothing to restore their composure. They were as nearly in tears as it is permissible to be during the luncheon hour in a really good restaurant. Financially speaking, they were well able to afford the luxury of an elaborate lunch, but their ideas on the subject of entertaining differed very sharply, according to the circumstances of whether they were dispensing or receiving hospitality. To have fed themselves liberally at their own expense was, perhaps, an extravagance to be deplored, but, at any rate, they had had something for their money; to have drawn an unknown and socially unremunerative Ellen Niggle into the net of their hospitality was a catastrophe that they could not contemplate with any degree of calmness.

The Smithly-Dubbs never quite recovered from their unnerving experience. They have given up politics and taken to doing good.

# A Young Turkish Catastrophe in Two Scenes

***Saki***

The Minister for Fine Arts (to whose Department had been lately added the new sub-section of Electoral Engineering) paid a business visit to the Grand Vizier. According to Eastern etiquette they discoursed for a while on indifferent subjects. The minister only checked himself in time from making a passing reference to the Marathon Race, remembering that the Vizier had a Persian grandmother and might consider any allusion to Marathon as somewhat tactless. Presently the Minister broached the subject of his interview.

"Under the new Constitution are women to have votes?" he asked suddenly.

"To have votes? Women?" exclaimed the Vizier in some astonishment. "My dear Pasha, the New Departure has a flavour of the absurd as it is; don't let's try and make it altogether ridiculous. Women have no souls and no intelligence; why on earth should they have votes?"

"I know it sounds absurd," said the Minister, "but they are seriously considering the idea in the West."

"Then they must have a larger equipment of seriousness than I gave them credit for. After a lifetime of specialised effort in maintaining my gravity I can scarcely restrain an inclination to smile at the suggestion. Why, out womenfolk in most cases don't know how to read or write. How could they perform the operation of voting?"

"They could be shown the names of the candidates and where to make their cross."

"I beg your pardon?" interrupted the Vizier.

"Their crescent, I mean," corrected the Minister. "It would

be to the liking of the Young Turkish Party," he added.

"Oh, well," said the Vizier, "if we are to do the thing at all we may as well go the whole h- " he pulled up just as he was uttering the name of an unclean animal, and continued, "the complete camel. I will issue instructions that womenfolk are to have votes."

* * *

The poll was drawing to a close in the Lakoumistan division. The candidate of the Young Turkish Party was known to be three or four hundred votes ahead, and he was already drafting his address, returning thanks to the electors. His victory had been almost a foregone conclusion, for he had set in motion all the approved electioneering machinery of the West. He had even employed motorcars. Few of his supporters had gone to the poll in these vehicles, but, thanks to the intelligent driving of his chauffeurs, many of his opponents had gone to their graves or to the local hospitals, or otherwise abstained from voting. And then something unlooked-for happened. The rival candidate, Ali the Blest, arrived on the scene with his wives and womenfolk, who numbered, roughly, six hundred. Ali had wasted little effort on election literature, but had been heard to remark that every vote given to his opponent meant another sack thrown into the Bosphorus. The Young Turkish candidate, who had conformed to the Western custom of one wife and hardly any mistresses, stood by helplessly while his adversary's poll swelled to a triumphant majority.

"Cristabel Columbus!" he exclaimed, invoking in some confusion the name of a distinguished pioneer; "who would have thought it?"

"Strange," mused Ali, "that one who harangued so clamorously about the Secret Ballot should have overlooked the Veiled Vote."

And, walking homeward with his constituents, he murmured in his beard an improvisation on the heretic poet of Persia:

"One, rich in metaphors, his cause contrives to urge with edged words, like Kabul knives; And I, who worst him in this sorry game, Was never rich in anything but–wives."

# The Sex That Doesn't Shop

***Saki***

The opening of a large new centre for West End shopping, particularly feminine shopping, suggests the reflection, Do women ever really shop? Of course, it is a well-attested fact that they go forth shopping as assiduously as a bee goes flower-visiting, but do they shop in the practical sense of the word? Granted the money, time, and energy, a resolute course of shopping transactions would naturally result in having one's ordinary domestic needs unfailingly supplied, whereas it is notorious that women servants (and housewives of all classes) make it almost a point of honour not to be supplied with everyday necessities. "We shall be out of starch by Thursday," they say with fatalistic foreboding, and by Thursday they are out of starch. They have predicted almost to a minute the moment when their supply would give out and if Thursday happens to be early closing day their triumph is complete. A shop where starch is stored for retail purposes possibly stands at their very door, but the feminine mind has rejected such an obvious source for replenishing a dwindling stock. "We don't deal there" places it at once beyond the pale of human resort. And it is noteworthy that, just as a sheep-worrying dog seldom molests the flocks in his near neighbourhood, so a woman rarely deals with shops in her immediate vicinity. The more remote the source of supply the more fixed seems to be the resolve to run short of the commodity. The Ark had probably not quitted its last moorings five minutes before some feminine voice gloatingly recorded a shortage of bird-seed. A few days ago two lady acquaintances of mine were confessing to some mental uneasiness because a friend had called just before lunch- time, and they had been unable to ask her to stop and share their meal, as (with a touch of legitimate pride) "there was nothing in the house." I pointed out that they lived in a street that bristled with provision shops and that it would have been easy to mobilise a very passable luncheon in less than five minutes. "That," they said with quiet dignity, "would not have occurred to us," and I felt that I had suggested something bordering on the indecent.

But it is in catering for her literary wants that a woman's shopping capacity breaks down most completely. If you have perchance produced a book which has met with some little measure of success, you are certain to get a letter from some lady whom you scarcely known to bow to, asking you "how it can be got." She knows the name of the book, its author, and who published it, but how to get into actual contact with it is still an unsolved problem to her. You write back pointing out that to have recourse to an ironmonger or a corn-dealer will only entail delay and disappointment, and suggest an application to a bookseller as the most hopeful thing you can think of. In a day or two she writes again: "It is all right; I have borrowed it from your aunt." Here, of course, we have an example of the Beyond-Shopper, one who has learned the Better Way, but the helplessness exists even when such bypaths of relief are closed. A lady who lives in the West End was expressing to me the other day her interest in West Highland terriers, and her desire to know more about the breed, so when, a few days later, I came across an exhaustive article on that subject in the current number of one of our best known outdoor-life weeklies, I mentioned that circumstance in a letter, giving the date of that number. "I cannot get the paper," was her telephoned response. And she couldn't. She lived in a city where newsagents are numbered, I suppose, by the thousand, and she must have passed dozens of such shops in her daily shopping excursions, but as far as she was concerned that article on West Highland terriers might as well have been written in a missal stored away in some Buddhist monastery in Eastern Thibet.

The brutal directness of the masculine shopper arouses a certain combative derision in the feminine onlooker. A cat that spreads one shrew-mouse over the greater part of a long summer afternoon, and then possibly loses him, doubtless feels the same contempt for the terrier who compresses his rat into ten seconds of the strenuous life. I was finishing off a short list of purchases a few afternoons ago when I was discovered by a lady of my acquaintance whom, swerving aside from the lead given us by her godparents thirty years ago, we will call Agatha.

"You're surely not buying blotting-paper HERE?" she exclaimed in an agitated whisper, and she seemed so genuinely concerned that I stayed my hand.

"Let me take you to Winks and Pinks," she said as soon as we were out of the building: "they've got such lovely shades of blotting- paper – pearl and heliotrope and momie and crushed – "

"But I want ordinary white blotting-paper," I said.

"Never mind. They know me at Winks and Pinks," she replied inconsequently. Agatha apparently has an idea that blotting-paper is only sold in small quantities to persons of known reputation, who may be trusted not to put it to dangerous or improper uses. After walking some two hundred yards she began to feel that her tea was of more immediate importance than my blotting-paper.

"What do you want blotting-paper for?" she asked suddenly. I explained patiently.

"I use it to dry up the ink of wet manuscript without smudging the writing. Probably a Chinese invention of the second century before Christ, but I'm not sure. The only other use for it that I can think of is to roll it into a ball for a kitten to play with."

"But you haven't got a kitten," said Agatha, with a feminine desire for stating the entire truth on most occasions.

"A stray one might come in at any moment," I replied.

Anyway, I didn't get the blotting-paper.

Reginald in Russia – Saki

Reginald sat in a corner of the Princess's salon and tried to forgive the furniture, which started out with an obvious intention of being Louis Quinze, but relapsed at frequent intervals into Wilhelm II.

He classified the Princess with that distinct type of woman that looks as if it habitually went out to feed hens in the rain.

Her name was Olga; she kept what she hoped and believed to be a fox- terrier, and professed what she thought were Socialist opinions. It is not necessary to be called Olga if you are a Russian Princess; in fact, Reginald knew quite a number who were called Vera; but the fox-terrier and the Socialism are essential.

"The Countess Lomshen keeps a bull-dog," said the Princess suddenly. "In England is it more chic to have a bull-dog than a fox-terrier?"

Reginald threw his mind back over the canine fashions of the last ten years and gave an evasive answer.

"Do you think her handsome, the Countess Lomshen?" asked the Princess.

Reginald thought the Countess's complexion suggested an exclusive diet of macaroons and pale sherry. He said so.

"But that cannot be possible," said the Princess triumphantly; "I've seen her eating fish-soup at Donon's."

The Princess always defended a friend's complexion if it was really bad. With her, as with a great many of her sex, charity began at homeliness and did not generally progress much farther.

Reginald withdrew his macaroon and sherry theory, and became interested in a case of miniatures.

"That?" said the Princess; "that is the old Princess Lorikoff. She lived in Millionaya Street, near the Winter Palace, and was one of the Court ladies of the old Russian school. Her knowledge of people and events was extremely limited; but she used to patronise every one who came in contact with her. There was a story that when she died and left the Millionaya for Heaven she addressed St. Peter in her formal staccato French: 'Je suis la Princesse Lor-i-koff. Il me donne grand plaisir a faire votre connaissance. Je vous en prie me presenter au Bon Dieu.' St. Peter made the desired introduction, and the Princess addressed le Bon Dieu: 'Je suis la Princesse Lor- i-koff. Il me donne grand plaisir a faire votre connaissance. On a souvent parle de vous a l'eglise de la rue Million.'"

"Only the old and the clergy of Established churches know how to be flippant gracefully," commented Reginald; "which reminds me that in the Anglican Church in a certain foreign capital, which shall be nameless, I was present the other day when one of the junior chaplains was preaching in aid of distressed somethings or other, and he brought a really eloquent passage to a close with the remark, 'The tears of the afflicted, to what shall I liken them – to diamonds?' The other junior chaplain, who had been dozing out of professional jealousy, awoke with a start and asked hurriedly, 'Shall I play to diamonds, partner?' It didn't improve matters when the senior chaplain remarked dreamily but with painful distinctness, 'Double diamonds.' Every one looked at the preacher, half expecting him to redouble, but he contented himself with scoring what points he could under the circumstances."

"You English are always so frivolous," said the Princess. "In Russia we have too many troubles to permit of our being lighthearted."

Reginald gave a delicate shiver, such as an Italian greyhound might give in contemplating the approach of an ice age of which he personally disapproved, and resigned himself to the inevitable political discussion.

"Nothing that you hear about us in England is true," was the Princess's hopeful beginning.

"I always refused to learn Russian geography at school," observed Reginald; "I was certain some of the names must be wrong."

"Everything is wrong with our system of government," continued the Princess placidly. "The Bureaucrats think only of their pockets, and the people are exploited and plundered in every direction, and everything is mismanaged."

"With us," said Reginald, "a Cabinet usually gets the credit of being depraved and worthless beyond the bounds of human conception by the time it has been in office about four years."

"But if it is a bad Government you can turn it out at the elections," argued the Princess.

"As far as I remember, we generally do," said Reginald.

"But here it is dreadful, every one goes to such extremes. In England you never go to extremes."

"We go to the Albert Hall," explained Reginald.

"There is always a see-saw with us between repression and violence," continued the Princess; "and the pity of it is the people are really not in the least inclined to be anything but peaceable. Nowhere will you find people more good-natured, or family circles where there is more affection."

"There I agree with you," said Reginald. "I know a boy who lives somewhere on the French Quay who is a case in point. His hair curls naturally, especially on Sundays, and he plays bridge well, even for a Russian, which is saying much. I don't think he has any other accomplishments, but his family affection is really of a very high order. When his maternal grandmother died he didn't go as far as to give up bridge altogether, but he declared on nothing but black suits for the next three months. That, I think, was really beautiful."

The Princess was not impressed.

"I think you must be very self-indulgent and live only for amusement," she said, "a life of pleasure-seeking and card-playing and dissipation brings only dissatisfaction. You will find that out some day."

"Oh, I know it turns out that way sometimes," assented Reginald. "Forbidden fizz is often the sweetest."

But the remark was wasted on the Princess, who preferred champagne that had at least a suggestion of dissolved barley-sugar.

"I hope you will come and see me again," she said, in a tone that prevented the hope from becoming too infectious; adding as a happy afterthought, "you must come to stay with us in the country."

Her particular part of the country was a few hundred versts the other side of Tamboff, with some fifteen miles of agrarian disturbance between her and the nearest neighbour. Reginald felt that there is some privacy which should be sacred from intrusion.

# Agafya

***Anton Chekov***

During my stay in the district of S. I often used to go to see the watchman Savva Stukatch, or simply Savka, in the kitchen gardens of Dubovo. These kitchen gardens were my favorite resort for so-called "mixed" fishing, when one goes out without knowing what day or hour one may return, taking with one every sort of fishing tackle as well as a store of provisions. To tell the truth, it was not so much the fishing that attracted me as the peaceful stroll, the meals at no set time, the talk with Savka, and being for so long face to face with the calm summer nights. Savka was a young man of five-and-twenty, well grown and handsome, and as strong as a flint. He had the reputation of being a sensible and reasonable fellow. He could read and write, and very rarely drank, but as a workman this strong and healthy young man was not worth a farthing. A sluggish, overpowering sloth was mingled with the strength in his muscles, which were strong as cords. Like everyone else in his village, he lived in his own hut, and had his share of land, but neither tilled it nor sowed it, and did not work at any sort of trade. His old mother begged alms at people's windows and he himself lived like a bird of the air; he did not know in the morning what he would eat at midday. It was not that he was lacking in will, or energy, or feeling for his mother; it was simply that he felt no inclination for work and did not recognize the advantage of it. His whole figure suggested unruffled serenity, an innate, almost artistic passion for living carelessly, never with his sleeves tucked up. When Savka's young, healthy body had a physical craving for muscular work, the young man abandoned himself completely for a brief interval to some free but nonsensical pursuit, such as sharpening skates not wanted for any special purpose, or racing about after the peasant women. His favorite attitude was one of concentrated immobility. He was capable of standing for hours at a stretch in the same place with his eyes fixed on the same spot without stirring. He never moved except on impulse, and then only when an occasion presented itself for some rapid and abrupt action: catching a running dog by the tail, pulling off a woman's k erchief, or jumping over a big hole. It need hardly be said that with such parsimony of movement Savka was as poor as a mouse and lived worse than any homeless outcast. As time went on, I suppose he accumulated arrears of taxes and, young and sturdy as he was, he was sent by the commune to do an old man's job – to be watchman and scarecrow in the kitchen gardens. However much they laughed at him for his premature senility he did not object to it. This position, quiet and convenient for motionless contemplation, exactly fitted his temperament.

It happened I was with this Savka one fine May evening. I remember I was lying on a torn and dirty sackcloth cover close to the shanty from which came a heavy, fragrant scent of hay. Clasping my hands under my head I looked before me. At my feet was lying a wooden fork. Behind it Savka's dog Kutka stood out like a black patch, and not a dozen feet from Kutka the ground ended abruptly in the steep bank of the little river. Lying down I could not see the river; I could only see the tops of the young willows growing thickly on the nearer bank, and the twisting, as it were gnawed away, edges of the opposite bank. At a distance beyond the bank on the dark hillside the huts of the village in which Savka lived lay huddling together like frightened young partridges. Beyond the hill the afterglow of sunset still lingered in the sky. One pale crimson streak was all that was left, and even that began to be covered by little clouds as a fire with ash.

A copse with alder-trees, softly whispering, and from time to time shuddering in the fitful breeze, lay, a dark blur, on the right of the kitchen gardens; on the left stretched the immense plain. In the distance, where the eye could not distinguish between the sky and the plain, there was a bright gleam of light. A little way off from me sat Savka. With his legs tucked under him like a Turk and his head hanging, he looked pensively at Kutka. Our hooks with live bait on them had long been in the river, and we had nothing left to do but to abandon ourselves to repose, which Savka, who was never exhausted and always rested, loved so much. The glow had not yet quite died away, but the summer night was already enfolding nature in its caressing, soothing embrace.

Everything was sinking into its first deep sleep except some night bird unfamiliar to me, which indolently uttered a long, protracted cry in several distinct notes like the phrase, "Have you seen Ni-ki-ta?" and immediately answered itself, "Seen him, seen him, seen him!"

"Why is it the nightingales aren't singing tonight?" I asked Savka.

He turned slowly towards me. His features were large, but his face was open, soft, and expressive as a woman's. Then he gazed with his mild, dreamy eyes at the copse, at the willows, slowly pulled a whistle out of his pocket, put it in his mouth and whistled the note of a hen-nightingale. And at once, as though in answer to his call, a landrail called on the opposite bank.

"There's a nightingale for you ..." laughed Savka. "Drag-drag! drag-drag! just like pulling at a hook, and yet I bet he thinks he is singing, too."

"I like that bird," I said. "Do you know, when the birds are migrating the landrail does not fly, but runs along the ground? It only flies over the rivers and the sea, but all the rest it does on foot."

"Upon my word, the dog ..." muttered Savka, looking with respect in the direction of the calling landrail.

Knowing how fond Savka was of listening, I told him all I had learned about the landrail from sportsman's books. From the landrail I passed imperceptibly to the migration of the birds. Savka listened attentively, looking at me without blinking, and smiling all the while with pleasure.

"And which country is most the bird's home? Ours or those foreign parts?" he asked.

"Ours, of course. The bird itself is hatched here, and it hatches out its little ones here in its native country, and they only fly off there to escape being frozen."

"It's interesting," said Savka. "Whatever one talks about it is always interesting. Take a bird now, or a man ... or take this little stone; there's something to learn about all of them ... Ah, sir, if I had known you were coming I wouldn't have told a woman to come here this evening ... She asked to come to-day."

"Oh, please don't let me be in your way," I said. "I can lie down in the wood ..."

"What next! She wouldn't have died if she hadn't come till to-morrow ... If only she would sit quiet and listen, but she always wants to be slobbering ... You can't have a good talk when she's here."

"Are you expecting Darya?" I asked, after a pause.

"No ... a new one has asked to come this evening ... Agafya, the signalman's wife."

Savka said this in his usual passionless, somewhat hollow voice, as though he were talking of tobacco or porridge, while I started with surprise. I knew Agafya ... She was quite a young peasant woman of nineteen or twenty, who had been married not more than a year before to a railway signalman, a fine young fellow. She lived in the village, and her husband came home there from the line every night.

"Your goings on with the women will lead to trouble, my boy," said I.

"Well, may be ..."

And after a moment's thought Savka added:

"I've said so to the women; they won't heed me ... They don't trouble about it, the silly things!"

Silence followed ... Meanwhile the darkness was growing thicker and thicker, and objects began to lose their contours. The streak behind the hill had completely died away, and the stars were growing brighter and more luminous ... The mournfully monotonous chirping of the grasshoppers, the call of the landrail, and the cry of the quail did not destroy the stillness of the night, but, on the contrary, gave it an added monotony. It seemed as though the soft sounds that enchanted the ear came, not from birds or insects, but from the stars looking down upon us from the sky ...

Savka was the first to break the silence. He slowly turned his eyes from black Kutka and said,

"I see you are dull, sir. Let's have supper."

And without waiting for my consent he crept on his stomach into the shanty, rummaged about there, making the whole edifice tremble like a leaf; then he crawled back and set before me my vodka and an earthenware bowl; in the bowl there were baked eggs, lard scones made of rye, pieces of black bread, and something else ... We had a drink from a little crooked glass that wouldn't stand, and then we fell upon the food ... Coarse grey salt, dirty, greasy cakes, eggs tough as india-rubber, but how nice it all was!

"You live all alone, but what lots of good things you have," I said, pointing to the bowl. "Where do you get them from?"

"The women bring them," mumbled Savka.

"What do they bring them to you for?"

"Oh ... from pity."

Not only Savka's menu, but his clothing, too, bore traces of feminine "pity." Thus I noticed that he had on, that evening, a new woven belt and a crimson ribbon on which a copper cross hung round his dirty neck. I knew of the weakness of the fair sex for Savka, and I knew that he did not like talking about it, and so I did not carry my inquiries any further. Besides there was not time to talk ... Kutka, who had been fidgeting about near us and patiently waiting for scraps, suddenly pricked up his ears and growled. We heard in the distance repeated splashing of water.

"Someone is coming by the ford," said Savka.

Three minutes later Kutka growled again and made a sound like a cough.

"Shsh!" his master shouted at him.

In the darkness there was a muffled thud of timid footsteps, and the silhouette of a woman appeared out of the copse. I recognized her, although it was dark – it was Agafya. She came up to us diffidently and stopped, breathing hard. She was breathless, probably not so much from walking as from fear and the unpleasant sensation everyone experiences in wading across a river at night. Seeing near the shanty not one but two persons, she uttered a faint cry and fell back a step.

"Ah ... that is you!" said Savka, stuffing a scone into his mouth.

"Ye-es ... I," she mutte red, dropping on the ground a bundle of some sort and looking sideways at me. "Yakov sent his greetings to you and told me to give you ... something here ..."

"Come, why tell stories? Yakov!" laughed Savka. "There is no need for lying; the gentleman knows why you have come! Sit down; you shall have supper with us."

Agafya looked sideways at me and sat down irresolutely.

"I thought you weren't coming this evening," Savka said, after a prolonged silence. "Why sit like that? Eat! Or shall I give you a drop of vodka?"

"What an idea!" laughed Agafya; "do you think you have got hold of a drunkard? ..."

"Oh, drink it up ... Your heart will feel warmer ... There!"

Savka gave Agafya the crooked glass. She slowly drank the vodka, ate nothing with it, but drew a deep breath when she had finished.

"You've brought something," said Savka, untying the bundle and throwing a condescending, jesting shade into his voice. "Women can never come without bringing something. Ah, pie and potatoes ... They live well," he sighed, turning to me. "They are the only ones in the whole village who have got potatoes left from the winter!"

In the darkness I did not see Agafya's face, but from the movement of her shoulders and head it seemed to me that she could not take her eyes off Savka's face. To avoid being the third person at this tryst, I decided to go for a walk and got up. But at that moment a nightingale in the wood suddenly uttered two low contralto notes. Half a minute later it gave a tiny high trill and then, having thus tried its voice, began singing. Savka jumped up and listened.

"It's the same one as yesterday," he said. "Wait a minute."

And, getting up, he went noiselessly to the wood.

"Why, what do you want with it?" I shouted out after him, "Stop!"

Savka shook his hand as much as to say, "Don't shout," and vanished into the darkness. Savka was an excellent sportsman and fisherman when he liked, but his talents in this direction were as completely thrown away as his strength. He was too slothful to do things in the routine way, and vented his passion for sport in useless tricks. For instance, he would catch nightingales only with his hands, would shoot pike with a fowling piece, he would spend whole hours by the river trying to catch little fish with a big hook.

Left alone with me, Agafya coughed and passed her hand several times over her forehead ... She began to feel a little drunk from the vodka.

"How are you getting on, Agasha?" I asked her, after a long silence, when it began to be awkward to remain mute any longer.

"Very well, thank God ... Don't tell anyone, sir, will you?" she added suddenly in a whisper.

"That's all right," I reassured her. "But how reckless you are, Agasha! ... What if Yakov finds out?"

"He won't find out."

But what if he does?"

"No ... I shall be at home before he is. He is on the line now, and he will come back when the mail train brings him, and from here I can hear when the train's coming ..."

Agafya once more passed her hand over her forehead and looked away in the direction in which Savka had vanished. The nightingale was singing. Some night bird flew low down close to the ground and, noticing us, was startled, fluttered its wings and flew across to the other side of the river.

Soon the nightingale was silent, but Savka did not come back. Agafya got up, took a few steps uneasily, and sat down again.

"What is he doing?" she could not refrain from saying. "The train's not coming in to-morrow! I shall have to go away directly."

"Savka," I shouted. "Savka."

I was not answered even by an echo. Agafya moved uneasily and sat down again.

"It's time I was going," she said in an agitated voice. "The train will be here directly! I know when the trains come in."

The poor woman was not mistaken. Before a quarter of an hour had passed a sound was heard in the distance.

Agafya kept her eyes fixed on the copse for a long time and moved her hands impatiently.

"Why, where can he be?" she said, laughing nervously. "Where has the devil carried him? I am going! I really must be going."

Meanwhile the noise was growing more and more distinct.

By now one could distinguish the rumble of the wheels from the heavy gasps of the engine. Then we heard the whistle, the train crossed the bridge with a hollow rumble ... another minute and all was still.

"I'll wait one minute more," said Agafya, sitting down resolutely. "So be it, I'll wait."

At last Savka appeared in the darkness. He walked noiselessly on the crumbling earth of the kitchen gardens and hummed something softly to himself.

"Here's a bit of luck; what do you say to that now?" he said gaily. "As soon as I got up to the bush and began taking aim with my hand it left off singing! Ah, the bald dog! I waited and waited to see when it would begin again, but I had to give it up."

Savka flopped clumsily down to the ground beside Agafya and, to keep his balance, clutched at her waist with both hands.

"Why do you look cross, as though your aunt were your mother?" he asked.

With all his soft-heartedness and good-nature, Savka despised women. He behaved carelessly, condescendingly with them, and even stooped to scornful laughter of their feelings for himself. God knows, perhaps this careless, contemptuous manner was one of the causes of his irresistible attraction for the village Dulcineas. He was handsome and well-built; in his eyes there was always a soft friendliness, even when he was looking at the women he so despised, but the fascination was not to be explained by merely external qualities. Apart from his happy exterior and original manner, one must suppose that the touching position of Savka as an acknowledged failure and an unhappy exile from his own hut to the kitchen gardens also had an influence upon the women.

"Tell the gentleman what you have come here for!" Savka went on, still holding Agafya by the waist. "Come, tell him, you good married woman! Ho-ho! Shall we have another drop of vodka, friend Agasha?"

I got up and, threading my way between the plots, I walked the length of the kitchen garden. The dark beds looked like flattened-out graves. They smelt of dug earth and the tender dampness of plants beginning to be covered with dew ... A red light was still gleaming on the left. It winked genially and seemed to smile.

I heard a happy laugh. It was Agafya laughing.

"And the train?" I thought. "The train has come in long ago."

Waiting a little longer, I went back to the shanty. Savka was sitting motionless, his legs crossed like a Turk, and was softly, scarcely audibly humming a song consisting of words of one syllable something like: "Out on you, fie on you ... I and you." Agafya, intoxicated by the vodka, by Savka's scornful caresses, and by the stifling warmth of the night, was lying on the earth beside him, pressing her face convulsively to his knees. She was so carried away by her feelings that she did not even notice my arrival.

"Agasha, the train has been in a long time," I said.

"It's time – it's time you were gone," Savka, tossing his head, took up my thought. "What are you sprawling here for? You shameless hussy!"

Agafya started, took her head from his knees, glanced at me, and sank down beside him again.

"You ought to have gone long ago," I said.

Agafya turned round and got up on one knee ... She was unhappy ... For half a minute her whole figure, as far as I could distinguish it through the darkness, expressed conflict and hesitation. There was an instant when, seeming to come to herself, she drew herself up to get upon her feet, but then some invincible and implacable force seemed to push her whole body, and she sank down beside Savka again.

"Bother him!" she said, with a wild, guttural laugh, and reckless determination, impotence, and pain could be heard in that laugh.

I strolled quietly away to the copse, and from there down to the river, where our fishing lines were set. The river slept. Some soft, fluffy-petalled flower on a tall stalk touched my cheek tenderly like a child who wants to let one know it's awake. To pass the time I felt for one of the lines and pulled at it. It yielded e asily and hung limply – nothing had been caught ... The further bank and the village could not be seen. A light gleamed in one hut, but soon went out. I felt my way along the bank, found a hollow place which I had noticed in the daylight, and sat down in it as in an arm-chair. I sat there a long time ... I saw the stars begin to grow misty and lose their brightness; a cool breath passed over the earth like a faint sigh and touched the leaves of the slumbering osiers ...

"A-ga-fya!" a hollow voice called from the village. "Agafya!"

It was the husband, who had returned home, and in alarm was looking for his wife in the village. At that moment there came the sound of unrestrained laughter: the wife, forgetful of everything, sought in her intoxication to make up by a few hours of happiness for the misery awaiting her next day.

I dropped asleep.

When I woke up Savka was sitting beside me and lightly shaking my shoulder. The river, the copse, both banks, green and washed, trees and fields – all were bathed in bright morning light. Through the slim trunks of the trees the rays of the newly risen sun beat upon my back.

"So that's how you catch fish?" laughed Savka. "Get up!"

I got up, gave a luxurious stretch, and began greedily drinking in the damp and fragrant air.

"Has Agasha gone?" I asked.

"There she is," said Savka, pointing in the direction of the ford.

I glanced and saw Agafya. Dishevelled, with her kerchief dropping off her head, she was crossing the river, holding up her skirt. Her legs were scarcely moving ...

"The cat knows whose meat it has eaten," muttered Savka, screwing up his eyes as he looked at her. "She goes with her tail hanging down ... They are sly as cats, these women, and timid as hares ... She didn't go, silly thing, in the evening when we told her to! Now she will catch it, and they'll flog me again at the peasant court ... all on account of the women ..."

Agafya stepped upon the bank and went across the fields to the village. At first she walked fairly boldly, but soon terror and excitement got the upper hand; she turned round fearfully, stopped and took breath.

"Yes, you are frightened!" Savka laughed mournfully, looking at the bright green streak left by Agafya in the dewy grass. "She doesn't want to go! Her husband's been standing waiting for her for a good hour ... Did you see him?"

Savka said the last words with a smile, but they sent a chill to my heart. In the village, near the furthest hut, Yakov was standing in the road, gazing fixedly at his returning wife. He stood without stirring, and was as motionless as a post. What was he thinking as he looked at her? What words was he preparing to greet her with? Agafya stood still a little while, looked round once more as though expecting help from us, and went on. I have never seen anyone, drunk or sober, move as she did. Agafya seemed to be shrivelled up by her husband's eyes. At one time she moved in zigzags, then she moved her feet up and down without going forward, bending her knees and stretching out her hands, then she staggered back. When she had gone another hundred paces she looked round once more and sat down.

"You ought at least to hide behind a bush ..." I said to Savka. "If the husband sees you ..."

"He knows, anyway, who it is Agafya has come from ... The women don't go to the kitchen garden at night for cabbages – we all know that."

I glanced at Savka's face. It was pale and puckered up with a look of fastidious pity such as one sees in the faces of people watching tortured animals.

"What's fun for the cat is tears for the mouse ..." he muttered.

Agafya suddenly jumped up, shook her head, and with a bold step went towards her husband. She had evidently plucked up her courage and made up her mind.

# About Love

### *Anton Chekhov*

At lunch next day there were very nice pies, crayfish, and mutton cutlets; and while we were eating, Nikanor, the cook, came up to ask what the visitors would like for dinner. He was a man of medium height, with a puffy face and little eyes; he was close-shaven, and it looked as though his moustaches had not been shaved, but had been pulled out by the roots. Alehin told us that the beautiful Pelagea was in love with this cook. As he drank and was of a violent character, she did not want to marry him, but was willing to live with him without. He was very devout, and his religious convictions would not allow him to "live in sin"; he insisted on her marrying him, and would consent to nothing else, and when he was drunk he used to abuse her and even beat her. Whenever he got drunk she used to hide upstairs and sob, and on such occasions Alehin and the servants stayed in the house to be ready to defend her in case of necessity.

We began talking about love.

"How love is born," said Alehin, "why Pelagea does not love somebody more like herself in her spiritual and external qualities, and why she fell in love with Nikanor, that ugly snout – we all call him 'The Snout' – how far questions of personal happiness are of consequence in love – all that is known; one can take what view one likes of it. So far only one incontestable truth has been uttered about love: 'This is a great mystery.' Everything else that has been written or said about love is not a conclusion, but only a statement of questions which have remained unanswered. The explanation which would seem to fit one case does not apply in a dozen others, and the very best thing, to my mind, would be to explain every case individually without attempting to generalize. We ought, as the doctors say, to individualize each case."

"Perfectly true," Burkin assented.

"We Russians of the educated class have a partiality for these questions that remain unanswered. Love is usually poeticized, decorated with roses, nightingales; we Russians decorate our loves with these momentous questions, and select the most uninteresting of them, too. In Moscow, when I was a student, I had a friend who shared my life, a charming lady, and every time I took her in my arms she was thinking what I would allow her a month for housekeeping and what was the price of beef a pound. In the same way, when we are in love we are never tired of asking ourselves questions: whether it is honourable or dishonourable, sensible or stupid, what this love is leading up to, and so on. Whether it is a good thing or not I don't know, but that it is in the way, unsatisfactory, and irritating, I do know."

It looked as though he wanted to tell some story. People who lead a solitary existence always have something in their hearts which they are eager to talk about. In town bachelors visit the baths and the restaurants on purpose to talk, and sometimes tell the most interesting things to bath attendants and waiters; in the country, as a rule, they unbosom themselves to their guests. Now from the window we could see a grey sky, trees drenched in the rain; in such weather we could go nowhere, and there was nothing for us to do but to tell stories and to listen.

"I have lived at Sofino and been farming for a long time," Alehin began, "ever since I left the University. I am an idle gentleman by education, a studious person by disposition; but there was a big debt owing on the estate when I came here, and as my father was in debt partly because he had spent so much on my education, I resolved not to go away, but to work till I paid off the debt. I made up my mind to this and set to work, not, I must confess, without some repugnance. The land here does not yield much, and if one is not to farm at a loss one must employ serf labour or hired labourers, which is almost the same thing, or put it on a peasant footing – that is, work the fields oneself and with one's family. There is no middle path. But in those days I did not go into such subtleties. I did not leave a clod of earth unturned; I gathered together all the peasants, men and women, from the neighbouring villages; the work went on at a tremendous pace. I myself ploughed and sowed and reaped, and was bored doing it, and frowned with disgust, like a village cat driven by hunger to eat cucumbers in the kitchen-garden. My body ached, and I slept as I walked. At first it seemed to me that I could easily reconcile this life of toil with my cultured habits; to do so, I thought, all that is necessary is to maintain a certain external order in life. I established myself upstairs here in the best rooms, and ordered them to bring me there coffee and liquor after lunch and dinner, and when I went to bed I read every night the Yyesnik Evropi. But one day our priest, Father Ivan, came and drank up all my liquor at one sitting; and the Yyesnik Evropi went to the priest's daughters; as in the summer, especially at the haymaking, I did not succeed in getting to my bed at all, and slept in the sledge in the barn, or somewhere in the forester's lodge, what chance was there of reading? Little by little I moved downstairs, began dining in the servants' kitchen, and of my former luxury nothing is left but the servants who were in my father's service, and whom it would be painful to turn away.

"In the first years I was elected here an honourary justice of the peace. I used to have to go to the town and take part in the sessions of the congress and of the circuit court, and this was a pleasant change for me. When you live here for two or three months without a break, especially in the winter, you begin at last to pine for a black coat. And in the circuit court there were frock-coats, and uniforms, and dress-coats, too, all lawyers, men who have received a general education; I had some one to talk to. After sleeping in the sledge and dining in the kitchen, to sit in an arm-chair in clean linen, in thin boots, with a chain on one's waistcoat, is such luxury!

"I received a warm welcome in the town. I made friends eagerly. And of all my acquaintanceships the most intimate and, to tell the truth, the most agreeable to me was my acquaintance with Luganovitch, the vice-president of the circuit court. You both know him: a most charming personality. It all happened just after a celebrated case of incendiarism; the preliminary investigation lasted two days; we were exhausted. Luganovitch looked at me and said:

" 'Look here, come round to dinner with me.'

"This was unexpected, as I knew Luganovitch very little, only officially, and I had never been to his house. I only just went to my hotel room to change and went off to dinner. And here it was my lot to meet Anna Alexyevna, Luganovitch's wife. At that time she was still very young, not more than twenty-two, and her first baby had been born just six months before. It is all a thing of the past; and now I should find it difficult to define what there was so exceptional in her, what it was in her attracted me so much; at the time, at dinner, it was all perfectly clear to me. I saw a lovely young, good, intelligent, fascinating woman, such as I had never met before; and I felt her at once some one close and already familiar, as though that face, those cordial, intelligent eyes, I had seen somewhere in my childhood, in the album which lay on my mother's chest of drawers.

"Four Jews were charged with being incendiaries, were regarded as a gang of robbers, and, to my mind, quite groundlessly. At dinner I was very much excited, I was uncomfortable, and I don't know what I said, but Anna Alexyevna kept shaking her head and saying to her husband:

" 'Dmitry, how is this?'

"Luganovitch is a good-natured man, one of those simple-hearted people who firmly maintain the opinion that once a man is charged before a court he is guilty, and to express doubt of the correctness of a sentence cannot be done except in legal form on paper, and not at dinner and in private conversation.

" 'You and I did not set fire to the place,' he said softly, 'and you see we are not condemned, and not in prison.'

"And both husband and wife tried to make me eat and drink as much as possible. From some trifling details, from the way they made the coffee together, for instance, and from the way they understood each other at half a word, I could gather that they lived in harmony and comfort, and that they were glad of a visitor. After dinner they played a duet on the piano; then it got dark, and I went home. That was at the beginning of spring.

"After that I spent the whole summer at Sofino without a break, and I had no time to think of the town, either, but the memory of the graceful fair-haired woman remained in my mind all those days; I did not think of her, but it was as though her light shadow were lying on my heart.

"In the late autumn there was a theatrical performance for some charitable object in the town. I went into the governor's box (I was invited to go there in the interval); I looked, and there was Anna Alexyevna sitting beside the governor's wife; and again the same irresistible, thrilling impression of beauty and sweet, caressing eyes, and again the same feeling of nearness. We sat side by side, then went to the foyer.

" 'You've grown thinner,' she said; 'have you been ill?'

" 'Yes, I've had rheumatism in my shoulder, and in rainy weather I can't sleep.'

" 'You look dispirited. In the spring, when you came to dinner, you were younger, more confident. You were full of eagerness, and talked a great deal then; you were very interesting, and I really must confess I was a little carried away by you. For some reason you often came back to my memory during the summer, and when I was getting ready for the theatre today I thought I should see you.'

"And she laughed.

" 'But you look dispirited today,' she repeated; 'it makes you seem older.'

"The next day I lunched at the Luganovitchs'. After lunch they drove out to their summer villa, in order to make arrangements there for the winter, and I went with them. I returned with them to the town, and at midnight drank tea with them in quiet domestic surroundings, while the fire glowed, and the young mother kept going to see if her baby girl was asleep. And after that, every time I went to town I never failed to visit the Luganovitchs. They grew used to me, and I grew used to them. As a rule I went in unannounced, as though I were one of the family.

" 'Who is there?' I would hear from a faraway room, in the drawling voice that seemed to me so lovely.

" 'It is Pavel Konstantinovitch,' answered the maid or the nurse.

"Anna Alexyevna would come out to me with an anxious face, and would ask every time:

" 'Why is it so long since you have been? Has anything happened?'

"Her eyes, the elegant refined hand she gave me, her indoor dress, the way she did her hair, her voice, her step, always produced the same impression on me of something new and extraordinary in my life, and very important. We talked together for hours, were silent, thinking each our own thoughts, or she played for hours to me on the piano. If there were no one at home I stayed and waited, talked to the nurse, played with the child, or lay on the sofa in the study and read; and when Anna Alexyevna came back I met her in the hall, took all her parcels from her, and for some reason I carried those parcels every time with as much love, with as much solemnity, as a boy.

"There is a proverb that if a peasant woman has no troubles she will buy a pig. The Luganovitchs had no troubles, so they made friends with me. If I did not come to the town I must be ill or something must have happened to me, and both of them were extremely anxious. They were worried that I, an educated man with a knowledge of languages, should, instead of devoting myself to science or literary work, live in the country, rush round like a squirrel in a rage, work hard with never a penny to show for it. They fancied that I was unhappy, and that I only talked, laughed, and ate to conceal my sufferings, and even at cheerful moments when I felt happy I was aware of their searching eyes fixed upon me. They were particularly touching when I really was depressed, when I was being worried by some creditor or had not money enough to pay interest on the proper day. The two of them, husband and wife, would whisper together at the window; then he would come to me and say with a grave face:

" 'If you really are in need of money at the moment, Pavel Konstantinovitch, my wife and I beg you not to hesitate to borrow from us.'

"And he would blush to his ears with emotion. And it would happen that, after whispering in the same way at the window, he would come up to me, with red ears, and say:

" 'My wife and I earnestly beg you to accept this present.'

"And he would give me studs, a cigar-case, or a lamp, and I would send them game, butter, and flowers from the country. They both, by the way, had considerable means of their own. In early days I often borrowed money, and was not very particular about it – borrowed wherever I could – but nothing in the world would have induced me to borrow from the Luganovitchs. But why talk of it?

"I was unhappy. At home, in the fields, in the barn, I thought of her; I tried to understand the mystery of a beautiful, intelligent young woman's marrying some one so uninteresting, almost an old man (her husband was over forty), and having children by him; to understand the mystery of this uninteresting, good, simple-hearted man, who argued with such wearisome good sense, at balls and evening parties kept near the more solid people, looking listless and superfluous, with a submissive, uninterested expression, as though he had been brought there for sale, who yet believed in his right to be happy, to have children by her; and I kept trying to understand why she had met him first and not me, and why such a terrible mistake in our lives need have happened.

"And when I went to the town I saw every time from her eyes that she was expecting me, and she would confess to me herself that she had had a peculiar feeling all that day and had guessed that I should come. We talked a long time, and were silent, yet we did not confess our love to each other, but timidly and jealously concealed it. We were afraid of everything that might reveal our secret to ourselves. I loved her tenderly, deeply, but I reflected and kept asking myself what our love could lead to if we had not the strength to fight against it. It seemed to be incredible that my gentle, sad love could all at once coarsely break up the even tenor of the life of her husband, her children, and all the household in which I was so loved and trusted. Would it be honourable? She would go away with me, but where? Where could I take her? It would have been a different matter if I had had a beautiful, interesting life – if, for instance, I had been struggling for the emancipation of my country, or had been a celebrated man of science, an artist or a painter; but as it was it would mean taking her from one everyday humdrum life to another as humdrum or perhaps more so. And how long would our happiness last? What would happen to her in case I was ill, in case I died, or if we simply grew cold to one another?

"And she apparently reasoned in the same way. She thought

of her husband, her children, and of her mother, who loved the husband like a son. If she abandoned herself to her feelings she would have to lie, or else to tell the truth, and in her position either would have been equally terrible and inconvenient. And she was tormented by the question whether her love would bring me happiness – would she not complicate my life, which, as it was, was hard enough and full of all sorts of trouble? She fancied she was not young enough for me, that she was not industrious nor energetic enough to begin a new life, and she often talked to her husband of the importance of my marrying a girl of intelligence and merit who would be a capable housewife and a help to me – and she would immediately add that it would be difficult to find such a girl in the whole town.

"Meanwhile the years were passing. Anna Alexyevna already had two children. When I arrived at the Luganovitchs' the servants smiled cordially, the children shouted that Uncle Pavel Konstantinovitch had come, and hung on my neck; every one was overjoyed. They did not understand what was passing in my soul, and thought that I, too, was happy. Every one looked on me as a noble being. And grown-ups and children alike felt that a noble being was walking about their rooms, and that gave a peculiar charm to their manner towards me, as though in my presence their life, too, was purer and more beautiful. Anna Alexyevna and I used to go to the theatre together, always walking there; we used to sit side by side in the stalls, our shoulders touching. I would take the opera-glass from her hands without a word, and feel at that minute that she was near me, that she was mine, that we could not live without each other; but by some strange misunderstanding, when we came out of the theatre we always said good-bye and parted as though we were strangers. Goodness knows what people were saying about us in the town already, but there was not a word of truth in it all!

"In the latter years Anna Alexyevna took to going away for frequent visits to her mother or to her sister; she began to suffer from low spirits, she began to recognize that her life was spoilt and unsatisfied, and at times she did not care to see her husband nor her children. She was already being treated for neurasthenia.

"We were silent and still silent, and in the presence of

outsiders she displayed a strange irritation in regard to me; whatever I talked about, she disagreed with me, and if I had an argument she sided with my opponent. If I dropped anything, she would say coldly:

" 'I congratulate you.'

"If I forgot to take the opera-glass when we were going to the theatre, she would say afterwards:

" 'I knew you would forget it.'

"Luckily or unluckily, there is nothing in our lives that does not end sooner or later. The time of parting came, as Luganovitch was appointed president in one of the western provinces. They had to sell their furniture, their horses, their summer villa. When they drove out to the villa, and afterwards looked back as they were going away, to look for the last time at the garden, at the green roof, every one was sad, and I realized that I had to say goodbye not only to the villa. It was arranged that at the end of August we should see Anna Alexyevna off to the Crimea, where the doctors were sending her, and that a little later Luganovitch and the children would set off for the western province.

"We were a great crowd to see Anna Alexyevna off. When she had said good-bye to her husband and her children and there was only a minute left before the third bell, I ran into her compartment to put a basket, which she had almost forgotten, on the rack, and I had to say good-bye. When our eyes met in the compartment our spiritual fortitude deserted us both; I took her in my arms, she pressed her face to my breast, and tears flowed from her eyes. Kissing her face, her shoulders, her hands wet with tears – oh, how unhappy we were! – I confessed my love for her, and with a burning pain in my heart I realized how unnecessary, how petty, and how deceptive all that had hindered us from loving was. I understood that when you love you must either, in your reasonings about that love, start from what is highest, from what is more important than happiness or unhappiness, sin or virtue in their accepted meaning, or you must not reason at all.

"I kissed her for the last time, pressed her hand, and parted for ever. The train had already started. I went into the next compartment – it was empty – and until I reached the next station I sat there crying. Then I walked home to Sofino. . . ."

While Alehin was telling his story, the rain left off and the sun came out. Burkin and Ivan Ivanovitch went out on the balcony, from which there was a beautiful view over the garden and the mill-pond, which was shining now in the sunshine like a mirror. They admired it, and at the same time they were sorry that this man with the kind, clever eyes, who had told them this story with such genuine feeling, should be rushing round and round this huge estate like a squirrel on a wheel instead of devoting himself to science or something else which would have made his life more pleasant; and they thought what a sorrowful face Anna Alexyevna must have had when he said good-bye to her in the railway-carriage and kissed her face and shoulders. Both of them had met her in the town, and Burkin knew her and thought her beautiful.

# Aepyornis Island

## *H.G. Wells*

The man with the scarred face leant over the table and looked at my bundle.

'Orchids?' he asked.

'A few,' I said.

'Cypripediums,' he said.

'Chiefly,' said I.

'Anything new? I thought not. I did these islands twenty-five – twenty-seven years ago. If you find anything new here – well, it's brand new. I didn't leave much.'

'I'm not a collector,' said I.

'I was young then,' he went on. 'Lord! how I used to fly round.' He seemed to take my measure. 'I was in the East Indies two years and in Brazil seven. Then I went to Madagascar.'

'I know a few explorers by name,' I said, anticipating a yarn. 'Whom did you collect for?'

'Dawsons. I wonder if you've heard the name of Butcher ever?'

'Butcher – Butcher?' The name seemed vaguely present in my memory; then I recalled Butcher v. Dawson. 'Why!' said I, 'you are the man who sued them for four years' salary – got cast away on a desert island...'

'Your servant,' said the man with the scar, bowing. 'Funny case, wasn't it? Here was me, making a little fortune on that island, doing nothing for it neither, and them quite unable to give me notice. It often used to amuse me thinking over it while I was there. I did calculations of it – big – all over the blessed atoll in ornamental figuring.'

'How did it happen?' said I. 'I don't rightly remember the case.'

'Well...you've heard of the Aepyornis?'

'Rather. Andrews was telling me of a new species he was

working on only a month or so ago. Just before I sailed. They've got a thigh-bone, it seems, nearly a yard long. Monster the thing must have been!'

'I believe you,' said the man with the scar. 'It was a monster. Sindbad's roc was just a legend of 'em. But when did they find these bones?'

'Three or four years ago – '91, I fancy. Why?'

'Why? because I found them – Lord! – it's nearly twenty years ago. If Dawsons' hadn't been silly about that salary they might have made a perfect ring in 'em.... I couldn't help the infernal boat going adrift.'

He paused. 'I suppose it's the same place. A kind of swamp about ninety miles north of Antananarivo. Do you happen to know? You have to go to it along the coast by boats. You don't happen to remember, perhaps?'

'I don't. I fancy Andrews said something about a swamp.'

'It must be the same. It's on the east coast. And somehow there's something in the water that keeps things from decaying. Like creosote it smells. It reminded me of Trinidad. Did they get any more eggs? Some of the eggs I found were a foot and a half long. The swamp goes circling round, you know, and cuts off this bit. It's mostly salt, too. Well.... What a time I had of it! I found the things quite by accident. We went for eggs, me and two native chaps, in one of those rum canoes all tied together, and found the bones at the same time. We had a tent and provisions for four days, and we pitched on one of the firmer places. To think of it brings that old tarry smell back even now. It's funny work. You go probing into the mud with iron rods, you know. Usually the egg gets smashed. I wonder how long it is since these Aepyornises really lived. The missionaries say the natives have legends about when they were alive, but I never heard any such stories myself. But certainly those eggs we got were as fresh as if they had been new laid. Fresh! Carrying them down to the boat one of my n - chaps dropped one on a rock and it smashed. How I lammed into the beggar! But sweet it was, as if it was new laid, not even smelly, and its mother dead these four hundred years, perhaps. Said a centipede had bit him. However, I'm getting off the straight with the story.

It had taken us all day to dig into the slush and gets these eggs out unbroken, and we were all covered with beastly black mud, and naturally I was cross. As far as I knew they were the only eggs that have ever been got out not even cracked. I went afterwards to see the ones at the Natural History Museum in London; all of them were cracked and just stuck together like a mosaic, and bits missing. Mine were perfect, and I meant to blow them when I got back. Naturally I was annoyed at the silly duffer dropping three hours' work just on account of a centipede. I hit him about rather.'

The man with the scar took out a clay pipe. I placed my pouch before him. He filled up absent-mindedly.

'How about the others? Did you get those home? I don't remember'

'That's the queer part of the story. I had three others. Perfectly fresh eggs. Well, we put 'em in the boat, and then I went up to the tent to make some coffee, leaving my two heathens down on the beach – the one fooling about with his sting and the other helping him. It never occurred to me that the beggar would take advantage of the peculiar position I was in to pick a quarrel. But I suppose the centipede poison and the kicking I had given him had upset the one – he was always a cantankerous sort – and he persuaded the other.

'I remember I was sitting and smoking and boiling up the water over a spirit-lamp business I used to take on these expeditions. Incidentally I was admiring the swamp under the sunset. All black and blood-red it was, in streaks – a beautiful sight. And up beyond the land rose grey and hazy to the hills, and the sky behind them was red, like a furnace mouth. And fifty yards behind the back of me was these blessed heathen – quite regardless of the tranquil air of things – plotting to cut off with the boat and leave me all alone with three days' provisions and a canvas tent, and nothing to drink whatsoever beyond a little keg of water. I heard a kind of yelp behind me, and there they were in this canoe affair – it wasn't properly a boat – and, perhaps, twenty yards from land. I realized what was up in a moment. My gun was in the tent, and, besides, I had no bullets – only duck shot. They knew that. But I had a little revolver in my pocket, and I pulled that out as I ran down to the beach.

' "Come back!" says I, flourishing it.

'They jabbered something at me, and the man that broke the egg jeered. I aimed at the other – because he was unwounded and had the paddle, and I missed. They laughed. However, I wasn't beat. I knew I had to keep cool, and I tried him again and made him jump with the whang of it. He didn't laugh that time. The third time I got his head, and over he went, and the paddle with him. It was a precious lucky shot for a revolver. I reckon it was fifty yards. He went right under. I don't know if he was shot, or simply stunned and drowned. The I began to shout to the other chap to come back, but he huddled up in the canoe and refused to answer. So I fired out my revolver at him and never got near him.

'I felt a precious fool, I can tell you. There I was on this rotten black beach, flat swamp all behind me, and the flat sea, cold after the sun set, and just this black canoe drifting steadily out to sea. I tell you I damned Dawsons' and Jamrach's and Museums and all the rest of it just to rights. I bawled to this n – – - to come back, until my voice went up into a scream.

'There was nothing for it but to swim after him and take my luck with the sharks. So I opened my clasp-knife and put it in my mouth, and took off my clothes and waded in. As soon as I was in the water I lost sight of the canoe, but I aimed, as I judged, to head it off. I hoped the man in it was too bad to navigate it, and that it would keep on drifting in the same direction. Presently it came up over the horizon again to the south-westward about. The afterglow of sunset was well over now and the dim of night creeping up. The stars were coming through the blue. I swum like a champion, though my legs and arms were soon aching.

'However, I came up to him by the time the stars were fairly out. As it got darker I began to see all manner of glowing things in the water – phosphorescence, you know. At times it made me giddy. I hardly knew which was stars and which was phosphorescence, and whether I was swimming on my head or my heels. The canoe was as black as sin, and the ripple under the bows like liquid fire. I was naturally chary of clambering up into it. I was anxious to see what he was up to first. He seemed to be lying cuddled up in a lump in the bows, and the stern was all out of water. The thing kept turning round slowly as it drifted – kind of waltzing, don't you know. I went to the stern and pulled it down, expecting him to wake up. Then I began to clamber in with my knife in my hand, and ready for a rush. But he never stirred. So there I sat in the stern of the little canoe, drifting away over the calm phosphorescent sea and with all the host of the stars above me, waiting for something to happen.

'After a long time I called him by name, but he never answered. I was too tired to take any risks by going along to him. So we sat there. I fancy I dozed once or twice. When the dawn came I saw he was as dead as a door-nail and all puffed up and purple. My three eggs and the bones were lying in the middle of the canoe, and the keg of water and some coffee and biscuits wrapped in a Cape Argus by his feet, and a tin of methylated spirit underneath him. There was no paddle, nor, in fact, anything except the spirit tin that I could use as one, so I settled to drift until I was picked up. I held an inquest on him, brought in a verdict against some snake, scorpion, or centipede unknown, and sent him overboard.

'After that I had a drink of water and a few biscuits, and took a look round. I suppose a man low down as I was don't see very far; leastways, Madagascar was clean out of sight, and any trace of land at all. I saw a sail going south-westward – looked like a schooner but her hull never came up. Presently the sun got high in the sky and began to beat down upon me. Lord! It pretty near made my brains boil. I tried dipping my head in the sea, but after a while my eye fell on the Cape Argus, and I lay down flat in the canoe and spread this over me. Wonderful things these newspapers! I never read one thoroughly before, but it's odd what you get up to when you're alone, as I was. I suppose I read that blessed old Cape Argus twenty times. The pitch in the canoe simply reeked with the heat and rose up into big blisters

'I drifted ten days,' said the man with the scar. 'It's a little thing in the telling, isn't it? Every day was like the last. Except in the morning and the evening, I never kept a lookout even –

the blaze was so infernal. I didn't see a sail after the first three days, and those I saw took no notice of me. About the sixth night a ship went by scarcely half a mile away from me, with all its lights ablaze and its ports open, looking like a big firefly. There was music aboard. I stood up and shouted and screamed at it. The second day I broached one of the Aepyornis eggs, scraped the shell away at the end bit by bit, and tried it, and I was glad to find it was good enough to eat. A bit flavoury – not bad, I mean – but with something of the taste of a duck's egg. There was a kind of circular patch, about six inches across, on one side of the yolk, and with streaks of blood and a white mark like a ladder in it that I thought queer, but I did not understand what this meant at the time, and I wasn't inclined to be particular. The egg lasted me three days, with biscuits and a drink of water. I chewed coffee-berries too – invigorating stuff. The second egg I opened about the eighth day, and it scared me.'

The man with the scar paused. 'Yes,' he said, 'developing.'

'I dare say you find it hard to believe. I did, with the thing before me. There the egg had been, sunk in that cold black mud, perhaps three hundred years. But there was no mistaking it. There was the – what is it? – embryo, with its big head and curved back, and its heart beating under its throat, and the yolk shrivelled up and great membranes spreading inside of the shell and all over the yolk. Here was I hatching out the eggs of the biggest of all extinct birds, in a little canoe in the midst of the Indian Ocean. If old Dawson had known that! It was worth four years' salary. What do you think?

'However, I had to eat that precious thing up, every bit of it, before I sighted the reef, and some of the mouthfuls were beastly unpleasant. I left the third one alone. I held it up to the light, but the shell was too thick for me to get any notion of what might be happening inside; and though I fancied I heard blood pulsing, it might have been the rustle in my own ears, like what you listen to in a seashell.

'Then came the atoll. Came out of the sunrise, as it were, suddenly, close up to me. I drifted straight towards it until I was about half a mile from shore, not more, and then the current took a turn, and I had to paddle as hard as I could with my hands and bits of the Aepyornis shell to make the place. However, I got there. It was just a common atoll about four miles round, with a few trees growing and a spring in one place, and the lagoon full of parrot-fish. I took the egg ashore and put it in a good place, well above the tide lines and in the sun, to give it all the chance I could, and pulled the canoe up safe, and loafed about prospecting. It's rum how dull an atoll is. As soon as I had found a spring all the interest seemed to vanish. When I was a kid I thought nothing could be finer or more adventurous than the Robinson Crusoe business, but that place was as monotonous as a book of sermons. I went round finding eatable things and generally thinking; but I tell you I was bored to death before the first day was out. It shows my luck – the very day I landed the weather changed. A thunderstorm went by to the north and flicked its wing over the island, and in the night there came a drencher and a howling wind slap over us. It wouldn't have taken much, you know, to upset that canoe.

'I was sleeping under the canoe, and the egg was luckily among the sand higher up the beach, and the first thing I remember was a sound like a hundred pebbles hitting the boat at once, and a rush of water over my body. I'd been dreaming of Antananarivo, and I sat up and halloed to Intoshi to ask her what the devil was up, and clawed out at the chair where the matches used to be. Then I remembered where I was. There were phosphorescent waves rolling up as if they meant to eat me, and all the rest of the night as black as pitch. The air was simply yelling. The clouds seemed down on your head almost, and the rain fell as if heaven was sinking and they were bailing out the waters above the firmament. One great roller came writhing at me, like a fiery serpent, and I bolted. Then I thought of the canoe, and ran down to it as the water went hissing back again; but the thing had gone. I wondered about the egg, then, and felt my way to it. It was all right and well out of reach of the maddest waves, so I sat down beside it and cuddled it for company. Lord! What a night that was!

'The storm was over before the morning. There wasn't a rag of cloud left in the sky when the dawn came, and all along the beach there were bits of plank scattered – which was the disarticulated skeleton, so to speak, of my canoe. However, that gave me something to do, for taking advantage of two of the trees being together, I rigged up a kind of storm-shelter with these vestiges. And that day the egg hatched.

'Hatched, sir, when my head was pillowed on it and I was asleep. I heard a whack and felt a jar and sat up, and there was the end of the egg pecked out and a rum little brown head looking out at me. "Lord!" I said, "you're welcome'; and with a little difficulty he came out.

'He was a nice friendly little chap at first, about the size of a small hen – very much like most other young birds, only bigger. His plumage was a dirty brown to begin with, with a sort of grey scab that fell off it very soon, and scarcely feathers – a kind of downy hair. I can hardly express how pleased I was to see him. I tell you, Robinson Crusoe don't make near enough of his loneliness. But here was interesting company. He looked at me and winked his eye from the front backward, like a hen, and gave a chirp and began to peck about at once, as though being hatched three hundred years too late was just nothing. "Glad to see you, Man Friday!" says I, for I had naturally settled he was to be called Man Friday if he ever was hatched, as soon as ever I found the egg in the canoe had developed. I was a bit anxious about his feed, so I gave him a lump of raw parrot-fish at once. He took it, and opened his beak for more. I was glad of that, for, under the circumstances, if he'd been at all fanciful, I should have had to eat him after all.

'And he grew. You could almost see him grow. And as I was never much of a society man, his quiet, friendly ways suited me to a T. For nearly two years we were as happy as we could be on that island. I had no business worries, for I knew my salary was mounting up at Dawsons'. We would see a sail now and then, but nothing ever came near us. I amused myself, too, by decorating the island with designs worked in sea-urchins and fancy shells of various kinds. I put AEPYORNIS ISLAND all around the place very nearly, in big letters, like what you see done with coloured stones at railway stations in the old country, and mathematical calculations and drawings of various sorts. And I used to lie watching the blessed bird stalking round and growing, growing; and think how I could make a living out of him by showing him about if I ever got taken off. After his first moult he began to get handsome, with a crest and a blue wattle, and a lot of green feathers at the behind of him. And then I used to puzzle whether Dawsons' had any right to claim him or not. Stormy weather and in the rainy season we lay snug under the shelter I had made out of the old canoe, and I used to tell him lies about my friends at home. And after a storm we would go round the island together to see if there was any drift. It was a kind of idyll, you might say. If only I had had some tobacco it would have been simply just like heaven.

'It was about the end of the second year our little paradise went wrong. Friday was then about fourteen feet high to the bill of him, with a big, broad head like the end of a pickaxe, and two huge brown eyes with yellow rims, set together like a man's – not out of sight of each other like a hen's. His plumage was fine – none of the half-mourning style of your ostrich – more like a cassowary as far as colour and texture go. And then it was he began to cock his comb at me and give himself airs, and show signs of a nasty temper...

'At last came a time when my fishing had been rather unlucky, and he began to hang about me in a queer, meditative way. I thought he might have been eating sea-cucumbers or something, but it was really just discontent on his part. I was hungry, too, and when at last I landed a fish I wanted it for myself. Tempers were short that morning on both sides. He pecked at it and grabbed it, and I gave him a whack on the head to make him leave go. And at that he went for me. Lord!...

'He gave me this in the face.' The man indicated his scar. 'Then he kicked me. It was like a cart-horse. I got up, and, seeing he hadn't finished, I started off full tilt with my arms doubled up over my face. But he ran on those gawky legs of his faster than a racehorse, and kept landing out at me with sledgehammer kicks and bringing his pickaxe down on the back of my head. I made for the lagoon, and went in up to my neck. He stopped at the water, for he hated getting his feet wet, and began to make a shindy, something like a peacock's, only hoarser. He started strutting up and down the beach. I'll admit I felt small to see this blessed fossil lording it there. And my head and face were all bleeding, and – well, my body just one jelly of bruises.

'I decided to swim across the lagoon and leave him alone for a bit, until the affair blew over. I shinned up the tallest palm-tree, and sat there thinking of it all. I don't suppose I ever felt so hurt by anything before or since. It was the brutal ingratitude of the creature. I'd been more than a brother to him. A great gawky, out-of-date bird! And me a human being – heir of the ages and all that.

'I thought after a time he'd begin to see things in that light himself, and feel a little sorry for his behaviour. I thought if I was to catch some nice little bits of fish, perhaps, and go to him presently in a casual kind of way, and offer them to him, he might do the sensible thing. It took me some time to learn how unforgiving and cantankerous an extinct bird can be. Malice!

'I won't tell you all the little devices I tried to get that bird round again. I simply can't. It makes my cheek burn with shame even now to think of the snubs and buffets I had from this infernal curiosity. I tried violence. I chucked lumps of coral at him from a safe distance, but he only swallowed them. I shied my open knife at him and almost lost it, though it was too big for him to swallow. I tried starving him out and struck fishing, but he took to picking along the beach at low water after worms, and rubbed along on that. Half my time I spent up to my neck in the lagoon, and the rest up the palm-trees. One of them was scarcely high enough, and when he caught me up it he had a regular Bank Holiday with the calves of my legs. It got unbearable. I don't know if you have ever tried sleeping up a palm-tree. It gave me the most horrible nightmares. Think of the shame of it, too! Here was this extinct animal mooning about my island like a sulky duke, and me not allowed to rest the sole of my foot on the place. I used to cry with weariness and vexation. I told him straight that I didn't mean to be chased about a desert island by any damned anachronisms. I told him to go and peck a navigator of his own age. But he only snapped his beak at me. Great ugly bird, all legs and neck!

'I shouldn't like to say how long that went on altogether. I'd have killed him sooner if I'd known how. However, I hit on a way of settling him at last. It is a South American dodge. I joined all my fishing-lines together with stems of seaweed and things, and made a stoutish string, perhaps twelve yards in length or more, and I fastened two lumps of coral rock to the ends of this. It took me some time to do, because every now and then I had to go into the lagoon or up a tree as the fancy took me. This I whirled rapidly round my head, and then let it go at him. The first time I missed, but the next time the string caught his legs beautifully, and wrapped round them again and again. Over he went. I threw it standing waist-deep in the lagoon, and as soon as he went down I was out of the water and sawing at his neck with my knife...

'I don't like to think of that even now. I felt like a murderer while I did it, though my anger was hot against him. When I stood over him and saw him bleeding on the white sand, and his beautiful great legs and neck writhing in his last agony...Pah!

'With that tragedy loneliness came upon me like a curse. Good Lord! You can't imagine how I missed that bird. I sat by his corpse and sorrowed over him, and shivered as I looked round the desolate, silent reef. I thought of what a jolly little bird he had been when he was hatched, and of a thousand pleasant tricks he had played before he went wrong. I thought if I'd only wounded him I might have nursed him round into a better understanding. If I'd had any means of digging into the coral rock I'd have buried him. I felt exactly as if he was human. As it was, I couldn't think of eating him, so I put him in the lagoon, and the little fishes picked him clean. I didn't even save the feathers. Then one day a chap cruising about in a yacht had a fancy to see if my atoll still existed.

'He didn't come a moment too soon, for I was about sick enough of the desolation of it, and only hesitating whether I should walk out into the sea and finish up the business that way, or fall back on the green things...

'I sold the bones to a man named Winslow – a dealer near the British Museum, and he says he sold them to old Havers. It seems Havers didn't understand they were extra large, and it was only after his death they attracted attention. They called 'em Aepyornis – what was it?'

'Aepyornis vastus,' said I. 'It's funny the very thing was mentioned to me by a friend of mine. When they found an Aepyornis with a thigh a yard long, they thought they had reached the top of the scale, and called him Aepyornis maximus. Then someone turned up another thigh-bone four feet six or more, and that they called Aepyornis titan. Then your vastus was found after old Havers died, in his collection, and then a vastissimus turned up.'

'Winslow was telling me as much,' said the man with the scar. 'If they get any more Aepyornises, he reckons some scientific swell will go and burst a blood-vessel. But it was a queer thing to happen to a man; wasn't it – altogether?'

# The Magic Shop

*H.G. Wells*

I had seen the Magic Shop from afar several times; I had passed it once or twice, a shop window of alluring little objects, magic balls, magic hens, wonderful cones, ventriloquist dolls, the material of the basket trick, packs of cards that looked all right, and all that sort of thing, but never had I thought of going in until one day, almost without warning, Gip hauled me by my finger right up to the window, and so conducted himself that there was nothing for it but to take him in. I had not thought the place was there, to tell the truth – a modest-sized frontage in Regent Street, between the picture shop and the place where the chicks run about just out of patent incubators, but there it was sure enough. I had fancied it was down nearer the Circus, or round the corner in Oxford Street, or even in Holborn; always over the way and a little inaccessible it had been, with something of the mirage in its position; but here it was now quite indisputably, and the fat end of Gip's pointing finger made a noise upon the glass.

"If I was rich," said Gip, dabbing a finger at the Disappearing Egg, "I'd buy myself that. And that" – which was The Crying Baby, Very Human – and that," which was a mystery, and called, so a neat card asserted, "Buy One and Astonish Your Friends."

"Anything," said Gip, "will disappear under one of those cones. I have read about it in a book.

"And there, dadda, is the Vanishing Halfpenny, only they've put it this way up so's we can't see how it's done."

Gip, dear boy, inherits his mother's breeding, and he did not propose to enter the shop or worry in any way; only, you know, quite unconsciously he lugged my finger doorward, and he made his interest clear.

"That," he said, and pointed to the Magic Bottle.

"If you had that?" I said; at which promising inquiry he

looked up with a sudden radiance.

"I could show it to Jessie," he said, thoughtful as ever of others.

"It's less than a hundred days to your birthday, Gibbles," I said, and laid my hand on the door-handle.

Gip made no answer, but his grip tightened on my finger, and so we came into the shop.

It was no common shop this; it was a magic shop, and all the prancing precedence Gip would have taken in the matter of mere toys was wanting. He left the burthen of the conversation to me.

It was a little, narrow shop, not very well lit, and the door-bell pinged again with a plaintive note as we closed it behind us. For a moment or so we were alone and could glance about us. There was a tiger in papier-mache on the glass case that covered the low counter – a grave, kind-eyed tiger that waggled his head in a methodical manner; there were several crystal spheres, a china hand holding magic cards, a stock of magic fish-bowls in various sizes, and an immodest magic hat that shamelessly displayed its springs. On the floor were magic mirrors; one to draw you out long and thin, one to swell your head and vanish your legs, and one to make you short and fat like a draught; and while we were laughing at these the shopman, as I suppose, came in.

At any rate, there he was behind the counter – a curious, sallow, dark man, with one ear larger than the other and a chin like the toe-cap of a boot.

"What can we have the pleasure?" he said, spreading his long, magic fingers on the glass case; and so with a start we were aware of him.

"I want," I said, "to buy my little boy a few simple tricks."

"Legerdemain?" he asked. "Mechanical? Domestic?"

"Anything amusing?" said I.

"Um!" said the shopman, and scratched his head for a moment as if thinking. Then, quite distinctly, he drew from his head a glass ball. "Something in this way?" he said, and held it out.

The action was unexpected. I had seen the trick done at entertainments endless times before – it's part of the common stock of conjurers – but I had not expected it here.

"That's good," I said, with a laugh.

"Isn't it?" said the shopman.

Gip stretched out his disengaged hand to take this object and found merely a blank palm.

"It's in your pocket," said the shopman, and there it was!

"How much will that be?" I asked.

"We make no charge for glass balls," said the shopman politely. "We get them," – he picked one out of his elbow as he spoke – "free." He produced another from the back of his neck, and laid it beside its predecessor on the counter. Gip regarded his glass ball sagely, then directed a look of inquiry at the two on the counter, and finally brought his round-eyed scrutiny to the shopman, who smiled.

"You may have those too," said the shopman, "and, if you don't mind, one from my mouth. So!"

Gip counselled me mutely for a moment, and then in a profound silence put away the four balls, resumed my reassuring finger, and nerved himself for the next event.

"We get all our smaller tricks in that way," the shopman remarked.

I laughed in the manner of one who subscribes to a jest. "Instead of going to the wholesale shop," I said. "Of course, it's cheaper."

"In a way," the shopman said. "Though we pay in the end. But not so heavily – as people suppose. Our larger tricks, and our daily provisions and all the other things we want, we get out of that hat... And you know, sir, if you'll excuse my saying it, there isn't a wholesale shop, not for Genuine Magic goods, sir. I don't know if you noticed our inscription – the Genuine Magic shop." He drew a business-card from his cheek and handed it to me. "Genuine," he said, with his finger on the word, and added, "There is absolutely no deception, sir."

He seemed to be carrying out the joke pretty thoroughly, I thought.

He turned to Gip with a smile of remarkable affability. "You, you know, are the Right Sort of Boy."

I was surprised at his knowing that, because, in the interests of discipline, we keep it rather a secret even at home; but Gip received it in unflinching silence, keeping a steadfast eye on him.

"It's only the Right Sort of Boy gets through that doorway."

And, as if by way of illustration, there came a rattling at the door, and a squeaking little voice could be faintly heard. "Nyar! I warn 'a go in there, dadda, I warn 'a go in there. Ny-a-a-ah!" and then the accents of a down-trodden parent, urging consolations and propitiations. "It's locked, Edward," he said.

"But it isn't," said I.

"It is, sir," said the shopman, "always – for that sort of child," and as he spoke we had a glimpse of the other youngster, a little, white face, pallid from sweet-eating and over-sapid food, and distorted by evil passions, a ruthless little egotist, pawing at the enchanted pane. "It's no good, sir," said the shopman, as I moved, with my natural helpfulness, doorward, and presently the spoilt child was carried off howling.

"How do you manage that?" I said, breathing a little more freely.

"Magic!" said the shopman, with a careless wave of the hand, and behold! sparks of coloured fire flew out of his fingers and vanished into the shadows of the shop.

"You were saying," he said, addressing himself to Gip, "before you came in, that you would like one of our 'Buy One and Astonish your Friends' boxes?"

Gip, after a gallant effort, said "Yes."

"It's in your pocket."

And leaning over the counter – he really had an extraordinarily long body – this amazing person produced the article in the customary conjurer's manner. "Paper," he said, and took a sheet out of the empty hat with the springs; "string," and behold his mouth was a string-box, from which he drew an unending thread, which when he had tied his parcel he bit off – and, it seemed to me, swallowed the ball of string. And then he lit a candle at the nose of one of the ventriloquist's dummies, stuck one of his fingers (which had become sealing-wax red) into the flame, and so sealed the parcel. "Then there was the Disappearing Egg," he remarked, and produced one from within my coat-breast and packed it, and also The Crying Baby, Very Human. I handed each parcel to Gip as it was ready, and he clasped them to his chest.

He said very little, but his eyes were eloquent; the clutch of his arms was eloquent. He was the playground of unspeakable emotions. These, you know, were real Magics. Then, with a start, I discovered something moving about in my hat – something soft and jumpy. I whipped it off, and a ruffled pigeon – no doubt a confederate – dropped out and ran on the counter, and went, I fancy, into a cardboard box behind the papier-mache tiger.

"Tut, tut!" said the shopman, dexterously relieving me of my headdress; "careless bird, and – as I live – nesting!"

He shook my hat, and shook out into his extended hand two or three eggs, a large marble, a watch, about half-a-dozen of the inevitable glass balls, and then crumpled, crinkled paper, more and more and more, talking all the time of the way in which people neglect to brush their hats inside as well as out, politely, of course, but with a certain personal application. "All sorts of things accumulate, sir. Not you, of course, in particular. . . . Nearly every customer. . . . Astonishing what they carry about with them." The crumpled paper rose and billowed on the counter more and more and more, until he was nearly hidden from us, until he was altogether hidden, and still his voice went on and on. "We none of us know what the fair semblance of a human being may conceal, sir. Are we all then no better than brushed exteriors, whited sepulchres – "

His voice stopped – exactly like when you hit a neighbour's gramophone with a well-aimed brick, the same instant silence, and the rustle of the paper stopped, and everything was still.

"Have you done with my hat?" I said, after an interval.

There was no answer.

I stared at Gip, and Gip stared at me, and there were our distortions in the magic mirrors, looking very rum, and grave, and quiet.

"I think we'll go now," I said. "Will you tell me how much all this comes to?

"I say," I said, on a rather louder note, "I want the bill; and my hat, please."

It might have been a sniff from behind the paper pile.

"Let's look behind the counter, Gip," I said. "He's making fun of us."

I led Gip round the head-wagging tiger, and what do you

think there was behind the counter? No one at all! Only my hat on the floor, and a common conjurer's lop-eared white rabbit lost in meditation, and looking as stupid and crumpled as only a conjurer's rabbit can do. I resumed my hat, and the rabbit lolloped a lollop or so out of my way.

"Dadda!" said Gip, in a guilty whisper.

"What is it, Gip?" said I.

"I do like this shop, dadda."

"So should I," I said to myself, "if the counter wouldn't suddenly extend itself to shut one off from the door." But I didn't call Gip's attention to that. "Pussy!" he said, with a hand out to the rabbit as it came lolloping past us; "Pussy, do Gip a magic!" and his eyes followed it as it squeezed through a door I had certainly not remarked a moment before. Then this door opened wider, and the man with one ear larger than the other appeared again. He was smiling still, but his eye met mine with something between amusement and defiance. "You'd like to see our show-room, sir," he said, with an innocent suavity. Gip tugged my finger forward. I glanced at the counter and met the shopman's eye again. I was beginning to think the magic just a little too genuine. "We haven't VERY much time," I said. But somehow we were inside the show-room before I could finish that.

"All goods of the same quality," said the shopman, rubbing his flexible hands together, "and that is the Best. Nothing in the place that isn't genuine Magic, and warranted thoroughly rum. Excuse me, sir!"

I felt him pull at something that clung to my coat-sleeve, and then I saw he held a little, wriggling red demon by the tail – the little creature bit and fought and tried to get at his hand – and in a moment he tossed it carelessly behind a counter. No doubt the thing was only an image of twisted indiarubber, but for the moment – ! And his gesture was exactly that of a man who handles some petty biting bit of vermin. I glanced at Gip, but Gip was looking at a magic rocking- horse. I was glad he hadn't seen the thing. "I say," I said, in an undertone, and indicating Gip and the red demon with my eyes, "you haven't many things like that about, have you?"

"None of ours! Probably brought it with you," said the

shopman – also in an undertone, and with a more dazzling smile than ever. "Astonishing what people will carry about with them unawares!" And then to Gip, "Do you see anything you fancy here?"

There were many things that Gip fancied there.

He turned to this astonishing tradesman with mingled confidence and respect. "Is that a Magic Sword?" he said.

"A Magic Toy Sword. It neither bends, breaks, nor cuts the fingers. It renders the bearer invincible in battle against any one under eighteen. Half-a-crown to seven and sixpence, according to size. These panoplies on cards are for juvenile knights-errant and very useful – shield of safety, sandals of swiftness, helmet of invisibility."

"Oh, daddy!" gasped Gip.

I tried to find out what they cost, but the shopman did not heed me. He had got Gip now; he had got him away from my finger; he had embarked upon the exposition of all his confounded stock, and nothing was going to stop him. Presently I saw with a qualm of distrust and something very like jealousy that Gip had hold of this person's finger as usually he has hold of mine. No doubt the fellow was interesting, I thought, and had an interestingly faked lot of stuff, really good faked stuff, still –

I wandered after them, saying very little, but keeping an eye on this prestidigital fellow. After all, Gip was enjoying it. And no doubt when the time came to go we should be able to go quite easily.

It was a long, rambling place, that show-room, a gallery broken up by stands and stalls and pillars, with archways leading off to other departments, in which the queerest-looking assistants loafed and stared at one, and with perplexing mirrors and curtains. So perplexing, indeed, were these that I was presently unable to make out the door by which we had come.

The shopman showed Gip magic trains that ran without steam or clockwork, just as you set the signals, and then some very, very valuable boxes of soldiers that all came alive directly you took off the lid and said – . I myself haven't a very quick ear and it was a tongue- twisting sound, but Gip – he has his mother's ear – got it in no time. "Bravo!" said the shopman, putting the men back into the box unceremoniously and handing it to Gip. "Now," said the shopman, and in a moment Gip had made them all alive again.

"You'll take that box?" asked the shopman.

"We'll take that box," said I, "unless you charge its full value. In which case it would need a Trust Magnate – "

"Dear heart! No!" and the shopman swept the little men back again, shut the lid, waved the box in the air, and there it was, in brown paper, tied up and – with Gip's full name and address on the paper!

The shopman laughed at my amazement.

"This is the genuine magic," he said. "The real thing."

"It's a little too genuine for my taste," I said again.

After that he fell to showing Gip tricks, odd tricks, and still odder the way they were done. He explained them, he turned them inside out, and there was the dear little chap nodding his busy bit of a head in the sagest manner.

I did not attend as well as I might. "Hey, presto!" said the Magic Shopman, and then would come the clear, small "Hey, presto!" of the boy. But I was distracted by other things. It was being borne in upon me just how tremendously rum this place was; it was, so to speak, inundated by a sense of rumness. There was something a little rum about the fixtures even, about the ceiling, about the floor, about the casually distributed chairs. I had a queer feeling that whenever I wasn't looking at them straight they went askew, and moved about, and played a noiseless puss-in-the-corner behind my back. And the cornice had a serpentine design with masks – masks altogether too expressive for proper plaster.

Then abruptly my attention was caught by one of the odd-looking assistants. He was some way off and evidently unaware of my presence – I saw a sort of three-quarter length of him over a pile of toys and through an arch – and, you know, he was leaning against a pillar in an idle sort of way doing the most horrid things with his features! The particular horrid thing he did was with his nose. He did it just as though he was idle and wanted to amuse himself. First of all it was a short, blobby nose, and then suddenly he shot it out like a telescope, and then out it flew and became thinner and thinner until it was like a long, red, flexible whip. Like a thing in a nightmare it was! He flourished it about and flung it forth as a fly-fisher flings his line.

My instant thought was that Gip mustn't see him. I turned about, and there was Gip quite preoccupied with the shopman, and thinking no evil. They were whispering together and looking at me. Gip was standing on a little stool, and the shopman was holding a sort of big drum in his hand.

"Hide and seek, dadda!" cried Gip. "You're He!"

And before I could do anything to prevent it, the shopman had clapped the big drum over him. I saw what was up directly. "Take that off," I cried, "this instant! You'll frighten the boy. Take it off!"

The shopman with the unequal ears did so without a word, and held the big cylinder towards me to show its emptiness. And the little stool was vacant! In that instant my boy had utterly disappeared? . . .

You know, perhaps, that sinister something that comes like a hand out of the unseen and grips your heart about. You know it takes your common self away and leaves you tense and deliberate, neither slow nor hasty, neither angry nor afraid. So it was with me.

I came up to this grinning shopman and kicked his stool aside. "Stop this folly!" I said. "Where is my boy?"

"You see," he said, still displaying the drum's interior, "there is no deception."

I put out my hand to grip him, and he eluded me by a dexterous movement. I snatched again, and he turned from me and pushed open a door to escape. "Stop!" I said, and he laughed, receding. I leapt after him – into utter darkness.

THUD!

"Lor' bless my 'eart! I didn't see you coming, sir!"

I was in Regent Street, and I had collided with a decent-looking working man; and a yard away, perhaps, and looking a little perplexed with himself, was Gip. There was some sort of apology, and then Gip had turned and come to me with a bright little smile, as though for a moment he had missed me.

And he was carrying four parcels in his arm!

He secured immediate possession of my finger.

For the second I was rather at a loss. I stared round to see the door of the magic shop, and, behold, it was not there! There was no door, no shop, nothing, only the common pilaster between the shop where they sell pictures and the window with the chicks! . . .

I did the only thing possible in that mental tumult; I walked straight to the kerbstone and held up my umbrella for a cab.

"'Ansoms," said Gip, in a note of culminating exultation.

I helped him in, recalled my address with an effort, and got in also. Something unusual proclaimed itself in my tail-coat pocket, and I felt and discovered a glass ball. With a petulant expression I flung it into the street.

Gip said nothing.

For a space neither of us spoke.

"Dada!" said Gip, at last, "that was a proper shop!"

I came round with that to the problem of just how the whole thing had seemed to him. He looked completely undamaged – so far, good; he was neither scared nor unhinged, he was simply tremendously satisfied with the afternoon's entertainment, and there in his arms were the four parcels.

Confound it! What could be in them?

"Um!" I said. "Little boys can't go to shops like that every day."

He received this with his usual stoicism, and for a moment I was sorry I was his father and not his mother, and so couldn't suddenly there, coram publico, in our hansom, kiss him. After all, I thought, the thing wasn't so very bad.

But it was only when we opened the parcels that I really began to be reassured. Three of them contained boxes of soldiers, quite ordinary lead soldiers, but of so good a quality as to make Gip altogether forget that originally these parcels had been Magic Tricks of the only genuine sort, and the fourth contained a kitten, a little living white kitten, in excellent health and appetite and temper.

I saw this unpacking with a sort of provisional relief. I hung about in the nursery for quite an unconscionable time. . . .

That happened six months ago. And now I am beginning to

believe it is all right. The kitten had only the magic natural to all kittens, and the soldiers seem as steady a company as any colonel could desire. And Gip – ?

The intelligent parent will understand that I have to go cautiously with Gip.

But I went so far as this one day. I said, "How would you like your soldiers to come alive, Gip, and march about by themselves?"

"Mine do," said Gip. "I just have to say a word I know before I open the lid."

"Then they march about alone?"

"Oh, quite, dadda. I shouldn't like them if they didn't do that."

I displayed no unbecoming surprise, and since then I have taken occasion to drop in upon him once or twice, unannounced, when the soldiers were about, but so far I have never discovered them performing in anything like a magical manner.

It's so difficult to tell.

There's also a question of finance. I have an incurable habit of paying bills. I have been up and down Regent Street several times, looking for that shop. I am inclined to think, indeed, that in that matter honour is satisfied, and that, since Gip's name and address are known to them, I may very well leave it to these people, whoever they may be, to send in their bill in their own time.

# Chun Ah Chun

***Jack London***

There was nothing striking in the appearance of Chun Ah Chun. He was rather undersized, as Chinese go, and the Chinese narrow shoulders and spareness of flesh were his. The average tourist, casually glimpsing him on the streets of Honolulu, would have concluded that he was a good-natured little Chinese, probably the proprietor of a prosperous laundry or tailorshop. In so far as good nature and prosperity went, the judgment would be correct, though beneath the mark; for Ah Chun was as good-natured as he was prosperous, and of the latter no man knew a tithe the tale. It was well known that he was enormously wealthy, but in his case "enormous" was merely the symbol for the unknown.

Ah Chun had shrewd little eyes, black and beady and so very little that they were like gimlet-holes. But they were wide apart, and they sheltered under a forehead that was patently the forehead of a thinker. For Ah Chun had his problems, and had had them all his life. Not that he ever worried over them. He was essentially a philosopher, and whether as coolie, or multi-millionaire and master of many men, his poise of soul was the same. He lived always in the high equanimity of spiritual repose, undeterred by good fortune, unruffled by ill fortune. All things went well with him, whether they were blows from the overseer in the cane field or a slump in the price of sugar when he owned those cane fields himself. Thus, from the steadfast rock of his sure content he mastered problems such as are given to few men to consider, much less to a Chinese peasant.

He was precisely that – a Chinese peasant, born to labour in the fields all his days like a beast, but fated to escape from the fields like the prince in a fairy tale. Ah Chun did not remember his father, a small farmer in a district not far from Canton; nor did he remember much of his mother, who had died when he was six. But he did remember his respected uncle, Ah Kow, for him had he served as a slave from his sixth year to his twenty-fourth. It was then that he escaped by contracting himself as a coolie to labour for three years on the sugar plantations of Hawaii for fifty cents a day.

Ah Chun was observant. He perceived little details that not one man in a thousand ever noticed. Three years he worked in the field, at the end of which time he knew more about cane-growing than the overseers or even the superintendent, while the superintendent would have been astounded at the knowledge the weazened little coolie possessed of the reduction processes in the mill. But Ah Chun did not study only sugar processes. He studied to find out how men came to be owners of sugar mills and plantations. One judgment he achieved early, namely, that men did not become rich from the labour of their own hands. He knew, for he had laboured for a score of years himself. The men who grew rich did so from the labour of the hands of others. That man was richest who had the greatest number of his fellow creatures toiling for him.

So, when his term of contract was up, Ah Chun invested his savings in a small importing store, going into partnership with one, Ah Yung. The firm ultimately became the great one of "Ah Chun and Ah Yung," which handled anything from India silks and ginseng to guano islands and blackbird brigs. In the meantime, Ah Chun hired out as cook. He was a good cook, and in three years he was the highest-paid chef in Honolulu. His career was assured, and he was a fool to abandon it, as Dantin, his employer, told him; but Ah Chun knew his own mind best, and for knowing it was called a triple-fool and given a present of fifty dollars over and above the wages due him.

The firm of Ah Chun and Ah Yung was prospering. There was no need for Ah Chun longer to be a cook. There were boom times in Hawaii. Sugar was being extensively planted, and labour was needed. Ah Chun saw the chance, and went into the labour-importing business. He brought thousands of Cantonese coolies into Hawaii, and his wealth began to grow. He made investments. His beady black eyes saw bargains where other men saw bankruptcy. He bought a fish-pond for a song, which later paid five hundred per cent and was the opening wedge by which he monopolized the fish market of Honolulu. He did not talk for publication, nor figure in politics, nor play at revolutions, but he forecast events more clearly and farther ahead than did the men who engineered them. In his mind's eye he saw Honolulu a modern, electric-lighted city at a time when it straggled, unkempt and sand-tormented, over a barren reef of uplifted coral rock. So he bought land. He bought land from merchants who needed ready cash, from impecunious natives, from riotous traders' sons, from widows and orphans and the lepers deported to Molokai; and, somehow, as the years went by, the pieces of land he had bought proved to be needed for warehouses, or coffee buildings, or hotels. He leased, and rented, sold and bought, and resold again.

But there were other things as well. He put his confidence and his money into Parkinson, the renegade captain whom nobody would trust. And Parkinson sailed away on mysterious voyages in the little Vega. Parkinson was taken care of until he died, and years afterward Honolulu was astonished when the news leaked out that the Drake and Acorn guano islands had been sold to the British Phosphate Trust for three-quarters of a million. Then there were the fat, lush days of King Kalakaua, when Ah Chun paid three hundred thousand dollars for the opium licence. If he paid a third of a million for the drug monopoly, the investment was nevertheless a good one, for the dividends bought him the Kalalau Plantation, which, in turn, paid him thirty per cent for seventeen years and was ultimately sold by him for a million and a half.

It was under the Kamehamehas, long before, that he had served his own country as Chinese Consul – a position that was not altogether unlucrative; and it was under Kamehameha IV that he changed his citizenship, becoming an Hawaiian subject in order to marry Stella Allendale, herself a subject of the brown-skinned king, though more of Anglo-Saxon blood ran in her veins than of Polynesian. In fact, the random breeds in her were so attenuated that they were valued at eighths and sixteenths. In the latter proportions was the blood of her great-grandmother, Paahao – the Princess Paahao, for she came of the royal line.

Stella Allendale's great-grandfather had been a Captain Blunt, an English adventurer who took service under Kamehameha I and was made a tabu chief himself. Her grandfather had been a New Bedford whaling captain, while through her own father had been introduced a remote blend of Italian and Portuguese which had been grafted upon his own English stock. Legally a Hawaiian, Ah Chun's spouse was more of any one of three other nationalities.

And into this conglomerate of the races, Ah Chun introduced the Mongolian mixture. Thus, his children by Mrs. Ah Chun were one thirty-second Polynesian, one-sixteenth Italian, one sixteenth Portuguese, one-half Chinese, and eleven thirty-seconds English and American. It might well be that Ah Chun would have refrained from matrimony could he have foreseen the wonderful family that was to spring from this union. It was wonderful in many ways. First, there was its size. There were fifteen sons and daughters, mostly daughters. The sons had come first, three of them, and then had followed, in unswerving sequence, a round dozen of girls. The blend of the race was excellent. Not alone fruitful did it prove, for the progeny, without exception, was healthy and without blemish. But the most amazing thing about the family was its beauty. All the girls were beautiful – delicately, ethereally beautiful. Mamma Ah Chun's rotund lines seemed to modify papa Ah Chun's lean angles, so that the daughters were willowy without being lathy, round-muscled without being chubby. In every feature of every face were haunting reminiscences of Asia, all manipulated over and disguised by Old England, New England, and South of Europe. No observer, without information, would have guessed, the heavy Chinese strain in their veins; nor could any observer, after being informed, fail to note immediately the Chinese traces.

As beauties, the Ah Chun girls were something new. Nothing like them had been seen before. They resembled nothing so much as they resembled one another, and yet each girl was sharply individual. There was no mistaking one for another. On the other hand, Maud, who was blue-eyed and yellow-haired, would remind one instantly of Henrietta, an olive brunette with large, languishing dark eyes and hair that was blue-black. The hint of resemblance that ran through them all, reconciling every differentiation, was Ah Chun's contribution. He had furnished the groundwork upon which had been traced the blended patterns of the races. He had furnished the slim-boned Chinese frame, upon which had been builded the delicacies and subtleties of Saxon, Latin, and Polynesian flesh.

Mrs. Ah Chun had ideas of her own to which Ah Chun gave credence, though never permitting them expression when they conflicted with his own philosophic calm. She had been used all her life to living in European fashion. Very well. Ah Chun gave her a European mansion. Later, as his sons and daughters grew able to advise, he built a bungalow, a spacious, rambling affair, as unpretentious as it was magnificent. Also, as time went by, there arose a mountain house on Tantalus, to which the family could flee when the "sick wind" blew from the south. And at Waikiki he built a beach residence on an extensive site so well chosen that later on, when the United States government condemned it for fortification purposes, an immense sum accompanied the condemnation. In all his houses were billiard and smoking rooms and guest rooms galore, for Ah Chun's wonderful progeny was given to lavish entertainment. The furnishing was extravagantly simple. Kings' ransoms were expended without display – thanks to the educated tastes of the progeny.

Ah Chun had been liberal in the matter of education. "Never mind expense," he had argued in the old days with Parkinson when that slack mariner could see no reason for making the Vega seaworthy; "you sail the schooner, I pay the bills." And so with his sons and daughters. It had been for them to get the education and never mind the expense. Harold, the eldest-born, had gone to Harvard and Oxford; Albert and Charles had gone through Yale in the same classes. And the daughters, from the eldest down, had undergone their preparation at Mills Seminary in California and passed on to Vassar, Wellesley, or Bryn Mawr. Several, having so desired, had had the finishing touches put on in Europe. And from all the world Ah Chun's sons and daughters returned to him to suggest and advise in the garnishment of the chaste magnificence of his residences. Ah Chun himself preferred the voluptuous glitter of Oriental display; but he was a philosopher, and he clearly saw that his children's tastes were correct according to Western standards.

Of course, his children were not known as the Ah Chun children. As he had evolved from a coolie labourer to a multimillionaire, so had his name evolved. Mamma Ah Chun had spelled it A'Chun, but her wiser offspring had elided the apostrophe and spelled it Achun. Ah Chun did not object. The spelling of his name interfered no whit with his comfort nor his philosophic calm. Besides, he was not proud. But when his children arose to the height of a starched shirt, a stiff collar, and a frock coat, they did interfere with his comfort and calm. Ah Chun would have none of it. He preferred the loose-flowing robes of China, and neither could they cajole nor bully him into making the change. They tried both courses, and in the latter one failed especially disastrously. They had not been to America for nothing. They had learned the virtues of the boycott as employed by organized labour, and he, their father, Chun Ah Chun, they boycotted in his own house, Mamma Achun aiding and abetting. But Ah Chun himself, while unversed in Western culture, was thoroughly conversant with Western labour conditions. An extensive employer of labour himself, he knew how to cope with its tactics. Promptly he imposed a lockout on his rebellious progeny and erring spouse. He discharged his scores of servants, locked up his stables, closed his houses, and went to live in the Royal Hawaiian Hotel, in which enterprise he happened to be the heaviest stockholder. The family fluttered distractedly on visits about with friends, while Ah Chun calmly managed his many affairs, smoked his long pipe with the tiny silver bowl, and pondered the problem of his wonderful progeny.

This problem did not disturb his calm. He knew in his philosopher's soul that when it was ripe he would solve it. In the meantime he enforced the lesson that complacent as he might be, he was nevertheless the absolute dictator of the Achun destinies. The family held out for a week, then returned, along with Ah Chun and the many servants, to occupy the bungalow once more. And thereafter no question was raised when Ah Chun elected to enter his brilliant drawing-room in blue silk robe, wadded slippers, and black silk skull-cap with red button peak, or when he chose to draw at his slender-stemmed silver-bowled pipe among the cigarette- and cigar- smoking officers and civilians on the broad verandas or in the smoking room.

Ah Chun occupied a unique position in Honolulu. Though he did not appear in society, he was eligible anywhere. Except among the Chinese merchants of the city, he never went out; but he received, and he always was the centre of his household and the head of his table. Himself peasant, born Chinese, he presided over an atmosphere of culture and refinement second to none in all the islands. Nor were there any in all the islands too proud to cross his threshold and enjoy his hospitality. First of all, the Achun bungalow was of irreproachable tone. Next, Ah Chun was a power. And finally, Ah Chun was a moral paragon and an honest business man. Despite the fact that business morality was higher than on the mainland, Ah Chun outshone the business men of Honolulu in the scrupulous rigidity of his honesty. It was a saying that his word was as good as his bond. His signature was never needed to bind him. He never broke his word. Twenty years after Hotchkiss, of Hotchkiss, Morterson Company, died, they found among mislaid papers a memorandum of a loan of thirty thousand dollars to Ah Chun. It had been incurred when Ah Chun was Privy Councillor to Kamehameha II. In the bustle and confusion of those heyday, money-making times, the affair had slipped Ah Chun's mind. There was no note, no legal claim against him, but he settled in full with the Hotchkiss' Estate, voluntarily paying a compound interest that dwarfed the principal. Likewise, when he verbally guaranteed the disastrous Kakiku Ditch Scheme, at a time when the least sanguine did not dream a guarantee necessary – "Signed his cheque for two hundred thousand without a quiver, gentlemen, without a quiver," was the report of the secretary of the defunct enterprise, who had been sent on the forlorn hope of finding out Ah Chun's intentions. And on top of the many similar actions that were true of his word, there was scarcely a man of repute in the islands that at one time or another had not experienced the helping financial hand of Ah Chun.

So it was that Honolulu watched his wonderful family grow up into a perplexing problem and secretly sympathized with him, for it was beyond any of them to imagine what he was going to do with it. But Ah Chun saw the problem more clearly than they. No one knew as he knew the extent to which he was an alien in his family. His own family did not guess it. He saw that there was no place for him amongst this marvellous seed of his loins, and he looked forward to his declining years and knew that he would grow more and more alien. He did not understand his children. Their conversation was of things that did not interest him and about which he knew nothing. The culture of the West had passed him by. He was Asiatic to the last fibre, which meant that he was heathen. Their Christianity was to him so much nonsense. But all this he would have ignored as extraneous and irrelevant, could he have but understood the young people themselves. When Maud, for instance, told him that the housekeeping bills for the month were thirty thousand – that he understood, as he understood Albert's request for five thousand with which to buy the schooner yacht Muriel and become a member of the Hawaiian Yacht Club. But it was their remoter, complicated desires and mental processes that obfuscated him. He was not slow in learning that the mind of each son and daughter was a secret labyrinth which he could never hope to tread. Always he came upon the wall that divides East from West. Their souls were inaccessible to him, and by the same token he knew that his soul was inaccessible to them.

Besides, as the years came upon him, he found himself harking back more and more to his own kind. The reeking smells of the Chinese quarter were spicy to him. He sniffed them with satisfaction as he passed along the street, for in his mind they carried him back to the narrow tortuous alleys of Canton swarming with life and movement. He regretted that he had cut off his queue to please Stella Allendale in the prenuptial days, and he seriously considered the advisability of shaving his crown and growing a new one. The dishes his highly paid chef concocted for him failed to tickle his reminiscent palate in the way that the weird messes did in the stuffy restaurant down in the Chinese quarter. He enjoyed vastly more a half-hour's smoke and chat with two or three Chinese chums, than to preside at the lavish and elegant dinners for which his bungalow was famed, where the pick of the Americans and Europeans sat at the long table, men and women on equality, the women with jewels that blazed in the subdued light against white necks and arms, the men in evening dress, and all chattering and laughing over topics and witticisms that, while they were not exactly Greek to him, did not interest him nor entertain.

But it was not merely his alienness and his growing desire to return to his Chinese flesh-pots that constituted the problem. There was also his wealth. He had looked forward to a placid old age. He had worked hard. His reward should have been peace and repose. But he knew that with his immense fortune peace and repose could not possibly be his. Already there were signs and omens. He had seen similar troubles before. There was his old employer, Dantin, whose children had wrested from him, by due process of law, the management of his property, having the Court appoint guardians to administer it for him. Ah Chun knew, and knew thoroughly well, that had Dantin been a poor man, it would have been found that he could quite rationally manage his own affairs. And old Dantin had had only three children and half a million, while he, Chun Ah Chun, had fifteen children and no one but himself knew how many millions.

"Our daughters are beautiful women," he said to his wife, one evening. "There are many young men. The house is always full of young men. My cigar bills are very heavy. Why are there no marriages?"

Mamma Achun shrugged her shoulders and waited.

"Women are women and men are men – it is strange there are no marriages. Perhaps the young men do not like our daughters."

"Ah, they like them well enough," Mamma Chun answered; "but you see, they cannot forget that you are your daughters' father."

"Yet you forgot who my father was," Ah Chun said gravely. "All you asked was for me to cut off my queue."

"The young men are more particular than I was, I fancy."

"What is the greatest thing in the world?" Ah Chun demanded with abrupt irrelevance.

Mamma Achun pondered for a moment, then replied: "God."

He nodded. "There are gods and gods. Some are paper, some

are wood, some are bronze. I use a small one in the office for a paper- weight. In the Bishop Museum are many gods of coral rock and lava stone."

"But there is only one God," she announced decisively, stiffening her ample frame argumentatively.

Ah Chun noted the danger signal and sheered off.

"What is greater than God, then?" he asked. "I will tell you. It is money. In my time I have had dealings with Jews and Christians, Mohammedans and Buddhists, and with little black men from the Solomons and New Guinea who carried their god about them, wrapped in oiled paper. They possessed various gods, these men, but they all worshipped money. There is that Captain Higginson. He seems to like Henrietta."

"He will never marry her," retorted Mamma Achun. "He will be an admiral before he dies – "

"A rear-admiral," Ah Chun interpolated.

"Yes, I know. That is the way they retire."

"His family in the United States is a high one. They would not like it if he married . . . if he did not marry an American girl."

Ah Chun knocked the ashes out of his pipe, thoughtfully refilling the silver bowl with a tiny pleget of tobacco. He lighted it and smoked it out before he spoke.

"Henrietta is the oldest girl. The day she marries I will give her three hundred thousand dollars. That will fetch that Captain Higginson and his high family along with him. Let the word go out to him. I leave it to you."

And Ah Chun sat and smoked on, and in the curling smoke-wreaths he saw take shape the face and figure of Toy Shuey – Toy Shuey, the maid of all work in his uncle's house in the Cantonese village, whose work was never done and who received for a whole year's work one dollar. And he saw his youthful self arise in the curling smoke, his youthful self who had toiled eighteen years in his uncle's field for little more. And now he, Ah Chun, the peasant, dowered his daughter with three hundred thousand years of such toil. And she was but one daughter of a dozen. He was not elated at the thought. It struck him that it was a funny, whimsical world, and he chuckled aloud and startled Mamma Achun from a revery which he knew lay deep in the hidden crypts of her being where he had never penetrated.

But Ah Chun's word went forth, as a whisper, and Captain Higginson forgot his rear-admiralship and his high family and took to wife three hundred thousand dollars and a refined and cultured girl who was one thirty-second Polynesian, one-sixteenth Italian, one- sixteenth Portuguese, eleven thirty-seconds English and Yankee, and one-half Chinese.

Ah Chun's munificence had its effect. His daughters became suddenly eligible and desirable. Clara was the next, but when the Secretary of the Territory formally proposed for her, Ah Chun informed him that he must wait his turn, that Maud was the oldest and that she must be married first. It was shrewd policy. The whole family was made vitally interested in marrying off Maud, which it did in three months, to Ned Humphreys, the United States immigration commissioner. Both he and Maud complained, for the dowry was only two hundred thousand. Ah Chun explained that his initial generosity had been to break the ice, and that after that his daughters could not expect otherwise than to go more cheaply.

Clara followed Maud, and thereafter, for a space of two years; there was a continuous round of weddings in the bungalow. In the meantime Ah Chun had not been idle. Investment after investment was called in. He sold out his interests in a score of enterprises, and step by step, so as not to cause a slump in the market, he disposed of his large holdings in real estate. Toward the last he did precipitate a slump and sold at sacrifice. What caused this haste were the squalls he saw already rising above the horizon. By the time Lucille was married, echoes of bickerings and jealousies were already rumbling in his ears. The air was thick with schemes and counter-schemes to gain his favour and to prejudice him against one or another or all but one of his sons-in-law. All of which was not conducive to the peace and repose he had planned for his old age.

He hastened his efforts. For a long time he had been in correspondence with the chief banks in Shanghai and Macao. Every steamer for several years had carried away drafts drawn in favour of one, Chun Ah Chun, for deposit in those Far Eastern banks. The drafts now became heavier. His two youngest daughters were not yet married. He did not wait, but dowered them with a hundred thousand each, which sums lay in the Bank of Hawaii, drawing interest and awaiting their wedding day. Albert took over the business of the firm of Ah Chun and Ah Yung, Harold, the eldest, having elected to take a quarter of a million and go to England to live. Charles, the youngest, took a hundred thousand, a legal guardian, and a course in a Keeley institute. To Mamma Achun was given the bungalow, the mountain House on Tantalus, and a new seaside residence in place of the one Ah Chun sold to the government. Also, to Mamma Achun was given half a million in money well invested.

Ah Chun was now ready to crack the nut of the problem. One fine morning when the family was at breakfast – he had seen to it that all his sons-in-law and their wives were present – he announced that he was returning to his ancestral soil. In a neat little homily he explained that he had made ample provision for his family, and he laid down various maxims that he was sure, he said, would enable them to dwell together in peace and harmony. Also, he gave business advice to his sons-in-law, preached the virtues of temperate living and safe investments, and gave them the benefit of his encyclopedic knowledge of industrial and business conditions in Hawaii. Then he called for his carriage, and, in the company of the weeping Mamma Achun, was driven down to the Pacific Mail steamer, leaving behind him a panic in the bungalow. Captain Higginson clamoured wildly for an injunction. The daughters shed copious tears. One of their husbands, an ex-Federal judge, questioned Ah Chun's sanity, and hastened to the proper authorities to inquire into it. He returned with the information that Ah Chun had appeared before the commission the day before, demanded an examination, and passed with flying colours. There was nothing to be done, so they went down and said good-bye to the little old man, who waved farewell from the promenade deck as the big steamer poked her nose seaward through the coral reef.

But the little old man was not bound for Canton. He knew his own country too well, and the squeeze of the Mandarins, to venture into it with the tidy bulk of wealth that remained to him. He went to Macao. Now Ah Chun had long exercised the power of a king and he was as imperious as a king. When he landed at Macao and went into the office of the biggest European hotel to register, the clerk closed the book on him. Chinese were not permitted. Ah Chun called for the manager and was treated with contumely. He drove away, but in two hours he was back again. He called the clerk and manager in, gave them a month's salary, and discharged them. He had made himself the owner of the hotel; and in the finest suite he settled down during the many months the gorgeous palace in the suburbs was building for him. In the meantime, with the inevitable ability that was his, he increased the earnings of his big hotel from three per cent to thirty.

The troubles Ah Chun had flown began early. There were sons-in-law that made bad investments, others that played ducks and drakes with the Achun dowries. Ah Chun being out of it, they looked at Mamma Ah Chun and her half million, and, looking, engendered not the best of feeling toward one another. Lawyers waxed fat in the striving to ascertain the construction of trust deeds. Suits, cross-suits, and counter-suits cluttered the Hawaiian courts. Nor did the police courts escape. There were angry encounters in which harsh words and harsher blows were struck. There were such things as flower pots being thrown to add emphasis to winged words. And suits for libel arose that dragged their way through the courts and kept Honolulu agog with excitement over the revelations of the witnesses.

In his palace, surrounded by all dear delights of the Orient, Ah Chun smokes his placid pipe and listens to the turmoil overseas. By each mail steamer, in faultless English, typewritten on an American machine, a letter goes from Macao to Honolulu, in which, by admirable texts and precepts, Ah Chun advises his family to live in unity and harmony. As for himself, he is out of it all, and well content. He has won to peace and repose. At times he chuckles and rubs his hands, and his slant little black eyes twinkle merrily at the thought of the funny world. For out of all his living and philosophizing, that remains to him – the conviction that it is a very funny world.

# The Enemy of All the World

### *Jack London*

It was Silas Bannerman who finally ran down that scientific wizard and arch-enemy of mankind, Emil Gluck. Gluck's confession, before he went to the electric chair, threw much light upon the series of mysterious events, many apparently unrelated, that so perturbed the world between the years 1933 and 1941. It was not until that remarkable document was made public that the world dreamed of there being any connection between the assassination of the King and Queen of Portugal and the murders of the New York City police officers. While the deeds of Emil Gluck were all that was abominable, we cannot but feel, to a certain extent, pity for the unfortunate, malformed, and maltreated genius. This side of his story has never been told before, and from his confession and from the great mass of evidence and the documents and records of the time we are able to construct a fairly accurate portrait of him, and to discern the factors and pressures that moulded him into the human monster he became and that drove him onward and downward along the fearful path he trod. Emil Gluck was born in Syracuse, New York, in 1895. His father, Josephus Gluck, was a special policeman and night watchman, who, in the year 1900, died suddenly of pneumonia. The mother, a pretty, fragile creature, who, before her marriage, had been a milliner, grieved herself to death over the loss of her husband. This sensitiveness of the mother was the heritage that in the boy became morbid and horrible.

In 1901, the boy, Emil, then six years of age, went to live with his aunt, Mrs. Ann Bartell. She was his mother's sister, but in her breast was no kindly feeling for the sensitive, shrinking boy. Ann Bartell was a vain, shallow, and heartless woman. Also, she was cursed with poverty and burdened with a husband who was a lazy, erratic ne'er-do-well. Young Emil Gluck was not wanted, and Ann Bartell could be trusted to impress this fact sufficiently upon him. As an illustration of the treatment he received in that early, formative period, the following instance is given.

When he had been living in the Bartell home a little more than a year, he broke his leg. He sustained the injury through playing on the forbidden roof – as all boys have done and will continue to do to the end of time. The leg was broken in two places between the knee and thigh. Emil, helped by his frightened playmates, managed to drag himself to the front sidewalk, where he fainted. The children of the neighbourhood were afraid of the hard-featured shrew who presided over the Bartell house; but, summoning their resolution, they rang the bell and told Ann Bartell of the accident. She did not even look at the little lad who lay stricken on the sidewalk, but slammed the door and went back to her wash- tub. The time passed. A drizzle came on, and Emil Gluck, out of his faint, lay sobbing in the rain. The leg should have been set immediately. As it was, the inflammation rose rapidly and made a nasty case of it. At the end of two hours, the indignant women of the neighbourhood protested to Ann Bartell. This time she came out and looked at the lad. Also she kicked him in the side as he lay helpless at her feet, and she hysterically disowned him. He was not her child, she said, and recommended that the ambulance be called to take him to the city receiving hospital. Then she went back into the house.

It was a woman, Elizabeth Shepstone, who came along, learned the situation, and had the boy placed on a shutter. It was she who called the doctor, and who, brushing aside Ann Bartell, had the boy carried into the house. When the doctor arrived, Ann Bartell promptly warned him that she would not pay him for his services. For two months the little Emil lay in bed, the first month on his back without once being turned over; and he lay neglected and alone, save for the occasional visits of the unremunerated and over-worked physician. He had no toys, nothing with which to beguile the long and tedious hours. No kind word was spoken to him, no soothing hand laid upon his brow, no single touch or act of loving tenderness – naught but the reproaches and harshness of Ann Bartell, and the continually reiterated information that he was not wanted. And it can well be understood, in such environment, how there was generated in the lonely, neglected boy much of the bitterness and hostility for his kind that later was to express itself in deeds so frightful as to terrify the world.

It would seem strange that, from the hands of Ann Bartell, Emil Gluck should have received a college education; but the explanation is simple. Her ne'er-do-well husband, deserting her, made a strike in the Nevada goldfields, and returned to her a many-times millionaire. Ann Bartell hated the boy, and immediately she sent him to the Farristown Academy, a hundred miles away. Shy and sensitive, a lonely and misunderstood little soul, he was more lonely than ever at Farristown. He never came home, at vacation, and holidays, as the other boys did. Instead, he wandered about the deserted buildings and grounds, befriended and misunderstood by the servants and gardeners, reading much, it is remembered, spending his days in the fields or before the fire-place with his nose poked always in the pages of some book. It was at this time that he over-used his eyes and was compelled to take up the wearing of glasses, which same were so prominent in the photographs of him published in the newspapers in 1941.

He was a remarkable student. Application such as his would have taken him far; but he did not need application. A glance at a text meant mastery for him. The result was that he did an immense amount of collateral reading and acquired more in half a year than did the average student in half-a-dozen years. In 1909, barely fourteen years of age, he was ready – "more than ready" the headmaster of the academy said – to enter Yale or Harvard. His juvenility prevented him from entering those universities, and so, in 1909, we find him a freshman at historic Bowdoin College. In 1913 he graduated with highest honours, and immediately afterward followed Professor Bradlough to Berkeley, California. The one friend that Emil Gluck discovered in all his life was Professor Bradlough. The latter's weak lungs had led him to exchange Maine for California, the removal being facilitated by the offer of a professorship in the State University. Throughout the year 1914, Emil Gluck resided in Berkeley and took special scientific courses. Toward the end of that year two deaths changed his prospects and his relations with life. The death of Professor Bradlough took from him the one friend he was ever to know, and the death of Ann Bartell left him penniless. Hating the unfortunate lad to the last, she cut him off with one hundred dollars.

The following year, at twenty years of age, Emil Gluck was enrolled as an instructor of chemistry in the University of California. Here the years passed quietly; he faithfully performed the drudgery that brought him his salary, and, a student always, he took half-a-dozen degrees. He was, among other things, a Doctor of Sociology, of Philosophy, and of Science, though he was known to the world, in later days, only as Professor Gluck.

He was twenty-seven years old when he first sprang into prominence in the newspapers through the publication of his book, SEX AND PROGRESS. The book remains to-day a milestone in the history and philosophy of marriage. It is a heavy tome of over seven hundred pages, painfully careful and accurate, and startlingly original. It was a book for scientists, and not one calculated to make a stir. But Gluck, in the last chapter, using barely three lines for it, mentioned the hypothetical desirability of trial marriages. At once the newspapers seized these three lines, "played them up yellow," as the slang was in those days, and set the whole world laughing at Emil Gluck, the bespectacled young professor of twenty- seven. Photographers snapped him, he was besieged by reporters, women's clubs throughout the land passed resolutions condemning him and his immoral theories; and on the floor of the California Assembly, while discussing the state appropriation to the University, a motion demanding the expulsion of Gluck was made under threat of withholding the appropriation – of course, none of his persecutors had read the book; the twisted newspaper version of only three lines of it was enough for them. Here began Emil Gluck's hatred for newspaper men. By them his serious and intrinsically valuable work of six years had been made a laughing- stock and a notoriety. To his dying day, and to their everlasting regret, he never forgave them.

It was the newspapers that were responsible for the next disaster that befell him. For the five years following the publication of his book he had remained silent, and silence for a lonely man is not good. One can conjecture sympathetically the awful solitude of Emil Gluck in that populous University; for he was without friends and without sympathy. His only recourse was books, and he went on reading and studying enormously. But in 1927 he accepted an invitation to appear before the Human Interest Society of Emeryville. He did not trust himself to speak, and as we write we have before us a copy of his learned paper. It is sober, scholarly, and scientific, and, it must also be added, conservative. But in one place he dealt with, and I quote his words, "the industrial and social revolution that is taking place in society." A reporter present seized upon the word "revolution," divorced it from the text, and wrote a garbled account that made Emil Gluck appear an anarchist. At once, "Professor Gluck, anarchist," flamed over the wires and was appropriately "featured" in all the newspapers in the land.

He had attempted to reply to the previous newspaper attack, but now he remained silent. Bitterness had already corroded his soul. The University faculty appealed to him to defend himself, but he sullenly declined, even refusing to enter in defence a copy of his paper to save himself from expulsion. He refused to resign, and was discharged from the University faculty. It must be added that political pressure had been put upon the University Regents and the President.

Persecuted, maligned, and misunderstood, the forlorn and lonely man made no attempt at retaliation. All his life he had been sinned against, and all his life he had sinned against no one. But his cup of bitterness was not yet full to overflowing. Having lost his position, and being without any income, he had to find work. His first place was at the Union Iron Works, in San Francisco, where he proved a most able draughtsman. It was here that he obtained his firsthand knowledge of battleships and their construction. But the reporters discovered him and featured him in his new vocation. He immediately resigned and found another place; but after the reporters had driven him away from half-a-dozen positions, he steeled himself to brazen out the newspaper persecution. This occurred when he started his electroplating establishment – in Oakland, on Telegraph Avenue. It was a small shop, employing three men and two boys. Gluck himself worked long hours. Night after night, as Policeman Carew testified on the stand, he did not leave the shop till one and two in the morning. It was during this period that he perfected the improved ignition device for gas- engines, the royalties from which ultimately made him wealthy.

He started his electroplating establishment early in the spring of 1928, and it was in the same year that he formed the disastrous love attachment for Irene Tackley. Now it is not to be imagined that an extraordinary creature such as Emil Gluck could be any other than an extraordinary lover. In addition to his genius, his loneliness, and his morbidness, it must be taken into consideration that he knew nothing about women. Whatever tides of desire flooded his being, he was unschooled in the conventional expression of them; while his excessive timidity was bound to make his love- making unusual. Irene Tackley was a rather pretty young woman, but shallow and light-headed. At the time she worked in a small candy store across the street from Gluck's shop. He used to come in and drink ice-cream sodas and lemon-squashes, and stare at her. It seems the girl did not care for him, and merely played with him. He was "queer," she said; and at another time she called him a crank when describing how he sat at the counter and peered at her through his spectacles, blushing and stammering when she took notice of him, and often leaving the shop in precipitate confusion.

Gluck made her the most amazing presents – a silver tea-service, a diamond ring, a set of furs, opera-glasses, a ponderous HISTORY OF THE WORLD in many volumes, and a motor-cycle all silver-plated in his own shop. Enters now the girl's lover, putting his foot down, showing great anger, compelling her to return Gluck's strange assortment of presents. This man, William Sherbourne, was a gross and stolid creature, a heavy-jawed man of the working class who had become a successful building-contractor in a small way. Gluck did not understand. He tried to get an explanation, attempting to speak with the girl when she went home from work in the evening. She complained to Sherbourne, and one night he gave Gluck a beating. It was a very severe beating, for it is on the records of the Red Cross Emergency Hospital that Gluck was treated there that night and was unable to leave the hospital for a week.

Still Gluck did not understand. He continued to seek an explanation from the girl. In fear of Sherbourne, he applied to the Chief of Police for permission to carry a revolver, which permission was refused, the newspapers as usual playing it up sensationally. Then came the murder of Irene Tackley, six days before her contemplated marriage with Sherbourne. It was on a Saturday night. She had worked late in the candy store, departing after eleven o'clock with her week's wages in her purse. She rode on a San Pablo Avenue surface car to Thirty-fourth Street, where she alighted and started to walk the three blocks to her home. That was the last seen of her alive. Next morning she was found, strangled, in a vacant lot.

Emil Gluck was immediately arrested. Nothing that he could do could save him. He was convicted, not merely on circumstantial evidence, but on evidence "cooked up" by the Oakland police. There is no discussion but that a large portion of the evidence was manufactured. The testimony of Captain Shehan was the sheerest perjury, it being proved long afterward that on the night in question he had not only not been in the vicinity of the murder, but that he had been out of the city in a resort on the San Leandro Road. The unfortunate Gluck received life imprisonment in San Quentin, while the newspapers and the public held that it was a miscarriage of justice – that the death penalty should have been visited upon him.

Gluck entered San Quentin prison on April 17, 1929. He was then thirty-four years of age. And for three years and a half, much of the time in solitary confinement, he was left to meditate upon the injustice of man. It was during that period that his bitterness corroded home and he became a hater of all his kind. Three other things he did during the same period: he wrote his famous treatise, HUMAN MORALS, his remarkable brochure, THE CRIMINAL SANE, and he worked out his awful and monstrous scheme of revenge. It was an episode that had occurred in his electroplating establishment that suggested to him his unique weapon of revenge. As stated in his confession, he worked every detail out theoretically during his imprisonment, and was able, on his release, immediately to embark on his career of vengeance.

His release was sensational. Also it was miserably and criminally delayed by the soulless legal red tape then in vogue. On the night of February 1, 1932, Tim Haswell, a hold-up man, was shot during an attempted robbery by a citizen of Piedmont Heights. Tim Haswell lingered three days, during which time he not only confessed to the murder of Irene Tackley, but furnished conclusive proofs of the same. Bert Danniker, a convict dying of consumption in Folsom Prison, was implicated as accessory, and his confession followed. It is inconceivable to us of to-day – the bungling, dilatory processes of justice a generation ago. Emil Gluck was proved in February to be an innocent man, yet he was not released until the following October. For eight months, a greatly wronged man, he was compelled to undergo his unmerited punishment. This was not conducive to sweetness and light, and we can well imagine how he ate his soul with bitterness during those dreary eight months.

He came back to the world in the fall of 1932, as usual a "feature" topic in all the newspapers. The papers, instead of expressing heartfelt regret, continued their old sensational persecution. One paper did more – the SAN FRANCISCO INTELLIGENCER. John Hartwell, its editor, elaborated an ingenious theory that got around the confessions of the two criminals and went to show that Gluck was responsible, after all, for the murder of Irene Tackley. Hartwell died. And Sherbourne died too, while Policeman Phillipps was shot in the leg and discharged from the Oakland police force.

The murder of Hartwell was long a mystery. He was alone in his editorial office at the time. The reports of the revolver were heard by the office boy, who rushed in to find Hartwell expiring in his chair. What puzzled the police was the fact, not merely that he had been shot with his own revolver, but that the revolver had been exploded in the drawer of his desk. The bullets had torn through the front of the drawer and entered his body. The police scouted the theory of suicide, murder was dismissed as absurd, and the blame was thrown upon the Eureka Smokeless Cartridge Company. Spontaneous explosion was the police explanation, and the chemists of the cartridge company were well bullied at the inquest. But what the police did not know was that across the street, in the Mercer Building, Room 633, rented by Emil Gluck, had been occupied by Emil Gluck at the very moment Hartwell's revolver so mysteriously exploded.

At the time, no connection was made between Hartwell's death and the death of William Sherbourne. Sherbourne had continued to live in the home he had built for Irene Tackley, and one morning in January, 1933, he was found dead. Suicide was the verdict of the coroner's inquest, for he had been shot by his own revolver. The curious thing that happened that night was the shooting of Policeman Phillipps on the sidewalk in front of Sherbourne's house. The policeman crawled to a police telephone on the corner and rang up for an ambulance. He claimed that some one had shot him from behind in the leg. The leg in question was so badly shattered by three '38 calibre bullets that amputation was necessary. But when the police discovered that the damage had been done by his own revolver, a great laugh went up, and he was charged with having been drunk. In spite of his denial of having touched a drop, and of his persistent assertion that the revolver had been in his hip pocket and that he had not laid a finger to it, he was discharged from the force. Emil Gluck's confession, six years later, cleared the unfortunate policeman of disgrace, and he is alive to-day and in good health, the recipient of a handsome pension from the city.

Emil Gluck, having disposed of his immediate enemies, now sought a wider field, though his enmity for newspaper men and for the police remained always active. The royalties on his ignition device for gasoline-engines had mounted up while he lay in prison, and year by year the earning power of his invention increased. He was independent, able to travel wherever he willed over the earth and to glut his monstrous appetite for revenge. He had become a monomaniac and an anarchist – not a philosophic anarchist, merely, but a violent anarchist. Perhaps the word is misused, and he is better described as a nihilist, or an annihilist. It is known that he affiliated with none of the groups of terrorists. He operated wholly alone, but he created a thousandfold more terror and achieved a thousandfold more destruction than all the terrorist groups added together.

He signalised his departure from California by blowing up Fort Mason. In his confession he spoke of it as a little experiment – he was merely trying his hand. For eight years he wandered over the earth, a mysterious terror, destroying property to the tune of hundreds of millions of dollars, and destroying countless lives. One good result of his awful deeds was the destruction he wrought among the terrorists themselves. Every time he did anything the terrorists in the vicinity were gathered in by the police dragnet, and many of them were executed. Seventeen were executed at Rome alone, following the assassination of the Italian King.

Perhaps the most world-amazing achievement of his was the assassination of the King and Queen of Portugal. It was their wedding day. All possible precautions had been taken against the terrorists, and the way from the cathedral, through Lisbon's streets, was double-banked with troops, while a squad of two hundred mounted troopers surrounded the carriage. Suddenly the amazing thing happened. The automatic rifles of the troopers began to go off, as well as the rifles, in the immediate vicinity, of the double-banked infantry. In the excitement the muzzles of the exploding rifles were turned in all directions. The slaughter was terrible – horses, troops, spectators, and the King and Queen, were riddled with bullets. To complicate the affair, in different parts of the crowd behind the foot-soldiers, two terrorists had bombs explode on their persons. These bombs they had intended to throw if they got the opportunity. But who was to know this? The frightful havoc wrought by the bursting bombs but added to the confusion; it was considered part of the general attack.

One puzzling thing that could not be explained away was the conduct of the troopers with their exploding rifles. It seemed impossible that they should be in the plot, yet there were the hundreds their flying bullets had slain, including the King and Queen. On the other hand, more baffling than ever was the fact that seventy per cent. of the troopers themselves had been killed or wounded. Some explained this on the ground that the loyal foot-soldiers, witnessing the attack on the royal carriage, had opened fire on the traitors. Yet not one bit of evidence to verify this could be drawn from the survivors, though many were put to the torture. They contended stubbornly that they had not discharged their rifles at all, but that their rifles had discharged themselves. They were laughed at by the chemists, who held that, while it was just barely probable that a single cartridge, charged with the new smokeless powder, might spontaneously explode, it was beyond all probability and possibility for all the cartridges in a given area, so charged, spontaneously to explode. And so, in the end, no explanation of the amazing occurrence was reached. The general opinion of the rest of the world was that the whole affair was a blind panic of the feverish Latins, precipitated, it was true, by the bursting of two terrorist bombs; and in this connection was recalled the laughable encounter of long years before between the Russian fleet and the English fishing boats.

And Emil Gluck chuckled and went his way. He knew. But how was the world to know? He had stumbled upon the secret in his old electroplating shop on Telegraph Avenue in the city of Oakland. It happened, at that time, that a wireless telegraph station was established by the Thurston Power Company close to his shop. In a short time his electroplating vat was put out of order. The vat- wiring had many bad joints, and, on investigation, Gluck discovered minute welds at the joints in the wiring. These, by lowering the resistance, had caused an excessive current to pass through the solution, "boiling" it and spoiling the work. But what had caused the welds? was the question in Gluck's mind. His reasoning was simple. Before the establishment of the wireless station, the vat had worked well. Not until after the establishment of the wireless station had the vat been ruined. Therefore the wireless station had been the cause. But how? He quickly answered the question. If an electric discharge was capable of operating a coherer across three thousand miles of ocean, then, certainly, the electric discharges from the wireless station four hundred feet away could produce coherer effects on the bad joints in the vat-wiring.

Gluck thought no more about it at the time. He merely re-wired his vat and went on electroplating. But afterwards, in prison, he remembered the incident, and like a flash there came into his mind the full significance of it. He saw in it the silent, secret weapon with which to revenge himself on the world. His great discovery, which died with him, was control over the direction and scope of the electric discharge. At the time, this was the unsolved problem of wireless telegraphy – as it still is to-day – but Emil Gluck, in his prison cell, mastered it. And, when he was released, he applied it. It was fairly simple, given the directing power that was his, to introduce a spark into the powder-magazines of a fort, a battleship, or a revolver. And not alone could he thus explode powder at a distance, but he could ignite conflagrations. The great Boston fire was started by him – quite by accident, however, as he stated in his confession, adding that it was a pleasing accident and that he had never had any reason to regret it.

It was Emil Gluck that caused the terrible German-American War, with the loss of 800,000 lives and the consumption of almost incalculable treasure. It will be remembered that in 1939, because of the Pickard incident, strained relations existed between the two countries. Germany, though aggrieved, was not anxious for war, and, as a peace token, sent the Crown Prince and seven battleships on a friendly visit to the United States. On the night of February 15, the seven warships lay at anchor in the Hudson opposite New York City. And on that night Emil Gluck, alone, with all his apparatus on board, was out in a launch. This launch, it was afterwards proved, was bought by him from the Ross Turner Company, while much of the apparatus he used that night had been purchased from the Columbia Electric Works. But this was not known at the time. All that was known was that the seven battleships blew up, one after another, at regular four-minute intervals. Ninety per cent. of the crews and officers, along with the Crown Prince, perished. Many years before, the American battleship Maine had been blown up in the harbour of Havana, and war with Spain had immediately followed – though there has always existed a reasonable doubt as to whether the explosion was due to conspiracy or accident. But accident could not explain the blowing up of the seven battleships on the Hudson at four-minute intervals. Germany believed that it had been done by a submarine, and immediately declared war. It was six months after Gluck's confession that she returned the

Philippines and Hawaii to the United States.

In the meanwhile Emil Gluck, the malevolent wizard and arch-hater, travelled his whirlwind path of destruction. He left no traces. Scientifically thorough, he always cleaned up after himself. His method was to rent a room or a house, and secretly to install his apparatus – which apparatus, by the way, he so perfected and simplified that it occupied little space. After he had accomplished his purpose he carefully removed the apparatus. He bade fair to live out a long life of horrible crime.

The epidemic of shooting of New York City policemen was a remarkable affair. It became one of the horror mysteries of the time. In two short weeks over a hundred policemen were shot in the legs by their own revolvers. Inspector Jones did not solve the mystery, but it was his idea that finally outwitted Gluck. On his recommendation the policemen ceased carrying revolvers, and no more accidental shootings occurred.

It was in the early spring of 1940 that Gluck destroyed the Mare Island navy-yard. From a room in Vallejo he sent his electric discharges across the Vallejo Straits to Mare Island. He first played his flashes on the battleship Maryland. She lay at the dock of one of the mine-magazines. On her forward deck, on a huge temporary platform of timbers, were disposed over a hundred mines. These mines were for the defence of the Golden Gate. Any one of these mines was capable of destroying a dozen battleships, and there were over a hundred mines. The destruction was terrific, but it was only Gluck's overture. He played his flashes down the Mare Island shore, blowing up five torpedo boats, the torpedo station, and the great magazine at the eastern end of the island. Returning westward again, and scooping in occasional isolated magazines on the high ground back from the shore, he blew up three cruisers and the battleships Oregon, Delaware, New Hampshire, and Florida – the latter had just gone into dry-dock, and the magnificent dry-dock was destroyed along with her.

It was a frightful catastrophe, and a shiver of horror passed through the land. But it was nothing to what was to follow. In the late fall of that year Emil Gluck made a clean sweep of the Atlantic seaboard from Maine to Florida. Nothing escaped. Forts, mines, coast defences of all sorts, torpedo stations, magazines – everything went up. Three months afterward, in midwinter, he smote the north shore of the Mediterranean from Gibraltar to Greece in the same stupefying manner. A wail went up from the nations. It was clear that human agency was behind all this destruction, and it was equally clear, through Emil Gluck's impartiality, that the destruction was not the work of any particular nation. One thing was patent, namely, that whoever was the human behind it all, that human was a menace to the world. No nation was safe. There was no defence against this unknown and all-powerful foe. Warfare was futile – nay, not merely futile but itself the very essence of the peril. For a twelve-month the manufacture of powder ceased, and all soldiers and sailors were withdrawn from all fortifications and war vessels. And even a world-disarmament was seriously considered at the Convention of the Powers, held at The Hague at that time.

And then Silas Bannerman, a secret service agent of the United States, leaped into world-fame by arresting Emil Gluck. At first Bannerman was laughed at, but he had prepared his case well, and in a few weeks the most sceptical were convinced of Emil Gluck's guilt. The one thing, however, that Silas Bannerman never succeeded in explaining, even to his own satisfaction, was how first he came to connect Gluck with the atrocious crimes. It is true, Bannerman was in Vallejo, on secret government business, at the time of the destruction of Mare Island; and it is true that on the streets of Vallejo Emil Gluck was pointed out to him as a queer crank; but no impression was made at the time. It was not until afterward, when on a vacation in the Rocky Mountains and when reading the first published reports of the destruction along the Atlantic Coast, that suddenly Bannerman thought of Emil Gluck. And on the instant there flashed into his mind the connection between Gluck and the destruction. It was only an hypothesis, but it was sufficient. The great thing was the conception of the hypothesis, in itself an act of unconscious cerebration – a thing as unaccountable as the flashing, for instance, into Newton's mind of the principle of gravitation.

The rest was easy. Where was Gluck at the time of the destruction along the Atlantic sea-board? was the question that formed in Bannerman's mind. By his own request he was put upon the case. In no time he ascertained that Gluck had himself been up and down the Atlantic Coast in the late fall of 1940. Also he ascertained that Gluck had been in New York City during the epidemic of the shooting of police officers. Where was Gluck now? was Bannerman's next query. And, as if in answer, came the wholesale destruction along the Mediterranean. Gluck had sailed for Europe a month before – Bannerman knew that. It was not necessary for Bannerman to go to Europe. By means of cable messages and the co-operation of the European secret services, he traced Gluck's course along the Mediterranean and found that in every instance it coincided with the blowing up of coast defences and ships. Also, he learned that Gluck had just sailed on the Green Star liner Plutonic for the United States.

The case was complete in Bannerman's mind, though in the interval of waiting he worked up the details. In this he was ably assisted by George Brown, an operator employed by the Wood's System of Wireless Telegraphy. When the Plutonic arrived off Sandy Hook she was boarded by Bannerman from a Government tug, and Emil Gluck was made a prisoner. The trial and the confession followed. In the confession Gluck professed regret only for one thing, namely, that he had taken his time. As he said, had he dreamed that he was ever to be discovered he would have worked more rapidly and accomplished a thousand times the destruction he did. His secret died with him, though it is now known that the French Government managed to get access to him and offered him a billion francs for his invention wherewith he was able to direct and closely to confine electric discharges. "What!" was Gluck's reply – "to sell to you that which would enable you to enslave and maltreat suffering Humanity?" And though the war departments of the nations have continued to experiment in their secret laboratories, they have so far failed to light upon the slightest trace of the secret. Emil Gluck was executed on December 4, 1941, and so died, at the age of forty-six, one of the world's most unfortunate geniuses, a man of tremendous intellect, but whose mighty powers, instead of making toward good, were so twisted and warped that he became the most amazing of criminals.

# "Party Cries" In Ireland

***Mark Twain***

Belfast is a peculiarly religious community. This may be said of the whole of the North of Ireland. About one-half of the people are Protestants and the other half Catholics. Each party does all it can to make its own doctrines popular and draw the affections of the irreligious toward them. One hears constantly of the most touching instances of this zeal. A week ago a vast concourse of Catholics assembled at Armagh to dedicate a new Cathedral; and when they started home again the roadways were lined with groups of meek and lowly Protestants who stoned them till all the region round about was marked with blood. I thought that only Catholics argued in that way, but it seems to be a mistake.

Every man in the community is a missionary and carries a brick to admonish the erring with. The law has tried to break this up, but not with perfect success. It has decreed that irritating "party cries" shall not be indulged in, and that persons uttering them shall be fined forty shillings and costs. And so, in the police court reports every day, one sees these fines recorded. Last week a girl of twelve years old was fined the usual forty shillings and costs for proclaiming in the public streets that she was "a Protestant." The usual cry is, "To hell with the Pope!" or "To hell with the Protestants!" according to the utterer's system of salvation.

One of Belfast's local jokes was very good. It referred to the uniform and inevitable fine of forty shillings and costs for uttering a party cry – and it is no economical fine for a poor man, either, by the way. They say that a policeman found a drunken man lying on the ground, up a dark alley, entertaining himself with shouting, "To hell with!" "To hell with!" The officer smelt a fine – informers get half.

"What's that you say?"

"To hell with!"

"To hell with who? To hell with what?"

"Ah, bedad, ye can finish it yourself – it's too expansive for me!"

I think the seditious disposition, restrained by the economical instinct, is finely put in that.

# The Five Boons of Life

*Mark Twain*

**Chapter I**

In the morning of life came a good fairy with her basket, and said:

"Here are gifts. Take one, leave the others. And be wary, chose wisely; oh, choose wisely! for only one of them is valuable."

The gifts were five: Fame, Love, Riches, Pleasure, Death. The youth said, eagerly:

"There is no need to consider"; and he chose Pleasure.

He went out into the world and sought out the pleasures that youth delights in. But each in its turn was short-lived and disappointing, vain and empty; and each, departing, mocked him. In the end he said: "These years I have wasted. If I could but choose again, I would choose wisely."

**Chapter II**

The fairy appeared, and said:

"Four of the gifts remain. Choose once more; and oh, remember– time is flying, and only one of them is precious."

The man considered long, then chose Love; and did not mark the tears that rose in the fairy's eyes.

After many, many years the man sat by a coffin, in an empty home. And he communed with himself, saying: "One by one they have gone away and left me; and now she lies here, the dearest and the last. Desolation after desolation has swept over me; for each hour of happiness the treacherous trader, Love, as sold me I have paid a thousand hours of grief. Out of my heart of hearts I curse him."

**Chapter III**

"Choose again." It was the fairy speaking.

"The years have taught you wisdom – surely it must be so. Three gifts remain. Only one of them has any worth – remember it, and choose warily."

The man reflected long, then chose Fame; and the fairy, sighing, went her way.

Years went by and she came again, and stood behind the man where he sat solitary in the fading day, thinking. And she knew his thought:

"My name filled the world, and its praises were on every tongue, and it seemed well with me for a little while. How little a while it was! Then came envy; then detraction; then calumny; then hate; then persecution. Then derision, which is the beginning of the end. And last of all came pity, which is the funeral of fame. Oh, the bitterness and misery of renown! target for mud in its prime, for contempt and compassion in its decay."

**Chapter IV**

"Chose yet again." It was the fairy's voice.

"Two gifts remain. And do not despair. In the beginning there was but one that was precious, and it is still here."

"Wealth – which is power! How blind I was!" said the man. "Now, at last, life will be worth the living. I will spend, squander, dazzle. These mockers and despisers will crawl in the dirt before me, and I will feed my hungry heart with their envy. I will have all luxuries, all joys, all enchantments of the spirit, all contentments of the body that man holds dear. I will buy, buy, buy! deference, respect, esteem, worship – every pinchbeck grace of life the market of a trivial world can furnish forth. I have lost much time, and chosen badly heretofore, but let that pass; I was ignorant then, and could but take for best what seemed so."

Three short years went by, and a day came when the man sat shivering in a mean garret; and he was gaunt and wan and hollow-eyed, and clothed in rags; and he was gnawing a dry crust and mumbling:

"Curse all the world's gifts, for mockeries and gilded lies! And miscalled, every one. They are not gifts, but merely lendings. Pleasure, Love, Fame, Riches: they are but temporary disguises for lasting realities – Pain, Grief, Shame, Poverty. The fairy said true; in all her store there was but one gift which was precious, only one that was not valueless. How poor and cheap and mean I know those others now to be, compared with that inestimable one, that dear and sweet and kindly one, that steeps in dreamless and enduring sleep the pains that persecute the body, and the shames and griefs that eat the mind and heart. Bring it! I am weary, I would rest."

**Chapter V**

The fairy came, bringing again four of the gifts, but Death was wanting. She said:

"I gave it to a mother's pet, a little child. It was ignorant, but trusted me, asking me to choose for it. You did not ask me to choose."

"Oh, miserable me! What is left for me?"

"What not even you have deserved: the wanton insult of Old Age."

# A Ghost Story

***Mark Twain***

I took a large room, far up Broadway, in a huge old building whose upper stories had been wholly unoccupied for years until I came. The place had long been given up to dust and cobwebs, to solitude and silence. I seemed groping among the tombs and invading the privacy of the dead, that first night I climbed up to my quarters. For the first time in my life a superstitious dread came over me; and as I turned a dark angle of the stairway and an invisible cobweb swung its hazy woof in my face and clung there, I shuddered as one who had encountered a phantom.

I was glad enough when I reached my room and locked out the mold and the darkness. A cheery fire was burning in the grate, and I sat down before it with a comforting sense of relief. For two hours I sat there, thinking of bygone times; recalling old scenes, and summoning half-forgotten faces out of the mists of the past; listening, in fancy, to voices that long ago grew silent for all time, and to once familiar songs that nobody sings now. And as my reverie softened down to a sadder and sadder pathos, the shrieking of the winds outside softened to a wail, the angry beating of the rain against the panes diminished to a tranquil patter, and one by one the noises in the street subsided, until the hurrying footsteps of the last belated straggler died away in the distance and left no sound behind.

The fire had burned low. A sense of loneliness crept over me. I arose and undressed, moving on tiptoe about the room, doing stealthily what I had to do, as if I were environed by sleeping enemies whose slumbers it would be fatal to break. I covered up in bed, and lay listening to the rain and wind and the faint creaking of distant shutters, till they lulled me to sleep.

I slept profoundly, but how long I do not know. All at once I found myself awake, and filled with a shuddering expectancy.

All was still. All but my own heart—I could hear it beat. Presently the bedclothes began to slip away slowly toward the foot of the bed, as if some one were pulling them! I could not stir; I could not speak. Still the blankets slipped deliberately away, till my breast was uncovered. Then with a great effort I seized them and drew them over my head. I waited, listened, waited. Once more that steady pull began, and once more I lay torpid a century of dragging seconds till my breast was naked again. At last I roused my energies and snatched the covers back to their place and held them with a strong grip. I waited. By and by I felt a faint tug, and took a fresh grip. The tug strengthened to a steady strain—it grew stronger and stronger. My hold parted, and for the third time the blankets slid away. I groaned. An answering groan came from the foot of the bed! Beaded drops of sweat stood upon my forehead. I was more dead than alive. Presently I heard a heavy footstep in my room—the step of an elephant, it seemed to me—it was not like anything human. But it was moving from me—there was relief in that. I heard it approach the door—pass out without moving bolt or lock—and wander away among the dismal corridors, straining the floors and joists till they creaked again as it passed—and then silence reigned once more.

When my excitement had calmed, I said to myself, "This is a dream—simply a hideous dream." And so I lay thinking it over until I convinced myself that it was a dream, and then a comforting laugh relaxed my lips and I was happy again. I got up and struck a light; and when I found that the locks and bolts were just as I had left them, another soothing laugh welled in my heart and rippled from my lips. I took my pipe and lit it, and was just sitting down before the fire, when—down went the pipe out of my nerveless fingers, the blood forsook my cheeks, and my placid breathing was cut short with a gasp! In the ashes on the hearth, side by side with my own bare footprint, was another, so vast that in comparison mine was but an infant's! Then I had had a visitor, and the elephant tread was explained.

I put out the light and returned to bed, palsied with fear. I lay a long time, peering into the darkness, and listening. Then I heard a grating noise overhead, like the dragging of a heavy body across the floor; then the throwing down of the body, and the shaking of my windows in response to the concussion. In distant parts of the building I heard the muffled slamming of doors. I heard, at intervals, stealthy footsteps creeping in and out among the corridors, and up and down the stairs. Sometimes these noises approached my door, hesitated, and went away again. I heard the clanking of chains faintly, in remote passages, and listened while the clanking grew nearer—while it wearily climbed the stairways, marking each move by the loose surplus of chain that fell with an accented rattle upon each succeeding step as the goblin that bore it advanced. I heard muttered sentences; half uttered screams that seemed smothered violently; and the swish of invisible garments, the rush of invisible wings. Then I became conscious that my chamber was invaded—that I was not alone. I heard sighs and breathings about my bed, and mysterious whisperings. Three little spheres of soft phosphorescent light appeared on the ceiling directly over my head, clung and glowed there a moment, and then dropped—two of them upon my face and one upon the pillow. They spattered, liquidly, and felt warm. Intuition told me they had turned to gouts of blood as they fell—I needed no light to satisfy myself of that. Then I saw pallid faces, dimly luminous, and white uplifted hands, floating bodiless in the air—floating a moment and then disappearing. The whispering ceased, and the voices and the sounds, and a solemn stillness followed. I waited and listened. I felt that I must have light or die. I was weak with fear. I slowly raised myself toward a sitting posture, and my face came in contact with a clammy hand! All strength went from me apparently, and I fell back like a stricken invalid. Then I heard the rustle of a garment—it seemed to pass to the door and go out.

When everything was still once more, I crept out of bed, sick and feeble, and lit the gas with a hand that trembled as if it were aged with a hundred years. The light brought some little cheer to my spirits. I sat down and fell into a dreamy contemplation of that great footprint in the ashes. By and by its outlines began to waver and grow dim. I glanced up and the broad gas flame was slowly wilting away. In the same moment I heard that elephantine tread again. I noted its approach, nearer and nearer, along the musty halls, and dimmer and dimmer the light waned. The tread reached my very door and paused—the light had dwindled to a sickly blue, and all things about me lay in a spectral twilight. The door did not open, and yet I felt a faint gust of air fan my cheek, and presently was conscious of a huge, cloudy presence before me. I watched it with fascinated eyes. A pale glow stole over the Thing; gradually its cloudy folds took shape—an arm appeared, then legs, then a body, and last a great sad face looked out of the vapor. Stripped of its filmy housings, naked, muscular and comely, the majestic Cardiff Giant loomed above me!

All my misery vanished—for a child might know that no harm could come with that benignant countenance. My cheerful spirits returned at once, and in sympathy with them the gas flamed up brightly again. Never a lonely outcast was so glad to welcome company as I was to greet the friendly giant. I said:

"Why, is it nobody but you? Do you know, I have been scared to death for the last two or three hours? I am most honestly glad to see you. I wish I had a chair—Here, here, don't try to sit down in that thing—"

But it was too late. He was in it before I could stop him and down he went—I never saw a chair shivered so in my life.

"Stop, stop, you'll ruin ev—"

Too late again. There was another crash, and another chair was resolved into its original elements.

"Confound it, haven't you got any judgment at all? Do you want to ruin all the furniture in the place? Here, here, you petrified fool—"

But it was no use. Before I could arrest him he had sat down on the bed, and it was a melancholy ruin.

"Now what sort of a way is that to do? First you come lumbering about the place bringing a legion of vagabond goblins along with you to worry me to death, and then when I overlook an indelicacy of costume which would not be tolerated anywhere by cultivated people except in a respectable theater, and not even there if the nudity were of your sex, you repay me by wrecking all the furniture you can find to sit down on. And why will you? You damage yourself as much as you do me. You have broken off the end of your spinal column, and littered up the floor with chips of your hams till the place looks like a marble yard. You ought to be ashamed of yourself—you are big enough to know better."

"Well, I will not break any more furniture. But what am I to do? I have not had a chance to sit down for a century." And the tears came into his eyes.

"Poor devil," I said, "I should not have been so harsh with you. And you are an orphan, too, no doubt. But sit down on the floor here—nothing else can stand your weight—and besides, we cannot be sociable with you away up there above me; I want you down where I can perch on this high counting house stool and gossip with you face to face." So he sat down on the floor, and lit a pipe which I gave him, threw one of my red blankets over his shoulders, inverted my sitzbath on his head, helmet fashion, and made himself picturesque and comfortable. Then he crossed his ankles, while I renewed the fire, and exposed the flat, honeycombed bottoms of his prodigious feet to the grateful warmth.

"What is the matter with the bottom of your feet and the back of your legs, that they are gouged up so?"

"Infernal chilblains—I caught them clear up to the back of my head, roosting out there under Newell's farm. But I love the place; I love it as one loves his old home. There is no peace for me like the peace I feel when I am there."

We talked along for half an hour, and then I noticed that he looked tired, and spoke of it.

"Tired?" he said. "Well, I should think so. And now I will tell you all about it, since you have treated me so well. I am the spirit of the Petrified Man that lies across the street there in the museum. I am the ghost of the Cardiff Giant. I can have no rest, no peace, till they have given that poor body burial again. Now what was the most natural thing for me to do, to make men satisfy this wish? Terrify them into it! Haunt the place where the body lay! So I haunted the museum night after night. I even got other spirits to help me. But it did no good, for nobody ever came to the museum at midnight. Then it occurred to me to come over the way and haunt this place a little. I felt that if

I ever got a hearing I must succeed, for I had the most efficient company that perdition could furnish. Night after night we have shivered around through these mildewed halls, dragging chains, groaning, whispering, tramping up and down stairs, till, to tell you the truth, I am almost worn out. But when I saw a light in your room tonight I roused my energies again and went at it with a deal of the old freshness. But I am tired out—entirely fagged out. Give me, I beseech you, give me some hope!"

I lit off my perch in a burst of excitement, and exclaimed:

"This transcends everything! Everything that ever did occur! Why you poor blundering old fossil, you have had all your trouble for nothing—you have been haunting a plaster cast of yourself—the real Cardiff Giant is in Albany! [A fact. The original was ingeniously and fraudulently duplicated and exhibited in New York as the "only genuine" Cardiff Giant (to the unspeakable disgust of the owners of the real colossus) at the very same time that the real giant was drawing crowds at a museum in Albany.] Confound it, don't you know your own remains?"

I never saw such an eloquent look of shame, of pitiable humiliation, overspread a countenance before.

The Petrified Man rose slowly to his feet, and said:

"Honestly, is that true?"

"As true as I am sitting here."

He took the pipe from his mouth and laid it on the mantel, then stood irresolute a moment (unconsciously, from old habit, thrusting his hands where his pantaloons pockets should have been, and meditatively dropping his chin on his breast); and finally said:

"Well—I never felt so absurd before. The Petrified Man has sold everybody else, and now the mean fraud has ended by selling its own ghost! My son, if there is any charity left in your heart for a poor friendless phantom like me, don't let this get out. Think how you would feel if you had made such an ass of yourself."

I heard his stately tramp die away, step by step down the stairs and out into the deserted street, and felt sorry that he was gone, poor fellow—and sorrier still that he had carried off my red blanket and my bathtub.

# Concerning the American Language

*Mark Twain*

There was as Englishman in our compartment, and he complimented me on – on what? But you would never guess. He complimented me on my English. He said Americans in general did not speak the English language as correctly as I did. I said I was obliged to him for his compliment, since I knew he meant it for one, but that I was not fairly entitled to it, for I did not speak English at all – I only spoke American.

He laughed, and said it was a distinction without a difference. I said no, the difference was not prodigious, but still it was considerable. We fell into a friendly dispute over the matter. I put my case as well as I could, and said:

"The languages were identical several generations ago, but our changed conditions and the spread of our people far to the south and far to the west have made many alterations in our pronunciation, and have introduced new words among us and changed the meanings of many old ones. English people talk through their noses; we do not. We say know, English people say nao; we say cow, the Briton says kaow; we – "

"Oh, come! that is pure Yankee; everybody knows that."

"Yes, it is pure Yankee; that is true. One cannot hear it in America outside of the little corner called New England, which is Yankee land. The English themselves planted it there, two hundred and fifty years ago, and there it remains; it has never spread. But England talks through her nose yet; the Londoner and the backwoods New-Englander pronounce 'know' and 'cow' alike, and then the Briton unconsciously satirizes himself by making fun of the Yankee's pronunciation."

We argued this point at some length; nobody won; but no matter, the fact remains Englishmen say nao and kaow for "know" and "cow," and that is what the rustic inhabitant of a very small section of America does.

"You conferred your 'a' upon New England, too, and there it remains; it has not traveled out of the narrow limits of those six little states in all these two hundred and fifty years. All England uses it, New England's small population – say four millions – use it, but we have forty-five millions who do not use it. You say 'glahs of wawtah,' so does New England; at least, New England says 'glahs.' America at large flattens the 'a', and says 'glass of water.' These sounds are pleasanter than yours; you may think they are not right – well, in English they are not right, but 'American' they are. You say 'flahsk' and 'bahsket,' and 'jackahss'; we say 'flask,' 'basket,' 'jackass' – sounding the 'a' as it is in 'tallow,' 'fallow,' and so on. Up to as late as 1847 Mr. Webster's Dictionary had the impudence to still pronounce 'basket' bahsket, when he knew that outside of his little New England all America shortened the 'a' and paid no attention to his English broadening of it. However, it called itself an English Dictionary, so it was proper enough that it should stick to English forms, perhaps. It still calls itself an English Dictionary today, but it has quietly ceased to pronounce 'basket' as if it were spelt 'bahsket.' In the American language the 'h' is respected; the 'h' is not dropped or added improperly."

"The same is the case in England – I mean among the educated classes, of course."

"Yes, that is true; but a nation's language is a very large matter. It is not simply a manner of speech obtaining among the educated handful; the manner obtaining among the vast uneducated multitude must be considered also. Your uneducated masses speak English, you will not deny that; our uneducated masses speak American it won't be fair for you to deny that, for you can see, yourself, that when your stable-boy says, 'It isn't the 'unting that 'urts the 'orse, but the 'ammer, 'ammer, 'ammer on the 'ard 'ighway,' and our stable-boy makes the same remark without suffocating a single h, these two people are manifestly talking two different languages. But if the signs are to be trusted, even your educated classes used to drop the 'h.' They say humble, now, and heroic, and historic etc., but I judge that they used to drop those h's because your writers still keep up the fashion of patting an before those words instead of a. This is what Mr. Darwin might call a 'rudimentary' sign that as an was justifiable once, and useful when your educated classes used to say 'umble, and 'eroic, and 'istorical. Correct writers of the American language do not put an before three words."

The English gentleman had something to say upon this matter, but never mind what he said – I'm not arguing his case. I have him at a disadvantage, now. I proceeded:

"In England you encourage an orator by exclaiming, 'H'yaah! 'yaah!' We pronounce it heer in some sections, 'h'yer' in others, and so on; but our whites do not say 'h'yaah,' pronouncing the a's like the a in ah. I have heard English ladies say 'don't you' – making two separate and distinct words of it; your Mr. Burnand has satirized it. But we always say 'dontchu.' This is much better. Your ladies say, 'Oh, it's oful nice!' Ours say, 'Oh, it's awful nice!' We say, 'Four hundred,' you say 'For' – as in the word or. Your clergymen speak of 'the Lawd,' ours of 'the Lord'; yours speak of 'the gawds of the heathen,' ours of 'the gods of the heathen.' When you are exhausted, you say you are 'knocked up.' We don't. When you say you will do a thing 'directly,' you mean 'immediately'; in the American language – generally speaking – the word signifies 'after a little.' When you say 'clever,' you mean 'capable'; with us the word used to mean 'accommodating,' but I don't know what it means now. Your word 'stout' means 'fleshy'; our word 'stout' usually means 'strong.' Your words 'gentleman' and 'lady' have a very restricted meaning; with us they include the barmaid, butcher, burglar, harlot, and horse-thief. You say, 'I haven't got any stockings on,' 'I haven't got any memory,' 'I haven't got any money in my purse; we usually say, 'I haven't any stockings on,' 'I haven't any memory!' 'I haven't any money in my purse.' You say 'out of window'; we always put in a the. If one asks 'How old is that man?' the Briton answers, 'He will be about forty'; in the American language we should say, 'He is about forty.' However, I won't tire you, sir; but if I wanted to, I could pile up differences here until I not only convinced you that English and American are separate languages, but that when I speak my native tongue in its utmost purity an Englishman can't understand me at all."

"I don't wish to flatter you, but it is about all I can do to understand you now."

That was a very pretty compliment, and it put us on the pleasantest terms directly – I use the word in the English sense.

[Later – 1882. Esthetes in many of our schools are now beginning to teach the pupils to broaden the 'a,' and to say "don't you," in the elegant foreign way.]

# After-Dinner Speech

*Mark Twain*

[AT A FOURTH OF JULY GATHERING, IN LONDON, OF AMERICANS]

MR. CHAIRMAN AND LADIES AND GENTLEMEN: I thank you for the compliment which has just been tendered me, and to show my appreciation of it I will not afflict you with many words. It is pleasant to celebrate in this peaceful way, upon this old mother soil, the anniversary of an experiment which was born of war with this same land so long ago, and wrought out to a successful issue by the devotion of our ancestors. It has taken nearly a hundred years to bring the English and Americans into kindly and mutually appreciative relations, but I believe it has been accomplished at last. It was a great step when the two last misunderstandings were settled by arbitration instead of cannon. It is another great step when England adopts our sewing-machines without claiming the invention – as usual. It was another when they imported one of our sleeping-cars the other day. And it warmed my heart more than I can tell, yesterday, when I witnessed the spectacle of an Englishman ordering an American sherry cobbler of his own free will and accord – and not only that but with a great brain and a level head reminding the barkeeper not to forget the strawberries. With a common origin, a common language, a common literature, a common religion and – common drinks, what is longer needful to the cementing of the two nations together in a permanent bond of brotherhood?

This is an age of progress, and ours is a progressive land. A great and glorious land, too – a land which has developed a Washington, a Franklin, a William M. Tweed, a Longfellow, a Motley, a Jay Gould, a Samuel C. Pomeroy, a recent Congress which has never had its equal (in some respects), and a United

States Army which conquered sixty Indians in eight months by tiring them out – which is much better than uncivilized slaughter, God knows. We have a criminal jury system which is superior to any in the world; and its efficiency is only marred by the difficulty of finding twelve men every day who don't know anything and can't read. And I may observe that we have an insanity plea that would have saved Cain. I think I can say, – and say with pride, that we have some legislatures that bring higher prices than any in the world.

I refer with effusion to our railway system, which consents to let us live, though it might do the opposite, being our owners. It only destroyed three thousand and seventy lives last year by collisions, and twenty-seven thousand two hundred and sixty by running over heedless and unnecessary people at crossings. The companies seriously regretted the killing of these thirty thousand people, and went so far as to pay for some of them – voluntarily, of course, for the meanest of us would not claim that we possess a court treacherous enough to enforce a law against a railway company. But, thank Heaven, the railway companies are generally disposed to do the right and kindly thing without compulsion. I know of an instance which greatly touched me at the time. After an accident the company sent home the remains of a dear distant old relative of mine in a basket, with the remark, "Please state what figure you hold him at – and return the basket." Now there couldn't be anything friendlier than that.

But I must not stand here and brag all night. However, you won't mind a body bragging a little about his country on the fourth of July. It is a fair and legitimate time to fly the eagle. I will say only one more word of brag – and a hopeful one. It is this. We have a form of government which gives each man a fair chance and no favor. With us no individual is born with a right to look down upon his neighbor and hold him in contempt. Let such of us as are not dukes find our consolation in that. And we may find hope for the future in the fact that as unhappy as is the condition of our political morality to-day, England has risen up out of a far fouler since the days when Charles I. ennobled courtesans and all political place was a matter of bargain and sale. There is hope for us yet.

[At least the above is the speech which I was going to make, but our minister, General Schenck, presided, and after the blessing, got up and made a great long inconceivably dull harangue, and wound up by saying that inasmuch as speech-making did not seem to exhilarate the guests much, all further oratory would be dispensed with during the evening, and we could just sit and talk privately to our elbow- neighbors and have a good sociable time. It is known that in consequence of that remark forty-four perfected speeches died in the womb. The depression, the gloom, the solemnity that reigned over the banquet from that time forth will be a lasting memory with many that were there. By that one thoughtless remark General Schenck lost forty-four of the best friends he had in England. More than one said that night, "And this is the sort of person that is sent to represent us in a great sister empire!"]

# How to Tell a Story

*Mark Twain*

The Humorous Story An American Development. – Its Difference from Comic and Witty Stories.

I do not claim that I can tell a story as it ought to be told. I only claim to know how a story ought to be told, for I have been almost daily in the company of the most expert storytellers for many years.

There are several kinds of stories, but only one difficult kind – the humorous. I will talk mainly about that one. The humorous story is American, the comic story is English, the witty story is French. The humorous story depends for its effect upon the manner of the telling; the comic story and the witty story upon the matter.

The humorous story may be spun out to great length, and may wander around as much as it pleases, and arrive nowhere in particular; but the comic and witty stories must be brief and end with a point. The humorous story bubbles gently along, the others burst.

The humorous story is strictly a work of art, – high and delicate art, – and only an artist can tell it; but no art is necessary in telling the comic and the witty story; anybody can do it. The art of telling a humorous story – understand, I mean by word of mouth, not print – was created in America, and has remained at home.

The humorous story is told gravely; the teller does his best to conceal the fact that he even dimly suspects that there is anything funny about it; but the teller of the comic story tells you beforehand that it is one of the funniest things he has ever heard, then tells it with eager delight, and is the first person to laugh when he gets through. And sometimes, if he has had good success, he is so glad and happy that he will repeat the "nub" of it and glance around from face to face, collecting applause, and then repeat it again. It is a pathetic thing to see.

Very often, of course, the rambling and disjointed humorous story finishes with a nub, point, snapper, or whatever you like to call it. Then the listener must be alert, for in many cases the teller will divert attention from that nub by dropping it in a carefully casual and indifferent way, with the pretense that he does not know it is a nub.

Artemus Ward used that trick a good deal; then when the belated audience presently caught the joke he would look up with innocent surprise, as if wondering what they had found to laugh at. Dan Setchell used it before him, Nye and Riley and others use it to-day.

But the teller of the comic story does not slur the nub; he shouts at you – every time. And when he prints it, in England, France, Germany and Italy, he italicises it, puts some whooping exclamation-points after it, and sometimes explains it in a parenthesis. All of which is very depressing, and makes one want to renounce joking and lead a better life.

Let me set down an instance of the comic method, using an anecdote which has been popular all over the world for twelve or fifteen hundred years. The teller tells it in this way:

THE WOUNDED SOLDIER

In the course of a certain battle a soldier whose leg had been shot off appealed to another soldier who was hurrying by to carry him to the rear, informing him at the same time of the loss which he had sustained; whereupon the generous son of Mars, shouldering the unfortunate, proceeded to carry out his desire. The bullets and cannon-balls were flying in all directions, and presently one of the latter took the wounded man's head off – without, however, his deliverer being aware of it. In no long time he was hailed by an officer, who said:

"Where are you going with that carcass?"

"To the rear, sir – he's lost his leg!"

"His leg, forsooth?" responded the astonished officer; "you mean his head, you booby."

Whereupon the soldier dispossessed himself of his burden,

and stood looking down upon it in great perplexity. At length he said:

"It is true, sir, just as you have said." Then after a pause he added, "But he TOLD me IT WAS HIS LEG!!!!!"

Here the narrator bursts into explosion after explosion of thunderous horse-laughter, repeating that nub from time to time through his gaspings and shriekings and suffocatings.

It takes only a minute and a half to tell that in its comic-story form; and isn't worth the telling, after all. Put into the humorous-story form it takes ten minutes, and is about the funniest thing I have ever listened to – as James Whitcomb Riley tells it.

He tells it in the character of a dull-witted old farmer who has just heard it for the first time, thinks it unspeakably funny, and is trying to repeat it to a neighbor. But he can't remember it; so he gets it all mixed up and wanders helplessly round and round, putting in tedious details that don't belong in the tale and only retard it; taking them out conscientiously and putting in others that are just as useless; making minor mistakes now and then and stopping to correct them and explain how he came to make them; remembering things which he forgot to put in in their proper place and going back to put them in there; stopping his narrative a good while in order to try to recall the name of the soldier that was hurt, and finally remembering that the soldier's name was not mentioned, and remarking placidly that the name is of no real importance, after all, – and so on, and so on, and so on.

The teller is innocent and happy and pleased with himself, and has to stop every little while to hold himself in and keep from laughing outright; and does hold in, but his body quakes in a jelly-like way with interior chuckles; and at the end of the ten minutes the audience have laughed until they are exhausted, and the tears are running down their faces.

The simplicity and innocence and sincerity and unconsciousness of the old farmer are perfectly simulated, and the result is a performance which is thoroughly charming and delicious. This is art – and fine and beautiful, and only a master can compass it; but a machine could tell the other story.

To string incongruities and absurdities together in a wandering and sometimes purposeless way, and seem innocently unaware that they are absurdities, is the basis of the American art, if my position is correct. Another feature is the slurring of the point. A third is the dropping of a studied remark apparently without knowing it, as if one were thinking aloud. The fourth and last is the pause.

Artemus Ward dealt in numbers three and four a good deal. He would begin to tell with great animation something which he seemed to think was wonderful; then lose confidence, and after an apparently absent-minded pause add an incongruous remark in a soliloquizing way; and that was the remark intended to explode the mine – and it did.

For instance, he would say eagerly, excitedly, "I once knew a man in New Zealand who hadn't a tooth in his head" – here his animation would die out; a silent, reflective pause would follow, then he would say dreamily, and as if to himself, "and yet that man could beat a drum better than any man I ever saw."

The pause is an exceedingly important feature in any kind of story, and a frequently recurring feature, too. It is a dainty thing, and delicate, and also uncertain and treacherous; for it must be exactly the right length – no more and no less – or it fails of its purpose and makes trouble. If the pause is too short the impressive point is passed, and the audience have had time to divine that a surprise is intended – and then you can't surprise them, of course.

On the platform I used to tell a negro ghost story that had a pause in front of the snapper on the end, and that pause was the most important thing in the whole story. If I got it the right length precisely, I could spring the finishing ejaculation with effect enough to make some impressionable girl deliver a startled little yelp and jump out of her seat – and that was what I was after. This story was called "The Golden Arm," and was told in this fashion. You can practise with it yourself – and mind you look out for the pause and get it right.

**THE GOLDEN ARM**

Once 'pon a time dey wuz a monsus mean man, en he live 'way out in de prairie all 'lone by hisself, 'cep'n he had a wife.

En bimeby she died, en he tuck en toted her way out dah in de prairie en buried her. Well, she had a golden arm – all solid gold, fum de shoulder down. He wuz pow'ful mean – pow'ful; en dat night he couldn't sleep, caze he want dat golden arm so bad.

When it come midnight he couldn't stan' it no mo'; so he git up, he did, en tuck his lantern en shoved out thoo de storm en dug her up en got de golden arm; en he bent his head down 'gin de win', en plowed en plowed en plowed thoo de snow. Den all on a sudden he stop (make a considerable pause here, and look startled, and take a listening attitude) en say: "My lan', what's dat!"

En he listen – en listen – en de win' say (set your teeth together and imitate the wailing and wheezing singsong of the wind), "Bzzz-z-zzz" – en den, way back yonder what de grave is, he hear a voice! – he hear a voice all mix' up in de win' – can't hardly tell 'em 'part – "Bzzz-zzz – W-h-o – g-o-t – m-y – g-o-l-d-e-n – arm? – zzz – zzz – W-h-o g-o-t m-y g-o-l-d-e-n arm?" (You must begin to shiver violently now.)

En he begin to shiver en shake, en say, "Oh, my! Oh, my lan'!" en de win' blow de lantern out, en de snow en sleet blow in his face en mos' choke him, en he start a-plowin' knee-deep toward home mos' dead, he so sk'yerd – en pooty soon he hear de voice agin, en (pause) it 'us comin' after him! "Bzzz – zzz – zzz – W-h-o – g-o-t – m-y g-o-l-d-e-n – arm?"

When he git to de pasture he hear it agin – closter now, en a-comin'! – a-comin' back dah in de dark en de storm – (repeat the wind and the voice). When he git to de house he rush up-stairs en jump in de bed en kiver up, head and years, en lay dah shiverin' en shakin' – en den way out dah he hear it again! – en a-comin'! En bimeby he hear (pause – awed, listening attitude) – pat – pat – pat – hit's a-comin' up-stairs! Den he hear de latch, en he know it's in de room!

Den pooty soon he know it's a-stannin' by de bed! (Pause.) Den – he know it's a – bendin' down over him – en he cain't skasely git his breath! Den – den – he seem to feel someth'n c-o-l-d, right down 'most agin his head! (Pause.)

Den de voice say, right at his year – "W-h-o – g-o-t – m-y – g-o-l-d-e-n arm?" (You must wail it out very plaintively and accusingly; then you stare steadily and impressively into the face of the farthest-gone auditor, – a girl, preferably, – and let that awe-inspiring pause begin to build itself in the deep hush. When it has reached exactly the right length, jump suddenly at that girl and yell, "You've got it!"

If you've got the pause right, she'll fetch a dear little yelp and spring right out of her shoes. But you must get the pause right; and you will find it the most troublesome and aggravating and uncertain thing you ever undertook.)

– October 1895

# Italian Without A Master

***Mark Twain***

It is almost a fortnight now that I am domiciled in a medieval villa in the country, a mile or two from Florence. I cannot speak the language; I am too old not to learn how, also too busy when I am busy, and too indolent when I am not; wherefore some will imagine that I am having a dull time of it. But it is not so. The "help" are all natives; they talk Italian to me, I answer in English; I do not understand them, they do not understand me, consequently no harm is done, and everybody is satisfied. In order to be just and fair, I throw in an Italian word when I have one, and this has a good influence. I get the word out of the morning paper. I have to use it while it is fresh, for I find that Italian words do not keep in this climate. They fade toward night, and next morning they are gone. But it is no matter; I get a new one out of the paper before breakfast, and thrill the domestics with it while it lasts. I have no dictionary, and I do not want one; I can select words by the sound, or by orthographic aspect. Many of them have French or German or English look, and these are the ones I enslave for the day's service. That is, as a rule. Not always. If I find a learnable phrase that has an imposing look and warbles musically along I do not care to know the meaning of it; I pay it out to the first applicant, knowing that if I pronounce it carefully he will understand it, and that's enough.

Yesterday's word was avanti. It sounds Shakespearian, and probably means Avaunt and quit my sight. Today I have a whole phrase: Sono dispiacentissimo. I do not know what it means, but it seems to fit in everywhere and give satisfaction. Although as a rule my words and phrases are good for one day and train only, I have several that stay by me all the time, for some unknown reason, and these come very handy when I get into a long conversation and need things to fire up with in monotonous stretches. One of the best ones is dov' 'e il gatto. It nearly always produces a pleasant surprise, therefore I save it up for places where I want to express applause or admiration. The fourth word has a French sound, and I think the phrase means "that takes the cake."

During my first week in the deep and dreamy stillness of this woodsy and flowery place I was without news of the outside world, and was well content without it. It has been four weeks since I had seen a newspaper, and this lack seemed to give life a new charm and grace, and to saturate it with a feeling verging upon actual delight. Then came a change that was to be expected: the appetite for news began to rise again, after this invigorating rest. I had to feed it, but I was not willing to let it make me its helpless slave again; I determined to put it on a diet, and a strict and limited one. So I examined an Italian paper, with the idea of feeding it on that, and on that exclusively. On that exclusively, and without help of a dictionary. In this way I should surely be well protected against overloading and indigestion.

A glance at the telegraphic page filled me with encouragement. There were no scare-heads. That was good – supremely good. But there were headings – one-liners and two-liners – and that was good too; for without these, one must do as one does with a German paper – pay our precious time in finding out what an article is about, only to discover, in many cases, that there is nothing in it of interest to you. The headline is a valuable thing.

Necessarily we are all fond of murders, scandals, swindles, robberies, explosions, collisions, and all such things, when we knew the people, and when they are neighbors and friends, but when they are strangers we do not get any great pleasure out of them, as a rule. Now the trouble with an American paper is that it has no discrimination; it rakes the whole earth for blood and garbage, and the result is that you are daily overfed and suffer a surfeit. By habit you stow this muck every day, but you come by and by to take no vital interest in it – indeed, you almost get tired of it. As a rule, forty-nine-fiftieths of it concerns strangers only – people away off yonder, a thousand miles, two thousand miles, ten thousand miles from where you are. Why, when you come to think of it, who cares what becomes of those people?

I would not give the assassination of one personal friend for a whole massacre of those others. And, to my mind, one relative or neighbor mixed up in a scandal is more interesting than a whole Sodom and Gomorrah of outlanders gone rotten. Give me the home product every time.

Very well. I saw at a glance that the Florentine paper would suit me: five out of six of its scandals and tragedies were local; they were adventures of one's very neighbors, one might almost say one's friends. In the matter of world news there was not too much, but just about enough. I subscribed. I have had no occasion to regret it. Every morning I get all the news I need for the day; sometimes from the headlines, sometimes from the text. I have never had to call for a dictionary yet. I read the paper with ease. Often I do not quite understand, often some of the details escape me, but no matter, I get the idea. I will cut out a passage or two, then you see how limpid the language is:

Il ritorno dei Beati d'Italia

Elargizione del Re all' Ospedale italiano

The first line means that the Italian sovereigns are coming back – they have been to England. The second line seems to mean that they enlarged the King at the Italian hospital. With a banquet, I suppose. An English banquet has that effect. Further:

Il ritorno dei Sovrani

a Roma

Roma, 24, ore 22,50. – I Sovrani e le Principessine Reali si attendono a Roma domani alle ore 15,51.

Return of the sovereigns to Rome, you see. Date of the telegram, Rome, November 24, ten minutes before twenty-three o'clock. The telegram seems to say, "The Sovereigns and the Royal Children expect themselves at Rome tomorrow at fifty-one minutes after fifteen o'clock."

I do not know about Italian time, but I judge it begins at midnight and runs through the twenty-four hours without breaking bulk. In the following ad, the theaters open at half-past twenty. If these are not matinees, 20.30 must mean 8.30 P.M., by my reckoning.

Spettacolli del di 25

Teatro della Pergola – (Ore 20,30) – Opera. Boh'eme.

Teatro Alfieri. – Compagnia drammatica Drago – (Ore 20,30) – La Legge. Alhambra – (Ore 20,30) – Spettacolo variato. Sala Edison – Grandiosoo spettacolo Cinematografico: Quo Vadis? – Inaugurazione della Chiesa Russa – In coda al Direttissimo – Vedute di Firenze con gran movimeno – America: Transporto tronchi giganteschi – I ladri in casa del Diavolo – Scene comiche. Cinematografo – Via Brunelleschi n. 4. – Programma straordinario, Don Chisciotte – Prezzi populari.

The whole of that is intelligible to me – and sane and rational, too – except the remark about the Inauguration of a Russian Chinese. That one oversizes my hand. Give me five cards.

This is a four-page paper; and as it is set in long primer leaded and has a page of advertisements, there is no room for the crimes, disasters, and general sweepings of the outside world – thanks be! Today I find only a single importation of the off-color sort:

Una Principessa

che fugge con un cocchiere

Parigi, 24. – Il Matin ha da Berlino che la principessa Schovenbare-Waldenbure scomparve il 9 novembre. Sarebbe partita col suo cocchiere.

La Principassa ha 27 anni.

Twenty-seven years old, and scomparve – scampered – on the 9th November. You see by the added detail that she departed with her coachman. I hope Sarebbe has not made a mistake, but I am afraid the chances are that she has. Sono Dispiacentissimo.

There are several fires: also a couple of accidents. This is one of them:

Grave disgrazia sul Ponte Vecchio

Stammattina, circe le 7,30, mentre Giuseppe Sciatti, di anni 55, di Casellina e Torri, passava dal Ponte Vecchio, stando seduto sopra un barroccio carico di verdura, perse l' equilibrio e cadde al suolo, rimanendo con la gamba destra sotto una ruota del veicolo.

Lo Sciatti fu subito raccolto da alcuni cittadini, che, per mezzo della pubblica vettura n. 365, lo transporto a San Giovanni di Dio.

Ivi il medico di guardia gli riscontro la frattura della gamba destra e alcune lievi escoriazioni giudicandolo guaribile in 50 giorni salvo complicazioni.

What it seems to say is this: "Serious Disgrace on the Old Old Bridge. This morning about 7.30, Mr. Joseph Sciatti, aged 55, of Casellina and Torri, while standing up in a sitting posture on top of a carico barrow of vedure (foliage? hay? vegetables?), lost his equilibrium and fell on himself, arriving with his left leg under one of the wheels of the vehicle.

"Said Sciatti was suddenly harvested (gathered in?) by several citizens, who by means of public cab No. 365 transported to St. John of God."

Paragraph No. 3 is a little obscure, but I think it says that the medico set the broken left leg – right enough, since there was nothing the matter with the other one – and that several are encouraged to hope that fifty days well fetch him around in quite giudicandolo-guaribile way, if no complications intervene.

I am sure I hope so myself.

There is a great and peculiar charm about reading news-scraps in a language which you are not acquainted with – the charm that always goes with the mysterious and the uncertain. You can never be absolutely sure of the meaning of anything you read in such circumstances; you are chasing an alert and gamy riddle all the time, and the baffling turns and dodges of the prey make the life of the hunt. A dictionary would spoil it. Sometimes a single word of doubtful purport will cast a veil of dreamy and golden uncertainty over a whole paragraph of cold and practical certainties, and leave steeped in a haunting and adorable mystery an incident which had been vulgar and commonplace but for that benefaction. Would you be wise to draw a dictionary on that gracious word? Would you be properly grateful?

After a couple of days' rest I now come back to my subject and seek a case in point. I find it without trouble, in the morning paper; a cablegram from Chicago and Indiana by way of Paris. All the words save one are guessable by a person ignorant of Italian:

Revolverate in teatro

Parigi, 27. – La Patrie ha da Chicago:

Il guardiano del teatro dell'opera di Walace (Indiana), avendo voluto espellare uno spettatore che continuava a fumare malgrado il diviety, questo spalleggiato dai suoi amici tir'o diversi colpi di rivoltella. Il guardiano ripose. Nacque una scarica generale.

Grande panico tra gli spettatori. Nessun ferito.

Translation. – "Revolveration in Theater. Paris, 27th. La Patrie has from Chicago: The cop of the theater of the opera of Wallace, Indiana, had willed to expel a spectator which continued to smoke in spite of the prohibition, who, spalleggiato by his friends, tir'o (Fr. tir'e, Anglice pulled) manifold revolver-shots; great panic among the spectators. Nobody hurt."

It is bettable that that harmless cataclysm in the theater of the opera of Wallace, Indiana, excited not a person in Europe but me, and so came near to not being worth cabling to Florence by way of France. But it does excite me. It excites me because I cannot make out, for sure, what it was that moved the spectator to resist the officer. I was gliding along smoothly and without obstruction or accident, until I came to that word "spalleggiato," then the bottom fell out. You notice what a rich gloom, what a somber and pervading mystery, that word sheds all over the whole Wallachian tragedy. That is the charm of the thing, that is the delight of it. This is where you begin, this is where you revel. You can guess and guess, and have all the fun you like; you need not be afraid there will be an end to it; none is possible, for no amount of guessing will ever furnish you a meaning for that word that you can be sure is the right one. All the other words give you hints, by their form, their sound, or their spelling – this one doesn't, this one throws out no hints, this one keeps its secret. If there is even the slightest slight shadow of a hint anywhere, it lies in the very meagerly suggestive fact that "spalleggiato" carries our word "egg" in its stomach. Well, make the most out of it, and then where are you at? You conjecture that the spectator which was smoking in spite of the prohibition and become reprohibited by the guardians, was "egged on" by his friends, and that was owing to that evil influence that he initiated the revolveration in theater that has galloped under the sea and come crashing through the European press without exciting anybody but me. But are you sure, are you dead sure, that that was the way of it? No. Then the uncertainty remains, the mystery abides, and with it the charm. Guess again.

If I had a phrase-book of a really satisfactory sort I would study it, and not give all my free time to undictionarial readings, but there is no such work on the market. The existing phrase-books are inadequate. They are well enough as far as they go, but when you fall down and skin your leg they don't tell you what to say.

# Doctor Marigold

***Charles Dickens***

I am a Cheap Jack, and my own father's name was Willum Marigold. It was in his lifetime supposed by some that his name was William, but my own father always consistently said, no, it was Willum. On which point I content myself with looking at the argument this way: If a man is not allowed to know his own name in a free country, how much is he allowed to know in a land of slavery? As to looking at the argument through the medium of the Register, Willum Marigold come into the world before Registers come up much, – and went out of it too. They wouldn't have been greatly in his line neither, if they had chanced to come up before him.

I was born on the Queen's highway, but it was the King's at that time. A doctor was fetched to my own mother by my own father, when it took place on a common; and in consequence of his being a very kind gentleman, and accepting no fee but a tea-tray, I was named Doctor, out of gratitude and compliment to him. There you have me. Doctor Marigold.

I am at present a middle-aged man of a broadish build, in cords, leggings, and a sleeved waistcoat the strings of which is always gone behind. Repair them how you will, they go like fiddle-strings. You have been to the theatre, and you have seen one of the violin-players screw up his wiolin, after listening to it as if it had been whispering the secret to him that it feared it was out of order, and then you have heard it snap. That's as exactly similar to my waistcoat as a waistcoat and a wiolin can be like one another.

I am partial to a white hat, and I like a shawl round my neck wore loose and easy. Sitting down is my favourite posture. If I have a taste in point of personal jewelry, it is mother-of-pearl buttons. There you have me again, as large as life.

The doctor having accepted a tea-tray, you'll guess that my father was a Cheap Jack before me. You are right. He was. It was a pretty tray. It represented a large lady going along a serpentining up-hill gravel-walk, to attend a little church. Two swans had likewise come astray with the same intentions. When I call her a large lady, I don't mean in point of breadth, for there she fell below my views, but she more than made it up in heighth; her heighth and slimness was – in short the heighth of both.

I often saw that tray, after I was the innocently smiling cause (or more likely screeching one) of the doctor's standing it up on a table against the wall in his consulting-room. Whenever my own father and mother were in that part of the country, I used to put my head (I have heard my own mother say it was flaxen curls at that time, though you wouldn't know an old hearth-broom from it now till you come to the handle, and found it wasn't me) in at the doctor's door, and the doctor was always glad to see me, and said, "Aha, my brother practitioner! Come in, little M.D. How are your inclinations as to sixpence?"

You can't go on for ever, you'll find, nor yet could my father nor yet my mother. If you don't go off as a whole when you are about due, you're liable to go off in part, and two to one your head's the part. Gradually my father went off his, and my mother went off hers. It was in a harmless way, but it put out the family where I boarded them. The old couple, though retired, got to be wholly and solely devoted to the Cheap Jack business, and were always selling the family off. Whenever the cloth was laid for dinner, my father began rattling the plates and dishes, as we do in our line when we put up crockery for a bid, only he had lost the trick of it, and mostly let 'em drop and broke 'em. As the old lady had been used to sit in the cart, and hand the articles out one by one to the old gentleman on the footboard to sell, just in the same way she handed him every item of the family's property, and they disposed of it in their own imaginations from morning to night. At last the old gentleman, lying bedridden in the same room with the old lady, cries out in the old patter, fluent, after having been silent for two days and nights: "Now here, my jolly companions every one, – which the Nightingale club in a village was held, At the sign of the

Cabbage and Shears, Where the singers no doubt would have greatly excelled, But for want of taste, voices and ears, – now, here, my jolly companions, every one, is a working model of a used-up old Cheap Jack, without a tooth in his head, and with a pain in every bone: so like life that it would be just as good if it wasn't better, just as bad if it wasn't worse, and just as new if it wasn't worn out. Bid for the working model of the old Cheap Jack, who has drunk more gunpowder-tea with the ladies in his time than would blow the lid off a washerwoman's copper, and carry it as many thousands of miles higher than the moon as naught nix naught, divided by the national debt, carry nothing to the poor-rates, three under, and two over. Now, my hearts of oak and men of straw, what do you say for the lot? Two shillings, a shilling, tenpence, eightpence, sixpence, fourpence. Twopence? Who said twopence? The gentleman in the scarecrow's hat? I am ashamed of the gentleman in the scarecrow's hat. I really am ashamed of him for his want of public spirit. Now I'll tell you what I'll do with you. Come! I'll throw you in a working model of a old woman that was married to the old Cheap Jack so long ago that upon my word and honour it took place in Noah's Ark, before the Unicorn could get in to forbid the banns by blowing a tune upon his horn. There now! Come! What do you say for both? I'll tell you what I'll do with you. I don't bear you malice for being so backward. Here! If you make me a bid that'll only reflect a little credit on your town, I'll throw you in a warming-pan for nothing, and lend you a toasting-fork for life. Now come; what do you say after that splendid offer? Say two pound, say thirty shillings, say a pound, say ten shillings, say five, say two and six. You don't say even two and six? You say two and three? No. You shan't have the lot for two and three. I'd sooner give it to you, if you was good-looking enough. Here! Missis! Chuck the old man and woman into the cart, put the horse to, and drive 'em away and bury 'em!" Such were the last words of Willum Marigold, my own father, and they were carried out, by him and by his wife, my own mother, on one and the same day, as I ought to know, having followed as mourner.

My father had been a lovely one in his time at the Cheap Jack work, as his dying observations went to prove. But I top him. I don't say it because it's myself, but because it has been universally acknowledged by all that has had the means of comparison. I have worked at it. I have measured myself against other public speakers, – Members of Parliament, Platforms, Pulpits, Counsel learned in the law, – and where I have found 'em good, I have took a bit of imagination from 'em, and where I have found 'em bad, I have let 'em alone. Now I'll tell you what. I mean to go down into my grave declaring that of all the callings ill used in Great Britain, the Cheap Jack calling is the worst used. Why ain't we a profession? Why ain't we endowed with privileges? Why are we forced to take out a hawker's license, when no such thing is expected of the political hawkers? Where's the difference betwixt us? Except that we are Cheap Jacks and they are Dear Jacks, I don't see any difference but what's in our favour.

For look here! Say it's election time. I am on the footboard of my cart in the market-place, on a Saturday night. I put up a general miscellaneous lot. I say: "Now here, my free and independent woters, I'm a going to give you such a chance as you never had in all your born days, nor yet the days preceding. Now I'll show you what I am a going to do with you. Here's a pair of razors that'll shave you closer than the Board of Guardians; here's a flat-iron worth its weight in gold; here's a frying-pan artificially flavoured with essence of beefsteaks to that degree that you've only got for the rest of your lives to fry bread and dripping in it and there you are replete with animal food; here's a genuine chronometer watch in such a solid silver case that you may knock at the door with it when you come home late from a social meeting, and rouse your wife and family, and save up your knocker for the postman; and here's half-a- dozen dinner plates that you may play the cymbals with to charm baby when it's fractious. Stop! I'll throw in another article, and I'll give you that, and it's a rolling-pin; and if the baby can only get it well into its mouth when its teeth is coming and rub the gums once with it, they'll come through double, in a fit of laughter equal to being tickled. Stop again! I'll throw you in another article, because I don't like the looks of you, for you haven't the appearance of buyers unless I lose by you, and because I'd rather lose than not take money to-night, and that's a looking-glass in which you may see how ugly you look when you don't bid. What do you say now? Come! Do you say a pound? Not you, for you haven't got it. Do you say ten shillings? Not you, for you owe more to the tallyman. Well then, I'll tell you what I'll do with you. I'll heap 'em all on the footboard of the cart, – there they are! razors, flat watch, dinner plates, rolling-pin, and away for four shillings, and I'll give you sixpence for your trouble!" This is me, the Cheap Jack. But on the Monday morning, in the same market-place, comes the Dear Jack on the hustings – his cart – and, what does he say? "Now my free and independent woters, I am a going to give you such a chance" (he begins just like me) "as you never had in all your born days, and that's the chance of sending Myself to Parliament. Now I'll tell you what I am a going to do for you. Here's the interests of this magnificent town promoted above all the rest of the civilised and uncivilised earth. Here's your railways carried, and your neighbours' railways jockeyed. Here's all your sons in the Post-office. Here's Britannia smiling on you. Here's the eyes of Europe on you. Here's uniwersal prosperity for you, repletion of animal food, golden cornfields, gladsome homesteads, and rounds of applause from your own hearts, all in one lot, and that's myself. Will you take me as I stand? You won't? Well, then, I'll tell you what I'll do with you. Come now! I'll throw you in anything you ask for. There! Church-rates, abolition of more malt tax, no malt tax, universal education to the highest mark, or uniwersal ignorance to the lowest, total abolition of flogging in the army or a dozen for every private once a month all round, Wrongs of Men or Rights of Women – only say which it shall be, take 'em or leave 'em, and I'm of your opinion altogether, and the lot's your own on your own terms. There! You won't take it yet! Well, then, I'll tell you what I'll do with you. Come! You are such free and independent woters, and I am so proud of you, – you are such a noble and enlightened constituency, and I am so ambitious of the honour and dignity of being your member, which is by far the highest level to which the wings of the human mind can soar, – that I'll tell you what I'll do with you. I'll throw you in all the public-houses in your magnificent town for nothing. Will that content you? It won't? You won't take the lot yet? Well, then, before I put the horse in and drive away, and make the offer to the next most magnificent town that can be discovered, I'll tell you what I'll do. Take the lot, and I'll drop two thousand pound in the streets of your magnificent town for them to pick up that can. Not enough? Now look here. This is the very furthest that I'm a going to. I'll make it two thousand five hundred. And still you won't? Here, missis! Put the horse – no, stop half a moment, I shouldn't like to turn my back upon you neither for a trifle, I'll make it two thousand seven hundred and fifty pound. There! Take the lot on your own terms, and I'll count out two thousand seven hundred and fifty pound on the foot- board of the cart, to be dropped in the streets of your magnificent town for them to pick up that can. What do you say? Come now! You won't do better, and you may do worse. You take it? Hooray! Sold again, and got the seat!"

These Dear Jacks soap the people shameful, but we Cheap Jacks don't. We tell 'em the truth about themselves to their faces, and scorn to court 'em. As to wenturesomeness in the way of puffing up the lots, the Dear Jacks beat us hollow. It is considered in the Cheap Jack calling, that better patter can be made out of a gun than any article we put up from the cart, except a pair of spectacles. I often hold forth about a gun for a quarter of an hour, and feel as if I need never leave off. But when I tell 'em what the gun can do, and what the gun has brought down, I never go half so far as the Dear Jacks do when they make speeches in praise of their guns – their great guns that set 'em on to do it. Besides, I'm in business for myself: I ain't sent down into the market-place to order, as they are. Besides, again, my guns don't know what I say in their laudation, and their guns do, and the whole concern of 'em have reason to be sick and ashamed all round. These are some of my arguments for declaring that the Cheap Jack calling is treated ill in Great Britain, and for turning warm when I think of the other Jacks in question setting themselves up to pretend to look down upon it.

I courted my wife from the footboard of the cart. I did indeed. She was a Suffolk young woman, and it was in Ipswich marketplace right opposite the corn-chandler's shop. I had noticed her up at a window last Saturday that was, appreciating highly. I had took to her, and I had said to myself, "If not already disposed of, I'll have that lot." Next Saturday that come, I pitched the cart on the same pitch, and I was in very high feather indeed, keeping 'em laughing the whole of the time, and getting off the goods briskly. At last I took out of my waistcoat-pocket a small lot wrapped in soft paper, and I put it this way (looking up at the window where she was). "Now here, my blooming English maidens, is an article, the last article of the present evening's sale, which I offer to only you, the lovely Suffolk Dumplings biling over with beauty, and I won't take a bid of a thousand pounds for from any man alive. Now what is it? Why, I'll tell you what it is. It's made of fine gold, and it's not broke, though there's a hole in the middle of it, and it's stronger than any fetter that ever was forged, though it's smaller than any finger in my set of ten. Why ten? Because, when my parents made over my property to me, I tell you true, there was twelve sheets, twelve towels, twelve table-cloths, twelve knives, twelve forks, twelve tablespoons, and twelve teaspoons, but my set of fingers was two short of a dozen, and could never since be matched. Now what else is it? Come, I'll tell you. It's a hoop of solid gold, wrapped in a silver curl-paper, that I myself took off the shining locks of the ever beautiful old lady in Threadneedle Street, London city; I wouldn't tell you so if I hadn't the paper to show, or you mightn't believe it even of me. Now what else is it? It's a man-trap and a handcuff, the parish stocks and a leg-lock, all in gold and all in one. Now what else is it? It's a wedding- ring. Now I'll tell you what I'm a going to do with it. I'm not a going to offer this lot for money; but I mean to give it to the next of you beauties that laughs, and I'll pay her a visit to-morrow morning at exactly half after nine o'clock as the chimes go, and I'll take her out for a walk to put up the banns." She laughed, and got the ring handed up to her. When I called in the morning, she says, "O dear! It's never you, and you never mean it?" "It's ever me," says I, "and I am ever yours, and I ever mean it." So we got married, after being put up three times – which, by the bye, is quite in the Cheap Jack way again, and shows once more how the Cheap Jack customs pervade society.

She wasn't a bad wife, but she had a temper. If she could

have parted with that one article at a sacrifice, I wouldn't have swopped her away in exchange for any other woman in England. Not that I ever did swop her away, for we lived together till she died, and that was thirteen year. Now, my lords and ladies and gentlefolks all, I'll let you into a secret, though you won't believe it. Thirteen year of temper in a Palace would try the worst of you, but thirteen year of temper in a Cart would try the best of you. You are kept so very close to it in a cart, you see. There's thousands of couples among you getting on like sweet ile upon a whetstone in houses five and six pairs of stairs high, that would go to the Divorce Court in a cart. Whether the jolting makes it worse, I don't undertake to decide; but in a cart it does come home to you, and stick to you. Wiolence in a cart is so wiolent, and aggrawation in a cart is so aggrawating.

We might have had such a pleasant life! A roomy cart, with the large goods hung outside, and the bed slung underneath it when on the road, an iron pot and a kettle, a fireplace for the cold weather, a chimney for the smoke, a hanging-shelf and a cupboard, a dog and a horse. What more do you want? You draw off upon a bit of turf in a green lane or by the roadside, you hobble your old horse and turn him grazing, you light your fire upon the ashes of the last visitors, you cook your stew, and you wouldn't call the Emperor of France your father. But have a temper in the cart, flinging language and the hardest goods in stock at you, and where are you then? Put a name to your feelings.

My dog knew as well when she was on the turn as I did. Before she broke out, he would give a howl, and bolt. How he knew it, was a mystery to me; but the sure and certain knowledge of it would wake him up out of his soundest sleep, and he would give a howl, and bolt. At such times I wished I was him.

The worst of it was, we had a daughter born to us, and I love children with all my heart. When she was in her furies she beat the child. This got to be so shocking, as the child got to be four or five year old, that I have many a time gone on with my whip over my shoulder, at the old horse's head, sobbing and crying worse than ever little Sophy did. For how could I prevent it? Such a thing is not to be tried with such a temper –

in a cart – without coming to a fight. It's in the natural size and formation of a cart to bring it to a fight. And then the poor child got worse terrified than before, as well as worse hurt generally, and her mother made complaints to the next people we lighted on, and the word went round, "Here's a wretch of a Cheap Jack been a beating his wife."

Little Sophy was such a brave child! She grew to be quite devoted to her poor father, though he could do so little to help her. She had a wonderful quantity of shining dark hair, all curling natural about her. It is quite astonishing to me now, that I didn't go tearing mad when I used to see her run from her mother before the cart, and her mother catch her by this hair, and pull her down by it, and beat her.

Such a brave child I said she was! Ah! with reason.

"Don't you mind next time, father dear," she would whisper to me, with her little face still flushed, and her bright eyes still wet; "if I don't cry out, you may know I am not much hurt. And even if I do cry out, it will only be to get mother to let go and leave off." What I have seen the little spirit bear – for me – without crying out!

Yet in other respects her mother took great care of her. Her clothes were always clean and neat, and her mother was never tired of working at 'em. Such is the inconsistency in things. Our being down in the marsh country in unhealthy weather, I consider the cause of Sophy's taking bad low fever; but however she took it, once she got it she turned away from her mother for evermore, and nothing would persuade her to be touched by her mother's hand. She would shiver and say, "No, no, no," when it was offered at, and would hide her face on my shoulder, and hold me tighter round the neck.

The Cheap Jack business had been worse than ever I had known it, what with one thing and what with another (and not least with railroads, which will cut it all to pieces, I expect, at last), and I was run dry of money. For which reason, one night at that period of little Sophy's being so bad, either we must have come to a dead-lock for victuals and drink, or I must have pitched the cart as I did.

I couldn't get the dear child to lie down or leave go of me, and indeed I hadn't the heart to try, so I stepped out on the footboard with her holding round my neck. They all set up a laugh when they see us, and one chuckle-headed Joskin (that I hated for it) made the bidding, "Tuppence for her!"

"Now, you country boobies," says I, feeling as if my heart was a heavy weight at the end of a broken sashline, "I give you notice that I am a going to charm the money out of your pockets, and to give you so much more than your money's worth that you'll only persuade yourselves to draw your Saturday night's wages ever again arterwards by the hopes of meeting me to lay 'em out with, which you never will, and why not? Because I've made my fortunes by selling my goods on a large scale for seventy-five per cent. less than I give for 'em, and I am consequently to be elevated to the House of Peers next week, by the title of the Duke of Cheap and Markis Jackaloorul. Now let's know what you want to-night, and you shall have it. But first of all, shall I tell you why I have got this little girl round my neck? You don't want to know? Then you shall. She belongs to the Fairies. She's a fortune-teller. She can tell me all about you in a whisper, and can put me up to whether you're going to buy a lot or leave it. Now do you want a saw? No, she says you don't, because you're too clumsy to use one. Else here's a saw which would be a lifelong blessing to a handy man, at four shillings, at three and six, at three, at two and six, at two, at eighteen-pence. But none of you shall have it at any price, on account of your well-known awkwardness, which would make it manslaughter. The same objection applies to this set of three planes which I won't let you have neither, so don't bid for 'em. Now I am a going to ask her what you do want." (Then I whispered, "Your head burns so, that I am afraid it hurts you bad, my pet," and she answered, without opening her heavy eyes, "Just a little, father.") "O! This little fortune-teller says it's a memorandum- book you want. Then why didn't you mention it? Here it is. Look at it. Two hundred superfine hot-pressed wire-wove pages – if you don't believe me, count 'em – ready ruled for your expenses, an everlastingly pointed pencil to put 'em down with, a double-bladed penknife to scratch 'em out with, a book of printed tables to calculate your income with, and a camp-stool to sit down upon while you give your mind to it! Stop! And an umbrella to keep the moon off when you give your mind to it on a pitch-dark night. Now I won't ask you how much for the lot, but how little? How little are you thinking of? Don't be ashamed to mention it, because my fortune-teller knows already." (Then making believe to whisper, I kissed her, – and she kissed me.) "Why, she says you are thinking of as little as three and threepence! I couldn't have believed it, even of you, unless she told me. Three and threepence! And a set of printed tables in the lot that'll calculate your income up to forty thousand a year! With an income of forty thousand a year, you grudge three and sixpence. Well then, I'll tell you my opinion. I so despise the threepence, that I'd sooner take three shillings. There. For three shillings, three shillings, three shillings! Gone. Hand 'em over to the lucky man."

As there had been no bid at all, everybody looked about and grinned at everybody, while I touched little Sophy's face and asked her if she felt faint, or giddy. "Not very, father. It will soon be over." Then turning from the pretty patient eyes, which were opened now, and seeing nothing but grins across my lighted grease-pot, I went on again in my Cheap Jack style. "Where's the butcher?" (My sorrowful eye had just caught sight of a fat young butcher on the outside of the crowd.) "She says the good luck is the butcher's. Where is he?" Everybody handed on the blushing butcher to the front, and there was a roar, and the butcher felt himself obliged to put his hand in his pocket, and take the lot. The party so picked out, in general, does feel obliged to take the lot – good four times out of six. Then we had another lot, the counterpart of that one, and sold it sixpence cheaper, which is always wery much enjoyed. Then we had the spectacles. It ain't a special profitable lot, but I put 'em on, and I see what the Chancellor of the Exchequer is going to take off the taxes, and I see what the sweetheart of the young woman in the shawl is doing at home, and I see what the Bishops has got for dinner, and a deal more that seldom fails to fetch em 'up in their spirits; and the better their spirits, the better their bids. Then we had the ladies' lot – the teapot, tea- caddy, glass sugar-basin, half-a-dozen spoons, and caudle-cup – and all the time I was making similar excuses to give a look or two and say a word or two to my poor child. It was while the second ladies' lot was holding 'em enchained that I felt her lift herself a little on my shoulder, to look across the dark street. "What troubles you, darling?" "Nothing troubles me, father. I am not at all troubled. But don't I see a pretty churchyard over there?" "Yes, my dear." "Kiss me twice, dear father, and lay me down to rest upon that churchyard grass so soft and green." I staggered back into the cart with her head dropped on my shoulder, and I says to her mother, "Quick. Shut the door! Don't let those laughing people see!" "What's the matter?" she cries. "O woman, woman," I tells her, "you'll never catch my little Sophy by her hair again, for she has flown away from you!"

Maybe those were harder words than I meant 'em; but from that time forth my wife took to brooding, and would sit in the cart or walk beside it, hours at a stretch, with her arms crossed, and her eyes looking on the ground. When her furies took her (which was rather seldomer than before) they took her in a new way, and she banged herself about to that extent that I was forced to hold her. She got none the better for a little drink now and then, and through some years I used to wonder, as I plodded along at the old horse's head, whether there was many carts upon the road that held so much dreariness as mine, for all my being looked up to as the King of the Cheap Jacks. So sad our lives went on till one summer evening, when, as we were coming into Exeter, out of the farther West of England, we saw a woman beating a child in a cruel manner, who screamed, "Don't beat me! O mother, mother, mother!" Then my wife stopped her ears, and ran away like a wild thing, and next day she was found in the river.

Me and my dog were all the company left in the cart now; and the dog learned to give a short bark when they wouldn't bid, and to give another and a nod of his head when I asked him, "Who said half a crown? Are you the gentleman, sir, that offered half a crown?" He attained to an immense height of popularity, and I shall always believe taught himself entirely out of his own head to growl at any person in the crowd that bid as low as sixpence. But he got to be well on in years, and one night when I was conwulsing York with the spectacles, he took a conwulsion on his own account upon the very footboard by me, and it finished him.

Being naturally of a tender turn, I had dreadful lonely feelings on me arter this. I conquered 'em at selling times, having a reputation to keep (not to mention keeping myself), but they got me down in private, and rolled upon me. That's often the way with us public characters. See us on the footboard, and you'd give pretty well anything you possess to be us. See us off the footboard, and you'd add a trifle to be off your bargain. It was under those circumstances that I come acquainted with a giant. I might have been too high to fall into conversation with him, had it not been for my lonely feelings. For the general rule is, going round the country, to draw the line at dressing up. When a man can't trust his getting a living to his undisguised abilities, you consider him below your sort. And this giant when on view figured as a Roman.

He was a languid young man, which I attribute to the distance betwixt his extremities. He had a little head and less in it, he had weak eyes and weak knees, and altogether you couldn't look at him without feeling that there was greatly too much of him both for his joints and his mind. But he was an amiable though timid young man (his mother let him out, and spent the money), and we come acquainted when he was walking to ease the horse betwixt two fairs. He was called Rinaldo di Velasco, his name being Pickleson.

This giant, otherwise Pickleson, mentioned to me under the seal of confidence that, beyond his being a burden to himself, his life was made a burden to him by the cruelty of his master towards a step- daughter who was deaf and dumb. Her mother was dead, and she had no living soul to take her part, and was used most hard. She travelled with his master's caravan only because there was nowhere to leave her, and this giant, otherwise Pickleson, did go so far as to believe that his master often tried to lose her. He was such a very languid young man, that I don't know how long it didn't take him to get this story out, but it passed through his defective circulation to his top extremity in course of time.

When I heard this account from the giant, otherwise Pickleson, and likewise that the poor girl had beautiful long dark hair, and was often pulled down by it and beaten, I couldn't see the giant through what stood in my eyes. Having wiped 'em, I give him sixpence (for he was kept as short as he was long), and he laid it out in two three-penn'orths of gin-and-water, which so brisked him up, that he sang the Favourite Comic of Shivery Shakey, ain't it cold? – a popular effect which his master had tried every other means to get out of him as a Roman wholly in vain.

His master's name was Mim, a wery hoarse man, and I knew him to speak to. I went to that Fair as a mere civilian, leaving the cart outside the town, and I looked about the back of the Vans while the performing was going on, and at last, sitting dozing against a muddy cart-wheel, I come upon the poor girl who was deaf and dumb. At the first look I might almost have judged that she had escaped from the Wild Beast Show; but at the second I thought better of her, and thought that if she was more cared for and more kindly used she would be like my child. She was just the same age that my own daughter would have been, if her pretty head had not fell down upon my shoulder that unfortunate night.

To cut it short, I spoke confidential to Mim while he was beating the gong outside betwixt two lots of Pickleson's publics, and I put it to him, "She lies heavy on your own hands; what'll you take for her?" Mim was a most ferocious swearer. Suppressing that part of his reply which was much the longest part, his reply was, "A pair of braces." "Now I'll tell you," says I, "what I'm a going to do with you. I'm a going to fetch you half-a-dozen pair of the primest braces in the cart, and then to take her away with me." Says Mim (again ferocious), "I'll believe it when I've got the goods, and no sooner." I made all the haste I could, lest he should think twice of it, and the bargain was completed, which Pickleson he was thereby so relieved in his mind that he come out at his little back door, longways like a serpent, and give us Shivery Shakey in a whisper among the wheels at parting.

It was happy days for both of us when Sophy and me began to travel in the cart. I at once give her the name of Sophy, to put her ever towards me in the attitude of my own daughter. We soon made out to begin to understand one another, through the goodness of the Heavens, when she knowed that I meant true and kind by her. In a very little time she was wonderful fond of me. You have no idea what it is to have anybody wonderful fond of you, unless you have been got down and rolled upon by the lonely feelings that I have mentioned as having once got the better of me.

You'd have laughed – or the rewerse – it's according to your disposition – if you could have seen me trying to teach Sophy. At first I was helped – you'd never guess by what – milestones. I got some large alphabets in a box, all the letters separate on bits of bone, and saying we was going to Windsor, I give her those letters in that order, and then at every milestone I showed her those same letters in that same order again, and pointed towards the abode of royalty. Another time I give her cart, and then chalked the same upon the cart. Another time I give her Doctor Marigold, and hung a corresponding inscription outside my waistcoat. People that met us might stare a bit and laugh, but what did I care, if she caught the idea? She caught it after long patience and trouble, and then we did begin to get on swimmingly, I believe you! At first she was a little given to consider me the cart, and the cart the abode of royalty, but that soon wore off.

We had our signs, too, and they was hundreds in number. Sometimes she would sit looking at me and considering hard how to communicate with me about something fresh, – how to ask me what she wanted explained, – and then she was (or I thought she was; what does it signify?) so like my child with those years added to her, that I half-believed it was herself, trying to tell me where she had been to up in the skies, and what she had seen since that unhappy night when she flied away. She had a pretty face, and now that there was no one to drag at her bright dark hair, and it was all in order, there was a something touching in her looks that made the cart most peaceful and most quiet, though not at all melancholy. [N.B. In the Cheap Jack patter, we generally sound it lemonjolly, and it gets a laugh.]

The way she learnt to understand any look of mine was truly surprising. When I sold of a night, she would sit in the cart unseen by them outside, and would give a eager look into my eyes when I looked in, and would hand me straight the precise article or articles I wanted. And then she would clap her hands, and laugh for joy. And as for me, seeing her so bright, and remembering what she was when I first lighted on her, starved and beaten and ragged, leaning asleep against the muddy cart-wheel, it give me such heart that I gained a greater heighth of reputation than ever, and I put Pickleson down (by the name of Mim's Travelling Giant otherwise Pickleson) for a fypunnote in my will.

This happiness went on in the cart till she was sixteen year old. By which time I began to feel not satisfied that I had done my whole duty by her, and to consider that she ought to have better teaching than I could give her. It drew a many tears on both sides when I commenced explaining my views to her; but what's right is right, and you can't neither by tears nor laughter do away with its character.

So I took her hand in mine, and I went with her one day to the Deaf and Dumb Establishment in London, and when the gentleman come to speak to us, I says to him: "Now I'll tell you what I'll do with you, sir. I am nothing but a Cheap Jack, but of late years I have laid by for a rainy day notwithstanding. This is my only daughter (adopted), and you can't produce a deafer nor a dumber. Teach her the most that can be taught her in the shortest separation that can be named, – state the figure for it, – and I am game to put the money down. I won't bate you a single farthing, sir, but I'll put down the money here and now, and I'll thankfully throw you in a pound to take it. There!" The gentleman smiled, and then, "Well, well," says he, "I must first know what she has learned already. How do you communicate with her?" Then I showed him, and she wrote in printed writing many names of things and so forth; and we held some sprightly conversation, Sophy and me, about a little story in a book which the gentleman showed her, and which she was able to read. "This is most extraordinary," says the gentleman; "is it possible that you have been her only teacher?" "I have been her only teacher, sir," I says, "besides herself." "Then," says the gentleman, and more acceptable words was never spoke to me, "you're a clever fellow, and a good fellow." This he makes known to Sophy, who kisses his hands, claps her own, and laughs and cries upon it.

We saw the gentleman four times in all, and when he took down my name and asked how in the world it ever chanced to be Doctor, it come out that he was own nephew by the sister's side, if you'll believe me, to the very Doctor that I was called after. This made our footing still easier, and he says to me:

"Now, Marigold, tell me what more do you want your adopted daughter to know?"

"I want her, sir, to be cut off from the world as little as can be, considering her deprivations, and therefore to be able to read whatever is wrote with perfect ease and pleasure."

"My good fellow," urges the gentleman, opening his eyes wide, "why I can't do that myself!"

I took his joke, and gave him a laugh (knowing by experience how flat you fall without it), and I mended my words accordingly.

"What do you mean to do with her afterwards?" asks the gentleman, with a sort of a doubtful eye. "To take her about the country?"

"In the cart, sir, but only in the cart. She will live a private life, you understand, in the cart. I should never think of bringing her infirmities before the public. I wouldn't make a show of her for any money."

The gentleman nodded, and seemed to approve.

"Well," says he, "can you part with her for two years?"

"To do her that good, – yes, sir."

"There's another question," says the gentleman, looking towards her, – "can she part with you for two years?"

I don't know that it was a harder matter of itself (for the other was hard enough to me), but it was harder to get over. However, she was pacified to it at last, and the separation betwixt us was settled. How it cut up both of us when it took place, and when I left her at the door in the dark of an evening, I don't tell. But I know this; remembering that night, I shall never pass that same establishment without a heartache and a swelling in the throat; and I couldn't put you up the best of lots in sight of it with my usual spirit, – no, not even the gun, nor the pair of spectacles, – for five hundred pound reward from the Secretary of State for the Home Department, and throw in the honour of putting my legs under his mahogany arterwards.

Still, the loneliness that followed in the cart was not the old loneliness, because there was a term put to it, however long to look forward to; and because I could think, when I was anyways down, that she belonged to me and I belonged to her. Always planning for her coming back, I bought in a few months' time another cart, and what do you think I planned to do with it? I'll tell you. I planned to fit it up with shelves and books for her reading, and to have a seat in it where I could sit and see her read, and think that I had been her first teacher. Not hurrying over the job, I had the fittings knocked together in contriving ways under my own inspection, and here was her bed in a berth with curtains, and there was her reading-table, and here was her writing-desk, and elsewhere was her books in rows upon rows, picters and no picters, bindings and no bindings, gilt-edged and plain, just as I could pick 'em up for her in lots up and down the country, North and South and West and East, Winds liked best and winds liked least, Here and there and gone astray, Over the hills and far away. And when I had got together pretty well as many books as the cart would neatly hold, a new scheme come into my head, which, as it turned out, kept my time and attention a good deal employed, and helped me over the two years' stile.

Without being of an awaricious temper, I like to be the owner of things. I shouldn't wish, for instance, to go partners with yourself in the Cheap Jack cart. It's not that I mistrust you, but that I'd rather know it was mine. Similarly, very likely you'd rather know it was yours. Well! A kind of a jealousy began to creep into my mind when I reflected that all those books would have been read by other people long before they was read by her. It seemed to take away from her being the owner of 'em like. In this way, the question got into my head: Couldn't I have a book new-made express for her, which she should be the first to read?

It pleased me, that thought did; and as I never was a man to let a thought sleep (you must wake up all the whole family of thoughts you've got and burn their nightcaps, or you won't do in the Cheap Jack line), I set to work at it. Considering that I was in the habit of changing so much about the country, and that I should have to find out a literary character here to make a deal with, and another literary character there to make a deal with, as opportunities presented, I hit on the plan that this same book should be a general miscellaneous lot, – like the razors, flat-iron, chronometer watch, dinner plates, rolling-pin, and looking-glass, – and shouldn't be offered as a single indiwidual article, like the spectacles or the gun. When I had come to that conclusion, I come to another, which shall likewise be yours.

Often had I regretted that she never had heard me on the footboard, and that she never could hear me. It ain't that I am vain, but that you don't like to put your own light under a bushel. What's the worth of your reputation, if you can't convey the reason for it to the person you most wish to value it? Now I'll put it to you. Is it worth sixpence, fippence, fourpence, threepence, twopence, a penny, a halfpenny, a farthing? No, it ain't. Not worth a farthing. Very well, then. My conclusion was that I would begin her book with some account of myself. So that, through reading a specimen or two of me on the footboard, she might form an idea of my merits there. I was aware that I couldn't do myself justice. A man can't write his eye (at least I don't know how to), nor yet can a man write his voice, nor the rate of his talk, nor the quickness of his action, nor his general spicy way. But he can write his turns of speech, when he is a public speaker, – and indeed I have heard that he very often does, before he speaks 'em.

Well! Having formed that resolution, then come the question of a name. How did I hammer that hot iron into shape? This way. The most difficult explanation I had ever had with her was, how I come to be called Doctor, and yet was no Doctor. After all, I felt that I had failed of getting it correctly into her mind, with my utmost pains. But trusting to her improvement in the two years, I thought that I might trust to her understanding it when she should come to read it as put down by my own hand. Then I thought I would try a joke with her and watch how it took, by which of itself I might fully judge of her understanding it. We had first discovered the mistake we had dropped into, through her having asked me to prescribe for her when she had supposed me to be a Doctor in a medical point of view; so thinks I, "Now, if I give this book the name of my Prescriptions, and if she catches the idea that my only Prescriptions are for her amusement and interest, – to make her laugh in a pleasant way, or to make her cry in a pleasant way, – it will be a delightful proof to both of us that we have got over our difficulty." It fell out to absolute perfection. For when she saw the book, as I had it got up, – the printed and pressed book, – lying on her desk in her cart, and saw the title, Doctor Marigold's Prescriptions, she looked at me for a moment with astonishment, then fluttered the leaves, then broke out a laughing in the charmingest way, then felt her pulse and shook her head, then turned the pages pretending to read them most attentive, then kissed the book to me, and put it to her bosom with both her hands. I never was better pleased in all my life!

But let me not anticipate. (I take that expression out of a lot of romances I bought for her. I never opened a single one of 'em – and I have opened many – but I found the romancer saying "let me not anticipate." Which being so, I wonder why he did anticipate, or who asked him to it.) Let me not, I say, anticipate. This same book took up all my spare time. It was no play to get the other articles together in the general miscellaneous lot, but when it come to my own article! There! I couldn't have believed the blotting, nor yet the buckling to at it, nor the patience over it. Which again is like the footboard. The public have no idea.

At last it was done, and the two years' time was gone after all the other time before it, and where it's all gone to, who knows? The new cart was finished, – yellow outside, relieved with wermilion and brass fittings, – the old horse was put in it, a new 'un and a boy being laid on for the Cheap Jack cart, – and I cleaned myself up to go and fetch her. Bright cold weather it was, cart-chimneys smoking, carts pitched private on a piece of waste ground over at Wandsworth, where you may see 'em from the Sou'western Railway when not upon the road. (Look out of the right-hand window going down.)

"Marigold," says the gentleman, giving his hand hearty, "I am very glad to see you."

"Yet I have my doubts, sir," says I, "if you can be half as glad to see me as I am to see you."

"The time has appeared so long, – has it, Marigold?"

"I won't say that, sir, considering its real length; but – "

"What a start, my good fellow!"

Ah! I should think it was! Grown such a woman, so pretty, so intelligent, so expressive! I knew then that she must be really like my child, or I could never have known her, standing quiet by the door.

"You are affected," says the gentleman in a kindly manner.

"I feel, sir," says I, "that I am but a rough chap in a sleeved waistcoat."

"I feel," says the gentleman, "that it was you who raised her from misery and degradation, and brought her into communication with her kind. But why do we converse alone together, when we can converse so well with her? Address her in your own way."

"I am such a rough chap in a sleeved waistcoat, sir," says I, "and she is such a graceful woman, and she stands so quiet at the door!"

"Try if she moves at the old sign," says the gentleman.

They had got it up together o' purpose to please me! For when I give her the old sign, she rushed to my feet, and dropped upon her knees, holding up her hands to me with pouring tears of love and joy; and when I took her hands and lifted her, she clasped me round the neck, and lay there; and I don't know what a fool I didn't make of myself, until we all three settled down into talking without sound, as if there was a something soft and pleasant spread over the whole world for us.

[A portion is here omitted from the text, having reference to the sketches contributed by other writers; but the reader will be pleased to have what follows retained in a note:

"Now I'll tell you what I am a-going to do with you. I am a-going to offer you the general miscellaneous lot, her own book, never read by anybody else but me, added to and completed by me after her first reading of it, eight-and-forty printed pages, six-and-ninety columns, Whiting's own work, Beaufort House to wit, thrown off by the steam-ingine, best of paper, beautiful green wrapper, folded like clean linen come home from the clear-starcher's, and so exquisitely stitched that, regarded as a piece of needlework alone, it's better than the sampler of a seamstress undergoing a Competitive examination for Starvation before the Civil Service Commissioners – and I offer the lot for what? For eight pound? Not so much. For six pound? Less. For four pound. Why, I hardly expect you to believe me, but that's the sum. Four pound! The stitching alone cost half as much again. Here's forty-eight original pages, ninety-six original columns, for four pound. You want more for the money? Take it. Three whole pages of advertisements of thrilling interest thrown in for nothing. Read 'em and believe 'em. More? My best of wishes for your merry Christmases and your happy New Years, your long lives and your true prosperities. Worth twenty pound good if they are delivered as I send them. Remember! Here's a final prescription added, "To be taken for life," which will tell you how the cart broke down, and where the journey ended. You think Four Pound too much? And still you think so? Come! I'll tell you what then. Say Four Pence, and keep the secret."]

So every item of my plan was crowned with success. Our reunited life was more than all that we had looked forward to. Content and joy went with us as the wheels of the two carts went round, and the same stopped with us when the two carts stopped. I was as pleased and as proud as a Pug-Dog with his muzzle black-leaded for a evening party, and his tail extra curled by machinery.

But I had left something out of my calculations. Now, what had I left out? To help you to guess I'll say, a figure. Come. Make a guess and guess right. Nought? No. Nine? No. Eight? No. Seven? No. Six? No. Five? No. Four? No. Three? No. Two? No. One? No. Now I'll tell you what I'll do with you. I'll say it's another sort of figure altogether. There. Why then, says you, it's a mortal figure. No, nor yet a mortal figure. By such means you got yourself penned into a corner, and you can't help guessing a immortal figure. That's about it. Why didn't you say so sooner?

Yes. It was a immortal figure that I had altogether left out of my Calculations. Neither man's, nor woman's, but a child's. Girl's or boy's? Boy's. "I, says the sparrow with my bow and arrow." Now you have got it.

We were down at Lancaster, and I had done two nights more than fair average business (though I cannot in honour recommend them as a quick audience) in the open square there, near the end of the street where Mr. Sly's King's Arms and Royal Hotel stands. Mim's travelling giant, otherwise Pickleson, happened at the self-same time to be trying it on in the town. The genteel lay was adopted with him. No hint of a van. Green baize alcove leading up to Pickleson in a Auction Room. Printed poster, "Free list suspended, with the exception of that proud boast of an enlightened country, a free press. Schools admitted by private arrangement. Nothing to raise a blush in the cheek of youth or shock the most fastidious." Mim swearing most horrible and terrific, in a pink calico pay-place, at the slackness of the public. Serious handbill in the shops, importing that it was all but impossible to come to a right understanding of the history of David without seeing Pickleson.

I went to the Auction Room in question, and I found it entirely empty of everything but echoes and mouldiness, with the single exception of Pickleson on a piece of red drugget. This suited my purpose, as I wanted a private and confidential word with him, which was: "Pickleson. Owing much happiness to you, I put you in my will for a fypunnote; but, to save trouble, here's fourpunten down, which may equally suit your views, and let us so conclude the transaction." Pickleson, who up to that remark had had the dejected appearance of a long Roman rushlight that couldn't anyhow get lighted, brightened up at his top extremity, and made his acknowledgments in a way which (for him) was parliamentary eloquence. He likewise did add, that, having ceased to draw as a Roman, Mim had made proposals for his going in as a conwerted Indian Giant worked upon by The Dairyman's Daughter. This, Pickleson, having no acquaintance with the tract named after that young woman, and not being willing to couple gag with his serious views, had declined to do, thereby leading to words and the total stoppage of the unfortunate young man's beer. All of which, during the whole of the interview, was confirmed by the ferocious growling of Mim down below in the pay-place, which shook the giant like a leaf.

But what was to the present point in the remarks of the travelling giant, otherwise Pickleson, was this: "Doctor Marigold," – I give his words without a hope of conweying their feebleness,

– "who is the strange young man that hangs about your carts?" – "The strange young man?" I gives him back, thinking that he meant her, and his languid circulation had dropped a syllable. "Doctor," he returns, with a pathos calculated to draw a tear from even a manly eye, "I am weak, but not so weak yet as that I don't know my words. I repeat them, Doctor. The strange young man." It then appeared that Pickleson, being forced to stretch his legs (not that they wanted it) only at times when he couldn't be seen for nothing, to wit in the dead of the night and towards daybreak, had twice seen hanging about my carts, in that same town of Lancaster where I had been only two nights, this same unknown young man.

It put me rather out of sorts. What it meant as to particulars I no more foreboded then than you forebode now, but it put me rather out of sorts. Howsoever, I made light of it to Pickleson, and I took leave of Pickleson, advising him to spend his legacy in getting up his stamina, and to continue to stand by his religion. Towards morning I kept a look out for the strange young man, and – what was more – I saw the strange young man. He was well dressed and well looking. He loitered very nigh my carts, watching them like as if he was taking care of them, and soon after daybreak turned and went away. I sent a hail after him, but he never started or looked round, or took the smallest notice.

We left Lancaster within an hour or two, on our way towards Carlisle. Next morning, at daybreak, I looked out again for the strange young man. I did not see him. But next morning I looked out again, and there he was once more. I sent another hail after him, but as before he gave not the slightest sign of being anyways disturbed. This put a thought into my head. Acting on it I watched him in different manners and at different times not necessary to enter into, till I found that this strange young man was deaf and dumb.

The discovery turned me over, because I knew that a part of that establishment where she had been was allotted to young men (some of them well off), and I thought to myself, "If she favours him, where am I? and where is all that I have worked and planned for?" Hoping- -I must confess to the selfishness – that she might not favour him, I set myself to find out. At last I was by accident present at a meeting between them in the open air, looking on leaning behind a fir-tree without their knowing of it. It was a moving meeting for all the three parties concerned. I knew every syllable that passed between them as well as they did. I listened with my eyes, which had come to be as quick and true with deaf and dumb conversation as my ears with the talk of people that can speak. He was a-going out to China as clerk in a merchant's house, which his father had been before him. He was in circumstances to keep a wife, and he wanted her to marry him and go along with him. She persisted, no. He asked if she didn't love him. Yes, she loved him dearly, dearly; but she could never disappoint her beloved, good, noble, generous, and I-don't-know-what-all father (meaning me, the Cheap Jack in the sleeved waistcoat) and she would stay with him, Heaven bless him! though it was to break her heart. Then she cried most bitterly, and that made up my mind.

While my mind had been in an unsettled state about her favouring this young man, I had felt that unreasonable towards Pickleson, that it was well for him he had got his legacy down. For I often thought, "If it hadn't been for this same weak-minded giant, I might never have come to trouble my head and wex my soul about the young man." But, once that I knew she loved him, – once that I had seen her weep for him, – it was a different thing. I made it right in my mind with Pickleson on the spot, and I shook myself together to do what was right by all.

She had left the young man by that time (for it took a few minutes to get me thoroughly well shook together), and the young man was leaning against another of the fir-trees, – of which there was a cluster, -with his face upon his arm. I touched him on the back. Looking up and seeing me, he says, in our deaf-and-dumb talk, "Do not be angry."

"I am not angry, good boy. I am your friend. Come with me."

I left him at the foot of the steps of the Library Cart, and I went up alone. She was drying her eyes.

"You have been crying, my dear."

"Yes, father."

"Why?"

"A headache."

"Not a heartache?"

"I said a headache, father."

"Doctor Marigold must prescribe for that headache."

She took up the book of my Prescriptions, and held it up with a forced smile; but seeing me keep still and look earnest, she softly laid it down again, and her eyes were very attentive.

"The Prescription is not there, Sophy."

"Where is it?"

"Here, my dear."

I brought her young husband in, and I put her hand in his, and my only farther words to both of them were these: "Doctor Marigold's last Prescription. To be taken for life." After which I bolted.

When the wedding come off, I mounted a coat (blue, and bright buttons), for the first and last time in all my days, and I give Sophy away with my own hand. There were only us three and the gentleman who had had charge of her for those two years. I give the wedding dinner of four in the Library Cart. Pigeon-pie, a leg of pickled pork, a pair of fowls, and suitable garden stuff. The best of drinks. I give them a speech, and the gentleman give us a speech, and all our jokes told, and the whole went off like a sky- rocket. In the course of the entertainment I explained to Sophy that I should keep the Library Cart as my living-cart when not upon the road, and that I should keep all her books for her just as they stood, till she come back to claim them. So she went to China with her young husband, and it was a parting sorrowful and heavy, and I got the boy I had another service; and so as of old, when my child and wife were gone, I went plodding along alone, with my whip over my shoulder, at the old horse's head.

Sophy wrote me many letters, and I wrote her many letters. About the end of the first year she sent me one in an unsteady hand: "Dearest father, not a week ago I had a darling little daughter, but I am so well that they let me write these words to you. Dearest and best father, I hope my child may not be deaf and dumb, but I do not yet know." When I wrote back, I hinted the question; but as Sophy never answered that question, I felt it to be a sad one, and I never repeated it. For a long time our letters were regular, but then they got irregular, through Sophy's husband being moved to another station, and through my being always on the move. But we were in one another's thoughts, I was equally sure, letters or no letters.

Five years, odd months, had gone since Sophy went away. I was still the King of the Cheap Jacks, and at a greater height of popularity than ever. I had had a first-rate autumn of it, and on the twenty-third of December, one thousand eight hundred and sixty-four, I found myself at Uxbridge, Middlesex, clean sold out. So I jogged up to London with the old horse, light and easy, to have my Christmas- eve and Christmas-day alone by the fire in the Library Cart, and then to buy a regular new stock of goods all round, to sell 'em again and get the money.

I am a neat hand at cookery, and I'll tell you what I knocked up for my Christmas-eve dinner in the Library Cart. I knocked up a beefsteak-pudding for one, with two kidneys, a dozen oysters, and a couple of mushrooms thrown in. It's a pudding to put a man in good humour with everything, except the two bottom buttons of his waistcoat. Having relished that pudding and cleared away, I turned the lamp low, and sat down by the light of the fire, watching it as it shone upon the backs of Sophy's books.

Sophy's books so brought Sophy's self, that I saw her touching face quite plainly, before I dropped off dozing by the fire. This may be a reason why Sophy, with her deaf-and-dumb child in her arms, seemed to stand silent by me all through my nap. I was on the road, off the road, in all sorts of places, North and South and West and East, Winds liked best and winds liked least, Here and there and gone astray, Over the hills and far away, and still she stood silent by me, with her silent child in her arms. Even when I woke with a start, she seemed to vanish, as if she had stood by me in that very place only a single instant before.

I had started at a real sound, and the sound was on the steps of the cart. It was the light hurried tread of a child, coming clambering up. That tread of a child had once been so familiar to me, that for half a moment I believed I was a-going to see a little ghost.

But the touch of a real child was laid upon the outer handle of the door, and the handle turned, and the door opened a little way, and a real child peeped in. A bright little comely girl with large dark eyes.

Looking full at me, the tiny creature took off her mite of a straw hat, and a quantity of dark curls fell about her face. Then she opened her lips, and said in a pretty voice,

"Grandfather!"

"Ah, my God!" I cries out. "She can speak!"

"Yes, dear grandfather. And I am to ask you whether there was ever any one that I remind you of?"

In a moment Sophy was round my neck, as well as the child, and her husband was a-wringing my hand with his face hid, and we all had to shake ourselves together before we could get over it. And when we did begin to get over it, and I saw the pretty child a-talking, pleased and quick and eager and busy, to her mother, in the signs that I had first taught her mother, the happy and yet pitying tears fell rolling down my face.

# Fanny and Annie

## *D.H. Lawrence*

Flame-lurid his face as he turned among the throng of flame-lit and dark faces upon the platform. In the light of the furnace she caught sight of his drifting countenance, like a piece of floating fire. And the nostalgia, the doom of homecoming went through her veins like a drug. His eternal face, flame-lit now! The pulse and darkness of red fire from the furnace towers in the sky, lighting the desultory, industrial crowd on the wayside station, lit him and went out.

Of course he did not see her. Flame-lit and unseeing! Always the same, with his meeting eyebrows, his common cap, and his red-and-black scarf knotted round his throat. Not even a collar to meet her! The flames had sunk, there was shadow.

She opened the door of her grimy, branch-line carriage, and began to get down her bags. The porter was nowhere, of course, but there was Harry, obscure, on the outer edge of the little crowd, missing her, of course.

'Here! Harry!' she called, waving her umbrella in the twilight. He hurried forward.

'Tha's come, has ter?' he said, in a sort of cheerful welcome. She got down, rather flustered, and gave him a peck of a kiss.

'Two suit-cases!' she said.

Her soul groaned within her, as he clambered into the carriage after her bags. Up shot the fire in the twilight sky, from the great furnace behind the station. She felt the red flame go across her face. She had come back, she had come back for good. And her spirit groaned dismally. She doubted if she could bear it.

There, on the sordid little station under the furnaces, she stood, tall and distinguished, in her well-made coat and skirt and her broad grey velour hat. She held her umbrella, her bead chatelaine, and a little leather case in her grey-gloved hands, while Harry staggered out of the ugly little train with her bags.

'There's a trunk at the back,' she said in her bright voice. But she was not feeling bright. The twin black cones of the iron foundry blasted their sky-high fires into the night. The whole scene was lurid. The train waited cheerfully. It would wait another ten minutes. She knew it. It was all so deadly familiar.

Let us confess it at once. She was a lady's maid, thirty years old, come back to marry her first-love, a foundry worker: after having kept him dangling, off and on, for a dozen years. Why had she come back? Did she love him? No. She didn't pretend to. She had loved her brilliant and ambitious cousin, who had jilted her, and who had died. She had had other affairs which had come to nothing. So here she was, come back suddenly to marry her first-love, who had waited – or remained single – all these years.

'Won't a porter carry those?' she said, as Harry strode with his workman's stride down the platform towards the guard's van.

'I can manage,' he said.

And with her umbrella, her chatelaine, and her little leather case, she followed him.

The trunk was there.

'We'll get Heather's greengrocer's cart to fetch it up,' he said.

'Isn't there a cab?' said Fanny, knowing dismally enough that there wasn't.

'I'll just put it aside o' the penny-in-the-slot, and Heather's greengrocers'll fetch it about half past eight,' he said.

He seized the box by its two handles and staggered with it across the level-crossing, bumping his legs against it as he waddled. Then he dropped it by the red sweet-meats machine.

'Will it be safe there?' she said.

'Ay – safe as houses,' he answered. He returned for the two bags. Thus laden, they started to plod up the hill, under the great long black building of the foundry. She walked beside him – workman of workmen he was, trudging with that luggage. The red lights flared over the deepening darkness. From the foundry came the horrible, slow clang, clang, clang of iron, a great noise, with an interval just long enough to make it unendurable.

Compare this with the arrival at Gloucester: the carriage for her mistress, the dog-cart for herself with the luggage; the drive out past the river, the pleasant trees of the carriage-approach; and herself sitting beside Arthur, everybody so polite to her.

She had come home – for good! Her heart nearly stopped beating as she trudged up that hideous and interminable hill, beside the laden figure. What a come-down! What a come-down! She could not take it with her usual bright cheerfulness. She knew it all too well. It is easy to bear up against the unusual, but the deadly familiarity of an old stale past!

He dumped the bags down under a lamp-post, for a rest. There they stood, the two of them, in the lamplight. Passers-by stared at her, and gave good-night to Harry. Her they hardly knew, she had become a stranger.

'They're too heavy for you, let me carry one,' she said.

'They begin to weigh a bit by the time you've gone a mile,' he answered.

'Let me carry the little one,' she insisted.

'Tha can ha'e it for a minute, if ter's a mind,' he said, handing over the valise.

And thus they arrived in the streets of shops of the little ugly town on top of the hill. How everybody stared at her; my word, how they stared! And the cinema was just going in, and the queues were tailing down the road to the corner. And everybody took full stock of her. 'Night, Harry!' shouted the fellows, in an interested voice.

However, they arrived at her aunt's – a little sweet-shop in a side street. They 'pinged' the door-bell, and her aunt came running forward out of the kitchen.

'There you are, child! Dying for a cup of tea, I'm sure. How are you?'

Fanny's aunt kissed her, and it was all Fanny could do to refrain from bursting into tears, she felt so low. Perhaps it was her tea she wanted.

'You've had a drag with that luggage,' said Fanny's aunt to Harry.

'Ay – I'm not sorry to put it down,' he said, looking at his hand which was crushed and cramped by the bag handle.

Then he departed to see about Heather's greengrocery cart.

When Fanny sat at tea, her aunt, a grey-haired, fair-faced little woman, looked at her with an admiring heart, feeling bitterly sore for her. For Fanny was beautiful: tall, erect, finely coloured, with her delicately arched nose, her rich brown hair, her large lustrous grey eyes. A passionate woman – a woman to be afraid of. So proud, so inwardly violent! She came of a violent race.

It needed a woman to sympathize with her. Men had not the courage. Poor Fanny! She was such a lady, and so straight and magnificent. And yet everything seemed to do her down. Every time she seemed to be doomed to humiliation and disappointment, this handsome, brilliantly sensitive woman, with her nervous, overwrought laugh.

'So you've really come back, child?' said her aunt.

'I really have, Aunt,' said Fanny.

'Poor Harry! I'm not sure, you know, Fanny, that you're not taking a bit of an advantage of him.'

'Oh, Aunt, he's waited so long, he may as well have what he's waited for.' Fanny laughed grimly.

'Yes, child, he's waited so long, that I'm not sure it isn't a bit hard on him. You know, I like him, Fanny – though as you know quite well, I don't think he's good enough for you. And I think he thinks so himself, poor fellow.'

'Don't you be so sure of that, Aunt. Harry is common, but he's not humble. He wouldn't think the Queen was any too good for him, if he'd a mind to her.'

'Well – It's as well if he has a proper opinion of himself.'

'It depends what you call proper,' said Fanny. 'But he's got his good points – '

'Oh, he's a nice fellow, and I like him, I do like him. Only, as I tell you, he's not good enough for you.'

'I've made up my mind, Aunt,' said Fanny, grimly.

'Yes,' mused the aunt. 'They say all things come to him who waits – '

'More than he's bargained for, eh, Aunt?' laughed Fanny rather bitterly.

The poor aunt, this bitterness grieved her for her niece.

They were interrupted by the ping of the shop-bell, and Harry's call of 'Right!' But as he did not come in at once, Fanny, feeling solicitous for him presumably at the moment, rose and went into the shop. She saw a cart outside, and went to the door.

And the moment she stood in the doorway, she heard a woman's common vituperative voice crying from the darkness of the opposite side of the road:

'Tha'rt theer, ar ter? I'll shame thee, Mester. I'll shame thee, see if I dunna.'

Startled, Fanny stared across the darkness, and saw a woman in a black bonnet go under one of the lamps up the side street.

Harry and Bill Heather had dragged the trunk off the little dray, and she retreated before them as they came up the shop step with it.

'Wheer shalt ha'e it?' asked Harry.

'Best take it upstairs,' said Fanny.

She went up first to light the gas.

When Heather had gone, and Harry was sitting down having tea and pork pie, Fanny asked:

'Who was that woman shouting?'

'Nay, I canna tell thee. To somebody, Is'd think,' replied Harry. Fanny looked at him, but asked no more.

He was a fair-haired fellow of thirty-two, with a fair moustache. He was broad in his speech, and looked like a foundry-hand, which he was. But women always liked him. There was something of a mother's lad about him – something warm and playful and really sensitive.

He had his attractions even for Fanny. What she rebelled against so bitterly was that he had no sort of ambition. He was a moulder, but of very commonplace skill. He was thirty-two years old, and hadn't saved twenty pounds. She would have to provide the money for the home. He didn't care. He just didn't care. He had no initiative at all. He had no vices – no obvious ones. But he was just indifferent, spending as he went, and not caring. Yet he did not look happy. She remembered his face in the fire-glow: something haunted, abstracted about it. As he sat there eating his pork pie, bulging his cheek out, she felt he was like a doom to her. And she raged against the doom of him. It wasn't that he was gross. His way was common, almost on purpose. But he himself wasn't really common. For instance, his food was not particularly important to him, he was not greedy. He had a charm, too, particularly for women, with his blondness and his sensitiveness and his way of making a woman feel that she was a higher being. But Fanny knew him, knew the peculiar obstinate limitedness of him, that would nearly send her mad.

He stayed till about half past nine. She went to the door with him.

'When are you coming up?' he said, jerking his head in the direction, presumably, of his own home.

'I'll come tomorrow afternoon,' she said brightly. Between Fanny and Mrs. Goodall, his mother, there was naturally no love lost.

Again she gave him an awkward little kiss, and said good-night.

'You can't wonder, you know, child, if he doesn't seem so very keen,' said her aunt. 'It's your own fault.'

'Oh, Aunt, I couldn't stand him when he was keen. I can do with him a lot better as he is.'

The two women sat and talked far into the night. They understood each other. The aunt, too, had married as Fanny was marrying: a man who was no companion to her, a violent man, brother of Fanny's father. He was dead, Fanny's father was dead.

Poor Aunt Lizzie, she cried woefully over her bright niece, when she had gone to bed.

Fanny paid the promised visit to his people the next afternoon. Mrs. Goodall was a large woman with smooth-parted hair, a common, obstinate woman, who had spoiled her four lads and her one vixen of a married daughter. She was one of those old-fashioned powerful natures that couldn't do with looks or education or any form of showing off. She fairly hated the sound of correct English. She thee'd and tha'd her prospective daughter-in-law, and said:

'I'm none as ormin' as I look, seest ta.'

Fanny did not think her prospective mother-in-law looked at all orming, so the speech was unnecessary.

'I towd him mysen,' said Mrs. Goodall, ''Er's held back all this long, let 'er stop as 'er is. 'E'd none ha' had thee for my tellin' – tha hears. No, 'e's a fool, an' I know it. I says to him,

'Tha looks a man, doesn't ter, at thy age, goin' an' openin' to her when ter hears her scrat' at th' gate, after she's done gallivantin' round wherever she'd a mind. That looks rare an' soft.' But it's no use o' any talking: he answered that letter o' thine and made his own bad bargain.'

But in spite of the old woman's anger, she was also flattered at Fanny's coming back to Harry. For Mrs. Goodall was impressed by Fanny – a woman of her own match. And more than this, everybody knew that Fanny's Aunt Kate had left her two hundred pounds: this apart from the girl's savings.

So there was high tea in Princes Street when Harry came home black from work, and a rather acrid odour of cordiality, the vixen Jinny darting in to say vulgar things. Of course Jinny lived in a house whose garden end joined the paternal garden. They were a clan who stuck together, these Goodalls.

It was arranged that Fanny should come to tea again on the Sunday, and the wedding was discussed. It should take place in a fortnight's time at Morley Chapel. Morley was a hamlet on the edge of the real country, and in its little Congregational Chapel Fanny and Harry had first met.

What a creature of habit he was! He was still in the choir of Morley Chapel – not very regular. He belonged just because he had a tenor voice, and enjoyed singing. Indeed his solos were only spoilt to local fame because when he sang he handled his aitches so hopelessly.

'And I saw 'eaven hopened
And be'old, a wite 'orse-'

This was one of Harry's classics, only surpassed by the fine outburst of his heaving:

'Hangels – hever bright an' fair-'

It was a pity, but it was inalterable. He had a good voice, and he sang with a certain lacerating fire, but his pronunciation made it all funny. And nothing could alter him.

So he was never heard save at cheap concerts and in the little, poorer chapels. The others scoffed.

Now the month was September, and Sunday was Harvest Festival at Morley Chapel, and Harry was singing solos. So that Fanny was to go to afternoon service, and come home to a grand spread of Sunday tea with him. Poor Fanny! One of the most wonderful afternoons had been a Sunday afternoon service, with her cousin Luther at her side, Harvest Festival in Morley Chapel. Harry had sung solos then – ten years ago. She remembered his pale blue tie, and the purple asters and the great vegetable marrows in which he was framed, and her cousin Luther at her side, young, clever, come down from London, where he was getting on well, learning his Latin and his French and German so brilliantly.

However, once again it was Harvest Festival at Morley Chapel, and once again, as ten years before, a soft, exquisite September day, with the last roses pink in the cottage gardens, the last dahlias crimson, the last sunflowers yellow. And again the little old chapel was a bower, with its famous sheaves of corn and corn-plaited pillars, its great bunches of grapes, dangling like tassels from the pulpit corners, its marrows and potatoes and pears and apples and damsons, its purple asters and yellow Japanese sunflowers. Just as before, the red dahlias round the pillars were dropping, weak-headed among the oats. The place was crowded and hot, the plates of tomatoes seemed balanced perilously on the gallery front, the Rev. Enderby was weirder than ever to look at, so long and emaciated and hairless.

The Rev. Enderby, probably forewarned, came and shook hands with her and welcomed her, in his broad northern, melancholy singsong before he mounted the pulpit. Fanny was handsome in a gauzy dress and a beautiful lace hat. Being a little late, she sat in a chair in the side-aisle wedged in, right in front of the chapel. Harry was in the gallery above, and she could only see him from the eyes upwards. She noticed again how his eyebrows met, blond and not very marked, over his nose. He was attractive too: physically lovable, very. If only – if only her pride had not suffered! She felt he dragged her down.

'Come, ye thankful people come,
Raise the song of harvest-home.
All is safely gathered in
Ere the winter storms begin – '

Even the hymn was a falsehood, as the season had been wet, and half the crops were still out, and in a poor way.

Poor Fanny! She sang little, and looked beautiful through that inappropriate hymn. Above her stood Harry – mercifully in a dark suit and dark tie, looking almost handsome. And his lacerating, pure tenor sounded well, when the words were drowned in the general commotion. Brilliant she looked, and brilliant she felt, for she was hot and angrily miserable and inflamed with a sort of fatal despair. Because there was about him a physical attraction which she really hated, but which she could not escape from. He was the first man who had ever kissed her. And his kisses, even while she rebelled from them, had lived in her blood and sent roots down into her soul. After all this time she had come back to them. And her soul groaned, for she felt dragged down, dragged down to earth, as a bird which some dog has got down in the dust. She knew her life would be unhappy. She knew that what she was doing was fatal. Yet it was her doom. She had to come back to him.

He had to sing two solos this afternoon: one before the 'address' from the pulpit and one after. Fanny looked at him, and wondered he was not too shy to stand up there in front of all the people. But no, he was not shy. He had even a kind of assurance on his face as he looked down from the choir gallery at her: the assurance of a common man deliberately entrenched in his commonness. Oh, such a rage went through her veins as she saw the air of triumph, laconic, indifferent triumph which sat so obstinately and recklessly on his eyelids as he looked down at her. Ah, she despised him! But there he stood up in that choir gallery like Balaam's ass in front of her, and she could not get beyond him. A certain winsomeness also about him. A certain physical winsomeness, and as if his flesh were new and lovely to touch. The thorn of desire rankled bitterly in her heart.

He, it goes without saying, sang like a canary this particular afternoon, with a certain defiant passion which pleasantly crisped the blood of the congregation. Fanny felt the crisp flames go through her veins as she listened. Even the curious loud-mouthed vernacular had a certain fascination. But, oh, also, it was so repugnant. He would triumph over her, obstinately he would drag her right back into the common people: a doom, a vulgar doom.

The second performance was an anthem, in which Harry sang the solo parts. It was clumsy, but beautiful, with lovely words.

'They that sow in tears shall reap in joy,

He that goeth forth and weepeth, bearing precious seed

Shall doubtless come again with rejoicing, bringing his sheaves with

him – '

'Shall doubtless come, Shall doubtless come – ' softly intoned the altos – 'Bringing his she-e-eaves with him,' the trebles flourished brightly, and then again began the half-wistful solo:

'They that sow in tears shall reap in joy – '

Yes, it was effective and moving.

But at the moment when Harry's voice sank carelessly down to his close, and the choir, standing behind him, were opening their mouths for the final triumphant outburst, a shouting female voice rose up from the body of the congregation. The organ gave one startled trump, and went silent; the choir stood transfixed.

'You look well standing there, singing in God's holy house,' came the loud, angry female shout. Everybody turned electrified. A stoutish, red-faced woman in a black bonnet was standing up denouncing the soloist. Almost fainting with shock, the congregation realized it. 'You look well, don't you, standing there singing solos in God's holy house, you, Goodall. But I said I'd shame you. You look well, bringing your young woman here with you, don't you? I'll let her know who she's dealing with. A scamp as won't take the consequences of what he's done.' The hard-faced, frenzied woman turned in the direction of Fanny. 'That's what Harry Goodall is, if you want to know.'

And she sat down again in her seat. Fanny, startled like all the rest, had turned to look. She had gone white, and then a burning red, under the attack. She knew the woman: a Mrs. Nixon, a devil of a woman, who beat her pathetic, drunken, red-nosed second husband, Bob, and her two lanky daughters, grown-up as they were. A notorious character. Fanny turned round again, and sat motionless as eternity in her seat.

There was a minute of perfect silence and suspense. The audience was open-mouthed and dumb; the choir stood like Lot's wife; and Harry, with his music-sheet, stood there uplifted, looking down with a dumb sort of indifference on Mrs. Nixon, his face naive and faintly mocking. Mrs. Nixon sat defiant in her seat, braving them all.

Then a rustle, like a wood when the wind suddenly catches the leaves. And then the tall, weird minister got to his feet, and in his strong, bell-like, beautiful voice – the only beautiful thing about him – he said with infinite mournful pathos:

'Let us unite in singing the last hymn on the hymn-sheet; the last hymn on the hymn-sheet, number eleven.

'Fair waved the golden corn,
In Canaan's pleasant land.'

The organ tuned up promptly. During the hymn the offertory was taken. And after the hymn, the prayer.

Mr. Enderby came from Northumberland. Like Harry, he had never been able to conquer his accent, which was very broad. He was a little simple, one of God's fools, perhaps, an odd bachelor soul, emotional, ugly, but very gentle.

'And if, O our dear Lord, beloved Jesus, there should fall a shadow of sin upon our harvest, we leave it to Thee to judge, for Thou art judge. We lift our spirits and our sorrow, Jesus, to Thee, and our mouths are dumb. O, Lord, keep us from forward speech, restrain us from foolish words and thoughts, we pray Thee, Lord Jesus, who knowest all and judgest all.'

Thus the minister said in his sad, resonant voice, washed his hands before the Lord. Fanny bent forward open-eyed during the prayer. She could see the roundish head of Harry, also bent forward. His face was inscrutable and expressionless. The shock left her bewildered. Anger perhaps was her dominating emotion.

The audience began to rustle to its feet, to ooze slowly and excitedly out of the chapel, looking with wildly-interested eyes at Fanny, at Mrs. Nixon, and at Harry. Mrs. Nixon, shortish, stood defiant in her pew, facing the aisle, as if announcing that, without rolling her sleeves up, she was ready for anybody. Fanny sat quite still. Luckily the people did not have to pass her. And Harry, with red ears, was making his way sheepishly out of the gallery. The loud noise of the organ covered all the downstairs commotion of exit.

The minister sat silent and inscrutable in his pulpit, rather like a death's-head, while the congregation filed out. When the last lingerers had unwillingly departed, craning their necks to stare at the still seated Fanny, he rose, stalked in his hooked fashion down the little country chapel and fastened the door. Then he returned and sat down by the silent young woman.

'This is most unfortunate, most unfortunate!' he moaned. 'I am so sorry, I am so sorry, indeed, indeed, ah, indeed!' he sighed himself to a close.

'It's a sudden surprise, that's one thing,' said Fanny brightly.

'Yes – yes – indeed. Yes, a surprise, yes. I don't know the woman, I don't know her.'

'I know her,' said Fanny. 'She's a bad one.'

'Well! Well!' said the minister. 'I don't know her. I don't understand. I don't understand at all. But it is to be regretted, it is very much to be regretted. I am very sorry.'

Fanny was watching the vestry door. The gallery stairs communicated with the vestry, not with the body of the chapel. She knew the choir members had been peeping for information.

At last Harry came – rather sheepishly – with his hat in his hand.

'Well!' said Fanny, rising to her feet.

'We've had a bit of an extra,' said Harry.

'I should think so,' said Fanny.

'A most unfortunate circumstance – a most unfortunate circumstance. Do you understand it, Harry? I don't understand it at all.'

'Ah, I understand it. The daughter's goin' to have a childt, an' 'er lays it on to me.'

'And has she no occasion to?' asked Fanny, rather censorious.

'It's no more mine than it is some other chap's,' said Harry, looking aside.

There was a moment of pause.

'Which girl is it?' asked Fanny.

'Annie – the young one – '

There followed another silence.

'I don't think I know them, do I?' asked the minister.

'I shouldn't think so. Their name's Nixon – mother married old Bob for her second husband. She's a tanger – 's driven the gel to what she is. They live in Manners Road.'

'Why, what's amiss with the girl?' asked Fanny sharply. 'She was all right when I knew her.'

'Ay – she's all right. But she's always in an' out o' th' pubs, wi' th' fellows,' said Harry.

'A nice thing!' said Fanny.

Harry glanced towards the door. He wanted to get out.

'Most distressing, indeed!' The minister slowly shook his head.

'What about tonight, Mr. Enderby?' asked Harry, in rather a small voice. 'Shall you want me?'

Mr. Enderby looked up painedly, and put his hand to his brow. He studied Harry for some time, vacantly. There was the faintest sort of a resemblance between the two men.

'Yes,' he said. 'Yes, I think. I think we must take no notice, and cause as little remark as possible.'

Fanny hesitated. Then she said to Harry.

'But will you come?'

He looked at her.

'Ay, I s'll come,' he said.

Then he turned to Mr. Enderby.

'Well, good-afternoon, Mr. Enderby,' he said.

'Good-afternoon, Harry, good-afternoon,' replied the mournful minister. Fanny followed Harry to the door, and for some time they walked in silence through the late afternoon.

'And it's yours as much as anybody else's?' she said.

'Ay,' he answered shortly.

And they went without another word, for the long mile or so, till they came to the corner of the street where Harry lived. Fanny hesitated. Should she go on to her aunt's? Should she? It would mean leaving all this, for ever. Harry stood silent.

Some obstinacy made her turn with him along the road to his own home. When they entered the house-place, the whole family was there, mother and father and Jinny, with Jinny's husband and children and Harry's two brothers.

'You've been having yours ears warmed, they tell me,' said Mrs. Goodall grimly.

'Who telled thee?' asked Harry shortly.

'Maggie and Luke's both been in.'

'You look well, don't you!' said interfering Jinny.

Harry went and hung his hat up, without replying.

'Come upstairs and take your hat off,' said Mrs. Goodall to Fanny, almost kindly. It would have annoyed her very much if Fanny had dropped her son at this moment.

'What's 'er say, then?' asked the father secretly of Harry, jerking his head in the direction of the stairs whence Fanny had disappeared.

'Nowt yet,' said Harry.

'Serve you right if she chucks you now,' said Jinny. 'I'll bet it's right about Annie Nixon an' you.'

'Tha bets so much,' said Harry.

'Yi – but you can't deny it,' said Jinny.

'I can if I've a mind.'

His father looked at him inquiringly.

'It's no more mine than it is Bill Bower's, or Ted Slaney's, or six or seven on 'em,' said Harry to his father.

And the father nodded silently.

'That'll not get you out of it, in court,' said Jinny.

Upstairs Fanny evaded all the thrusts made by his mother, and did not declare her hand. She tidied her hair, washed her hands, and put the tiniest bit of powder on her face, for coolness, there in front of Mrs. Goodall's indignant gaze. It was like a declaration of independence. But the old woman said nothing.

They came down to Sunday tea, with sardines and tinned salmon and tinned peaches, besides tarts and cakes. The chatter was general. It concerned the Nixon family and the scandal.

'Oh, she's a foul-mouthed woman,' said Jinny of Mrs. Nixon. 'She may well talk about God's holy house, she had. It's first time she's set foot in it, ever since she dropped off from being converted. She's a devil and she always was one. Can't you remember how she treated Bob's children, mother, when we lived down in the Buildings? I can remember when I was a little girl she used to bathe them in the yard, in the cold, so that they shouldn't splash the house. She'd half kill them if they made a mark on the floor, and the language she'd use! And one Saturday I can remember Garry, that was Bob's own girl, she ran off when her stepmother was going to bathe her – ran off without a rag of clothes on – can you remember, mother? And she hid in Smedley's closes – it was the time of mowing-grass – and nobody could find her. She hid out there all night, didn't she, mother? Nobody could find her. My word, there was a talk. They found her on Sunday morning – '

'Fred Coutts threatened to break every bone in the woman's body, if she touched the children again,' put in the father.

'Anyhow, they frightened her,' said Jinny. 'But she was nearly as bad with her own two. And anybody can see that she's driven old Bob till he's gone soft.'

'Ah, soft as mush,' said Jack Goodall. ''E'd never addle a week's wage, nor yet a day's if th' chaps didn't make it up to him.'

'My word, if he didn't bring her a week's wage, she'd pull his head off,' said Jinny.

'But a clean woman, and respectable, except for her foul mouth,' said Mrs. Goodall. 'Keeps to herself like a bull-dog. Never lets anybody come near the house, and neighbours with nobody.'

'Wanted it thrashed out of her,' said Mr. Goodall, a silent, evasive sort of man.

'Where Bob gets the money for his drink from is a mystery,' said Jinny.

'Chaps treats him,' said Harry.

'Well, he's got the pair of frightenedest rabbit-eyes you'd wish to see,' said Jinny.

'Ay, with a drunken man's murder in them, I think,' said Mrs. Goodall.

So the talk went on after tea, till it was practically time to start off to chapel again.

'You'll have to be getting ready, Fanny,' said Mrs. Goodall.

'I'm not going tonight,' said Fanny abruptly. And there was a sudden halt in the family. 'I'll stop with you tonight, Mother,' she added.

'Best you had, my gel,' said Mrs. Goodall, flattered and assured.

# The Coffee-House of Surat

***Leo Tolstoy***

(After Bernardin de Saint-Pierre)

In the town of Surat, in India, was a coffee-house where many travellers and foreigners from all parts of the world met and conversed.

One day a learned Persian theologian visited this coffee-house. He was a man who had spent his life studying the nature of the Deity, and reading and writing books upon the subject. He had thought, read, and written so much about God, that eventually he lost his wits, became quite confused, and ceased even to believe in the existence of a God. The Shah, hearing of this, had banished him from Persia.

After having argued all his life about the First Cause, this unfortunate theologian had ended by quite perplexing himself, and instead of understanding that he had lost his own reason, he began to think that there was no higher Reason controlling the universe.

This man had an African slave who followed him everywhere. When the theologian entered the coffee-house, the slave remained outside, near the door, sitting on a stone in the glare of the sun, and driving away the flies that buzzed around him. The Persian having settled down on a divan in the coffee-house, ordered himself a cup of opium. When he had drunk it and the opium had begun to quicken the workings of his brain, he addressed his slave through the open door:

"Tell me, wretched slave," said he, "do you think there is a God, or not?"

"Of course there is," said the slave, and immediately drew from under his girdle a small idol of wood.

"There," said he, "that is the God who has guarded me from the day of my birth. Every one in our country worships the fetish tree, from the wood of which this God was made."

This conversation between the theologian and his slave was listened to with surprise by the other guests in the coffee-house. They were astonished at the master's question, and yet more so at the slave's reply.

One of them, a Brahmin, on hearing the words spoken by the slave, turned to him and said:

"Miserable fool! Is it possible you believe that God can be carried under a man's girdle? There is one God – Brahma, and he is greater than the whole world, for he created it. Brahma is the One, the mighty God, and in His honour are built the temples on the Ganges' banks, where his true priests, the Brahmins, worship him. They know the true God, and none but they. A thousand score of years have passed, and yet through revolution after revolution these priests have held their sway, because Brahma, the one true God, has protected them."

So spoke the Brahmin, thinking to convince every one; but a Jewish broker who was present replied to him, and said:

"No! the temple of the true God is not in India. Neither does God protect the Brahmin caste. The true God is not the God of the Brahmins, but of Abraham, Isaac, and Jacob. None does He protect but His chosen people, the Israelites. From the commencement of the world, our nation has been beloved of Him, and ours alone. If we are now scattered over the whole earth, it is but to try us; for God has promised that He will one day gather His people together in Jerusalem. Then, with the Temple of Jerusalem – the wonder of the ancient world – restored to its splendor, shall Israel be established a ruler over all nations."

So spoke the Jew, and burst into tears. He wished to say more, but an Italian missionary who was there interrupted him.

"What you are saying is untrue," said he to the Jew. "You attribute injustice to God. He cannot love your nation above the rest. Nay rather, even if it be true that of old He favored the Israelites, it is now nineteen hundred years since they angered Him, and caused Him to destroy their nation and scatter them over the earth, so that their faith makes no converts and has died out except here and there. God shows preference to no nation, but calls all who wish to be saved to the bosom of the Catholic

Church of Rome, the one outside whose borders no salvation can be found."

So spoke the Italian. But a Protestant minister, who happened to be present, growing pale, turned to the Catholic missionary and exclaimed:

"How can you say that salvation belongs to your religion? Those only will be saved, who serve God according to the Gospel, in spirit and in truth, as bidden by the word of Christ."

Then a Turk, an office-holder in the custom-house at Surat, who was sitting in the coffee-house smoking a pipe, turned with an air of superiority to both the Christians.

"Your belief in your Roman religion is vain," said he. "It was superseded twelve hundred years ago by the true faith: that of Mohammed! You cannot but observe how the true Mohammed faith continues to spread both in Europe and Asia, and even in the enlightened country of China. You say yourselves that God has rejected the Jews; and, as a proof, you quote the fact that the Jews are humiliated and their faith does not spread. Confess then the truth of Mohammedanism, for it is triumphant and spreads far and wide. None will be saved but the followers of Mohammed, God's latest prophet; and of them, only the followers of Omar, and not of Ali, for the latter are false to the faith."

To this the Persian theologian, who was of the sect of Ali, wished to reply; but by this time a great dispute had arisen among all the strangers of different faiths and creeds present. There were Abyssinian Christians, Llamas from Thibet, Ismailians and Fireworshippers. They all argued about the nature of God, and how He should be worshipped. Each of them asserted that in his country alone was the true God known and rightly worshipped.

Every one argued and shouted, except a Chinaman, a student of Confucius, who sat quietly in one corner of the coffee-house, not joining in the dispute. He sat there drinking tea and listening to what the others said, but did not speak himself.

The Turk noticed him sitting there, and appealed to him, saying:

"You can confirm what I say, my good Chinaman. You hold your peace, but if you spoke I know you would uphold my opinion. Traders from your country, who come to me for assistance, tell me that though many religions have been introduced into China, you Chinese consider Mohammedanism the best of all, and adopt it willingly. Confirm, then, my words, and tell us your opinion of the true God and of His prophet."

"Yes, yes," said the rest, turning to the Chinaman, "let us hear what you think on the subject."

The Chinaman, the student of Confucius, closed his eyes, and thought a while. Then he opened them again, and drawing his hands out of the wide sleeves of his garment, and folding them on his breast, he spoke as follows, in a calm and quiet voice.

Sirs, it seems to me that it is chiefly pride that prevents men agreeing with one another on matters of faith. If you care to listen to me, I will tell you a story which will explain this by an example.

I came here from China on an English steamer which had been round the world. We stopped for fresh water, and landed on the east coast of the island of Sumatra. It was midday, and some of us, having landed, sat in the shade of some cocoanut palms by the seashore, not far from a native village. We were a party of men of different nationalities.

As we sat there, a blind man approached us. We learned afterwards that he had gone blind from gazing too long and too persistently at the sun, trying to find out what it is, in order to seize its light.

He strove a long time to accomplish this, constantly looking at the sun; but the only result was that his eyes were injured by its brightness, and he became blind.

Then he said to himself:

"The light of the sun is not a liquid; for if it were a liquid it would be possible to pour it from one vessel into another, and it would be moved, like water, by the wind. Neither is it fire; for if it were fire, water would extinguish it. Neither is light a spirit, for it is seen by the eye; nor is it matter, for it cannot be moved. Therefore, as the light of the sun is neither liquid, nor fire, nor spirit, nor matter, it is – nothing!"

So he argued, and, as a result of always looking at the sun and always thinking about it, he lost both his sight and his reason. And when he went quite blind, he became fully convinced that the sun did not exist.

With this blind man came a slave, who after placing his master in the shade of a cocoanut tree, picked up a cocoanut from the ground, and began making it into a night-light. He twisted a wick from the fibre of the cocoanut: squeezed oil from the nut in the shell, and soaked the wick in it.

As the slave sat doing this, the blind man sighed and said to him:

"Well, slave, was I not right when I told you there is no sun? Do you not see how dark it is? Yet people say there is a sun. But if so, what is it?"

"I do not know what the sun is," said the slave. "That is no business of mine. But I know what light is. Here I have made a night-light, by the help of which I can serve you and find anything I want in the hut."

And the slave picked up the cocoanut shell, saying:

"This is my sun."

A lame man with crutches, who was sitting near by, heard these words, and laughed:

"You have evidently been blind all your life," said he to the blind man, "not to know what the sun is. I will tell you what it is. The sun is a ball of fire, which rises every morning out of the sea and goes down again among the mountains of our island each evening. We have all seen this, and if you had had your eyesight you too would have seen it."

A fisherman, who had been listening to the conversation said:

"It is plain enough that you have never been beyond your own island. If you were not lame, and if you had been out as I have in a fishing-boat, you would know that the sun does not set among the mountains of our island, but as it rises from the ocean every morning so it sets again in the sea every night. What I am telling you is true, for I see it every day with my own eyes."

Then an Indian who was of our party, interrupted him by saying:

"I am astonished that a reasonable man should talk such nonsense. How can a ball of fire possibly descend into the water and not be extinguished? The sun is not a ball of fire at all, it is the Deity named Deva, who rides for ever in a chariot round the golden mountain, Meru. Sometimes the evil serpents Ragu and Ketu attack Deva and swallow him: and then the earth is dark. But our priests pray that the Deity may be released, and then he is set free. Only such ignorant men as you, who have never been beyond their own island, can imagine that the sun shines for their country alone."

Then the master of an Egyptian vessel, who was present, spoke in his turn.

"No," said he, "you also are wrong. The sun is not a Deity, and does not move only round India and its golden mountain. I have sailed much on the Black Sea, and along the coasts of Arabia, and have been to Madagascar and to the Philippines. The sun lights the whole earth, and not India alone. It does not circle round one mountain, but rises far in the East, beyond the Isles of Japan, and sets far, far away in the West, beyond the islands of England. That is why the Japanese call their country 'Nippon,' that is, 'the birth of the sun.' I know this well, for I have myself seen much, and heard more from my grandfather, who sailed to the very ends of the sea."

He would have gone on, but an English sailor from our ship interrupted him.

"There is no country," he said "where people know so much about the sun's movements as in England. The sun, as every one in England knows, rises nowhere and sets nowhere. It is always moving round the earth. We can be sure of this for we have just been round the world ourselves, and nowhere knocked up against the sun. Wherever we went, the sun showed itself in the morning and hid itself at night, just as it does here."

And the Englishman took a stick and, drawing circles on the sand, tried to explain how the sun moves in the heavens and goes round the world. But he was unable to explain it clearly, and pointing to the ship's pilot said:

"This man knows more about it than I do. He can explain it properly."

The pilot, who was an intelligent man, had listened in silence to the talk till he was asked to speak. Now every one turned to him, and he said:

"You are all misleading one another, and are yourselves

deceived. The sun does not go round the earth, but the earth goes round the sun, revolving as it goes, and turning towards the sun in the course of each twenty-four hours, not only Japan, and the Philippines, and Sumatra where we now are, but Africa, and Europe, and America, and many lands besides. The sun does not shine for some one mountain, or for some one island, or for some one sea, nor even for one earth alone, but for other planets as well as our earth. If you would only look up at the heavens, instead of at the ground beneath your own feet, you might all understand this, and would then no longer suppose that the sun shines for you, or for your country alone."

Thus spoke the wise pilot, who had voyaged much about the world, and had gazed much upon the heavens above.

"So on matters of faith," continued the Chinaman, the student of Confucius, "it is pride that causes error and discord among men. As with the sun, so it is with God. Each man wants to have a special God of his own, or at least a special God for his native land. Each nation wishes to confine in its own temples Him, whom the world cannot contain.

"Can any temple compare with that which God Himself has built to unite all men in one faith and one religion?

"All human temples are built on the model of this temple, which is God's own world. Every temple has its fonts, its vaulted roof, its lamps, its pictures or sculptures, its inscriptions, its books of the law, its offerings, its altars and its priests. But in what temple is there such a font as the ocean; such a vault as that of the heavens; such lamps as the sun, moon, and stars; or any figures to be compared with living, loving, mutually-helpful men? Where are there any records of God's goodness so easy to understand as the blessings which God has strewn abroad for man's happiness? Where is there any book of the law so clear to each man as that written in his heart? What sacrifices equal the self-denials which loving men and women make for one another? And what altar can be compared with the heart of a good man, on which God Himself accepts the sacrifice?

"The higher a man's conception of God, the better will he know Him. And the better he knows God, the nearer will he draw to Him, imitating His goodness, His mercy, and His love of man.

"Therefore, let him who sees the sun's whole light filling the world, refrain from blaming or despising the superstitious man, who in his own idol sees one ray of that same light. Let him not despise even the unbeliever who is blind and cannot see the sun at all."

So spoke the Chinaman, the student of Confucius; and all who were present in the coffee-house were silent, and disputed no more as to whose faith was the best.

# God Sees the Truth, But Waits

*Leo Tolstoy*

In the town of Vladimir lived a young merchant named Ivan Dmitrich Aksionov. He had two shops and a house of his own.

Aksionov was a handsome, fair-haired, curly-headed fellow, full of fun, and very fond of singing. When quite a young man he had been given to drink, and was riotous when he had had too much; but after he married he gave up drinking, except now and then.

One summer Aksionov was going to the Nizhny Fair, and as he bade good-bye to his family, his wife said to him, "Ivan Dmitrich, do not start to-day; I have had a bad dream about you."

Aksionov laughed, and said, "You are afraid that when I get to the fair I shall go on a spree."

His wife replied: "I do not know what I am afraid of; all I know is that I had a bad dream. I dreamt you returned from the town, and when you took off your cap I saw that your hair was quite grey."

Aksionov laughed. "That's a lucky sign," said he. "See if I don't sell out all my goods, and bring you some presents from the fair."

So he said good-bye to his family, and drove away.

When he had travelled half-way, he met a merchant whom he knew, and they put up at the same inn for the night. They had some tea together, and then went to bed in adjoining rooms.

It was not Aksionov's habit to sleep late, and, wishing to travel while it was still cool, he aroused his driver before dawn, and told him to put in the horses.

Then he made his way across to the landlord of the inn (who lived in a cottage at the back), paid his bill, and continued his journey.

When he had gone about twenty-five miles, he stopped for

the horses to be fed. Aksionov rested awhile in the passage of the inn, then he stepped out into the porch, and, ordering a samovar to be heated, got out his guitar and began to play.

Suddenly a troika drove up with tinkling bells and an official alighted, followed by two soldiers. He came to Aksionov and began to question him, asking him who he was and whence he came. Aksionov answered him fully, and said, "Won't you have some tea with me?" But the official went on cross-questioning him and asking him. "Where did you spend last night? Were you alone, or with a fellow-merchant? Did you see the other merchant this morning? Why did you leave the inn before dawn?"

Aksionov wondered why he was asked all these questions, but he described all that had happened, and then added, "Why do you cross-question me as if I were a thief or a robber? I am travelling on business of my own, and there is no need to question me."

Then the official, calling the soldiers, said, "I am the police-officer of this district, and I question you because the merchant with whom you spent last night has been found with his throat cut. We must search your things."

They entered the house. The soldiers and the police-officer unstrapped Aksionov's luggage and searched it. Suddenly the officer drew a knife out of a bag, crying, "Whose knife is this?"

Aksionov looked, and seeing a blood-stained knife taken from his bag, he was frightened.

"How is it there is blood on this knife?"

Aksionov tried to answer, but could hardly utter a word, and only stammered: "I – don't know – not mine." Then the police-officer said: "This morning the merchant was found in bed with his throat cut. You are the only person who could have done it. The house was locked from inside, and no one else was there. Here is this blood-stained knife in your bag and your face and manner betray you! Tell me how you killed him, and how much money you stole?"

Aksionov swore he had not done it; that he had not seen the merchant after they had had tea together; that he had no money except eight thousand rubles of his own, and that the knife was not his. But his voice was broken, his face pale, and he trembled with fear as though he went guilty.

The police-officer ordered the soldiers to bind Aksionov and to put him in the cart. As they tied his feet together and flung him into the cart, Aksionov crossed himself and wept. His money and goods were taken from him, and he was sent to the nearest town and imprisoned there. Enquiries as to his character were made in Vladimir. The merchants and other inhabitants of that town said that in former days he used to drink and waste his time, but that he was a good man. Then the trial came on: he was charged with murdering a merchant from Ryazan, and robbing him of twenty thousand rubles.

His wife was in despair, and did not know what to believe. Her children were all quite small; one was a baby at her breast. Taking them all with her, she went to the town where her husband was in jail. At first she was not allowed to see him; but after much begging, she obtained permission from the officials, and was taken to him. When she saw her husband in prison-dress and in chains, shut up with thieves and criminals, she fell down, and did not come to her senses for a long time. Then she drew her children to her, and sat down near him. She told him of things at home, and asked about what had happened to him. He told her all, and she asked, "What can we do now?"

"We must petition the Czar not to let an innocent man perish."

His wife told him that she had sent a petition to the Czar, but it had not been accepted.

Aksionov did not reply, but only looked downcast.

Then his wife said, "It was not for nothing I dreamt your hair had turned grey. You remember? You should not have started that day." And passing her fingers through his hair, she said: "Vanya dearest, tell your wife the truth; was it not you who did it?"

"So you, too, suspect me!" said Aksionov, and, hiding his face in his hands, he began to weep. Then a soldier came to say that the wife and children must go away; and Aksionov said good-bye to his family for the last time.

When they were gone, Aksionov recalled what had been said, and when he remembered that his wife also had suspected him, he said to himself, "It seems that only God can know the truth; it is to Him alone we must appeal, and from Him alone expect mercy."

And Aksionov wrote no more petitions; gave up all hope, and only prayed to God.

Aksionov was condemned to be flogged and sent to the mines. So he was flogged with a knot, and when the wounds made by the knot were healed, he was driven to Siberia with other convicts.

For twenty-six years Aksionov lived as a convict in Siberia. His hair turned white as snow, and his beard grew long, thin, and grey. All his mirth went; he stooped; he walked slowly, spoke little, and never laughed, but he often prayed.

In prison Aksionov learnt to make boots, and earned a little money, with which he bought The Lives of the Saints. He read this book when there was light enough in the prison; and on Sundays in the prison-church he read the lessons and sang in the choir; for his voice was still good.

The prison authorities liked Aksionov for his meekness, and his fellow-prisoners respected him: they called him "Grandfather," and "The Saint." When they wanted to petition the prison authorities about anything, they always made Aksionov their spokesman, and when there were quarrels among the prisoners they came to him to put things right, and to judge the matter.

No news reached Aksionov from his home, and he did not even know if his wife and children were still alive.

One day a fresh gang of convicts came to the prison. In the evening the old prisoners collected round the new ones and asked them what towns or villages they came from, and what they were sentenced for. Among the rest Aksionov sat down near the newcomers, and listened with downcast air to what was said.

One of the new convicts, a tall, strong man of sixty, with a closely-cropped grey beard, was telling the others what be had been arrested for.

"Well, friends," he said, "I only took a horse that was tied to a sledge, and I was arrested and accused of stealing. I said I had only taken it to get home quicker, and had then let it go; besides, the driver was a personal friend of mine. So I said, 'It's all right.' 'No,' said they, 'you stole it.' But how or where I stole it they could not say. I once really did something wrong, and ought by rights to have come here long ago, but that time I was not found out. Now I have been sent here for nothing at all... Eh, but it's lies I'm telling you; I've been to Siberia before, but I did not stay long."

"Where are you from?" asked some one.

"From Vladimir. My family are of that town. My name is Makar, and they also call me Semyonich."

Aksionov raised his head and said: "Tell me, Semyonich, do you know anything of the merchants Aksionov of Vladimir? Are they still alive?"

"Know them? Of course I do. The Aksionovs are rich, though their father is in Siberia: a sinner like ourselves, it seems! As for you, Gran'dad, how did you come here?"

Aksionov did not like to speak of his misfortune. He only sighed, and said, "For my sins I have been in prison these twenty-six years."

"What sins?" asked Makar Semyonich.

But Aksionov only said, "Well, well – I must have deserved it!" He would have said no more, but his companions told the newcomers how Aksionov came to be in Siberia; how some one had killed a merchant, and had put the knife among Aksionov's things, and Aksionov had been unjustly condemned.

When Makar Semyonich heard this, he looked at Aksionov, slapped his own knee, and exclaimed, "Well, this is wonderful! Really wonderful! But how old you've grown, Gran'dad!"

The others asked him why he was so surprised, and where he had seen Aksionov before; but Makar Semyonich did not reply. He only said: "It's wonderful that we should meet here, lads!"

These words made Aksionov wonder whether this man knew who had killed the merchant; so he said, "Perhaps, Semyonich, you have heard of that affair, or maybe you've seen me before?"

"How could I help hearing? The world's full of rumours. But it's a long time ago, and I've forgotten what I heard."

"Perhaps you heard who killed the merchant?" asked Aksionov.

Makar Semyonich laughed, and replied: "It must have been him in whose bag the knife was found! If some one else hid the knife there, 'He's not a thief till he's caught,' as the saying is. How could any one put a knife into your bag while it was under your head? It would surely have woke you up."

When Aksionov heard these words, he felt sure this was the man who had killed the merchant. He rose and went away. All that night Aksionov lay awake. He felt terribly unhappy, and all sorts of images rose in his mind. There was the image of his wife as she was when he parted from her to go to the fair. He saw her as if she were present; her face and her eyes rose before him; he heard her speak and laugh. Then he saw his children, quite little, as they: were at that time: one with a little cloak on, another at his mother's breast. And then he remembered himself as he used to be-young and merry. He remembered how he sat playing the guitar in the porch of the inn where he was arrested, and how free from care he had been. He saw, in his mind, the place where he was flogged, the executioner, and the people standing around; the chains, the convicts, all the twenty-six years of his prison life, and his premature old age. The thought of it all made him so wretched that he was ready to kill himself.

"And it's all that villain's doing!" thought Aksionov. And his anger was so great against Makar Semyonich that he longed for vengeance, even if he himself should perish for it. He kept repeating prayers all night, but could get no peace. During the day he did not go near Makar Semyonich, nor even look at him.

A fortnight passed in this way. Aksionov could not sleep at night, and was so miserable that he did not know what to do.

One night as he was walking about the prison he noticed some earth that came rolling out from under one of the shelves on which the prisoners slept. He stopped to see what it was. Suddenly Makar Semyonich crept out from under the shelf, and looked up at Aksionov with frightened face. Aksionov tried to pass without looking at him, but Makar seized his hand and told him that he had dug a hole under the wall, getting rid of the earth by putting it into his high-boots, and emptying it out every day on the road when the prisoners were driven to their work.

"Just you keep quiet, old man, and you shall get out too. If you blab, they'll flog the life out of me, but I will kill you first."

Aksionov trembled with anger as he looked at his enemy. He

drew his hand away, saying, "I have no wish to escape, and you have no need to kill me; you killed me long ago! As to telling of you – I may do so or not, as God shall direct."

Next day, when the convicts were led out to work, the convoy soldiers noticed that one or other of the prisoners emptied some earth out of his boots. The prison was searched and the tunnel found. The Governor came and questioned all the prisoners to find out who had dug the hole. They all denied any knowledge of it. Those who knew would not betray Makar Semyonich, knowing he would be flogged almost to death. At last the Governor turned to Aksionov whom he knew to be a just man, and said:

"You are a truthful old man; tell me, before God, who dug the hole?"

Makar Semyonich stood as if he were quite unconcerned, looking at the Governor and not so much as glancing at Aksionov. Aksionov's lips and hands trembled, and for a long time he could not utter a word. He thought, "Why should I screen him who ruined my life? Let him pay for what I have suffered. But if I tell, they will probably flog the life out of him, and maybe I suspect him wrongly. And, after all, what good would it be to me?"

"Well, old man," repeated the Governor, "tell me the truth: who has been digging under the wall?"

Aksionov glanced at Makar Semyonich, and said, "I cannot say, your honour. It is not God's will that I should tell! Do what you like with me; I am your hands."

However much the Governor! Aksionov would say no more, and so the matter had to be left.

That night, when Aksionov was lying on his bed and just beginning to doze, some one came quietly and sat down on his bed. He peered through the darkness and recognised Makar.

"What more do you want of me?" asked Aksionov. "Why have you come here?"

Makar Semyonich was silent. So Aksionov sat up and said, "What do you want? Go away, or I will call the guard!"

Makar Semyonich bent close over Aksionov, and whispered, "Ivan Dmitrich, forgive me!"

"What for?" asked Aksionov.

"It was I who killed the merchant and hid the knife among

your things. I meant to kill you too, but I heard a noise outside, so I hid the knife in your bag and escaped out of the window."

Aksionov was silent, and did not know what to say. Makar Semyonich slid off the bed-shelf and knelt upon the ground. "Ivan Dmitrich," said he, "forgive me! For the love of God, forgive me! I will confess that it was I who killed the merchant, and you will be released and can go to your home."

"It is easy for you to talk," said Aksionov, "but I have suffered for you these twenty-six years. Where could I go to now?... My wife is dead, and my children have forgotten me. I have nowhere to go..."

Makar Semyonich did not rise, but beat his head on the floor. "Ivan Dmitrich, forgive me!" he cried. "When they flogged me with the knot it was not so hard to bear as it is to see you now ... yet you had pity on me, and did not tell. For Christ's sake forgive me, wretch that I am!" And he began to sob.

When Aksionov heard him sobbing he, too, began to weep. "God will forgive you!" said he. "Maybe I am a hundred times worse than you." And at these words his heart grew light, and the longing for home left him. He no longer had any desire to leave the prison, but only hoped for his last hour to come.

In spite of what Aksionov had said, Makar Semyonich confessed his guilt. But when the order for his release came, Aksionov was already dead.

# The Babus of Nayanjore

*Rabindranath Tagore*

I

Once upon a time the Babus at Nayanjore were famous landholders. They were noted for their princely extravagance. They would tear off the rough border of their Dacca muslin, because it rubbed against their delicate skin. They could spend many thousands of rupees over the wedding of a kitten. And on a certain grand occasion it is alleged that in order to turn night into day they lighted numberless lamps and showered silver threads from the sky to imitate sunlight.

Those were the days before the flood. The flood came. The line of succession among these old-world Babus, with their lordly habits, could not continue for long. Like a lamp with too many wicks burning, the oil flared away quickly, and the light went out.

Kailas Babu, our neighbour, is the last relic of this extinct magnificence. Before he grew up, his family had very nearly reached its lowest ebb. When his father died, there was one dazzling outburst of funeral extravagance, and then insolvency. The property was sold to liquidate the debt. What little ready money was left over was altogether insufficient to keep up the past ancestral splendours.

Kailas Babu left Nayanjore and came to Calcutta. His son did not remain long in this world of faded glory. He died, leaving behind him an only daughter.

In Calcutta we are Kailas Babu's neighbours. Curiously enough our own family history is just the opposite of his. My father got his money by his own exertions, and prided himself on never spending a penny more than was needed. His clothes were those of a working man, and his hands also. He never had any inclination to earn the title of Babu by extravagant display; and I myself, his only son, owe him gratitude for that. He gave me the very best education, and I was able to make my way in the world. I am not ashamed of the fact that I am a self-made man. Crisp bank-notes in my safe are dearer to me than a long pedigree in an empty family chest.

I believe this was why I disliked seeing Kailas Babu drawing his heavy cheques on the public credit from the bankrupt bank of his ancient Babu reputation. I used to fancy that he looked down on me, because my father had earned money with his own hands.

I ought to have noticed that no one showed any vexation towards Kailas Babu except myself. Indeed it would have been difficult to find an old man who did less harm than he. He was always ready with his kindly little acts of courtesy in times of sorrow and joy. He would join in all the ceremonies and religious observances of his neighbours. His familiar smile would greet young and old alike. His politeness in asking details about domestic affairs was untiring. The friends who met him in the street were perforce ready to be button-holed, while a long string of questions of this kind followed one another from his lips:

"My dear friend, I am delighted to see you. Are you quite well? How is Shashi? And Dada—is he all right? Do you know, I've only just heard that Madhu's son has got fever. How is he? Have you heard? And Hari Charan Babu—I have not seen him for a long time—I hope he is not ill. What's the matter with Rakkhal? And er—er, how are the ladies of your family?"

Kailas Babu was spotlessly neat in his dress on all occasions, though his supply of clothes was sorely limited. Every day he used to air his shirts and vests and coats and trousers carefully, and put them out in the sun, along with his bed-quilt, his pillowcase, and the small carpet on which he always sat. After airing them he would shake them, and brush them, and put them carefully away. His little bits of furniture made his small room decent, and hinted that there was more in reserve if needed. Very often, for want of a servant, he would shut up his house for a while. Then he would iron out his shirts and linen with his own hands, and do other little menial tasks. After this he would open his door and receive his friends again.

Though Kailas Babu, as I have said, had lost all his landed

property, he had still some family heirlooms left. There was a silver cruet for sprinkling scented water, a otto-of-roses, a small gold salver, a costly ancient shawl, and the old-fashioned ceremonial dress and ancestral turban. These he had rescued with the greatest difficulty from the money-lenders' clutches. On every suitable occasion he would bring them out in state, and thus try to save the world-famed dignity of the Babus of Nayanjore. At heart the most modest of men, in his daily speech he regarded it as a sacred duty, owed to his rank, to give free play to his family pride. His friends would encourage this trait in his character with kindly good-humour, and it gave them great amusement.

The neighbourhood soon learnt to call him their Thakur Dada. They would flock to his house and sit with him for hours together. To prevent his incurring any expense, one or other of his friends would bring him tobacco and say: "Thakur Dada, this morning some tobacco was sent to me from Gaya. Do take it and see how you like it."

Thakur Dada would take it and say it was excellent. He would then go on to tell of a certain exquisite tobacco which they once smoked in the old days of Nayanjore at the cost of a guinea an ounce.

"I wonder," he used to say, "if any one would like to try it now. I have some left, and can get it at once."

Every one knew that, if they asked for it, then somehow or other the key of the cupboard would be missing; or else Ganesh, his old family servant, had put it away somewhere.

"You never can be sure," he would add, "where things go to when servants are about. Now, this Ganesh of mine,—I can't tell you what a fool he is, but I haven't the heart to dismiss him."

Ganesh, for the credit of the family, was quite ready to bear all the blame without a word.

One of the company usually said at this point: "Never mind, Thakur Dada. Please don't trouble to look for it. This tobacco we're smoking will do quite well. The other would be too strong."

Then Thakur Dada would be relieved and settle down again, and the talk would go on.

When his guests got up to go away, Thakur Dada would

accompany them to the door and say to them on the door-step: "Oh, by the way, when are you all coming to dine with me?"

One or other of us would answer: "Not just yet, Thakur Dada, not just yet. We'll fix a day later."

"Quite right," he would answer. "Quite right. We had much better wait till the rains come. It's too hot now. And a grand rich dinner such as I should want to give you would upset us in weather like this."

But when the rains did come, every one was very careful not to remind him of his promise. If the subject was brought up, some friend would suggest gently that it was very inconvenient to get about when the rains were so severe, and therefore it would be much better to wait till they were over. Thus the game went on.

Thakur Dada's poor lodging was much too small for his position, and we used to condole with him about it. His friends would assure him they quite understood his difficulties: it was next to impossible to get a decent house in Calcutta. Indeed, they had all been looking out for years for a house to suit him. But, I need hardly add, no friend had been foolish enough to find one. Thakur Dada used to say, with a sigh of resignation: "Well, well, I suppose I shall have to put up with this house after all." Then he would add with a genial smile: "But, you know, I could never bear to be away from my friends. I must be near you. That really compensates for everything."

Somehow I felt all this very deeply indeed. I suppose the real reason was, that when a man is young, stupidity appears to him the worst of crimes. Kailas Babu was not really stupid. In ordinary business matters every one was ready to consult him. But with regard to Nayanjore his utterances were certainly void of common sense. Because, out of amused affection for him, no one contradicted his impossible statements, he refused to keep them in bounds. When people recounted in his hearing the glorious history of Nayanjore with absurd exaggerations, he would accept all they said with the utmost gravity, and never doubted, even in his dreams, that any one could disbelieve it.

## II

When I sit down and try to analyse the thoughts and feelings that I had towards Kailas Babu, I see that there was a still deeper reason for my dislike. I will now explain.

Though I am the son of a rich man, and might have wasted time at college, my industry was such that I took my M.A. degree in Calcutta University when quite young. My moral character was flawless. In addition, my outward appearance was so handsome, that if I were to call myself beautiful, it might be thought a mark of self-estimation, but could not be considered an untruth.

There could be no question that among the young men of Bengal I was regarded by parents generally as a very eligible match. I was myself quite clear on the point and had determined to obtain my full value in the marriage market. When I pictured my choice, I had before my mind's eye a wealthy father's only daughter, extremely beautiful and highly educated. Proposals came pouring in to me from far and near; large sums in cash were offered. I weighed these offers with rigid impartiality in the delicate scales of my own estimation. But there was no one fit to be my partner. I became convinced, with the poet Bhabavuti, that,

In this world's endless time and boundless space One may be born at last to match my sovereign grace.

But in this puny modern age, and this contracted space of modern Bengal, it was doubtful if the peerless creature existed as yet.

Meanwhile my praises were sung in many tunes, and in different metres, by designing parents.

Whether I was pleased with their daughters or not, this worship which they offered was never unpleasing. I used to regard it as my proper due, because I was so good. We are told that when the gods withhold their boons from mortals they still expect their worshippers to pay them fervent honour and are angry if it is withheld. I had that divine expectance strongly developed in myself.

I have already mentioned that Thakur Dada had an only grand-daughter. I had seen her many times, but had never mistaken her for beautiful. No thought had ever entered my mind that she would be a possible partner for myself. All the same, it seemed quite certain to me that some day or other Kailas Babu would offer her, with all due worship, as an oblation at my shrine. Indeed—this was the inner secret of my dislike—I was thoroughly annoyed that he had not done so already.

I heard that Thakur Dada had told his friends that the Babus of Nayanjore never craved a boon. Even if the girl remained unmarried, he would not break the family tradition. It was this arrogance of his that made me angry. My indignation smouldered for some time. But I remained perfectly silent and bore it with the utmost patience, because I was so good.

As lightning accompanies thunder, so in my character a flash of humour was mingled with the mutterings of my wrath. It was, of course, impossible for me to punish the old man merely to give vent to my rage; and for a long time I did nothing at all. But suddenly one day such an amusing plan came into my head, that I could not resist the temptation of carrying it into effect.

I have already said that many of Kailas Babu's friends used to flatter the old man's vanity to the full. One, who was a retired Government servant, had told him that whenever he saw the Chota Lât Sahib he always asked for the latest news about the Babus of Nayanjore, and the Chota Lât had been heard to say that in all Bengal the only really respectable families were those of the Maharaja of Cossipore and the Babus of Nayanjore. When this monstrous falsehood was told to Kailas Babu he was extremely gratified and often repeated the story. And wherever after that he met this Government servant in company he would ask, along with other questions:

"Oh! er—by the way, how is the Chota Lât Sahib? Quite well, did you say? Ah, yes, I am so delighted to hear it! And the dear Mem Sahib, is she quite well too? Ah, yes! and the little children—are they quite well also? Ah, yes! that's very good news! Be sure and give them my compliments when you see them."

Kailas Babu would constantly express his intention of going some day and paying a visit to the Lord Sahib. But it may be taken for granted that many Chota Lâts and Burra Lâts also would come and go, and much water would pass down the Hoogly, before the family coach of Nayanjore would be furbished up to pay a visit to Government House.

One day I took Kailas Babu aside and told him in a whisper: "Thakur Dada, I was at the Levee yesterday, and the Chota

Lât Sahib happened to mention the Babus of Nayanjore. I told him that Kailas Babu had come to town. Do you know, he was terribly hurt because you hadn't called. He told me he was going to put etiquette on one side and pay you a private visit himself this very afternoon."

Anybody else could have seen through this plot of mine in a moment. And, if it had been directed against another person, Kailas Babu would have understood the joke. But after all that he had heard from his friend the Government servant, and after all his own exaggerations, a visit from the Lieutenant-Governor seemed the most natural thing in the world. He became highly nervous and excited at my news. Each detail of the coming visit exercised him greatly,—most of all his own ignorance of English. How on earth was that difficulty to be met? I told him there was no difficulty at all: it was aristocratic not to know English: and, besides, the Lieutenant-Governor always brought an interpreter with him, and he had expressly mentioned that this visit was to be private.

About midday, when most of our neighbours are at work, and the rest are asleep, a carriage and pair stopped before the lodging of Kailas Babu. Two flunkeys in livery came up the stairs, and announced in a loud voice, "The Chota Lât Sahib has arrived!" Kailas Babu was ready, waiting for him, in his old-fashioned ceremonial robes and ancestral turban, and Ganesh was by his side, dressed in his master's best suit of clothes for the occasion.

When the Chota Lât Sahib was announced, Kailas Babu ran panting and puffing and trembling to the door, and led in a friend of mine, in disguise, with repeated salaams, bowing low at each step and walking backward as best he could. He had his old family shawl spread over a hard wooden chair and he asked the Lât Sahib to be seated. He then made a high-flown speech in Urdu, the ancient Court language of the Sahibs, and presented on the golden salver a string of gold mohurs, the last relics of his broken fortune. The old family servant Ganesh, with an expression of awe bordering on terror, stood behind with the scent-sprinkler, drenching the Lât Sahib, and touched him gingerly from time to time with the otto-of-roses from the filigree box.

Kailas Babu repeatedly expressed his regret at not being able to receive His Honour Bahadur with all the ancestral magnificence of his own family estate at Nayanjore. There he could have welcomed him properly with due ceremonial. But in Calcutta he was a mere stranger and sojourner,—in fact a fish out of water.

My friend, with his tall silk hat on, very gravely nodded. I need hardly say that according to English custom the hat ought to have been removed inside the room. But my friend did not dare to take it off for fear of detection: and Kailas Babu and his old servant Ganesh were sublimely unconscious of the breach of etiquette.

After a ten minutes' interview, which consisted chiefly of nodding the head, my friend rose to his feet to depart. The two flunkeys in livery, as had been planned beforehand, carried off in state the string of gold mohurs, the gold salver, the old ancestral shawl, the silver scent-sprinkler, and the otto-of-roses filigree box; they placed them ceremoniously in the carriage. Kailas Babu regarded this as the usual habit of Chota Lât Sahibs.

I was watching all the while from the next room. My sides were aching with suppressed laughter. When I could hold myself in no longer, I rushed into a further room, suddenly to discover, in a corner, a young girl sobbing as if her heart would break. When she saw my uproarious laughter she stood upright in passion, flashing the lightning of her big dark eyes in mine, and said with a tear-choked voice: "Tell me! What harm has my grandfather done to you? Why have you come to deceive him? Why have you come here? Why?"

She could say no more. She covered her face with her hands and broke into sobs.

My laughter vanished in a moment. It had never occurred to me that there was anything but a supremely funny joke in this act of mine, and here I discovered that I had given the cruellest pain to this tenderest little heart. All the ugliness of my cruelty rose up to condemn me. I slunk out of the room in silence, like a kicked dog.

Hitherto I had only looked upon Kusum, the grand-daughter of Kailas Babu, as a somewhat worthless commodity in the marriage market, waiting in vain to attract a husband. But now I found, with a shock of surprise, that in the corner of that room a human heart was beating.

The whole night through I had very little sleep. My mind was in a tumult. On the next day, very early in the morning, I took all those stolen goods back to Kailas Babu's lodgings, wishing to hand them over in secret to the servant Ganesh. I waited outside the door, and, not finding any one, went upstairs to Kailas Babu's room. I heard from the passage Kusum asking her grandfather in the most winning voice: "Dada, dearest, do tell me all that the Chota Lât Sahib said to you yesterday. Don't leave out a single word. I am dying to hear it all over again."

And Dada needed no encouragement. His face beamed over with pride as he related all manner of praises which the Lât Sahib had been good enough to utter concerning the ancient families of Nayanjore. The girl was seated before him, looking up into his face, and listening with rapt attention. She was determined, out of love for the old man, to play her part to the full.

My heart was deeply touched, and tears came to my eyes. I stood there in silence in the passage, while Thakur Dada finished all his embellishments of the Chota Lât Sahib's wonderful visit. When he left the room at last, I took the stolen goods and laid them at the feet of the girl and came away without a word.

Later in the day I called again to see Kailas Babu himself. According to our ugly modern custom, I had been in the habit of making no greeting at all to this old man when I came into the room. But on this day I made a low bow and touched his feet. I am convinced the old man thought that the coming of the Chota Lât Sahib to his house was the cause of my new politeness. He was highly gratified by it, and an air of benign serenity shone from his eyes. His friends had looked in, and he had already begun to tell again at full length the story of the Lieutenant-Governor's visit with still further adornments of a most fantastic kind. The interview was already becoming an epic, both in quality and in length.

When the other visitors had taken their leave, I made my proposal to the old man in a humble manner. I told him that, "though I could never for a moment hope to be worthy of marriage connection with such an illustrious family, yet ... etc. etc."

When I made clear my proposal of marriage, the old man

embraced me and broke out in a tumult of joy: "I am a poor man, and could never have expected such great good fortune."

That was the first and last time in his life that Kailas Babu confessed to being poor. It was also the first and last time in his life that he forgot, if only for a single moment, the ancestral dignity that belongs to the Babus of Nayanjore.

# Living or Dead

***Rabindranath Tagore***

## Part 1

The widow in the house of Saradasankar, the Ranihat zemindar, had no kinsmen of her father's family. One after another all had died. Nor had she in her husband's family any one she could call her own, neither husband nor son. The child of her brother-in-law Saradasankar was her darling. Far a long time after his birth, his mother had been very ill, and the widow, his aunt Kadambini, had fostered him. If a woman fosters another's child, her love for him is all the stronger because she has no claim upon him-no claim of kinship, that is, but simply the claim of love. Love cannot prove its claim by any document which society accepts, and does not wish to prove it; it merely worships with double passion its life's uncertain treasure. Thus all the widow's thwarted love went out to wards this little child. One night in Sraban Kadambini died suddenly. For some reason her heart stopped beating. Everywhere else the world held on its course; only m this gentle little breast, suffering with love, the watch of time stood still for ever.

Lest they should be harassed by the poike, four of the zemindar's Brahmin servants took away the body, without ceremony, to be burned. The burning-ground of Ranihat was very far from the village. There was a hut beside a tank, a huge banian near it, and nothing more. Formerly a river, now completely dried up, ran through the ground, and part of the watercourse had been dug out to make a tank for the performance of funeral rites. The people considered the tank as part of the river and reverenced it as such.

Taking the body into the hut, the four men sat down to wait for the wood. The time seemed so long that two of the four grew restless, and went to see why it did not come. Nitai and Gurucharan being gone, Bidhu and Banamali remained to watch over the body.

It was a dark night of Sraban. Heavy clouds hung In a starless sky. The two men sat silent in the dark room. Their matches and lamp were useless. The matches were damp, and would not light, for all their efforts, and the lantern went out.

After a long silence, one said: "Brother, it would be good if we had a bowl of tobacco. In our hurry we brought none."

The other answered: "I can run and bring all we want."

Understanding why Banarnali wanted to go (From fear of ghosts, the burning-ground being considered haunted.), Bidhu said: "I daresay! Meanwhile, I suppose I am to sit here alone!"

Conversation ceased again. Five minutes seemed like an hour. In their minds they cursed the two, who had gone to fetch the wood, and they began to suspect that they sat gossiping in some pleasant nook. There was no sound anywhere, except the incessant noise of frogs and crickets from the tank. Then suddenly they fancied that the bed shook slightly, as if the dead body had turned on its side. Bidhu and Banamali trembled, and began muttering: "Ram, Ram." A deep sigh was heard in the room. In a moment the watchers leapt out of the hut, and raced for the village.

After running aboat three miles, they met their colleagues coming back with a lantern. As a matter of fact, they had gone to smoke, and knew nothing about the wood. But they declared that a tree had been cut down, and that, when it was split up, it would be brought along at once. Then Bidhu and Banamali told them what had happened in the hut. Nitai and Gurucharan scoffed at the story, and abused Bidhu and Banamali angrily for leaving their duty.

Without delay all four returned to the hut. As they entered, they saw at once that the body was gone; nothing but an empty bed remained. They stared at one another. Could a jackal have taken it? But there was no scrap of clothing anywhere. Going outside, they saw that on the mud that had collected at the door of the but there were a woman's tiny footprints, newly made. Saradasankar was no fool, and they could hardly persuade him to believe in this ghost story. So after much discussion the four decided that it would be best to say that the body had been burnt.

Towards dawn, when the men with the wood arrived they were told that, owing to their delay, the work had been done without them; there had been some wood in the but after all. No one was likely to question this, since a dead body is not such a valuable property that any one would steal it.

## Part 2

Every one knows that, even when there is no sign, life is often secretly present, and may begin again in an apparently dead body. Kadambini was not dead; only the machine of her life had for some reason suddenly stopped.

When consciousness returned, she saw dense darkness on all sides. It occurred to her that she was not lying in her usual place. She called out " Sister," but no answer came from the darkness. As she sat up, terror-stricken, she remembered her death-bed, the sudden pain at her breast, the beginning of a choking sensation. Her elder sister-in-law was warming some milk for the child, when Kadambini became faint, and fell on the bed, saying with a choking voice: "Sister, bring the child here. I am worried." After that everything was black, as when an inkpot is upset over an exercise-book. Kadambini's memory and consciousness, all the letters of the world's book, in a moment became formless. The widow could not remember whether the child, in the sweet voice of love, called her " Auntie," as if for the last time, or not; she could not remember whether, as she left the world she knew for death's endless unknown journey, she had received a parting gift of affection, love's passage-money for the silent land. At first, I fancy, she thought the lonely dark place was the House of Yama, where there is nothing to see, nothing to hear, nothing to do, only an eternal watch. But when a cold damp wind drove through the open door, and she heard the croaking of frogs, she remembered vividly and in a moment all the rains of her short life, and could feel her kinship with the earth. Then came a flash of lightning, and she saw the tank, the banian, the great plain, the far-off trees. She remembered how at full moon she had sometimes come to bathe in this tank, and how dreadful death had seemed when she saw a corpse on the burning-ground.

Her first thought was to return home. But then she reflected: "I am dead. How can I return home? That would bring disaster on them. I have left the kingdom of the living; I am my own ghost!" If this were not so, she reasoned, how could she have got out of Saradasankar's well-guarded zenana, and come to this distant burningground at midnight? Also, if her funeral rites had not been finished, where had the men gone who should burn her? Recalling her death-moment in Saradasankar's brightly-lit house, she now found herself alone in a distant, deserted, dark burning. ground. Surely she was no member of earthly society! Surely she was a creature of horror, of ill-omen, her own ghost!

At this thought, all the bonds were snapped which bound her to the world. She felt that she had marvelous strength, endless freedom. She could do what she liked, go where she pleased. Mad with the inspiration of this new idea, she rushed from the but like a gust of wind, and stood upon the burning. ground. All trace of shame or fear had left her.

But as she walked on and on, her feet grew tired, her body weak. The plain stretched on endlessly; here and there were paddy-fields; sometimes she found herself standing knee-deep in water.

At the first glimmer of dawn she heard one or two birds cry from the bamboo clumps 6y the distant houses. Then terror seized her. She could not tell in what new relation she stood to the earth and to living folk. So long as she had been on the plain, on the burning-ground, covered by the dark night of Sraban, so long she had been fearless, a denizen of her own kingdom. By daylight the homes of men filled her with fear. Men and ghosts dread each other, for their tribes inhabit different banks of the river of death.

## Part 3

Her clothes were clotted in the mud; strange thoughts and walking by night had given her the aspect of a madwoman; truly, her apparition was such that folk might have been afraid of her, and children might have stoned her or run away. Luckily, the first to catch sight of her was a traveler. He came up, and said: "Mother, you look a respectable woman. Wherever are you going, alone and in this guise?"

Kadambini, unable to collect her thoughts, stared at him in silence. She could not think that she was still in touch with the world, that she looked like a respectable woman, that a traveler was asking her questions.

Again the min said: "Come, mother, I will see you home. Tell me where you live."

Kadambini thought. To return to her father-in-law's house would be absurd, and she had no father's house. Then she remembered the friend of her childhood. She had not seen Jogmaya since the days of her youth, but from time to time they had exchanged letters. Occasionally there had been quarrels between them, as was only right, since Kadambini wished to make it dear that her love for Jogmaya was unbounded, while her friend complained that Kadambini did not return a love equal to her own. They were both sure that, if they once met, they would be inseparable.

Kadambini said to the traveler: "I will go to Sripati's house at Nisindapur."

As he was going to Calcutta, Nisindapur, though not near, was on his way. So he took Kadambini to Sripati s house, and the friends met again. At first they did not recognize one another, but gradually each recognized the features of the other's childhood.

"What luck!" said Jogmaya. "I never dreamt that I should see you again. But how hate you come here, sister? Your father-in-law's folk surely didn't let you go!"

Kadambini remained silent, and at last said: "Sister, do not ask about my father-in-law. Give me a corner, and treat me as a servant: I will do your work."

"What?" cried Jogmaya. "Keep you like a servant! Why, you are my closest friend, you are my –" and so on and so on.

Just then Sripati came in. Kadambini stared at him for some time, and then went out very slowly. She kept her head uncovered, and showed not the slightest modesty or respect. Jogmaya, fearing that Sripati would be prejudiced against her friend, began an elaborate explanation. But Sripati, who readily agreed to anything Jogmaya said, cut short her story, and left his wife uneasy in her mind.

Kadambini had come, but she was not at one with her friend: death was between them. She could feel no intimacy for others so long as her existence perplexed her and consciousness remained. Kadambini would look at Jogmaya, and brood. She would think: "She has her husband and her work, she lives in a world far away from mine. She shares affection and duty with the people of the world; I am an empty shadow. She is among the living; I am in eternity."

Jogmaya also was uneasy, but could not explain why. Women do not love mystery, because, though uncertainty may be transmuted into poetry, into heroism, into scholarship, it cannot be turned to account in household work. So, when a woman cannot understand a thing, she either destroys and forgets it, or she shapes it anew for her own use; if she fails to deal with it in one of these ways, she loses her temper with it. The greater Kadambini's abstraction became, the more impatient was Jogmaya with her, wondering what trouble weighed upon her mind.

Then a new danger arose. Kadambini was afraid of herself; yet she could not flee from herself. Those who fear ghosts fear those who are behind them; wherever they cannot see there is fear. But Kadambini's chief terror lay in herself, for she dreaded nothing external. At the dead of night, when alone in her room, she screamed; in the evening, when she saw her shadow in the lamp-light, her whole body shook. Watching her fearfulness, the rest of the house fell into a sort of terror. The servants and Jogmaya herself began to see ghosts.

One midnight, Kadambini came out from her bedroom weeping, and wailed at Jogmaya's door: "Sister, sister, let me lie at your feet! Do not put me by myself!"

Jogmaya's anger was no less than her fear. She would have liked to drive Kadambini from the house that very second. The good-natured Sripati, after much effort, succeeded in quieting their guest, and put her in the next room.

Next day Sripati was unexpectedly summoned to his wife's apartments. She began to upbraid him: " You, do you call yourself a man? A woman runs away from her father-in-law, and enters your house; a month passes, and you haven't hinted that she should go away, nor have I heard the slightest protest from you. I should cake it as a favor if you would explain yourself. You men are all alike."

Men, as a race, have a natural partiality for womankind in general, foe which women themselves hold them accountable. Although Sripati was prepared to touch Jogmaya's body, and swear that his kind feeling towards the helpless but beautiful Kadambini was no whit greater than it should be, he could not prove it by his behavior. He thought that her father-in-law's people must have treated this forlorn widow abominably, if she could bear it no longer, and was driven to take refuge with him. As she had neither father nor mother, how could he desert her? So saying, he let the matter drop, far he had no mind to distress Kadambini by asking her unpleasant questions.

His wife, then, tried other means of her sluggish lord, until at last he saw that for the sake of peace he must send word to Kadambini's father-in-law. The result of a letter, he thought, might not be satisfactory; so he resolved to go to Ranihat, and act on what he learnt.

So Sripati went, and Jogmaya on her part said to Kadambini "Friend, it hardly seems proper for you to stop here any longer. What will people say?"

Kadambini stared solemnly at Jogmaya, and said: "What have I to do with people?"

Jogmaya was astounded. Then she said sharply: "If you have nothing to do with people, we have. How can we explain the detention of a woman belonging to another house?"

Kadambini said: "Where is my father-in-law's house?"

"Confound it!" thought Jogmaya. "What will the wretched woman say next?"

Very slowly Kadambini said: "What have I to do with you? Am I of the earth? You laugh, weep, love; each grips and holds his own; I merely look. You are human, I a shadow. I cannot understand why God has kept me in this world of yours."

So strange were her look and speech that Jogmaya understood something of her drift, though not all. Unable either to dismiss her, or to ask her any more questions, she went away, oppressed with thought.

Part 4

It was nearly ten o'clock at night when Sripati returned from Ranihat. The earth was drowned in torrents of rain. It seemed that the downpour would never stop, that the night would never end.

Jogmaya asked: "Well?"

"I've lots to say, presently."

So saying, Sripati changed his clothes, and sat down to supper; then he lay dawn for a smoke. His mind was perplexed.

His wife stilled her curiosity for a long time; then she came to his couch and demanded: "What did you hear?"

"That you have certainly made a mistake."

Jogmaya was nettled. Women never make mistakes, or, if they do, a sensible man never mentions them; it is better to take them on his own shoulders. Jogmaya snapped: "May I be permitted to hear how?"

Sripati replied: "The woman you have taken into your house is not your Kadambini."

Hearing this, she was greatly annoyed, especially since it was her husband who said it. "What! I don't know my own friend? I must come to you to recognize her! You are clever, indeed!"

Sripati explained that there was no need to quarrel about his cleverness. He could prove what he said. There was no doubt that Jogmaya's Kadambini was dead.

Jogmaya replied: "Listen! You've certainly made some huge mistake. You've been to the wrong house, or are confused as to what you have heard. Who told you to go yourself? Write a letter, and everything will be cleared up."

Sripati was hurt by his wife's lack of faith in his executive ability; he produced all sorts of proof, without result. Midnight found them still asserting and contradicting. Although they were both agreed now that Kadambini should be got out of the house, although Sripati believed that their guest had deceived his wife all the time by a pretended acquaintance, and Jogmaya that she was a prostitute, yet in the present discussion neither would acknowledge defeat. By degrees their voices became so loud that they forgot that Kadambini was sleeping in the next room.

The one said: "We're in a nice fix! I tell you, I heard it with my own ears!" And the other answered angrily: "What do I care about that? I can see with my own eyes, surely."

At length Jogmaya said: "Very well. Tell me when Kadambini died." She thought that if she could find a discrepancy between the day of death and the date of some letter from Kadambini, she could prove that Sripati erred.

He told her the date of Kadambini's death, and they both saw that it fell on the very day before she came to their house. Jogmaya's heart trembled, even Sripati was not unmoved.

Just then the door flew open; a damp wind swept in and blew the lamp out. The darkness rushed after it, and filled the whole house. Kadambini stood in the room. It was nearly one o'clock, the rain was pelting outside.

Kadambini spoke: "Friend, I am your Kadambini, but I am no longer living. I am dead."

Jogmaya screamed with terror; Sripati could speak.

"But, save in being dead, I have done you no wrong. If I have no place among the living, I have none among the dead. Oh! whither shall I go?"

Crying as if to wake the sleeping Creator in the dense night of rain, she asked again: "Oh! whither shall I go?"

So saying Kadambini left her friend fainting in the dark house, and went out into the world, seeking her own place.

## Part 5

It is hard to say how Kadambini reached Ranihat. At first she showed herself to no one, but spent the whole day in a ruined temple, starving. When the untimely afternoon of the rains was pitch-black, and people huddled into their houses for fear of the impending storm, then Kadambini came forth. Her heart trembled as she reached her father-in- law's house; and when, drawing a thick veil over her face, she entered, none of the doorkeepers objected, since they took her for a servant. And the rain was pouring down, and the wind howled.

The mistress, Saradasankar's wife, was playing cards with her widowed sister. A servant was in the kitchen, the sick child was sleeping in the bedroom. Kadambini, escaping every one's notice, entered this room. I do not know why she had come to her father-in-law's house; she herself did not know; she felt only that she wanted to see her child again. She had no thought where to go next, or what to do.

In the lighted room she saw the child sleeping, his fists clenched, his body wasted with fever. At sight of him, her heart became parched and thirsty. If only she could press that tortured body to her breast! Immediately the thought followed: "I do not exist. Who would see it? His mother loves company, loves gossip and cards. All the time that she left me in charge, she was herself free from anxiety, nor was she troubled about him in the least. Who will look after him now as I did?"

The child turned on his side, and cried, half-asleep: "Auntie, give me water." Her darling had not yet forgotten his auntie! In a fever of excitement, she poured out some water, and, taking him to her breast, she gave it him.

As long as he was asleep, the child felt no strangeness in taking water from the accustomed hand. But when Kadambini satisfied her long-starved longing, and kissed him and began rocking him asleep again, he awoke and embraced her. "Did you die, Auntie?" he asked.

"Yes, darling."

"And you have come back? Do not die again."

Before she could answer disaster overtook her. One of the maidservants coming in with a cup of sago dropped it, and fell down. At the crash the mistress left her cards, and entered the room. She stood like a pillar of wood, unable to flee or speak. Seeing all this, the child, too, became terrified, and burst out weeping: " Go away, Auntie," he said, "go away!"

Now at last Kadambini understood that she had not died. The old room, the old things, the same child, the same love, all returned to their living state, without change or difference between her and them. In her friend's house she had felt that her childhood's companion was dead. In her child's room she knew that the boy's "Auntie" was not dead at all. In anguished tones she said: "Sister, why do you dread me? See, I am as you knew me."

Her sister-in-law could endure no longer, and fell into a faint.

Saradasankar himself entered the zenana. With folded hands, he said piteously: "Is this right? Satis is my only son. Why do you show yourself to him? Are we not your own kin? Since you went, he has wasted away daily; his fever has been incessant; day and night he cries: 'Auntie, Auntie.' You have left the world; break these bonds of maya (Illusory affection binding a soul to the world). We will perform all funeral honors."

Kadambini could bear no more. She said: "Oh, I am not dead, I am not dead. Oh, how can I persuade you that I am not dead? I am living, living!" She lifted a brass pot from the ground and dashed it against her forehead. The blood ran from her brow. "Look!" she cried, "I am living!" Saradasankar stood like an image; the child screamed with fear, the two fainting women lay still.

Then Kadambini, shouting "I am not dead, I am not dead," went down the steps to the zenana well, and plunged in. From the upper storey Saradasankar heard the splash.

All night the rain poured; it poured next day at dawn, was pouring still at noon. By dying, Kadambini had given proof that she was not dead.

# The Postmaster

## *Rabindranath Tagore*

The postmaster first took up his duties in the village of Ulapur. Though the village was a small one, there was an indigo factory near by, and the proprietor, an Englishman, had managed to get a post office established.

Our postmaster belonged to Calcutta. He felt like a fish out of water in this remote village. His office and living-room were in a dark thatched shed, not far from a green, slimy pond, surrounded on all sides by a dense growth.

The men employed in the indigo factory had no leisure; moreover, they were hardly desirable companions for decent folk. Nor is a Calcutta boy an adept in the art of associating with others. Among strangers he appears either proud or ill at ease. At any rate, the postmaster had but little company; nor had he much to do.

At times he tried his hand at writing a verse or two. That the movement of the leaves and the clouds of the sky were enough to fill life with joy—such were the sentiments to which he sought to give expression. But God knows that the poor fellow would have felt it as the gift of a new life, if some genie of the Arabian Nights had in one night swept away the trees, leaves and all, and replaced them with a macadamised road, hiding the clouds from view with rows of tall houses.

The postmaster's salary was small. He had to cook his own meals, which he used to share with Ratan, an orphan girl of the village, who did odd jobs for him.

When in the evening the smoke began to curl up from the village cowsheds, and the cicalas chirped in every bush; when the mendicants of the Baül sect sang their shrill songs in their daily meeting-place, when any poet, who had attempted to watch the movement of the leaves in the dense bamboo thickets, would have felt a ghostly shiver run down his back, the postmaster would light his little lamp, and call out "Ratan."

Ratan would sit outside waiting for this call, and, instead of coming in at once, would reply, "Did you call me, sir?"

"What are you doing?" the postmaster would ask.

"I must be going to light the kitchen fire," would be the answer.

And the postmaster would say: "Oh, let the kitchen fire be for awhile; light me my pipe first."

At last Ratan would enter, with puffed-out cheeks, vigorously blowing into a flame a live coal to light the tobacco. This would give the postmaster an opportunity of conversing. "Well, Ratan," perhaps he would begin, "do you remember anything of your mother?" That was a fertile subject. Ratan partly remembered, and partly didn't. Her father had been fonder of her than her mother; him she recollected more vividly. He used to come home in the evening after his work, and one or two evenings stood out more clearly than others, like pictures in her memory. Ratan would sit on the floor near the postmaster's feet, as memories crowded in upon her. She called to mind a little brother that she had—and how on some bygone cloudy day she had played at fishing with him on the edge of the pond, with a twig for a make-believe fishing-rod. Such little incidents would drive out greater events from her mind. Thus, as they talked, it would often get very late, and the postmaster would feel too lazy to do any cooking at all. Ratan would then hastily light the fire, and toast some unleavened bread, which, with the cold remnants of the morning meal, was enough for their supper.

On some evenings, seated at his desk in the corner of the big empty shed, the postmaster too would call up memories of his own home, of his mother and his sister, of those for whom in his exile his heart was sad,—memories which were always haunting him, but which he could not talk about with the men of the factory, though he found himself naturally recalling them aloud in the presence of the simple little girl. And so it came about that the girl would allude to his people as mother, brother, and sister, as if she had known them all her life. In fact, she had a complete picture of each one of them painted in her little heart.

One noon, during a break in the rains, there was a cool soft breeze blowing; the smell of the damp grass and leaves in the hot sun felt like the warm breathing of the tired earth on one's body. A persistent bird went on all the afternoon repeating the burden of its one complaint in Nature's audience chamber.

The postmaster had nothing to do. The shimmer of the freshly washed leaves, and the banked-up remnants of the retreating rain-clouds were sights to see; and the postmaster was watching them and thinking to himself: "Oh, if only some kindred soul were near—just one loving human being whom I could hold near my heart!" This was exactly, he went on to think, what that bird was trying to say, and it was the same feeling which the murmuring leaves were striving to express. But no one knows, or would believe, that such an idea might also take possession of an ill-paid village postmaster in the deep, silent mid-day interval of his work.

The postmaster sighed, and called out "Ratan." Ratan was then sprawling beneath the guava-tree, busily engaged in eating unripe guavas. At the voice of her master, she ran up breathlessly, saying: "Were you calling me, Dada?" "I was thinking," said the postmaster, "of teaching you to read." And then for the rest of the afternoon he taught her the alphabet.

Thus, in a very short time, Ratan had got as far as the double consonants.

It seemed as though the showers of the season would never end. Canals, ditches, and hollows were all overflowing with water. Day and night the patter of rain was heard, and the croaking of frogs. The village roads became impassable, and marketing had to be done in punts.

One heavily clouded morning, the postmaster's little pupil had been long waiting outside the door for her call, but, not hearing it as usual, she took up her dog-eared book, and slowly entered the room. She found her master stretched out on his bed, and, thinking that he was resting, she was about to retire on tip-toe, when she suddenly heard her name—"Ratan!" She turned at once and asked: "Were you sleeping, Dada?" The postmaster in a plaintive voice said: "I am not well. Feel my head; is it very hot?"

In the loneliness of his exile, and in the gloom of the rains, his ailing body needed a little tender nursing. He longed to remember the touch on the forehead of soft hands with tinkling bracelets, to imagine the presence of loving womanhood, the nearness of mother and sister. And the exile was not disappointed. Ratan ceased to be a little girl. She at once stepped into the post of mother, called in the village doctor, gave the patient his pills at the proper intervals, sat up all night by his pillow, cooked his gruel for him, and every now and then asked: "Are you feeling a little better, Dada?"

It was some time before the postmaster, with weakened body, was able to leave his sick-bed. "No more of this," said he with decision. "I must get a transfer." He at once wrote off to Calcutta an application for a transfer, on the ground of the unhealthiness of the place.

Relieved from her duties as nurse, Ratan again took up her old place outside the door. But she no longer heard the same old call. She would sometimes peep inside furtively to find the postmaster sitting on his chair, or stretched on his bed, and staring absent-mindedly into the air. While Ratan was awaiting her call, the postmaster was awaiting a reply to his application. The girl read her old lessons over and over again,—her great fear was lest, when the call came, she might be found wanting in the double consonants. At last, after a week, the call did come one evening. With an overflowing heart Ratan rushed into the room with her—"Were you calling me, Dada?"

The postmaster said: "I am going away to-morrow, Ratan."

"Where are you going, Dada?"

"I am going home."

"When will you come back?"

"I am not coming back."

Ratan asked no other question. The postmaster, of his own accord, went on to tell her that his application for a transfer had been rejected, so he had resigned his post and was going home.

For a long time neither of them spoke another word. The lamp went on dimly burning, and from a leak in one corner of the thatch water dripped steadily into an earthen vessel on the floor beneath it.

After a while Ratan rose, and went off to the kitchen to prepare the meal; but she was not so quick about it as on other days. Many new things to think of had entered her little brain. When the postmaster had finished his supper, the girl suddenly asked him: "Dada, will you take me to your home?"

The postmaster laughed. "What an idea!" said he; but he did not think it necessary to explain to the girl wherein lay the absurdity.

That whole night, in her waking and in her dreams, the postmaster's laughing reply haunted her—"What an idea!"

On getting up in the morning, the postmaster found his bath ready. He had stuck to his Calcutta habit of bathing in water drawn and kept in pitchers, instead of taking a plunge in the river as was the custom of the village. For some reason or other, the girl could not ask him about the time of his departure, so she had fetched the water from the river long before sunrise, that it should be ready as early as he might want it. After the bath came a call for Ratan. She entered noiselessly, and looked silently into her master's face for orders. The master said: "You need not be anxious about my going away, Ratan; I shall tell my successor to look after you." These words were kindly meant, no doubt: but inscrutable are the ways of a woman's heart!

Ratan had borne many a scolding from her master without complaint, but these kind words she could not bear. She burst out weeping, and said: "No, no, you need not tell anybody anything at all about me; I don't want to stay on here."

The postmaster was dumbfounded. He had never seen Ratan like this before.

The new incumbent duly arrived, and the postmaster, having given over charge, prepared to depart. Just before starting he called Ratan and said: "Here is something for you; I hope it will keep you for some little time." He brought out from his pocket the whole of his month's salary, retaining only a trifle for his travelling expenses. Then Ratan fell at his feet and cried: "Oh, Dada, I pray you, don't give me anything, don't in any way trouble about me," and then she ran away out of sight.

The postmaster heaved a sigh, took up his carpet bag, put his umbrella over his shoulder, and, accompanied by a man carrying his many-coloured tin trunk, he slowly made for the boat.

When he got in and the boat was under way, and the rain-swollen river, like a stream of tears welling up from the earth, swirled and sobbed at her bows, then he felt a pain at heart; the grief-stricken face of a village girl seemed to represent for him the great unspoken pervading grief of Mother Earth herself. At one time he had an impulse to go back, and bring away along with him that lonesome waif, forsaken of the world. But the wind had just filled the sails, the boat had got well into the middle of the turbulent current, and already the village was left behind, and its outlying burning-ground came in sight.

So the traveller, borne on the breast of the swift-flowing river, consoled himself with philosophical reflections on the numberless meetings and partings going on in the world—on death, the great parting, from which none returns.

But Ratan had no philosophy. She was wandering about the post office in a flood of tears. It may be that she had still a lurking hope in some corner of her heart that her Dada would return, and that is why she could not tear herself away. Alas for our foolish human nature! Its fond mistakes are persistent. The dictates of reason take a long time to assert their own sway. The surest proofs meanwhile are disbelieved. False hope is clung to with all one's might and main, till a day comes when it has sucked the heart dry and it forcibly breaks through its bonds and departs. After that comes the misery of awakening, and then once again the longing to get back into the maze of the same mistakes.

# The Cabuliwallah

## *Rabindranath Tagore*

My five years' old daughter Mini cannot live without chattering. I really believe that in all her life she has not wasted a minute in silence. Her mother is often vexed at this, and would stop her prattle, but I would not. To see Mini quiet is unnatural, and I cannot bear it long. And so my own talk with her is always lively.

One morning, for instance, when I was in the midst of the seventeenth chapter of my new novel, my little Mini stole into the room, and putting her hand into mine, said: "Father! Ramdayal the door-keeper calls a crow a krow! He doesn't know anything, does he?"

Before I could explain to her the differences of language in this world, she was embarked on the full tide of another subject. "What do you think, Father? Bhola says there is an elephant in the clouds, blowing water out of his trunk, and that is why it rains!"

And then, darting off anew, while I sat still making ready some reply to this last saying: "Father! what relation is Mother to you?"

With a grave face I contrived to say: "Go and play with Bhola, Mini! I am busy!"

The window of my room overlooks the road. The child had seated herself at my feet near my table, and was playing softly, drumming on her knees. I was hard at work on my seventeenth chapter, where Pratap Singh, the hero, had just caught Kanchanlata, the heroine, in his arms, and was about to escape with her by the third-story window of the castle, when all of a sudden Mini left her play, and ran to the window, crying: "A Cabuliwallah! A Cabuliwallah!" Sure enough in the street below was a Cabuliwallah, passing slowly along. He wore the loose, soiled clothing of his people, with a tall turban; there was a bag on his back, and he carried boxes of grapes in his hand.

I cannot tell what were my daughter's feelings at the sight of this man, but she began to call him loudly. "Ah!" I thought, "he will come in, and my seventeenth chapter will never be finished!" At which exact moment the Cabuliwallah turned, and looked up at the child. When she saw this, overcome by terror, she fled to her mother's protection and disappeared. She had a blind belief that inside the bag, which the big man carried, there were perhaps two or three other children like herself. The pedlar meanwhile entered my doorway and greeted me with a smiling face.

So precarious was the position of my hero and my heroine, that my first impulse was to stop and buy something, since the man had been called. I made some small purchases, and a conversation began about Abdurrahman, the Russians, the English, and the Frontier Policy.

As he was about to leave, he asked: "And where is the little girl, sir?"

And I, thinking that Mini must get rid of her false fear, had her brought out.

She stood by my chair, and looked at the Cabuliwallah and his bag. He offered her nuts and raisins, but she would not be tempted, and only clung the closer to me, with all her doubts increased.

This was their first meeting.

One morning, however, not many days later, as I was leaving the house, I was startled to find Mini, seated on a bench near the door, laughing and talking, with the great Cabuliwallah at her feet. In all her life, it appeared, my small daughter had never found so patient a listener, save her father. And already the corner of her little sari was stuffed with almonds and raisins, the gift of her visitor. "Why did you give her those?" I said, and taking out an eight-anna bit, I handed it to him. The man accepted the money without demur, and slipped it into his pocket.

Alas, on my return an hour later, I found the unfortunate coin had made twice its own worth of trouble! For the Cabuliwallah had given it to Mini; and her mother, catching sight of the bright round object, had pounced on the child with: "Where did you get that eight-anna bit?"

"The Cabuliwallah gave it me," said Mini cheerfully.

"The Cabuliwallah gave it you!" cried her mother much shocked. "O Mini! how could you take it from him?"

I, entering at the moment, saved her from impending disaster, and proceeded to make my own inquiries.

It was not the first or second time, I found, that the two had met. The Cabuliwallah had overcome the child's first terror by a judicious bribery of nuts and almonds, and the two were now great friends.

They had many quaint jokes, which afforded them much amusement. Seated in front of him, looking down on his gigantic frame in all her tiny dignity, Mini would ripple her face with laughter and begin: "O Cabuliwallah! Cabuliwallah! What have you got in your bag?"

And he would reply, in the nasal accents of the mountaineer: "An elephant!" Not much cause for merriment, perhaps; but how they both enjoyed the fun! And for me, this child's talk with a grown-up man had always in it something strangely fascinating.

Then the Cabuliwallah, not to be behindhand, would take his turn: "Well, little one, and when are you going to the father-in-law's house?"

Now most small Bengali maidens have heard long ago about the father-in-law's house; but we, being a little new-fangled, had kept these things from our child, and Mini at this question must have been a trifle bewildered. But she would not show it, and with ready tact replied: "Are you going there?"

Amongst men of the Cabuliwallah's class, however, it is well known that the words father-in-law's house have a double meaning. It is a euphemism for jail, the place where we are well cared for, at no expense to ourselves. In this sense would the sturdy pedlar take my daughter's question. "Ah," he would say, shaking his fist at an invisible policeman, "I will thrash my father-in-law!" Hearing this, and picturing the poor discomfited relative, Mini would go off into peals of laughter, in which her formidable friend would join.

These were autumn mornings, the very time of year when kings of old went forth to conquest; and I, never stirring from my little corner in Calcutta, would let my mind wander over the whole world. At the very name of another country, my heart would go out to it, and at the sight of a foreigner in the streets, I would fall to weaving a network of dreams,—the mountains, the glens, and the forests of his distant home, with his cottage in its setting, and the free and independent life of far-away wilds. Perhaps the scenes of travel conjure themselves up before me and pass and repass in my imagination all the more vividly, because I lead such a vegetable existence that a call to travel would fall upon me like a thunder-bolt. In the presence of this Cabuliwallah I was immediately transported to the foot of arid mountain peaks, with narrow little defiles twisting in and out amongst their towering heights. I could see the string of camels bearing the merchandise, and the company of turbanned merchants carrying some their queer old firearms, and some their spears, journeying downward towards the plains. I could see—. But at some such point Mini's mother would intervene, imploring me to "beware of that man."

Mini's mother is unfortunately a very timid lady. Whenever she hears a noise in the street, or sees people coming towards the house, she always jumps to the conclusion that they are either thieves, or drunkards, or snakes, or tigers, or malaria, or cockroaches, or caterpillars. Even after all these years of experience, she is not able to overcome her terror. So she was full of doubts about the Cabuliwallah, and used to beg me to keep a watchful eye on him.

I tried to laugh her fear gently away, but then she would turn round on me seriously, and ask me solemn questions:—

Were children never kidnapped?

Was it, then, not true that there was slavery in Cabul?

Was it so very absurd that this big man should be able to carry off a tiny child?

I urged that, though not impossible, it was highly improbable. But this was not enough, and her dread persisted. As it was indefinite, however, it did not seem right to forbid the man the house, and the intimacy went on unchecked.

Once a year in the middle of January Rahmun, the Cabuliwallah, was in the habit of returning to his country, and as the time approached he would be very busy, going from house to house collecting his debts. This year, however, he could always find time to come and see Mini. It would have seemed to an outsider that there was some conspiracy between the two, for when he could not come in the morning, he would appear in the evening.

Even to me it was a little startling now and then, in the corner of a dark room, suddenly to surprise this tall, loose-garmented, much bebagged man; but when Mini would run in smiling, with her "O Cabuliwallah! Cabuliwallah!" and the two friends, so far apart in age, would subside into their old laughter and their old jokes, I felt reassured.

One morning, a few days before he had made up his mind to go, I was correcting my proof sheets in my study. It was chilly weather. Through the window the rays of the sun touched my feet, and the slight warmth was very welcome. It was almost eight o'clock, and the early pedestrians were returning home with their heads covered. All at once I heard an uproar in the street, and, looking out, saw Rahmun being led away bound between two policemen, and behind them a crowd of curious boys. There were blood-stains on the clothes of the Cabuliwallah, and one of the policemen carried a knife. Hurrying out, I stopped them, and inquired what it all meant. Partly from one, partly from another, I gathered that a certain neighbour had owed the pedlar something for a Rampuri shawl, but had falsely denied having bought it, and that in the course of the quarrel Rahmun had struck him. Now, in the heat of his excitement, the prisoner began calling his enemy all sorts of names, when suddenly in a verandah of my house appeared my little Mini, with her usual exclamation: "O Cabuliwallah! Cabuliwallah!" Rahmun's face lighted up as he turned to her. He had no bag under his arm to-day, so she could not discuss the elephant with him. She at once therefore proceeded to the next question: "Are you going to the father-in-law's house?" Rahmun laughed and said: "Just where I am going, little one!" Then, seeing that the reply did not amuse the child, he held up his fettered hands. "Ah!" he said, "I would have thrashed that old father-in-law, but my hands are bound!"

On a charge of murderous assault, Rahmun was sentenced

to some years' imprisonment.

Time passed away and he was not remembered. The accustomed work in the accustomed place was ours, and the thought of the once free mountaineer spending his years in prison seldom or never occurred to us. Even my light-hearted Mini, I am ashamed to say, forgot her old friend. New companions filled her life. As she grew older, she spent more of her time with girls. So much time indeed did she spend with them that she came no more, as she used to do, to her father's room. I was scarcely on speaking terms with her.

Years had passed away. It was once more autumn and we had made arrangements for our Mini's marriage. It was to take place during the Puja Holidays. With Durga returning to Kailas, the light of our home also was to depart to her husband's house, and leave her father's in the shadow.

The morning was bright. After the rains, there was a sense of ablution in the air, and the sun-rays looked like pure gold. So bright were they, that they gave a beautiful radiance even to the sordid brick walls of our Calcutta lanes. Since early dawn that day the wedding-pipes had been sounding, and at each beat my own heart throbbed. The wail of the tune, Bhairavi, seemed to intensify my pain at the approaching separation. My Mini was to be married that night.

From early morning noise and bustle had pervaded the house. In the courtyard the canopy had to be slung on its bamboo poles; the chandeliers with their tinkling sound must be hung in each room and verandah. There was no end of hurry and excitement. I was sitting in my study, looking through the accounts, when some one entered, saluting respectfully, and stood before me. It was Rahmun the Cabuliwallah. At first I did not recognise him. He had no bag, nor the long hair, nor the same vigour that he used to have. But he smiled, and I knew him again.

"When did you come, Rahmun?" I asked him.

"Last evening," he said, "I was released from jail."

The words struck harsh upon my ears. I had never before talked with one who had wounded his fellow, and my heart shrank within itself when I realised this; for I felt that the day would have been better-omened had he not turned up.

"There are ceremonies going on," I said, "and I am busy. Could you perhaps come another day?"

At once he turned to go; but as he reached the door he hesitated, and said: "May I not see the little one, sir, for a moment?" It was his belief that Mini was still the same. He had pictured her running to him as she used, calling "O Cabuliwallah! Cabuliwallah!" He had imagined too that they would laugh and talk together, just as of old. In fact, in memory of former days he had brought, carefully wrapped up in paper, a few almonds and raisins and grapes, obtained somehow from a countryman; for his own little fund was dispersed.

I said again: "There is a ceremony in the house, and you will not be able to see any one to-day."

The man's face fell. He looked wistfully at me for a moment, then said "Good morning," and went out.

I felt a little sorry, and would have called him back, but I found he was returning of his own accord. He came close up to me holding out his offerings with the words: "I brought these few things, sir, for the little one. Will you give them to her?"

I took them and was going to pay him, but he caught my hand and said: "You are very kind, sir! Keep me in your recollection. Do not offer me money!—You have a little girl: I too have one like her in my own home. I think of her, and bring fruits to your child—not to make a profit for myself."

Saying this, he put his hand inside his big loose robe, and brought out a small and dirty piece of paper. With great care he unfolded this, and smoothed it out with both hands on my table. It bore the photograph. Not a drawing. The impression of an ink-smeared hand laid flat on the paper. This touch of his own little daughter had been always on his heart, as he had come year after year to Calcutta to sell his wares in the streets.

Tears came to my eyes. I forgot that he was a poor Cabuli fruit-seller, while I was—. But no, what was I more than he? He also was a father.

That impression of the hand of his little Pārbati in her distant mountain home reminded me of my own little Mini.

I sent for Mini immediately from the inner apartment. Many difficulties were raised, but I would not listen. Clad in the red silk of her wedding-day, with the sandal paste on her forehead, and adorned as a young bride, Mini came, and stood bashfully before me.

The Cabuliwallah looked a little staggered at the apparition. He could not revive their old friendship. At last he smiled and said: "Little one, are you going to your father-in-law's house?"

But Mini now understood the meaning of the word "father-in-law," and she could not reply to him as of old. She flushed up at the question, and stood before him with her bride-like face turned down.

I remembered the day when the Cabuliwallah and my Mini had first met, and I felt sad. When she had gone, Rahmun heaved a deep sigh, and sat down on the floor. The idea had suddenly come to him that his daughter too must have grown in this long time, and that he would have to make friends with her anew. Assuredly he would not find her as he used to know her. And besides, what might not have happened to her in these eight years?

The marriage-pipes sounded, and the mild autumn sun streamed round us. But Rahmun sat in the little Calcutta lane, and saw before him the barren mountains of Afghanistan.

I took out a bank-note and gave it to him, saying: "Go back to your own daughter, Rahmun, in your own country, and may the happiness of your meeting bring good fortune to my child!"

Having made this present, I had to curtail some of the festivities. I could not have the electric lights I had intended, nor the military band, and the ladies of the house were despondent at it. But to me the wedding-feast was all the brighter for the thought that in a distant land a long-lost father met again with his only child.

# The Kingdom of Cards

***Rabindranath Tagore***

1

Once upon a time there was a lonely island in a distant sea where lived the Kings and Queens, the Aces and the Knaves, in the Kingdom of Cards. The Tens and Nines, with the Twos and Threes, and all the other members, had long ago settled there also. But these were not twice-born people, like the famous Court Cards.

The Ace, the King, and the Knave were the three highest castes. The fourth Caste was made up of a mixture of the lower Cards. The Twos and Threes were lowest of all. These inferior Cards were never allowed to sit in the same row with the great Court Cards.

Wonderful indeed were the regulations and rules of that island kingdom. The particular rank of each individual had been settled from time immemorial. Every one had his own appointed work, and never did anything else. An unseen hand appeared to be directing them wherever they went, –according to the Rules.

No one in the Kingdom of Cards had any occasion to think: no one had any need to come to any decision: no one was ever required to debate any new subject. The citizens all moved along in a listless groove without speech. When they fell, they made no noise. They lay down on their backs, and gazed upward at the sky with each prim feature firmly fixed for ever.

There was a remarkable stillness in the Kingdom of Cards. Satisfaction and contentment were complete in all their rounded wholeness. There was never any uproar or violence. There was never any excitement or enthusiasm.

The great ocean, crooning its lullaby with one unceasing melody, lapped the island to sleep with a thousand soft touches of its wave's white hands. The vast sky, like the outspread azure wings of the brooding mother-bird, nestled the island round with its downy plume. For on the distant horizon a deep blue line betokened another shore. But no sound of quarrel or strife could reach the Island of Cards, to break its calm repose.

2

In that far-off foreign land, across the sea, there lived a young Prince whose mother was a sorrowing queen. This queen had fallen from favor, and was living with her only son on the seashore. The Prince passed his childhood alone and forlorn, sitting by his forlorn mother, weaving the net of his big desires. He longed to go in search of the Flying Horse, the Jewel in the Cobra's hood, the Rose of Heaven, the Magic Roads, or to find where the Princess Beauty was sleeping in the Ogre's castle over the thirteen rivers and across the seven seas.

From the Son of the Merchant at school the young Prince learnt the stories of foreign kingdoms. From the Son of the Kotwal he learnt the adventures of the Two Genii of the Lamp. And when the rain came beating down, and the clouds covered the sky, he would sit on the threshold that faces the sea, and say to his sorrowing mother: "Tell me, mother, a story of some very far-off land."

And his mother would tell him an endless tale she had heard in her childhood of a wonderful country beyond the sea where dwelt the Princess Beauty. And the heart of the young Prince would become sick with longing, as he sat on the threshold, looking out on the ocean, listening to his mother's wonderful story, while the rain outside came beating down and the grey clouds covered the sky.

One day the Son of the Merchant came to the Prince, and said boldly: "Comrade, my studies are over. I am now setting out on my travels to seek my fortunes on the sea. I have come to bid you good-bye."

The Prince said; "I will go with you."

And the Son of Kotwal said also: "Comrades, trusty and true, you will not leave me behind. I also will be your companion."

Then the young Prince said to his sorrowing mother; "Mother,

I am now setting out on my travels to seek my fortune. When I come back once more, I shall surely have found some way to remove all your sorrow."

So the Three Companions set out on their travels together. In the harbor were anchored the twelve ships of the merchant, and the Three Companions got on board. The south wind was blowing, and the twelve ships sailed away, as fast as the desires which rose in the Prince's breast.

At the Conch Shell Island they filled one ship with conchs. At the Sandal Wood Island they filled a second ship with sandal-wood, and at the Coral Island they filled a third ship with coral.

Four years passed away, and they filled four more ships, one with ivory, one with musk, one with cloves, and one with nutmegs.

But when these ships were all loaded a terrible tempest arose. The ships were all of them sunk, with their cloves and nutmeg, and musk and ivory, and coral and sandal-wood and conchs. But the ship with the Three Companions struck on an island reef, buried them safe ashore, and itself broke in pieces.

This was the famous Island of Cards, where lived the Ace and King and Queen and Knave, with the Nines and Tens and all the other Members– according to the Rules.

3

Up till now there had been nothing to disturb that island stillness. No new thing had ever happened. No discussion had ever been held.

And then, of a sudden, the Three Companions appeared, thrown up by the sea,–and the Great Debate began. There were three main points of dispute.

First, to what caste should these unclassed strangers belong? Should they rank with the Court Cards? Or were they merely lower-caste people, to be ranked with the Nines and Tens? No precedent could be quoted to decide this weighty question.

Secondly, what was their clan? Had they the fairer hue and bright complexion of the Hearts, or was theirs the darker complexion of the Clubs? Over this question there were interminable disputes. The whole marriage system of the island, with its intricate regulations, would depend on its nice adjustment.

Thirdly, what food should they take? With whom should they live and sleep ? And should their heads be placed south-west, north-west, or only north-east? In all the Kingdom of Cards a series of problems so vital and critical had never been debated before.

But the Three Companions grew desperately hungry. They had to get food in some way or other. So while this debate went on, with its interminable silence and pauses, and while the Aces called their own meeting, and formed themselves into a Committee, to find some obsolete dealing with the question, the Three Companions themselves were eating all they could find, and drinking out of every vessel, and breaking all regulations.

Even the Twos and Threes were shocked at this outrageous behavior. The Threes said; "Brother Twos, these people are openly shameless!" And the Twos said: "Brother Threes, they are evidently of lower caste than ourselves! "After their meal was over, the Three Companions went for a stroll in the city.

When they saw the ponderous people moving in their dismal processions with prim and solemn faces, then the Prince turned to the Son of the Merchant and the Son of the Kotwal, and threw back his head, and gave one stupendous laugh.

Down Royal Street and across Ace Square and along the Knave Embankment ran the quiver of this strange, unheard-of laughter, the laughter that, amazed at itself, expired in the vast vacuum of silence.

The Son of the Kotwal and the Son of the Merchant were chilled through to the bone by the ghost-like stillness around them. They turned to the Prince, and said: "Comrade, let us away. Let us not stop for a moment in this awful land of ghosts."

But the Prince said: "Comrades, these people resemble men, so I am going to find out, by shaking them upside down and outside in, whether they have a single drop of warm living blood left in their veins."

4

The days passed one by one, and the placid existence of the Island went on almost without a ripple. The Three Companions obeyed no rules nor regulations. They never did anything correctly either in sitting or standing or turning themselves round or lying on their back. On the contrary, wherever they saw these things going on precisely and exactly according to the Rules, they gave way to inordinate laughter. They remained unimpressed altogether by the eternal gravity of those eternal regulations.

One day the great Court Cards came to the Son of the Kotwal and the Son of the Merchant and the Prince.

"Why," they asked slowly, "are you not moving according to the Rules?"

The Three Companions answered: "Because that is our Ichcha (wish)."

The great Court Cards with hollow, cavernous voices, as if slowly awakening from an age-long dream, said together: "Ich-cha! And pray who is Ich-cha?"

They could not understand who Ichcha was then, but the whole island was to understand it by-and-by. The first glimmer of light passed the threshold of their minds when they found out, through watching the actions of the Prince, that they might move in a straight line in an opposite direction from the one in which they had always gone before. Then they made another startling discovery, that there was another side to the Cards which they had never yet noticed with attention. This was the beginning of the change.

Now that the change had begun, the Three Companions were able to initiate them more and more deeply into the mysteries of Ichcha. The Cards gradually became aware that life was not bound by regulations. They began to feel a secret satisfaction in the kingly power of choosing for themselves.

But with this first impact of Ichcha the whole pack of cards began to totter slowly, and then tumble down to the ground. The scene was like that of some huge python awaking from a long sleep, as it slowly unfolds its numberless coils with a quiver that runs through its whole frame.

## 5

Hitherto the Queens of Spades and Clubs and Diamonds and Hearts had remained behind curtains with eyes that gazed vacantly into space, or else remained fixed upon the ground.

And now, all of a sudden, on an afternoon in spring the Queen of Hearts from the balcony raised her dark eyebrows for a moment, and cast a single glance upon the Prince from the corner of her eye.

"Great God," cried the Prince, "I thought they were all painted images. But I am wrong. They are women after all."

Then the young Prince called to his side his two Companions, and said in a meditative voice; "My comrades! There is a charm about these ladies that I never noticed before. When I saw that glance of the Queen's dark, luminous eyes, brightening with new emotion, it seemed to me like the first faint streak of dawn in a newly created world."

The two Companions smiled a knowing smile, and said: "Is that really so, Prince?"

And the poor Queen of Hearts from that day went from bad to worse. She began to forget all rules in a truly scandalous manner. If, for instance, her place in the row was beside the Knave, she suddenly found herself quite accidentally standing beside the Prince instead. At this, the Knave, with motionless face and solemn voice, would say: "Queen, you have made a mistake."

And the poor Queen of Hearts' red cheeks would get redder than ever. But the Prince would come gallantly to her rescue and say: "No! There is no mistake. From to-day I am going to be Knave!"

Now it came to pass that, while every one was trying to correct the improprieties of the guilty Queen of Hearts, they began to make mistakes themselves. The Aces found themselves elbowed out by the Kings. The Kings got muddled up with the Knaves. The Nines and Tens assumed airs as though they belonged to the Great Court Cards. The Twos and Threes were found secretly taking the places specially resented for the Fours and Fives. Confusion had never been so confounded before.

Many spring seasons had come and gone in that Island of Cards. The Kokil, the bird of Spring, had sung its song year after year. But it had never stirred the blood as it stirred it now. In days gone by the sea had sung its tireless melody. But, then, it had proclaimed only the inflexible monotony of the Rule. And suddenly its waves were telling, through all their flashing light and luminous shade and myriad voices, the deepest yearnings of the heart of love!

6

Where are vanished now their prim, round, regular, complacent features? Here is a face full of love-sick longing. Here is a heart heating wild with regrets. Here is a mind racked sore with doubts. Music and sighing, and smiles and tears, are filling the air. Life is throbbing; hearts are breaking; passions are kindling.

Every one is now thinking of his own appearance, and comparing himself with others. The Ace of Clubs is musing to himself, that the King of Spades may be just passably good-looking. "But," says he, "when I walk down the street you have only to see how people's eyes turn towards me." The King of Spades is saying; "Why on earth is that Ace of Clubs always straining his neck and strutting about like a peacock? He imagines all the Queens are dying of love for him, while the real fact is "Here he pauses, and examines his face in the glass.

But the Queens were the worst of all. They began to spend all their time in dressing themselves up to the Nines. And the Nines would become their hopeless and abject slaves. But their cutting remarks about one another were more shocking still.

So the young men would sit listless on the leaves under the trees, lolling with outstretched limbs in the forest shade. And the young maidens, dressed in pale-blue robes, would come walking accidentally to the same shade of the same forest by the same trees, and turn their eyes as though they saw no one there, and look as though they came out to see nothing at all. And then one young man more forward than the rest in a fit of madness would dare to go near to a maiden in blue. But, as he drew near, speech would forsake him. He would stand there tongue-tied and foolish, and the favorable moment would pass.

The Kokil birds were singing in the boughs overhead. The mischievous South wind was blowing; it disarrayed the hair, it whispered in the ear, and stirred the music in the blood. The leaves of the trees were murmuring with rustling delight. And the ceaseless sound of the ocean made all the mute longings of the heart of man and maid surge backwards and forwards on the full springtide of love.

The Three Companions had brought into the dried-up channels of the Kingdom of Cards the full flood-tide of a new life.

7

And, though the tide was full, there -was a pause as though the rising waters would not break into foam but remain suspended for ever. There were no outspoken words, only a cautious going forward one step and receding two. All seemed busy heaping up their unfulfilled desires like castles in the air, or fortresses of sand. They were pale and speechless; their eyes were burning, their lips trembling with unspoken secrets.

The Prince saw what was wrong. He summoned every one on the Island and said: "Bring hither the flutes and the cymbals, the pipes and drums. Let all be played together, and raise loud shouts of rejoicing. For the Queen of Hearts this very night is going to choose her Mate!"

So the Tens and Nines began to blow on their flutes and pipes; the Eights and Sevens played on their sackbuts and viols; and even the Twos and Threes began to beat madly on their drums.

When this tumultuous gust of music came, it swept away at one blast all those sighing's and moping's. And then what a torrent of laughter and words poured forth! There were daring proposals and locking refusals, and gossip and chatter, and jests and merriment. It was like the swaying and shaking, and rustling and soughing, in a summer gale, of a million leaves and branches in the depth of the primeval forest.

But the Queen of Hearts, in a rose-red robe, sat silent in the shadow of her secret bower, and listened to the great uproarious sound of music and mirth, that came floating towards her. She shut her eyes, and dreamt her dream of lore. And when she opened them she found the Prince seated on the ground before her gazing up at her face. And she covered her eyes with both hands, and shrank back quivering with an inward tumult of joy.

And the Prince passed the whole day alone, walking by the side of the surging sea. He carried in his mind that startled look, that shrinking gesture of the Queen, and his heart beat high with hope.

That night the serried, gaily-dressed ranks of young men and maidens waited with smiling faces at the Palace Gates. The Palace Hall was lighted with fairy lamps and festooned with the flowers of spring. Slowly the Queen of Hearts entered, and the whole assembly rose to greet her. With a jasmine garland in her hand, she stood before the Prince with downcast eyes. In her lowly bashfulness she could hardly raise the garland to the neck of the Mate she had chosen. But the Prince bowed his head, and the garland slipped to its place. The assembly of youths and maidens had waited her choice with eager, expectant hush. And when the choice was made, the whole vast concourse rocked and swayed with a tumult of wild delight. And the sound of their shouts was heard in every part of the island, and by ships far out at sea. Never had such a shout been raised in the Kingdom of Cards before.

And they carried the Prince and his Bride, and seated them on the throne, and crowned them then and there in the Ancient Island of Cards.

And the sorrowing Mother Queen, on the 'far-off island shore on the other side of the sea, came sailing to her son's new kingdom in a ship adorned with gold.

And the citizens are no longer regulated according to the Rules, but are good or bad, or both, according to their Ichcha.

# The Victory

***Rabindranath Tagore***

She was the Princess Ajita. And the court poet of King Nârâyan had never seen her. On the day he recited a new poem to the king he would raise his voice just to that pitch which could be heard by unseen hearers in the screened balcony high above the hall. He sent up his song towards the star-land out of his reach, where, circled with light, the planet who ruled his destiny shone unknown and out of ken.

He would espy some shadow moving behind the veil. A tinkling sound would come to his ear from afar, and would set him dreaming of the ankles whose tiny golden bells sang at each step. Ah, the rosy red tender feet that walked the dust of the earth like God's mercy on the fallen! The poet had placed them on the altar of his heart, where he wove his songs to the tune of those golden bells. Doubt never arose in his mind as to whose shadow it was that moved behind the screen, and whose anklets they were that sang to the time of his beating heart. Manjari, the maid of the princess, passed by the poet's house on her way to the river, and she never missed a day to have a few words with him on the sly. When she found the road deserted, and the shadow of dusk on the land, she would boldly enter his room, and sit at the corner of his carpet. There was a suspicion of an added care in the choice of the colour of her veil, in the setting of the flower in her hair.

People smiled and whispered at this, and they were not to blame. For Shekhar the poet never took the trouble to hide the fact that these meetings were a pure joy to him.

The meaning of her name was the spray of flowers. One must confess that for an ordinary mortal it was sufficient in its sweetness. But Shekhar made his own addition to this name, and called her the Spray of Spring Flowers. And ordinary mortals shook their heads and said, Ah, me!

In the spring songs that the poet sang the praise of the spray of spring flowers was conspicuously reiterated; and the king winked and smiled at him when he heard it, and the poet smiled in answer. The king would put him the question:

"Is it the business of the bee merely to hum in the court of the spring?"

The poet would answer: "No, but also to sip the honey of the spray of spring flowers."

And they all laughed in the king's hall. And it was rumoured that the Princess Ajita also laughed at her maid's accepting the poet's name for her, and Manjari felt glad in her heart.

Thus truth and falsehood mingle in life – and to what God builds man adds his own decoration.

Only those were pure truths which were sung by the poet. The theme was Krishna, the lover god, and Râdhâ, the beloved, the Eternal Man and the Eternal Woman, the sorrow that comes from the beginning of time, and the joy without end. The truth of these songs was tested in his inmost heart by everybody from the beggar to the king himself. The poet's songs were on the lips of all. At the merest glimmer of the moon and the faintest whisper of the summer breeze his songs would break forth in the land from windows and courtyards, from sailing-boats, from shadows of the wayside trees, in numberless voices.

Thus passed the days happily. The poet recited, the king listened, the hearers applauded, Manjari passed and repassed by the poet's room on her way to the river – the shadow flitted behind the screened balcony, and the tiny golden bells tinkled from afar.

Just then set forth from his home in the south a poet on his path of conquest. He came to King Nârâyan, in the kingdom of Amarapur. He stood before the throne, and uttered a verse in praise of the king. He had challenged all the court poets on his way, and his career of victory had been unbroken.

The king received him with honour, and said:

"Poet, I offer you welcome."

Pundarik, the poet, proudly replied: "Sire, I ask for war."

Shekhar, the court poet of the king did not know how the battle of the muse was to be waged. He had no sleep at night. The mighty figure of the famous Pundarik, his sharp nose curved like a scimitar, and his proud head tilted on one side, haunted the poet's vision in the dark.

With a trembling heart Shekhar entered the arena in the morning. The theatre was filled with the crowd.

The poet greeted his rival with a smile and a bow. Pundarik returned it with a slight toss of his head, and turned his face towards his circle of adoring followers with a meaning smile.

Shekhar cast his glance towards the screened balcony high above, and saluted his lady in his mind, saying: "If I am the winner at the combat to-day, my lady, thy victorious name shall be glorified."

The trumpet sounded. The great crowd stood up, shouting victory to the king. The king, dressed in an ample robe of white, slowly came into the hall like a floating cloud of autumn, and sat on his throne.

Pundarik stood up, and the vast hall became still. With his head raised high and chest expanded, he began in his thundering voice to recite the praise of King Nârâyan. His words burst upon the walls of the hall like breakers of the sea, and seemed to rattle against the ribs of the listening crowd. The skill with which he gave varied meanings to the name Nârâyan, and wove each letter of it through the web of his verses in all manner of combinations, took away the breath of his amazed hearers.

For some minutes after he took his seat his voice continued to vibrate among the numberless pillars of the king's court and in thousands of speechless hearts. The learned professors who had come from distant lands raised their right hands, and cried, Bravo!

The king threw a glance on Shekhar's face, and Shekhar in answer raised for a moment his eyes full of pain towards his master, and then stood up like a stricken deer at bay. His face was pale, his bashfulness was almost that of a woman, his slight youthful figure, delicate in its outline, seemed like a tensely strung vina ready to break out in music at the least touch.

His head was bent, his voice was low, when he began. The

first few verses were almost inaudible. Then he slowly raised his head, and his clear sweet voice rose into the sky like a quivering flame of fire. He began with the ancient legend of the kingly line lost in the haze of the past, and brought it down through its long course of heroism and matchless generosity to the present age. He fixed his gaze on the king's face, and all the vast and unexpressed love of the people for the royal house rose like incense in his song, and enwreathed the throne on all sides. These were his last words when, trembling, he took his seat: "My master, I may be beaten in play of words, but not in my love for thee."

Tears filled the eyes of the hearers, and the stone walls shook with cries of victory.

Mocking this popular outburst of feeling, with an august shake of his head and a contemptuous sneer, Pundarik stood up, and flung this question to the assembly: "What is there superior to words?" In a moment the hall lapsed into silence again.

Then with a marvellous display of learning, he proved that the Word was in the beginning, that the Word was God. He piled up quotations from scriptures, and built a high altar for the Word to be seated above all that there is in heaven and in earth. He repeated that question in his mighty voice: "What is there superior to words?"

Proudly he looked around him. None dared to accept his challenge, and he slowly took his seat like a lion who had just made a full meal of its victim. The pandits shouted, Bravo! The king remained silent with wonder, and the poet Shekhar felt himself of no account by the side of this stupendous learning. The assembly broke up for that day.

Next day Shekhar began his song. It was of that day when the pipings of love's flute startled for the first time the hushed air of the Vrinda forest. The shepherd women did not know who was the player or whence came the music. Sometimes it seemed to come from the heart of the south wind, and sometimes from the straying clouds of the hilltops. It came with a message of tryst from the land of the sunrise, and it floated from the verge of sunset with its sigh of sorrow. The stars seemed to be the stops of the instrument that flooded the dreams of the night with melody. The music seemed to burst all at once from all sides, from fields and groves, from the shady lanes and lonely roads, from the melting blue of the sky, from the shimmering green of the grass. They neither knew its meaning nor could they find words to give utterance to the desire of their hearts. Tears filled their eyes, and their life seemed to long for a death that would be its consummation.

Shekhar forgot his audience, forgot the trial of his strength with a rival. He stood alone amid his thoughts that rustled and quivered round him like leaves in a summer breeze, and sang the Song of the Flute. He had in his mind the vision of an image that had taken its shape from a shadow, and the echo of a faint tinkling sound of a distant footstep.

He took his seat. His hearers trembled with the sadness of an indefinable delight, immense and vague, and they forgot to applaud him. As this feeling died away Pundarik stood up before the throne and challenged his rival to define who was this Lover and who was the Beloved. He arrogantly looked around him, he smiled at his followers and then put the question again: "Who is Krishna, the lover, and who is Râdhâ, the beloved?"

Then he began to analyse the roots of those names, – and various interpretations of their meanings. He brought before the bewildered audience all the intricacies of the different schools of metaphysics with consummate skill. Each letter of those names he divided from its fellow, and then pursued them with a relentless logic till they fell to the dust in confusion, to be caught up again and restored to a meaning never before imagined by the subtlest of word-mongers.

The pandits were in ecstasy; they applauded vociferously; and the crowd followed them, deluded into the certainty that they had witnessed, that day, the last shred of the curtains of Truth torn to pieces before their eyes by a prodigy of intellect. The performance of his tremendous feat so delighted them that they forgot to ask themselves if there was any truth behind it after all.

The king's mind was overwhelmed with wonder. The atmosphere was completely cleared of all illusion of music, and the vision of the world around seemed to be changed from its freshness of tender green to the solidity of a high road levelled and made hard with crushed stones.

To the people assembled their own poet appeared a mere boy in comparison with this giant, who walked with such ease, knocking down difficulties at each step in the world of words and thoughts. It became evident to them for the first time that the poems Shekhar wrote were absurdly simple, and it must be a mere accident that they did not write them themselves. They were neither new, nor difficult, nor instructive, nor necessary.

The king tried to goad his poet with keen glances, silently inciting him to make a final effort. But Shekhar took no notice, and remained fixed to his seat.

The king in anger came down from his throne – took off his pearl chain and put it on Pundarik's head. Everybody in the hall cheered. From the upper balcony came a slight sound of the movements of rustling robes and waist-chains hung with golden bells. Shekhar rose from his seat and left the hall.

It was a dark night of waning moon. The poet Shekhar took down his MSS. from his shelves and heaped them on the floor. Some of them contained his earliest writings, which he had almost forgotten. He turned over the pages, reading passages here and there. They all seemed to him poor and trivial – mere words and childish rhymes!

One by one he tore his books to fragments, and threw them into a vessel containing fire, and said: "To thee, to thee, O my beauty, my fire! Thou hast been burning in my heart all these futile years. If my life were a piece of gold it would come out of its trial brighter, but it is a trodden turf of grass, and nothing remains of it but this handful of ashes."

The night wore on. Shekhar opened wide his windows. He spread upon his bed the white flowers that he loved, the jasmines, tuberoses and chrysanthemums, and brought into his bedroom all the lamps he had in his house and lighted them. Then mixing with honey the juice of some poisonous root he drank it and lay down on his bed.

Golden anklets tinkled in the passage outside the door, and a subtle perfume came into the room with the breeze. The poet, with his eyes shut, said:

"My lady, have you taken pity upon your servant at last and come to see him?"

The answer came in a sweet voice: "My poet, I have come."

Shekhar opened his eyes – and saw before his bed the figure of a woman.

His sight was dim and blurred. And it seemed to him that the image made of a shadow that he had ever kept throned in the secret shrine of his heart had come into the outer world in his last moment to gaze upon his face.

The woman said:

"I am the Princess Ajita."

The poet with a great effort sat up on his bed.

The princess whispered into his ear: "The king has not done you justice. It was you who won at the combat, my poet, and I have come to crown you with the crown of victory."

She took the garland of flowers from her own neck, and put it on his hair, and the poet fell down upon his bed stricken by death.

# The Gift of the Magi

***O. Henry***

One dollar and eighty-seven cents. That was all. And sixty cents of it was in pennies. Pennies saved one and two at a time by bulldozing the grocer and the vegetable man and the butcher until one's cheeks burned with the silent imputation of parsimony that such close dealing implied. Three times Della counted it. One dollar and eighty- seven cents. And the next day would be Christmas.

There was clearly nothing to do but flop down on the shabby little couch and howl. So Della did it. Which instigates the moral reflection that life is made up of sobs, sniffles, and smiles, with sniffles predominating.

While the mistress of the home is gradually subsiding from the first stage to the second, take a look at the home. A furnished flat at $8 per week. It did not exactly beggar description, but it certainly had that word on the lookout for the mendicancy squad.

In the vestibule below was a letter-box into which no letter would go, and an electric button from which no mortal finger could coax a ring. Also appertaining there unto was a card bearing the name "Mr. James Dillingham Young."

The "Dillingham" had been flung to the breeze during a former period of prosperity when its possessor was being paid $30 per week. Now, when the income was shrunk to $20, though, they were thinking seriously of contracting to a modest and unassuming D. But whenever Mr. James Dillingham Young came home and reached his flat above he was called "Jim" and greatly hugged by Mrs. James Dillingham Young, already introduced to you as Della. Which is all very good.

Della finished her cry and attended to her cheeks with the powder rag. She stood by the window and looked out dully at a gray cat walking a gray fence in a gray backyard. Tomorrow would be Christmas Day, and she had only $1.87 with which to buy Jim a present. She had been saving every penny she could for months, with this result. Twenty dollars a week doesn't go far. Expenses had been greater than she had calculated. They always are. Only $1.87 to buy a present for Jim. Her Jim. Many a happy hour she had spent planning for something nice for him. Something fine and rare and sterling – something just a little bit near to being worthy of the honor of being owned by Jim.

There was a pier-glass between the windows of the room. Perhaps you have seen a pier-glass in an $8 flat. A very thin and very agile person may, by observing his reflection in a rapid sequence of longitudinal strips, obtain a fairly accurate conception of his looks. Della, being slender, had mastered the art.

Suddenly she whirled from the window and stood before the glass. her eyes were shining brilliantly, but her face had lost its color within twenty seconds. Rapidly she pulled down her hair and let it fall to its full length.

Now, there were two possessions of the James Dillingham Youngs in which they both took a mighty pride. One was Jim's gold watch that had been his father's and his grandfather's. The other was Della's hair. Had the queen of Sheba lived in the flat across the airshaft, Della would have let her hair hang out the window some day to dry just to depreciate Her Majesty's jewels and gifts. Had King Solomon been the janitor, with all his treasures piled up in the basement, Jim would have pulled out his watch every time he passed, just to see him pluck at his beard from envy.

So now Della's beautiful hair fell about her rippling and shining like a cascade of brown waters. It reached below her knee and made itself almost a garment for her. And then she did it up again nervously and quickly. Once she faltered for a minute and stood still while a tear or two splashed on the worn red carpet.

On went her old brown jacket; on went her old brown hat. With a whirl of skirts and with the brilliant sparkle still in her eyes, she fluttered out the door and down the stairs to the street.

Where she stopped the sign read: "Mne. Sofronie. Hair Goods of All Kinds." One flight up Della ran, and collected herself, panting. Madame, large, too white, chilly, hardly looked the "Sofronie."

"Will you buy my hair?" asked Della.

"I buy hair," said Madame. "Take yer hat off and let's have a sight at the looks of it."

Down rippled the brown cascade.

"Twenty dollars," said Madame, lifting the mass with a practised hand.

"Give it to me quick," said Della.

Oh, and the next two hours tripped by on rosy wings. Forget the hashed metaphor. She was ransacking the stores for Jim's present.

She found it at last. It surely had been made for Jim and no one else. There was no other like it in any of the stores, and she had turned all of them inside out. It was a platinum fob chain simple and chaste in design, properly proclaiming its value by substance alone and not by meretricious ornamentation – as all good things should do. It was even worthy of The Watch. As soon as she saw it she knew that it must be Jim's. It was like him. Quietness and value – the description applied to both. Twenty-one dollars they took from her for it, and she hurried home with the 87 cents. With that chain on his watch Jim might be properly anxious about the time in any company. Grand as the watch was, he sometimes looked at it on the sly on account of the old leather strap that he used in place of a chain.

When Della reached home her intoxication gave way a little to prudence and reason. She got out her curling irons and lighted the gas and went to work repairing the ravages made by generosity added to love. Which is always a tremendous task, dear friends – a mammoth task.

Within forty minutes her head was covered with tiny, close-lying curls that made her look wonderfully like a truant schoolboy. She looked at her reflection in the mirror long, carefully, and critically.

"If Jim doesn't kill me," she said to herself, "before he takes a second look at me, he'll say I look like a Coney Island chorus girl. But what could I do – oh! What could I do with a dollar and eighty- seven cents?"

At 7 o'clock the coffee was made and the frying-pan was on the back of the stove hot and ready to cook the chops.

Jim was never late. Della doubled the fob chain in her hand and sat on the corner of the table near the door that he always entered. Then she heard his step on the stair away down on the first flight, and she turned white for just a moment. She had a habit for saying little silent prayer about the simplest everyday things, and now she whispered: "Please God, make him think I am still pretty."

The door opened and Jim stepped in and closed it. He looked thin and very serious. Poor fellow, he was only twenty-two – and to be burdened with a family! He needed a new overcoat and he was without gloves.

Jim stopped inside the door, as immovable as a setter at the scent of quail. His eyes were fixed upon Della, and there was an expression in them that she could not read, and it terrified her. It was not anger, nor surprise, nor disapproval, nor horror, nor any of the sentiments that she had been prepared for. He simply stared at her fixedly with that peculiar expression on his face.

Della wriggled off the table and went for him.

"Jim, darling," she cried, "don't look at me that way. I had my hair cut off and sold because I couldn't have lived through Christmas without giving you a present. It'll grow out again – you won't mind, will you? I just had to do it. My hair grows awfully fast. Say 'Merry Christmas!' Jim, and let's be happy. You don't know what a nice – what a beautiful, nice gift I've got for you."

"You've cut off your hair?" asked Jim, laboriously, as if he had not arrived at that patent fact yet even after the hardest mental labor.

"Cut it off and sold it," said Della. "Don't you like me just as well, anyhow? I'm me without my hair, ain't I?"

Jim looked about the room curiously.

"You say your hair is gone?" he said, with an air almost of idiocy.

"You needn't look for it," said Della. "It's sold, I tell you – sold and gone, too. It's Christmas Eve, boy. Be good to me, for it went for you. Maybe the hairs of my head were numbered," she went on with sudden serious sweetness, "but nobody could ever count my love for you. Shall I put the chops on, Jim?"

Out of his trance Jim seemed quickly to wake. He enfolded his Della. For ten seconds let us regard with discreet scrutiny some inconsequential object in the other direction. Eight dollars a week or a million a year – what is the difference? A mathematician or a wit would give you the wrong answer. The magi brought valuable gifts, but that was not among them. This dark assertion will be illuminated later on.

Jim drew a package from his overcoat pocket and threw it upon the table.

"Don't make any mistake, Dell," he said, "about me. I don't think there's anything in the way of a haircut or a shave or a shampoo that could make me like my girl any less. But if you'll unwrap that package you may see why you had me going a while at first."

White fingers and nimble tore at the string and paper. And then an ecstatic scream of joy; and then, alas! a quick feminine change to hysterical tears and wails, necessitating the immediate employment of all the comforting powers of the lord of the flat.

For there lay The Combs – the set of combs, side and back, that Della had worshipped long in a Broadway window. Beautiful combs, pure tortoise shell, with jewelled rims – just the shade to wear in the beautiful vanished hair. They were expensive combs, she knew, and her heart had simply craved and yearned over them without the least hope of possession. And now, they were hers, but the tresses that should have adorned the coveted adornments were gone.

But she hugged them to her bosom, and at length she was able to look up with dim eyes and a smile and say: "My hair grows so fast, Jim!"

And them Della leaped up like a little singed cat and cried, "Oh, oh!"

Jim had not yet seen his beautiful present. She held it out to him eagerly upon her open palm. The dull precious metal seemed to flash with a reflection of her bright and ardent spirit.

"Isn't it a dandy, Jim? I hunted all over town to find it. You'll have to look at the time a hundred times a day now. Give me your watch. I want to see how it looks on it."

Instead of obeying, Jim tumbled down on the couch and put his hands under the back of his head and smiled.

"Dell," said he, "let's put our Christmas presents away and keep 'em a while. They're too nice to use just at present. I sold the watch to get the money to buy your combs. And now suppose you put the chops on."

The magi, as you know, were wise men – wonderfully wise men – who brought gifts to the Babe in the manger. They invented the art of giving Christmas presents. Being wise, their gifts were no doubt wise ones, possibly bearing the privilege of exchange in case of duplication. And here I have lamely related to you the uneventful chronicle of two foolish children in a flat who most unwisely sacrificed for each other the greatest treasures of their house. But in a last word to the wise of these days let it be said that of all who give gifts these two were the wisest. O all who give and receive gifts, such as they are wisest. Everywhere they are wisest. They are the magi.

# The Adventures of Shamrock Jolnes

***O. Henry***

I am so fortunate as to count Shamrock Jolnes, the great New York detective, among my muster of friends. Jolnes is what is called the "inside man" of the city detective force. He is an expert in the use of the typewriter, and it is his duty, whenever there is a "murder mystery" to be solved, to sit at a desk telephone at headquarters and take down the messages of "cranks" who 'phone in their confessions to having committed the crime.

But on certain "off" days when confessions are coming in slowly and three or four newspapers have run to earth as many different guilty persons, Jolnes will knock about the town with me, exhibiting, to my great delight and instruction, his marvellous powers of observation and deduction.

The other day I dropped in at Headquarters and found the great detective gazing thoughtfully at a string that was tied tightly around his little finger.

"Good morning, Whatsup," he said, without turning his head. "I'm glad to notice that you've had your house fitted up with electric lights at last."

"Will you please tell me," I said, in surprise, "how you knew that? I am sure that I never mentioned the fact to any one, and the wiring was a rush order not completed until this morning."

"Nothing easier," said Jolnes, genially. "As you came in I caught the odour of the cigar you are smoking. I know an expensive cigar; and I know that not more than three men in New York can afford to smoke cigars and pay gas bills too at the present time. That was an easy one. But I am working just now on a little problem of my own."

"Why have you that string on your finger?" I asked.

"That's the problem," said Jolnes. "My wife tied that on this morning to remind me of something I was to send up to the house. Sit down, Whatsup, and excuse me for a few moments."

The distinguished detective went to a wall telephone, and stood with the receiver to his ear for probably ten minutes.

"Were you listening to a confession?" I asked, when he had returned to his chair.

"Perhaps," said Jolnes, with a smile, "it might be called something of the sort. To be frank with you, Whatsup, I've cut out the dope. I've been increasing the quantity for so long that morphine doesn't have much effect on me any more. I've got to have something more powerful. That telephone I just went to is connected with a room in the Waldorf where there's an author's reading in progress. Now, to get at the solution of this string."

After five minutes of silent pondering, Jolnes looked at me, with a smile, and nodded his head.

"Wonderful man!" I exclaimed; "already?"

"It is quite simple," he said, holding up his finger. "You see that knot? That is to prevent my forgetting. It is, therefore, a forget-me-knot. A forget-me-not is a flower. It was a sack of flour that I was to send home!"

"Beautiful!" I could not help crying out in admiration.

"Suppose we go out for a ramble," suggested Jolnes.

"There is only one case of importance on hand just now. Old man McCarty, one hundred and four years old, died from eating too many bananas. The evidence points so strongly to the Mafia that the police have surrounded the Second Avenue Katzenjammer Gambrinus Club No. 2, and the capture of the assassin is only the matter of a few hours. The detective force has not yet been called on for assistance."

Jolnes and I went out and up the street toward the corner, where we were to catch a surface car.

Half-way up the block we met Rheingelder, an acquaintance of ours, who held a City Hall position.

"Good morning, Rheingelder," said Jolnes, halting.

"Nice breakfast that was you had this morning." Always on the lookout for the detective's remarkable feats of deduction, I saw Jolnes's eye flash for an instant upon a long yellow splash on the shirt bosom and a smaller one upon the chin of Rheingelder – both undoubtedly made by the yolk of an egg.

"Oh, dot is some of your detectiveness," said Rheingelder, shaking all over with a smile. "Vell, I pet you trinks und cigars all round dot you cannot tell vot I haf eaten for breakfast."

"Done," said Jolnes. "Sausage, pumpernickel and coffee."

Rheingelder admitted the correctness of the surmise and paid the bet. When we had proceeded on our way I said to Jolnes:

"I thought you looked at the egg spilled on his chin and shirt front."

"I did," said Jolnes. "That is where I began my deduction. Rheingelder is a very economical, saving man. Yesterday eggs dropped in the market to twenty-eight cents per dozen. To-day they are quoted at forty-two. Rheingelder ate eggs yesterday, and to-day he went back to his usual fare. A little thing like this isn't anything, Whatsup; it belongs to the primary arithmetic class."

When we boarded the street car we found the seats all occupied – principally by ladies. Jolnes and I stood on the rear platform.

About the middle of the car there sat an elderly man with a short, gray beard, who looked to be the typical, well-dressed New Yorker. At successive corners other ladies climbed aboard, and soon three or four of them were standing over the man, clinging to straps and glaring meaningly at the man who occupied the coveted seat. But he resolutely retained his place.

"We New Yorkers," I remarked to Jolnes, "have about lost our manners, as far as the exercise of them in public goes."

"Perhaps so," said Jolnes, lightly; "but the man you evidently refer to happens to be a very chivalrous and courteous gentleman from Old Virginia. He is spending a few days in New York with his wife and two daughters, and he leaves for the South to-night."

"You know him, then?" I said, in amazement.

"I never saw him before we stepped on the car," declared the detective, smilingly.

"By the gold tooth of the Witch of Endor!" I cried, "if you can construe all that from his appearance you are dealing in nothing else than black art."

"The habit of observation – nothing more," said Jolnes. "If the old gentleman gets off the car before we do, I think I can demonstrate to you the accuracy of my deduction."

Three blocks farther along the gentleman rose to leave the car. Jolnes addressed him at the door: "Pardon me, sir, but are you not Colonel Hunter, of Norfolk, Virginia?"

"No, suh," was the extremely courteous answer. "My name, suh, is Ellison – Major Winfield R. Ellison, from Fairfax County, in the same state. I know a good many people, suh, in Norfolk – the Goodriches, the Tollivers, and the Crabtrees, suh, but I never had the pleasure of meeting yo' friend, Colonel Hunter. I am happy to say, suh, that I am going back to Virginia to-night, after having spent a week in yo' city with my wife and three daughters. I shall be in Norfolk in about ten days, and if you will give me yo' name, suh, I will take pleasure in looking up Colonel Hunter and telling him that you inquired after him, suh."

"Thank you," said Jolnes; "tell him that Reynolds sent his regards, if you will be so kind."

I glanced at the great New York detective and saw that a look of intense chagrin had come upon his clear-cut features. Failure in the slightest point always galled Shamrock Jolnes.

"Did you say your three daughters?" he asked of the Virginia gentleman.

"Yes, suh, my three daughters, all as fine girls as there are in Fairfax County," was the answer.

With that Major Ellison stopped the car and began to descend the step.

Shamrock Jolnes clutched his arm.

"One moment, sir," he begged, in an urbane voice in which I alone detected the anxiety – "am I not right in believing that one of the young ladies is an adopted daughter?"

"You are, suh," admitted the major, from the ground, "but how the devil you knew it, suh, is mo' than I can tell."

"And mo' than I can tell, too," I said, as the car went on.

Jolnes was restored to his calm, observant serenity by having wrested victory from his apparent failure; so after we got off the car he invited me into a cafe, promising to reveal the process of his latest wonderful feat.

"In the first place," he began after we were comfortably seated, "I knew the gentleman was no New Yorker because he was flushed and uneasy and restless on account of the ladies that were standing, although he did not rise and give them his seat. I decided from his appearance that he was a Southerner rather than a Westerner.

"Next I began to figure out his reason for not relinquishing his seat to a lady when he evidently felt strongly, but not overpoweringly, impelled to do so. I very quickly decided upon that. I noticed that one of his eyes had received a severe jab in one corner, which was red and inflamed, and that all over his face were tiny round marks about the size of the end of an uncut lead pencil. Also upon both of his patent leather shoes were a number of deep imprints shaped like ovals cut off square at one end.

"Now, there is only one district in New York City where a man is bound to receive scars and wounds and indentations of that sort – and that is along the sidewalks of Twenty-third Street and a portion of Sixth Avenue south of there. I knew from the imprints of trampling French heels on his feet and the marks of countless jabs in the face from umbrellas and parasols carried by women in the shopping district that he had been in conflict with the amazonian troops. And as he was a man of intelligent appearance, I knew he would not have braved such dangers unless he had been dragged thither by his own women folk. Therefore, when he got on the car his anger at the treatment he had received was sufficient to make him keep his seat in spite of his traditions of Southern chivalry."

"That is all very well," I said, "but why did you insist upon daughters – and especially two daughters? Why couldn't a wife alone have taken him shopping?"

"There had to be daughters," said Jolnes, calmly. "If he had only a wife, and she near his own age, he could have bluffed her into going alone. If he had a young wife she would prefer to go alone. So there you are."

"I'll admit that," I said; "but, now, why two daughters? And how, in the name of all the prophets, did you guess that one was adopted when he told you he had three?"

"Don't say guess," said Jolnes, with a touch of pride in his air; "there is no such word in the lexicon of ratiocination. In Major Ellison's buttonhole there was a carnation and a rosebud backed by a geranium leaf. No woman ever combined a carnation and a rosebud into a boutonniere. Close your eyes, Whatsup, and give the logic of your imagination a chance. Cannot you see the lovely Adele fastening the carnation to the lapel so that papa may be gay upon the street? And then the romping Edith May dancing up with sisterly jealousy to add her rosebud to the adornment?"

"And then," I cried, beginning to feel enthusiasm, "when he declared that he had three daughters" –

"I could see," said Jolnes, "one in the background who added no flower; and I knew that she must be – "

"Adopted!" I broke in. "I give you every credit; but how did you know he was leaving for the South to-night?"

"In his breast pocket," said the great detective, "something large and oval made a protuberance. Good liquor is scarce on trains, and it is a long journey from New York to Fairfax County."

"Again, I must bow to you," I said. "And tell me this, so that my last shred of doubt will be cleared away; why did you decide that he was from Virginia?"

"It was very faint, I admit," answered Shamrock Jolnes, "but no trained observer could have failed to detect the odour of mint in the car."

# A Bird of Bagdad

***O. Henry***

Without a doubt much of the spirit and genius of the Caliph Harun Al Rashid descended to the Margrave August Michael von Paulsen Quigg.

Quigg's restaurant is in Fourth Avenue – that street that the city seems to have forgotten in its growth. Fourth Avenue – born and bred in the Bowery – staggers northward full of good resolutions.

Where it crosses Fourteenth Street it struts for a brief moment proudly in the glare of the museums and cheap theatres. It may yet become a fit mate for its high-born sister boulevard to the west, or its roaring, polyglot, broad-waisted cousin to the east. It passes Union Square; and here the hoofs of the dray horses seem to thunder in unison, recalling the tread of marching hosts – Hooray! But now come the silent and terrible mountains – buildings square as forts, high as the clouds, shutting out the sky, where thousands of slaves bend over desks all day. On the ground floors are only little fruit shops and laundries and book shops, where you see copies of "Littell's Living Age" and G. W. M. Reynold's novels in the windows. And next – poor Fourth Avenue! – the street glides into a mediaeval solitude. On each side are shops devoted to "Antiques."

Let us say it is night. Men in rusty armor stand in the windows and menace the hurrying cars with raised, rusty iron gauntlets. Hauberks and helms, blunderbusses, Cromwellian breastplates, matchlocks, creeses, and the swords and daggers of an army of dead-and-gone gallants gleam dully in the ghostly light. Here and there from a corner saloon (lit with Jack-o'-lanterns or phosphorus), stagger forth shuddering, home-bound citizens, nerved by the tankards within to their fearsome journey adown that eldrich avenue lined with the bloodstained weapons of the fighting dead. What street could live inclosed by these mortuary relics, and trod by these spectral citizens in whose sunken hearts scarce one good whoop or tra-la-la remained?

Not Fourth Avenue. Not after the tinsel but enlivening glories of the Little Rialto – not after the echoing drum-beats of Union Square. There need be no tears, ladies and gentlemen; 'tis but the suicide of a street. With a shriek and a crash Fourth Avenue dives headlong into the tunnel at Thirty-fourth and is never seen again.

Near the sad scene of the thoroughfare's dissolution stood the modest restaurant of Quigg. It stands there yet if you care to view its crumbling red-brick front, its show window heaped with oranges, tomatoes, layer cakes, pies, canned asparagus – its papier-mache lobster and two Maltese kittens asleep on a bunch of lettuce – if you care to sit at one of the little tables upon whose cloth has been traced in the yellowest of coffee stains the trail of the Japanese advance – to sit there with one eye on your umbrella and the other upon the bogus bottle from which you drop the counterfeit sauce foisted upon us by the cursed charlatan who assumes to be our dear old lord and friend, the "Nobleman in India."

Quigg's title came through his mother. One of her ancestors was a Margravine of Saxony. His father was a Tammany brave. On account of the dilution of his heredity he found that he could neither become a reigning potentate nor get a job in the City Hall. So he opened a restaurant. He was a man full of thought and reading. The business gave him a living, though he gave it little attention. One side of his house bequeathed to him a poetic and romantic adventure. The other have him the restless spirit that made him seek adventure. By day he was Quigg, the restaurateur. By night he was the Margrave – the Caliph – the Prince of Bohemia – going about the city in search of the odd, the mysterious, the inexplicable, the recondite.

One night at 9, at which hour the restaurant closed, Quigg set forth upon his quest. There was a mingling of the foreign, the military and the artistic in his appearance as he buttoned his coat high up under his short-trimmed brown and gray beard and turned westward toward the more central life conduits of the city. In his pocket he had stored an assortment of cards, written upon, without which he never stirred out of doors. Each of those cards was good at his own restaurant for its face value. Some called simply for a bowl of soup or sandwiches and coffee; others entitled their bearer to one, two, three or more days of full meals; a few were for single regular meals; a very few were, in effect, meal tickets good for a week.

Of riches and power Margrave Quigg had none; but he had a Caliph's heart – it may be forgiven him if his head fell short of the measure of Harun Al Rashid's. Perhaps some of the gold pieces in Bagdad had put less warmth and hope into the complainants among the bazaars than had Quigg's beef stew among the fishermen and one-eyed calenders of Manhattan.

Continuing his progress in search of romance to divert him, or of distress that he might aid, Quigg became aware of a fast-gathering crowd that whooped and fought and eddied at a corner of Broadway and the crosstown street that he was traversing. Hurrying to the spot he beheld a young man of an exceedingly melancholy and preoccupied demeanor engaged in the pastime of casting silver money from his pockets in the middle of the street. With each motion of the generous one's hand the crowd huddled upon the falling largesse with yells of joy. Traffic was suspended. A policman in the centre of the mob stooped often to the ground as he urged the blockaders to move on.

The Margrave saw at a glance that here was food for his hunger after knowledge concerning abnormal working of the human heart. He made his way swiftly to the young man's side and took his arm. "Come with me at once," he said, in the low but commanding voice that his waiters had learned to fear.

"Pinched," remarked the young man, looking up at him with expressionless eyes. "Pinched by a painless dentist. Take me away, flatty, and give me gas. Some lay eggs and some lay none. When is a hen?"

Still deeply seized by some inward grief, but tractable, he allowed Quigg to lead him away and down the street to a little park.

There, seated on a bench, he upon whom a corner of the great Caliph's mantle has descended, spake with kindness and discretion, seeking to know what evil had come upon the other, disturbing his soul and driving him to such ill-considered and ruinous waste of his substance and stores.

"I was doing the Monte Cristo act as adapted by Pompton, N. J., wasn't I?" asked the young man.

"You were throwing small coins into the street for the people to scramble after," said the Margrave.

"That's it. You buy all the beer you can hold, and then you throw chicken feed to – Oh, curse that word chicken, and hens, feathers, roosters, eggs, and everything connected with it!"

"Young sir," said the Margrave kindly, but with dignity, "though I do not ask your confidence, I invite it. I know the world and I know humanity. Man is my study, though I do not eye him as the scientist eyes a beetle or as the philanthropist gazes at the objects of his bounty – through a veil of theory and ignorance. It is my pleasure and distraction to interest myself in the peculiar and complicated misfortunes that life in a great city visits upon my fellow-men. You may be familiar with the history of that glorious and immortal ruler, the Caliph Harun Al Rashid, whose wise and beneficent excursions among his people in the city of Bagdad secured him the privilege of relieving so much of their distress. In my humble way I walk in his footsteps. I seek for romance and adventure in city streets – not in ruined castles or in crumbling palaces. To me the greatest marvels of magic are those that take place in men's hearts when acted upon by the furious and diverse forces of a crowded population. In your strange behavior this evening I fancy a story lurks. I read in your act something deeper than the wanton wastefulness of a spendthrift. I observe in your countenance the certain traces of consuming grief or despair. I repeat – I invite your confidence. I am not without some power to alleviate and advise. Will you not trust me?"

"Gee, how you talk!" exclaimed the young man, a gleam of admiration supplanting for a moment the dull sadness of his eyes. "You've got the Astor Library skinned to a synopsis of preceding chapters. I mind that old Turk you speak of. I read 'The Arabian Nights' when I was a kid. He was a kind of Bill Devery and Charlie Schwab rolled into one. But, say, you might wave enchanted dishrags and make copper bottles smoke up coon giants all night without ever touching me. My case won't yield to that kind of treatment."

"If I could hear your story," said the Margrave, with his lofty, serious smile.

"I'll spiel it in about nine words," said the young man, with a deep sigh, "but I don't think you can help me any. Unless you're a peach at guessing it's back to the Bosphorous for you on your magic linoleum." THE STORY OF THE YOUNG MAN AND THE HARNESS MAKER'S RIDDLE

"I work in Hildebrant's saddle and harness shop down in Grant Street. I've worked there five years. I get $18 a week. That's enough to marry on, ain't it? Well, I'm not going to get married. Old Hildebrant is one of these funny Dutchmen – you know the kind – always getting off bum jokes. He's got about a million riddles and things that he faked from Rogers Brothers' great-grandfather. Bill Watson works there, too. Me and Bill have to stand for them chestnuts day after day. Why do we do it? Well, jobs ain't to be picked off every Anheuser bush – And then there's Laura.

"What? The old man's daughter. Comes in the shop every day. About nineteen, and the picture of the blonde that sits on the palisades of the Rhine and charms the clam-diggers into the surf. Hair the color of straw matting, and eyes as black and shiny as the best harness blacking – think of that!

"Me? well, it's either me or Bill Watson. She treats us both equal. Bill is all to the psychopathic about her; and me? – well, you saw me plating the roadbed of the Great Maroon Way with silver tonight. That was on account of Laura. I was spiflicated, Your Highness, and I wot not of what I wouldst.

"How? Why, old Hildebrandt say to me and Bill this afternoon: 'Boys, one riddle have I for you gehabt haben. A young man who cannot riddles antworten, he is not so good by business for ein family to provide – is not that – hein?' And he hands us a riddle – a conundrum, some calls it – and he chuckles interiorly and gives both of us till to-morrow morning to work out the answer to it. And he says whichever of us guesses the repartee end of it goes to his house o' Wednesday night to his daughter's birthday party. And it means Laura for whichever of us goes, for she's naturally aching for a husband, and it's either me or Bill Watson, for old Hildebrant likes us both, and wants her to marry somebody that'll carry on the business after he's stitched his last pair of traces.

"The riddle? Why, it was this: 'What kind of a hen lays the longest? Think of that! What kind of a hen lays the longest? Ain't it like a Dutchman to risk a man's happiness on a fool proposition like that? Now, what's the use? What I don't know about hens would fill several incubators. You say you're giving imitations of the old Arab guy that gave away – libraries in Bagdad. Well, now, can you whistle up a fairy that'll solve this hen query, or not?"

When the young man ceased the Margrave arose and paced to and fro by the park bench for several minutes. Finally he sat again, and said, in grave and impressive tones:

"I must confess, sir, that during the eight years that I have spent in search of adventure and in relieving distress I have never encountered a more interesting or a more perplexing case. I fear that I have overlooked hens in my researches and observations. As to their habits, their times and manner of laying, their many varieties and cross-breedings, their span of life, their -"

"Oh, don't make an Ibsen drama of it!" interrupted the young man, flippantly. "Riddles – especially old Hildebrant's riddles – don't have to be worked out seriously. They are light themes such as Sim Ford and Harry Thurston Peck like to handle. But, somehow, I can't strike just the answer. Bill Watson may, and he may not. To-morrow will tell. Well, Your Majesty, I'm glad anyhow that you butted in and whiled the time away. I guess Mr. Al Rashid himself would have bounced back if one of his constituents had conducted him up against this riddle. I'll say good night. Peace fo' yours, and what-you-may-call-its of Allah."

The Margrave, still with a gloomy air, held out his hand.

"I cannot exppress my regret," he said, sadly. "Never before have I found myself unable to assist in some way. 'What kind of a hen lays the longest? It is a baffling problem. There is a hen, I believe, called the Plymouth Rock that -"

"Cut it out," said the young man. "The Caliph trade is a

mighty serious one. I don't suppose you'd even see anything funny in a preacher's defense of John D. Rockefeller. Well, good night, Your Nibs."

From habit the Margrave began to fumble in his pockets. He drew forth a card and handed it to the young man.

"Do me the favor to accept this, anyhow," he said. "The time may come when it might be of use to you."

"Thanks!" said the young man, pocketing it carelessly. "My name is Simmons."

*

Shame to him who would hint that the reader's interest shall altogether pursue the Margrave August Michael von Paulsen Quigg. I am indeed astray if my hand fail in keeping the way where my peruser's heart would follow. Then let us, on the morrow, peep quickly in at the door of Hildebrant, harness maker.

Hildebrant's 200 pounds reposed on a bench, silverbuckling a raw leather martingale.

Bill Watson came in first.

"Vell," said Hildebrant, shaking all over with the vile conceit of the joke-maker, "haf you guessed him? 'Vat kind of a hen lays der longest?'"

"Er – why, I think so," said Bill, rubbing a servile chin. "I think so, Mr. Hildebrant – the one that lives the longest – Is that right?"

"Nein!" said Hildebrant, shaking his head violently. "You haf not guessed der answer."

Bill passed on and donned a bed-tick apron and bachelorhood.

In came the young man of the Arabian Night's fiasco – pale, melancholy, hopeless.

"Vell," said Hildebrant, "haf you guessed him? 'Vat kind of a hen lays der longest?'"

Simmons regarded him with dull savagery in his eye. Should he curse this mountain of pernicious humor – curse him and die? Why should – But there was Laura.

Dogged, speechless, he thrust his hands into his coat pockets and stood. His hand encountered the strange touch of the Margrave's card. He drew it out and looked at it, as men about to be hanged look at a crawling fly. There was written on it in

Quigg's bold, round hand: "Good for one roast chicken to bearer."

Simmons looked up with a flashing eye.

"A dead one!" said he.

"Goot!" roared Hildebrant, rocking the table with giant glee. "Dot is right! You gome at mine house at 8 o'clock to der party."

# The Model Millionaire

***Oscar Wilde***

Unless one is wealthy there is no use in being a charming fellow. Romance is the privilege of the rich, not the profession of the unemployed. The poor should be practical and prosaic. It is better to have a permanent income than to be fascinating. These are the great truths of modern life which Hughie Erskine never realised. Poor Hughie! Intellectually, we must admit, he was not of much importance. He never said a brilliant or even an ill-natured thing in his life. But then he was wonderfully good-looking, with his crisp brown hair, his clear-cut profile, and his grey eyes. He was as popular with men as he was with women, and he had every accomplishment except that of making money. His father had bequeathed him his cavalry sword, and a History of the Peninsular War in fifteen volumes. Hughie hung the first over his looking-glass, put the second on a shelf between Ruff's Guide and Bailey's Magazine, and lived on two hundred a year that an old aunt allowed him. He had tried everything. He had gone on the Stock Exchange for six months; but what was a butterfly to do among bulls and bears? He had been a tea-merchant for a little longer, but had soon tired of pekoe and souchong. Then he had tried selling dry sherry. That did not answer; the sherry was a little too dry. Ultimately he became nothing, a delightful, ineffectual young man with a perfect profile and no profession.

To make matters worse, he was in love. The girl he loved was Laura Merton, the daughter of a retired Colonel who had lost his temper and his digestion in India, and had never found either of them again. Laura adored him, and he was ready to kiss her shoe-strings. They were the handsomest couple in London, and had not a penny-piece between them. The Colonel was very fond of Hughie, but would not hear of any engagement.

'Come to me, my boy, when you have got ten thousand

pounds of your own, and we will see about it,' he used to say; and Hughie looked very glum on those days, and had to go to Laura for consolation.

One morning, as he was on his way to Holland Park, where the Mertons lived, he dropped in to see a great friend of his, Alan Trevor. Trevor was a painter. Indeed, few people escape that nowadays. But he was also an artist, and artists are rather rare. Personally he was a strange rough fellow, with a freckled face and a red ragged beard. However, when he took up the brush he was a real master, and his pictures were eagerly sought after. He had been very much attracted by Hughie at first, it must be acknowledged, entirely on account of his personal charm. 'The only people a painter should know,' he used to say, 'are people who are bete and beautiful, people who are an artistic pleasure to look at and an intellectual repose to talk to. Men who are dandies and women who are darlings rule the world, at least they should do so.' However, after he got to know Hughie better, he liked him quite as much for his bright buoyant spirits and his generous reckless nature, and had given him the permanent entree to his studio.

When Hughie came in he found Trevor putting the finishing touches to a wonderful life-size picture of a beggar-man. The beggar himself was standing on a raised platform in a corner of the studio. He was a wizened old man, with a face like wrinkled parchment, and a most piteous expression. Over his shoulders was flung a coarse brown cloak, all tears and tatters; his thick boots were patched and cobbled, and with one hand he leant on a rough stick, while with the other he held out his battered hat for alms.

'What an amazing model!' whispered Hughie, as he shook hands with his friend.

'An amazing model?' shouted Trevor at the top of his voice; 'I should think so! Such beggars as he are not to be met with every day. A trouvaille, mort cher; a living Velasquez! My stars! what an etching Rembrandt would have made of him!'

'Poor old chap! said Hughie, 'how miserable he looks! But I suppose, to you painters, his face is his fortune?'

'Certainly,' replied Trevor, 'you don't want a beggar to look happy, do you?'

'How much does a model get for sitting?' asked Hughie, as he found himself a comfortable seat on a divan.

'A shilling an hour.'

'And how much do you get for your picture, Alan?'

'Oh, for this I get two thousand!'

'Pounds?'

'Guineas. Painters, poets, and physicians always get guineas.'

'Well, I think the model should have a percentage,' cried Hughie, laughing; 'they work quite as hard as you do.'

'Nonsense, nonsense! Why, look at the trouble of laying on the paint alone, and standing all day long at one's easel! It's all very well, Hughie, for you to talk, but I assure you that there are moments when Art almost attains to the dignity of manual labour. But you mustn't chatter; I'm very busy. Smoke a cigarette, and keep quiet.'

After some time the servant came in, and told Trevor that the frame-maker wanted to speak to him.

'Don't run away, Hughie,' he said, as he went out, 'I will be back in a moment.'

The old beggar-man took advantage of Trevor's absence to rest for a moment on a wooden bench that was behind him. He looked so forlorn and wretched that Hughie could not help pitying him, and felt in his pockets to see what money he had. All he could find was a sovereign and some coppers. 'Poor old fellow', he thought to himself, 'he wants it more than I do, but it means no hansoms for a fortnight'; and he walked across the studio and slipped the sovereign into the beggar's hand.

The old man started, and a faint smile flitted across his withered lips. 'Thank you, sir,' he said, 'thank you.'

Then Trevor arrived, and Hughie took his leave, blushing a little at what he had done. He spent the day with Laura, got a charming scolding for his extravagance, and had to walk home.

That night he strolled into the Palette Club about eleven o'clock, and found Trevor sitting by himself in the smoking-room drinking hock and seltzer.

'Well, Alan, did you get the picture finished all right?' he said, as he lit his cigarette.

'Finished and framed, my boy!' answered Trevor; 'and, by-the-bye, you have made a conquest. That old model you saw is quite devoted to you. I had to tell him all about you – who you are, where you live, what your income is, what prospects you have – '

'My dear Alan,' cried Hughie, 'I shall probably find him waiting for me when I go home. But of course you are only joking. Poor old wretch! I wish I could do something for him. I think it is dreadful that any one should be so miserable. I have got heaps of old clothes at home – do you think he would care for any of them? Why, his rags were falling to bits.'

'But he looks splendid in them,' said Trevor. 'I wouldn't paint him in a frock-coat for anything. What you call rags I call romance. What seems poverty to you is picturesqueness to me. However, I'll tell him of your offer.'

'Alan,' said Hughie seriously, 'you painters are a heartless lot.'

'An artist's heart is his head,' replied Trevor; 'and besides, our business is to realise the world as we see it, not to reform it as we know it. A chacun son métier. And now tell me how Laura is. The old model was quite interested in her.'

'You don't mean to say you talked to him about her?' said Hughie.

'Certainly I did. He knows all about the relentless colonel, the lovely Laura, and the £10,000.'

'You told that old beggar all my private affairs?' cried Hughie, looking very red and angry.

'My dear boy,' said Trevor, smiling, 'that old beggar, as you call him, is one of the richest men in Europe. He could buy all London to-morrow without overdrawing his account. He has a house in every capital, dines off gold plate, and can prevent Russia going to war when he chooses.'

'What on earth do you mean?' exclaimed Hughie.

'What I say,' said Trevor. 'The old man you saw to-day in the studio was Baron Hausberg. He is a great friend of mine, buys all my pictures and that sort of thing, and gave me a commission a month ago to paint him as a beggar. Que voulez-vous? La fantaisie d'un millionnaire! And I must say he made a magnificent figure in his rags, or perhaps I should say in my rags; they are an old suit I got in Spain.'

'Baron Hausberg!' cried Hughie. 'Good heavens! I gave him a sovereign!' and he sank into an armchair the picture of dismay.

'Gave him a sovereign!' shouted Trevor, and he burst into a roar of laughter. 'My dear boy, you'll never see it again. Son affaire c'est l'argent des autres.'

'I think you might have told me, Alan,' said Hughie sulkily, 'and not have let me make such a fool of myself.'

'Well, to begin with, Hughie,' said Trevor, 'it never entered my mind that you went about distributing alms in that reckless way. I can understand your kissing a pretty model, but your giving a sovereign to an ugly one – by Jove, no! Besides, the fact is that I really was not at home to-day to any one; and when you came in I didn't know whether Hausberg would like his name mentioned. You know he wasn't in full dress.'

'What a duffer he must think me!' said Hughie.

'Not at all. He was in the highest spirits after you left; kept chuckling to himself and rubbing his old wrinkled hands together. I couldn't make out why he was so interested to know all about you; but I see it all now. He'll invest your sovereign for you, Hughie, pay you the interest every six months, and have a capital story to tell after dinner.'

'I am an unlucky devil,' growled Hughie. 'The best thing I can do is to go to bed; and, my dear Alan, you mustn't tell any one. I shouldn't dare show my face in the Row.'

'Nonsense! It reflects the highest credit on your philanthropic spirit, Hughie. And don't run away. Have another cigarette, and you can talk about Laura as much as you like.'

However, Hughie wouldn't stop, but walked home, feeling very unhappy, and leaving Alan Trevor in fits of laughter.

The next morning, as he was at breakfast, the servant brought him up a card on which was written, 'Monsieur Gustave Naudin, de la part de M. le Baron Hausberg.'

'I suppose he has come for an apology,' said Hughie to himself; and he told the servant to show the visitor up.

An old gentleman with gold spectacles and grey hair came into the room, and said, in a slight French accent, 'Have I the honour of addressing Monsieur Erskine?'

Hughie bowed.

'I have come from Baron Hausberg,' he continued. 'The Baron – '

'I beg, sir, that you will offer him my sincerest apologies,' stammered Hughie.

'The Baron,' said the old gentleman, with a smile, 'has commissioned me to bring you this letter;' and he extended a sealed envelope.

On the outside was written, 'A wedding present to Hugh Erskine and Laura Merton, from an old beggar,' and inside was a cheque for £10,000.

When they were married Alan Trevor was the best-man, and the Baron made a speech at the wedding-breakfast.

'Millionaire models,' remarked Alan, 'are rare enough; but, by Jove, model millionaires are rarer still!'

# The Devoted Friend

***Oscar Wilde***

One morning the old Water-rat put his head out of his hole. He had bright beady eyes and stiff grey whiskers, and his tail was like a long bit of black india-rubber. The little ducks were swimming about in the pond, looking just like a lot of yellow canaries, and their mother, who was pure white with real red legs, was trying to teach them how to stand on their heads in the water.

'You will never be in the best society unless you can stand on your heads,' she kept saying to them; and every now and then she showed them how it was done. But the little ducks paid no attention to her. They were so young that they did not know what an advantage it is to be in society at all.

'What disobedient children!' cried the old Water-rat; 'they really deserve to be drowned.'

'Nothing of the kind,' answered the Duck, 'every one must make a beginning, and parents cannot be too patient.'

'Ah! I know nothing about the feelings of parents,' said the Water-rat; 'I am not a family man. In fact, I have never been married, and I never intend to be. Love is all very well in its way, but friendship is much higher. Indeed, I know of nothing in the world that is either nobler or rarer than a devoted friendship.'

'And what, pray, is your idea of the duties of a devoted friend?' asked a Green Linnet, who was sitting in a willow-tree hard by, and had overheard the conversation.

'Yes, that is just what I want to know,' said the Duck, and she swam away to the end of the pond, and stood upon her head, in order to give her children a good example.

'What a silly question!' cried the Water-rat. 'I should expect my devoted friend to be devoted to me, of course.'

'And what would you do in return?' said the little bird,

swinging upon a silver spray, and flapping his tiny wings.

'I don't understand you,' answered the Water-rat.

'Let me tell you a story on the subject,' said the Linnet.

'Is the story about me?' asked the Water-rat. If so, I will listen to it, for I am extremely fond of fiction.'

'It is applicable to you,' answered the Linnet; and he flew down, and alighting upon the bank, he told the story of The Devoted Friend.

'Once upon a time,' said the Linnet, 'there was an honest little fellow named Hans.'

'Was he very distinguished?' asked the Water-rat.

'No,' answered the Linnet, 'I don't think he was distinguished at all, except for his kind heart, and his funny round good-humoured face. He lived in a tiny cottage all by himself, and every day he worked in his garden. In all the country-side there was no garden so lovely as his. Sweet-william grew there, and Gilly-flowers, and Shepherds'-purses, and Fair-maids of France. There were damask Roses, and yellow Roses, lilac Crocuses, and gold, purple Violets and white. Columbine and Ladysmock, Marjoram and Wild Basil, the Cowslip and the Flower-de-luce, the Daffodil and the Clove-Pink bloomed or blossomed in their proper order as the months went by, one flower taking another flower's place, so that there were always beautiful things to look at, and pleasant odours to smell.

'Little Hans had a great many friends, but the most devoted friend of all was big Hugh the Miller. Indeed, so devoted was the rich Miller to little Hans, that he [Hans] would never go by his garden without leaning over the wall and plucking a large nosegay, or a handful of sweet herbs, or filling his pockets with plums and cherries if it was the fruit season.

'"Real friends should have everything in common," the Miller used to say, and little Hans nodded and smiled, and felt very proud of having a friend with such noble ideas.

'Sometimes, indeed, the neighbours thought it strange that the rich Miller never gave little Hans anything in return, though he had a hundred sacks of flour stored away in his mill, and six milk cows, and a large stock of woolly sheep; but Hans never troubled his head about these things, and nothing gave him greater pleasure than to listen to all the wonderful things the Miller used to say about the unselfishness of true friendship.

'So little Hans worked away in his garden. During the spring, the summer, and the autumn he was very happy, but when the winter came, and he had no fruit or flowers to bring to the market, he suffered a good deal from cold and hunger, and often had to go to bed without any supper but a few dried pears or some hard nuts. Jn the winter, also, he was extremely lonely, as the Miller never came to see him then.

'"There is no good in my going to see little Hans as long as the snow lasts," the Miller used to say to his wife, "for when people are in trouble they should be left alone, and not be bothered by visitors. That at least is my idea about friendship, and I am sure I am right. So I shall wait till the spring comes, and then I shall pay him a visit, and he will be able to give me a large basket of primroses, and that will make him so happy."

"You are certainly very thoughtful about others," answered the Wife, as she sat in her comfortable armchair by the big pinewood fire; "very thoughtful indeed. It is quite a treat to hear you talk about friendship. I am sure the clergyman himself could not say such beautiful things as you do, though he does live in a three-storied house, and wears a gold ring on his little finger."

'"But could We not ask little Hans up here?" said the Miller's youngest son. "If poor Hans is in trouble I will give him half my porridge, and show him my white rabbits."

"What a silly boy you are!" cried the Miller; "I really don't know what is the use of sending you to school. You seem not to learn anything. Why, if little Hans came up here, and saw our warm fire, and our good supper, and our great cask of red wine, he might get envious, and envy is a most terrible thing, and would spoil anybody's nature. I certainly will not allow Hans's nature to be spoiled. I am his best friend, and I will always watch over him, and see that he is not led into any temptations. Besides, if Hans came here, he might ask me to let him have some flour on credit, and that I could not do. Flour is one thing, and friendship is another, and they should not be confused. Why, the words are spelt differently, and mean quite different things. Everybody can see that."

'"How well you talk!" said the Miller's Wife, pouring herself out a large glass of warm ale; "really I feel quite drowsy. It is just like being in church."

"Lots of people act well," answered the Miller; "but very few people talk well, which shows that talking is much the more difficult thing of the two, and much the finer thing also;" and he looked sternly across the table at his little son, who felt so ashamed of himself that he hung his head down, and grew quite scarlet, and began to cry into his tea. However, he was so young that you must excuse him.'

'Is that the end of the story?' asked the Water-rat.

'Certainly not,' answered the Linnet, that is the beginning.

'Then you are quite behind the age,' said the Water-rat. 'Every good story-teller nowadays starts with the end, and then goes on to the beginning, and concludes with the middle. That is the new method. I heard all about it the other day from a critic who was walking round the pond with a young man. He spoke of the matter at great length, and I am sure he must have been right, for he had blue spectacles and a bald head, and whenever the young man made any remark, he always answered "Pooh!" But pray go on with your story. I like the Miller immensely. I have all kinds of beautiful sentiments myself, so there is a great sympathy between us.

'Well,' said the Linnet, hopping now on one leg and now on the other, 'as soon as the winter was over, and the primroses began to open their pale yellow stars, the Miller said to his wife that he would go down and see little Hans.

'"Why, what a good heart you have!" cried his wife; "you are always thinking of others. And mind you take the big basket with you for the flowers."

'So the Miller tied the sails of the windmill together with a strong iron chain, and went down the hill with the basket on his arm.

'"Good morning, little Hans," said the Miller.

'"Good morning," said Hans, leaning on his spade, and smiling from ear to ear.

'"And how have you been all the winter?" said the Miller. "Well, really," cried Hans, "it is very good of you to ask, very good indeed. I am afraid I had rather a hard time of it, but now the spring has come, and I am quite happy, and all my flowers are doing well."

'"We often talked of you during the winter, Hans," said the Miller, "and wondered how you were getting on."

'"That was kind of you," said Hans; "I was half afraid you had forgotten me."

'"Hans, I am surprised at you," said the Miller; "friendship never forgets. That is the wonderful thing about it, but I am afraid you don't understand the poetry of life. How lovely your primroses are looking, by-the-by!"

'"They are certainly very lovely," said Hans, "and it is a most lucky thing for me that I have so many. I am going to bring them into the market and sell them to the Burgomaster's daughter, and buy back my wheelbarrow with the money."

'"Buy back your wheelbarrow? You don't mean to say you have sold it? What a very stupid thing to do!"

'"Well, the fact is," said Hans, "that I was obliged to. You see the winter was a very bad time for me, and I really had no money at all to buy bread with. So I first sold the silver buttons off my Sunday coat, and then I sold my silver chain, and then I sold my big pipe, and at last I sold my wheelbarrow. But I am going to buy them all back again now."

'"Hans," said the Miller, "I will give you my wheelbarrow. It is not in very good repair; indeed, one side is gone, and there is something wrong with the wheel-spokes; but in spite of that I will give it to you. I know it is very generous of me, and a great many people would think me extremely foolish for parting with it, but I am not like the rest of the world. I think that generosity is the essence of friendship, and, besides, I have got a new wheelbarrow for myself. Yes, you may set your mind at ease, I will give you my wheelbarrow."

'"Well, really, that is generous of you," said little Hans, and his funny round face glowed all over with pleasure. "I can easily put it in repair, as I have a plank of wood in the house."

'"A plank of wood" said the Miller; "why, that is just what I want for the roof of my barn. There is a very large hole in it, and the corn will all get damp if I don't stop it up. How lucky you mentioned it! It is quite remarkable how one good action always breeds another. I have given you my wheelbarrow, and now you are going to give me your plank. Of course, the wheelbarrow is worth far more than the plank, but true friendship never notices things like that. Pray get it at once, and I will set to work at my barn this very day."

'"Certainly," cried little Hans, and he ran into the shed and dragged the plank out.

'"It is not a very big plank," said the Miller, looking at it, "and I am afraid that after I have mended my barn-roof there won't be any left for you to mend the wheelbarrow with; but, of course, that is not my fault. And now, as I have given you my wheelbarrow, I am sure you would like to give me some flowers in return. Here is the basket, and mind you fill it quite full."

'"Quite full?" said little Hans, rather sorrowfully, for it was really a very big basket, and he knew that if he filled it he would have no flowers left for the market, and he was very anxious to get his silver buttons back.

'"Well, really," answered the Miller, "as I have given you my wheelbarrow, I don't think that it is much to ask you for a few flowers. I may be wrong, but I should have thought that friendship, true friendship, was quite free from selfishness of any kind."

'"My dear friend, my best friend," cried little Hans, "you are welcome to all the flowers in my garden. I would much sooner have your good opinion than my silver buttons, any day;" and he ran and plucked all his pretty primroses, and filled the Miller's basket.

'"Good-bye, little Hans," said the Miller, as he went up the hill with the plank on his shoulder, and the big basket in his hand.

'"Good-bye," said little Hans, and he began to dig away quite merrily, he was so pleased about the wheelbarrow.

'The next day he was nailing up some honeysuckle against the porch, when he heard the Miller's voice calling to him from the road. So he jumped off the ladder, and ran down the garden, and looked over the wall.

'There was the Miller with a large sack of flour on his back.

'"Dear little Hans," said the Miller, "would you mind carrying this sack of flour for me to market?"

'"Oh, I am so sorry," said Hans,"but I am really very busy to-day. I have got all my creepers to nail up, and all my flowers to water, and all my grass to roll."

'"Well, really," said the Miller, "I think that, considering that I am going to give you my wheelbarrow, it is rather unfriendly of you to refuse."

'"Oh, don't say that," cried little Hans, "I wouldn't be unfriendly for the whole world"; and he ran in for his cap, and trudged off with the big sack on his shoulders.

'It was a very hot day, and the road was terribly dusty, and before Hans had reached the sixth milestone he was so tired that he had to sit down and rest. However, he went on bravely, and at last he reached the market. After he had waited there some time, he sold the sack of flour for a very good price, and then he returned home at once, for he was afraid that if he stopped too late he might meet some robbers on the way.

"It has certainly been a hard day," said little Hans to himself as he was going to bed, "but I am glad I did not refuse the Miller, for he is my best friend, and, besides, he is going to give me his wheelbarrow."

'Early the next morning the Miller came down to get the money for his sack of flour, but little Hans was so tired that he was still in bed.

'"Upon my word," said the Miller, "you are very lazy. Really, considering that I am going to give you my wheelbarrow, I think you might work harder. Idleness is a great sin, and I certainly don't like any of my friends to be idle or sluggish. You must not mind my speaking quite plainly to you. Of course I should not dream of doing so if I were not your friend. But what is the good of friendship if one cannot say exactly what one means? Anybody can say charming things and try to please and to flatter, but a true friend always says unpleasant things, and does not mind giving pain. Indeed, if he is a really true friend he prefers it, for he knows that then he is doing good."

'"I am very sorry," said little Hans, rubbing his eyes and pulling off his night-cap, "but I was so tired that I thought I would lie in bed for a little time, and listen to the birds singing.

Do you know that I always work better after hearing the birds sing?"

'"Well, I am glad of that," said the Miller, clapping little Hans on the back, "for I want you to come up to the mill as soon as you are dressed, and mend my barn-roof for me."

'Poor little Hans was very anxious to go and work in his garden, for his flowers had not been watered for two days, but he did not like to refuse the Miller, as he was such a good friend to him.

'"Do you think it would be unfriendly of me if I said I was busy?" he inquired in a shy and timid voice.

'"Well, really," answered the Miller, "I do not think it is much to ask of you, considering that I am going to give you my wheelbarrow; but of course if you refuse I will go and do it myself."

'"Oh! on no account," cried little Hans; and he jumped out of bed, and dressed himself, and went up to the barn.

'He worked there all day long, till sunset, and at sunset the Miller came to see how he was getting on.

'"Have you mended the hole in the roof yet, little Hans?" cried the Miller in a cheery voice.

'"It is quite mended," answered little Hans, coming down the ladder.

'"Ah!" said the Miller, "there is no work so delightful as the work one does for others."

'"It is certainly a great privilege to hear you talk," answered little Hans, sitting down and wiping his forehead, "a very great privilege. But I am afraid I shall never have such beautiful ideas as you have."

'"Oh! they will come to you," said the Miller, "but you must take more pains. At present you have only the practice of friendship; some day you will have the theory also."

'"Do you really think I shall?" asked little Hans.

'"I have no doubt of it," answered the Miller; "but now that you have mended the roof, you had better go home and rest, for I want you to drive my sheep to the mountain to-morrow."

'Poor little Hans was afraid to say anything to this, and early the next morning the Miller brought his sheep round to the cottage, and Hans started off with them to the mountain. It took him the whole day to get there and back; and when he returned he was so tired that he went off to sleep in his chair, and did not wake up till it was broad daylight.

'"What a delightful time I shall have in my garden," he said, and he went to work at once.

'But somehow he was never able to look after his flowers at all, for his friend the Miller was always coming round and sending him off on long errands, or getting him to help at the mill. Little Hans was very much distressed at times, as he was afraid his flowers would think he had forgotten them, but he consoled himself by the reflection that the Miller was his best friend. "Besides," he used to say, "he is going to give me his wheelbarrow, and that is an act of pure generosity."

'So little Hans worked away for the Miller, and the Miller said all kinds of beautiful things about friendship, which Hans took down in a note-book, and used to read over at night, for he was a very good scholar.

'Now it happened that one evening little Hans was sitting by his fireside when a loud rap came at the door. It was a very wild night, and the wind was blowing and roaring round the house so terribly that at first he thought it was merely the storm. But a second rap came, and then a third, louder than either of the others.

'"It is some poor traveller," said little Hans to himself, and he ran to the door.

'There stood the Miller with a lantern in one hand and a big stick in the other.

'"Dear little Hans," cried the Miller, "I am in great trouble. My little boy has fallen off a ladder and hurt himself, and I am going for the Doctor. But he lives so far away, and it is such a bad night, that it has just occurred to me that it would be much better if you went instead of me. You know I am going to give you my wheelbarrow, and so it is only fair that you should do something for me in return."

'"Certainly," cried little Hans, "I take it quite as a compliment your coming to me, and I will start off at once. But you must lend me your lantern, as the night is so dark that I am afraid I might fall into the ditch."

'"I am very sorry," answered the Miller, "but it is my new lantern, and it would be a great loss to me if anything happened to it."

'"Well, never mind, I will do without it," cried little Hans, and he took down his great fur coat, and his warm scarlet cap, and tied a muffler round his throat, and started off.

'What a dreadful storm it was! The night was so black that little Hans could hardly see, and the wind was so strong that he could scarcely stand. However, he was very courageous, and after he had been walking about three hours, he arrived at the Doctor's house, and knocked at the door.

'"Who is there?"' cried the Doctor, putting his head out of his bedroom window.

'"Little Hans, Doctor."

'"What do you want, little Hans?"

'"The Miller's son has fallen from a ladder, and has hurt himself, and the Miller wants you to come at once."

'"All right!" said the Doctor; and he ordered his horse, and his big boots, and his lantern, and came downstairs, and rode off in the direction of the Miller's house, little Hans trudging behind him.

'But the storm grew worse and worse, and the rain fell in torrents, and little Hans could not see where he was going, or keep up with the horse. At last he lost his way, and wandered off on the moor, which was a very dangerous place, as it was full of deep holes, and there poor little Hans was drowned. His body was found the next day by some goatherds, floating in a great pool of water, and was brought back by them to the cottage. 'Everybody went to little Hans's funeral, as he was so popular, and the Miller was the chief mourner.

'"As I was his best friend," said the Miller, "it is only fair that I should have the best place;" so he walked at the head of the procession in a long black cloak, and every now and then he wiped his eyes with a big pocket-handkerchief.

'"Little Hans is certainly a great loss to every one," said the Blacksmith, when the funeral was over, and they were all seated comfortably in the inn, drinking spiced wine and eating sweet cakes.

'"A great loss to me at any rate," answered the Miller; "why, I had as good as given him my wheelbarrow, and now I really don't know what to do with it. It is very much in my way at home, and it is in such bad repair that I could not get anything for it if I sold it. I will certainly take care not to give away anything again. One always suffers for being generous."

'Well?' said the Water-rat, after a long pause. 'Well, that is the end,' said the Linnet.

'But what became of the Miller?' asked the Water-rat. 'Oh! I really don't know,' replied the Linnet, 'and I am sure that I don't care.'

'It is quite evident then that you have no sympathy in your nature,' said the Water-rat.

'I am afraid you don't quite see the moral of the story,' remarked the Linnet.

'The what?' screamed the Water-rat.

'The moral.'

'Do you mean to say that the story has a moral?'

'Certainly,' said the Linnet.

'Well, really,' said the Water-rat, in a very angry manner, 'I think you should have told me that before you began. If you had done so, I certainly would not have listened to you; in fact, I should have said "Pooh," like the critic. However, I can say it now;' so he shouted out 'Pooh' at the top of his voice, gave a whisk with his tail, and went back into his hole.

'And how do you like the Water-rat?' asked the Duck, who came paddling up some minutes afterwards. 'He has a great many good points, but for my own part I have a mother's feelings, and I can never look at a confirmed bachelor without the tears coming into my eyes.'

'I am rather afraid that I have annoyed him,' answered the Linnet. 'The fact is, that I told him a story with a moral.'

'Ah! that is always a very dangerous thing to do,' said the Duck.

And I quite agree with her.

# The Nightingale and the Rose

*Oscar Wilde*

'She said that she would dance with me if I brought her red roses,' cried the young Student; 'but in all my garden there is no red rose.'

From her nest in the holm-oak tree the Nightingale heard him, and she looked out through the leaves, and wondered.

'No red rose in all my garden!' he cried, and his beautiful eyes filled with tears. 'Ah, on what little things does happiness depend! I have read all that the wise men have written, and all the secrets of philosophy are mine, yet for want of a red rose is my life made wretched.'

'Here at last is a true lover,' said the Nightingale. 'Night after night have I sung of him, though I knew him not: night after night have I told his story to the stars, and now I see him. His hair is dark as the hyacinth-blossom, and his lips are red as the rose of his desire; but passion has made his lace like pale Ivory, and sorrow has set her seal upon his brow.'

'The Prince gives a ball to-morrow night,' murmured the young Student, 'and my love will be of the company. If I bring her a red rose she will dance with me till dawn. If I bring her a red rose, I shall hold her in my arms, and she will lean her head upon my shoulder, and her hand will be clasped in mine. But there is no red rose in my garden, so I shall sit lonely, and she will pass me by. She will have no heed of me, and my heart will break.'

'Here indeed is the true lover,' said the Nightingale. 'What I sing of he suffers: what is joy to me, to him is pain. Surely Love is a wonderful thing. It is more precious than emeralds, and dearer than fine opals. Pearls and pomegranates cannot buy it, nor is it set forth in the market-place. it may not be purchased of the merchants, 'or can it be weighed out in the balance for gold.'

'The musicians will sit in their gallery,' said the young Student, 'and play upon their stringed instruments, and my love will dance to the sound of the harp and the violin. She will dance so lightly that her feet will not touch the floor, and the courtiers in their gay dresses will throng round her. But with me she will not dance, for I have no red rose to give her'; and he flung himself down on the grass, and buried his face in his hands, and wept.

'Why is he weeping?' asked a little Green Lizard, as he ran past him with his tail in the air.

'Why, indeed?' said a Butterfly, who was fluttering about after a sunbeam.

'Why, indeed?' whispered a Daisy to his neighbour, in a soft, low voice.

'He is weeping for a red rose,' said the Nightingale.

'For a red rose!' they cried; 'how very ridiculous!' and the little Lizard, who was something of a cynic, laughed outright.

But the Nightingale understood the secret of the Student's sorrow, and she sat silent in the oak-tree, and thought about the mystery of Love.

Suddenly she spread her brown wings for flight, and soared into the air. She passed through the grove like a shadow, and like a shadow she sailed across the garden.

In the centre of the grass-plot was standing a beautiful Rose-tree, and when she saw it, she flew over to it, and lit upon a spray.

'Give me a red rose,' she cried, 'and I will sing you my sweetest song.'

But the Tree shook its head.

'My roses are white,' it answered; 'as white as the foam of the sea, and whiter than the snow upon the mountain. But go to my brother who grows round the old sun-dial, and perhaps he will give you what you want.'

So the Nightingale flew over to the Rose-tree that was growing round the old sun-dial.

'Give me a red rose,' she cried, 'and I will sing you my sweetest song.'

But the Tree shook its head.

'My roses are yellow,' it answered; 'as yellow as the hair of the mermaiden who sits upon an amber throne, and yellower than the daffodil that blooms in the meadow before the mower comes with his scythe. But go to my brother who grows beneath the Student's window, and perhaps he will give you what you want.'

So the Nightingale flew over to the Rose-tree that was growing beneath the Student's window.

'Give me a red rose,' she cried, 'and I will sing you my sweetest song.'

But the Tree shook its head.

'My roses are red,' it answered, 'as red as the feet of the dove, and redder than the great fans of coral that wave and wave in the ocean-cavern. But the winter has chilled my veins, and the frost has nipped my buds, and the storm has broken my branches, and I shall have no roses at all this year.'

'One red rose is all I want,' cried the Nightingale, 'only one red rose! Is there no way by which I can get it?'

'There is a way,' answered the Tree; 'but it is so terrible that I dare not tell it to you.'

'Tell it to me,' said the Nightingale, 'I am not afraid.'

'If you want a red rose,' said the Tree, 'you must build it out of music by moonlight, and stain it with your own heart's-blood. You must sing to me with your breast against a thorn. All night long you must sing to me, and the thorn must pierce your heart, and your life-blood must flow into my veins, and become mine.'

'Death is a great price to pay for a red rose,' cried the Nightingale, 'and Life is very dear to all. It is pleasant to sit in the green wood, and to watch the Sun in his chariot of gold, and the Moon in her chariot of pearl. Sweet is the scent of the hawthorn, and sweet are the bluebells that hide in the valley, and the heather that blows on the hill. Yet Love is better than Life, and what is the heart of a bird compared to the heart of a man?'

So she spread her brown wings for flight, and soared into the air. She swept over the garden like a shadow, and like a shadow she sailed through the grove.

The young Student was still lying on the grass, where she had left him, and the tears were not yet dry in his beautiful eyes.

'Be happy,' cried the Nightingale, 'be happy; you shall have your red rose. I will build it out of music by moonlight, and stain it with my own heart's-blood. All that I ask of you in return is that you will be a true lover, for Love is wiser than Philosophy, though she is wise, and mightier than Power, though he is mighty. Flame-coloured are his wings, and coloured like flame is his body. His lips are sweet as honey, and his breath is like frankincense.'

The Student looked up from the grass, and listened, but he could not understand what the Nightingale was saying to him, for he only knew the things that are written down in books.

But the Oak-tree understood, and felt sad, for he was very fond of the little Nightingale who had built her nest in his branches.

'Sing me one last song,' he whispered; 'I shall feel very lonely when you are gone.'

So the Nightingale sang to the Oak-tree, and her voice was like water bubbling from a silver jar.

When she had finished her song the Student got lip, and pulled a note-book and a lead-pencil out of his pocket.

'She has form,' he said to himself, as he walked away through the grove – 'that cannot be denied to her; but has she got feeling? I am afraid not. In fact, she is like most artists; she is all style, without any sincerity. She would not sacrifice herself for others. She thinks merely of music, and everybody knows that the arts are selfish. Still, it must be admitted that she has some beautiful notes in her voice. What a pity it is that they do not mean anything, or do any practical good.' And he went into his room, and lay down on his little pallet-bed, and began to think of his love; and, after a time, he fell asleep.

And when the Moon shone in the heavens the Nightingale flew to the Rose-tree, and set her breast against the thorn. All night long she sang with her breast against the thorn, and the cold crystal Moon leaned down and listened. All night long she sang, and the thorn went deeper and deeper into her breast, and her life-blood ebbed away from her.

She sang first of the birth of love in the heart of a boy and a girl. And on the topmost spray of the Rose-tree there blossomed a marvellous rose, petal following petal, as song followed song.

Yale was it, at first, as the mist that hangs over the river – pale as the feet of the morning, and silver as the wings of the dawn. As the shadow of a rose in a mirror of silver, as the shadow of a rose in a water-pool, so was the rose that blossomed on the topmost spray of the Tree.

But the Tree cried to the Nightingale to press closer against the thorn. 'Press closer, little Nightingale,' cried the Tree, 'or the Day will come before the rose is finished.'

So the Nightingale pressed closer against the thorn, and louder and louder grew her song, for she sang of the birth of passion in the soul of a man and a maid.

And a delicate flush of pink came into the leaves of the rose, like the flush in the face of the bridegroom when he kisses the lips of the bride. But the thorn had not yet reached her heart, so the rose's heart remained white, for only a Nightingale's heart's-blood can crimson the heart of a rose.

And the Tree cried to the Nightingale to press closer against the thorn. 'Press closer, little Nightingale,' cried the Tree, 'or the Day will come before the rose is finished.'

So the Nightingale pressed closer against the thorn, and the thorn touched her heart, and a fierce pang of pain shot through her. Bitter, bitter was the pain, and wilder and wilder grew her song, for she sang of the Love that is perfected by Death, of the Love that dies not in the tomb.

And the marvellous rose became crimson, like the rose of the eastern sky. Crimson was the girdle of petals, and crimson as a ruby was the heart.

But the Nightingale's voice grew fainter, and her little wings began to beat, and a film came over her eyes. Fainter and fainter grew her song, and she felt something choking her in her throat.

Then she gave one last burst of music. The white Moon heard it, and she forgot the dawn, and lingered on in the sky. The red rose heard it, and it trembled all over with ecstasy, and opened its petals to the cold morning air. Echo bore it to her purple cavern in the hills, and woke the sleeping shepherds from their dreams. It floated through the reeds of the river, and they carried its message to the sea.

'Look, look!' cried the Tree, 'the rose is finished now;' but the Nightingale made no answer, for she was lying dead in the long grass, with the thorn in her heart.

And at noon the Student opened his window and looked out.

'Why, what a wonderful piece of luck! he cried; 'here is a red rose! I have never seen any rose like it in all my life. It is so beautiful that I am sure it has a long Latin name'; and he leaned down and plucked it.

Then he put on his hat, and ran up to the Professor's house with the rose in his hand.

The daughter of the Professor was sitting in the doorway winding blue silk on a reel, and her little dog was lying at her feet.

'You said that you would dance with me if I brought you a red rose,' cried the Student. Here is the reddest rose in all the world. You will wear it to-night next your heart, and as we dance together it will tell you how I love you.'

But the girl frowned.

'I am afraid it will not go with my dress,' she answered; 'and, besides, the Chamberlain's nephew has sent me some real jewels, and everybody knows that jewels cost far more than flowers.'

'Well, upon my word, you are very ungrateful,' said the Student angrily; and he threw the rose into the street, where it fell into the gutter, and a cart-wheel went over it.

'Ungrateful!' said the girl. 'I tell you what, you are very rude; and, after all, who are you? Only a Student. Why, I don't believe you have even got silver buckles to your shoes as the Chamberlain's nephew has;' and she got up from her chair and went into the house.

'What a silly thing Love is,' said the Student as he walked away. 'It is not half as useful as Logic, for it does not prove anything, and it is always telling one of things that are not going to happen, and making one believe things that are not true. In fact, it is quite unpractical, and, as in this age to be practical is everything, I shall go back to Philosophy and study Metaphysics.'

So he returned to his room and pulled out a great dusty book, and began to read.

# The Happy Price

***Oscar Wilde***

High above the city, on a tall column, stood the statue of the Happy Prince. He was gilded all over with thin leaves of fine gold, for eyes he had two bright sapphires, and a large red ruby glowed on his sword-hilt.

He was very much admired indeed. "He is as beautiful as a weathercock," remarked one of the Town Councillors who wished to gain a reputation for having artistic tastes; "only not quite so useful," he added, fearing lest people should think him unpractical, which he really was not.

"Why can't you be like the Happy Prince?" asked a sensible mother of her little boy who was crying for the moon. "The Happy Prince never dreams of crying for anything."

"I am glad there is some one in the world who is quite happy," muttered a disappointed man as he gazed at the wonderful statue.

"He looks just like an angel," said the Charity Children as they came out of the cathedral in their bright scarlet cloaks and their clean white pinafores.

"How do you know?" said the Mathematical Master, "you have never seen one."

"Ah! But we have, in our dreams," answered the children; and the Mathematical Master frowned and looked very severe, for he did not approve of children dreaming.

One night there flew over the city a little Swallow. His friends had gone away to Egypt six weeks before, but he had stayed behind, for he was in love with the most beautiful Reed. He had met her early in the spring as he was flying down the river after a big yellow moth, and had been so attracted by her slender waist that he had stopped to talk to her.

"Shall I love you?" said the Swallow, who liked to come to the point at once, and the Reed made him a low bow. So he flew round and round her, touching the water with his wings, and making silver ripples. This was his courtship, and it lasted all through the summer.

"It is a ridiculous attachment," twittered the other Swallows; "she has no money, and far too many relations"; and indeed the river was quite full of Reeds. Then, when the autumn came they all flew away.

After they had gone he felt lonely, and began to tire of his lady-love. "She has no conversation," he said, "and I am afraid that she is a coquette, for she is always flirting with the wind." And certainly, whenever the wind blew, the Reed made the most graceful curtseys. "I admit that she is domestic," he continued, "but I love travelling, and my wife, consequently, should love travelling also."

"Will you come away with me?" he said finally to her; but the Reed shook her head, she was so attached to her home.

"You have been trifling with me," he cried. "I am off to the Pyramids. Good-bye!" and he flew away.

All day long he flew, and at night-time he arrived at the city. "Where shall I put up?" he said; "I hope the town has made preparations."

Then he saw the statue on the tall column.

"I will put up there," he cried; "it is a fine position, with plenty of fresh air." So he alighted just between the feet of the Happy Prince.

"I have a golden bedroom," he said softly to himself as he looked round, and he prepared to go to sleep; but just as he was putting his head under his wing a large drop of water fell on him. "What a curious thing!" he cried; "there is not a single cloud in the sky, the stars are quite clear and bright, and yet it is raining. The climate in the north of Europe is really dreadful. The Reed used to like the rain, but that was merely her selfishness."

Then another drop fell.

"What is the use of a statue if it cannot keep the rain off?" he said; "I must look for a good chimney-pot," and he determined to fly away.

But before he had opened his wings, a third drop fell, and

he looked up, and saw—Ah! what did he see?

The eyes of the Happy Prince were filled with tears, and tears were running down his golden cheeks. His face was so beautiful in the moonlight that the little Swallow was filled with pity.

"Who are you?" he said.

"I am the Happy Prince."

"Why are you weeping then?" asked the Swallow; "you have quite drenched me."

"When I was alive and had a human heart," answered the statue, "I did not know what tears were, for I lived in the Palace of Sans-Souci, where sorrow is not allowed to enter. In the daytime I played with my companions in the garden, and in the evening I led the dance in the Great Hall. Round the garden ran a very lofty wall, but I never cared to ask what lay beyond it, everything about me was so beautiful. My courtiers called me the Happy Prince, and happy indeed I was, if pleasure be happiness. So I lived, and so I died. And now that I am dead they have set me up here so high that I can see all the ugliness and all the misery of my city, and though my heart is made of lead yet I cannot chose but weep."

"What! Is he not solid gold?" said the Swallow to himself. He was too polite to make any personal remarks out loud.

"Far away," continued the statue in a low musical voice, "far away in a little street there is a poor house. One of the windows is open, and through it I can see a woman seated at a table. Her face is thin and worn, and she has coarse, red hands, all pricked by the needle, for she is a seamstress. She is embroidering passion-flowers on a satin gown for the loveliest of the Queen's maids-of-honour to wear at the next Court-ball. In a bed in the corner of the room her little boy is lying ill. He has a fever, and is asking for oranges. His mother has nothing to give him but river water, so he is crying. Swallow, Swallow, little Swallow, will you not bring her the ruby out of my sword-hilt? My feet are fastened to this pedestal and I cannot move."

"I am waited for in Egypt," said the Swallow. "My friends are flying up and down the Nile, and talking to the large lotus-flowers. Soon they will go to sleep in the tomb of the great King. The King is there himself in his painted coffin. He is wrapped in yellow linen, and embalmed with spices. Round his neck is a chain of pale green jade, and his hands are like withered leaves."

"Swallow, Swallow, little Swallow," said the Prince, "will you not stay with me for one night, and be my messenger? The boy is so thirsty, and the mother so sad."

"I don't think I like boys," answered the Swallow. "Last summer, when I was staying on the river, there were two rude boys, the miller's sons, who were always throwing stones at me. They never hit me, of course; we swallows fly far too well for that, and besides, I come of a family famous for its agility; but still, it was a mark of disrespect."

But the Happy Prince looked so sad that the little Swallow was sorry. "It is very cold here," he said; "but I will stay with you for one night, and be your messenger."

"Thank you, little Swallow," said the Prince.

So the Swallow picked out the great ruby from the Prince's sword, and flew away with it in his beak over the roofs of the town.

He passed by the cathedral tower, where the white marble angels were sculptured. He passed by the palace and heard the sound of dancing. A beautiful girl came out on the balcony with her lover. "How wonderful the stars are," he said to her, "and how wonderful is the power of love!"

"I hope my dress will be ready in time for the State-ball," she answered; "I have ordered passion-flowers to be embroidered on it; but the seamstresses are so lazy."

He passed over the river, and saw the lanterns hanging to the masts of the ships. He passed over the Ghetto, and saw the old Jews bargaining with each other, and weighing out money in copper scales. At last he came to the poor house and looked in. The boy was tossing feverishly on his bed, and the mother had fallen asleep, she was so tired. In he hopped, and laid the great ruby on the table beside the woman's thimble. Then he flew gently round the bed, fanning the boy's forehead with his wings. "How cool I feel," said the boy, "I must be getting better"; and he sank into a delicious slumber.

Then the Swallow flew back to the Happy Prince, and told him what he had done. "It is curious," he remarked, "but I feel quite warm now, although it is so cold."

"That is because you have done a good action," said the Prince. And the little Swallow began to think, and then he fell asleep. Thinking always made him sleepy.

When day broke he flew down to the river and had a bath. "What a remarkable phenomenon," said the Professor of Ornithology as he was passing over the bridge. "A swallow in winter!" And he wrote a long letter about it to the local newspaper. Every one quoted it, it was full of so many words that they could not understand.

"To-night I go to Egypt," said the Swallow, and he was in high spirits at the prospect. He visited all the public monuments, and sat a long time on top of the church steeple. Wherever he went the Sparrows chirruped, and said to each other, "What a distinguished stranger!" so he enjoyed himself very much.

When the moon rose he flew back to the Happy Prince. "Have you any commissions for Egypt?" he cried; "I am just starting."

"Swallow, Swallow, little Swallow," said the Prince, "will you not stay with me one night longer?"

"I am waited for in Egypt," answered the Swallow. "To-morrow my friends will fly up to the Second Cataract. The river-horse couches there among the bulrushes, and on a great granite throne sits the God Memnon. All night long he watches the stars, and when the morning star shines he utters one cry of joy, and then he is silent. At noon the yellow lions come down to the water's edge to drink. They have eyes like green beryls, and their roar is louder than the roar of the cataract."

"Swallow, Swallow, little Swallow," said the Prince, "far away across the city I see a young man in a garret. He is leaning over a desk covered with papers, and in a tumbler by his side there is a bunch of withered violets. His hair is brown and crisp, and his lips are red as a pomegranate, and he has large and dreamy eyes. He is trying to finish a play for the Director of the Theatre, but he is too cold to write any more. There is no fire in the grate, and hunger has made him faint."

"I will wait with you one night longer," said the Swallow, who really had a good heart. "Shall I take him another ruby?"

"Alas! I have no ruby now," said the Prince; "my eyes are

all that I have left. They are made of rare sapphires, which were brought out of India a thousand years ago. Pluck out one of them and take it to him. He will sell it to the jeweller, and buy food and firewood, and finish his play."

"Dear Prince," said the Swallow, "I cannot do that"; and he began to weep.

"Swallow, Swallow, little Swallow," said the Prince, "do as I command you."

So the Swallow plucked out the Prince's eye, and flew away to the student's garret. It was easy enough to get in, as there was a hole in the roof. Through this he darted, and came into the room. The young man had his head buried in his hands, so he did not hear the flutter of the bird's wings, and when he looked up he found the beautiful sapphire lying on the withered violets.

"I am beginning to be appreciated," he cried; "this is from some great admirer. Now I can finish my play," and he looked quite happy.

The next day the Swallow flew down to the harbour. He sat on the mast of a large vessel and watched the sailors hauling big chests out of the hold with ropes. "Heave a-hoy!" they shouted as each chest came up. "I am going to Egypt"! cried the Swallow, but nobody minded, and when the moon rose he flew back to the Happy Prince.

"I am come to bid you good-bye," he cried.

"Swallow, Swallow, little Swallow," said the Prince, "will you not stay with me one night longer?"

"It is winter," answered the Swallow, "and the chill snow will soon be here. In Egypt the sun is warm on the green palm-trees, and the crocodiles lie in the mud and look lazily about them. My companions are building a nest in the Temple of Baalbec, and the pink and white doves are watching them, and cooing to each other. Dear Prince, I must leave you, but I will never forget you, and next spring I will bring you back two beautiful jewels in place of those you have given away. The ruby shall be redder than a red rose, and the sapphire shall be as blue as the great sea."

"In the square below," said the Happy Prince, "there stands a little match-girl. She has let her matches fall in the gutter, and they are all spoiled. Her father will beat her if she does not bring home some money, and she is crying. She has no shoes or stockings, and her little head is bare. Pluck out my other eye, and give it to her, and her father will not beat her."

"I will stay with you one night longer," said the Swallow, "but I cannot pluck out your eye. You would be quite blind then."

"Swallow, Swallow, little Swallow," said the Prince, "do as I command you."

So he plucked out the Prince's other eye, and darted down with it. He swooped past the match-girl, and slipped the jewel into the palm of her hand. "What a lovely bit of glass," cried the little girl; and she ran home, laughing.

Then the Swallow came back to the Prince. "You are blind now," he said, "so I will stay with you always."

"No, little Swallow," said the poor Prince, "you must go away to Egypt."

"I will stay with you always," said the Swallow, and he slept at the Prince's feet.

All the next day he sat on the Prince's shoulder, and told him stories of what he had seen in strange lands. He told him of the red ibises, who stand in long rows on the banks of the Nile, and catch gold-fish in their beaks; of the Sphinx, who is as old as the world itself, and lives in the desert, and knows everything; of the merchants, who walk slowly by the side of their camels, and carry amber beads in their hands; of the King of the Mountains of the Moon, who is as black as ebony, and worships a large crystal; of the great green snake that sleeps in a palm-tree, and has twenty priests to feed it with honey-cakes; and of the pygmies who sail over a big lake on large flat leaves, and are always at war with the butterflies.

"Dear little Swallow," said the Prince, "you tell me of marvellous things, but more marvellous than anything is the suffering of men and of women. There is no Mystery so great as Misery. Fly over my city, little Swallow, and tell me what you see there."

So the Swallow flew over the great city, and saw the rich making merry in their beautiful houses, while the beggars were sitting at the gates. He flew into dark lanes, and saw the white faces of starving children looking out listlessly at the black streets. Under the archway of a bridge two little boys were lying in one another's arms to try and keep themselves warm. "How hungry we are!" they said. "You must not lie here," shouted the Watchman, and they wandered out into the rain.

Then he flew back and told the Prince what he had seen.

"I am covered with fine gold," said the Prince, "you must take it off, leaf by leaf, and give it to my poor; the living always think that gold can make them happy."

Leaf after leaf of the fine gold the Swallow picked off, till the Happy Prince looked quite dull and grey. Leaf after leaf of the fine gold he brought to the poor, and the children's faces grew rosier, and they laughed and played games in the street. "We have bread now!" they cried.

Then the snow came, and after the snow came the frost. The streets looked as if they were made of silver, they were so bright and glistening; long icicles like crystal daggers hung down from the eaves of the houses, everybody went about in furs, and the little boys wore scarlet caps and skated on the ice.

The poor little Swallow grew colder and colder, but he would not leave the Prince, he loved him too well. He picked up crumbs outside the baker's door when the baker was not looking and tried to keep himself warm by flapping his wings.

But at last he knew that he was going to die. He had just strength to fly up to the Prince's shoulder once more. "Good-bye, dear Prince!" he murmured, "will you let me kiss your hand?"

"I am glad that you are going to Egypt at last, little Swallow," said the Prince, "you have stayed too long here; but you must kiss me on the lips, for I love you."

"It is not to Egypt that I am going," said the Swallow. "I am going to the House of Death. Death is the brother of Sleep, is he not?"

And he kissed the Happy Prince on the lips, and fell down dead at his feet.

At that moment a curious crack sounded inside the statue, as if something had broken. The fact is that the leaden heart had snapped right in two. It certainly was a dreadfully hard frost.

Early the next morning the Mayor was walking in the square

below in company with the Town Councillors. As they passed the column he looked up at the statue: "Dear me! how shabby the Happy Prince looks!" he said.

"How shabby indeed!" cried the Town Councillors, who always agreed with the Mayor; and they went up to look at it.

"The ruby has fallen out of his sword, his eyes are gone, and he is golden no longer," said the Mayor in fact, "he is litttle better than a beggar!"

"Little better than a beggar," said the Town Councillors.

"And here is actually a dead bird at his feet!" continued the Mayor. "We must really issue a proclamation that birds are not to be allowed to die here." And the Town Clerk made a note of the suggestion.

So they pulled down the statue of the Happy Prince. "As he is no longer beautiful he is no longer useful," said the Art Professor at the University.

Then they melted the statue in a furnace, and the Mayor held a meeting of the Corporation to decide what was to be done with the metal. "We must have another statue, of course," he said, "and it shall be a statue of myself."

"Of myself," said each of the Town Councillors, and they quarrelled. When I last heard of them they were quarrelling still.

"What a strange thing!" said the overseer of the workmen at the foundry. "This broken lead heart will not melt in the furnace. We must throw it away." So they threw it on a dust-heap where the dead Swallow was also lying.

"Bring me the two most precious things in the city," said God to one of His Angels; and the Angel brought Him the leaden heart and the dead bird.

"You have rightly chosen," said God, "for in my garden of Paradise this little bird shall sing for evermore, and in my city of gold the Happy Prince shall praise me."

# The Sphinx without a Secret

***Oscar Wilde***

One afternoon I was sitting outside the Cafe de la Paix, watching the splendour and shabbiness of Parisian life, and wondering over my vermouth at the strange panorama of pride and poverty that was passing before me, when I heard some one call my name. I turned round, and saw Lord Murchison. We had not met since we had been at college together, nearly ten years before, so I was delighted to come across him again, and we shook hands warmly. At Oxford we had been great friends. I had liked him immensely, he was so handsome, so high-spirited, and so honourable. We used to say of him that he would be the best of fellows, if he did not always speak the truth, but I think we really admired him all the more for his frankness. I found him a good deal changed. He looked anxious and puzzled, and seemed to be in doubt about something. I felt it could not be modern scepticism, for Murchison was the stoutest of Tories, and believed in the Pentateuch as firmly as he believed in the House of Peers; so I concluded that it was a woman, and asked him if he was married yet.

'I don't understand women well enough,' he answered.

'My dear Gerald,' I said, 'women are meant to be loved, not to be understood.'

'I cannot love where I cannot trust,' he replied.

'I believe you have a mystery in your life, Gerald,' I exclaimed; 'tell me about it.'

'Let us go for a drive,' he answered, 'it is too crowded here. No, not a yellow carriage, any other colour – there, that dark-green one will do;' and in a few moments we were trotting down the boulevard in the direction of the Madeleine.

'Where shall we go to?' I said.

'Oh, anywhere you like!' he answered – 'to the restaurant

in the Bois; we will dine there, and you shall tell me all about yourself.'

'I want to hear about you first,' I said. 'Tell me your mystery.'

He took from his pocket a little silver-clasped morocco case, and handed it to me. I opened it. Inside there was the photograph of a woman. She was tall and slight, and strangely picturesque with her large vague eyes and loosened hair. She looked like a clairvoyante, and was wrapped in rich furs.

'What do you think of that face?' he said; 'is it truthful?'

I examined it carefully. It seemed to me the face of some one who had a secret, but whether that secret was good or evil I could not say. Its beauty was a beauty moulded out of many mysteries – the beauty, in face, which is psychological, not plastic – and the faint smile that just played across the lips was far too subtle to be really sweet.

'Well,' he cried impatiently, 'what do you say?'

'She is the Gioconda in sables,' I answered. 'Let me know all about her.'

'Not now,' he said; 'after dinner;' and began to talk of other things.

When the waiter brought us our coffee and cigarettes I reminded Gerald of his promise. He rose from his seat, walked two or three times up and down the room, and, sinking into an armchair, told me the following story: -

'One evening,' he said, 'I was walking down Bond Street about five o'clock. There was a terrific crush of carriages, and the traffic was almost stopped. Close to the pavement was standing a little yellow brougham, which, for some reason or other, attracted my attention. As I passed by there looked out from it the face I showed you this afternoon. I fascinated me immediately. All that night I kept thinking of it, and all the next day. I wandered up and down that wretched Row, peering into every carriage, and waiting for the yellow brougham; but I could not find ma belle inconnue, and at last I began to think she was merely a dream. About a week afterwards I was dining with Madame de Rastail. Dinner was for eight o'clock; but at half-past eight we were still waiting in the drawing-room. Finally the servant threw open the door, and announced Lady Alroy. It was the woman

I had been looking for. She came in very slowly, looking like a moon-beam in grey lace, and, to my intense delight, I was asked to take her in to dinner. After we had sat down I remarked quite innocently, "I think I caught sight of you in Bond Street some time ago, Lady Alroy." She grew very pale, and said to me in a low voice, "Pray do not talk so loud; you may be overheard." I felt miserable at having made such a bad beginning, and plunged recklessly into the subject of French plays. She spoke very little, always in the same low musical voice, and seemed as if she was afraid of some one listening. I fell passionately, stupidly in love, and the indefinable atmosphere of mystery that surrounded her excited my most ardent curiosity. When she was going away, which she did very soon after dinner, I asked her if I might call and see her. She hesitated for a moment, glanced round to see if any one was near us, and then said, "Yes; to-morrow at a quarter to five." I begged Madame de Rastail to tell me about her; but all that I could learn was that she was a window with a beautiful house in Park Lane, and as some scientific bore began a dissertation of widows, as exemplifying the survival of the matrimonially fittest, I left and went home.

'The next day I arrived at Park Lane punctual to the moment, but was told by the butler that Lady Alroy had just gone out. I went down to the club quite unhappy and very much puzzled, and after long consideration wrote her a letter, asking if I might be allowed to try my chance some other afternoon. I had no answer for several days, but at last I got a little note saying she would be at home on Sunday at four, and with this extraordinary postscript: "Please do not write to me here again; I will explain when I see you." On Sunday she received me, and was perfectly charming; but when I was going away she begged of me, if I ever had occasion to write to her again, to address my letter to "Mrs. Knox, care of Whittaker's Library, Green Street." "There are reasons," she said, " why I cannot receive letters in my own house."

'All through the season I saw a great deal of her, and the atmosphere of mystery never left her. Sometimes I thought that she was in the power of some man, but she looked so unapproachable that I could not believe it. It was really very difficult for me to come to any conclusion, for she was like one of those strange crystals that one sees in museums, which are at one moment clear, and at another clouded. At last I determined to ask her to be my wife: I was sick and tired of the incessant secrecy that she imposed on all my visits, and on the few letters I sent her. I wrote to her at the library to ask her if she could see me the following Monday at six. She answered yes, and I was in the seventh heaven of delight. I was infatuated with her: in spite of the mystery, I thought then – in consequence of it, I see now. No; it was the woman herself I loved. The mystery troubled me, maddened me. Why did chance put me in its track?'

'You discovered it, then?' I cried.

'I fear so,' he answered. 'You can judge for yourself.'

'When Monday came round I went to lunch with my uncle, and about four o'clock found myself in the Marylebone Road. My uncle, you know, lives in Regent's Park. I wanted to get to Piccadilly, and took a short cut through a lot of shabby little streets. Suddenly I saw in front of me Lady Alroy, deeply veiled and walking very fast. On coming to the last house in the street, she went up the steps, took out a latch-key, and let herself in. "Here is the mystery," I said to myself; and I hurried on and examined the house. It seemed a sort of place for letting lodgings. On the doorstep lay her handkerchief, which she had dropped. I picked it up and put it in my pocket. Then I began to consider what I should do. I came to the conclusion that I had no right to spy on her, and I drove down to the club. At six I called to see her. She was lying on a sofa, in a tea-gown of silver tissue looped up by some strange moonstones that she always wore. She was looking quite lovely. "I am so glad to see you," she said; "I have not been out all day." I stared at her in amazement, and pulling the handkerchief out of my pocket, handed it to her. "You dropped this in Cumnor Street this afternoon, Lady Alroy," I said very calmly. She looked at me in terror, but made no attempt to take the handkerchief. "What were you doing there?" I asked. "What right have you to question me?" she answered. "The right of a man who loves you," I replied; "I came here to ask you to be my wife." She hid her face in her hands, and burst into floods of tears. "You must tell me," I continued. She stood up, and , looking me straight in the face, said, "Lord Murchison, there is nothing to tell you." – "You went to meet some one," I cried; "this is your mystery." She grew dreadfully white, and said, "I went to meet no one," – "Can't you tell the truth?" I exclaimed. "I have told it," she replied. I was mad, frantic; I don't know what I said, but I said terrible things to her. Finally I rushed out of the house. She wrote me a letter the next day; I sent it back unopened, and started for Norway with Alan Colville. After a month I came back, and the first thing I saw in the Morning Post was the death of Lady Alroy. She had caught a chill at the Opera, and had died in five days of congestion of the lungs. I shut myself up and saw no one. I had loved her so much, I had loved her so madly. good god! how I had loved that woman!'

'You went to the street, to the house in it?' I said.

'Yes,' he answered.

'One day I went to Cumnor Street. I could not help it; I was tortured with doubt. I knocked at the door, and a respectable-looking woman opened it to me. I asked her if she had any rooms to let. "Well, sir," she replied, "the drawing-rooms are supposed to be let; but I have not seen the lady for three months, and as rent is owing on them, you can have them." – "Is this the lady?" I said, showing the photograph. "That's her, sure enough," she exclaimed; "and when is she coming back, sir?" – "The lady is dead," I replied. "Oh, sir, I hope not!" said the woman; "she was my best lodger. She paid me three guineas a week merely to sit in my drawing-rooms now and then." – "She met some one here?" I said; but the woman assured me that it was not so, that she always came alone, and saw no one. "What on earth did she do here?" I cried. "She simply sat in the drawing-room, sir, reading books, and sometimes had tea," the woman answered. I did not know what to say, so I have her a sovereign and went away. Now, what do you think it all meant? You don't believe the woman was telling the truth?'

'I do.'

'Then why did Lady Alroy go there?'

'My dear Gerald,' I answered, 'Lady Alroy was simply a woman with a mania for mystery. She took these rooms for the pleasure of going there with her veil down, and imagining she was a heroine. She had a passion for secrecy, but she herself was merely a Sphinx without a secret.'

'Do you really think so?'

'I am sure of it,' I replied.

He took out the morocco case, opened it, and looked at the photograph. 'I wonder?' he said at last.

# A Fight with a Cannon

***Victor Hugo***

La Vieuville was suddenly cut short by a cry of despair, and a the same time a noise was heard wholly unlike any other sound. The cry and sounds came from within the vessel.

The captain and lieutenant rushed toward the gun-deck but could not get down. All the gunners were pouring up in dismay.

Something terrible had just happened.

One of the carronades of the battery, a twenty-four pounder, had broken loose.

This is the most dangerous accident that can possibly take place on shipboard. Nothing more terrible can happen to a sloop of was in open sea and under full sail.

A cannon that breaks its moorings suddenly becomes some strange, supernatural beast. It is a machine transformed into a monster. That short mass on wheels moves like a billiard-ball, rolls with the rolling of the ship, plunges with the pitching goes, comes, stops, seems to meditate, starts on its course again, shoots like an arrow from one end of the vessel to the other, whirls around, slips away, dodges, rears, bangs, crashes, kills, exterminates. It is a battering ram capriciously assaulting a wall. Add to this the fact that the ram is of metal, the wall of wood.

It is matter set free; one might say, this eternal slave was avenging itself; it seems as if the total depravity concealed in what we call inanimate things has escaped, and burst forth all of a sudden; it appears to lose patience, and to take a strange mysterious revenge; nothing more relentless than this wrath of the inanimate. This enraged lump leaps like a panther, it has the clumsiness of an elephant, the nimbleness of a mouse, the obstinacy of an ox, the uncertainty of the billows, the zigzag of the lightning, the deafness of the grave. It weighs ten thousand pounds, and it rebounds like a child's ball. It spins and then abruptly darts off at right angles.

And what is to be done? How put an end to it? A tempest ceases, a cyclone passes over, a wind dies down, a broken mast can be replaced, a leak can be stopped, a fire extinguished, but that will become of this enormous brute of bronze. How can it be captured? You can reason with a bulldog, astonish a bull, fascinate a boa, frighten a tiger, tame a lion; but you have no resource against this monster, a loose cannon. You can not kill it, it is dead; and at the same time it lives. It lives with a sinister life which comes to it from the infinite. The deck beneath it gives it full swing. It is moved by the ship, which is moved by the sea, which is moved by the wind. This destroyer is a toy. The ship, the waves, the winds, all play with it, hence its frightful animation. What is to be done with this apparatus? How fetter this stupendous engine of destruction? How anticipate its comings and goings, its returns, its stops, its shocks? Any one of its blows on the side of the ship may stave it in. How foretell its frightful meanderings? It is dealing with a projectile, which alters its mind, which seems to have ideas, and changes its direction every instant. How check the course of what must be avoided? The horrible cannon struggles, advances, backs, strikes right, strikes left, retreats, passes by, disconcerts expectation, grinds p obstacles, crushes men like flies. All the terror of the situation is in the fluctuations of the flooring. How fight an inclined plane subject to caprices? The ship has, so to speak, in its belly, an imprisoned thunderstorm, striving to escape; something like a thunderbolt rumbling above an earthquake.

In an instant the whole crew was on foot. It was the fault of the gun captain, who had neglected to fasten the screw-nut of the mooring-chain, and had insecurely clogged the four wheels of the gun carriage; this gave play to the sole and the framework, separated the two platforms, and the breeching. The tackle had given way, so that the cannon was no longer firm on its carriage. The stationary breeching, which prevents recoil, was not in use at this time. A heavy sea struck the port, the carronade, insecurely fastened, had recoiled and broken its chain, and began its terrible course over the deck.

To form an idea of this strange sliding, let one imagine a

drop of water running over a glass.

At the moment when the fastenings gave way, the gunners were in the battery, some in groups, others scattered about, busied with the customary work among sailors getting ready for a signal for action. The carronade, hurled forward by the pitching of the vessel, made a gap in this crowd of men and crushed four at the first blow; then sliding back and shot out again as the ship rolled, it cut in two a fifth unfortunate, and knocked a piece of the battery against the larboard side with such force as to unship it. This caused the cry of distress just heard. All the men rushed to the companion-way. The gun-deck was vacated in a twinkling.

The enormous gun was left alone. It was given up to itself. It was its own master and master of the ship. It could do what it pleased. This whole crew, accustomed to laugh in time of battle, now trembled. To describe the terror is impossible.

Captain Boisberthelot and Lieutenant la Vieuville, although both dauntless men, stopped at the head of the companion-way and, dumb, pale, and hesitating, looked down on the deck below. Some one elbowed past and went down.

It was their passenger, the peasant, the man of whom they had just been speaking a moment before.

Reaching the foot of the companion-way, he stopped.

The cannon was rushing back and forth on the deck. One might have supposed it to be the living chariot of the Apocalypse. The marine lantern swinging overhead added a dizzy shifting of light and shade to the picture. The form of the cannon disappeared in the violence of its course, and it looked now black in the light, now mysteriously white in the darkness.

It went on in its destructive work. It had already shattered four other guns and made two gaps in the side of the ship, fortunately above the water-line, but where the water would come in, in case of heavy weather. It rushed frantically against the framework; the strong timbers withstood the shock; the curved shape of the wood gave them great power of resistance; but they creaked beneath the blows of this huge club, beating on all sides at once, with a strange sort of ubiquity. The percussions of a grain of shot shaken in a bottle are not swifter or more senseless. The four wheels passed back and forth over the dead men, cutting them, carving them, slashing them, till the five corpses were a score of stumps rolling across the deck; the heads of the dead men seemed to cry out; streams of blood curled over the deck with the rolling of the vessel; the planks, damaged in several places, began to gape open. The whole ship was filled with the horrid noise and confusion.

The captain promptly recovered his presence of mind and ordered everything that could check and impede the cannon's mad course to be thrown through the hatchway down on the gun-deck – mattresses, hammocks, spare sails, rolls of cordage, bags belonging to the crew, and bales of counterfeit assignats, of which the corvette carried a large quantity – a characteristic piece of English villainy regarded as legitimate warfare.

But what could these rags do? As nobody dared to go below to dispose of them properly, they were reduced to lint in a few minutes.

There was just sea enough to make the accident as bad as possible. A tempest would have been desirable, for it might have upset the cannon, and with its four wheels once in the air there would be some hope of getting it under control. Meanwhile, the havoc increased.

There were splits and fractures in the masts, which are set into the framework of the keel and rise above the decks of ships like great, round pillars. The convulsive blows of the cannon had cracked the mizzenmast, and had cut into the mainmast.

The battery was being ruined. Ten pieces out of thirty were disabled; the breaches in the side of the vessel were increasing, and the corvette was beginning to leak.

The old passenger having gone down to the gun-deck, stood like a man of stone at the foot of the steps. He cast a stern glance over this scene of devastation. He did not move. It seemed impossible to take a step forward. Every movement of the loose carronade threatened the ship's destruction. A few moments more and shipwreck would be inevitable.

They must perish or put a speedy end to the disaster; some course must be decided on; but what? What an opponent was this carronade! Something must be done to stop this terrible madness

– to capture this lightning – to overthrow this thunderbolt.

Boisberthelot said to La Vieuville:

"Do you believe in God, chevalier?"

La Vieuville replied:

"Yes – no. Sometimes."

"During a tempest?"

"Yes, and in moments like this."

"God alone can save us from this," said Boisberthelot.

Everybody was silent, letting the carronade continue its horrible din.

Outside, the waves beating against the ship responded with their blows to the shocks of the cannon. It was like two hammers alternating.

Suddenly, in the midst of this inaccessible ring, where the escaped cannon was leaping, a man was seen to appear, with an iron bar in his hand. He was the author of the catastrophe, the captain of the gun, guilty of criminal carelessness, and the cause of the accident, the master of the carronade. Having done the mischief, he was anxious to repair it. He had seized the iron bar in one hand, a tiller-rope with a slip-noose in the other, and jumped, down the hatchway to the gun-deck.

Then began an awful sight; a Titanic scene; the contest between gun and gunner; the battle of matter and intelligence; the duel between man and the inanimate.

The man stationed himself in a corner, and, with bar and rope in his two hands, he leaned against one of the riders, braced himself on his legs, which seemed two steel posts; and livid, calm, tragic, as if rooted to the deck, he waited.

He waited for the cannon to pass by him.

The gunner knew his gun, and it seemed to him as if the gun ought to know him. He had lived long with it. How many times he had thrust his hand into its mouth! It was his own familiar monster. He began to speak to it as if it were his dog.

"Come!" he said. Perhaps he loved it.

He seemed to wish it to come to him.

But to come to him was to come upon him. And then he would be lost. How could he avoid being crushed? That was the question. All looked on in terror.

Not a breast breathed freely, unless perhaps that of the old man, who was alone in the battery with the two contestants, a stern witness.

He might be crushed himself by the cannon. He did not stir.

Beneath them the sea blindly directed the contest.

At the moment when the gunner, accepting this frightful hand-to-hand conflict, challenged the cannon, some chance rocking of the sea caused the carronade to remain for an instant motionless and as if stupefied. "Come, now!" said the man.

It seemed to listen.

Suddenly it leaped toward him. The man dodged the blow.

The battle began. Battle unprecedented. Frailty struggling against the invulnerable. The gladiator of flesh attacking the beast of brass. On one side, brute force; on the other, a human soul.

All this was taking place in semi-darkness. It was like the shadowy vision of a miracle.

A soul – strange to say, one would have thought the cannon also had a soul; but a soul full of hatred and rage. This sightless thing seemed to have eyes. The monster appeared to lie in wait for the man. One would have at least believed that there was craft in this mass. It also chose its time.

It was a strange, gigantic insect of metal, having or seeming to have the will of a demon. For a moment this colossal locust would beat against the low ceiling overhead, then it would come down on its four wheels like a tiger on its four paws, and begin to run at the man. He, supple, nimble, expert, writhed away like an adder from all these lightning movements. He avoided a collision, but the blows which he parried fell against the, vessel, and continued their work of destruction.

An end of broken chain was left hanging to the carronade. This chain had in some strange way become twisted about the screw of the cascabel. One end of the chain was fastened to the gun-carriage. The other, left loose, whirled desperately about the cannon, making all its blows more dangerous.

The screw held it in a firm grip, adding a thong to a battering-ram, making a terrible whirlwind around the cannon, an iron lash in a brazen hand. This chain complicated the contest.

However, the man went on fighting. Occasionally, it was

the man who attacked the cannon; he would creep along the side of the vessel, bar and rope in hand; and the cannon, as if it understood, and as though suspecting some snare, would flee away. The man, bent on victory, pursued it.

Such things can not long continue. The cannon seemed to say to itself, all of a sudden, "Come, now! Make an end of it!" and it stopped. One felt that the crisis was at hand. The cannon, as if in suspense, seemed to have, or really had – for to all it was a living being – a ferocious malice prepense. It made a sudden, quick dash at the gunner. The gunner sprang out of the way, let it pass by, and cried out to it with a laugh, "Try it again!" The cannon, as if enraged, smashed a carronade on the port side; then, again seized by the invisible sling which controlled it, it was hurled to the starboard side at the man, who made his escape. Three carronades gave way under the blows of the cannon; then, as if blind and not knowing what more to do, it turned its back on the man, rolled from stern to bow, injured the stern and made a breach in the planking of the prow. The man took refuge at the foot of the steps, not far from the old man who was looking on. The gunner held his iron bar in rest. The cannon seemed to notice it, and without taking the trouble to turn around, slid back on the man, swift as the blow of an axe. The man, driven against the side of the ship, was lost. The whole crew cried out with horror.

But the old passenger, till this moment motionless, darted forth more quickly than any of this wildly swift rapidity. He seized a package of counterfeit assignats, and, at the risk of being crushed, succeeded in throwing it between the wheels of the carronade. This decisive and perilous movement could not have been made with more exactness and precision by a man trained in all the exercises described in Durosel's "Manual of Gun Practice at Sea."

The package had the effect of a clog. A pebble may stop a log, the branch of a tree turn aside an avalanche. The carronade stumbled. The gunner, taking advantage of this critical opportunity, plunged his iron bar between the spokes of one of the hind wheels. The cannon stopped. It leaned forward. The man, using the bar as a lever, held it in equilibrium. The heavy mass was overthrown, with the crash of a falling bell, and the man, rushing with all his might, dripping with perspiration, passed the slipnoose around the bronze neck of the subdued monster.

It was ended. The man had conquered. The ant had control over the mastodon; the pygmy had taken the thunderbolt prisoner.

The mariners and sailors clapped their hands.

The whole crew rushed forward with cables and chains, and in an instant the cannon was secured.

The gunner saluted the passenger.

"Sir," he said, "you have saved my life."

The old man had resumed his impassive attitude, and made no reply.

The man had conquered, but the cannon might be said to have conquered as well. Immediate shipwreck had been avoided, but the corvette was not saved. The damage to the vessel seemed beyond repair. There were five breaches in her sides, one, very large, in the bow; twenty of the thirty carronades lay useless in their frames. The one which had just been captured and chained again was disabled; the screw of the cascabel was sprung, and consequently leveling the gun made impossible. The battery was reduced to nine pieces. The ship was leaking. It was necessary to repair the damages at once, and to work the pumps.

The gun-deck, now that one could look over it, was frightful to behold. The inside of an infuriated elephant's cage would not be more completely demolished.

However great might be the necessity of escaping observation, the necessity of immediate safety was still more imperative to the corvette. They had been obliged to light up the deck with lanterns hung here and there on the sides.

However, all the while this tragic play was going on, the crew were absorbed by a question of life and death, and they were wholly ignorant of what was taking place outside the vessel. The fog had grown thicker; the weather had changed; the wind had worked its pleasure with the ship; they were out of their course, with Jersey and Guernsey close at hand, further to the south than they ought to have been, and in the midst of a heavy sea. Great billows kissed the gaping wounds of the vessel – kisses full of danger. The rocking of the sea threatened destruction. The breeze had become a gale. A squall, a tempest, perhaps, was brewing. It was impossible to see four waves ahead.

While the crew were hastily repairing the damages to the gun-deck, stopping the leaks, and putting in place the guns which had been uninjured in the disaster, the old passenger had gone on deck again.

He stood with his back against the mainmast.

He had not noticed a proceeding which had taken place on the vessel. The Chevalier de la Vieuville had drawn up the marines in line on both sides of the mainmast, and at the sound of the boatswain's whistle the sailors formed in line, standing on the yards.

The Count de Boisberthelot approached the passenger.

Behind the captain walked a man, haggard, out of breath, his dress disordered, but still with a look of satisfaction on his face.

It was the gunner who had just shown himself so skilful in subduing monsters, and who had gained the mastery over the cannon.

The count gave the military salute to the old man in peasant's dress, and said to him:

"General, there is the man."

The gunner remained standing, with downcast eyes, in military attitude.

The Count de Boisberthelot continued:

"General, in consideration of what this man has done, do you not think there is something due him from his commander?"

"I think so," said the old man.

"Please give your orders," replied Boisberthelot.

"It is for you to give them, you are the captain."

"But you are the general," replied Boisberthelot.

The old man looked at the gunner.

"Come forward," he said.

The gunner approached.

The old man turned toward the Count de Boisberthelot, took off the cross of Saint-Louis from the captain's coat and fastened it on the gunner's jacket.

"Hurrah!" cried the sailors.

The mariners presented arms.

And the old passenger, pointing to the dazzled gunner, added: "Now, have this man shot."

Dismay succeeded the cheering.

Then in the midst of the death-like stillness, the old man raised his voice and said:

"Carelessness has compromised this vessel. At this very hour it is perhaps lost. To be at sea is to be in front of the enemy. A ship making a voyage is an army waging war. The tempest is concealed, but it is at hand. The whole sea is an ambuscade. Death is the penalty of any misdemeanor committed in the face of the enemy. No fault is reparable. Courage should be rewarded, and negligence punished."

These words fell one after another, slowly, solemnly, in a sort of inexorable metre, like the blows of an axe upon an oak.

And the man, looking at the soldiers, added:

"Let it be done."

The man on whose jacket hung the shining cross of Saint-Louis bowed his head.

At a signal from Count de Boisberthelot, two sailors went below and came back bringing the hammock-shroud; the chaplain, who since they sailed had been at prayer in the officers' quarters, accompanied the two sailors; a sergeant detached twelve marines from the line and arranged them in two files, six by six; the gunner, without uttering a word, placed himself between the two files. The chaplain, crucifix in hand, advanced and stood beside him. "March," said the sergeant. The platoon marched with slow steps to the bow of the vessel. The two sailors, carrying the shroud, followed. A gloomy silence fell over the vessel. A hurricane howled in the distance.

A few moments later, a light flashed, a report sounded through the darkness, then all was still, and the sound of a body falling into the sea was heard.

The old passenger, still leaning against the mainmast, had crossed his arms, and was buried in thought.

Boisberthelot pointed to him with the forefinger of his left hand, and said to La Vieuville in a low voice:

"La Vendée has a head."

# The Final Problem

*Sir Arthur Conan Doyle*

It is with a heavy heart that I take up my pen to write these the last words in which I shall ever record the singular gifts by which my friend Mr. Sherlock Holmes was distinguished. In an incoherent and, as I deeply feel, an entirely inadequate fashion, I have endeavored to give some account of my strange experiences in his company from the chance which first brought us together at the period of the "Study in Scarlet," up to the time of his interference in the matter of the "Naval Treaty"—and interference which had the unquestionable effect of preventing a serious international complication.

It was my intention to have stopped there, and to have said nothing of that event which has created a void in my life which the lapse of two years has done little to fill. My hand has been forced, however, by the recent letters in which Colonel James Moriarty defends the memory of his brother, and I have no choice but to lay the facts before the public exactly as they occurred. I alone know the absolute truth of the matter, and I am satisfied that the time has come when on good purpose is to be served by its suppression.

As far as I know, there have been only three accounts in the public press: that in the Journal de Genève on May 6th, 1891, the Reuters dispatch in the English papers on May 7th, and finally the recent letter to which I have alluded. Of these the first and second were extremely condensed, while the last is, as I shall now show, an absolute perversion of the facts. It lies with me to tell for the first time what really took place between Professor Moriarty and Mr. Sherlock Holmes. It may be remembered that after my marriage, and my subsequent start in private practice, the very intimate relations which had existed between Holmes and myself became to some extent modified. He still came to me from time to time when he desired a companion in his investigation, but these occasions grew more and more seldom, until I find that in the year 1890 there were only three cases of which I retain any record. During the winter of that year and the early spring of 1891, I saw in the papers that he had been engaged by the French government upon a matter of supreme importance, and I received two notes from Holmes, dated from Narbonne and from Nimes, from which I gathered that his stay in France was likely to be a long one.

It was with some surprise, therefore, that I saw him walk into my consulting-room upon the evening of April 24th. It struck me that he was looking even paler and thinner than usual. "Yes, I have been using myself up rather too freely," he remarked, in answer to my look rather than to my words; "I have been a little pressed of late. Have you any objection to my closing your shutters?"

The only light in the room came from the lamp upon the table at which I had been reading. Holmes edged his way round the wall and flinging the shutters together, he bolted them securely.

"You are afraid of something?" I asked.

"Well, I am."

"Of what?"

"Of air-guns."

"My dear Holmes, what do you mean?"

"I think that you know me well enough, Watson, to understand that I am by no means a nervous man. At the same time, it is stupidity rather than courage to refuse to recognize danger when it is close upon you. Might I trouble you for a match?" He drew in the smoke of his cigarette as if the soothing influence was grateful to him.

"I must apologize for calling so late," said he, "and I must further beg you to be so unconventional as to allow me to leave your house presently by scrambling over your back garden wall."

"But what does it all mean?" I asked.

He held out his hand, and I saw in the light of the lamp that two of his knuckles were burst and bleeding. "It is not an airy nothing, you see," said he, smiling. "On the contrary, it is solid enough for a man to break his hand over. Is Mrs. Watson in?"

"She is away upon a visit."

"Indeed! You are alone?"

"Quite."

"Then it makes it the easier for me to propose that you should come away with me for a week to the Continent."

"Where?"

"Oh, anywhere. It's all the same to me."

There was something very strange in all this. It was not Holmes's nature to take an aimless holiday, and something about his pale, worn face told me that his nerves were at their highest tension.

He saw the question in my eyes, and, putting his fingertips together and his elbows upon his knees, he explained the situation. "You have probably never heard of Professor Moriarty?" said he.

"Never."

"Aye, there's the genius and the wonder of the thing!" he cried. "The man pervades London, and no one has heard of him. That's what puts him on a pinnacle in the records of crime. I tell you, Watson, in all seriousness, that if I could beat that man, if I could free society of him, I should feel that my own career had reached its summit, and I should be prepared to turn to some more placid line in life. Between ourselves, the recent cases in which I have been of assistance to the royal family of Scandinavia, and to the French republic, have left me in such a position that I could continue to live in the quiet fashion which is most congenial to me, and to concentrate my attention upon my chemical researches. But I could not rest, Watson, I could not sit quiet in my chair, if I thought that such a man as Professor Moriarty were walking the streets of London unchallenged."

"What has he done, then?"

"His career has been an extraordinary one. He is a man of good birth and excellent education, endowed by nature with a phenomenal mathematical faculty. At the age of twenty-one he wrote a treatise upon the Binomial Theorem, which has had a European vogue. On the strength of it he won the Mathematical Chair at one of our smaller universities, and had, to all appearance, a most brilliant career before him. But the man had hereditary tendencies of the most diabolical kind. A criminal strain ran in his blood, which, instead of being modified, was increased and rendered infinitely more dangerous by his extraordinary mental powers. Dark rumors gathered round him in the university town, and eventually he was compelled to resign his chair and to come down to London, where he set up as an army coach. So much is known to the world, but what I am telling you now is what I have myself discovered.

"As you are aware, Watson, there is no one who knows the higher criminal world of London so well as I do. For years past I have continually been conscious of some power behind the malefactor, some deep organizing power which forever stands in the way of the law, and throws its shield over the wrongdoer. Again and again in cases of the most varying sorts—forgery cases, robberies, murders—I have felt the presence of this force, and I have deduced its action in many of those undiscovered crimes in which I have not been personally consulted. For years I have endeavored to break through the veil which shrouded it, and at last the time came when I seized my thread and followed it, until it led me, after a thousand cunning windings, to ex-Professor Moriarty of mathematical celebrity.

"He is the Napoleon of crime, Watson. He is the organizer of half that is evil and of nearly all that is undetected in this great city. He is a genius, a philosopher, an abstract thinker. He has a brain of the first order. He sits motionless, like a spider in the center of its web, but that web has a thousand radiations, and he knows well every quiver of each of them. He does little himself. He only plans. But his agents are numerous and splendidly organized. Is there a crime to be done, a paper to be abstracted, we will say, a house to be rifled, a man to be removed—the word is passed to the Professor, the matter is organized and carried out. The agent may be caught. In that case money is found for his bail or his defense But the central power which uses the agent is never caught—never so much as suspected. This was the organization which I deduced, Watson, and which I devoted my whole energy to exposing and breaking up.

"But the Professor was fenced round with safeguards so cunningly devised that, do what I would, it seemed impossible to get evidence which would convict in a court of law. You know my powers, my dear Watson, and yet at the end of three months I was forced to confess that I had at last met an antagonist who was my intellectual equal. My horror at his crimes was lost in my admiration at his skill. But at last he made a trip—only a little, little trip—but it was more than he could afford when I was so close upon him. I had my chance, and, starting from that point, I have woven my net round him until now it is all ready to close. In three days—that is to say, on Monday next—matters will be ripe, and the Professor, with all the principal members of his gang, will be in the hands of the police. Then will come the greatest criminal trial of the century, the clearing up of over forty mysteries, and the rope for all of them; but if we move at all prematurely, you understand, they may slip out of our hands even at the last moment.

"Now, if I could have done this without the knowledge of Professor Moriarty, all would have been well. But he was too wily for that. He saw every step which I took to draw my toils round him. Again and again he strove to break away, but I as often headed him off. I tell you, my friend, that if a detailed account of that silent contest could be written, it would take its place as the most brilliant bit of thrust-and-parry work in the history of detection. Never have I risen to such a height, and never have I been so hard pressed by an opponent. He cut deep, and yet I just undercut him. This morning the last steps were taken, and three days only were wanted to complete the business. I was sitting in my room thinking the matter over, when the door opened and Professor Moriarty stood before me.

"My nerves are fairly proof, Watson, but I must confess to a start when I saw the very man who had been so much in my thoughts standing there on my threshold. His appearance was quite familiar to me. He is extremely tall and thin, his forehead domes out in a white curve, and his two eyes are deeply sunken in this head. He is clean-shaven, pale, and ascetic-looking, retaining something of the professor in his features. His shoulders are rounded from much study, and his face protrudes forward, and is forever slowly oscillating from side to side in a curiously reptilian fashion. He peered at me with great curiosity in his puckered eyes.

"'You have less frontal development that I should have expected,' said he, at last. 'It is a dangerous habit to finger loaded firearms in the pocket of one's dressing-gown.'

"The fact is that upon his entrance I had instantly recognized the extreme personal danger in which I lay. The only conceivable escape for him lay in silencing my tongue. In an instant I had slipped the revolved from the drawer into my pocket, and was covering him through the cloth. At his remark I drew the weapon out and laid it cocked upon the table. He still smiled and blinked, but there was something about his eyes which made me feel very glad that I had it there.

"'You evidently don't know me,' said he.

"'On the contrary,' I answered, 'I think it is fairly evident that I do. Pray take a chair. I can spare you five minutes if you have anything to say.'

" 'All that I have to say has already crossed your mind,' said he.

"'Then possibly my answer has crossed yours,' I replied. "'You stand fast?'

"'Absolutely.'

"He clapped his hand into his pocket, and I raised the pistol from the table. But he merely drew out a memorandum-book in which he had scribbled some dates.

" 'You crossed my patch on the 4th of January,' said he. 'On the 23d you incommoded me; by the middle of February I was seriously inconvenienced by you; at the end of March I was absolutely hampered in my plans; and now, at the close of April, I find myself placed in such a position through your continual persecution that I am in positive danger of losing my liberty. The situation is becoming an impossible one.'

" 'Have you any suggestion to make?' I asked.

" 'You must drop it, Mr. Holmes,' said he, swaying his face about. 'You really must, you know.'

" 'After Monday,' said I.

" 'Tut, tut,' said he. 'I am quite sure that a man of your intelligence will see that there can be but one outcome to this affair. It is necessary that you should withdraw. You have worked things in such a fashion that we have only one resource left. It has been an intellectual treat to me to see the way in which you have grappled with this affair, and I say, unaffectedly, that it would be a grief to me to be forced to take any extreme measure. You smile, sir, abut I assure you that it really would.'

"'Danger is part of my trade,' I remarked.

" 'That is not danger,' said he. 'It is inevitable destruction. You stand in the way not merely of an individual, but of a mighty organization, the full extent of which you, with all your cleverness, have been unable to realize. You must stand clear, Mr. Holmes, or be trodden under foot.'

" 'I am afraid,' said I, rising, 'that in the pleasure of this conversation I am neglecting business of importance which awaits me elsewhere.'

"He rose also and looked at me in silence, shaking his head sadly.

" 'Well, well,' said he, at last. 'It seems a pity, but I have done what I could. I know every move of your game. You can do nothing before Monday. It has been a duel between you and me, Mr. Holmes. You hope to place me in the dock. I tell you that I will never stand in the dock. You hope to beat me. I tell you that you will never beat me. If you are clever enough to bring destruction upon me, rest assured that I shall do as much to you.'

" 'You have paid me several compliments, Mr. Moriarty,' said I. 'Let me pay you one in return when I say that if I were assured of the former eventuality I would, in the interests of the public, cheerfully accept the latter.'

" 'I can promise you the one, but not the other,' he snarled, and so turned his rounded back upon me, and went peering and blinking out of the room.

"That was my singular interview with Professor Moriarty. I confess that it left an unpleasant effect upon my mind. His soft, precise fashion of speech leaves a conviction of sincerity which a mere bully could not produce. Of course, you will say: 'Why not take police precautions against him?' the reason is that I am well convinced that it is from his agents the blow will fall. I have the best proofs that it would be so."

"You have already been assaulted?"

"My dear Watson, Professor Moriarty is not a man who lets the grass grow under his feet. I went out about midday to transact some business in Oxford Street. As I passed the corner which leads from Bentinck Street on to the Welbeck Street crossing a two-horse van furiously driven whizzed round and was on me like a flash. I sprang for the footpath and saved myself by the fraction of a second. The van dashed round by Marylebone Lane and was gone in an instant. I kept to the pavement after that, Watson, but as I walked down Vere Street a brick came down from the roof of one of the houses, and was shattered to fragments at my feet. I called the police and had the place examined. There were slates and bricks piled up on the roof preparatory to some repairs, and they would have me believe that the wind had toppled over one of these. Of course I knew better, but I could prove nothing. I took a cab after that and reached my brother's rooms in Pall Mall, where I spent the day. Now I have come round to you, and on my way I was attacked by a rough with a bludgeon. I knocked him down, and the police have him in custody; but I can tell you with the most absolute confidence that no possible connection will ever be traced between the gentleman upon whose front teeth I have barked my knuckles and the retiring mathematical coach, who is, I dare say, working out problems upon a blackboard ten miles away. You will not wonder, Watson, that my first act on entering your rooms was to close your shutters, and that I have been compelled to ask your permission to leave the house by some less conspicuous exit than the front door."

I had often admired my friend's courage, but never more than now, as he sat quietly checking off a series of incidents which must have combined to make up a day of horror.

"You will spend the night here?" I said.

"No, my friend, you might find me a dangerous guest. I have my plans laid, and all will be well. Matters have gone so far now that they can move without my help as far as the arrest goes, though my presence is necessary for a conviction. It is obvious, therefore, that I cannot do better than get away for the few days which remain before the police are at liberty to act. It would be a great pleasure to me, therefore, if you could come on to the Continent with me."

"The practice is quiet," said I, "and I have an accommodating neighbor. I should be glad to come."

"And to start tomorrow morning?"

"If necessary."

"Oh yes, it is most necessary. Then these are your instructions, and I beg, my dear Watson, that you will obey them to the letter, for you are now playing a double-handed game with me against the cleverest rogue and the most powerful syndicate of criminals in Europe. Now listen! You will dispatch whatever luggage you intend to take by a trusty messenger unaddressed to Victoria tonight In the morning you will send for a hansom, desiring your man to take neither the first nor the second which may present itself. Into this hansom you will jump, and you will drive to the Strand end of the Lowther Arcade, handling the address to the cabman upon a slip of paper, with a request that he will not throw it away. Have your fare ready, and the instant that your cab stops, dash through the Arcade, timing yourself to reach the other side at a quarter-past nine. You will find a small brougham waiting close to the curb, driven by a fellow with a heavy black cloak tipped at the collar with red. Into this you will step, and you will reach Victoria in time for the Continental express."

"Where shall I meet you?"

"At the station. The second first-class carriage from the front will be reserved for us."

"The carriage is our rendezvous, then?"

"Yes."

It was in vain that I asked Holmes to remain for the evening. It was evident to me that he though he might bring trouble to the roof he was under, and that that was the motive which impelled him to go. With a few hurried words as to our plans for the morrow he rose and came out with me into the garden, clambering over the wall which leads into Mortimer Street, and immediately whistling for a hansom, in which I heard him drive away.

In the morning I obeyed Holmes's injunctions to the letter. A hansom was procured with such precaution as would prevent its being one which was placed ready for us, and I drove immediately after breakfast to the Lowther Arcade, through which I hurried at the top of my speed. A brougham was waiting with a very massive driver wrapped in a dark cloak, who, the instant that I had stepped in, whipped up the horse and rattled off to Victoria Station. On my alighting there he turned the carriage, and dashed away again without so much as a look in my direction.

So far all had gone admirably. My luggage was waiting for me, and I had no difficulty in finding the carriage, which Holmes had indicated, the less so as it was the only one in the train which was marked "Engaged." My only source of anxiety now was the nonappearance of Holmes. The station clock marked only seven minutes from the time when we were due to start. In vain I searched among the groups of travelers and leave-takers for the little figure of my friend. There was no sign of him. I spent a few minutes in assisting a venerable Italian priest, who was endeavoring to make a porter understand, in his broken English, that his luggage was to be booked through to Paris. Then, having taken another look round, I returned to my carriage, where I found that the porter, in spite of the ticket, had given me my decrepit Italian friend as a traveling companion. It was useless for me to explain to him that his presence was an intrusion, for my Italian was even more limited than his English, so I shrugged my shoulders resignedly, and continued to look out anxiously for my friend. A chill of fear had come over me, as I thought that his absence might mean that some blow had fallen during the night. Already the doors had all been shut and the whistle blown, when—

"My dear Watson," said a voice, "you have not even condescended to say good-morning."

I turned in uncontrollable astonishment. The aged ecclesiastic had turned his face towards me. For an instant the wrinkles were smoothed away, the nose drew away from the chin, the lower lip ceased to protrude and the mouth to mumble, the dull eyes regained their fire, the drooping figure expanded. The next the whole frame collapsed again, and Holmes had gone as quickly as he had come.

"Good heavens!" I cried; "how you startled me!"

"Every precaution is still necessary," he whispered.

"I have reason to think that they are hot upon our trail. Ah, there is Moriarty himself."

The train had already begun to move as Holmes spoke. Glancing back, I saw a tall man pushing his way furiously through the crowd, and waving his hand as if he desired to have the train stopped. It was too late, however, for we were rapidly gathering momentum, and an instant later had shot clear of the station.

"With all our precautions, you see that we have cut it rather fine," said Holmes, laughing. He rose, and throwing off the black cassock and hat which had formed his disguise, he packed them away in a handbag. "Have you seen the morning paper, Watson?"

"No."

"You haven't' seen about Baker Street, then?"

"Baker Street?"

"They set fire to our rooms last night. No great harm was done."

"Good heavens, Holmes! this is intolerable."

"They must have lost my track completely after their bludgeon-man was arrested. Otherwise they could not have imagined that I had returned to my rooms. They have evidently taken the precaution of watching you, however, and that is what has brought Moriarty to Victoria. You could not have made any slip in coming?"

"I did exactly what you advised."

"Did you find your brougham?"

"Yes, it was waiting."

"Did you recognize your coachman?"

"No."

"It was my brother Mycroft. It is an advantage to get about in such a case without taking a mercenary into your confidence. But we must plan what we are to do about Moriarty now."

"As this is an express, and as the boat runs in connection with it, I should think we have shaken him off very effectively."

"My dear Watson, you evidently did not realize my meaning when I said that this man may be taken as being quite on the same intellectual plane as myself. You do not imagine that if I were the pursuer I should allow myself to be baffled by so slight an obstacle. Why, then, should you think so meanly of him?"

"What will he do?"

"What I should do?"

"What would you do, then?"

"Engage a special."

"But it must be late."

"By no means. This train stops at Canterbury; and there is always at least a quarter of an hour's delay at the boat. He will catch us there."

"One would think that we were the criminals. Let us have him arrested on his arrival."

"It would be to ruin the work of three months. We should get the big fish, but the smaller would dart right and left out of the net. On Monday we should have them all. No, an arrest is inadmissible."

"What then?"

"We shall get out at Canterbury."

"And then?"

"Well, then we must make a cross-country journey to Newhaven, and so over to Dieppe. Moriarty will again do what I should do. He will get on to Paris, mark down our luggage, and wait for two days at the depot. In the meantime we shall treat ourselves to a couple of carpetbags, encourage the manufactures of the countries through which we travel, and make our way at our leisure into Switzerland, via Luxembourg and Basle."

At Canterbury, therefore, we alighted, only to find that we should have to wait an hour before we could get a train to Newhaven. I was still looking rather ruefully after the rapidly disappearing luggage-van which contained my wardrobe, when Holmes pulled my sleeve and pointed up the line.

"Already, you see," said he.

Far away, from among the Kentish woods there rose a thin spray of smoke. A minute later a carriage and engine could be seen flying along the open curve, which leads to the station. We had hardly time to take our place behind a pile of luggage when it passed with a rattle and a roar, beating a blast of hot air into our faces.

"There he goes," said Holmes, as we watched the carriage

swing and rock over the point. "There are limits, you see, to our friend's intelligence. It would have been a coup-de-maître had he deduced what I would deduce and acted accordingly."

"And what would he have done had he overtaken us?"

"There cannot be the least doubt that he would have made a murderous attack upon me. It is, however, a game at which two may play. The question, now is whether we should take a premature lunch here, or run our chance of starving before we reach the buffet at Newhaven."

We made our way to Brussels that night and spent two days there, moving on upon the third day as far as Strasburg.

On the Monday morning Holmes had telegraphed to the London police, and in the evening we found a reply waiting for us at our hotel. Holmes tore it open, and then with a bitter curse hurled it into the grate. "I might have known it!" he groaned. "He has escaped!"

"Moriarty?"

"They have secured the whole gang with the exception of him. He has given them the slip. Of course, when I had left the country there was no one to cope with him. But I did think that I had put the game in their hands. I think that you had better return to England, Watson."

"Why?"

"Because you will find me a dangerous companion now. This man's occupation is gone. He is lost if he returns to London. If I read his character right he will devote his whole energies to revenging himself upon me. He said as much in our short interview, and I fancy that he meant it. I should certainly recommend you to return to your practice."

It was hardly an appeal to be successful with one who was an old campaigner as well as an old friend. We sat in the Strasburg salle-à-manger arguing the question for half an hour, but the same night we had resumed our journey and were well on our way to Geneva. For a charming week we wandered up the Valley of the Rhone, and then, branching off at Leuk, we made our way over the Gemmi Pass, still deep in snow, and so, by way of Interlaken, to Meiringen.

It was a lovely trip, the dainty green of the spring below,

the virgin white of the winter above; but it was clear to me that never for one instant did Holmes forget the shadow which lay across him. In the homely Alpine villages or in the lonely mountain passes, I could tell by his quick glancing eyes and his sharp scrutiny of every face that passed us, that he was well convinced that, walk where we would, we could not walk ourselves clear of the danger which was dogging our footsteps.

Once, I remember, as we passed over the Gemmi, and walked along the border of the melancholy Daubensee, a large rock which had been dislodged from the ridge upon our right clattered down and roared into the lake behind us. In an instant Holmes had raced up on to the ridge, and, standing upon a lofty pinnacle, craned his neck in every direction. It was in vain that our guide assured him that a fall of stones was a common chance in the springtime at that spot. He said nothing, but he smiled at me with the air of a man who sees the fulfillment of that which he had expected.

And yet for all his watchfulness he was never depressed. On the contrary, I can never recollect having seen him in such exuberant spirits. Again and again he recurred to the fact that if he could be assured that society was freed from Professor Moriarty he would cheerfully bring his own career to a conclusion. "I think that I may go so far as to say, Watson, that I have not lived wholly in vain," he remarked. "If my record were closed tonight I could still survey it with equanimity. The air of London is the sweeter for my presence. In over a thousand cases I am not aware that I have ever used my powers upon the wrong side. Of late I have been tempted to look into the problems furnished by nature rather than those more superficial ones for which our artificial state of society is responsible. Your memoirs will draw to an end, Watson, upon the day that I crown my career by the capture or extinction of the most dangerous and capable criminal in Europe."

I shall be brief, and yet exact, in the little which remains for me to tell. It is not a subject on which I would willingly dwell, and yet I am conscious that a duty devolves upon me to omit no detail.

It was on the 3d of May that we reached the little village

of Meiringen, where we put up at the Englischer Hof, then kept by Peter Steiler the elder. Our landlord was an intelligent man, and spoke excellent English, having served for three years as waiter at the Grosvenor Hotel in London. At his advice, on the afternoon of the 4th we set off together, with the intention of crossing the hills and spending the night at the hamlet of Rosenlaui. We had strict injunctions, however, on no account to pass the falls of Reichenbach, which are about halfway up the hill, without making a small detour to see them. It is indeed, a fearful place. The torrent, swollen by the melting snow, plunges into a tremendous abyss, from which the spray rolls up like the smoke from a burning house. The shaft into which the river hurls itself is a immense chasm, lined by glistening coal-black rock, and narrowing into a creaming, boiling pit of incalculable depth, which brims over and shoots the stream onward over its jagged lip. The long sweep of green water roaring forever down, and the thick flickering curtain of spray hissing forever upward, turn a man giddy with their constant whirl and clamor.

We stood near the edge peering down at the gleam of the breaking water far below us against the black rocks, and listening to the half-human shout which came booming up with the spray out of the abyss. The path has been cut halfway round the fall to afford a complete view, but it ends abruptly, and the traveler has to return as he came. We had turned to do so, when we saw a Swiss lad come running along it with a letter in his hand. It bore the mark of the hotel which we had just left, and was addressed to me by the landlord. It appeared that within a very few minutes of our leaving, an English lady had arrived who was in the last stage of consumption. She had wintered at Davos Platz, and was journeying now to join her friends at Lucerne, when a sudden hemorrhage had overtaken her. It was thought that she could hardly live a few hours, but it would be a great consolation to her to see an English doctor, and, if I would only return, etc. The good Steiler assured me in a postscript that he would himself look upon my compliance as a very great favor, since the lady absolutely refused to see a Swiss physician, and he could not but feel that he was incurring a great responsibility.

The appeal was one which could not be ignored. It was

impossible to refuse the request of a fellow-countrywoman dying in a strange land. Yet I had my scruples about leaving Holmes. It was finally agreed, however, that he should retain the young Swiss messenger with him as guide and companion while I returned to Meiringen. My friend would stay some little time at the fall, he said, and would then walk slowly over the hill to Rosenlaui, where I was to rejoin him in the evening.

As I turned away I saw Holmes, with his back against a rock and his arms folded, gazing down at the rush of the waters. It was the last that I was ever destined to see of him in this world. When I was near the bottom of the descent I looked back. It was impossible, from that position, to see the fall, but I could see the curving path which winds over the shoulder of the hill and leads to it. Along this a man was, I remember, walking very rapidly. I could see his black figure clearly outlined against the green behind him. I noted him, and the energy with which he walked but he passed from my mind again as I hurried on upon my errand.

It may have been a little over an hour before I reached Meiringen. Old Steiler was standing at the porch of his hotel. "Well," said I, as I came hurrying up, "I trust that she is no worse?"

A look of surprise passed over his face, and at the first quiver of his eyebrows my heart turned to lead in my breast. "You did not write this?" I said, pulling the letter from my pocket. "There is no sick Englishwoman in the hotel?"

"Certainly not!" he cried. "But it has the hotel mark upon it! Ha, it must have been written by that tall Englishman who came in after you had gone. He said—"

But I waited for none of the landlord's explanations. In a tingle of fear I was already running down the village street, and making for the path which I had so lately descended. It had taken me an hour to come down. For all my efforts two more had passed before I found myself at the fall of Reichenbach once more. There was Holmes's Alpine-stock still leaning against the rock by which I had left him. But there was no sign of him, and it was in vain that I shouted. My only answer was my own voice reverberating in a rolling echo from the cliffs around me.

It was the sight of that Alpine-stock which turned me cold and sick. He had not gone to Rosenlaui, then. He had remained on that three-foot path, with sheer wall on one side and sheer drop on the other, until his enemy had overtaken him. The young Swiss had gone too. He had probably been in the pay of Moriarty, and had left the two men together.

And then what had happened? Who was to tell us what had happened then? I stood for a minute or two to collect myself, for I was dazed with the horror of the thing. Then I began to think of Holmes's own methods and to try to practice them in reading this tragedy. It was, alas, only too easy to do. During our conversation we had not gone to the end of the path, and the Alpine-stock marked the place where we had stood. The blackish soil is kept forever soft by the incessant drift of spray, and a bird would leave its tread upon it. Two lines of footmarks were clearly marked along the farther end of the path, both leading away from me. There were none returning.

A few yards from the end the soil was all plowed up into a patch of mud, and the branches and ferns which fringed the chasm were torn and bedraggled. I lay upon my face and peered over with the spray spouting up all around me. It had darkened since I left, and now I could only see here and there the glistening of moisture upon the black walls, and far away down at the end of the shaft the gleam of the broken water. I shouted; but only the same half-human cry of the fall was borne back to my ears.

But it was destined that I should after all have a last word of greeting from my friend and comrade. I have said that his Alpine-stock had been left leaning against a rock which jutted on to the path. From the top of this boulder the gleam of something bright caught my eye, and, raising my hand, I found that it came from the silver cigarette-case which he used to carry. As I took it up a small square of paper upon which it had lain fluttered down on to the ground. Unfolding it, I found that it consisted of three pages torn from his notebook and addressed to me. It was characteristic of the man that the direction was a precise, and the writing as firm and clear, as though it had been written in his study.

"My dear Watson [it said], I write these few lines through

the courtesy of Mr. Moriarty, who awaits my convenience for the final discussion of those questions which lie between us. He has been giving me a sketch of the methods by which he avoided the English police and kept himself informed of our movements. They certainly confirm the very high opinion which I had formed of his abilities. I am pleased to think that I shall be able to free society from any further effects of his presence, though I fear that it is at a cost which will give pain to my friends, and especially, my dear Watson, to you. I have already explained to you, however, that my career had in any case reached its crisis, and that no possible conclusion to it could be more congenial to me than this. Indeed, if I may make a full confession to you, I was quite convinced that the letter from Meiringen was a hoax, and I allowed you to depart on that errand under the persuasion that some development of this sort would follow. Tell Inspector Patterson that the papers which he needs to convict the gang are in pigeonhole M., done up in a blue envelope and inscribed "Moriarty." I made every disposition of my property before leaving England, and handed it to my brother Mycroft. Pray give my greetings to Mrs. Watson, and believe me to be, my dear fellow,

Very sincerely yours, Sherlock Holmes

A few words may suffice to tell the little that remains. An examination by experts leaves little doubt that a personal contest between the two men ended, as it could hardly fail to end in such a situation, in their reeling over, locked in each other's arms. Any attempt at recovering the bodies was absolutely hopeless, and there, deep down in that dreadful caldron of swirling water and seething foam, will lie for all time the most dangerous criminal and the foremost champion of the law of their generation. The Swiss youth was never found again, and there can be no doubt that he was one of the numerous agents whom Moriarty kept in this employ.

As to the gang, it will be within the memory of the public how completely the evidence which Holmes had accumulated exposed their organization, and how heavily the hand of the dead man weighted upon them. Of their terrible chief few details came out during the proceedings, and if I have now been compelled to make a clear statement of his career it is due to those injudicious champions who have endeavored to clear his memory by attacks upon him whom I shall ever regard as the best and the wisest man whom I have ever known.

# The Adventure of the Blue Carbuncle

*Sir Arthur Conan Doyle*

I had called upon my friend Sherlock Holmes upon the second morning after Christmas, with the intention of wishing him the compliments of the season. He was lounging upon the sofa in a purple dressing-gown, a pipe-rack within his reach upon the right, and a pile of crumpled morning papers, evidently newly studied, near at hand. Beside the couch was a wooden chair, and on the angle of the back hung a very seedy and disreputable hard-felt hat, much the worse for wear, and cracked in several places. A lens and a forceps lying upon the seat of the chair suggested that the hat had been suspended in this manner for the purpose of examination.

"You are engaged," said I; "perhaps I interrupt you."

"Not at all. I am glad to have a friend with whom I can discuss my results. The matter is a perfectly trivial one" – he jerked his thumb in the direction of the old hat – "but there are points in connection with it which are not entirely devoid of interest and even of instruction."

I seated myself in his armchair and warmed my hands before his crackling fire, for a sharp frost had set in, and the windows were thick with the ice crystals. "I suppose," I remarked, "that, homely as it looks, this thing has some deadly story linked on to it – that it is the clew which will guide you in the solution of some mystery and the punishment of some crime."

"No, no. No crime," said Sherlock Holmes, laughing. "Only one of those whimsical little incidents which will happen when you have four million human beings all jostling each other within the space of a few square miles. Amid the action and reaction of so dense a swarm of humanity, every possible combination of events may be expected to take place, and many a little problem will be presented which may be striking and bizarre without being criminal. We have already had experience of such."

"So much so," I remarked, "that of the last six cases which I have added to my notes, three have been entirely free of any legal crime."

"Precisely. You allude to my attempt to recover the Irene Adler papers, to the singular case of Miss Mary Sutherland, and to the adventure of the man with the twisted lip. Well, I have no doubt that this small matter will fall into the same innocent category. You know Peterson, the commissionaire?"

"Yes."

"It is to him that this trophy belongs."

"It is his hat."

"No, no, he found it. Its owner is unknown. I beg that you will look upon it not as a battered billycock but as an intellectual problem. And, first, as to how it came here. It arrived upon Christmas morning, in company with a good fat goose, which is, I have no doubt, roasting at this moment in front of Peterson's fire. The facts are these: about four o'clock on Christmas morning, Peterson, who, as you know, is a very honest fellow, was returning from some small jollification and was making his way homeward down Tottenham Court Road. In front of him he saw, in the gaslight, a tallish man, walking with a slight stagger, and carrying a white goose slung over his shoulder. As he reached the corner of Goodge Street, a row broke out between this stranger and a little knot of roughs. One of the latter knocked off the man's hat, on which he raised his stick to defend himself and, swinging it over his head, smashed the shop window behind him. Peterson had rushed forward to protect the stranger from his assailants; but the man, shocked at having broken the window, and seeing an official-looking person in uniform rushing towards him, dropped his goose, took to his heels, and vanished amid the labyrinth of small streets which lie at the back of Tottenham Court Road. The roughs had also fled at the appearance of Peterson, so that he was left in possession of the field of battle, and also of the spoils of victory in the shape of this battered hat and a most unimpeachable Christmas goose."

"Which surely he restored to their owner?"

"My dear fellow, there lies the problem. It is true that 'For

Mrs. Henry Baker' was printed upon a small card which was tied to the bird's left leg, and it is also true that the initials 'H. B.' are legible upon the lining of this hat, but as there are some thousands of Bakers, and some hundreds of Henry Bakers in this city of ours, it is not easy to restore lost property to any one of them."

"What, then, did Peterson do?"

"He brought round both hat and goose to me on Christmas morning, knowing that even the smallest problems are of interest to me. The goose we retained until this morning, when there were signs that, in spite of the slight frost, it would be well that it should be eaten without unnecessary delay. Its finder has carried it off, therefore, to fulfil the ultimate destiny of a goose, while I continue to retain the hat of the unknown gentleman who lost his Christmas dinner."

"Did he not advertise?"

"No."

"Then, what clew could you have as to his identity?"

"Only as much as we can deduce."

"From his hat?"

"Precisely."

"But you are joking. What can you gather from this old battered felt?"

"Here is my lens. You know my methods. What can you gather yourself as to the individuality of the man who has worn this article?"

I took the tattered object in my hands and turned it over rather ruefully. It was a very ordinary black hat of the usual round shape, hard and much the worse for wear. The lining had been of red silk, but was a good deal discolored. There was no maker's name; but, as Holmes had remarked, the initials "H. B." were scrawled upon one side. It was pierced in the brim for a hat-securer, but the elastic was missing. For the rest, it was cracked, exceedingly dusty, and spotted in several places, although there seemed to have been some attempt to hide the discolored patches by smearing them with ink.

"I can see nothing," said I, handing it back to my friend.

"On the contrary, Watson, you can see everything. You fail,

however, to reason from what you see. You are too timid in drawing your inferences."

"Then, pray tell me what it is that you can infer from this hat?"

He picked it up and gazed at it in the peculiar introspective fashion which was characteristic of him. "It is perhaps less suggestive than it might have been," he remarked, "and yet there are a few inferences which are very distinct, and a few others which represent at least a strong balance of probability. That the man was highly intellectual is of course obvious upon the face of it, and also that he was fairly well-to-do within the last three years, although he has now fallen upon evil days. He had foresight, but has less now than formerly, pointing to a moral retrogression, which, when taken with the decline of his fortunes, seems to indicate some evil influence, probably drink, at work upon him. This may account also for the obvious fact that his wife has ceased to love him."

"My dear Holmes!"

"He has, however, retained some degree of self-respect," he continued, disregarding my remonstrance. "He is a man who leads a sedentary life, goes out little, is out of training entirely, is middle-aged, has grizzled hair which he has had cut within the last few days, and which he anoints with lime-cream. These are the more patent facts which are to be deduced from his hat. Also, by the way, that it is extremely improbable that he has gas laid on in his house."

"You are certainly joking, Holmes."

"Not in the least. Is it possible that even now, when I give you these results, you are unable to see how they are attained?"

"I have no doubt that I am very stupid, but I must confess that I am unable to follow you. For example, how did you deduce that this man was intellectual?"

For answer Holmes clapped the hat upon his head. It came right over the forehead and settled upon the bridge of his nose. "It is a question of cubic capacity," said he; "a man with so large a brain must have something in it."

"The decline of his fortunes, then?"

"This hat is three years old. These flat brims curled at the edge came in then. It is a hat of the very best quality. Look at the band of ribbed silk and the excellent lining. If this man could afford to buy so expensive a hat three years ago, and has had no hat since, then he has assuredly gone down in the world."

"Well, that is clear enough, certainly. But how about the foresight and the moral retrogression?"

Sherlock Holmes laughed. "Here is the foresight," said he putting his finger upon the little disc and loop of the hat-securer. "They are never sold upon hats. If this man ordered one, it is a sign of a certain amount of foresight, since he went out of his way to take this precaution against the wind. But since we see that he has broken the elastic and has not troubled to replace it, it is obvious that he has less foresight now than formerly, which is a distinct proof of a weakening nature. On the other hand, he has endeavored to conceal some of these stains upon the felt by daubing them with ink, which is a sign that he has not entirely lost his self-respect."

"Your reasoning is certainly plausible."

"The further points, that he is middle-aged, that his hair is grizzled, that it has been recently cut, and that he uses limecream, are all to be gathered from a close examination of the lower part of the lining. The lens discloses a large number of hair-ends, clean cut by the scissors of the barber. They all appear to be adhesive, and there is a distinct odour of lime-cream. This dust, you will observe, is not the gritty, gray dust of the street but the fluffy brown dust of the house, showing that it has been hung up indoors most of the time, while the marks of moisture upon the inside are proof positive that the wearer perspired very freely, and could therefore, hardly be in the best of training."

"But his wife – you said that she had ceased to love him."

"This hat has not been brushed for weeks. When I see you, my dear Watson, with a week's accumulation of dust upon your hat, and when your wife allows you to go out in such a state, I shall fear that you also have been unfortunate enough to lose your wife's affection."

"But he might be a bachelor."

"Nay, he was bringing home the goose as a peace-offering to his wife. Remember the card upon the bird's leg."

"You have an answer to everything. But how on earth do you deduce that the gas is not laid on in his house?"

"One tallow stain, or even two, might come by chance; but when I see no less than five, I think that there can be little doubt that the individual must be brought into frequent contact with burning tallow – walks upstairs at night probably with his hat in one hand and a guttering candle in the other. Anyhow, he never got tallow-stains from a gas-jet. Are you satisfied?"

"Well, it is very ingenious," said I, laughing; "but since, as you said just now, there has been no crime committed, and no harm done save the loss of a goose, all this seems to be rather a waste of energy."

Sherlock Holmes had opened his mouth to reply, when the door flew open, and Peterson, the commissionaire, rushed into the apartment with flushed cheeks and the face of a man who is dazed with astonishment.

"The goose, Mr. Holmes! The goose, sir!" he gasped.

"Eh? What of it, then? Has it returned to life and flapped off through the kitchen window?" Holmes twisted himself round upon the sofa to get a fairer view of the man's excited face.

"See here, sir! See what my wife found in its crop!" He held out his hand and displayed upon the centre of the palm a brilliantly scintillating blue stone, rather smaller than a bean in size, but of such purity and radiance that it twinkled like an electric point in the dark hollow of his hand.

Sherlock Holmes sat up with a whistle. "By Jove, Peterson!" said he, "this is treasure trove indeed. I suppose you know what you have got?"

"A diamond, sir? A precious stone. It cuts into glass as though it were putty."

"It's more than a precious stone. It is the precious stone."

"Not the Countess of Morcar's blue carbuncle!" I ejaculated.

"Precisely so. I ought to know its size and shape, seeing that I have read the advertisement about it in The Times every day lately. It is absolutely unique, and its value can only be conjectured, but the reward offered of 1000 pounds is certainly not within a twentieth part of the market price."

"A thousand pounds! Great Lord of mercy!" The commissionaire plumped down into a chair and stared from one to the other of us.

"That is the reward, and I have reason to know that there are sentimental considerations in the background which would induce the Countess to part with half her fortune if she could but recover the gem."

"It was lost, if I remember aright, at the Hotel Cosmopolitan," I remarked.

"Precisely so, on December 22d, just five days ago. John Horner, a plumber, was accused of having abstracted it from the lady's jewel-case. The evidence against him was so strong that the case has been referred to the Assizes. I have some account of the matter here, I believe." He rummaged amid his newspapers, glancing over the dates, until at last he smoothed one out, doubled it over, and read the following paragraph:

"Hotel Cosmopolitan Jewel Robbery. John Horner, 26, plumber, was brought up upon the charge of having upon the 22d inst., abstracted from the jewel-case of the Countess of Morcar the valuable gem known as the blue carbuncle. James Ryder, upper-attendant at the hotel, gave his evidence to the effect that he had shown Horner up to the dressing-room of the Countess of Morcar upon the day of the robbery in order that he might solder the second bar of the grate, which was loose. He had remained with Horner some little time, but had finally been called away. On returning, he found that Horner had disappeared, that the bureau had been forced open, and that the small morocco casket in which, as it afterwards transpired, the Countess was accustomed to keep her jewel, was lying empty upon the dressing-table. Ryder instantly gave the alarm, and Horner was arrested the same evening; but the stone could not be found either upon his person or in his rooms. Catherine Cusack, maid to the Countess, deposed to having heard Ryder's cry of dismay on discovering the robbery, and to having rushed into the room, where she found matters as described by the last witness. Inspector Bradstreet, B division, gave evidence as to the arrest of Horner, who struggled frantically, and protested his innocence in the strongest terms. Evidence of a previous conviction for robbery having been given against the prisoner, the magistrate refused to deal summarily with the offence, but referred it to the Assizes. Horner, who had shown signs of intense emotion during the proceedings, fainted away at the conclusion and was carried out of court.

"Hum! So much for the police-court," said Holmes thoughtfully, tossing aside the paper. "The question for us now to solve is the sequence of events leading from a rifled jewel-case at one end to the crop of a goose in Tottenham Court Road at the other. You see, Watson, our little deductions have suddenly assumed a much more important and less innocent aspect. Here is the stone; the stone came from the goose, and the goose came from Mr. Henry Baker, the gentleman with the bad hat and all the other characteristics with which I have bored you. So now we must set ourselves very seriously to finding this gentleman and ascertaining what part he has played in this little mystery. To do this, we must try the simplest means first, and these lie undoubtedly in an advertisement in all the evening papers. If this fail, I shall have recourse to other methods."

"What will you say?"

"Give me a pencil and that slip of paper. Now, then: 'Found at the corner of Goodge Street, a goose and a black felt hat. Mr. Henry Baker can have the same by applying at 6:30 this evening at 221B, Baker Street.' That is clear and concise."

"Very. But will he see it?"

"Well, he is sure to keep an eye on the papers, since, to a poor man, the loss was a heavy one. He was clearly so scared by his mischance in breaking the window and by the approach of Peterson that he thought of nothing but flight, but since then he must have bitterly regretted the impulse which caused him to drop his bird. Then, again, the introduction of his name will cause him to see it, for everyone who knows him will direct his attention to it. Here you are, Peterson, run down to the advertising agency and have this put in the evening papers."

"In which, sir?"

"Oh, in the Globe, Star, Pall Mall, St. James's, Evening News Standard, Echo, and any others that occur to you."

"Very well, sir. And this stone?"

"Ah, yes, I shall keep the stone. Thank you. And, I say, Peterson, just buy a goose on your way back and leave it here with me, for we must have one to give to this gentleman in place of the one which your family is now devouring."

When the commissionaire had gone, Holmes took up the stone and held it against the light. "It's a bonny thing," said he. "Just see how it glints and sparkles. Of course it is a nucleus and focus of crime. Every good stone is. They are the devil's pet baits. In the larger and older jewels every facet may stand for a bloody deed. This stone is not yet twenty years old. It was found in the banks of the Amoy River in southem China and is remarkable in having every characteristic of the carbuncle, save that it is blue in shade instead of ruby red. In spite of its youth, it has already a sinister history. There have been two murders, a vitriol-throwing, a suicide, and several robberies brought about for the sake of this forty-grain weight of crystallized charcoal. Who would think that so pretty a toy would be a purveyor to the gallows and the prison? I'll lock it up in my strong box now and drop a line to the Countess to say that we have it."

"Do you think that this man Horner is innocent?"

"I cannot tell."

"Well, then, do you imagine that this other one, Henry Baker, had anything to do with the matter?"

"It is, I think, much more likely that Henry Baker is an absolutely innocent man, who had no idea that the bird which he was carrying was of considerably more value than if it were made of solid gold. That, however, I shall determine by a very simple test if we have an answer to our advertisement."

"And you can do nothing until then?"

"Nothing."

"In that case I shall continue my professional round. But I shall come back in the evening at the hour you have mentioned, for I should like to see the solution of so tangled a business."

"Very glad to see you. I dine at seven. There is a woodcock, I believe. By the way, in view of recent occurrences, perhaps I ought to ask Mrs. Hudson to examine its crop."

I had been delayed at a case, and it was a little after half-past six when I found myself in Baker Street once more. As I approached the house I saw a tall man in a Scotch bonnet with a coat which was buttoned up to his chin waiting outside in the bright semicircle which was thrown from the fanlight. Just as I arrived the door was opened, and we were shown up together to Holmes's room.

"Mr. Henry Baker, I believe," said he, rising from his armchair and greeting his visitor with the easy air of geniality which he could so readily assume. "Pray take this chair by the fire, Mr. Baker. It is a cold night, and I observe that your circulation is more adapted for summer than for winter. Ah, Watson, you have just come at the right time. Is that your hat, Mr. Baker?"

"Yes, sir, that is undoubtedly my hat."

He was a large man with rounded shoulders, a massive head, and a broad, intelligent face, sloping down to a pointed beard of grizzled brown. A touch of red in nose and cheeks, with a slight tremor of his extended hand, recalled Holmes's surmise as to his habits. His rusty black frock-coat was buttoned right up in front, with the collar turned up, and his lank wrists protruded from his sleeves without a sign of cuff or shirt. He spoke in a slow staccato fashion, choosing his words with care, and gave the impression generally of a man of learning and letters who had had ill-usage at the hands of fortune.

"We have retained these things for some days," said Holmes, "because we expected to see an advertisement from you giving your address. I am at a loss to know now why you did not advertise."

Our visitor gave a rather shamefaced laugh. "Shillings have not been so plentiful with me as they once were," he remarked. "I had no doubt that the gang of roughs who assaulted me had carried off both my hat and the bird. I did not care to spend more money in a hopeless attempt at recovering them."

"Very naturally. By the way, about the bird, we were compelled to eat it."

"To eat it!" Our visitor half rose from his chair in his excitement.

"Yes, it would have been of no use to anyone had we not done so. But I presume that this other goose upon the sideboard, which is about the same weight and perfectly fresh, will answer your purpose equally well?"

"Oh, certainly, certainly," answered Mr. Baker with a sigh of relief.

"Of course, we still have the feathers, legs, crop, and so on of your own bird, so if you wish – "

The man burst into a hearty laugh. "They might be useful to me as relics of my adventure," said he, "but beyond that I can hardly see what use the disjecta membra of my late acquaintance are going to be to me. No, sir, I think that, with your permission, I will confine my attentions to the excellent bird which I perceive upon the sideboard."

Sherlock Holmes glanced sharply across at me with a slight shrug of his shoulders.

"There is your hat, then, and there your bird," said he. "By the way, would it bore you to tell me where you got the other one from? I am somewhat of a fowl fancier, and I have seldom seen a better grown goose."

"Certainly, sir," said Baker, who had risen and tucked his newly gained property under his arm. "There are a few of us who frequent the Alpha Inn, near the Museum – we are to be found in the Museum itself during the day, you understand. This year our good host, Windigate by name, instituted a goose club, by which, on consideration of some few pence every week, we were each to receive a bird at Christmas. My pence were duly paid, and the rest is familiar to you. I am much indebted to you, sir, for a Scotch bonnet is fitted neither to my years nor my gravity." With a comical pomposity of manner he bowed solemnly to both of us and strode off upon his way.

"So much for Mr. Henry Baker," said Holmes when he had closed the door behind him. "It is quite certain that he knows nothing whatever about the matter. Are you hungry, Watson?"

"Not particularly."

"Then I suggest that we turn our dinner into a supper and follow up this clew while it is still hot."

"By all means."

It was a bitter night, so we drew on our ulsters and wrapped cravats about our throats. Outside, the stars were shining coldly in a cloudless sky, and the breath of the passers-by blew out into smoke like so many pistol shots. Our footfalls rang out crisply and loudly as we swung through the doctors' quarter, Wimpole Street, Harley Street, and so through Wigmore Street into Oxford

Street. In a quarter of an hour we were in Bloomsbury at the Alpha Inn, which is a small public-house at the corner of one of the streets which runs down into Holborn. Holmes pushed open the door of the private bar and ordered two glasses of beer from the ruddy-faced, white-aproned landlord.

"Your beer should be excellent if it is as good as your geese," said he.

"My geese!" The man seemed surprised.

"Yes. I was speaking only half an hour ago to Mr. Henry Baker, who was a member of your goose club."

"Ah! yes, I see. But you see, sir, them's not our geese."

"Indeed! Whose, then?"

"Well, I got the two dozen from a salesman in Covent Garden."

"Indeed? I know some of them. Which was it?"

"Breckinridge is his name."

"Ah! I don't know him. Well, here's your good health landlord, and prosperity to your house. Good-night.

"Now for Mr. Breckinridge," he continued, buttoning up his coat as we came out into the frosty air. "Remember, Watson that though we have so homely a thing as a goose at one end of this chain, we have at the other a man who will certainly get seven years' penal servitude unless we can establish his innocence. It is possible that our inquiry may but confirm his guilt but, in any case, we have a line of investigation which has been missed by the police, and which a singular chance has placed in our hands. Let us follow it out to the bitter end. Faces to the south, then, and quick march!"

We passed across Holborn, down Endell Street, and so through a zigzag of slums to Covent Garden Market. One of the largest stalls bore the name of Breckinridge upon it, and the proprietor a horsy-looking man, with a sharp face and trim side-whiskers was helping a boy to put up the shutters.

"Good-evening. It's a cold night," said Holmes.

The salesman nodded and shot a questioning glance at my companion.

"Sold out of geese, I see," continued Holmes, pointing at the bare slabs of marble.

"Let you have five hundred to-morrow morning."

"That's no good."

"Well, there are some on the stall with the gas-flare."

"Ah, but I was recommended to you."

"Who by?"

"The landlord of the Alpha."

"Oh, yes; I sent him a couple of dozen."

"Fine birds they were, too. Now where did you get them from?"

To my surprise the question provoked a burst of anger from the salesman.

"Now, then, mister," said he, with his head cocked and his arms akimbo, "what are you driving at? Let's have it straight, now."

"It is straight enough. I should like to know who sold you the geese which you supplied to the Alpha."

"Well then, I shan't tell you. So now!"

"Oh, it is a matter of no importance; but I don't know why you should be so warm over such a trifle."

"Warm! You'd be as warm, maybe, if you were as pestered as I am. When I pay good money for a good article there should be an end of the business; but it's 'Where are the geese?' and 'Who did you sell the geese to?' and 'What will you take for the geese?' One would think they were the only geese in the world, to hear the fuss that is made over them."

"Well, I have no connection with any other people who have been making inquiries," said Holmes carelessly. "If you won't tell us the bet is off, that is all. But I'm always ready to back my opinion on a matter of fowls, and I have a fiver on it that the bird I ate is country bred."

"Well, then, you've lost your fiver, for it's town bred," snapped the salesman.

"It's nothing of the kind."

"I say it is."

"I don't believe it."

"D'you think you know more about fowls than I, who have handled them ever since I was a nipper? I tell you, all those birds that went to the Alpha were town bred."

"You'll never persuade me to believe that."

"Will you bet, then?"

"It's merely taking your money, for I know that I am right. But I'll have a sovereign on with you, just to teach you not to be obstinate."

The salesman chuckled grimly. "Bring me the books, Bill," said he.

The small boy brought round a small thin volume and a great greasy-backed one, laying them out together beneath the hanging lamp.

"Now then, Mr. Cocksure," said the salesman, "I thought that I was out of geese, but before I finish you'll find that there is still one left in my shop. You see this little book?"

"Well?"

"That's the list of the folk from whom I buy. D'you see? Well, then, here on this page are the country folk, and the numbers after their names are where their accounts are in the big ledger. Now, then! You see this other page in red ink? Well, that is a list of my town suppliers. Now, look at that third name. Just read it out to me."

"Mrs. Oakshott, 117, Brixton Road – 249," read Holmes.

"Quite so. Now turn that up in the ledger."

Holmes turned to the page indicated. "Here you are, 'Mrs. Oakshott, 117, Brixton Road, egg and poultry supplier."

"Now, then, what's the last entry?"

"'December 22d. Twenty-four geese at 7s. 6d.'"

"Quite so. There you are. And underneath?"

"'Sold to Mr. Windigate of the Alpha, at 12s.'"

"What have you to say now?"

Sherlock Holmes looked deeply chagrined. He drew a sovereign from his pocket and threw it down upon the slab, turning away with the air of a man whose disgust is too deep for words. A few yards off he stopped under a lamp-post and laughed in the hearty, noiseless fashion which was peculiar to him.

"When you see a man with whiskers of that cut and the 'Pink 'un' protruding out of his pocket, you can always draw him by a bet," said he. "I daresay that if I had put 100 pounds down in front of him, that man would not have given me such complete information as was drawn from him by the idea that he was doing me on a wager. Well, Watson, we are, I fancy, nearing the end of our quest, and the only point which remains to be determined is whether we should go on to this Mrs. Oakshott to-night, or whether we should reserve it for to-morrow. It is clear from what that surly fellow said that there are others besides ourselves who are anxious about the matter, and I should – "

His remarks were suddenly cut short by a loud hubbub which broke out from the stall which we had just left. Turning round we saw a little rat-faced fellow standing in the centre of the circle of yellow light which was thrown by the swinging lamp, while Breckinridge, the salesman, framed in the door of his stall, was shaking his fists fiercely at the cringing figure.

"I've had enough of you and your geese," he shouted. "I wish you were all at the devil together. If you come pestering me any more with your silly talk I'll set the dog at you. You bring Mrs. Oakshott here and I'll answer her, but what have you to do with it? Did I buy the geese off you?"

"No; but one of them was mine all the same," whined the little man.

"Well, then, ask Mrs. Oakshott for it."

"She told me to ask you."

"Well, you can ask the King of Proosia, for all I care. I've had enough of it. Get out of this!" He rushed fiercely forward, and the inquirer flitted away into the darkness.

"Ha! this may save us a visit to Brixton Road," whispered Holmes. "Come with me, and we will see what is to be made of this fellow." Striding through the scattered knots of people who lounged round the flaring stalls, my companion speedily overtook the little man and touched him upon the shoulder. He sprang round, and I could see in the gas-light that every vestige of color had been driven from his face.

"Who are you, then? What do you want?" he asked in a quavering voice.

"You will excuse me," said Holmes blandly, "but I could not help overhearing the questions which you put to the salesman just now. I think that I could be of assistance to you."

"You? Who are you? How could you know anything of the matter?"

"My name is Sherlock Holmes. It is my business to know what other people don't know."

"But you can know nothing of this?"

"Excuse me, I know everything of it. You are endeavoring to trace some geese which were sold by Mrs. Oakshott, of Brixton Road, to a salesman named Breckinridge, by him in turn to Mr. Windigate, of the Alpha, and by him to his club, of which Mr. Henry Baker is a member."

"Oh, sir, you are the very man whom I have longed to meet," cried the little fellow with outstretched hands and quivering fingers. "I can hardly explain to you how interested I am in this matter."

Sherlock Holmes hailed a four-wheeler which was passing. "In that case we had better discuss it in a cosy room rather than in this wind-swept market-place," said he. "But pray tell me, before we go farther, who it is that I have the pleasure of assisting."

The man hesitated for an instant. "My name is John Robinson," he answered with a sidelong glance.

"No, no; the real name," said Holmes sweetly. "It is always awkward doing business with an alias."

A flush sprang to the white cheeks of the stranger. "Well then," said he, "my real name is James Ryder."

"Precisely so. Head attendant at the Hotel Cosmopolitan. Pray step into the cab, and I shall soon be able to tell you everything which you would wish to know."

The little man stood glancing from one to the other of us with half-frightened, half-hopeful eyes, as one who is not sure whether he is on the verge of a windfall or of a catastrophe. Then he stepped into the cab, and in half an hour we were back in the sitting-room at Baker Street. Nothing had been said during our drive, but the high, thin breathing of our new companion, and the claspings and unclaspings of his hands, spoke of the nervous tension within him.

"Here we are!" said Holmes cheerily as we filed into the room. "The fire looks very seasonable in this weather. You look cold, Mr. Ryder. Pray take the basket-chair. I will just put on my slippers before we settle this little matter of yours. Now, then! You want to know what became of those geese?"

"Yes, sir."

"Or rather, I fancy, of that goose. It was one bird, I imagine in which you were interested – white, with a black bar across the tail."

Ryder quivered with emotion. "Oh, sir," he cried, "can you tell me where it went to?"

"It came here."

"Here?"

"Yes, and a most remarkable bird it proved. I don't wonder that you should take an interest in it. It laid an egg after it was dead – the bonniest, brightest little blue egg that ever was seen. I have it here in my museum."

Our visitor staggered to his feet and clutched the mantelpiece with his right hand. Holmes unlocked his strong-box and held up the blue carbuncle, which shone out like a star, with a cold brilliant, many-pointed radiance. Ryder stood glaring with a drawn face, uncertain whether to claim or to disown it.

"The game's up, Ryder," said Holmes quietly. "Hold up, man, or you'll be into the fire! Give him an arm back into his chair, Watson. He's not got blood enough to go in for felony with impunity. Give him a dash of brandy. So! Now he looks a little more human. What a shrimp it is, to be sure!"

For a moment he had staggered and nearly fallen, but the brandy brought a tinge of color into his cheeks, and he sat staring with frightened eyes at his accuser.

"I have almost every link in my hands, and all the proofs which I could possibly need, so there is little which you need tell me. Still, that little may as well be cleared up to make the case complete. You had heard, Ryder, of this blue stone of the Countess of Morcar's?"

"It was Catherine Cusack who told me of it," said he in a crackling voice.

"I see – her ladyship's waiting-maid. Well, the temptation of sudden wealth so easily acquired was too much for you, as it has been for better men before you; but you were not very scrupulous in the means you used. It seems to me, Ryder, that there is the making of a very pretty villain in you. You knew that this man Horner, the plumber, had been concerned in some such matter before, and that suspicion would rest the more readily upon him. What did you do, then? You made some small job in my lady's room – you and your confederate Cusack – and you managed that he should be the man sent for. Then, when he had left, you rifled the jewel-case, raised the alarm, and had this unfortunate man arrested. You then – "

Ryder threw himself down suddenly upon the rug and clutched at my companion's knees. "For God's sake, have mercy!" he shrieked. "Think of my father! of my mother! It would break their hearts. I never went wrong before! I never will again. I swear it. I'll swear it on a Bible. Oh, don't bring it into court! For Christ's sake, don't!"

"Get back into your chair!" said Holmes sternly. "It is very well to cringe and crawl now, but you thought little enough of this poor Horner in the dock for a crime of which he knew nothing."

"I will fly, Mr. Holmes. I will leave the country, sir. Then the charge against him will break down."

"Hum! We will talk about that. And now let us hear a true account of the next act. How came the stone into the goose, and how came the goose into the open market? Tell us the truth, for there lies your only hope of safety."

Ryder passed his tongue over his parched lips. "I will tell you it just as it happened, sir," said he. "When Horner had been arrested, it seemed to me that it would be best for me to get away with the stone at once, for I did not know at what moment the police might not take it into their heads to search me and my room. There was no place about the hotel where it would be safe. I went out, as if on some commission, and I made for my sister's house. She had married a man named Oakshott, and lived in Brixton Road, where she fattened fowls for the market. All the way there every man I met seemed to me to be a policeman or a detective; and, for all that it was a cold night, the sweat was pouring down my face before I came to the Brixton Road. My sister asked me what was the matter, and why I was so pale; but I told her that I had been upset by the jewel robbery at the hotel. Then I went into the back yard and smoked a pipe and wondered what it would be best to do.

"I had a friend once called Maudsley, who went to the bad, and has just been serving his time in Pentonville. One day he had met me, and fell into talk about the ways of thieves, and how they could get rid of what they stole. I knew that he would be true to me, for I knew one or two things about him; so I made up my mind to go right on to Kilburn, where he lived, and take him into my confidence. He would show me how to turn the stone into money. But how to get to him in safety? I thought of the agonies I had gone through in coming from the hotel. I might at any moment be seized and searched, and there would be the stone in my waistcoat pocket. I was leaning against the wall at the time and looking at the geese which were waddling about round my feet, and suddenly an idea came into my head which showed me how I could beat the best detective that ever lived.

"My sister had told me some weeks before that I might have the pick of her geese for a Christmas present, and I knew that she was always as good as her word. I would take my goose now, and in it I would carry my stone to Kilburn. There was a little shed in the yard, and behind this I drove one of the birds – a fine big one, white, with a barred tail. I caught it, and prying its bill open, I thrust the stone down its throat as far as my finger could reach. The bird gave a gulp, and I felt the stone pass along its gullet and down into its crop. But the creature flapped and struggled, and out came my sister to know what was the matter. As I turned to speak to her the brute broke loose and fluttered off among the others.

"'Whatever were you doing with that bird, Jem?' says she.

"'Well,' said I, 'you said you'd give me one for Christmas, and I was feeling which was the fattest.'

"'Oh,' says she, 'we've set yours aside for you – Jem's bird, we call it. It's the big white one over yonder. There's twenty-six of them, which makes one for you, and one for us, and two dozen for the market.'

"'Thank you, Maggie,' says I; 'but if it is all the same to you, I'd rather have that one I was handling just now.'

"'The other is a good three pound heavier,' said she, 'and we fattened it expressly for you.'

"'Never mind. I'll have the other, and I'll take it now,' said I.

"'Oh, just as you like,' said she, a little huffed. 'Which is it you want, then?'

"'That white one with the barred tail, right in the middle of the flock.'

"'Oh, very well. Kill it and take it with you.'

"Well, I did what she said, Mr. Holmes, and I carried the bird all the way to Kilburn. I told my pal what I had done, for he was a man that it was easy to tell a thing like that to. He laughed until he choked, and we got a knife and opened the goose. My heart turned to water, for there was no sign of the stone, and I knew that some terrible mistake had occurred. I left the bird rushed back to my sister's, and hurried into the back yard. There was not a bird to be seen there.

"'Where are they all, Maggie?' I cried.

"'Gone to the dealer's, Jem.'

"'Which dealer's?'

"'Breckinridge, of Covent Garden.'

"'But was there another with a barred tail?' I asked, 'the same as the one I chose?'

"'Yes, Jem; there were two barred-tailed ones, and I could never tell them apart.'

"Well, then, of course I saw it all, and I ran off as hard as my feet would carry me to this man Breckinridge; but he had sold the lot at once, and not one word would he tell me as to where they had gone. You heard him yourselves to-night. Well, he has always answered me like that. My sister thinks that I am going mad. Sometimes I think that I am myself. And now – and now I am myself a branded thief, without ever having touched the wealth for which I sold my character. God help me! God help me!" He burst into convulsive sobbing, with his face buried in his hands.

There was a long silence, broken only by his heavy breathing and by the measured tapping of Sherlock Holmes's finger-tips upon the edge of the table. Then my friend rose and threw open the door.

"Get out!" said he.

"What, sir! Oh, Heaven bless you!"

"No more words. Get out!"

And no more words were needed. There was a rush, a clatter upon the stairs, the bang of a door, and the crisp rattle of running footfalls from the street.

"After all, Watson," said Holmes, reaching up his hand for his clay pipe, "I am not retained by the police to supply their deficiencies. If Horner were in danger it would be another thing; but this fellow will not appear against him, and the case must collapse. I suppose that I am commuting a felony. but it is just possible that I am saving a soul. This fellow will not go wrong again; he is too terribly frightened. Send him to jail now, and you make him a jail-bird for life. Besides, it is the season of forgiveness. Chance has put in our way a most singular and whimsical problem, and its solution is its own reward. If you will have the goodness to touch the bell, Doctor, we will begin another investigation, in which, also a bird will be the chief feature."

# A Scandal in Bohemia

## *Sir Arthur Conan Doyle*

### I

To Sherlock Holmes she is always the woman. I have seldom heard him mention her under any other name. In his eyes she eclipses and predominates the whole of her sex. It was not that he felt any emotion akin to love for Irene Adler. All emotions, and that one particularly, were abhorrent to his cold, precise but admirably balanced mind. He was, I take it, the most perfect reasoning and observing machine that the world has seen, but as a lover he would have placed himself in a false position. He never spoke of the softer passions, save with a gibe and a sneer. They were admirable things for the observer – excellent for drawing the veil from men's motives and actions. But for the trained teasoner to admit such intrusions into his own delicate and finely adjusted temperament was to introduce a distracting factor which might throw a doubt upon all his mental results. Grit in a sensitive instrument, or a crack in one of his own high-power lenses, would not be more disturbing than a strong emotion in a nature such as his. And yet there was but one woman to him, and that woman was the late Irene Adler, of dubious and questionable memory.

I had seen little of Holmes lately. My marriage had drifted us away from each other. My own complete happiness, and the home-centred interests which rise up around the man who first finds himself master of his own establishment, were sufficient to absorb all my attention, while Holmes, who loathed every form of society with his whole Bohemian soul, remained in our lodgings in Baker Street, buried among his old books, and alternating from week to week between cocaine and ambition, the drowsiness of the drug, and the fierce energy of his own keen nature. He was still, as ever, deeply attracted by the study of crime, and occupied his immense faculties and extraordinary powers of observation in following out those clews, and clearing up those mysteries which had been abandoned as hopeless by the official police. From time to time I heard some vague account of his doings: of his summons to Odessa in the case of the Trepoff murder, of his clearing up of the singular tragedy of the Atkinson brothers at Trincomalee, and finally of the mission which he had accomplished so delicately and successfully for the reigning family of Holland. Beyond these signs of his activity, however, which I merely shared with all the readers of the daily press, I knew little of my former friend and companion.

One night – it was on the twentieth of March, 1888 – I was returning from a journey to a patient (for I had now returned to civil practice), when my way led me through Baker Street. As I passed the well-remembered door, which must always be associated in my mind with my wooing, and with the dark incidents of the Study in Scarlet, I was seized with a keen desire to see Holmes again, and to know how he was employing his extraordinary powers. His rooms were brilliantly lit, and, even as I looked up, I saw his tall, spare figure pass twice in a dark silhouette against the blind. He was pacing the room swiftly, eagerly, with his head sunk upon his chest and his hands clasped behind him. To me, who knew his every mood and habit, his attitude and manner told their own story. He was at work again. He had risen out of his drug-created dreams and was hot upon the scent of some new problem. I rang the bell and was shown up to the chamber which had formerly been in part my own.

His manner was not effusive. It seldom was; but he was glad, I think, to see me. With hardly a word spoken, but with a kindly eye, he waved me to an armchair, threw across his case of cigars, and indicated a spirit case and a gasogene in the corner. Then he stood before the fire and looked me over in his singular introspective fashion.

"Wedlock suits you," he remarked. "I think, Watson, that you have put on seven and a half pounds since I saw you."

"Seven!" I answered.

"Indeed, I should have thought a little more. Just a trifle more, I fancy, Watson. And in practice again, I observe. You did not tell me that you intended to go into harness."

"Then, how do you know?"

"I see it, I deduce it. How do I know that you have been getting yourself very wet lately, and that you have a most clumsy and careless servant girl?"

"My dear Holmes," said I, "this is too much. You would certainly have been burned, had you lived a few centuries ago. It is true that I had a country walk on Thursday and came home in a dreadful mess, but as I have changed my clothes I can't imagine how you deduce it. As to Mary Jane, she is incorrigible, and my wife has given her notice, but there, again, I fail to see how you work it out."

He chuckled to himself and rubbed his long, nervous hands together.

"It is simplicity itself," said he; "my eyes tell me that on the inside of your left shoe, just where the firelight strikes it, the leather is scored by six almost parallel cuts. Obviously they have been caused by someone who has very carelessly scraped round the edges of the sole in order to remove crusted mud from it. Hence, you see, my double deduction that you had been out in vile weather, and that you had a particularly malignant boot-slitting specimen of the London slavey. As to your practice, if a gentleman walks into my rooms smelling of iodoform, with a black mark of nitrate of silver upon his right forefinger, and a bulge on the right side of his top-hat to show where he has secreted his stethoscope, I must be dull, indeed, if I do not pronounce him to be an active member of the medical profession."

I could not help laughing at the ease with which he explained his process of deduction. "When I hear you give your reasons," I remarked, "the thing always appears to me to be so ridiculously simple that I could easily do it myself, though at each successive instance of your reasoning I am baffled until you explain your process. And yet I believe that my eyes are as good as yours."

"Quite so," he answered, lighting a cigarette, and throwing himself down into an armchair. "You see, but you do not observe. The distinction is clear. For example, you have frequently seen the steps which lead up from the hall to this room."

"Frequently."

"How often?"

"Well, some hundreds of times."

"Then how many are there?"

"How many? I don't know."

"Quite so! You have not observed. And yet you have seen. That is just my point. Now, I know that there are seventeen steps, because I have both seen and observed. By-the-way, since you are interested in these little problems, and since you are good enough to chronicle one or two of my trifling experiences, you may be interested in this." He threw over a sheet of thick, pink-tinted note-paper which had been lying open upon the table. "It came by the last post," said he. "Read it aloud."

The note was undated, and without either signature or address.

"There will call upon you to-night, at a quarter to eight o'clock," it said, "a gentleman who desires to consult you upon a matter of the very deepest moment. Your recent services to one of the royal houses of Europe have shown that you are one who may safely be trusted with matters which are of an importance which can hardly be exaggerated. This account of you we have from all quarters received. Be in your chamber then at that hour, and do not take it amiss if your visitor wear a mask.

"This is indeed a mystery," I remarked. "What do you imagine that it means?"

"I have no data yet. It is a capital mistake to theorize before one has data. Insensibly one begins to twist facts to suit theories, instead of theories to suit facts. But the note itself. What do you deduce from it?"

I carefully examined the writing, and the paper upon which it was written.

"The man who wrote it was presumably well to do," I remarked, endeavoring to imitate my companion's processes. "Such paper could not be bought under half a crown a packet. It is peculiarly strong and stiff."

"Peculiar – that is the very word," said Holmes. "It is not an English paper at all. Hold it up to the light."

I did so, and saw a large "E" with a small "g," a "P," and a large "G" with a small "t" woven into the texture of the paper.

"What do you make of that?" asked Holmes.

"The name of the maker, no doubt; or his monogram, rather."

"Not at all. The 'G' with the small 't' stands for 'Gesellschaft,' which is the German for 'Company.' It is a customary contraction like our 'Co.' 'P,' of course, stands for 'Papier.' Now for the 'Eg.' Let us glance at our Continental Gazetteer." He took down a heavy brown volume from his shelves. "Eglow, Eglonitz – here we are, Egria. It is in a German-speaking country – in Bohemia, not far from Carlsbad. 'Remarkable as being the scene of the death of Wallenstein, and for its numerous glass-factories and paper-mills.' Ha, ha, my boy, what do you make of that?" His eyes sparkled, and he sent up a great blue triumphant cloud from his cigarette.

"The paper was made in Bohemia," I said.

"Precisely. And the man who wrote the note is a German. Do you note the peculiar construction of the sentence – 'This account of you we have from all quarters received.' A Frenchman or Russian could not have written that. It is the German who is so uncourteous to his verbs. It only remains, therefore, to discover what is wanted by this German who writes upon Bohemian paper and prefers wearing a mask to showing his face. And here he comes, if I am not mistaken, to resolve all our doubts."

As he spoke there was the sharp sound of horses' hoofs and grating wheels against the curb, followed by a sharp pull at the bell. Holmes whistled.

"A pair, by the sound," said he. "Yes," he continued, glancing out of the window. "A nice little brougham and a pair of beauties. A hundred and fifty guineas apiece. There's money in this case, Watson, if there is nothing else."

"I think that I had better go, Holmes."

"Not a bit, Doctor. Stay where you are. I am lost without my Boswell. And this promises to be interesting. It would be a pity to miss it."

"But your client – "

"Never mind him. I may want your help, and so may he. Here he comes. Sit down in that armchair, Doctor, and give us your best attention."

A slow and heavy step, which had been heard upon the stairs and in the passage, paused immediately outside the door.

Then there was a loud and authoritative tap.

"Come in!" said Holmes.

A man entered who could hardly have been less than six feet six inches in height, with the chest and limbs of a Hercules. His dress was rich with a richness which would, in England, be looked upon as akin to bad taste. Heavy bands of astrakhan were slashed across the sleeves and fronts of his double-breasted coat, while the deep blue cloak which was thrown over his shoulders was lined with flame-colored silk and secured at the neck with a brooch which consisted of a single flaming beryl. Boots which extended halfway up his calves, and which were trimmed at the tops with rich brown fur, completed the impression of barbaric opulence which was suggested by his whole appearance. He carried a broad-brimmed hat in his hand, while he wore across the upper part of his face, extending down past the cheekbones, a black vizard mask, which he had apparently adjusted that very moment, for his hand was still raised to it as he entered. From the lower part of the face he appeared to be a man of strong character, with a thick, hanging lip, and a long, straight chin suggestive of resolution pushed to the length of obstinacy.

"You had my note?" he asked with a deep harsh voice and a strongly marked German accent. "I told you that I would call." He looked from one to the other of us, as if uncertain which to address.

"Pray take a seat," said Holmes. "This is my friend and colleague, Dr. Watson, who is occasionally good enough to help me in my cases. Whom have I the honor to address?"

"You may address me as the Count Von Kramm, a Bohemian nobleman. I understand that this gentleman, your friend, is a man of honor and discretion, whom I may trust with a matter of the most extreme importance. If not, I should much prefer to communicate with you alone."

I rose to go, but Holmes caught me by the wrist and pushed me back into my chair. "It is both, or none," said he. "You may say before this gentleman anything which you may say to me."

The Count shrugged his broad shoulders. "Then I must begin," said he, "by binding you both to absolute secrecy for two years; at the end of that time the matter will be of no importance. At present it is not too much to say that it is of such weight it may have an influence upon European history."

"I promise," said Holmes.

"And I."

"You will excuse this mask," continued our strange visitor. "The august person who employs me wishes his agent to be unknown to you, and I may confess at once that the title by which I have just called myself is not exactly my own."

"I was aware of it," said Holmes drily.

"The circumstances are of great delicacy, and every precaution has to be taken to quench what might grow to be an immense scandal and seriously compromise one of the reigning families of Europe. To speak plainly, the matter implicates the great House of Ormstein, hereditary kings of Bohemia."

"I was also aware of that," murmured Holmes, settling himself down in his armchair and closing his eyes.

Our visitor glanced with some apparent surprise at the languid, lounging figure of the man who had been no doubt depicted to him as the most incisive reasoner and most energetic agent in Europe. Holmes slowly reopened his eyes and looked impatiently at his gigantic client.

"If your Majesty would condescend to state your case," he remarked, "I should be better able to advise you."

The man sprang from his chair and paced up and down the room in uncontrollable agitation. Then, with a gesture of desperation, he tore the mask from his face and hurled it upon the ground. "You are right," he cried; "I am the King. Why should I attempt to conceal it?"

"Why, indeed?" murmured Holmes. "Your Majesty had not spoken before I was aware that I was addressing Wilhelm Gottsreich Sigismond von Ormstein, Grand Duke of Cassel-Felstein, and hereditary King of Bohemia."

"But you can understand," said our strange visitor, sitting down once more and passing his hand over his high white forehead, "you can understand that I am not accustomed to doing such business in my own person. Yet the matter was so delicate that I could not confide it to an agent without putting myself in his power. I have come incognito from Prague for the purpose of consulting you."

"Then, pray consult," said Holmes, shutting his eyes once more.

"The facts are briefly these: Some five years ago, during a lengthy visit to Warsaw, I made the acquaintance of the wellknown adventuress, Irene Adler. The name is no doubt farmiliar to you."

"Kindly look her up in my index, Doctor," murmured Holmes without opening his eyes. For many years he had adopted a system of docketing all paragraphs concerning men and things, so that it was difficult to name a subject or a person on which he could not at once furnish information. In this case I found her biography sandwiched in between that of a Hebrew rabbi and that of a staff-commander who had written a monograph upon the deep-sea fishes.

"Let me see!" said Holmes. "Hum! Born in New Jersey in the year 1858. Contralto – hum! La Scala, hum! Prima donna Imperial Opera of Warsaw – yes! Retired from operatic stage – ha! Living in London – quite so! Your Majesty, as I understand, became entangled with this young person, wrote her some compromising letters, and is now desirous of getting those letters back."

"Precisely so. But how – "

"Was there a secret marriage?"

"None."

"No legal papers or certificates?"

"None."

"Then I fail to follow your Majesty. If this young person should produce her letters for blackmailing or other purposes, how is she to prove their authenticity?"

"There is the writing."

"Pooh, pooh! Forgery."

"My private note-paper."

"Stolen."

"My own seal."

"Imitated."

"My photograph."

"Bought."

"We were both in the photograph."

"Oh, dear! That is very bad! Your Majesty has indeed

committed an indiscretion."

"I was mad – insane."

"You have compromised yourself seriously."

"I was only Crown Prince then. I was young. I am but thirty now."

"It must be recovered."

"We have tried and failed."

"Your Majesty must pay. It must be bought."

"She will not sell."

"Stolen, then."

"Five attempts have been made. Twice burglars in my pay ransacked her house. Once we diverted her luggage when she travelled. Twice she has been waylaid. There has been no result."

"No sign of it?"

"Absolutely none."

Holmes laughed. "It is quite a pretty little problem," said he.

"But a very serious one to me," returned the King reproachfully.

"Very, indeed. And what does she propose to do with the photograph?"

"To ruin me."

"But how?"

"I am about to be married."

"So I have heard."

"To Clotilde Lothman von Saxe-Meningen, second daughter of the King of Scandinavia. You may know the stnct principles of her family. She is herself the very soul of delicacy. A shadow of a doubt as to my conduct would bring the matter to an end."

"And Irene Adler?"

"Threatens to send them the photograph. And she will do it. I know that she will do it. You do not know her, but she has a soul of steel. She has the face of the most beautiful of women, and the mind of the most resolute of men. Rather than I should marry another woman, there are no lengths to which she would not go – none."

"You are sure that she has not sent it yet?"

"I am sure."

"And why?"

"Because she has said that she would send it on the day

when the betrothal was publicly proclaimed. That will be next Monday."

"Oh, then we have three days yet," said Holmes with a yawn. "That is very fortunate, as I have one or two matters of importance to look into just at present. Your Majesty will, of course, stay in London for the present?"

"Certainly. You will find me at the Langham under the name of the Count Von Kramm."

"Then I shall drop you a line to let you know how we progress."

"Pray do so. I shall be all anxiety."

"Then, as to money?"

"You have carte blanche."

"Absolutely?"

"I tell you that I would give one of the provinces of my kingdom to have that photograph."

"And for present expenses?"

The King took a heavy chamois leather bag from under his cloak and laid it on the table.

"There are three hundred pounds in gold and seven hundred in notes," he said.

Holmes scribbled a receipt upon a sheet of his note-book and handed it to him.

"And Mademoiselle's address?" he asked.

"Is Briony Lodge, Serpentine Avenue, St. John's Wood."

Holmes took a note of it. "One other question," said he. "Was the photograph a cabinet?"

"It was."

"Then, good-night, your Majesty, and I trust that we shall soon have some good news for you. And good-night, Watson," he added, as the wheels of the royal brougham rolled down the street. "If you wlll be good enough to call to-morrow afternoon at three o'clock I should like to chat this little matter over with you."

## II

At three o'clock precisely I was at Baker Street, but Holmes had not yet returned. The landlady informed me that he had left the house shortly after eight o'clock in the morning. I sat down beside the fire, however, with the intention of awaiting him, however long he might be. I was already deeply interested in his inquiry, for, though it was surrounded by none of the grim and strange features which were associated with the two crimes which I have already recorded, still, the nature of the case and the exalted station of his client gave it a character of its own. Indeed, apart from the nature of the investigation which my friend had on hand, there was something in his masterly grasp of a situation, and his keen, incisive reasoning, which made it a pleasure to me to study his system of work, and to follow the quick, subtle methods by which he disentangled the most inextricable mysteries. So accustomed was I to his invariable success that the very possibility of his failing had ceased to enter into my head.

It was close upon four before the door opened, and a drunkenlooking groom, ill-kempt and side-whiskered, with an inflamed face and disreputable clothes, walked into the room. Accustomed as I was to my friend's amazing powers in the use of disguises, I had to look three times before I was certain that it was indeed he. With a nod he vanished into the bedroom, whence he emerged in five minutes tweed-suited and respectable, as of old. Putting his hands into his pockets, he stretched out his legs in front of the fire and laughed heartily for some minutes.

"Well, really!" he cried, and then he choked and laughed again until he was obliged to lie back, limp and helpless, in the chair.

"What is it?"

"It's quite too funny. I am sure you could never guess how I employed my morning, or what I ended by doing."

"I can't imagine. I suppose that you have been watching the habits, and perhaps the house, of Miss Irene Adler."

"Quite so; but the sequel was rather unusual. I will tell you, however. I left the house a little after eight o'clock this morning in the character of a groom out of work. There is a wonderful sympathy and freemasonry among horsy men. Be one of them, and you will know all that there is to know. I soon found Briony Lodge. It is a bijou villa, with a garden at the back. but built out in front right up to the road, two stories. Chubb lock to the door. Large sitting-room on the right side, well furnished, with long windows almost to the floor, and those preposterous English window fasteners which a child could open. Behind there was nothing remarkable, save that the passage window could be reached from the top of the coach-house. I walked round it and examined it closely from every point of view, but without noting anything else of interest.

"I then lounged down the street and found, as I expected, that there was a mews in a lane which runs down by one wall of the garden. I lent the ostlers a hand in rubbing down their horses, and received in exchange twopence, a glass of half and half, two fills of shag tobacco, and as much information as I could desire about Miss Adler, to say nothing of half a dozen other people in the neighborhood in whom I was not in the least interested, but whose biographies I was compelled to listen to."

"And what of Irene Adler?" I asked.

"Oh, she has turned all the men's heads down in that part. She is the daintiest thing under a bonnet on this planet. So say the Serpentine-mews, to a man. She lives quietly, sings at concerts, drives out at five every day, and returns at seven sharp for dinner. Seldom goes out at other times, except when she sings. Has only one male visitor, but a good deal of him. He is dark, handsome, and dashing, never calls less than once a day, and often twice. He is a Mr. Godfrey Norton, of the Inner Temple. See the advantages of a cabman as a confidant. They had driven him home a dozen times from Serpentine-mews, and knew all about him. When I had listened to all they had to tell, I began to walk up and down near Briony Lodge once more, and to think over my plan of campaign.

"This Godfrey Norton was evidently an important factor in the matter. He was a lawyer. That sounded ominous. What was the relation between them, and what the object of his repeated visits? Was she his client, his friend, or his mistress? If the former, she had probably transferred the photograph to his keeping. If the latter, it was less likely. On the issue of this question depended whether I should continue my work at Briony Lodge, or turn my attention to the gentleman's chambers in the Temple. It was a delicate point. and it widened the field of my inquiry. I fear that I bore you with these details, but I have to let you see my little difficulties, if you are to understand the situation."

"I am following you closely," I answered.

"I was still balancing the matter in my mind when a hansom cab drove up to Briony Lodge, and a gentleman sprang out. He was a remarkably handsome man, dark, aquiline, and moustached-evidently the man of whom I had heard. He appeared to be in a great hurry, shouted to the cabman to wait, and brushed past the maid who opened the door with the air of a man who was thoroughly at home.

"He was in the house about half an hour, and I could catch glimpses of him in the windows of the sitting-room, pacing up and down, talking excitedly, and waving his arms. Of her I could see nothing. Presently he emerged, looking even more flurried than before. As he stepped up to the cab, he pulled a gold watch from his pocket and looked at it earnestly, 'Drive like the devil,' he shouted, 'first to Gross & Hankey's in Regent Street, and then to the Church of St. Monica in the Edgeware Road. Half a guinea if you do it in twenty minutes!'

"Away they went, and I was just wondering whether I should not do well to follow them when up the lane came a neat little landau, the coachman with his coat only half-buttoned, and his tie under his ear, while all the tags of his harness were sticking out of the buckles. It hadn't pulled up before she shot out of the hall door and into it. I only caught a glimpse of her at the moment, but she was a lovely woman, with a face that a man might die for.

"'The Church of St. Monica, John,' she cried, 'and half a sovereign if you reach it in twenty minutes.'

"This was quite too good to lose, Watson. I was just balancing whether I should run for it, or whether I should perch behind her landau when a cab came through the street. The driver looked twice at such a shabby fare, but I jumped in before he could object. 'The Church of St. Monica,' said I, 'and half a sovereign if you reach it in twenty minutes.' It was twenty-five minutes to twelve, and of course it was clear enough what was in the wind.

"My cabby drove fast. I don't think I ever drove faster, but the others were there before us. The cab and the landau with their steaming horses were in front of the door when I arrived.

I paid the man and hurried into the church. There was not a soul there save the two whom I had followed and a surpliced clergyman, who seemed to be expostulating with them. They were all three standing in a knot in front of the altar. I lounged up the side aisle like any other idler who has dropped into a church. Suddenly, to my surprise, the three at the altar faced round to me, and Godfrey Norton came running as hard as he could towards me.

"Thank God," he cried. "You'll do. Come! Come!"

"What then?" I asked.

"Come, man, come, only three minutes, or it won't be legal."

I was half-dragged up to the altar, and before I knew where I was I found myself mumbling responses which were whispered in my ear. and vouching for things of which I knew nothing, and generally assisting in the secure tying up of Irene Adler, spinster, to Godfrey Norton, bachelor. It was all done in an instant, and there was the gentleman thanking me on the one side and the lady on the other, while the clergyman beamed on me in front. It was the most preposterous position in which I ever found myself in my life, and it was the thought of it that started me laughing just now. It seems that there had been some informality about their license, that the clergyman absolutely refused to marry them without a witness of some sort, and that my lucky appearance saved the bridegroom from having to sally out into the streets in search of a best man. The bride gave me a sovereign, and I mean to wear it on my watch-chain in memory of the occasion."

"This is a very unexpected turn of affairs," said I; "and what then?"

"Well, I found my plans very seriously menaced. It looked as if the pair might take an immediate departure, and so necessitate very prompt and energetic measures on my part. At the church door, however, they separated, he driving back to the Temple, and she to her own house. 'I shall drive out in the park at five as usual,' she said as she left him. I heard no more. They drove away in different directions, and I went off to make my own arrangements."

"Which are?"

"Some cold beef and a glass of beer," he answered, ringing the bell. "I have been too busy to think of food, and I am likely to be busier still this evening. By the way, Doctor, I shall want your cooperation."

"I shall be delighted."

"You don't mind breaking the law?"

"Not in the least."

"Nor running a chance of arrest?"

"Not in a good cause."

"Oh, the cause is excellent!"

"Then I am your man."

"I was sure that I might rely on you."

"But what is it you wish?"

"When Mrs. Turner has brought in the tray I will make it clear to you. Now," he said as he turned hungrily on the simple fare that our landlady had provided, "I must discuss it while I eat, for I have not much time. It is nearly five now. In two hours we must be on the scene of action. Miss Irene, or Madame, rather, returns from her drive at seven. We must be at Briony Lodge to meet her."

"And what then?"

"You must leave that to me. I have already arranged what is to occur. There is only one point on which I must insist. You must not interfere, come what may. You understand?"

"I am to be neutral?"

"To do nothing whatever. There will probably be some small unpleasantness. Do not join in it. It will end in my being conveyed into the house. Four or five minutes afterwards the sitting-room window will open. You are to station yourself close to that open window."

"Yes."

"You are to watch me, for I will be visible to you."

"Yes."

"And when I raise my hand – so – you will throw into the room what I give you to throw, and will, at the same time, raise the cry of fire. You quite follow me?"

"Entirely."

"It is nothing very formidable," he said, taking a long

cigarshaped roll from his pocket. "It is an ordinary plumber's smokerocket, fitted with a cap at either end to make it self-lighting. Your task is confined to that. When you raise your cry of fire, it will be taken up by quite a number of people. You may then walk to the end of the street, and I will rejoin you in ten minutes. I hope that I have made myself clear?"

"I am to remain neutral, to get near the window, to watch you, and at the signal to throw in this object, then to raise the cry of fire, and to wait you at the corner of the street."

"Precisely."

"Then you may entirely rely on me."

"That is excellent. I think, perhaps, it is almost time that I prepare for the new role I have to play."

He disappeared into his bedroom and returned in a few minutes in the character of an amiable and simple-minded Nonconformist clergyman. His broad black hat, his baggy trousers. his white tie, his sympathetic smile, and general look of peering and benevolent curiosity were such as Mr. John Hare alone could have equalled. It was not merely that Holmes changed his costume. His expression, his manner, his very soul seemed to vary with every fresh part that he assumed. The stage lost a fine actor, even as science lost an acute reasoner, when he became a specialist in crime.

It was a quarter past six when we left Baker Street, and it still wanted ten minutes to the hour when we found ourselves in Serpentine Avenue. It was already dusk, and the lamps were just being lighted as we paced up and down in front of Briony Lodge, waiting for the coming of its occupant. The house was just such as I had pictured it from Sherlock Holmes's succinct description, but the locality appeared to be less private than I expected. On the contrary, for a small street in a quiet neighborhood, it was remarkably animated. There was a group of shabbily dressed men smoking and laughing in a corner, a scissors-grinder with his wheel, two guardsmen who were flirting with a nurse-girl, and several well-dressed young men who were lounging up and down with cigars in their mouths.

"You see," remarked Holmes, as we paced to and fro in front of the house, "this marriage rather simplifies matters. The photograph becomes a double-edged weapon now. The chances are that she would be as averse to its being seen by Mr. Godfrey Norton, as our client is to its coming to the eyes of his princess. Now the question is, Where are we to find the photograph?"

"Where, indeed?"

"It is most unlikely that she carries it about with her. It is cabinet size. Too large for easy concealment about a woman's dress. She knows that the King is capable of having her waylaid and searched. Two attempts of the sort have already been made. We may take it, then, that she does not carry it about with her."

"Where, then?"

"Her banker or her lawyer. There is that double possibility. But I am inclined to think neither. Women are naturally secretive, and they like to do their own secreting. Why should she hand it over to anyone else? She could trust her own guardianship, but she could not tell what indirect or political influence might be brought to bear upon a business man. Besides, remember that she had resolved to use it within a few days. It must be where she can lay her hands upon it. It must be in her own house."

"But it has twice been burgled."

"Pshaw! They did not know how to look."

"But how will you look?"

"I will not look."

"What then?"

"I will get her to show me."

"But she will refuse."

"She will not be able to. But I hear the rumble of wheels. It is hcr carriage. Now carry out my orders to the letter."

As he spoke the gleam of the side-lights of a carriage came round the curve of the avenue. It was a smart little landau which rattled up to the door of Briony Lodge. As it pulled up, one of the loafing men at the corner dashed forward to open the door in the hope of earning a copper, but was elbowed away by another loafer, who had rushed up with the same intention. A fierce quarrel broke out, which was increased by the two guardsmen, who took sides with one of the loungers, and by the scissorsgrinder, who was equally hot upon the other side. A blow was struck, and in an instant the lady, who had stepped from her carriage, was the centre of a little knot of flushed and struggling men, who struck savagely at each other with their fists and sticks. Holmes dashed into the crowd to protect the lady; but just as he reached her he gave a cry and dropped to the ground, with the blood running freely down his face. At his fall the guardsmen took to their heels in one direction and the loungers in the other, while a number of better-dressed people, who had watched the scuffle without taking part in it, crowded in to help the lady and to attend to the injured man. Irene Adler, as I will still call her, had hurried up the steps; but she stood at the top with her superb figure outlined against the lights of the hall, looking back into the street.

"Is the poor gentleman much hurt?" she asked.

"He is dead," cried several voices.

"No, no, there's life in him!" shouted another. "But he'll be gone before you can get him to hospital."

"He's a brave fellow," said a woman. "They would have had the lady's purse and watch if it hadn't been for him. They were a gang, and a rough one, too. Ah, he's breathing now."

"He can't lie in the street. May we bring him in, marm?"

"Surely. Bring him into the sitting-room. There is a comfortable sofa. This way, please!"

Slowly and solemnly he was borne into Briony Lodge and laid out in the principal room, while I still observed the proceedings from my post by the window. The lamps had been lit, but the blinds had not been drawn, so that I could see Holmes as he lay upon the couch. I do not know whether he was seized with compunction at that moment for the part he was playing, but I know that I never felt more heartily ashamed of myself in my life than when I saw the beautiful creature against whom I was conspiring, or the grace and kindliness with which she waited upon the injured man. And yet it would be the blackest treachery to Holmes to draw back now from the part which he had intrusted to me. I hardened my heart, and took the smoke-rocket from under my ulster. After all, I thought, we are not injuring her. We are but preventing her from injuring another.

Holmes had sat up upon the couch, and I saw him motion like a man who is in need of air. A maid rushed across and threw open the window. At the same instant I saw him raise his hand and at the signal I tossed my rocket into the room with a cry of "Fire!" The word was no sooner out of my mouth than the whole crowd of spectators, well dressed and ill – gentlemen, ostlers, and servant-maids – joined in a general shriek of "Fire!" Thick clouds of smoke curled through the room and out at the open window. I caught a glimpse of rushing figures, and a moment later the voice of Holmes from within assuring them that it was a false alarm. Slipping through the shouting crowd I made my way to the corner of the street, and in ten minutes was rejoiced to find my friend's arm in mine, and to get away from the scene of uproar. He walked swiftly and in silence for some few minutes until we had turned down one of the quiet streets which lead towards the Edgeware Road.

"You did it very nicely, Doctor," he remarked. "Nothing could have been better. It is all right."

"You have the photograph?"

"I know where it is."

"And how did you find out?"

"She showed me, as I told you she would."

"I am still in the dark."

"I do not wish to make a mystery," said he, laughing. "The matter was perfectly simple. You, of course, saw that everyone in the street was an accomplice. They were all engaged for the evening."

"I guessed as much."

"Then, when the row broke out, I had a little moist red paint in the palm of my hand. I rushed forward, fell down. clapped my hand to my face, and became a piteous spectacle. It is an old trick."

"That also I could fathom."

"Then they carried me in. She was bound to have me in. What else could she do? And into her sitting-room. which was the very room which I suspected. It lay between that and her bedroom, and I was determined to see which. They laid me on a couch, I motioned for air, they were compelled to open the window. and you had your chance."

"How did that help you?"

"It was all-important. When a woman thinks that her house is on fire, her instinct is at once to rush to the thing which she values most. It is a perfectly overpowering impulse, and I have more than once taken advantage of it. In the case of the Darlington substitution scandal it was of use to me, and also in the Arnsworth Castle business. A married woman grabs at her baby; an unmarried one reaches for her jewel-box. Now it was clear to me that our lady of to-day had nothing in the house more precious to her than what we are in quest of. She would rush to secure it. The alarm of fire was admirably done. The smoke and shouting were enough to shake nerves of steel. She responded beautifully. The photograph is in a recess behind a sliding panel just above the right bell-pull. She was there in an instant, and I caught a glimpse of it as she half-drew it out. When I cried out that it was a false alarm, she replaced it, glanced at the rocket, rushed from the room, and I have not seen her since. I rose, and, making my excuses, escaped from the house. I hesitated whether to attempt to secure the photograph at once; but the coachman had come in, and as he was watching me narrowly it seemed safer to wait. A little over-precipitance may ruin all."

"And now?" I asked.

"Our quest is practically finished. I shall call with the King to-morrow, and with you, if you care to come with us. We will be shown into the sitting-room to wait for the lady; but it is probable that when she comes she may find neither us nor the photograph. It might be a satisfaction to his Majesty to regain it with his own hands."

"And when will you call?"

"At eight in the morning. She will not be up, so that we shall have a clear field. Besides, we must be prompt, for this marriage may mean a complete change in her life and habits. I must wire to the King without delay."

We had reached Baker Street and had stopped at the door. He was searching his pockets for the key when someone passing said:

"Good-night, Mister Sherlock Holmes."

There were several people on the pavement at the time, but the greeting appeared to come from a slim youth in an ulster who had hurried by.

"I've heard that voice before," said Holmes, staring down the dimly lit street. "Now, I wonder who the deuce that could have been."

III

I slept at Baker Street that night, and we were engaged upon our toast and coffee in the morning when the King of Bohemia rushed into the room.

"You have really got it!" he cried, grasping Sherlock Holmes by either shoulder and looking eagerly into his face.

"Not yet."

"But you have hopes?"

"I have hopes."

"Then, come. I am all impatience to be gone."

"We must have a cab."

"No, my brougham is waiting."

"Then that will simplify matters." We descended and started off once more for Briony Lodge.

"Irene Adler is married," remarked Holmes.

"Married! When?"

"Yesterday."

"But to whom?"

"To an English lawyer named Norton."

"But she could not love him."

"I am in hopes that she does."

"And why in hopes?"

"Because it would spare your Majesty all fear of future annoyance. If the lady loves her husband, she does not love your Majesty. If she does not love your Majesty, there is no reason why she should interfere with your Majesty's plan."

"It is true. And yet – Well! I wish she had been of my own station! What a queen she would have made!" He relapsed into a moody silence, which was not broken until we drew up in Serpentine Avenue.

The door of Briony Lodge was open, and an elderly woman stood upon the steps. She watched us with a sardonic eye as we stepped from the brougham.

"Mr. Sherlock Holmes, I believe?" said she.

"I am Mr. Holmes," answered my companion, looking at her with a questioning and rather startled gaze.

"Indeed! My mistress told me that you were likely to call. She left this morning with her husband by the 5:15 train from Charing Cross for the Continent."

"What!" Sherlock Holmes staggered back, white with chagrin and surprise. "Do you mean that she has left England?"

"Never to return."

"And the papers?" asked the King hoarsely. "All is lost."

"We shall see." He pushed past the servant and rushed into the drawing-room, followed by the King and myself. The furniture was scattered about in every direction, with dismantled shelves and open drawers, as if the lady had hurriedly ransacked them before her flight. Holmes rushed at the bell-pull, tore back a small sliding shutter, and, plunging in his hand, pulled out a photograph and a letter. The photograph was of Irene Adler herself in evening dress, the letter was superscribed to "Sherlock Holmes, Esq. To be left till called for." My friend tore it open and we all three read it together. It was dated at midnight of the preceding night and ran in this way:

MY DEAR MR. SHERLOCK HOLMES,

You really did it very well. You took me in completely. Until after the alarm of fire, I had not a suspicion. But then, when I found how I had betrayed myself, I began to think. I had been warned against you months ago. I had been told that if the King employed an agent it would certainly be you. And your address had been given me. Yet, with all this, you made me reveal what you wanted to know. Even after I became suspicious, I found it hard to think evil of such a dear, kind old clergyman. But, you know, I have been trained as an actress myself. Male costume is nothing new to me. I often take advantage of the freedom which it gives. I sent John, the coachman, to watch you, ran up stairs, got into my walking-clothes, as I call them, and came down just as you departed.

Well, I followed you to your door, and so made sure that I was really an object of interest to the celebrated Mr. Sherlock Holmes. Then I, rather imprudently, wished you good-night, and started for the Temple to see my husband. We both thought the best resource was flight, when pursued by so formidable an antagonist; so you will find the nest empty when you call to-morrow. As to the photograph, your client may rest in peace. I love and am loved by a better man than he. The King may do what he will without hindrance from one whom he has cruelly wronged. I keep it only to safeguard myself, and to preserve a weapon which will always secure me from any steps which he might take in the future. I leave a photograph which he might care to possess; and I remain, dear Mr. Sherlock Holmes,

Very truly yours,

IRENE NORTON, nee ADLER.

"What a woman – oh, what a woman!" cried the King of Bohemia, when we had all three read this epistle. "Did I not tell you how quick and resolute she was? Would she not have made an admirable queen? Is it not a pity that she was not on my level?"

"From what I have seen of the lady she seems indeed to be on a very different level to your Majesty," said Holmes coldly. "I am sorry that I have not been able to bring your Majesty's business to a more successful conclusion."

"On the contrary, my dear sir," cried the King; "nothing could be more successful. I know that her word is inviolate. The photograph is now as safe as if it were in the fire."

"I am glad to hear your Majesty say so."

"I am immensely indebted to you. Pray tell me in what way I can reward you. This ring – " He slipped an emerald snake ring from his finger and held it out upon the palm of his hand.

"Your Majesty has something which I should value even more highly," said Holmes.

"You have but to name it."

"This photograph!"

The King stared at him in amazement.

"Irene's photograph!" he cried. "Certainly, if you wish it."

"I thank your Majesty. Then there is no more to be done in the matter. I have the honor to wish you a very good-morning." He bowed, and, turning away without observing the hand which the King had stretched out to him, he set off in my company for his chambers.

And that was how a great scandal threatened to affect the kingdom of Bohemia, and how the best plans of Mr. Sherlock Holmes were beaten by a woman's wit. He used to make merry over the cleverness of women, but I have not heard him do it of late. And when he speaks of Irene Adler, or when he refers to her photograph, it is always under the honorable title of the woman.

# The "Slapping Sal"

### *Sir Arthur Conan Doyle*

It was in the days when France's power was already broken upon the seas, and when more of her three-deckers lay rotting in the Medway than were to be found in Brest harbour. But her frigates and corvettes still scoured the ocean, closely followed ever by those of her rival. At the uttermost ends of the earth these dainty vessels, with sweet names of girls or of flowers, mangled and shattered each other for the honour of the four yards of bunting which flapped from the end of their gaffs.

It had blown hard in the night, but the wind had dropped with the dawning, and now the rising sun tinted the fringe of the storm-wrack as it dwindled into the west and glinted on the endless crests of the long, green waves. To north and south and west lay a skyline which was unbroken save by the spout of foam when two of the great Atlantic seas dashed each other into spray. To the east was a rocky island, jutting out into craggy points, with a few scattered clumps of palm trees and a pennant of mist streaming out from the bare, conical hill which capped it. A heavy surf beat upon the shore, and, at a safe distance from it, the British 32-gun frigate Leda, Captain A. P. Johnson, raised her black, glistening side upon the crest of a wave, or swooped down into an emerald valley, dipping away to the nor'ard under easy sail. On her snow-white quarter-deck stood a stiff little brown-faced man, who swept the horizon with his glass.

"Mr. Wharton!" he cried, with a voice like a rusty hinge.

A thin, knock-kneed officer shambled across the poop to him.

"Yes, sir."

"I've opened the sealed orders, Mr. Wharton."

A glimmer of curiosity shone upon the meagre features of the first lieutenant. The Leda had sailed with her consort, the Dido, from Antigua the week before, and the admiral's orders had been contained in a sealed envelope.

"We were to open them on reaching the deserted island of Sombriero, lying in north latitude eighteen, thirty-six, west longitude sixty-three, twenty-eight. Sombriero bore four miles to the north-east from our port-bow when the gale cleared, Mr. Wharton."

The lieutenant bowed stiffly. He and the captain had been bosom friends from childhood. They had gone to school together, joined the navy together, fought again and again together, and married into each other's families, but so long as their feet were on the poop the iron discipline of the service struck all that was human out of them and left only the superior and the subordinate. Captain Johnson took from his pocket a blue paper, which crackled as he unfolded it.

"The 32-gun frigates Leda and Dido (Captains A. P. Johnson and James Munro) are to cruise from the point at which these instructions are read to the mouth of the Caribbean sea, in the hope of encountering the French frigate La Gloire (48), which has recently harassed our merchant ships in that quarter. H.M. frigates are also directed to hunt down the piratical craft known sometimes as the Slapping Sal and sometimes as the Hairy Hudson, which has plundered the British ships as per margin, inflicting barbarities upon their crews. She is a small brig, carrying ten light guns, with one twenty-four pound carronade forward. She was last seen upon the 23rd. ult. to the north-east of the island of Sombriero.

"(Signed) James Montgomery "(Rear-Admiral).

"H.M.S. Colossus, Antigua."

"We appear to have lost our consort," said Captain Johnson, folding up his instructions and again sweeping the horizon with his glass. "She drew away after we reefed down. It would be a pity if we met this heavy Frenchman without the Dido, Mr. Wharton. Eh?"

The lieutenant twinkled and smiled.

"She has eighteen-pounders on the main and twelves on the poop, sir," said the captain. "She carries four hundred to our two hundred and thirty-one. Captain de Milon is the smartest man in the French service. Oh, Bobby boy, I'd give my hopes of my flag to rub my side up against her!" He turned on his heel, ashamed of his momentary lapse. "Mr. Wharton," said he, looking back sternly over his shoulder, "get those square sails shaken out and bear away a point more to the west."

"A brig on the port-bow," came a voice from the forecastle.

"A brig on the port-bow," said the lieutenant.

The captain sprang upon the bulwarks and held on by the mizzen-shrouds, a strange little figure with flying skirts and puckered eyes. The lean lieutenant craned his neck and whispered to Smeaton, the second, while officers and men came popping up from below and clustered along the weather-rail, shading their eyes with their hands—for the tropical sun was already clear of the palm trees. The strange brig lay at anchor in the throat of a curving estuary, and it was already obvious that she could not get out without passing under the guns of the frigate. A long, rocky point to the north of her held her in.

"Keep her as she goes, Mr. Wharton," said the captain. "Hardly worth while our clearing for action, Mr. Smeaton, but the men can stand by the guns in case she tries to pass us. Cast loose the bow-chasers and send the small-arm men to the forecastle."

A British crew went to its quarters in those days with the quiet serenity of men on their daily routine. In a few minutes, without fuss or sound, the sailors were knotted round their guns, the marines were drawn up and leaning on their muskets, and the frigate's bowsprit pointed straight for her little victim.

"Is it the Slapping Sal, sir?"

"I have no doubt of it, Mr. Wharton."

"They don't seem to like the look of us, sir. They've cut their cable and are clapping on sail."

It was evident that the brig meant struggling for her freedom. One little patch of canvas fluttered out above another, and her people could be seen working like madmen in the rigging. She made no attempt to pass her antagonist, but headed up the estuary. The captain rubbed his hands.

"She's making for shoal water, Mr. Wharton, and we shall have to cut her out, sir. She's a footy little brig, but I should have thought a fore-and-after would have been more handy."

"It was a mutiny, sir."

"Ah, indeed!"

"Yes, sir, I heard of it at Manilla: a bad business, sir. Captain and two mates murdered. This Hudson, or Hairy Hudson as they call him, led the mutiny. He's a Londoner, sir, and a cruel villain as ever walked."

"His next walk will be to Execution Dock, Mr. Wharton. She seems heavily manned. I wish I could take twenty topmen out of her, but they would be enough to corrupt the crew of the ark, Mr. Wharton."

Both officers were looking through their glasses at the brig. Suddenly the lieutenant showed his teeth in a grin, while the captain flushed a deeper red.

"That's Hairy Hudson on the after-rail, sir."

"The low, impertinent blackguard! He'll play some other antics before we are done with him. Could you reach him with the long eighteen, Mr. Smeaton?"

"Another cable length will do it, sir."

The brig yawed as they spoke, and as she came round a spurt of smoke whiffed out from her quarter. It was a pure piece of bravado, for the gun could scarce carry half-way. Then with a jaunty swing the little ship came into the wind again, and shot round a fresh curve in the winding channel.

"The water's shoaling rapidly, sir," repeated the second lieutenant.

"There's six fathoms by the chart."

"Four by the lead, sir."

"When we clear this point we shall see how we lie. Ha! I thought as much! Lay her to, Mr. Wharton. Now we have got her at our mercy!"

The frigate was quite out of sight of the sea now at the head of this river-like estuary. As she came round the curve the two shores were seen to converge at a point about a mile distant. In the angle, as near shore as she could get, the brig was lying with her broadside towards her pursuer and a wisp of black cloth streaming from her mizzen. The lean lieutenant, who had reappeared upon deck with a cutlass strapped to his side and two pistols rammed into his belt, peered curiously at the ensign.

"Is it the Jolly Rodger, sir?" he asked.

But the captain was furious.

"He may hang where his breeches are hanging before I have done with him!" said he. "What boats will you want, Mr. Wharton?"

"We should do it with the launch and the jolly-boat."

"Take four and make a clean job of it. Pipe away the crews at once, and I'll work her in and help you with the long eighteens."

With a rattle of ropes and a creaking of blocks the four boats splashed into the water. Their crews clustered thickly into them: bare-footed sailors, stolid marines, laughing middies, and in the sheets of each the senior officers with their stern schoolmaster faces. The captain, his elbows on the binnacle, still watched the distant brig. Her crew were tricing up the boarding-netting, dragging round the starboard guns, knocking new portholes for them, and making every preparation for a desperate resistance. In the thick of it all a huge man, bearded to the eyes, with a red nightcap upon his head, was straining and stooping and hauling. The captain watched him with a sour smile, and then snapping up his glass he turned upon his heel. For an instant he stood staring.

"Call back the boats!" he cried in his thin, creaking voice. "Clear away for action there! Cast loose those main-deck guns. Brace back the yards, Mr. Smeaton, and stand by to go about when she has weigh enough."

Round the curve of the estuary was coming a huge vessel. Her great yellow bowsprit and white-winged figure-head were jutting out from the cluster of palm trees, while high above them towered three immense masts with the tricolour flag floating superbly from the mizzen. Round she came, the deep-blue water creaming under her fore foot, until her long, curving, black side, her line of shining copper beneath and of snow-white hammocks above, and the thick clusters of men who peered over her bulwarks were all in full view. Her lower yards were slung, her ports triced up, and her guns run out all ready for action. Lying behind one of the promontories of the island, the lookout men of the Gloire upon the shore had seen the cul de sac into which the British frigate was headed, so that Captain de Milon had served the Leda as Captain Johnson had the Slapping Sal.

But the splendid discipline of the British service was at its best in such a crisis. The boats flew back; their crews clustered aboard, they were swung up at the davits and the fall-ropes made fast. Hammocks were brought up and stowed, bulkheads sent down, ports and magazines opened, the fires put out in the galley, and the drums beat to quarters. Swarms of men set the head-sails and brought the frigate round, while the gun-crews threw off their jackets and shirts, tightened their belts, and ran out their eighteen-pounders, peering through the open portholes at the stately Frenchman. The wind was very light. Hardly a ripple showed itself upon the clear blue water, but the sails blew gently out as the breeze came over the wooded banks. The Frenchman had gone about also, and both ships were now heading slowly for the sea under fore-and-aft canvas, the Gloire a hundred yards in advance. She luffed up to cross the Leda's bows, but the British ship came round also, and the two rippled slowly on in such a silence that the ringing of ramrods as the French marines drove home their charges clanged quite loudly upon the ear.

"Not much sea-room, Mr. Wharton," remarked the captain.

"I have fought actions in less, sir."

"We must keep our distance and trust to our gunnery. She is very heavily manned, and if she got alongside we might find ourselves in trouble."

"I see the shakos of soldiers aboard of her."

"Two companies of light infantry from Martinique. Now we have her! Hard-a-port, and let her have it as we cross her stern!"

The keen eye of the little commander had seen the surface ripple, which told of a passing breeze. He had used it to dart across the big Frenchman and to rake her with every gun as he passed. But, once past her, the Leda had to come back into the wind to keep out of shoal water. The man[oe]uvre brought her on to the starboard side of the Frenchman, and the trim little frigate seemed to heel right over under the crashing broadside which burst from the gaping ports. A moment later her topmen were swarming aloft to set her topsails and royals, and she strove to cross the Gloire's bows and rake her again. The French captain, however, brought his frigate's head round, and the two rode side by side within easy pistol-shot, pouring broadsides into each other in one of those murderous duels which, could they all be recorded, would mottle our charts with blood.

In that heavy tropical air, with so faint a breeze, the smoke formed a thick bank round the two vessels, from which the topmasts only protruded. Neither could see anything of its enemy save the throbs of fire in the darkness, and the guns were sponged and trained and fired into a dense wall of vapour. On the poop and forecastle the marines, in two little red lines, were pouring in their volleys, but neither they nor the seamen-gunners could see what effect their fire was having. Nor, indeed, could they tell how far they were suffering themselves, for, standing at a gun, one could but hazily see that upon the right and the left. But above the roar of the cannon came the sharper sound of the piping shot, the crashing of riven planks, and the occasional heavy thud as spar or block came hurtling on to the deck. The lieutenants paced up and down the line of guns, while Captain Johnson fanned the smoke away with his cocked-hat and peered eagerly out.

"This is rare, Bobby!" said he, as the lieutenant joined him. Then, suddenly restraining himself, "What have we lost, Mr. Wharton?"

"Our maintopsail yard and our gaff, sir."

"Where's the flag?"

"Gone overboard, sir."

"They'll think we've struck! Lash a boat's ensign on the starboard arm of the mizzen cross-jackyard."

"Yes, sir."

A round-shot dashed the binnacle to pieces between them. A second knocked two marines into a bloody, palpitating mash. For a moment the smoke rose, and the English captain saw that his adversary's heavier metal was producing a horrible effect. The Leda was a shattered wreck. Her deck was strewed with corpses. Several of her portholes were knocked into one, and one of her eighteen-pounder guns had been thrown right back on to her breech, and pointed straight up to the sky. The thin line of marines still loaded and fired, but half the guns were silent, and their crews were piled thickly round them.

"Stand by to repel boarders!" yelled the captain.

"Cutlasses, lads, cutlasses!" roared Wharton.

"Hold your volley till they touch!" cried the captain of marines.

The huge loom of the Frenchman was seen bursting through the smoke. Thick clusters of boarders hung upon her sides and shrouds. A final broadside leapt from her ports, and the mainmast of the Leda, snapping short off a few feet above the deck, spun into the air and crashed down upon the port guns, killing ten men and putting the whole battery out of action. An instant later the two ships scraped together, and the starboard bower anchor of the Gloire caught the mizzen-chains of the Leda upon the port side. With a yell the black swarm of boarders steadied themselves for a spring.

But their feet were never to reach that blood-stained deck. From somewhere there came a well-aimed whiff of grape, and another, and another. The English marines and seamen, waiting with cutlass and musket behind the silent guns, saw with amazement the dark masses thinning and shredding away. At the same time the port broadside of the Frenchman burst into a roar.

"Clear away the wreck!" roared the captain. "What the devil are they firing at?"

"Get the guns clear!" panted the lieutenant. "We'll do them yet, boys!"

The wreckage was torn and hacked and splintered until first one gun and then another roared into action again. The Frenchman's anchor had been cut away, and the Leda had worked herself free from that fatal hug. But now, suddenly, there was a scurry up the shrouds of the Gloire, and a hundred Englishmen were shouting themselves hoarse: "They're running! They're running! They're running!"

And it was true. The Frenchman had ceased to fire, and was intent only upon clapping on every sail that he could carry. But that shouting hundred could not claim it all as their own. As the smoke cleared it was not difficult to see the reason. The ships had gained the mouth of the estuary during the fight, and there, about four miles out to sea, was the Leda's consort bearing down under full sail to the sound of the guns. Captain de Milon had done his part for one day, and presently the Gloire was drawing off swiftly to the north, while the Dido was bowling along at her skirts, rattling away with her bow-chasers, until a headland hid them both from view.

But the Leda lay sorely stricken, with her mainmast gone, her bulwarks shattered, her mizzen-topmast and gaff shot away, her sails like a beggar's rags, and a hundred of her crew dead and wounded. Close beside her a mass of wreckage floated upon the waves. It was the stern-post of a mangled vessel, and across it, in white letters on a black ground, was painted, "The Slapping Sal."

"By the Lord! it was the brig that saved us!" cried Mr. Wharton. "Hudson brought her into action with the Frenchman, and was blown out of the water by a broadside!"

The little captain turned on his heel and paced up and down the deck. Already his crew were plugging the shot-holes, knotting and splicing and mending. When he came back, the lieutenant saw a softening of the stern lines about his eyes and mouth.

"Are they all gone?"

"Every man. They must have sunk with the wreck."

The two officers looked down at the sinister name, and at the stump of wreckage which floated in the discoloured water. Something black washed to and fro beside a splintered gaff and a tangle of halliards. It was the outrageous ensign, and near it a scarlet cap was floating.

"He was a villain, but he was a Briton!" said the captain, at last. "He lived like a dog, but, by God, he died like a man!"

# The Three Strangers

*Thomas Hardy*

Among the few features of agricultural England which retain an appearance but little modified by the lapse of centuries, may be reckoned the high, grassy and furzy downs, coombs, or ewe-leases, as they are indifferently called, that fill a large area of certain counties in the south and southwest. If any mark of human occupation is met with hereon, it usually takes the form of the solitary cottage of some shepherd.

Fifty years ago such a lonely cottage stood on such a down, and may possibly be standing there now. In spite of its loneliness, however, the spot, by actual measurement, was not more than five miles from a county-town. Yet that affected it little. Five miles of irregular upland, during the long inimical seasons, with their sleets, snows, rains, and mists, afford withdrawing space enough to isolate a Timon or a Nebuchadnezzar; much less, in fair weather, to please that less repellent tribe, the poets, philosophers, artists, and others who "conceive and meditate of pleasant things."

Some old earthen camp or barrow, some clump of trees, at least some starved fragment of ancient hedge is usually taken advantage of in the erection of these forlorn dwellings. But, in the present case, such a kind of shelter had been disregarded. Higher Crowstairs, as the house was called, stood quite detached and undefended. The only reason for its precise situation seemed to be the crossing of two footpaths at right angles hard by, which may have crossed there and thus for a good five hundred years. Hence the house was exposed to the elements on all sides. But, though the wind up here blew unmistakably when it did blow, and the rain hit hard whenever it fell, the various weathers of the winter season were not quite so formidable on the coomb as they were imagined to be by dwellers on low ground. The raw rimes were not so pernicious as in the hollows, and the frosts were scarcely so severe. When the shepherd and his family who tenanted the house were pitied for their sufferings from the exposure, they said that upon the whole they were less inconvenienced by "wuzzes and flames" (hoarses and phlegms) than when they had lived by the stream of a snug neighboring valley.

The night of March 28, 182-, was precisely one of the nights that were wont to call forth these expressions of commiseration. The level rainstorm smote walls, slopes, and hedges like the clothyard shafts of Senlac and Crecy. Such sheep and outdoor animals as had no shelter stood with their buttocks to the winds; while the tails of little birds trying to roost on some scraggy thorn were blown inside-out like umbrellas. The gable-end of the cottage was stained with wet, and the eavesdroppings flapped against the wall. Yet never was commiseration for the shepherd more misplaced. For that cheerful rustic was entertaining a large party in glorification of the christening of his second girl.

The guests had arrived before the rain began to fall, and they were all now assembled in the chief or living room of the dwelling. A glance into the apartment at eight o'clock on this eventful evening would have resulted in the opinion that it was as cosy and comfortable a nook as could be wished for in boisterous weather. The calling of its inhabitant was proclaimed by a number of highly-polished sheep crooks without stems that were hung ornamentally over the fireplace, the curl of each shining crook varying from the antiquated type engraved in the patriarchal pictures of old family Bibles to the most approved fashion of the last local sheep-fair. The room was lighted by half-a-dozen candles, having wicks only a trifle smaller than the grease which enveloped them, in candlesticks that were never used but at high-days, holy-days, and family feasts. The lights were scattered about the room, two of them standing on the chimney-piece. This position of candles was in itself significant. Candles on the chimney-piece always meant a party.

On the hearth, in front of a back-brand to give substance, blazed a fire of thorns, that crackled "like the laughter of the fool."

Nineteen persons were gathered here. Of these, five women, wearing gowns of various bright hues, sat in chairs along the wall; girls shy and not shy filled the window-bench; four men, including Charley Jake the hedge-carpenter, Elijah New the parish-clerk, and John Pitcher, a neighboring dairyman, the shepherd's father-in-law, lolled in the settle; a young man and maid, who were blushing over tentative pourparlers on a life-companionship, sat beneath the corner-cupboard; and an elderly engaged man of fifty or upward moved restlessly about from spots where his betrothed was not to the spot where she was. Enjoyment was pretty general, and so much the more prevailed in being unhampered by conventional restrictions. Absolute confidence in each other's good opinion begat perfect ease, while the finishing stroke of manner, amounting to a truly princely serenity, was lent to the majority by the absence of any expression or trait denoting that they wished to get on in the world, enlarge their minds, or do any eclipsing thing whatever – which nowadays so generally nips the bloom and bonhomie of all except the two extremes of the social scale.

Shepherd Fennel had married well, his wife being a dairyman's daughter from a vale at a distance, who brought fifty guineas in her pocket – and kept them there, till they should be required for ministering to the needs of a coming family. This frugal woman had been somewhat exercised as to the character that should be given to the gathering. A sit-still party had its advantages; but an undisturbed position of ease in chairs and settles was apt to lead on the men to such an unconscionable deal of toping that they would sometimes fairly drink the house dry. A dancing-party was the alternative; but this, while avoiding the foregoing objection on the score of good drink, had a counterbalancing disadvantage in the matter of good victuals, the ravenous appetites engendered by the exercise causing immense havoc in the buttery. Shepherdess Fennel fell back upon the intermediate plan of mingling short dances with short periods of talk and singing, so as to hinder any ungovernable rage in either. But this scheme was entirely confined to her own gentle mind: the shepherd himself was in the mood to exhibit the most reckless phases of hospitality.

The fiddler was a boy of those parts, about twelve years of age, who had a wonderful dexterity in jigs and reels, though his fingers were so small and short as to necessitate a constant shifting for the high notes, from which he scrambled back to the first position with sounds not of unmixed purity of tone. At seven the shrill tweedle-dee of this youngster had begun, accompanied by a booming ground-bass from Elijah New, the parish-clerk, who had thoughtfully brought with him his favorite musical instrument, the serpent. Dancing was instantaneous, Mrs. Fennel privately enjoining the players on no account to let the dance exceed the length of a quarter of an hour.

But Elijah and the boy, in the excitement of their position, quite forgot the injunction. Moreover, Oliver Giles, a man of seventeen, one of the dancers, who was enamoured of his partner, a fair girl of thirty-three rolling years, had recklessly handed a new crown-piece to the musicians, as a bribe to keep going as long as they had muscle and wind. Mrs. Fennel, seeing the steam begin to generate on the countenances of her guests, crossed over and touched the fiddler's elbow and put her hand on the serpent's mouth. But they took no notice, and fearing she might lose her character of genial hostess if she were to interfere too markedly, she retired and sat down helpless. And so the dance whizzed on with cumulative fury, the performers moving in their planet-like courses, direct and retrograde, from apogee to perigee, till the hand of the well-kicked clock at the bottom of the room had travelled over the circumference of an hour.

While these cheerful events were in course of enactment within Fennel's pastoral dwelling, an incident having considerable bearing on the party had occurred in the gloomy night without. Mrs. Fennel's concern about the growing fierceness of the dance corresponded in point of time with the ascent of a human figure to the solitary hill of Higher Crowstairs from the direction of the distant town. This personage strode on through the rain without a pause, following the little-worn path which, further on in its course, skirted the shepherd's cottage.

It was nearly the time of full moon, and on this account, though the sky was lined with a uniform sheet of dripping cloud, ordinary objects out of doors were readily visible. The sad wan light revealed the lonely pedestrian to be a man of supple frame; his gait suggested that he had somewhat passed the period of perfect and instinctive agility, though not so far as to be otherwise than rapid of motion when occasion required. At a rough guess, he might have been about forty years of age. He appeared tall, but a recruiting sergeant, or other person accustomed to the judging of men's heights by the eye, would have discerned that this was chiefly owing to his gauntness, and that he was not more than five-feet-eight or nine.

Notwithstanding the regularity of his tread, there was caution in it, as in that of one who mentally feels his way; and despite the fact that it was not a black coat nor a dark garment of any sort that he wore, there was something about him which suggested that he naturally belonged to the black-coated tribes of men. His clothes were of fustian, and his boots hobnailed, yet in his progress he showed not the mud-accustomed bearing of hobnailed and fustianed peasantry.

By the time that he had arrived abreast of the shepherd's premises the rain came down, or rather came along, with yet more determined violence. The outskirts of the little settlement partially broke the force of wind and rain, and this induced him to stand still. The most salient of the shepherd's domestic erections was an empty sty at the forward corner of his hedgeless garden, for in these latitudes the principle of masking the homelier features of your establishment by a conventional frontage was unknown. The traveller's eye was attracted to this small building by the pallid shine of the wet slates that covered it. He turned aside, and, finding it empty, stood under the pent-roof for shelter.

While he stood, the boom of the serpent within the adjacent house, and the lesser strains of the fiddler, reached the spot as an accompaniment to the surging hiss of the flying rain on the sod, its louder beating on the cabbage-leaves of the garden, on the eight or ten beehives just discernible by the path, and its dripping from the eaves into a row of buckets and pans that had been placed under the walls of the cottage. For at Higher Crowstairs, as at all such elevated domiciles, the grand difficulty of housekeeping was an insufficiency of water; and a casual rainfall was utilized by turning out, as catchers, every utensil that the house contained. Some queer stories might be told of the contrivances for economy in suds and dishwaters that are absolutely necessitated in upland habitations during the droughts of summer. But at this season there were no such exigencies; a mere acceptance of what the skies bestowed was sufficient for an abundant store.

At last the notes of the serpent ceased and the house was silent. This cessation of activity aroused the solitary pedestrian from the reverie into which he had elapsed, and, emerging from the shed, with an apparently new intention, he walked up the path to the house-door. Arrived here, his first act was to kneel down on a large stone beside the row of vessels, and to drink a copious draught from one of them. Having quenched his thirst, he rose and lifted his hand to knock, but paused with his eye upon the panel. Since the dark surface of the wood revealed absolutely nothing, it was evident that he must be mentally looking through the door, as if he wished to measure thereby all the possibilities that a house of this sort might include, and how they might bear upon the question of his entry.

In his indecision he turned and surveyed the scene around. Not a soul was anywhere visible. The garden-path stretched downward from his feet, gleaming like the track of a snail; the roof of the little well (mostly dry), the well-cover, the top rail of the garden-gate, were varnished with the same dull liquid glaze; while, far away in the vale, a faint whiteness of more than usual extent showed that the rivers were high in the meads. Beyond all this winked a few bleared lamplights through the beating drops – lights that denoted the situation of the county-town from which he had appeared to come. The absence of all notes of life in that direction seemed to clinch his intentions, and he knocked at the door.

Within, a desultory chat had taken the place of movement and musical sound. The hedge-carpenter was suggesting a song to the company, which nobody just then was inclined to undertake, so that the knock afforded a not unwelcome diversion.

"Walk in!" said the shepherd, promptly.

The latch clicked upward, and out of the night our pedestrian appeared upon the door-mat. The shepherd arose, snuffed two of the nearest candles, and turned to look at him.

Their light disclosed that the stranger was dark in complexion and not unprepossessing as to feature. His hat, which for a moment he did not remove, hung low over his eyes, without concealing that they were large, open, and determined, moving with a flash rather than a glance round the room. He seemed pleased with his survey, and, baring his shaggy head, said, in a rich, deep voice: "The rain is so heavy, friends, that I ask leave to come in and rest awhile."

"To be sure, stranger," said the shepherd. "And faith, you've been lucky in choosing your time, for we are having a bit of a fling for a glad cause – though, to be sure, a man could hardly wish that glad cause to happen more than once a year."

"Nor less," spoke up a woman. "For 'tis best to get your family over and done with, as soon as you can, so as to be all the earlier out of the fag o't."

"And what may be this glad cause?" asked the stranger.

"A birth and christening," said the shepherd.

The stranger hoped his host might not be made unhappy either by too many or two few of such episodes, and being invited by a gesture to a pull at the mug, he readily acquiesced. His manner, which, before entering, had been so dubious, was now altogether that of a careless and candid man.

"Late to be traipsing athwart this coomb – hey?" said the engaged man of fifty.

"Late it is, master, as you say. – I'll take a seat in the chimney-corner, if you have nothing to urge against it, ma'am; for I am a little moist on the side that was next the rain."

Mrs. Shepherd Fennel assented, and made room for the self-invited comer, who, having got completely inside the chimney-corner, stretched out his legs and arms with the expansiveness of a person quite at home.

"Yes, I am rather cracked in the vamp," he said freely, seeing that the eyes of the shepherd's wife fell upon his boots, "and I am not well fitted either. I have had some rough times lately, and have been forced to pick up what I can get in the way of wearing, but I must find a suit better fit for working-days when I reach home."

"One of hereabouts?" she inquired.

"Not quite that – further up the country."

"I thought so. And so be I; and by your tongue you come

from my neighborhood."

"But you would hardly have heard of me," he said quickly. "My time would be long before yours, ma'am, you see."

This testimony to the youthfulness of his hostess had the effect of stopping her cross-examination.

"There is only one thing more wanted to make me happy," continued the new-comer, "and that is a little baccy, which I am sorry to say I am out of."

"I'll fill your pipe," said the shepherd.

"I must ask you to lend me a pipe likewise."

"A smoker, and no pipe about 'ee?"

"I have dropped it somewhere on the road."

The shepherd filled and handed him a new clay pipe, saying, as he did so, "Hand me your baccy-box – I'll fill that too, now I am about it."

The man went through the movement of searching his pockets.

"Lost that too?" said his entertainer, with some surprise.

"I am afraid so," said the man with some confusion. "Give it to me in a screw of paper." Lighting his pipe at the candle with a suction that drew the whole flame into the bowl, he resettled himself in the corner and bent his looks upon the faint steam from his damp legs, as if he wished to say no more.

Meanwhile the general body of guests had been taking little notice of this visitor by reason of an absorbing discussion in which they were engaged with the band about a tune for the next dance. The matter being settled, they were about to stand up when an interruption came in the shape of another knock at the door.

At sound of the same the man in the chimney-corner took up the poker and began stirring the brands as if doing it thoroughly were the one aim of his existence; and a second time the shepherd said, "Walk in!" In a moment another man stood upon the straw-woven door-mat. He too was a stranger.

This individual was one of a type radically different from the first. There was more of the commonplace in his manner, and a certain jovial cosmopolitanism sat upon his features. He was several years older than the first arrival, his hair being slightly frosted, his eyebrows bristly, and his whiskers cut back from his cheeks. His face was rather full and flabby, and yet it was not altogether a face without power. A few grog-blossoms marked the neighborhood of his nose. He flung back his long drab greatcoat, revealing that beneath it he wore a suit of cinder-gray shade throughout, large heavy seals, of some metal or other that would take a polish, dangling from his fob as his only personal ornament. Shaking the water-drops from his low-crowned glazed hat, he said, "I must ask for a few minutes' shelter, comrades, or I shall be wetted to my skin before I get to Casterbridge."

"Make yourself at home, master," said the shepherd, perhaps a trifle less heartily than on the first occasion. Not that Fennel had the least tinge of niggardliness in his composition; but the room was far from large, spare chairs were not numerous, and damp companions were not altogether desirable at close quarters for the women and girls in their bright-colored gowns.

However, the second comer, after taking off his greatcoat, and hanging his hat on a nail in one of the ceiling-beams as if he had been specially invited to put it there, advanced and sat down at the table. This had been pushed so closely into the chimney-corner, to give all available room to the dancers, that its inner edge grazed the elbow of the man who had ensconced himself by the fire; and thus the two strangers were brought into close companionship. They nodded to each other by way of breaking the ice of unacquaintance, and the first stranger handed his neighbor the family mug – a huge vessel of brown ware, having its upper edge worn away like a threshold by the rub of whole generations of thirsty lips that had gone the way of all flesh, and bearing the following inscription burnt upon its rotund side in yellow letters:

THERE IS NO FUN  UNTILL I CUM.

The other man, nothing loth, raised the mug to his lips, and drank on, and on, and on – till a curious blueness overspread the countenance of the shepherd's wife, who had regarded with no little surprise the first stranger's free offer to the second of what did not belong to him to dispense.

"I knew it!" said the toper to the shepherd with much satisfaction. "When I walked up your garden before coming in, and saw the hives all of a row, I said to myself, 'Where there's bees there's honey, and where there's honey there's mead,' But mead of such a truly comfortable sort as this I really didn't expect to meet in my older days." He took yet another pull at the mug, till it assumed an ominous elevation.

"Glad you enjoy it!" said the shepherd warmly.

"It is goodish mead," assented Mrs. Fennel, with an absence of enthusiasm which seemed to say that it was possible to buy praise for one's cellar at too heavy a price. "It is trouble enough to make – and really I hardly think we shall make any more. For honey sells well, and we ourselves can make shift with a drop o' small mead and metheglin for common use from the comb-washings."

"O, but you'll never have the heart!" reproachfully cried the stranger in cinder-gray, after taking up the mug a third time and setting it down empty. "I love mead, when 'tis old like this, as I love to go to church o' Sundays, or to relieve the needy any day of the week."

"Ha, ha, ha!" said the man in the chimney-corner, who, in spite of the taciturnity induced by the pipe of tobacco, could not or would not refrain from this slight testimony to his comrade's humor.

Now the old mead of those days, brewed of the purest first-year or maiden honey, four pounds to the gallon – with its due complement of white of eggs, cinnamon, ginger, cloves, mace, rosemary, yeast, and processes of working, bottling, and cellaring – tasted remarkably strong; but it did not taste so strong as it actually was. Hence, presently, the stranger in cinder-gray at the table, moved by its creeping influence, unbuttoned his waistcoat, threw himself back in his chair, spread his legs, and made his presence felt in various ways.

"Well, well, as I say," he resumed, "I am going to Casterbridge, and to Casterbridge I must go. I should have been almost there by this time; but the rain drove me into your dwelling, and I'm not sorry for it."

"You don't live in Casterbridge?" said the shepherd.

"Not as yet; though I shortly mean to move there."

"Going to set up in trade, perhaps?"

"No, no," said the shepherd's wife. "It is easy to see that the gentleman is rich, and don't want to work at anything."

The cinder-gray stranger paused, as if to consider whether he would accept that definition of himself. He presently rejected it by answering, "Rich is not quite the word for me, dame. I do work, and I must work. And even if I only get to Casterbridge by midnight I must begin work there at eight to-morrow morning. Yes, het or wet, blow or snow, famine or sword, my day's work to-morrow must be done."

"Poor man! Then, in spite o' seeming, you be off than we." replied the shepherd's wife.

"'Tis the nature of my trade, men and maidens. Tis the nature of my trade more than my poverty.... But really and truly I must up and off, or I shan't get a lodging in the town." However, the speaker did not move, and directly added, "There's time for one more draught of friendship before I go; and I'd perform it at once if the mug were not dry."

"Here's a mug o' small," said Mrs. Fennel. "Small, we call it, though to be sure 'tis only the first wash o' the combs."

"No," said the stranger, disdainfully. "I won't spoil your first kindness by partaking o' your second."

"Certainly not," broke in Fennel. "We don't increase and multiply every day, and I'll fill the mug again." He went away to the dark place under the stairs where the barrel stood. The shepherdess followed him.

"Why should you do this?" she said, reproachfully, as soon as they were alone. "He's emptied it once, though it held enough for ten people; and now he's not contented wi' the small, but must needs call for more o' the strong! And a stranger unbeknown to any of us. For my part, I don't like the look o' the man at all."

"But he's in the house, my honey; and 'tis a wet night, and a christening. Daze it, what's a cup of mead more or less? There'll be plenty more next bee-burning."

"Very well – this time, then," she answered, looking wistfully at the barrel. "But what is the man's calling, and where is he one of, that he should come in and join us like this?"

"I don't know. I'll ask him again."

The catastrophe of having the mug drained dry at one pull

by the stranger in cinder-gray was effectually guarded against this time by Mrs. Fennel. She poured out his allowance in a small cup, keeping the large one at a discreet distance from him. When he had tossed off his portion the shepherd renewed his inquiry about the stranger's occupation.

The latter did not immediately reply, and the man in the chimney-corner, with sudden demonstrativeness, said, "Anybody may know my trade – I'm a wheelwright."

"A very good trade for these parts," said the shepherd.

"And anybody may know mine – if they've the sense to find it out," said the stranger in cinder-gray.

"You may generally tell what a man is by his claws," observed the hedge-carpenter, looking at his own hands. "My fingers be as full of thorns as an old pin-cushion is of pins."

The hands of the man in the chimney-corner instinctively sought the shade, and he gazed into the fire as he resumed his pipe. The man at the table took up the hedge-carpenter's remark, and added smartly, "True; but the oddity of my trade is that, instead of setting a mark upon me, it sets a mark upon my customers."

No observation being offered by anybody in elucidation of this enigma, the shepherd's wife once more called for a song. The same obstacles presented themselves as at the former time – one had no voice, another had forgotten the first verse. The stranger at the table, whose soul had now risen to a good working temperature, relieved the difficulty by exclaiming that, to start the company, he would sing himself. Thrusting one thumb into the arm-hole of his waistcoat, he waved the other hand in the air, and, with an extemporizing gaze at the shining sheep-crooks above the mantelpiece, began:

"O my trade it is the rarest one, Simple shepherds all – My trade is a sight to see; For my customers I tie, and take them up on high, And waft 'em to a far countree!"

The room was silent when he had finished the verse – with one exception, that of the man in the chimney-corner, who, at the singer's word, "Chorus!" joined him in a deep bass voice of musical relish:

"And waft 'em to a far countree!"

Oliver Giles, John Pitcher the dairyman, the parish-clerk, the engaged man of fifty, the row of young women against the wall, seemed lost in thought not of the gayest kind. The shepherd looked meditatively on the ground, the shepherdess gazed keenly at the singer, and with some suspicion; she was doubting whether this stranger were merely singing an old song from recollection, or was composing one there and then for the occasion. All were as perplexed at the obscure revelation as the guests at Belshazzar's Feast, except the man in the chimney-corner, who quietly said, "Second verse, stranger," and smoked on.

The singer thoroughly moistened himself from his lips inward, and went on with the next stanza as requested:

"My tools are but common ones, Simple shepherds all – My tools are no sight to see: A little hempen string, and a post whereon to swing, Are implements enough for me!"

Shepherd Fennel glanced round. There was no longer any doubt that the stranger was answering his question rhythmically. The guests one and all started back with suppressed exclamations. The young woman engaged to the man of fifty fainted half-way, and would have proceeded, but finding him wanting in alacrity for catching her she sat down trembling.

"O, he's the – !" whispered the people in the background, mentioning the name of an ominous public officer. "He's come to do it! 'Tis to be at Casterbridge jail to-morrow – the man for sheep-stealing – the poor clock-maker we heard of, who used to live away at Shottsford and had no work to do – Timothy Summers, whose family were a-starving, and so he went out of Shottsford by the high-road, and took a sheep in open daylight, defying the farmer and the farmer's wife and the farmer's lad, and every man jack among 'em. He" (and they nodded toward the stranger of the deadly trade) "is come from up the country to do it because there's not enough to do in his own county-town, and he's got the place here now our own county man's dead; he's going to live in the same cottage under the prison wall."

The stranger in cinder-gray took no notice of this whispered string of observations, but again wetted his lips. Seeing that his friend in the chimney-corner was the only one who reciprocated his joviality in any way, he held out his cup toward that appreciative comrade, who also held out his own. They clinked together, the eyes of the rest of the room hanging upon the singer's actions. He parted his lips for the third verse; but at that moment another knock was audible upon the door. This time the knock was faint and hesitating.

The company seemed scared; the shepherd looked with consternation toward the entrance, and it was with some effort that he resisted his alarmed wife's deprecatory glance, and uttered for the third time the welcoming words, "Walk in!"

The door was gently opened, and another man stood upon the mat. He, like those who had preceded him, was a stranger. This time it was a short, small personage, of fair complexion, and dressed in a decent suit of dark clothes.

"Can you tell me the way to – ?" he began: when, gazing round the room to observe the nature of the company among whom he had fallen, his eyes lighted on the stranger in cinder-gray. It was just at the instant when the latter, who had thrown his mind into his song with such a will that he scarcely heeded the interruption, silenced all whispers and inquiries by bursting into his third verse:

"To-morrow is my working day, Simple shepherds all – To-morrow is a working day for me: For the farmer's sheep is slain, and the lad who did it ta'en, And on his soul may God ha' merc-y!"

The stranger in the chimney-corner, waving cups with the singer so heartily that his mead splashed over on the hearth, repeated in his bass voice as before:

"And on his soul may God ha' merc-y!"

All this time the third stranger had been standing in the doorway. Finding now that he did not come forward or go on speaking, the guests particularly regarded him. They noticed to their surprise that he stood before them the picture of abject terror – his knees trembling, his hand shaking so violently that the door-latch by which he supported himself rattled audibly: his white lips were parted, and his eyes fixed on the merry officer of justice in the middle of the room. A moment more and he had turned, closed the door, and fled.

"What a man can it be?" said the shepherd.

The rest, between the awfulness of their late discovery and the odd conduct of this third visitor, looked as if they knew not what to think, and said nothing. Instinctively they withdrew further and further from the grim gentleman in their midst, whom some of them seemed to take for the Prince of Darkness himself, till they formed a remote circle, an empty space of floor being left between them and him –

"... circulus, cujus centrum diabolus."

The room was so silent – though there were more than twenty people in it – that nothing could be heard but the patter of the rain against the window-shutters, accompanied by the occasional hiss of a stray drop that fell down the chimney into the fire, and the steady puffing of the man in the corner, who had now resumed his pipe of long clay.

The stillness was unexpectedly broken. The distant sound of a gun reverberated through the air – apparently from the direction of the county-town.

"Be jiggered!" cried the stranger who had sung the song, jumping up.

"What does that mean?" asked several.

"A prisoner escaped from the jail – that's what it means."

All listened. The sound was repeated, and none of them spoke but the man in the chimney-corner, who said quietly, "I've often been told that in this county they fire a gun at such times; but I never heard it till now."

"I wonder if it is _my_ man?" murmured the personage in cinder-gray.

"Surely it is!" said the shepherd involuntarily. "And surely we've zeed him! That little man who looked in at the door by now, and quivered like a leaf when he zeed ye and heard your song!"

"His teeth chattered, and the breath went out of his body," said the dairyman.

"And his heart seemed to sink within him like a stone," said Oliver Giles.

"And he bolted as if he'd been shot at," said the hedge-carpenter.

"True – his teeth chattered, and his heart seemed to sink;

and he bolted as if he'd been shot at," slowly summed up the man in the chimney-corner.

"I didn't notice it," remarked the hangman.

"We were all a-wondering what made him run off in such a fright," faltered one of the women against the wall, "and now 'tis explained!"

The firing of the alarm-gun went on at intervals, low and sullenly, and their suspicions became a certainty. The sinister gentleman in cinder-gray roused himself. "Is there a constable here?" he asked, in thick tones. "If so, let him step forward."

The engaged man of fifty stepped quavering out from the wall, his betrothed beginning to sob on the back of the chair.

"You are a sworn constable?"

"I be, sir."

"Then pursue the criminal at once, with assistance, and bring him back here. He can't have gone far."

"I will, sir, I will – when I've got my staff. I'll go home and get it, and come sharp here, and start in a body."

"Staff! – never mind your staff; the man'll be gone!"

"But I can't do nothing without my staff – can I, William, and John, and Charles Jake? No; for there's the king's royal crown a-painted on en in yaller and gold, and the lion and the unicorn, so as when I raise en up and hit my prisoner, 'tis made a lawful blow thereby. I wouldn't 'tempt to take up a man without my staff – no, not I. If I hadn't the law to gie me courage, why, instead o' my taking up him he might take up me!"

"Now, I'm a king's man myself, and can give you authority enough for this," said the formidable officer in gray. "Now then, all of ye, be ready. Have ye any lanterns?"

"Yes – have ye any lanterns? – I demand it!" said the constable.

"And the rest of you able-bodied – "

"Able-bodied men – yes – the rest of ye!" said the constable.

"Have you some good stout staves and pitchforks – "

"Staves and pitchforks – in the name o' the law! And take 'em in yer hands and go in quest, and do as we in authority tell ye!"

Thus aroused, the men prepared to give chase. The evidence was, indeed, though circumstantial, so convincing, that but little argument was needed to show the shepherd's guests that after what they had seen it would look very much like connivance if they did not instantly pursue the unhappy third stranger, who could not as yet have gone more than a few hundred yards over such uneven country.

A shepherd is always well provided with lanterns; and, lighting these hastily, and with hurdle-staves in their hands, they poured out of the door, taking a direction along the crest of the hill, away from the town, the rain having fortunately a little abated.

Disturbed by the noise, or possibly by unpleasant dreams of her baptism, the child who had been christened began to cry heart-brokenly in the room overhead. These notes of grief came down through the chinks of the floor to the ears of the women below, who jumped up one by one, and seemed glad of the excuse to ascend and comfort the baby, for the incidents of the last half-hour greatly oppressed them. Thus in the space of two or three minutes the room on the ground-floor was deserted quite.

But it was not for long. Hardly had the sound of footsteps died away when a man returned round the corner of the house from the direction the pursuers had taken. Peeping in at the door, and seeing nobody there, he entered leisurely. It was the stranger of the chimney-corner, who had gone out with the rest. The motive of his return was shown by his helping himself to a cut piece of skimmer-cake that lay on a ledge beside where he had sat, and which he had apparently forgotten to take with him. He also poured out half a cup more mead from the quantity that remained, ravenously eating and drinking these as he stood. He had not finished when another figure came in just as quietly – his friend in cinder-gray.

"O – you here?" said the latter, smiling. "I thought you had gone to help in the capture." And this speaker also revealed the object of his return by looking solicitously round for the fascinating mug of old mead.

"And I thought you had gone," said the other, continuing his skimmer-cake with some effort.

"Well, on second thoughts, I felt there were enough without me," said the first confidentially, "and such a night as it is, too. Besides, 'tis the business o' the Government to take care of its criminals – not mine."

"True; so it is. And I felt as you did, that there were enough without me."

"I don't want to break my limbs running over the humps and hollows of this wild country."

"Nor I neither, between you and me."

"These shepherd-people are used to it – simple-minded souls, you know, stirred up to anything in a moment. They'll have him ready for me before the morning, and no trouble to me at all."

"They'll have him, and we shall have saved ourselves all labor in the matter."

"True, true. Well, my way is to Casterbridge; and 'tis as much as my legs will do to take me that far. Going the same way?"

"No, I am sorry to say! I have to get home over there" (he nodded indefinitely to the right), "and I feel as you do, that it is quite enough for my legs to do before bedtime."

The other had by this time finished the mead in the mug, after which, shaking hands heartily at the door, and wishing each other well, they went their several ways.

In the meantime the company of pursuers had reached the end of the hog's-back elevation which dominated this part of the down. They had decided on no particular plan of action; and, finding that the man of the baleful trade was no longer in their company, they seemed quite unable to form any such plan now. They descended in all directions down the hill, and straightway several of the party fell into the snare set by Nature for all misguided midnight ramblers over this part of the cretaceous formation. The "lanchets," or flint slopes, which belted the escarpment at intervals of a dozen yards, took the less cautious ones unawares, and losing their footing on the rubbly steep they slid sharply downward, the lanterns rolling from their hands to the bottom, and there lying on their sides till the horn was scorched through.

When they had again gathered themselves together, the shepherd, as the man who knew the country best, took the lead, and guided them round these treacherous inclines. The lanterns, which seemed rather to dazzle their eyes and warn the fugitive than to assist them in the exploration, were extinguished, due silence was observed; and in this more rational order they plunged into the vale. It was a grassy, briery, moist defile, affording some shelter to any person who had sought it; but the party perambulated it in vain, and ascended on the other side. Here they wandered apart, and after an interval closed together again to report progress. At the second time of closing in they found themselves near a lonely ash, the single tree on this part of the coomb, probably sown there by a passing bird some fifty years before. And here, standing a little to one side of the trunk, as motionless as the trunk itself, appeared the man they were in quest of, his outline being well defined against the sky beyond. The band noiselessly drew up and faced him.

"Your money or your life!" said the constable sternly to the still figure.

"No, no," whispered John Pitcher. "'Tisn't our side ought to say that. That's the doctrine of vagabonds like him, and we be on the side of the law."

"Well, well," replied the constable, impatiently; "I must say something, mustn't I? and if you had all the weight o' this undertaking upon your mind, perhaps you'd say the wrong thing, too! – Prisoner at the bar, surrender, in the name of the Father – the Crown, I mane!"

The man under the tree seemed now to notice them for the first time, and, giving them no opportunity whatever for exhibiting their courage, he strolled slowly toward them. He was, indeed, the little man, the third stranger; but his trepidation had in a great measure gone.

"Well, travellers," he said, "did I hear you speak to me?"

"You did; you've got to come and be our prisoner at once!" said the constable. "We arrest 'ee on the charge of not biding in Casterbridge jail in a decent proper manner to be hung to-morrow morning. Neighbors, do your duty, and seize the culpet!"

On hearing the charge, the man seemed enlightened, and, saying not another word, resigned himself with preternatural civility to the search-party, who, with their staves in their hands, surrounded him on all sides, and marched him back toward the shepherd's cottage.

It was eleven o'clock by the time they arrived. The light

shining from the open door, a sound of men's voices within, proclaimed to them as they approached the house that some new events had arisen in their absence. On entering they discovered the shepherd's living-room to be invaded by two officers from Casterbridge jail, and a well-known magistrate who lived at the nearest country-seat, intelligence of the escape having become generally circulated.

"Gentlemen," said the constable, "I have brought back your man – not without risk and danger; but every one must do his duty! He is inside this circle of able-bodied persons, who have lent me useful aid, considering their ignorance of Crown work. Men, bring forward your prisoner!" And the third stranger was led to the light.

"Who is this?" said one of the officials.

"The man," said the constable.

"Certainly not," said the turnkey; and the first corroborated his statement.

"But how can it be otherwise?" asked the constable. "Or why was he so terrified at sight o' the singing instrument of the law who sat there?" Here he related the strange behavior of the third stranger on entering the house during the hangman's song.

"Can't understand it," said the officer coolly. "All I know is that it is not the condemned man. He's quite a different character from this one; a gauntish fellow, with dark hair and eyes, rather good-looking, and with a musical bass voice that if you heard it once you'd never mistake as long as you lived."

"Why, souls – 'twas the man in the chimney-corner!"

"Hey – what?" said the magistrate, coming forward after inquiring particulars from the shepherd in the background. "Haven't you got the man after all?"

"Well, sir," said the constable, "he's the man we were in search of, that's true; and yet he's not the man we were in search of. For the man we were in search of was not the man we wanted, sir, if you understand my every-day way; for 'twas the man in the chimney-corner!"

"A pretty kettle of fish altogether!" said the magistrate. "You had better start for the other man at once."

The prisoner now spoke for the first time. The mention of

the man in the chimney-corner seemed to have moved him as nothing else could do. "Sir," he said, stepping forward to the magistrate, "take no more trouble about me. The time is come when I may as well speak. I have done nothing; my crime is that the condemned man is my brother. Early this afternoon I left home at Shottsford to tramp it all the way to Casterbridge jail to bid him farewell. I was benighted, and called here to rest and ask the way. When I opened the door I saw before me the very man, my brother, that I thought to see in the condemned cell at Casterbridge. He was in this chimney-corner; and jammed close to him, so that he could not have got out if he had tried, was the executioner who'd come to take his life, singing a song about it and not knowing that it was his victim who was close by, joining in to save appearances. My brother looked a glance of agony at me, and I know he meant, 'Don't reveal what you see; my life depends on it.' I was so terror-struck that I could hardly stand, and, not knowing what I did, I turned and hurried away."

The narrator's manner and tone had the stamp of truth, and his story made a great impression on all around.

"And do you know where your brother is at the present time?" asked the magistrate.

"I do not. I have never seen him since I closed this door."

"I can testify to that, for we've been between ye ever since." said the constable.

"Where does he think to fly to? – what is his occupation?"

"He's a watch-and-clock-maker, sir."

"'A said 'a was a wheelwright – a wicked rogue," said the constable.

"The wheels of clocks and watches he meant, no doubt," said Shepherd Fennel. "I thought his hands were palish for's trade."

"Well, it appears to me that nothing can be gained by retaining this poor man in custody," said the magistrate; "your business lies with the other, unquestionably."

And so the little man was released off-hand; but he looked nothing the less sad on that account, it being beyond the power of magistrate or constable to raze out the written troubles in his brain, for they concerned another whom he regarded with more solicitude than himself. When this was done, and the man had gone his way, the night was found to be so far advanced that it was deemed useless to renew the search before the next morning.

Next day, accordingly, the quest for the clever sheep-stealer became general and keen, to all appearance at least. But the intended punishment was cruelly disproportioned to the transgression, and the sympathy of a great many country-folk in that district was strongly on the side of the fugitive. Moreover, his marvellous coolness and daring in hob-and-nobbing with the hangman, under the unprecedented circumstances of the shepherd's party, won their admiration. So that it may be questioned if all those who ostensibly made themselves so busy in exploring woods and fields and lanes were quite so thorough when it came to the private examination of their own lofts and outhouses. Stories were afloat of a mysterious figure being occasionally seen in some old overgrown trackway or other, remote from turnpike roads; but when a search was instituted in any of these suspected quarters nobody was found. Thus the days and weeks passed without tidings.

In brief, the bass-voiced man of the chimney-corner was never recaptured. Some said that he went across the sea, others that he did not, but buried himself in the depths of a populous city. At any rate, the gentleman in cinder-gray never did his morning's work at Casterbridge, nor met anywhere at all, for business purposes, the genial comrade with whom he had passed an hour of relaxation in the lonely house on the coomb.

The grass has long been green on the graves of Shepherd Fennel and his frugal wife; the guests who made up the christening party have mainly followed their entertainers to the tomb; the baby in whose honor they all had met is a matron in the sere and yellow leaf. But the arrival of the three strangers at the shepherd's that night, and the details connected therewith, is a story as well-known as ever in the country about Higher Crowstairs.

March, 1883.

# Rain

## *W. Somerset Maughan*

It was nearly bed-time and when they awoke next morning land would be in sight. Dr. Macphail lit his pipe and, leaning over the rail, searched the heavens for the Southern Cross. After two years at the front and a wound that had taken longer to heal than it should, he was glad to settle down quietly at Apia for twelve months at least, and he felt already better for the journey. Since some of the passengers were leaving the ship next day at Pago-Pago they had had a little dance that evening and in his ears hammered still the harsh notes of the mechanical piano. But the deck was quiet at last. A little way off he saw his wife in a long chair talking with the Davidsons, and he strolled over to her. When he sat down under the light and took off his hat you saw that he had very red hair, with a bald patch on the crown, and the red, freckled skin which accompanies red hair; he was a man of forty, thin, with a pinched face, precise and rather pedantic; and he spoke with a Scots accent in a very low, quiet voice.

Between the Macphails and the Davidsons, who were missionaries, there had arisen the intimacy of shipboard, which is due to propinquity rather than to any community of taste. Their chief tie was the disapproval they shared of the men who spent their days and nights in the smoking-room playing poker or bridge and drinking. Mrs. Macphail was not a little flattered to think that she and her husband were the only people on board with whom the Davidsons were willing to associate, and even the doctor, shy but no fool, half unconsciously acknowledged the compliment. It was only because he was of an argumentative mind that in their cabin at night he permitted himself to carp.

"Mrs. Davidson was saying she didn't know how they'd have got through the journey if it hadn't been for us," said Mrs.

Macphail, as she neatly brushed out her transformation. "She said we were really the only people on the ship they cared to know."

"I shouldn't have thought a missionary was such a big bug that he could afford to put on frills."

"It's not frills. I quite understand what she means. It wouldn't have been very nice for the Davidsons to have to mix with all that rough lot in the smoking-room."

"The founder of their religion wasn't so exclusive," said Dr. Macphail with a chuckle.

"I've asked you over and over again not to joke about religion," answered his wife. "I shouldn't like to have a nature like yours, Alec. You never look for the best in people."

He gave her a sidelong glance with his pale, blue eyes, but did not reply. After many years of married life he had learned that it was more conducive to peace to leave his wife with the last word. He was undressed before she was, and climbing into the upper bunk he settled down to read himself to sleep.

When he came on deck next morning they were close to land. He looked at it with greedy eyes. There was a thin strip of silver beach rising quickly to hills covered to the top with luxuriant vegetation. The coconut trees, thick and green, came nearly to the water's edge, and among them you saw the grass houses of the Samoaris; and here and there, gleaming white, a little church. Mrs. Davidson came and stood beside him. She was dressed in black, and wore round her neck a gold chain, from which dangled a small cross. She was a little woman, with brown, dull hair very elaborately arranged, and she had prominent blue eyes behind invisible pince-nez. Her face was long, like a sheep's, but she gave no impression of foolishness, rather of extreme alertness; she had the quick movements of a bird. The most remarkable thing about her was her voice, high, metallic, and without inflection; it fell on the ear with a hard monotony, irritating to the nerves like the pitiless clamour of the pneumatic drill.

"This must seem like home to you," said Dr. Macphail, with his thin, difficult smile.

"Ours are low islands, you know, not like these. Coral. These are volcanic. We've got another ten days' journey to reach them."

"In these parts that's almost like being in the next street at home," said Dr. Macphail facetiously.

"Well, that's rather an exaggerated way of putting it, but one does look at distances differently in the J South Seas. So far you're right."

Dr. Macphail sighed faintly.

"I'm glad we're not stationed here," she went on. "They say this is a terribly difficult place to work in. The steamers' touching makes the people unsettled; and then there's the naval station; that's bad for the natives. In our district we don't have difficulties like that to contend with. There are one or two traders, of course, but we take care to make them behave, and if they don't we make the place so hot for them they're glad to go."

Fixing the glasses on her nose she looked at the green island with a ruthless stare.

"It's almost a hopeless task for the missionaries here. I can never be sufficiently thankful to God that we are at least spared that."

Davidson's district consisted of a group of islands to the North of Samoa; they were widely separated and he had frequently to go long distances by canoe. At these times his wife remained at their headquarters and managed the mission. Dr. Macphail felt his heart sink when he considered the efficiency with which she certainly managed it. She spoke of the depravity of the natives in a voice which nothing could hush, but with a vehemently unctuous horror. Her sense of delicacy was singular. Early in their acquaintance she had said to him:

"You know, their marriage customs when we first settled in the islands were so shocking that I couldn't possibly describe them to you. But I'll tell Mrs. Macphail and she'll tell you."

Then he had seen his wife and Mrs. Davidson, their deck-chairs close together, in earnest conversation for about two hours. As he walked past them backwards and forwards for the sake of exercise, he had heard Mrs. Davidson's agitated whisper, like the distant flow of a mountain torrent, and he saw by his wife's open mouth and pale face that she was enjoying an alarming experience. At night in their cabin she repeated to him with bated breath all she had heard.

"Well, what did I say to you?" cried Mrs. Davidson, exultant, next morning. "Did you ever hear anything more dreadful? You don't wonder that I couldn't tell you myself, do you? Even though you are a doctor."

Mrs. Davidson scanned his face. She had a dramatic eagerness to see that she had achieved the desired effect.

"Can you wonder that when we first went there our hearts sank? You'll hardly believe me when I tell you it was impossible to find a single good girl in any of the villages."

She used the word good in a severely technical manner.

"Mr. Davidson and I talked it over, and we made up our minds the first thing to do was to put down the dancing. The natives were crazy about dancing."

"I was not averse to it myself when I was a young man," said Dr. Macphail.

"I guessed as much when I heard you ask Mrs. Macphail to have a turn with you last night. I don't think there's any real harm if a man dances with his wife, but I was relieved that she wouldn't. Under the circumstances I thought it better that we should keep ourselves to ourselves."

"Under what circumstances? "

Mrs. Davidson gave him a quick look through her pince-nez, but did not answer his question.

"But among white people it's not quite the same," she went on, "though I must say I agree with Mr. Davidson, who says he can't understand how a husband can stand by and see his wife in another man's arms, and as far as I'm concerned I've never danced a step since I married. But the native dancing is quite another matter. It's not only immoral in itself, but it distinctly leads to immorality. However, I'm thankful to God that we stamped it out, and I don't think I'm wrong in saying that no one has danced in our district for eight years."

But now they came to the mouth of the harbour and Mrs. Macphail joined them. The ship turned sharply and steamed slowly in. It was a great landlocked harbour big enough to hold a fleet of battleships; and all around it rose, high and steep, the green hills. Near the entrance, getting such breeze as blew from the sea, stood the governor's house in a garden. The Stars and

Stripes dangled languidly from a flagstaff. They passed two or three trim bungalows, and a tennis court, and then they came to the quay with its warehouses. Mrs. Davidson pointed out the schooner, moored two or three hundred yards from the side, which was to take them to Apia. There was a crowd of eager, noisy, and good-humoured natives come from all parts of the island, some from curiosity, others to barter with the travellers on their way to Sydney; and they brought pineapples and huge bunches of bananas, tapa cloths, necklaces of shells or sharks' teeth, kava-bowls, and models of war canoes. American sailors, neat and trim, clean-shaven and frank efface, sauntered among them, and there was a little group of officials. While their luggage was being landed the Macphails and Mrs. Davidson watched the crowd. Dr. Macphail looked at the yaws from which most of the children and the young boys seemed to suffer, disfiguring sores like torpid ulcers, and his professional eyes glistened when he saw for the first time in his experience cases of elephantiasis, men going about with a huge, heavy arm or dragging along a grossly disfigured leg. Men and women wore the lava-lava.

"It's a very indecent costume," said Mrs. Davidson. "Mr. Davidson thinks it should be prohibited by law. How can you expect people to be moral when they wear nothing but a strip of red cotton round their loins?"

"It's suitable enough to the climate," said the doctor, wiping the sweat off his head.

Now that they were on land the heat, though it was so early in the morning, was already oppressive. Closed in by its hills, not a breath of air came in to Pago-Pago.

"In our islands," Mrs. Davidson went on in her high-pitched tones, "we've practically eradicated the lava-lava. A few old men still continue to wear it, but that's all. The women have all taken to the Mother Hubbard, and the men wear trousers and singlets. At the very beginning of our stay Mr. Davidson said in one of his reports: the inhabitants of these islands will never be thoroughly Christianised till every boy of more than ten years is made to wear a pair of trousers."

But Mrs. Davidson had given two or three of her birdlike glances at heavy grey clouds that came floating over the mouth of the harbour. A few drops began to fall.

"We'd better take shelter," she said.

They made their way with all the crowd to a great shed of corrugated iron, and the rain began to fall in torrents. They stood there for some time and then were joined by Mr. Davidson. He had been polite enough to the Macphails during the journey, but he had not his wife's sociability, and had spent much of his time reading. He was a silent, rather sullen man, and you felt that his affability was a duty that he imposed upon himself Christianly; he was by nature reserved and even morose. His appearance was singular. He was very tall and thin, with long limbs loosely jointed; hollow cheeks and curiously high cheek-bones; he had so cadaverous an air that it surprised you to notice how full and sensual were his lips. He wore his hair very long. His dark eyes, set deep in their sockets, were large and tragic; and his hands with their big, long fingers, were finely shaped; they gave him a look of great strength. But the most striking thing about him was the feeling he gave you of suppressed fire. It was impressive and vaguely troubling. He was not a man with whom any intimacy was possible.

He brought now unwelcome news. There was an epidemic of measles, a serious and often fatal disease among the Kanakas, on the island, and a case had developed among the crew of the schooner which was to take them on their journey. The sick man had been brought ashore and put in hospital on the quarantine station, but telegraphic instructions had been sent from Apia to say that the schooner would not be allowed to enter the harbour till it was certain no other member of the crew was affected.

"It means we shall have to stay here for ten days at least."

"But I'm urgently needed a Apia," said Dr. Macphail.

"That can't be helped. If no more cases develop on board, the schooner will be allowed to sail with white passengers, but all native traffic is prohibited for three months."

"Is there a hotel here?" asked Mrs. Macphail.

Davidson gave a low chuckle.

"There's not."

"What shall we do then?"

"I've been talking to the governor. There's a trader along

the front who has rooms that he rents, and my proposition is that as soon as the rain lets up we should go along there and see what we can do. Don't expect comfort. You've just got to be thankful if we get a bed to sleep on and a roof over our heads."

But the rain showed no sign of stopping, and at length with umbrellas and waterproofs they set out. There was no town, but merely a group of official buildings, a store or two, and at the back, among the coconut trees and plantains, a few native dwellings. The house they sought was about five minutes' walk from the wharf. It was a frame house of two storeys, with broad verandahs on both floors and a roof of corrugated iron. The owner was a half-caste named Horn, with a native wife surrounded by little brown children, and on the ground-floor he had a store where he sold canned goods and cottons. The rooms he showed them were almost bare of furniture. In the Macphails' there was nothing but a poor, worn bed with a ragged mosquito net, a rickety chair, and a washstand. They looked round with dismay. The rain poured down without ceasing.

"I'm not going to unpack more than we actually need," said Mrs. Macphail.

Mrs. Davidson came into the room as she was unlocking a portmanteau. She was very brisk and alert. The cheerless surroundings had no effect on her.

"If you'll take my advice you'll get a needle and cotton and start right in to mend the mosquito net, she said, or you'll not be able to get a wink of sleep tonight."

"Will they be very bad?" asked Dr. Macphail.

"This is the season for them. When you're asked to a party at Government House at Apia you'll notice that all the ladies are given a pillow-slip to put their – their lower extremities in."

"I wish the rain would stop for a moment," said Mrs. Macphail. "I could try to make the place comfortable with more heart if the sun were shining."

"Oh, if you wait for that, you'll wait a long time. Pago-Pago is about the rainiest place in the Pacific. You see, the hills, and that bay, they attract the water, and one expects rain at this time of year anyway."

She looked from Macphail to his wife, standing helplessly

in different parts of the room, like lost souls, and she pursed her lips. She saw that she must take them in hand. Feckless people like that made her impatient, but her hands itched to put everything in the order which came so naturally to her.

"Here, you give me a needle and cotton and I'll mend that net of yours, while you go on with your unpacking. Dinner's at one. Dr. Macphail, you'd better go down to the wharf and see that your heavy luggage has been put in a dry place. You know what these natives are, they're quite capable of storing it where the rain will beat in on it all the time."

The doctor put on his waterproof again and went downstairs. At the door Mr. Horn was standing in conversation with the quartermaster of the ship they had just arrived in and a second-class passenger whom Dr. Macphail had seen several times on board. The quartermaster, a little, shrivelled man, extremely dirty, nodded to him as he passed.

"This is a bad job about the measles, doc," he said. "I see you've fixed yourself up already."

Dr. Macphail thought he was rather familiar, but he was a timid Man and he did not take offence easily.

"Yes, we've got a room upstairs."

"Miss Thompson was sailing with you to Apia, so I've brought her along here."

The quartermaster pointed with his thumb to the woman standing by his side. She was twenty-seven perhaps, plump, and in a coarse fashion pretty. She wore a white dress and a large white hat. Her fat calves in white cotton stockings bulged over the tops of long white boots in glace kid. She gave Macphail an ingratiating smile.

"The feller's tryin' to soak me a dollar and a half a day for the meanest sized room," she said in a hoarse voice.

"I tell you she's a friend of mine, Jo," said the quartermaster. "She can't pay more than a dollar, and you've sure got to take her for that."

The trader was fat and smooth and quietly smiling. "Well, if you put it like that, Mr. Swan, I'll see what I can do about it. I'll talk to Mrs. Horn and if we think we can make a reduction we will."

"Don't try to pull that stuff with me," said Miss Thompson. "We'll settle this right now. You get a dollar a day for the room and not one bean more."

Dr. Macphail smiled. He admired the effrontery with which she bargained. He was the sort of man who always paid what he was asked. He preferred to be over-charged than to haggle. The trader sighed.

"Well, to oblige Mr. Swan I'll take it."

"That's the goods," said Miss Thompson. "Come right in and have a shot of hooch. I've got some real good rye in that grip if you'll bring it' along, Mr. Swan. You come along too, doctor."

"Oh, I don't think I will, thank you," he answered. "I'm just going down to see that our luggage is all right."

He stepped out into the rain. It swept in from the opening of the harbour in sheets and the opposite shore was all blurred. He passed two or three natives clad in nothing but the lava-lava, with huge umbrellas over them. They walked finely, with leisurely movements, very upright; and they smiled and greeted him in a strange tongue as they went by.

It was nearly dinner-time when he got back, and their meal was laid in the trader's parlour. It was a room designed not to live in but for purposes of prestige, and it had a musty, melancholy air. A suite of stamped plush was arranged neatly round the walls, and from the middle of the ceiling, protected from the flies by yellow tissue paper, hung a gilt chandelier. Davidson did not come.

"I know he went to call on the governor," said Mrs. Davidson, "and I guess he's kept him to dinner."

A little native girl brought them a dish of Hamburger steak, and after a while the trader came up to see that they had everything they wanted.

"I see we have a fellow lodger, Mr. Horn." said Dr. Macphail.

"She's taken a room, that's all," answered the trader. "She's getting her own board."

He looked at the two ladies with an obsequious air.

"I put her downstairs so she shouldn't be in the way. She won't be any trouble to you."

"Is it someone who was on the boat?" asked Mrs. Macphail.

"Yes, ma'am, she was in the second cabin. She was going to Apia. She has a position as cashier waiting for her."

"Oh!"

When the trader was gone Macphail said:

"I shouldn't think she'd find it exactly cheerful having her meals in her room."

"If she was in the second cabin I guess she'd rather," answered Mrs. Davidson. "I don't exactly know who it can be."

"I happened to be there when the quartermaster brought her along. Her name's Thompson."

"It's not the woman who was dancing with the quartermaster last night? " asked Mrs. Davidson.

"That's who it must be," said Mrs. Macphail. "I wondered at the time what she was. She looked rather fast to me."

"Not good style at all," said Mrs. Davidson.

They began to talk of other things, and after dinner, tired with their early rise, they separated and slept. When they awoke, though the sky was still grey and the clouds hung low, it was not raining, and they went for a walk on the high road which the Americans had built along the bay.

On their return they found that Davidson had just come in.

We may be here for a fortnight, he said irritably. "I've argued it out with the governor, but he says there is nothing to be done."

"Mr. Davidson's just longing to get back to his work," said his wife, with an anxious glance at him.

"We've been away for a year," he said, walking up and down the verandah. "The mission has been in charge of native missionaries and I'm terribly nervous that they've let things slide. They're good men, I'm not saying a word against them, God-fearing, devout, and truly Christian men – their Christianity would put many so-called Christians at home to the blush – but they're pitifully lacking in energy, They can make a stand once, they can make a stand twice, but they can't make a stand all the time. If you leave a mission in charge of a native missionary, no matter how trust-worhy he seems, in course of time you'll find he's let abuses creep in."

Mr. Davidson stood still. With his tall, spare form, and his great eyes flashing out of his pale face, he was an impressive figure. His sincerity was obvious in the fire of his gestures and in his deep, ringing voice.

"I expect to have my work cut out for me. I shall act and I shall act promptly. If the tree is rotten it shall be cut down and cast into the flames."

And in the evening after the high tea which was their last meal, while they sat in the stiff parlour, the ladies working and Dr. Macphail smoking his pipe, the missionary told them of his work in the islands.

"When we went there they had no sense of sin at all," he said. "They broke the commandments one after the other and never knew they were doing wrong. And I think that was the most difficult part of my work, to instil into the natives the sense of sin."

The Macphails knew already that Davidson had worked in the Solomons for five years before he met his wife. She had been a missionary in China, and they had become acquainted in Boston, where they were both spending part of their leave to attend a missionary congress. On their marriage they had been appointed to the islands in which they had laboured ever since.

In the course of all the conversations they had had with Mr. Davidson one thing had shone out clearly and that was the man's unflinching courage. He was a medical missionary, and he was liable to be called at any time to one or other of the islands in the group. Even the whaleboat is not so very safe a conveyance in the stormy pacific of the wet season, but often he would be sent for in a canoe, and then the danger was great. In cases of illness or accident he never hesitated. A dozen times he had spent the whole night baling for his life, and more than once Mrs. Davidson had given him up for lost.

"I'd beg him not to go sometimes," she said, "or at least to wait till the weather was more settled, but he'd never listen. He's obstinate, and when he's once made up his mind, nothing can move him."

"How can I ask the natives to put their trust in the Lord if I am afraid to do so myself?" cried Davidson. "And I'm not, I'm not. They know that if they send for me in their trouble I'll come if it's humanly possible. And do you think the Lord is going to abandon me when I am on his business? The wind blows at his bidding and the waves toss and rage at his word."

Dr. Macphail was a timid man. He had never been able to get used to the hurtling of the shells over the trenches, and when he was operating in an advanced dressing-station the sweat poured from his brow and dimmed his spectacles in the effort he made to control his unsteady hand. He shuddered a little as he looked at the missionary.

"I wish I could say that I've never been afraid," he said.

"I wish you could say that you believed in God," retorted the other.

But for some reason, that evening the missionary's thoughts travelled back to the early days he and his wife had spent on the islands.

"Sometimes Mrs. Davidson and I would look at one another and the tears would stream down our cheeks. We worked without ceasing, day and night, and we seemed to make no progress. I don't know what I should have done without her then. When I felt my heart sink, when I was very near despair, she gave me courage and hope."

Mrs. Davidson looked down at her work, and a slight colour rose to her thin cheeks. Her hands trembled a little. She did not trust herself to speak.

"We had no one to help us. We were alone, thousands of miles from any of our own people, surrounded by darkness. When I was broken and weary she would put her work aside and take the Bible and read to me till peace came and settled upon me like sleep upon the eyelids of a child, and when at last she closed the book she'd say: 'We'll save them in spite of themselves.' And I felt strong again in the Lord, and I answered: 'Yes, with God's help I'll save them. I must save them.'"

He came over to the table and stood in front of it as though it were a lectern.

"You see, they were so naturally depraved that they couldn't be brought to see their wickedness. We had to make sins out of what they thought were natural actions. We had to make it a sin, not only to commit adultery and to lie and thieve, but to expose their bodies, and to dance and not to come to church. I made it a sin for a girl to show her bosom and a sin for a man not to wear trousers."

"How?" asked Dr. Macphail, not without surprise.

"I instituted fines. Obviously the only way to make people realise that an action is sinful is to punish them if they commit it. I fined them if they didn't come to church, and I fined them if they danced. I fined them if they were improperly dressed. I had a tariff, and every sin had to be paid for either in money or work. And at last I made them understand."

"But did they never refuse to pay?"

"How could they?" asked the missionary.

"It would be a brave man who tried to stand up against Mr. Davidson," said his wife, tightening her lips.

Dr. Macphail looked at Davidson with troubled eyes. What he heard shocked him, but he hesitated to express his disapproval.

"You must remember that in the last resort I could expel them from their church membership."

"Did they mind that?"

Davidson smiled a little and gently rubbed his hands.

"They couldn't sell their copra. When the men fished they got no share of the catch. It meant something very like starvation. Yes, they minded quite a lot."

"Tell him about Fred Ohlson," said Mrs. Davidson.

The missionary fixed his fiery eyes on Dr. Macphail.

"Fred Ohlson was a Danish trader who had been in the islands a good many years. He was a pretty rich man as traders go and he wasn't very pleased when we came. You see, he'd had things very much his own way. He paid the natives what he liked for their copra, and he paid in goods and whiskey. He had a native wife, but he was flagrantly unfaithful to her. He was a drunkard. I gave him a chance to mend his ways, but he wouldn't take it. He laughed at me."

Davidson's voice fell to a deep bass as he said the last words, and he was silent for a minute or two. The silence was heavy with menace.

"In two years he was a ruined man. He'd lost everything he'd saved in a quarter of a century. I broke him, and at last he was forced to come to me like a beggar and beseech me to give him a passage back to Sydney."

"I wish you could have seen him when he came to see Mr. Davidson," said the missionary's wife.

"He had been a fine, powerful man, with a lot of fat on him, and he had a great big voice, but now he was half the size, and he was shaking all over. He'd suddenly become an old man."

With abstracted gaze Davidson looked out into the night. The rain was falling again.

Suddenly from below came a sound, and Davidson turned and looked questioningly at his wife. It was the sound of a gramophone, harsh and loud, wheezing out a syncopated tune.

"What's that?" he asked.

Mrs. Davidson fixed her pince-nez more firmly on her nose.

"One of the second-class passengers has a room in the house. I guess it comes from there."

They listened in silence, and presently they heard the sound of dancing. Then the music stopped, and they heard the popping of corks and voices raised in animated conversation.

"I daresay she's giving a farewell party to her friends on board," said Dr. Macphail. "The ship sails at twelve, doesn't it?"

Davidson made no remark, but he looked at his watch.

"Are you ready?" he asked his wife.

She got up and folded her work.

"Yes, I guess I am," she answered.

"It's early to go to bed yet, isn't it?" said the doctor.

"We have a good deal of reading to do," explained Mrs. Davidson. "Wherever we are, we read a chapter of the Bible before retiring for the night and we study it with the commentaries, you know, and discuss it thoroughly. It's a wonderful training for the mind."

The two couples bade one another good night. Dr. and Mrs. Macphail were left alone. For two or three minutes they did not speak.

"I think I'll go and fetch the cards," the doctor said at last.

Mrs. Macphail looked at him doubtfully. Her conversation with the Davidsons had left her a little uneasy, but she did not like to say that she thought they had better not play cards when the Davidsons might come in at any moment. Dr. Macphail brought them and she watched him, though with a vague sense of guilt, while he laid out his patience. Below the sound of revelry continued.

It was fine enough next day, and the Macphails, condemned to spend a fortnight of idleness at Pago-Pago, set about making the best of things. They went down to the quay and got out of their boxes a number of books. The doctor called on the chief surgeon of the naval hospital and went round the beds with him. They left cards on the governor. They passed Miss Thompson on the road. The doctor took off his hat, and she gave him a "Good morning, doc.", in a loud, cheerful voice. She was dressed as on the day before, in a white frock, and her shiny white boots with their high heels, her fat legs bulging over the tops of them, were strange things on that exotic scene.

"I don't think she's very suitably dressed, I must say," said Mrs. Macphail. "She looks extremely common to me."

When they got back to their house, she was on the verandah playing with one of the trader's dark children.

"Say a word to her," Dr. Macphail whispered to his wife. "She's all alone here, and it seems rather unkind to ignore her."

Mrs. Macphail was shy, but she was in the habit of doing what her husband bade her.

"I think we're fellow lodgers here," she said rather foolishly.

"Terrible, ain't it, bein' cooped up in a one-horse burg like this?" answered Miss Thompson. "And they tell me I'm lucky to have gotten a room. I don't see myself livin' in a native house, and that's what some have to do. I don't know why they don't have a hotel."

They exchanged a few more words. Miss Thompson, loud-voiced and garrulous, was evidently quite willing to gossip, but Mrs. Macphail had a poor stock of small talk and presently she said:

"Well, I think we must go upstairs."

In the evening when they sat down to their high tea Davidson on coming in said:

"I see that woman downstairs has a couple of sailors sitting there. I wonder how she's gotten acquainted with them."

"She can't be very particular," said Mrs. Davidson.

They were all rather tired after the idle, aimless day.

"If there's going to be a fortnight of this I don't know what we shall feel like at the end of it," said Dr. Macphail.

"The only thing to do is to portion out the day to different activities," answered the missionary. "I shall set aside a certain number of hours to study and a certain number to exercise, rain or fine – in the wet season you can't afford to pay any attention to the rain – and a certain number to recreation."

Dr. Macphail looked at his companion with misgiving. Davidson's programme oppressed him. They were eating Hamburger steak again. It seemed the only dish the cook knew how to make. Then below the grama-phone began. Davidson started nervously when he heard it, but said nothing. Men's voices floated up. Miss Thompson's guests were joining in a well-known song and presently they heard her voice too, hoarse and loud. There was a good deal of shouting and laughing. The four people upstairs, trying to make conversation, listened despite themselves to the clink of glasses and the scrape of chairs. More people had evidently come. Miss Thompson was giving a party.

"I wonder how she gets them all in," said Mrs. Macphail, suddenly breaking into a medical conversation between the missionary and her husband.

It showed whither her thoughts were wandering. The twitch of Davidson's face proved that, though he spoke of scientific things, his mind was busy in the same direction. Suddenly, while the doctor was giving some experience of practice on the Flanders front, rather prosily, he sprang to his feet with a cry.

"What's the matter, Alfred?" asked Mrs. Davidson.

"Of course! It never occurred to me. She's out of Iwelei."

"She can't be."

"She came on board at Honolulu. It's obvious. And she's carrying on her trade here. Here."

He uttered the last word with a passion of indignation.

"What's Iwelei?" asked Mrs. Macphail.

He turned his gloomy eyes on her and his voice trembled with horror.

"The plague spot of Honolulu. The Red Light district. It was a blot on our civilisation."

Iwelei was on the edge of the city. You went down side streets by the harbour, in the darkness, across a rickety bridge, till you came to a deserted road, all ruts and holes, and then suddenly you came out into the light. There was parking room for motors on each side of the road, and there were saloons, tawdry and bright, each one noisy with its mechanical piano, and there were barbers' shops and tobacconists. There was a stir in the air and a sense of expectant gaiety. You turned down a narrow alley, either to the right or to the left, for the road divided Iwelei into two parts, and you found yourself in the district. There were rows of little bungalows, trim and neatly painted in green, and the pathway between them was broad and straight. It was laid out like a garden-city. In its respectable regularity, its order and spruceness, it gave an impression of sardonic horror; for never can the search for love have been so systematised and ordered. The pathways were lit by a rare lamp, but they would have been dark except for the lights that came from the open windows of the bungalows. Men wandered about, looking at the women who sat at their windows, reading or sewing, for the most part taking no notice of the passers-by; and like the women they were of all nationalities. There were Americans, sailors from the ships in port, enlisted men off the gunboats, sombrely drunk, and soldiers from the regiments, white and black, quartered on the island; there were Japanese, walking in twos and threes; Hawaiians, Chinese in long robes, and Filipinos in preposterous hats. They were silent and as it were oppressed. Desire is sad.

"It was the most crying scandal of the Pacific," exclaimed Davidson vehemently. "The missionaries had been agitating against it for years, and at last the local press took it up. The police refused to stir. You know their argument. They say that vice is inevitable and consequently the best thing is to localise and control it. The truth is, they were paid. Paid. They were paid by the saloon-keepers, paid by the bullies, paid by the women themselves. At last they were forced to move."

"I read about it in the papers that came on board in Honolulu," said Dr. Macphail.

"Iwelei, with its sin and shame, ceased to exist on the very day we arrived. The whole population was brought before the justices. I don't know why I didn't understand at once what that woman was."

"Now you come to speak of it," said Mrs. Macphail, "I remember seeing her come on board only a few minutes before the boat sailed. I remember thinking at the time she was cutting it rather fine."

"How dare she come here!" cried Davidson indignantly. "I'm not going to allow it."

He strode towards the door.

"What are you going to do?" asked Macphail.

"What do you expect me to do? I'm going to stop it. I'm not going to have this house turned into – into..."

He sought for a word that should not offend the ladies' ears. His eyes were flashing and his pale face was paler still in his emotion.

"It sounds as though there were three or four men down there," said the doctor. "Don't you think it's rather rash to go in just now?"

The missionary gave him a contemptuous look and without a word flung out of the room.

"You know Mr. Davidson very little if you think the fear of personal danger can stop him in the performance of his duty," said his wife.

She sat with her hands nervously clasped, a spot of colour on her high cheek bones, listening to what was about to happen below. They all listened. They heard him clatter down the wooden stairs and throw open the door. The singing stopped suddenly, but the gramophone continued to bray out its vulgar tune. They heard Davidson's voice and then the noise of something heavy falling. The music stopped. He had hurled the gramophone on the floor. Then again they heard Davidson's voice, they could not make out the words, then Miss Thompson's, loud and shrill, then a confused clamour as though several people were shouting together at the top of their lungs. Mrs. Davidson gave a little gasp, and she clenched her hands more tightly. Dr. Macphail looked uncertainly from her to his wife. He did not want to go down, but he wondered if they expected him to. Then there was something that sounded like a scuffle. The noise now was more distinct. It might be that Davidson was being thrown out of the room. The door was slammed. There was a moment's silence and they heard Davidson come up the stairs again. He went to his room.

"I think I'll go to him," said Mrs. Davidson.

She got up and went out.

"If you want me, just call," said Mrs. Macphail, and then when the other was gone: "I hope he isn't hurt."

"Why couldn't he mind his own business?" said Dr. Macphail.

They sat in silence for a minute or two and then they both started, for the gramophone began to play once more, defiantly, and mocking voices shouted hoarsely the words of an obscene song.

Next day Mrs. Davidson was pale and tired. She complained of headache, and she looked old and wizened. She told Mrs. Macphail that the missionary had not slept at all; he had passed the night in a state of frightful agitation and at five had got up and gone out. A glass of beer had been thrown over him and his clothes were stained and stinking. But a sombre fire glowed in Mrs. Davidson's eyes when she spoke of Miss Thompson.

"She'll bitterly rue the day when she flouted Mr. Davidson," she said. "Mr. Davidson has a wonderful heart and no one who is in trouble has ever gone to I him without being comforted, but he has no mercy for sin, and when his righteous wrath is excited he's terrible."

"Why, what will he do?" asked Mrs. Macphail.

"I don't know, but I wouldn't stand in that creature's shoes for anything in the world."

Mrs. Macphail shuddered. There was something positively alarming in the triumphant assurance of the little woman's manner. They were going out together that morning, and they went down the stairs side by side. Miss Thompson's door was open, and they saw her in a bedraggled dressing-gown, cooking something in a chafing – dish.

"Good morning," she called. "Is Mrs. Davidson better this morning?"

They passed her in silence, with their noses in the air, as if she did not exist. They flushed, however, when she burst into a shout of derisive laughter. Mrs. Davidson turned on her suddenly. "Don't you dare to speak to me," she screamed. "If you insult me I shall have you turned out of here."

"Say, did I ask M. Davidson to visit with me?"

"Don't answer her," whispered Mrs. Macphail hurriedly.

They walked on till they were out of earshot.

"She s brazen, brazen," burst from Mrs. Davidson.

Her anger almost suffocated her.

And on their way home they met her strolling towards the quay. She had all her finery on. Her great white hat with its vulgar, showy flowers was an affront. She called out cheerily to them as she went by, and a couple of American sailors who were standing there grinned as the ladies set their faces to an icy stare. They got in just before the rain began to fall again.

"I guess she'll get her fine clothes spoilt," said Mrs. Davidson with a bitter sneer.

Davidson did not come in till they were half way through dinner. He was wet through, but he would not change. He sat, morose and silent, refusing to eat more than a mouthful, and he stared at the slanting rain. When Mrs. Davidson told him of their two encounters with Miss Thompson he did not answer. His deepening frown alone showed that he had heard.

"Don't you think we ought to make Mr. Horn turn her out of here?" asked Mrs. Davidson. "We can't allow her to insult us."

"There doesn't seem to be any other place for her to go," said Macphail.

"She can live with one of the natives."

"In weather like this a native hut must be a rather uncomfortable place to live in."

"I lived in one for years," said the missionary.

When the little native girl brought in the fried bananas which formed the sweet they had every day, Davidson turned to her.

"Ask Miss Thompson when it would be convenient for me to see her," he said.

The girl nodded shyly and went out.

"What do you want to see her for, Alfred?" asked his wife.

"It's my duty to see her. I won't act till I've given her every chance."

"You don't know what she is. She'll insult you."

"Let her insult me. Let her spit on me. She has an immortal soul, and I must do all that is in my power to save it."

Mrs. Davidson's ears rang still with the harlot's mocking laughter.

"She's gone too far."

"Too far for the mercy of God?" His eyes lit up suddenly and his voice grew mellow and soft.

"Never. The sinner may be deeper in sin than the depth of hell itself, but the love of the Lord Jesus can reach him still."

The girl came back with the message.

"Miss Thompson's compliments and as long as Rev. Davidson don't come in business hours she'll be glad to see him any time."

The party received it in stony silence, and Dr. Macphail quickly effaced from his lips the smile which had come upon them. He knew his wife would be vexed with him if he found Miss Thompson's effrontery amusing.

They finished the meal in silence. When it was over the two ladies got up and took their work, Mrs. Macphail was making another of the innumerable comforters which she had turned out since the beginning of the war, and the doctor lit his pipe. But Davidson remained in his chair and with abstracted eyes stared at the table. At last he got up and without a word went out of the room. They heard him go down and they heard Miss Thompson's defiant "Come in" when he knocked at the door. He remained with her for an hour. And Dr. Macphail watched the rain. It was beginning to get on his nerves. It was not like our soft English rain that drops gently on the earth; it was unmerciful and somehow terrible; you felt in it the malignancy of the primitive powers of nature. It did not pour, it flowed. It was like a deluge from heaven, and it rattled on the roof of corrugated iron with a steady persistence that was maddening. It seemed to have a fury of its own. And sometimes you felt that you must scream if it did not stop, and then suddenly you felt powerless, as though your bones had suddenly become soft; and you were miserable and hopeless.

Macphail turned his head when the missionary came back. The two women looked up.

"I've given her every chance. I have exhorted her to repent. She is an evil woman."

He paused, and Dr. Macphail saw his eyes darken and his pale face grow hard and stern.

"Now I shall take the whips with which the Lord Jesus drove the usurers and the money changers out of the Temple of the Most High."

He walked up and down the room. His mouth was close set, and his black brows were frowning.

"If she fled to the uttermost parts of the earth I should pursue her."

With a sudden movement he turned round and strode out of the room. They heard him go downstairs again.

"What is he going to do?" asked Mrs. Macphail. If

"I don't know." Mrs. Davidson took off her pince-nez and wiped them. "When he is on the Lord's work I never ask him questions."

She sighed a little.

"What is the matter?"

"He'll wear himself out. He doesn't know what it is to spare himself."

Dr. Macphail learnt the first results of the missionary's activity from the half-caste trader in whose house they lodged. He stopped the doctor when he passed the store 'and came out to speak to him on the stoop. His fat face was worried.

"The Rev. Davidson has been at me for letting Miss Thompson have a room here," he said, "but I didn't know what she was when I rented it to her. When people come and ask if I can rent them a room all I want to know is if they've the money to pay for it. And she paid me for hers a week in advance."

Dr. Macphail did not want to commit himself. "When all's said and done it's your housed We're very much obliged to you for taking us in at all."

Horn looked at him doubtfully. He was not certain yet how definitely Macphail stood on the missionary's side.

"The missionaries are in with one another," he said, hesitatingly olf they get it in for a trader he may just as well shut up his store and quit."

"Did he want you to turn her out?"

"No, he said so long as she behaved herself he couldn't ask me to do that. He said he wanted to be just to me. I promised she shouldn't have no more visitors. I've just been and told her.

"How did she take it?"

"She gave me Hell."

The trader squirmed in his old ducks. He had found Miss Thompson a rough customer.

"Oh, well, I daresay she'll get out. I don't suppose she wants to stay here if she can't have anyone in."

"There's nowhere she can go, only a native house, and no native'll take her now, not now that the missionaries have got their knife in her."

Dr. Macphail looked at the falling rain.

"Well, I don't suppose it's any good waiting for it to clear up."

In the evening when they sat in the parlour Davidson talked to them of his early days at college. He had had no means and had worked his way through by doing odd jobs during the vacations. There was silence downstairs. Miss Thompson was sitting in her little room alone. But suddenly the gramophone began to play. She had set it on in defiance, to cheat her loneliness, but there was no one to sing, and it had a melancholy note. It was like a cry for help Davidson took no notice. He was in the middle of a long anecdote and without change of expression went on. The gramophone continued. Miss Thompson put on one reel after another. It looked as though the silence of the night were getting on her nerves. It was breathless and sultry. When the Macphails went to bed they could not sleep. They lay side by side with their eyes wide open, listening to the cruel singing of the mosquitoes outside their curtain.

"What's that?" whispered Mrs. Macphail at last.

They heard a voice, Davidson's voice, through the wooden partition. It went on with a monotonous, earnest insistence. He was praying aloud. He was praying for the soul of Miss Thompson.

Two or three days went by. Now when they passed Miss Thompson on the road she did not greet them with ironic cordiality or smile; she passed with her nose in the air, a sulky look on her painted face, frowning, as though she did not see them. The trader told Macphail that she had tried to get lodging elsewhere, but had failed. In the evening she played through the various reels of her gramophone, but the pretence of mirth was obvious now. The ragtime had a cracked, heart-broken rhythm as though it were a one-step of despair. When she began to play on Sunday Davidson sent Horn to beg her to stop at once since it was the Lord's day. The reel was taken off and the house was silent except for the steady pattering of the rain on the iron roof.

"I think she's getting a bit worked up," said the trader next day to Macphail. "She don't know what Mr. Davidson's up to and it makes her scared."

Macphail had caught a glimpse of her that morning and it struck him that her arrogant expression had changed. There was in her face a hunted look. The half-caste gave him a sidelong glance.

"I suppose you don't know what Mr. Davidson is doing about it?" he hazarded.

"No, I don't."

It was singular that Horn should ask him that question, for he also had the idea that the misssionary was mysteriously at work. He had an impression that he was weaving a net around the woman, carefully, systematically, and suddenly, when everything was ready, would pull the strings tight.

"He told me to tell her," said the trader, "that if at any time she wanted him she only had to send and he'd come."

"What did she say when you told her that?"

"She didn't say nothing. I didn't stop. I just said what he said I was to and then I beat it. I thought she might be going to start weepin'."

"I have no doubt the loneliness is getting on her nerves," said the doctor. "And the rain – that's enough to make anyone jumpy," he continued irritably. "Doesn't it ever stop in this confounded place?"

"It goes on pretty steady in the rainy season. We have three hundred inches in the year. You see, it's the shape of the bay. It seems to attract the rain from all over the Pacific."

"Damn the shape of the bay," said the doctor.

He scratched his mosquito bites. He felt very short-tempered.

When the rain stopped and the sun shone, it was like a hothouse, seething, humid, sultry, breathless, and you had a strange feeling that everything was growing with a savage violence. The natives, blithe and childlike by reputation, seemed then, with their tattooing an their dyed hair, to have something sinister in their appearance; and when they pattered along at your heels with their naked feet you looked back instinctively. You felt they might at any moment come behind you swiftly and thrust long knife between your shoulder blades. You could not tell what dark thoughts lurked behind their wide-set eyes. They had a little the look of ancient Egyptians painted on a temple wall, and there was about them the terror of what is immeasurably old.

The missionary came and went. He was busy, but the Macphails did not know what he was doing. Horn told the doctor that he saw the governor every day, and once Davidson mentioned him.

"He looks as if he had plenty of determination," he said, "but when you come down to brass tacks he has no backbone."

"I suppose that means he won't do exactly what you want," suggested the doctor facetiously.

The missionary did not smile.

"I want him to do what's right. It shouldn't be necessary to persuade a man to do that."

"But there may be differences of opinion about what is right."

"If a man had a gangrenous foot would you have patience with anyone who hesitated to amputate it?"

"Gangrene is a matter of fact."

"And Evil?"

What Davidson had done soon appeared. The four of them had just finished their midday meal, and they had not yet separated for the siesta which the heat imposed on the ladies and on the doctor. Davidson had little patience with the slothful habit. The door was suddenly flung open and Miss Thompson came in. She looked round the room and then went up to Davidson.

"You low-down skunk, what have you been saying about me to the governor?"

She was spluttering with rage. There was a moment's pause. Then the missionary drew forward a chair.

"Won't you be seated, Miss Thompson? I've been hoping to

have another talk with you."

"You poor low-life bastard."

She burst into a torrent of insult, foul and insolent. Davidson kept his grave eyes on her.

"I'm indifferent to the abuse you think fit to heap on me, Miss Thompson," he said, "but I must beg you to remember that ladies are present."

Tears by now were struggling with her anger. Her face was red and swollen as though she were choking.

"What has happened?" asked Dr. Macphail.

"A feller's just been in here and he says I gotter beat it on the next boat."

Was there a gleam in the missionary's eyes? His face remained impassive.

"You could hardly expect the governor to let you stay here under the circumstances."

"You done it," she shrieked. "You can't kid me. You done it."

"I don't want to deceive you. I urged the governor to take the only possible step consistent with his obligations."

"Why couldn't you leave me be? I wasn't doin' you no harm."

"You may be sure that if you had I should be the last man to resent it."

"Do you think I want to stay on in this poor imitation of a burg? I don't look no busher, do I?"

"In that case I don't see what cause of complaint you have," he answered.

She gave an inarticulate cry of rage and flung out of the room. There was a short silence.

"It's a relief to know that the governor has acted at last," said Davidson finally. "He's a weak man and he shilly-shallied. He said she was only here for a fortnight anyway, and if she went on to Apia that was under British jurisdiction and had nothing to do with him."

The missionary sprang to his feet and strode across the room.

"It's terrible the way the men who are in authority seek to evade their responsibility. They speak as though evil that was out of sight ceased to be evil. The very existence of that woman is a scandal and it does not help matters to shift it to another of the islands. In the end I had to speak straight from the shoulder."

Davidson's brow lowered, and he protruded his firm chin. He looked fierce and determined.

"What do you mean by that?"

"Our mission is not entirely without influence at Washington. I pointed out to the governor that it wouldn't do him any good if there was a complaint about the way he managed things here."

"When has she got to go?" asked the doctor, after a pause.

"The San Francisco boat is due here from Sydney next Tuesday. She's to sail on that."

That was in five days' time. It was next day, when he was coining back from the hospital where for want of something better to do Macphail spent most of his mornings, that the half-caste stopped him as he was going upstairs.

"Excuse me, Dr. Macphail, Miss Thompson's sick. Will you have a look at her."

"Certainly."

Horn led him to her room. She was sitting in a chair idly, neither reading nor sewing, staring in front of her. She wore her white dress and the large hat with the flowers on it. Macphail noticed that her skin was yellow and muddy under her powder, and her eyes were heavy.

"I'm sorry to hear you're not well," he said.

"Oh, I ain't sick really. I just said that, because I just had to see you. I've got to clear on a boat that's going to 'Frisco."

She looked at him and he saw that her eyes were suddenly startled. She opened and clenched her hands spasmodically. The trader stood at the door, listening.

"So I understand," said the doctor.

She gave a little gulp

"I guess it ain't very convenient for me to go to Frisco just now. T went to see the governor yesterday afternoon, but I couldn't get to him. I saw the secretary, and he told me I'd got to take that boat and that was all there was to it. I just had to see the governor, so I waited outside his house this morning, and when he come out I spoke to him. He didn't want to speak to me, I'll say, but I wouldn't let him shake me off, and at last he said he hadn't no objection to my staying here till the next boat to Sydney if the Rev. Davidson will stand for it."

She stopped and looked at Dr. Macphail anxiously.

"I don't know exactly what I can do," he said.

"Well, I thought maybe you wouldn't mind asking him. I swear to God I won't start anything here if he'll just only let me stay. I won't go out of the house if that'll suit him. It's no more'n a fortnight."

"I'll ask him."

"He won't stand for it," said Horn. "He'll have you out on Tuesday, so you may as well make up your mind to it."

"Tell him I can get work in Sydney, straight stuff, I mean. Tain't asking very much."

"I'll do what I can."

"And come and tell me right away, will you? I can't set down to a thing till I get the dope one way or the other."

It was not an errand that much pleased the doctor, and, characteristically perhaps, he went about it indirectly. He told his wife what Miss Thompson had said to him and asked her to speak to Mrs. Davidson. The missionary's attitude seemed rather arbitrary and it could do no harm if the girl were allowed to stay in Pago-Pago another fortnight. But he was not prepared for the result of his diplomacy. The missionary came to him straightway.

"Mrs. Davidson tells me that Thompson has been speaking to you."

Dr. Macphail, thus directly tackled, had the shy man's resentment at being forced out into the open. He felt his temper rising, and he flushed.

"I don't see that it can make any difference if she goes to Sydney rather than to San Francisco, and so long as she promises to behave while she's here it's dashed hard to persecute her."

The missionary fixed him with his stern eyes. "Why is she unwilling to go back to San Francisco?"

"I didn't inquire," answered the doctor with some asperity. "And I think one does better to mind one's own business."

Perhaps it was not a very tactful answer.

"The governor has ordered her to be deported by the first boat that leaves the island. He's only done his duty and I will not interfere. Her presence is a peril here."

"I think you're very harsh and tyrannical."

The two ladies looked up at the doctor with some alarm, but they need not have feared a quarrel, for the missionary smiled gently.

"I'm terribly sorry you should think that of Dr. Macphail. Believe me, my heart bleeds for the unfortunate woman, but I'm only trying to do my duty."

The doctor made no answer. He looked out of the window sullenly. For once it was not raining and across the bay you saw nestling among the trees the huts of a native village.

"I think I'll take advantage of the rain stopping to go out," he said.

"Please don't bear me malice because I can't accede to your wish," said Davidson, with a melancholy smile. "I respect you very much, doctor, and I should be sorry if you thought ill of me."

"I have no doubt you have a sufficiently good opinion of yourself to bear mine with equanimity," he retorted.

"That's one on me," chuckled Davidson.

When Dr. Macphail, vexed with himself because he had been uncivil to no purpose, went downstairs, Miss Thompson was waiting for him with her door ajar.

"Well," she said, "have you spoken to him?"

"Yes, I'm sorry, he won't do anything," he answered, not looking at her in his embarrassment.

But then he gave her a quick glance, for a sob broke from her. He saw that her face was white with fear. It gave him a shock of dismay. And suddenly he had an idea.

"But don't give up hope yet. I think it's a shame the way they're treating you and I'm going: to see the governor myself."

"Now?"

He nodded. Her face brightened.

"Say, that's real good of you. I'm sure he'll let me stay if you speak for me. I just won't do a thing I didn't ought all the time I'm here."

Dr. Macphail hardly knew why he had made up his mind to appeal to the governor. He was perfectly indifferent to Miss Thompson's affairs, the missionary had irritated him, and with him temper was a smouldering thing. He found the governor at home. He was a large, handsome man, a sailor, with a grey toothbrush moustache; and he wore a spotless uniform of white drill.

"I've come to see you about a woman who's lodging in the same house as we are," he said. "Her name's Thompson."

"I guess I've heard nearly enough about her, Dr. Macphail," said the governor, smiling. "I've given her the order to get out next Tuesday and that's all I can do."

"I wanted to ask you if you couldn't stretch a point and let her stay here till the boat comes in from San Francisco so that she can go to Sydney. I will guarantee her good behaviour."

The governor continued to smile, but his eyes grew small and serious.

"I'd be very glad to oblige you, Dr. Macphail, but I've given the order and it must stand."

The doctor put the case as reasonably as he could, but now the governor ceased to smile at all. He listened sullenly, with averted gaze. Macphail saw that he was making no impression.

"I'm sorry to cause any lady inconvenience, but she'll have to sail on Tuesday and that's all there is to it."

"But what difference can it make?"

"Pardon me, doctor, but I don't feel called upon to explain my official actions except to the, proper authorities."

Macphail looked at him shrewdly. He remembered Davidson's hint that he had used threats, and in the governor's attitude he read a singular embarrassment.

"Davidson's a damned busybody," he said hotly.

"Between ourselves, Dr. Macphail, I don't say that I have formed a very favourable opinion of Mr. Davidson, but I am bound to confess that he was within his rights in pointing out to me the danger that the presence of a woman of Miss Thompson's character was to a place like this where a number of enlisted men are stationed among a native population."

He got up and Dr. Macphail was obliged to do so too.

"I must ask you to excuse me. I have an engagement. Please give my respects to Mrs. Macphail."

The doctor left him crest-fallen. He knew that Miss Thompson would be waiting for him, and unwilling to tell her himself that he had failed, he went into the house by the back door and sneaked up the stairs as though he had something to hide.

At supper he was silent and ill-at-ease, but the missionary was jovial and animated. Dr. Macphail thought his eyes rested on him now and then with triumphant good-humour. It struck him suddenly that Davidson knew of his visit to the governor and of its ill success. But how on earth could he have heard of it? There was something sinister about the power of that man. After supper he saw Horn on the verandah and, as though to have a casual word with him, went out.

"She wants to know if you've seen the governor," the trader whispered.

"Yes. He wouldn't do anything. I'm awfully sorry, I can't do anything more."

"I knew he wouldn't. They daren't go against the missionaries."

"What are you talking about?" said Davidson affably, corning out to join them.

"I was just saying there was no chance of your getting over to Apia for at least another week," said the trader glibly.

He left them, and the two men returned into the parlour. Mr. Davidson devoted one hour after each meal to recreation. Presently a timid knock was heard at the door.

"Come in," said Mrs. Davidson, in her sharp voice.

The door was not opened. She got up and opened it. They saw Miss Thompson standing at the threshold. But the change in her appearance was extraordinary. This was no longer the flaunting hussy who had jeered at them in the road, but a broken, frightened woman. Her hair, as a rule so elaborately arranged, was tumbling untidily over her neck. She wore bedroom slippers and a skirt and blouse. They were unfresh and bedraggled. She stood at the door with the tears streaming down her face and did not dare to enter.

"What do you want?" said Mrs. Davidson harshly.

"May I speak to Mr. Davidson?" she said in a choking voice.

The missionary rose and went towards her.

"Come right in, Miss Thompson," he said in cordial tones. "What can I do for you?"

She entered the room.

"Say, I'm sorry for what I said to you the other day an' for – for everythin' else. I guess I was a bit lit up. I beg pardon."

"Oh, it was nothing. I guess my back's broad enough to bear a few hard words."

She stepped towards him with a movement that was horribly cringing.

"You've got me beat. I'm all in. You won't make me go back to 'Frisco?"

His genial manner vanished and his voice grew on a sudden hard and stern.

"Why don't you want to go back there?"

She cowered before him.

"I guess my people live there. I don't want them to see me like this. I'll go anywhere else you say."

"Why don't you want to go back to San Francisco?"

"I've told you."

He leaned forward, staring at her, and his great, shining eyes seemed to try to bore into her soul. He gave a sudden gasp.

"The penitentiary."

She screamed, and then she fell at his feet, clasping his legs.

"Don't send me back there. I swear to you before God I'll be a good woman. I'll give all this up."

She burst into a torrent of confused supplication and the tears coursed down her painted cheeks. He leaned over her and, lifting her face, forced her to look at him.

"Is that it, the penitentiary?"

"I beat it before they could get me, she gasped. "If the bulls grab me it's three years for mine."

He let go his hold of her and she fell in a heap on the floor, sobbing bitterly. Dr. Macphail stood up.

"This alters the whole thing," he said. "You can't make her go back when you know this. Give her another chance. She wants to turn over a new leaf."

"I'm going to give her the finest chance she's ever had. If she repents let her accept her punishment."

She misunderstood the words and looked up. There was a gleam of hope in her heavy eyes.

"You'll let me go?"

"No. You shall sail for San Francisco on Tuesday."

She gave a groan of horror and then burst into low, hoarse shrieks which sounded hardly human, and she beat her head passionately on the ground. Dr. Macphail sprang to her and lifted her up:

"Come on, you mustn't do that. You'd better go to your room and lie down. I'll get you something."

He raised her to her feet and partly dragging her, partly carrying her, got her downstairs. He was furious with Mrs. Davidson and with his wife because they made no effort to help. The half-caste was standing on the landing and with his assistanc he managed to get her on the bed. She was moaning and crying. She was almost insensible. He gave her a hypodermic injection. He was hot and exhausted when he went upstairs again.

"I've got her to lie down."

The two women and Davidson were in the same, positions as when he had left them. They could not have moved or spoken since he went.

"I was waiting for you," said Davidson, in a strange, distant voice. "I want you all to pray with me for the soul of our erring sister."

He took the Bible off a shelf, and sat down at the table at which they had supped. It had not been cleared, and he pushed the tea-pot out of the way. In a powerful voice, resonant and deep, he read to them the chapter in which is narrated the meeting of Jesus Christ with the woman taken in adultery.

"Now kneel with me and let us pray for the soul of our dear sister, Sadie Thompson."

He burst into a long, passionate prayer in which he implored God to have mercy on the sinful woman. Mrs. Macphail and Mrs. Davidson knelt with covered eyes. The doctor, taken by surprise, awkward and sheepish, knelt too. The missionary's prayer had a savage eloquence. He was extraordinarily moved, and as he spoke the tears ran down his cheeks. Outside, the pitiless rain fell, fell steadily, with a fierce malignity that was all too human.

At last he stopped. He paused for a moment and said:

"We will now repeat the Lord's prayer."

They said it and then, following him, they rose from their

knees. Mrs. Davidson's face was pale and restful. She was comforted and at peace, but the Macphails felt suddenly bashful. They did not know which way to look.

"I'll just go down and see how she is now," said Dr. Macphail.

When he knocked at her door it was opened for him by Horn. Miss Thompson was in a rocking-chair, sobbing quietly.

"What are you doing there?" exclaimed Macphail. " I told you to lie down."

"I can't lie down. I want to see Mr. Davidson."

"My poor child, what do you think is the good of it? You'll never move him."

"He said he'd come if I sent for him."

Macphail motioned to the trader.

"Go and fetch him."

He waited with her in silence while the trader went upstairs. Davidson came in.

"Excuse me for asking you to come here," she said, looking at him sombrely.

"I was expecting you to send for me. I knew the Lord would answer my prayer."

They stared at one another for a moment and then she looked away. She kept her eyes averted when she spoke.

"I've been a bad woman. I want to repent,"

"Thank God! thank God! He has heard our prayers."

He turned to the two men. "

"Leave me alone with her. Tell Mrs. Davidson that, our prayers have been answered."

They went out and closed the door behind them.

"Gee whizz," said the trader.

That night Dr. Macphail could not get to sleep till late, and when he heard the missionary come upstairs he looked at his watch. It was two o'clock. But even then he did not go to bed at once, for through the wooden partition that separated their rooms he heard him praying aloud, till he himself, exhausted, fell asleep.

When he saw him next morning he was surprised at his appearance. He was paler than ever, tired, but his eyes shone with an inhuman fire. It looked as though he were filled with an overwhelming joy.

"I want you to go down presently and see Sadie," he said. "I can't hope that her body is better, but her soul – her soul is transformed."

The doctor was feeling wan and nervous.

"You were with her very late last night," he said.

"Yes, she couldn't bear to have me leave her."

"You look as pleased as Punch," the doctor said irritably.

Davidson's eyes shone with ecstasy.

"A great mercy has been vouchsafed me. Last night I was privileged to bring a lost soul to the loving arms of Jesus."

Miss Thompson was again in the rocking-chair. The bed had not been made. The room was in disorder. She had not troubled to dress herself, but wore a dirty dressing-gown, and her hair was tied in a sluttish knot. She had given her face a dab with a wet towel, but it was all swollen and creased with crying. She looked a drab.

She raised her eyes dully when the doctor came in. She was cowed and broken.

"Where's Mr. Davidson?" she asked;

"He'll come presently if you want him," answered Macphail acidly. "I came here to see how you were."

"Oh, I guess I'm OK. You needn't worry about that"

"Have you had anything to eat?"

"Horn brought me some coffee."

She looked anxiously at the door.

"D'you think he'll come down soon? I feel as if it wasn't so terrible when he's with me."

"Are you still going on Tuesday?"

"Yes, he says I've got to go. Please tell him to come right along. You can't do me any good. He's the only one as can help me now."

"Very well," said Dr. Macphail.

During the next three days the missionary spent almost all his time with Sadie Thompson. He joined the others only to have his meals. Dr. Macphail noticed that he hardly ate.

"He's wearing himself out," said Mrs. Davidson pitifully. "He'll have a breakdown if he, doesn't take care, but he won't spare himself."

She herself was white and pale. She told Mrs. Macphail that she had no sleep. When the missionary came upstairs from Miss Thompson he prayed till he was exhausted, but even then he did not sleep for long. After an hour or two he got up and dressed himself, and went for a tramp along the bay. He had strange dreams.

"This morning he told me that he'd been dreaming about the mountains of Nebraska," said Mrs. Davidson.

"That's curious," said Dr. Macphail.

He remembered seeing them from the windows of the train when he crossed America. They were like huge mole-hills, rounded and smooth, an they rose from the plain abruptly. Dr. Macphail remembered how it struck him that they were like a woman's breasts.

Davidson's restlessness was intolerable even to himself. But he was buoyed up by a wonderful exhilaration. He was tearing out by the roots the last vestiges of sin that lurked in the hidden corners of that poor woman's heart. He read with her and prayed with her.

"It's wonderful," he said to them one day at supper. "It's a true rebirth. Her soul, which was black as night, is now pure and white like the new-fallen snow. I am humble and afraid. Her remorse for all her sins is beautiful. I am not worthy to touch the hem of her garment."

"Have you the heart to send her back to San Francisco?" said the doctor. "Three years in an American prison. I should have thought you might have saved her from that."

"Ah, but don't you see? It's necessary. Do you think my heart doesn't bleed for her? I love her as I love my wife and my sister. All the time that she is in prison I shall suffer all the pain that she suffers."

"Bunkum," cried the doctor impatiently.

"You don't understand because you're blind. She's sinned, and she must suffer. I know what she'll end-dure. She'll be starved and tortured and humiliated. I want her to accept the punishment of man as a sacrifice to God. I want her to accept it joyfully. She has an opportunity which is offered to very few of us. God is very good and very merciful."

Davidson's voice trembled with excitement. He could hardly articulate the words that tumbled passionately from his lips.

"All day I pray with her and when I leave her I pray again, I pray with all my might and main, so that Jesus may grant her this great mercy. I want to put in her heart the passionate desire to be punished so that at the end, even if I offered to let her go, she would refuse. I want her to feel that the bitter punishment of prison is the thank-offering that she places at the feet of our Blessed Lord, who gave his life for her."

The days passed slowly. The whole household, intent on the wretched, tortured woman down-stairs, lived in a state of unnatural excitement. She was like a victim that was being prepared for the savage rites of a bloody idolatry. Her terror numbed her. She could not bear to let Davidson out of her sight; it was only when he was with her that she had courage, and she hung upon him with a slavish dependence. She cried a great deal, and she read the Bible, and prayed. Sometimes she was exhausted and apathetic. Then she did indeed look forward to her ordeal, for it seemed to offer an escape, direct and concrete, from the anguish she was enduring. She could not bear much longer the vague terrors which now assailed her. With her sins she had put aside all personal vanity, and she slopped about her room, unkempt and dishevelled, in her tawdry dressing-gown. She had not taken off her nightdress for four days, nor put on stockings. Her room was littered and untidy. Meanwhile the rain fell with a cruel persistence. You felt that the heavens must at last be empty of water, but still it poured down, straight and heavy, with a maddening iteration, on the iron roof. Everything was damp and clammy. There was mildew on the wail and on the boots that stood on the floor. Through the sleepless nights the mosquitoes droned their angry chant.

"If it would only stop raining for a single day it wouldn't be so bad," said Dr. Macphail.

They all looked forward to the Tuesday when the boat for San Francisco was to arrive from Sydney. The strain was intolerable. So far as Dr. Macphail was concerned, his pity and his resentment were alike extinguished by his desire to be rid of the unfortunate woman. The inevitable must be accepted. He felt he would breathe more freely when the ship had sailed. Sadie Thompson was to be escorted on board by a clerk in the governor's office. This person called on the Monday evening and told Miss Thompson to be prepared at eleven in the morning. Davidson was with her.

"I'll see that everything is ready. I mean to come on board with her myself."

Miss Thompson did not speak.

When Dr. Macphail blew out his candle and crawled cautiously under his mosquito curtains, he gave a sigh of relief.

"Well, thank God that's over. By this time tomorrow she'll be gone."

"Mrs. Davidson will be glad too. She says he's wearing himself to a shadow," said Mrs. Macphail. "She's a different woman."

"Who?"

"Sadie, I should never have thought it possible. It makes one humble."

Dr. Macphail did not answer, and presently he fell asleep. He was tired out, and he slept more soundly than usual.

He was awakened in the morning by a hand placed on his arm, and, starting up, saw Horn by the side of his bed. The trader put his finger on his mouth to prevent any exclamation from Dr. Macphail and beckoned to him to come. As a rule he wore shabby ducks, but now he was barefoot and wore only the lava-lava of the natives. He looked suddenly savage, and Dr. Macphail, getting out of bed, saw that he was heavily tattooed. Horn made him a sign to come on to the verandah. Dr. Macphail got out of bed and followed the trader out.

"Don't make a noise," he whispered. "You're wanted. Put on a coat and some shoes. Quick."

Dr. Macphail's first thought was that something had happened to Miss Thompson.

"What is it? Shall I bring my instruments?"

"Hurry, please, hurry."

Dr. Macphail crept back into the bedroom, put on a waterproof over his pyjamas, and a pair of rubber-soled shoes. He rejoined the trader, and together they tiptoed down the stairs. The door leading out to the road was open and at it were standing half a dozen natives.

"What is it?" repeated the doctor.

"Come along with me," said Horn.

He walked out and the doctor followed him. The natives came after them in a little bunch. They crossed the road and came on to the beach. The doctor saw a group of natives standing round some object at the water's edge. They hurried along, a couple of dozen yards perhaps, and the natives opened out as the doctor came up. The trader pushed him forwards. Then he saw, lying half in the water and half out, a dreadful object, the body of Davidson. Dr. Macphail bent down – he was not a man to lose his head in an emergency – and turned the body over. The throat was cut from ear to ear, and in the right hand was still the razor with which the deed was done.

"He's quite cold," said the doctor. "He must have been dead some time."

"One of the boys saw him lying there on his way to work just now and came and told me. Do you think he did it himself?"

"Yes. Someone ought to go for the police."

Horn said something in the native tongue, and two youths started off.

"We must leave him here till they come," said the doctor.

"They mustn't take him into my house. I won't have him in my house."

"You'll do what the authorities say," replied the doctor sharply. "In point of fact I expect they'll take him to the mortuary."

They stood waiting where they were. The trader took a cigarette from a fold in his lava-lava and gave one to Dr. Macphail. They smoked while they stared at the corpse. Dr. Macphail could not understand.

"Why do you think he did it?" asked Horn.

The doctor shrugged his shoulders. In a little while native police came along, under the charge of a marine, with a stretcher, and immediately afterwards a couple of naval officers and a naval doctor. They managed everything in businesslike manner.

"What about the wife." said one of the officers.

"Now that you've come I'll go back to the house and get

some things on. I'll see that it's broken to her. She'd better not see him till he's been fixed up a little."

"I guess that's right," said the naval doctor. When Dr. Macphail went back he found his wife nearly dressed.

"Mrs. Davidson's in a dreadful state about her husband," she said to him as soon as he appeared. "He hasn't been to bed all night. She heard him leave Miss Thompson's room at two, but he went out. If he's been walking about since then he'll be absolutely dead."

Dr. Macphail told her what had happened and asked her to break the news to Mrs. Davidson.

"But why did he do it?" she asked, horror-stricken.

"I don't know."

"But I can't. I can't."

"You must."

She gave him a frightened look and went out He heard her go into Mrs. Davidson's room. He waited a minute to gather himself together and then began to shave and wash. When he was dressed he sat down on the bed and waited for his wife. At last she came.

"She wants to see him," she said.

"They've taken him to the mortuary. We'd better go down with her. How did she take it?"

"I think she's stunned. She didn't cry. But she's trembling like a leaf."

"We'd better go at once."

When they knocked at her door Mrs. Davidson came out. She was very pale, but dry-eyed. To the doctor she seemed unnaturally composed. No word was exchanged, and they set out in silence down the road. When they arrived at the mortuary Mrs. Davidson spoke.

"Let me go in and see him alone."

They stood aside. A native opened a door for her and closed it behind her. They sat down and waited. One or two white men came and talked to them in undertones. Dr. Macphail told them again what he knew of the tragedy. At last the door was quietly opened and Mrs. Davidson came out. Silence fell upon them.

"I'm ready to go back now," she said.

Her voice was hard and steady. Dr. Macphail could not understand the look in her eyes. Her pale face was very stern. They walked back slowly, never saying a word, and at last they came round the bend on the other side of which stood the ir house. Mrs. Davidson gave a gasp, and for moment they stopped still. An incredible sound assaulted their ears. The gramophone which had been silent for so long was playing, playing ragtime loud and harsh.

"What's that?" cried Mrs. Macphail with horror.

"Let's go on," said Mrs. Davidson.

They walked up the steps and entered the hall. Miss Thompson was standing at her door, chatting with a sailor. A sudden change had taken place in her. She was no longer the cowed drudge of the last days. She was dressed in all her finery, in her white dress, with the high shiny boots over which her fat legs bulged in their cotton stockings; her hair was elaborately arranged; and she wore that enormous hat covered with gaudy flowers. Her face was painted, her eyebrows were boldly black, and her lips were scarlet. She held herself erect. She was the flaunting quean that they had known at first. As they came in she broke into a loud, jeering laugh; and then, when Mrs. Davidson involuntarily stopped, she collected the spittle in her mouth and spat. Mrs. Davidson cowered back, and two red spots rose suddenly to her cheeks. Then, covering her face with her hands, she broke away and ran quickly up the stairs. Dr. Macphail was outraged. He pushed past the woman into her room.

"What the devil are you doing?" he cried. "Stop that, damned machine."

He went up to it and tore the record off. She turned on him.

"Say, doc, you can't do that stuff with me. What the hell are you doin' in my room? "

"What do you mean?" he cried. "What d'you mean?"

She gathered herself together. No one could describe the scorn of her expression or the contemptuous hatred she put into her answer.

"You men! You filthy, dirty pigs! You're all the same, all of you. Pigs! Pigs!"

Dr. Macphail gasped. He understood.

# A Haunted House

*Virginia Woolf*

Whatever hour you woke there was a door shutting. From room to room they went, hand in hand, lifting here, opening there, making sure – a ghostly couple.

"Here we left it," she said. And he added, "Oh, but here tool"

"It's upstairs," she murmured. "And in the garden," he whispered.

"Quietly," they said, "or we shall wake them."

But it wasn't that you woke us. Oh, no. "They're looking for it; they're drawing the curtain," one might say, and so read on a page or two. "Now they've found it,' one would be certain, stopping the pencil on the margin. And then, tired of reading, one might rise and see for oneself, the house all empty, the doors standing open, only the wood pigeons bubbling with content and the hum of the threshing machine sounding from the farm. "What did I come in here for? What did I want to find?" My hands were empty. "Perhaps its upstairs then?" The apples were in the loft. And so down again, the garden still as ever, only the book had slipped into the grass.

But they had found it in the drawing room. Not that one could ever see them. The windowpanes reflected apples, reflected roses; all the leaves were green in the glass. If they moved in the drawing room, the apple only turned its yellow side. Yet, the moment after, if the door was opened, spread about the floor, hung upon the walls, pendant from the ceiling – what? My hands were empty. The shadow of a thrush crossed the carpet; from the deepest wells of silence the wood pigeon drew its bubble of sound. "Safe, safe, safe" the pulse of the house beat softly. "The treasure buried; the room . . ." the pulse stopped short. Oh, was that the buried treasure?

A moment later the light had faded. Out in the garden then? But the trees spun darkness for a wandering beam of sun. So fine, so rare, coolly sunk beneath the surface the beam I sought always burned behind the glass. Death was the glass; death was between us, coming to the woman first, hundreds of years ago, leaving the house, sealing all the windows; the rooms were darkened. He left it, left her, went North, went East, saw the stars turned in the Southern sky; sought the house, found it dropped beneath the Downs. "Safe, safe, safe," the pulse of the house beat gladly. 'The Treasure yours."

The wind roars up the avenue. Trees stoop and bend this way and that. Moonbeams splash and spill wildly in the rain. But the beam of the lamp falls straight from the window. The candle burns stiff and still. Wandering through the house, opening the windows, whispering not to wake us, the ghostly couple seek their joy.

"Here we slept," she says. And he adds, "Kisses without number."

"Waking in the morning – "

"Silver between the trees – "

"Upstairs – " 'In the garden – "

"When summer came – " 'In winter snowtime – "

"The doors go shutting far in the distance, gently knocking like the pulse of a heart. Nearer they come, cease at the doorway. The wind falls, the rain slides silver down the glass. Our eyes darken, we hear no steps beside us; we see no lady spread her ghostly cloak. His hands shield the lantern. "Look," he breathes. "Sound asleep. Love upon their lips."

Stooping, holding their silver lamp above us, long they look and deeply. Long they pause. The wind drives straightly; the flame stoops slightly. Wild beams of moonlight cross both floor and wall, and, meeting, stain the faces bent; the faces pondering; the faces that search the sleepers and seek their hidden joy. "Safe, safe, safe," the heart of the house beats proudly. "Long years – " he sighs.

"Again you found me."

"Here," she murmurs, "sleeping; in the garden reading; laughing, rolling apples in the loft. Here we left our treasure – "

Stooping, their light lifts the lids upon my eyes. "Safe! safe! safe!" the pulse of the house beats wildly. Waking, I cry "Oh, is this your buried treasure? The light in the heart."

# How the Leopard Got His Spots

*Rudyard Kipling*

In the days when everybody started fair, Best Beloved, the Leopard lived in a place called the High Veldt. 'Member it wasn't the Low Veldt, or the Bush Veldt, or the Sour Veldt, but the 'sclusively bare, hot shiny High Veldt, where there was sand and sandy-coloured rock and 'sclusively tufts of sandy-yellowish grass. The Giraffe and the Zebra and the Eland and the Koodoo and the Hartebeest lived there: and they were 'sclusively sandy-yellow-brownish all over; but the Leopard, he was the 'sclusivest sandiest-yellowest-brownest of them all – a greyish-yellowish catty-shaped kind of beast, and he matched the 'sclusively yellowish-greyish-brownish colour of the High Veldt to one hair. This was very bad for the Giraffe and the Zebra and the rest of them: for he would lie down by a 'sclusively yellowish-greyish-brownish stone or clump of grass, and when the Giraffe or the Zebra or the Eland or the Koodoo or the Bush-Buck or the Bonte-Buck came by he would surprise them out of their jumpsome lives. He would indeed! And, also, there was an Ethiopian with bows and arrows (a 'sclusively greyish-brownish-yellowish man he was then), who lived on the High Veldt with the Leopard: and the two used to hunt together – the Ethiopian with his bows and arrows, and the Leopard 'sclusively with his teeth and claws – till the Giraffe and the Eland and the Koodoo and the Quagga and all the rest of them didn't know which way to jump, Best Beloved. They didn't indeed!

After a long time – things lived for ever so long in those days – they learned to avoid anything that looked like a Leopard or an Ethiopian: and bit by bit – the Giraffe began it, because his legs were the longest – they went away from the High Veldt. They scuttled for days and days till they came to a great forest, 'sclusively full of trees and bushes and stripy, speckly, patchyblatchy shadows, and there they hid: and after another long time, what with standing half in the shade and half out of it, and what with the slippery-slidy shadows of the trees falling on them, the Giraffe grew blotchy, and the Zebra grew stripy, and the Eland and the Koodoo grew darker, with little wavy grey lines on their backs like bark on a tree-trunk: and so, though you could hear them and smell them, you could very seldom see them, and then only when you knew precisely where to look. They had a beautiful time in the 'sclusively speckly-spickly shadows of the forest, while the Leopard and the Ethiopian ran about over the 'sclusively greyish-yellowish-reddish High Veldt outside, wondering where all their breakfasts and their dinners and their teas had gone. At last they were so hungry that they ate rats and beetles and rock-rabbits, the Leopard and the Ethiopian, and then they had the Big Tummy-ache, both together: and then they met Baviaan – the dog-headed, barking baboon, who is Quite the Wisest Animal in All South Africa.

Said the Leopard to Baviaan (and it was a very hot day), 'Where has all the game gone?'

And Baviaan winked. He knew.

Said Ethiopian to Baviaan, 'Can you tell me the present habitat of the aboriginal Fauna?' (That meant just the same thing, but the Ethiopian always used long words. He was a grown-up.)

And Baviaan winked. He knew.

Then said Baviaan, 'The game has gone into other spots: and my advice to you, Leopard, is to go into other spots as soon as you can.'

And the Ethiopian said, 'That is all very fine, but I wish to know whither the aboriginal Fauna has migrated.'

Then said Baviaan, 'The aboriginal Fauna has joined the aboriginal Flora because it was high time for a change; and my advice to you, Ethiopian, is to change as soon as you can.'

That puzzled the Leopard and the Ethiopian, but they set off to look for the aboriginal Flora, and presently, after ever so many days, they saw a great, high, tall forest full of tree-trunks all 'sclusively speckled and sprottled and spottled, dotted and splashed and slashed and hatched and cross-hatched with shadows. (Say that quickly aloud, and you will see how very shadowy the forest must have been.)

'What is this,' said the Leopard, 'that is so 'sclusively dark, and yet so full of little pieces of light?'

'I don't know,' said the Ethiopian, 'but it ought to be the aboriginal Flora. I can smell Giraffe, and I can hear Giraffe, but I can't see Giraffe.'

'That's curious,' said the Leopard. 'I suppose it is because we have just come in out of the sunshine. I can smell Zebra, and I can hear Zebra, but I can't see Zebra.'

'Wait a bit,' said the Ethiopian. 'It's a long time since we've hunted 'em. Perhaps we've forgotten what they were like.'

'Fiddle!' said the Leopard. I remember them perfectly on the High Veldt, especially their marrow- bones. Giraffe is about seventeen feet high, of a 'sclusively fulvous golden-yellow from head to heel: and Zebra is about four and a half feet high, of a 'sclusively grey-fawn colour from head to heel.'

'Umm,' said the Ethiopian, looking into the speckly-spickly shadows of the aboriginal Flora-forest. 'Then they ought to show up in this dark place like ripe bananas in a smoke-house.'

But they didn't. The Leopard and the Ethiopian hunted all day; and though they could smell them and hear them, they never saw one of them.

'For goodness' sake,' said the Leopard at tea-time, 'let us wait till it gets dark. This daylight hunting is a perfect scandal.'

So they waited till dark, and then the Leopard heard something breathing sniffily in the starlight that fell all stripy through the branches, and he jumped at the noise, and it smelt like Zebra, and it felt like Zebra, and when he knocked it down it kicked like Zebra, but he couldn't see it. So he said, 'Be quiet, O you person without any form. I am going to sit on your head till morning, because there is something about you that I don't understand.'

Presently he heard a grunt and a crash and a scramble, and the Ethiopian called out, 'I've caught a thing that I can't see. It smells like Giraffe, and it kicks like Giraffe, but it hasn't any form.'

'Don't you trust it, said the Leopard. 'Sit on its head till the morning – same as me. They haven't any form – any of 'em.'

So they sat down on them hard till bright morning-time, and then Leopard said, 'What have you at your end of the table, Brother?'

The Ethiopian scratched his head and said, 'It ought to be 'sclusively a rich fulvous orange-tawny from head to heel, and it ought to be Giraffe; but it is covered all over with chestnut blotches. What have you at your end of the table, Brother?'

And the Leopard scratched his head and said, 'It ought to be 'sclusively a delicate greyish-fawn, and it ought to be Zebra; but it is covered all over with black and purple stripes. What in the world have you been doing to yourself, Zebra? Don't you know that if you were on the High Veldt I could see you ten miles off? You haven't any form.'

'Yes,' said the Zebra, 'but this isn't the High Veldt. Can't you see?'

'I can now,' said the Leopard, 'But I couldn't all yesterday. How is it done?'

'Let us up,' said the Zebra, 'and we will show you.'

They let the Zebra and the Giraffe get up; and Zebra moved away to some little thorn-bushes where the sunlight fell all stripy, and the Giraffe moved off to some tallish trees where the shadows fell all blotchy.

'Now watch,' said the Zebra and the Giraffe. 'This is the way it's done. One – two – three! And where's your breakfast?'

Leopard stared, and Ethiopian stared, but all they could see were stripy shadows and blotched shadows in the forest, but never a sign of Zebra and Giraffe. They had just walked off and hidden themselves in the shadowy forest.

'Hi! Hi!' said the Ethiopian. 'That's a trick worth learning. Take a lesson by it, Leopard. You show up in this dark place like a bar of soap in a coal-scuttle.'

'Ho! Ho!' said the Leopard. 'Would it surprise you very much to know that you show up in this dark place like a mustard-plaster on a sack of coals?'

'Well, calling names won't catch dinner,' said the Ethiopian. 'The long and the little of it is that we don't match our backgrounds. I'm going to take Baviaan's advice. He told me I ought to change: and as I've nothing to change except my skin I'm going to change that.'

'What to?' said the Leopard, tremendously excited.

'To a nice working blackish-brownish colour, with a little purple in it, and touches of slaty-blue. It will be the very thing for hiding in hollows and behind trees.'

So he changed his skin then and there, and the Leopard was more excited than ever: he had never seen a man change his skin before.

'But what about me?' she said, when the Ethiopian had worked his last little finger into his fine new black skin.

'You take Baviaan's advice too. He told you to go into spots.'

'So I did,' said the Leopard. 'I went into other spots as fast as I could. I went into this spot with you, and a lot of good it has done me.'

'Oh,' said the Ethiopian. 'Baviaan didn't mean spots in South Africa. he meant spots on your skin.'

'What's the use of that?' said the Leopard.

'Think of Giraffe,' said the Ethiopian. 'Or if you prefer stripes, think of Zebra. They find their spots and stripes give them per-fect satisfaction.'

'Umm,' said the Leopard. 'I wouldn't look like Zebra – not for ever so.'

'Well, make up your mind,' said the Ethiopian, 'because I'd hate to go hunting without you, but I must if you insist on looking like a sunflower against a tarred fence.'

'I'll take spots, then,' said the Leopard; 'but don't make 'em too vulgar-big. I wouldn't look like Giraffe – not for ever so.'

'I'll make 'em with the tips of my fingers,' said the Ethiopian. 'There's plenty of black left on my skin still. Stand over!'

Then the Ethiopian put his five fingers close together (there was plenty of black left on his new skin still) and pressed them all over the Leopard, and wherever the five fingers touched they left five little black marks, all close together. You can see them on any Leopard's skin you like, Best Beloved. Sometimes the fingers slipped and the marks got a little blurred; but if you look closely at any Leopard now you will see that there are always five spots – off five black finger-tips.

'Now you are a beauty!' said the Ethiopian. 'You can lie out on the bare ground and look like a heap of pebbles. You can lie out on the naked rocks and look like a piece of pudding-stone.

You can lie out on a leafy branch and look like sunshine sifting through the leaves; and you can lie right across the centre of a path and look like nothing in particular. Think of that and purr!'

'But if I'm all this,' said the Leopard, 'why didn't you go spotty too?'

'Oh, plain black's best,' said the Ethiopian. 'Now come along and we'll see if we can't get even with Mr One-Two-Three-Where's-your-Breakfast!'

So they went away and lived happily ever afterwards, Best Beloved. That is all.

Oh, now and then you will hear grown-ups say, 'Can the Ethiopian change his skin or the Leopard his spots?' I don't think even grown-ups would keep on saying such a silly thing if the Leopard and the Ethiopian hadn't done it once – do you? But they will never do it again, Best Beloved. They are quite contented as they are.

# The Comprehension of Private Copper

*Rudyard Kipling*

PRIVATE COPPER'S father was a Southdown shepherd; in early youth Copper had studied under him. Five years' army service had somewhat blunted Private Copper's pastoral instincts, but it occurred to him as a memory of the Chalk that sheep, or in this case buck, do not move towards one across turf, or in this case, the Colesberg kopjes unless a stranger, or in this case an enemy, is in the neighbourhood. Copper, helmet back-first, advanced with caution, leaving his mates of the picket full a mile behind. The picket, concerned for its evening meal, did not protest. A year ago it would have been an officer's command, moving as such. To-day it paid casual allegiance to a Canadian, nominally a sergeant, actually a trooper of Irregular Horse, discovered convalescent in Naauwport Hospital, and forthwith employed on odd jobs. Private Copper crawled up the side of a bluish rock-strewn hill thinly fringed with brush a-top, and remembering how he had peered at Sussex conies through the edge of furze-clumps, cautiously parted the dry stems before his face. At the foot of the long slope sat three farmers smoking. To his natural lust for tobacco was added personal wrath because spiky plants were pricking his belly, and Private Copper slid the backsight up to fifteen hundred yards . . . .

'Good evening, khaki. Please don't move,' said a voice on his left, and as he jerked his head round he saw entirely down the barrel of a well-kept Lee-Metford protruding from an insignificant tuft of thorn. Very few graven images have moved less than did Private Copper through the next ten seconds.

'It's nearer seventeen hundred than fifteen,' said a young man in an obviously ready-made suit of grey tweed, possessing himself of Private Copper's rifle. 'Thank you. We've got a post of thirty-seven men out yonder. You've eleven—eh? We don't want to kill 'em. We have no quarrel with poor uneducated khakis, and we do not want prisoners we do not keep. It is demoralising to both sides—eh?'

Private Copper did not feel called upon to lay down the conduct of guerilla warfare. This dark-skinned, dark-haired, and dark-eyed stranger was his first intimate enemy. He spoke, allowing for a clipped cadence that recalled to Copper vague memories of Umballa, in precisely the same offensive accent that the young squire of Wilmington had used fifteen years ago when he caught and kicked Alf Copper, a rabbit in each pocket, out of the ditches of Cuckmere. The enemy looked Copper up and down, folded and repocketed a copy of an English weekly which he had been reading, and said: 'You seem an inarticulate sort of swinel—ike the rest of them—eh?'

'You,' said Copper, thinking, somehow, of the crushing answers he had never given to the young squire, 'are a renegid. Why, you ain't Dutch. You're English, same as me.'

'No, khaki. If you cannot talk civilly to a gentleman I will blow your head off.'

Copper cringed, and the action overbalanced him so that he rolled some six or eight feet downhill, under the lee of a rough rock. His brain was working with a swiftness and clarity strange in all his experience of Alf Copper. While he rolled he spoke, and the voice from his own jaws amazed him: 'If you did, 'twouldn't make you any less of a renegid.' As a useful afterthought he added 'I've sprained my ankle.'

The young man was at his side in a flash. Copper made no motion to rise, but, cross-legged under the rock, grunted: ''Ow much did old Krujer pay you for this? What was you wanted for at 'ome? Where did you desert from?'

'Khaki,' said the young man, sitting down in his turn, 'you are a shade better than your mates. You did not make much more noise than a yoke of oxen when you tried to come up this hill, but you are an ignorant diseased beast like the rest of your people—eh? When you were at the Ragged Schools did they teach you any history, Tommy—'istory, I mean?'

'Don't need no schoolin' to know a renegid,' said Copper. He had made three yards down the hill—out of sight, unless they could see through rocks, of the enemy's smoking party.

The young man laughed; and tossed the soldier a black sweating stick of 'True Affection.' (Private Copper had not smoked a pipe for three weeks.)

'You don't get this—eh?' said the young man. 'We do. We take it from the trains as we want it. You can keep the cake—you po-ah Tommee.' Copper rammed the good stuff into his long-cold pipe and puffed luxuriously. Two years ago the sister of gunner-guard De Souza, East India Railway, had, at a dance given by the sergeants to the Allahabad Railway Volunteers, informed Copper that she could not think of waltzing with 'a poo-ah Tommee.' Private Copper wondered why that memory should have returned at this hour.

'I'm going to waste a little trouble on you before I send you back to your picket quite naked—eh? Then you can say how you were overpowered by twenty of us and fired off your last round—like the men we picked up at the drift playing cards at Stryden's farm-eh? What's your name—eh?'

Private Copper thought for a moment of a faraway housemaid who might still, if the local postman had not gone too far, be interested in his fate. On the other hand, he was, by temperament, economical of the truth. 'Pennycuik,' he said, 'John Pennycuik.'

'Thank you. Well, Mr. John Pennycuik, I'm going to teach you a little 'istory, as you'd call it—eh?'

'Ow !' said Copper, stuffing his left hand in his mouth. 'So long since I've smoked I've burned my 'and—an' the pipe's dropped too. No objection to my movin' down to fetch it, is there—Sir?'

'I've got you covered,' said the young man, graciously, and Private Copper, hopping on one leg, because of his sprain, recovered the pipe yet another three yards downhill and squatted under another rock slightly larger than the first. A roundish boulder made a pleasant rest for his captor, who sat cross-legged once more, facing Copper, his rifle across his knee, his hand on the trigger-guard.

'Well, Mr. Pennycuik, as I was going to tell you. A little after you were born in your English workhouse, your kind, honourable, brave country, England, sent an English gentleman, who could not tell a lie, to say that so long as the sun rose and the rivers ran in their courses the Transvaal would belong to England. Did you ever hear that, khaki—eh?'

'Oh no, Sir,' said Copper. This sentence about the sun and the rivers happened to be a very aged jest of McBride, the professional humorist of D Company, when they discussed the probable length of the war. Copper had thrown beef-tins at McBride in the grey dawn of many wet and dry camps for intoning it.

'Of course you would not. Now, mann, I tell you, listen.' He spat aside and cleared his throat. 'Because of that little promise, my father he moved into the Transvaal and bought a farm—a little place of twenty or thirty thousand acres, don't—you—know.'

The tone, in spite of the sing-song cadence fighting with the laboured parody of the English drawl, was unbearably like the young Wilmington squire's, and Copper found himself saying: 'I ought to. I've 'elped burn some.'

'Yes, you'll pay for that later. And he opened a store.'

'Ho! Shopkeeper was he?'

'The kind you call "Sir" and sweep the floor for, Pennycuik . . . . You see, in those days one used to believe in the British Government. My father did. Then the Transvaal wiped thee earth with the English. They beat them six times running. You know thatt—eh?'

'Isn't what we've come 'ere for.'

'But my father (he knows better now) kept on believing in the English. I suppose it was the pretty talk about rivers and suns that cheated him—eh? Anyhow, he believed in his own country. Inn his own country. So—you see—he was a little startled when he found himself handed over to the Transvaal as a prisoner of war. That's what it came to, Tommy—a prisoner of war. You know what that is—eh? England was too honourable and too gentlemanly to take trouble. There were no terms made for my father.'

'So 'e made 'em 'imself. Useful old bird.' Private Copper sliced up another pipeful and looked out across the wrinkled sea of kopjes, through which came the roar of the rushing Orange River, so unlike quiet Cuckmere.

The young man's face darkened. 'I think I shall sjambok you

myself when I've quite done with you. No, my father (he was a fool) made no terms for eight years—ninety-six months—and for every day of them the Transvaal made his life hell for my father and—his people.'

'I'm glad to hear that,' said the impenitent Copper.

'Are you? You can think of it when I'm taking the skin off your back—eh? . . . My father, he lost everything—everything down to his self-respect. You don't know what thatt means—eh?'

'Why?' said Copper. 'I'm smokin' baccy stole by a renegid. Why wouldn't I know?'

If it came to a flogging on that hillside there might be a chance of reprisals. Of course, he might be marched to the Boer camp in the next valley and there operated upon; but Army life teaches no man to cross bridges unnecessarily.

'Yes, after eight years, my father, cheated by your bitch of a country, he found out who was the upper dog in South Africa.'

'That's me,' said Copper valiantly. 'If it takes another 'alf-century, it's me an' the likes of me.'

'You? Heaven help you! You'll be screaming at a wagon-wheel in an hour . . . . Then it struck my father that he'd like to shoot the people who'd betrayed him. You—you—you! He told his son all about it. He told him never to trust the English. He told him to do them all the harm he could. Mann, I tell you, I don't want much telling. I was born in the Transvaal—I'm a burgher. If my father didn't love the English, by the Lord, mann, I tell you, I hate them from the bottom of my soul.'

The voice quavered and ran high. Once more, for no conceivable reason, Private Copper found his inward eye turned upon Umballa cantonments of a dry dusty afternoon, when the saddle-coloured son of a local hotel-keeper came to the barracks to complain of a theft of fowls. He saw the dark face, the plover's-egg-tinted eyeballs, and the thin excited hands. Above all, he remembered the passionate, queerly-strung words. Slowly he returned to South Africa, using the very sentence his sergeant had used to the poultry man.

'Go on with your complaint. I'm listenin'.'

'Complaint! Complaint about you, you ox! We strip and kick your sort by thousands.'

The young man rocked to and fro above the rifle, whose muzzle thus deflected itself from the pit of Private Copper's stomach. His face was dusky with rage.

'Yess, I'm a Transvaal burgher. It took us about twenty years to find out how rotten you were. We know and you know it now. Your Army—it is the laughing-stock of the Continent.' He tapped the newspaper in his pocket. 'You think you're going to win, you poor fools! Your people—your own people—your silly rotten fools of people will crawl out of it as they did after Majuba. They are beginning now. Look what your own working classes, the diseased, lying, drinking white stuff that you come out of, are saying.' He thrust the English weekly, doubled at the leading article, on Copper's knee. 'See what dirty dogs your masters are. They do not even back you in your dirty work. We cleared the country down to Ladysmith—to Estcourt. We cleared the country down to Colesberg.'

'Yes. We 'ad to clean up be'ind you. Messy, I call it.'

'You've had to stop farm-burning because your people daren't do it. They were afraid. You daren't kill a spy. You daren't shoot a spy when you catch him in your own uniform. You daren't touch our loyal people in Cape Town! Your masters won't let you. You will feed our women and children till we are quite ready to take them back. You can't put your cowardly noses out of the towns you say you've occupied. You daren't move a convoy twenty miles. You think you've done something? You've done nothing, and you've taken a quarter of a million of men to do it! There isn't a nigger in South Africa that doesn't obey us if we lift our finger. You pay the stuff four pounds a month and they lie to you. We flog 'em, as I shall flog you.'

He clasped his hands together and leaned forward his out-thrust chin within two feet of Copper's left or pipe hand.

'Yuss,' said Copper, 'it's a fair knock-out.' The fist landed to a hair on the chin-point, the neck snicked like a gun-lock, and the back of the head crashed on the boulder behind.

Copper grabbed up both rifles, unshipped the cross-bandoliers, drew forth the English weekly, and picking up the lax hands, looked long and intently at the finger-nails.

'No! Not a sign of it there,' he said. ''Is nails are as clean as mine—but he talks just like 'em though. And he's a landlord too! A landed proprietor! Shockin', I call it.'

The arms began to flap with returning consciousness. Private Copper rose up and whispered 'If you open your head, I'll bash it.' There was no suggestion of sprain in the flung-back left boot. 'Now walk m front of me, both arms perpendicularly elevated. I'm only a third-class shot, so, if you don't object, I'll rest the muzzle of my rifle lightly but firmly on your collar-button—coverin' the serviceable vertebrae. If your friends see us thus engaged, you pray— 'ard.'

Private and prisoner staggered downhill. No shots broke the peace of the afternoon, but once the young man checked and was sick.

'There's a lot of things I could say to you,' Copper observed, at the close of the paroxysm, 'but it doesn't matter. Look 'ere, you call me "pore Tommy"again.'

The prisoner hesitated.

'Oh, I ain't goin' to do anythin' to you. I'm reconnoiterin' on my own. Say "pore Tommy" 'alf-a-dozen times.'

The prisoner obeyed.

'That's what's been puzzlin' me since I 'ad the pleasure o' meetin' you,' said Copper. 'You ain't 'alf-caste, but you talk chee-chee—pukka bazar chee-chee. Proceed.'

'Hullo,' said the Sergeant of the picket, twenty minutes later, 'where did you round him up?'

'On the top o' yonder craggy mounting. There's a mob of 'em sitting round their Bibles seventeen 'undred yards (you said it was seventeen 'undred ?) t'other side—an' I want some coffee.' He sat down on the smoke-blackened stones by the fire.

''Ow did you get 'im ?' said McBride, professional humorist, quietly filching the English weekly from under Copper's armpit.

'On the chin—while 'e was waggin' it at me.'

'What is 'e? 'Nother Colonial rebel to be 'orribly disenfranchised, or a Cape Minister, or only a loyal farmer with dynamite in both boots? Tell us all about it, Burjer!'

'You leave my prisoner alone,' said Private Copper. ''E's 'ad losses an' trouble; an' it's in the family too. 'E thought I never read the papers, so 'e kindly lent me his very own Jerrold's

Weekly—an' 'e explained it to me as patronisin' as a—as a militia subaltern doin' Railway Staff Officer. 'E's a left-over from Majuba—one of the worst kind, an' 'earin' the evidence as I did, I don't exactly blame 'im. It was this way.'

To the picket Private Copper held forth for ten minutes on the life-history of his captive. Allowing for some purple patches, it was an absolutely fair rendering.

'But what I dis-liked was this baccy-priggin' beggar, 'oo's people, on 'is own showin', couldn't 'ave been more than thirty or forty years in the coun—on this Gawd-forsaken dust-'eap, comin' the squire over me. They're all parsons—we know that, but parson an' squire is a bit too thick for Alf Copper. Why, I caught 'im in the shameful act of tryin' to start a aristocracy on a gun an' a wagon an' a shambuk! Yes; that's what it was: a bloomin' aristocracy.'

'No, it weren't,' said McBride, at length, on the dirt, above the purloined weekly. 'You're the aristocrat, Alf. Old Jerrold's givin' it you lot. You're the uneducated 'ireling of a calcallous aristocracy which 'as sold itself to the 'Ebrew financeer. Meantime, Ducky'—he ran his finger down a column of assorted paragraphs—'you're slakin' your brutal instincks in furious excesses. Shriekin' women an' desolated 'omesteads is what you enjoy, Alf . . . . Halloa! What's a smokin' 'ektacomb?'

''Ere! Let's look. 'Aven't seen a proper spicy paper for a year. Good old Jerrold's!' Pinewood and Moppet, reservists, flung themselves on McBride's shoulders, pinning him to the ground.

'Lie over your own bloomin' side of the bed, an' we can all look,' he protested.

'They're only po-ah Tommies,' said Copper, apologetically, to the prisoner. 'Po-ah unedicated khakis. They don't know what they're fightin' for. They're lookin' for what the diseased, lying, drinkin' white stuff that they come from is sayin' about 'em!'

The prisoner set down his tin of coffee and stared helplessly round the circle.

'I—I don't understand them.'

The Canadian sergeant, picking his teeth with a thorn, nodded sympathetically.

'If it comes to that, we don't in my country! . . . Say, boys, when you're through with your English mail you might 's well provide an escort for your prisoner. He's waitin'.'

'Arf a mo' Sergeant,' said McBride, still reading. ''Ere's Old Barbarity on the ramp again with some of 'is lady friends, 'oo don't like concentration camps. Wish they'd visit ours. Pinewood's a married man. He'd know how to be'ave!'

'Well, I ain't goin' to amuse my prisoner alone. 'E's gettin' 'omesick,' cried Copper. 'One of you thieves read out what's vexin' Old Barbarity an' 'is 'arem these days. You'd better listen, Burjer, because, afterwards, I'm goin' to fall out an' perpetrate those nameless barbarities all over you to keep up the reputation of the British Army.'

From that English weekly, to bar out which a large and perspiring staff of Press censors toiled seven days of the week at Cape Town, did Pinewood of the Reserve read unctuously excerpts of the speeches of the accredited leaders of His Majesty's Opposition. The night-picket arrived in the middle of it, but stayed entranced without paying any compliments, till Pinewood had entirely finished the leading article, and several occasional notes.

'Gentlemen of the jury,' said Alf Copper, hitching up what war had left to him of trousers—'you've 'eard what 'e's been fed up with. Do you blame the beggar? 'Cause I don't! . . . Leave 'im alone, McBride. He's my first and only cap-ture, an' I'm goin' to walk 'ome with 'im, ain't I, Ducky? . . . Fall in, Burjer. It's Bermuda, or Umballa, or Ceylon for you—and I'd give a month's pay to be in your little shoes.'

As not infrequently happens, the actual moving off the ground broke the prisoner's nerve. He stared at the tinted hills round him, gasped and began to struggle—kicking, swearing, weeping, and fluttering all together.

'Pore beggar—oh, pore, pore beggar!' said Alf, leaning in on one side of him, while Pinewood blocked him on the other.

'Let me go! Let me go! Mann, I tell you, let me go——'

''E screams like a woman!' said McBride. 'They'll 'ear 'im five miles off.'

'There's one or two ought to 'ear 'im—in England,' said Copper, putting aside a wildly waving arm.

'Married, ain't 'e?' said Pinewood. 'I've seen 'em go like

this before just at the last. 'Old on, old man. No one's goin' to 'urt you.'

The last of the sun threw the enormous shadow of a kopje over the little, anxious, wriggling group.

'Quit that,' said the Sergeant of a sudden. 'You're only making him worse. Hands up, prisoner! Now you get a holt of yourself, or this'll go off.'

And indeed the revolver-barrel square at the man's panting chest seemed to act like a tonic; he choked, recovered himself, and fell in between Copper and Pinewood.

As the picket neared the camp it broke into song that was heard among the officers' tents:

'E sent us 'is blessin' from London town
(The beggar that kep' the cordite down),
But what do we care if 'e smile or frown,
The beggar that kep' the cordite down?
The mildly nefarious
Wildly barbarious
Beggar that kep' the cordite down!

Said a captain a mile away: 'Why are they singing that? We haven't had a mail for a month, have we?'

An hour later the same captain said to his servant: 'Jenkins, I understand the picket have got a—got a newspaper off a prisoner to-day. I wish you could lay hands on it, Jenkins. Copy of the Times, I think.'

'Yes, Sir. Copy of the Times, Sir,' said Jenkins, without a quiver, and went forth to make his own arrangements.

'Copy of the Times?' said the blameless Alf, from beneath his blanket. 'I ain't a member of the Soldiers' Institoot. Go an' look in the reg'mental Readin'-room—Veldt Row, Kopje Street, second turnin' to the left between 'ere an' Naauwport.'

Jenkins summarised briefly in a tense whisper the thing that Alf Copper need not be.

'But my particular copy of the Times is specially pro'ibited by the censor from corruptin' the morals of the Army. Get a written order from K. o' K., properly countersigned, an' I'll think about it.'

'I've got all you want,' said Jenkins. ''Urry up. I want to 'ave a squint myself.'

Something gurgled in the darkness, and Private Copper fell back smacking his lips.

'Gawd bless my prisoner, and make me a good boy. Amen. 'Ere you are, Jenkins. It's dirt cheap at a tot.'

# The Amir's Homily

***Rudyard Kipling***

HIS Royal Highness Abdur Rahman, Amir of Afghanistan, G.C.S.I., and trusted ally of Her Imperial Majesty the Queen of England and Empress of India, is a gentleman for whom all right-thinking people should have a profound regard. Like most other rulers, he governs not as he would, but as he can, and the mantle of his authority covers the most turbulent race under the stars. To the Afghan neither life, property, law, nor kingship are sacred when his own lusts prompt him to rebel. He is a thief by instinct, a murderer by heredity and training, and frankly and bestially immoral by all three. None the less he has his own crooked notions of honour, and his character is fascinating to study. On occasion he will fight without reason given till he is hacked in pieces; on other occasions he will refuse to show fight till he is driven into a corner. Herein he is as unaccountable as the gray wolf, who is his blood-brother.

And these men His Highness rules by the only weapon that they understand the fear of death, which among some Orientals is the beginning of wisdom. Some say that the Amir's authority reaches no farther than a rifle bullet can range; but as none are quite certain when their king may be in their midst, and as he alone holds every one of the threads of Government, his respect is increased among men. Gholam Hyder, the Commander-in-chief of the Afghan army, is feared reasonably, for he can impale; all Kabul city fears the Governor of Kabul, who has power of life and death through all the wards; but the Amir of Afghanistan, though outlying tribes pretend otherwise when his back is turned, is dreaded beyond chief and governor together. His word is red law; by the gust of his passion falls the leaf of man's life, and his favour is terrible. He has suffered many things, and been a hunted fugitive before he came to the throne, and he understands all the classes of his people. By the custom of the East any man or woman having a complaint to make, or an enemy against whom to be avenged, has the right of speaking face to face with the king at the daily public audience. This is personal government, as it was in the days of Harun al Raschid of blessed memory, whose times exist still and will exist long after the English have passed away.

The privilege of open speech is of course exercised at certain personal risk. The king may be pleased, and raise the speaker to honour for that very bluntness of speech which three minutes later brings a too imitative petitioner to the edge of the ever ready blade. And the people love to have it so, for it is their right.

It happened upon a day in Kabul that the Amir chose to do his day's work in the Baber Gardens, which lie a short distance from the city of Kabul. A light table stood before him, and round the table in the open air were grouped generals and finance ministers according to their degree. The Court and the long tail of feudal chiefs men of blood, fed and cowed by blood stood in an irregular semicircle round the table, and the wind from the Kabul orchards blew among them. All day long sweating couriers dashed in with letters from the outlying districts with rumours of rebellion, intrigue, famine, failure of payments, or announcements of treasure on the road; and all day long the Amir would read the dockets, and pass such of these as were less private to the officials whom they directly concerned, or call up a waiting chief for a word of explanation. It is well to speak clearly to the ruler of Afghanistan. Then the grim head, under the black astrachan cap with the diamond star in front, would nod gravely, and that chief would return to his fellows. Once that afternoon a woman clamoured for divorce against her husband, who was bald, and the Amir, hearing both sides of the case, bade her pour curds over the bare scalp, and lick them, off, that the hair might grow again, and she be contented. Here the Court laughed, and the woman withdrew, cursing her king under her breath.

But when twilight was falling, and the order of the Court was a little relaxed, there came before the king, in custody, a trembling haggard wretch, sore with much buffeting, but of stout enough build, who had stolen three rupees of such small matters does His Highness take cognisance.

"Why did you steal?" said he; and when the king asks questions they do themselves service who answer directly.

"I was poor, and no one gave. Hungry, and there was no food."

"Why did you not work?"

"I could find no work, Protector of the Poor, and I was starving."

"You lie. You stole for drink, for lust, for idleness, for anything but hunger, since any man who will may find work and daily bread."

The prisoner dropped his eyes. He had attended the Court before, and he knew the ring of the death-tone.

"Any man may get work. Who knows this so well as I do? for I too have been hungered—not like you, bastard scum, but as any honest man may be, by the turn of Fate and the will of God."

Growing warm, the Amir turned to his nobles all arow and thrust the hilt of his sabre aside with his elbow.

"You have heard this Son of Lies? Hear me tell a true tale. I also was once starved, and tightened my belt on the sharp belly-pinch. Nor was I alone, for with me was another, who did not fail me in my evil days, when I was hunted, before ever I came to this throne. And wandering like a houseless dog by Kandahar, my money melted, melted, melted till—" He flung out a bare palm before the audience. "And day upon day, faint and sick, I went back to that one who waited, and God knows how we lived, till on a day I took our best lihaf silk it was, fine work of Iran, such as no needle now works, warm, and a coverlet for two, and all that we had. I brought it to a money-lender in a by-lane, and I asked for three rupees upon it. He said to me, who am now the King, 'You are a thief. This is worth three hundred.'—'I am no thief,' I answered, 'but a prince of good blood, and I am hungry.'—'Prince of wandering beggars," said that money-lender, 'I have no money with me, but go to my house with my clerk and he will give you two rupees eight annas, for that is all I will lend." So I went with the clerk to the house, and we talked on the way, and he gave me the money.

We lived on it till it was spent, and we fared hard. And then that clerk said, being a young man of a good heart, 'Surely the money-lender will lend yet more on that lihaf," and he offered me two rupees. These I refused, saying, 'Nay; but get me some work." And he got me work, and I, even I, Abdur Rahman, Amir of Afghanistan, wrought day by day as a coolie, bearing burdens, and labouring of my hands, receiving four annas wage a day for my sweat and backache. But he, this bastard son of naught, must steal! For a year and four months I worked, and none dare say that I lie, for I have a witness, even that clerk who is now my friend."

Then there rose in his place among the Sirdars and the nobles one clad in silk, who folded his hands and said, "This is the truth of God, for I, who by the favour of God and the Amir, am such as you know, was once clerk to that money-lender."

There was a pause, and the Amir cried hoarsely to the prisoner, throwing scorn upon him, till he ended with the dread 'Dar arid,' which clinches justice.

So they led the thief away, and the whole of him was seen no more together; and the Court rustled out of its silence, whispering, "Before God and the Prophet, but this is a man!"

# His Majesty the King

*Rudyard Kipling*

"YETH! And Chimo to sleep at ve foot of ve bed, and ve pink pikky-book, and ve bwead – 'cause I will be hungwy in ve night – and vat's all, Miss Biddums. And now give me one kiss and I'll go to sleep. – So! Kite quiet. Ow! Ve pink pikky-book has slidded under ve pillow and ve bwead is cwumbling! Miss Biddums! Miss Biddums! I'm so uncomfy! Come and tuck me up, Miss Biddums."

His Majesty the King was going to bed; and poor, patient Miss Biddums, who had advertised herself humbly as a "young person, European, accustomed to the care of little children," was forced to wait upon his royal caprices. The going to bed was always a lengthy process, because His Majesty had a convenient knack of forgetting which of his many friends, from the mehter's son to the Commissioner's daughter, he had prayed for, and, lest the Deity should take offence, was used to toil through his little prayers, in all reverence, five times in one evening. His Majesty the King believed in the efficacy of prayer as devoutly as he believed in Chimo the patient spaniel, or Miss Biddums, who could reach him down his gun – "with cursuffun caps – reel ones" – from the upper shelves of the big nursery cupboard.

At the door of the nursery his authority stopped. Beyond lay the empire of his father and mother – two very terrible people who had no time to waste upon His Majesty the King. His voice was lowered when he passed the frontier of his own dominions, his actions were fettered, and his soul was filled with awe because of the grim man who lived among a wilderness of pigeon-holes and the most fascinating pieces of red tape, and the wonderful woman who was always getting into or stepping out of the big carriage.

To the one belonged the mysteries of the "duftar-room";

to the other the great, reflected wilderness of the "Memsahib's room" where the shiny, scented dresses hung on pegs, miles and miles up in the air, and the just-seen plateau of the toilet-table revealed an acreage of speckly combs, broidered "hanafitch bags," and "white-headed" brushes.

There was no room for His Majesty the King either in official reserve or mundane gorgeousness. He had discovered that, ages and ages ago – before even Chimo came to the house, or Miss Biddums had ceased grizzling over a packet of greasy letters which appeared to be her chief treasure on earth. His Majesty the King, therefore, wisely confined himself to his own territories, where only Miss Biddums, and she feebly, disputed his sway.

From Miss Biddums he had picked up his simple theology and welded it to the legends of gods and devils that he had learned in the servants' quarters.

To Miss Biddums he confided with equal trust his tattered garments and his more serious griefs. She would make everything whole. She knew exactly how the Earth had been born, and had reassured the trembling soul of His Majesty the King that terrible time in July when it rained continuously for seven days and seven nights, and – there was no Ark ready and all the ravens had flown away! She was the most powerful person with whom he was brought into contact – always excepting the two remote and silent people beyond the nursery door.

How was His Majesty the King to know that, six years ago, in the summer of his birth, Mrs. Austell, turning over her husband's papers, had come upon the intemperate letter of a foolish woman who had been carried away by the silent man's strength and personal beauty? How could he tell what evil the overlooked slip of note-paper had wrought in the mind of a desperately jealous wife? How could he, despite his wisdom, guess that his mother had chosen to make of it excuse for a bar and a division between herself and her husband, that strengthened and grew harder to break with each year; that she, having unearthed this skeleton in the cupboard, had trained it into a household God which should be about their path and about their bed, and poison all their ways?

These things were beyond the province of His Majesty the

King. He only knew that his father was daily absorbed in some mysterious work for a thing called the Sirkar and that his mother was the victim alternately of the Nautch and the Burrakhana. To these entertainments she was escorted by a Captain-Man for whom His Majesty the King had no regard.

"He doesn't laugh," he argued with Miss Biddums, who would fain have taught him charity. "He only makes faces wiv his mouf, and when he wants to o-muse me I am not o-mused." And His Majesty the King shook his head as one who knew the deceitfulness of this world.

Morning and evening it was his duty to salute his father and mother – the former with a grave shake of the hand, and the latter with an equally grave kiss. Once, indeed, he had put his arms round his mother's neck, in the fashion he used toward Miss Biddums. The openwork of his sleeve-edge caught in an earring, and the last stage of His Majesty's little overture was a suppressed scream and summary dismissal to the nursery.

"It's w'ong," thought His Majesty the King, "to hug Memsahibs wiv fings in veir ears. I will amember." He never repeated the experiment.

Miss Biddums, it must be confessed, spoiled him as much as his nature admitted, in some sort of recompense for what she called "the hard ways of his Papa and Mamma." She, like her charge, knew nothing of the trouble between man and wife – the savage contempt for a woman's stupidity on the one side, or the dull, rankling anger on the other. Miss Biddums had looked after many little children in her time, and served in many establishments. Being a discreet woman, she observed little and said less, and, when her pupils went over the sea to the Great Unknown which she, with touching confidence in her hearers, called "Home," packed up her slender belongings and sought for employment afresh, lavishing all her love on each successive batch of ingrates. Only His Majesty the King had repaid her affection with interest; and in his uncomprehending ears she had told the tale of nearly all her hopes, her aspirations, the hopes that were dead, and the dazzling glories of her ancestral home in "Calcutta, close to Wellington Square."

Everything above the average was in the eyes of His Majesty

the King "Calcutta good." When Miss Biddums had crossed his royal will, he reversed the epithet to vex that estimable lady, and all things evil were, until the tears of repentance swept away spite, "Calcutta bad."

Now and again Miss Biddums begged for him the rare pleasure of a day in the society of the Commissioner's child – the wilful four-year-old Patsie, who, to the intense amazement of His Majesty the King, was idolized by her parents. On thinking the question out at length, by roads unknown to those who have left childhood behind, he came to the conclusion that Patsie was petted because she wore a big blue sash and yellow hair.

This precious discovery he kept to himself. The yellow hair was absolutely beyond his power, his own tousled wig being potato-brown; but something might be done toward the blue sash. He tied a large knot in his mosquito-curtains in order to remember to consult Patsie on their next meeting. She was the only child he had ever spoken to, and almost the only one that he had ever seen. The little memory and the very large and ragged knot held good.

"Patsie, lend me your blue wiband," said His Majesty the King.

"You'll bewy it," said Patsie, doubtfully, mindful of certain fearful atrocities committed on her doll.

"No, I won't – twoofanhonor. It's for me to wear."

"Pooh!" said Patsie. "Boys don't wear sa-ashes. Zey's only for dirls."

"I didn't know." The face of His Majesty the King fell.

"Who wants ribands? Are you playing horses, chickabiddies?" said the Commissioner's wife, stepping into the veranda.

"Toby wanted my sash," explained Patsie.

"I don't now," said His Majesty the King, hastily, feeling that with one of these terrible "grown-ups" his poor little secret would be shamelessly wrenched from him, and perhaps – most burning desecration of all – laughed at.

"I'll give you a cracker-cap," said the Commissioner's wife. "Come along with me, Toby, and we'll choose it."

The cracker-cap was a stiff, three-pointed vermilion-and-tinsel splendor. His Majesty the King fitted it on his royal brow. The Commissioner's wife had a face that children instinctively trusted, and her action, as she adjusted the toppling middle spike, was tender.

"Will it do as well?" stammered His Majesty the King.

"As what, little one?"

"As ve wiban?"

"Oh, quite. Go and look at yourself in the glass."

The words were spoken in all sincerity and to help forward any absurd "dressing-up" amusement that the children might take into their minds. But the young savage has a keen sense of the ludicrous. His Majesty the King swung the great cheval-glass down, and saw his head crowned with the staring horror of a fool's cap – a thing which his father would rend to pieces if it ever came into his office. He plucked it off, and burst into tears.

"Toby," said the Commissioner's wife, gravely, "you shouldn't give way to temper. I am very sorry to see it. It's wrong."

His Majesty the King sobbed inconsolably, and the heart of Patsie's mother was touched. She drew the child on to her knee. Clearly it was not temper alone.

"What is it, Toby? Won't you tell me? Aren't you well?"

The torrent of sobs and speech met, and fought for a time, with chokings and gulpings and gasps. Then, in a sudden rush, His Majesty the King was delivered of a few inarticulate sounds, followed by the words: – "Go a – way you – dirty – little debbil!"

"Toby! What do you mean?"

"It's what he'd say. I know it is! He said vat when vere was only a little, little eggy mess, on my t-t-unic; and he'd say it again, and laugh, if I went in wif vat on my head."

"Who would say that?"

"M-m-my Papa! And I fought if I had ve blue wiban, he'd let me play in ve waste-paper basket under ve table."

"What blue riband, childie?"

"Ve same vat Patsie had – ve big blue wiban w-w-wound my t-ttummy!"

"What is it, Toby? There's something on your mind. Tell me all about it, and perhaps I can help."

"Isn't anyfing," sniffed His Majesty, mindful of his manhood, and raising his head from the motherly bosom upon which it was resting. "I only fought vat you – you petted Patsie 'cause she had ve blue wiban, and – and if I'd had ve blue wiban too, m-my Papa w-would pet me."

The secret was out, and His Majesty the King sobbed bitterly in spite of the arms round him, and the murmur of comfort on his heated little forehead.

Enter Patsie tumultuously, embarrassed by several lengths of the Commissioner's pet mahseer-rod. "Tum along, Toby! Zere's a chu-chu lizard in ze chick, and I've told Chimo to watch him till we turn. If we poke him wiz zis his tail will go wiggle-wiggle and fall off. Tum along! I can't weach."

"I'm comin'," said His Majesty the King, climbing down from the Commissioner's wife's knee after a hasty kiss.

Two minutes later, the chu-chu lizard's tail was wriggling on the matting of the veranda, and the children were gravely poking it with splinters from the chick, to urge its exhausted vitality into "just one wiggle more, 'cause it doesn't hurt chu-chu."

The Commissioner's wife stood in the doorway and watched: – "Poor little mite! A blue sash ... and my own precious Patsie! I wonder if the best of us, or we who love them best, ever understand what goes on in their topsy-turvy little heads."

A big tear splashed on the Commissioner's wife's wedding-ring, and she went indoors to devise a tea for the benefit of His Majesty the King.

"Their souls aren't in their tummies at that age in this climate," said the Commissioner's wife, "but they are not far off. I wonder if I could make Mrs. Austell understand. Poor little fellow!"

With simple craft, the Commissioner's wife called on Mrs. Austell and spoke long and lovingly about children; inquiring specially for His Majesty the King.

"He's with his governess," said Mrs. Austell, and the tone intimated that she was not interested.

The Commissioner's wife, unskilled in the art of war, continued her questionings. "I don't know," said Mrs. Austell. "These things are left to Miss Biddums, and, of course, she does not ill-treat the child."

The Commissioner's wife left hastily. The last sentence jarred upon her nerves. "Doesn't ill-treat the child! As if that were all! I wonder what Tom would say if I only 'didn't ill-treat' Patsie!"

Thenceforward, His Majesty the King was an honored guest at the Commissioner's house, and the chosen friend of Patsie, with whom he blundered into as many scrapes as the compound and the servants' quarters afforded. Patsie's Mamma was always ready to give counsel, help, and sympathy, and, if need were and callers few, to enter into their games with an abandon that would have shocked the sleek-haired subalterns who squirmed painfully in their chairs when they came to call on her whom they profanely nicknamed "Mother Bunch."

Yet, in spite of Patsie and Patsie's Mamma, and the love that these two lavished upon him, His Majesty the King fell grievously from grace, and committed no less a sin than that of theft – unknown, it is true, but burdensome.

There came a man to the door one day, when His Majesty was playing in the hall and the bearer had gone to dinner, with a packet for his Majesty's Mamma. And he put it upon the hall-table, said that there was no answer, and departed.

Presently, the pattern of the dado ceased to interest His Majesty, while the packet, a white, neatly wrapped one of fascinating shape, interested him very much indeed. His Mamma was out, so was Miss Biddums, and there was pink string round the packet. He greatly desired pink string. It would help him in many of his little businesses – the haulage across the floor of his small cane-chair, the torturing of Chimo, who could never understand harness – and so forth. If he took the string it would be his own, and nobody would be any the wiser. He certainly could not pluck up sufficient courage to ask Mamma for it. Wherefore, mounting upon a chair, he carefully untied the string and, behold, the stiff white paper spread out in four directions, and revealed a beautiful little leather box with gold lines upon it! He tried to replace the string, but that was a failure. So he opened the box to get full satisfaction for his iniquity, and saw a most beautiful Star that shone and winked, and was altogether lovely and desirable.

"Vat," said His Majesty, meditatively, "is a 'parkle cwown, like what I will wear when I go to heaven. I will wear it on my head – Miss Biddums says so. I would like to wear it now. I would like to play wiv it. I will take it away and play wiv it, very careful, until Mamma asks for it. I fink it was bought for me to play wiv – same as my cart."

His Majesty the King was arguing against his conscience, and he knew it, for he thought immediately after: "Never mind. I will keep it to play wiv until Mamma says where is it, and then I will say: – 'I tookt it and I am sorry.' I will not hurt it because it is a 'parkle cwown. But Miss Biddums will tell me to put it back. I will not show it to Miss Biddums."

If Mamma had come in at that moment all would have gone well. She did not, and His Majesty the King stuffed paper, case, and jewel into the breast of his blouse and marched to the nursery.

"When Mamma asks I will tell," was the salve that he laid upon his conscience. But Mamma never asked, and for three whole days His Majesty the King gloated over his treasure. It was of no earthly use to him, but it was splendid, and, for aught he knew, something dropped from the heavens themselves. Still Mamma made no inquiries, and it seemed to him, in his furtive peeps, as though the shiny stones grew dim. What was the use of a 'parkle cwown if it made a little boy feel all bad in his inside? He had the pink string as well as the other treasure, but greatly he wished that he had not gone beyond the string. It was his first experience of iniquity, and it pained him after the flush of possession and secret delight in the "'parkle cwown" had died away.

Each day that he delayed rendered confession to the people beyond the nursery doors more impossible. Now and again he determined to put himself in the path of the beautifully attired lady as she was going out, and explain that he and no one else was the possessor of a "'parkle cwown," most beautiful and quite uninquired for. But she passed hurriedly to her carriage, and the opportunity was gone before His Majesty the King could draw the deep breath which clinches noble resolve. The dread secret cut him off from Miss Biddums, Patsie, and the Commissioner's wife, and – doubly hard fate – when he brooded over it Patsie said, and told her mother, that he was cross.

The days were very long to His Majesty the King, and the nights longer still. Miss Biddums had informed him, more than once, what was the ultimate destiny of "fieves," and when he passed the interminable mud flanks of the Central Jail, he shook in his little strapped shoes.

But release came after an afternoon spent in playing boats by the edge of the tank at the bottom of the garden. His Majesty the King went to tea, and, for the first time in his memory, the meal revolted him. His nose was very cold, and his cheeks were burning hot. There was a weight about his feet, and he pressed his head several times to make sure that it was not swelling as he sat.

"I feel vevy funny," said His Majesty the King, rubbing his nose. "Vere's a buzz-buzz in my head."

He went to bed quietly. Miss Biddums was out and the bearer undressed him.

The sin of the "'parkle cwown" was forgotten in the acuteness of the discomfort to which he roused after a leaden sleep of some hours, He was thirsty, and the bearer had forgotten to leave the drinking-water. "Miss Biddums! Miss Biddums! I'm so kirsty!"

No answer, Miss Biddums had leave to attend the wedding of a Calcutta schoolmate. His Majesty the King had forgotten that.

"I want a dwink of water!" he cried, but his voice was dried up in his throat. "I want a dwink! Vere is ve glass?"

He sat up in bed and looked round. There was a murmur of voices from the other side of the nursery door. It was better to face the terrible unknown than to choke in the dark. He slipped out of bed, but his feet were strangely wilful, and he reeled once or twice. Then he pushed the door open and staggered – a puffed and purple-faced little figure – into the brilliant light of the dining-room full of pretty ladies.

"I'm vevy hot! I'm vevy uncomfitivle," moaned His Majesty the King, clinging to the portière, "and vere's no water in ve glass, and I'm so kirsty. Give me a dwink of water."

An apparition in black and white – His Majesty the King could hardly see distinctly – lifted him up to the level of the table, and felt his wrists and forehead. The water came, and he drank deeply, his teeth chattering against the edge of the tumbler. Then every one seemed to go away – everyone except the huge man in black and white, who carried him back to his bed; the mother and father following. And the sin of the "'parkle cwown" rushed back and took possession of the terrified soul.

"I'm a fief!" he gasped. "I want to tell Miss Biddums vat I'm a fief. Vere is Miss Biddums?"

Miss Biddums had come and was bending over him. "I'm a fief," he whispered. "A fief – like ve men in the pwison. But I'll tell now, I tookt ... I tookt ve 'parkle cwown when the man that came left it in ve hall. I bwoke ve paper and ve little bwown box, and it looked shiny, and I tookt it to play wif, and I was afwaid. It's in ve dooly-box at ve bottom. No one never asked for it, but I was afwaid. Oh, go an' get ve dooly-box!"

Miss Biddums obediently stooped to the lowest shelf of the almirah and unearthed the big paper box in which His Majesty the King kept his dearest possessions. Under the tin soldiers, and a layer of mud pellets for a pellet-bow, winked and blazed a diamond star, wrapped roughly in a half-sheet of note-paper whereon were a few words.

Somebody was crying at the head of the bed, and a man's hand touched the forehead of His Majesty the King, who grasped the packet and spread it on the bed.

"Vat is ve 'parkle cwown," he said, and wept bitterly; for now that he had made restitution he would fain have kept the shining splendor with him.

"It concerns you too," said a voice at the head of the bed. "Read the note. This is not the time to keep back anything."

The note was curt, very much to the point, and signed by a single initial. "If you wear this to-morrow night I shall know what to expect." The date was three weeks old.

A whisper followed, and the deeper voice returned: "And you drifted as far apart as that! I think it makes us quits now, doesn't it? Oh, can't we drop this folly once and for all? Is it worth it, darling?"

"Kiss me too," said His Majesty the King, dreamily. "You isn't vevy angwy, is you?"

The fever burned itself out, and His Majesty the King slept.

When he waked, it was in a new world – peopled by his father and mother as well as Miss Biddums: and there was much love in that world and no morsel of fear, and more petting than was good for several little boys. His Majesty the King was too young to moralize on the uncertainty of things human, or he would have been impressed with the singular advantages of crime – ay, black sin. Behold, he had stolen the "'parkle cwown," and his reward was Love, and the right to play in the waste-paper basket under the table "for always".

* * * * * * *

He trotted over to spend an afternoon with Patsie, and the Commissioner's wife would have kissed him. "No, not vere," said His Majesty the King, with superb insolence, fencing one corner of his mouth with his hand, "Vat's my Mamma's place – vere she kisses me,"

"Oh!" said the Commissioner's wife, briefly. Then to herself: "Well, I suppose I ought to be glad for his sake. Children are selfish little grubs and – I've got my Patsie.

# My Own True Ghost Story

***Rudyard Kipling***

As I came through the Desert thus it was —

*As I came through the Desert.*— The City of Dreadful Night.

Somewhere in the Other World, where there are books and pictures and plays and shop windows to look at, and thousands of men who spend their lives in building up all four, lives a gentleman who writes real stories about the real insides of people; and his name is Mr. Walter Besant. But he will insist upon treating his ghosts — he has published half a workshopful of them — with levity. He makes his ghost-seers talk familiarly, and, in some cases, flirt outrageously, with the phantoms. You may treat anything, from a Viceroy to a Vernacular Paper, with levity; but you must behave reverently toward a ghost, and particularly an Indian one.

There are, in this land, ghosts who take the form of fat, cold, pobby corpses, and hide in trees near the roadside till a traveler passes. Then they drop upon his neck and remain. There are also terrible ghosts of women who have died in child-bed. These wander along the pathways at dusk, or hide in the crops near a village, and call seductively. But to answer their call is death in this world and the next. Their feet are turned backward that all sober men may recognize them. There are ghosts of little children who have been thrown into wells. These haunt well curbs and the fringes of jungles, and wail under the stars, or catch women by the wrist and beg to be taken up and carried. These and the corpse ghosts, however, are only vernacular articles and do not attack Sahibs. No native ghost has yet been authentically reported to have frightened an Englishman; but many English ghosts have scared the life out of both white and black.

Nearly every other Station owns a ghost. There are said to be two at Simla, not counting the woman who blows the bellows at Syree dâk-bungalow on the Old Road; Mussoorie has a house haunted of a very lively Thing; a White Lady is supposed to do night-watchman round a house in Lahore; Dalhousie says that one of her houses "repeats" on autumn evenings all the incidents of a horrible horse-and-precipice accident; Murree has a merry ghost, and, now that she has been swept by cholera, will have room for a sorrowful one; there are Officers' Quarters in Mian Mir whose doors open without reason, and whose furniture is guaranteed to creak, not with the heat of June but with the weight of Invisibles who come to lounge in the chairs; Peshawur possesses houses that none will willingly rent; and there is something — not fever — wrong with a big bungalow in Allahabad. The older Provinces simply bristle with haunted houses, and march phantom armies along their main thoroughfares.

Some of the dâk-bungalows on the Grand Trunk Road have handy little cemeteries in their compound — witnesses to the "changes and chances of this mortal life" in the days when men drove from Calcutta to the Northwest. These bungalows are objectionable places to put up in. They are generally very old, always dirty, while the khansamah is as ancient as the bungalow. He either chatters senilely, or falls into the long trances of age. In both moods he is useless. If you get angry with him, he refers to some Sahib dead and buried these thirty years, and says that when he was in that Sahib's service not a khansamah in the Province could touch him. Then he jabbers and mows and trembles and fidgets among the dishes, and you repent of your irritation.

In these dâk-bungalows, ghosts are most likely to be found, and when found, they should be made a note of. Not long ago it was my business to live in dâk-bungalows. I never inhabited the same house for three nights running, and grew to be learned in the breed. I lived in Government-built ones with red brick walls and rail ceilings, an inventory of the furniture posted in every room, and an excited snake at the threshold to give welcome. I lived in "converted" ones — old houses officiating as dâk-bungalows — where nothing was in its proper place and there wasn't even a fowl for dinner. I lived in second-hand palaces where the wind blew through open-work marble tracery just as uncomfortably as through a broken pane. I lived in dâk-bungalows where the last entry in the visitors' book was fifteen months old, and where they slashed off the curry-kid's head with a sword. It was my good luck to meet all sorts of men, from sober traveling missionaries and deserters flying from British Regiments, to drunken loafers who threw whisky bottles at all who passed; and my still greater good fortune just to escape a maternity case. Seeing that a fair proportion of the tragedy of our lives out here acted itself in dâk-bungalows, I wondered that I had met no ghosts. A ghost that would voluntarily hang about a dâk-bungalow would be mad of course; but so many men have died mad in dâk-bungalows that there must be a fair percentage of lunatic ghosts.

In due time I found my ghost, or ghosts rather, for there were two of them. Up till that hour I had sympathized with Mr. Besant's method of handling them, as shown in "The Strange Case of Mr. Lucraft and Other Stories." I am now in the Opposition.

We will call the bungalow Katmal dâk-bungalow. But THAT was the smallest part of the horror. A man with a sensitive hide has no right to sleep in dâk-bungalows. He should marry. Katmal dâk-bungalow was old and rotten and unrepaired. The floor was of worn brick, the walls were filthy, and the windows were nearly black with grime. It stood on a bypath largely used by native Sub–Deputy Assistants of all kinds, from Finance to Forests; but real Sahibs were rare. The khansamah, who was nearly bent double with old age, said so.

When I arrived, there was a fitful, undecided rain on the face of the land, accompanied by a restless wind, and every gust made a noise like the rattling of dry bones in the stiff toddy palms outside. The khansamah completely lost his head on my arrival. He had served a Sahib once. Did I know that Sahib? He gave me the name of a well-known man who has been buried for more than a quarter of a century, and showed me an ancient daguerreotype of that man in his prehistoric youth. I had seen a steel engraving of him at the head of a double volume of Memoirs a month before, and I felt ancient beyond telling.

The day shut in and the khansamah went to get me food. He did not go through the pretense of calling it "khana"— man's victuals. He said "ratub," and that means, among other things, "grub"— dog's rations. There was no insult in his choice of the term. He had forgotten the other word, I suppose.

While he was cutting up the dead bodies of animals, I settled myself down, after exploring the dâk-bungalow. There were three rooms, beside my own, which was a corner kennel, each giving into the other through dingy white doors fastened with long iron bars. The bungalow was a very solid one, but the partition walls of the rooms were almost jerry-built in their flimsiness. Every step or bang of a trunk echoed from my room down the other three, and every footfall came back tremulously from the far walls. For this reason I shut the door. There were no lamps — only candles in long glass shades. An oil wick was set in the bathroom.

For bleak, unadulterated misery that dâk-bungalow was the worst of the many that I had ever set foot in. There was no fireplace, and the windows would not open; so a brazier of charcoal would have been useless. The rain and the wind splashed and gurgled and moaned round the house, and the toddy palms rattled and roared. Half a dozen jackals went through the compound singing, and a hyena stood afar off and mocked them. A hyena would convince a Sadducee of the Resurrection of the Dead — the worst sort of Dead. Then came the ratub — a curious meal, half native and half English in composition — with the old khansamah babbling behind my chair about dead and gone English people, and the wind-blown candles playing shadow-bo-peep with the bed and the mosquito-curtains. It was just the sort of dinner and evening to make a man think of every single one of his past sins, and of all the others that he intended to commit if he lived.

Sleep, for several hundred reasons, was not easy. The lamp in the bath-room threw the most absurd shadows into the room, and the wind was beginning to talk nonsense.

Just when the reasons were drowsy with blood-sucking I heard the regular —"Let-us-take-and-heave-him-over" grunt of doolie-bearers in the compound. First one doolie came in, then a second, and then a third. I heard the doolies dumped on the ground, and the shutter in front of my door shook. "That's some one trying to come in," I said. But no one spoke, and I persuaded myself that it was the gusty wind. The shutter of the room next to mine was attacked, flung back, and the inner door opened. "That's some Sub–Deputy Assistant," I said, "and he has brought his friends with him. Now they'll talk and spit and smoke for an hour."

But there were no voices and no footsteps. No one was putting his luggage into the next room. The door shut, and I thanked Providence that I was to be left in peace. But I was curious to know where the doolies had gone. I got out of bed and looked into the darkness. There was never a sign of a doolie. Just as I was getting into bed again, I heard, in the next room, the sound that no man in his senses can possibly mistake — the whir of a billiard ball down the length of the slates when the striker is stringing for break. No other sound is like it. A minute afterwards there was another whir, and I got into bed. I was not frightened — indeed I was not. I was very curious to know what had become of the doolies. I jumped into bed for that reason.

Next minute I heard the double click of a cannon and my hair sat up. It is a mistake to say that hair stands up. The skin of the head tightens and you can feel a faint, prickly, bristling all over the scalp. That is the hair sitting up.

There was a whir and a click, and both sounds could only have been made by one thing — a billiard ball. I argued the matter out at great length with myself; and the more I argued the less probable it seemed that one bed, one table, and two chairs — all the furniture of the room next to mine — could so exactly duplicate the sounds of a game of billiards. After another cannon, a three-cushion one to judge by the whir, I argued no more. I had found my ghost and would have given worlds to have escaped from that dâk-bungalow. I listened, and with each listen the game grew clearer. There was whir on whir and click on click. Sometimes there was a double click and a whir and another click. Beyond any sort of doubt, people were playing billiards in the next room. And the next room was not big enough to hold a billiard table!

Between the pauses of the wind I heard the game go forward — stroke after stroke. I tried to believe that I could not hear voices; but that attempt was a failure.

Do you know what fear is? Not ordinary fear of insult, injury or death, but abject, quivering dread of something that you cannot see — fear that dries the inside of the mouth and half of the throat — fear that makes you sweat on the palms of the hands, and gulp in order to keep the uvula at work? This is a fine Fear — a great cowardice, and must be felt to be appreciated. The very improbability of billiards in a dâk-bungalow proved the reality of the thing. No man — drunk or sober — could imagine a game at billiards, or invent the spitting crack of a "screw-cannon."

A severe course of dâk-bungalows has this disadvantage — it breeds infinite credulity. If a man said to a confirmed dâk-bungalow-haunter:—"There is a corpse in the next room, and there's a mad girl in the next but one, and the woman and man on that camel have just eloped from a place sixty miles away," the hearer would not disbelieve because he would know that nothing is too wild, grotesque, or horrible to happen in a dâk-bungalow.

This credulity, unfortunately, extends to ghosts. A rational person fresh from his own house would have turned on his side and slept. I did not. So surely as I was given up as a bad carcass by the scores of things in the bed because the bulk of my blood was in my heart, so surely did I hear every stroke of a long game at billiards played in the echoing room behind the iron-barred door. My dominant fear was that the players might want a marker. It was an absurd fear; because creatures who could play in the dark would be above such superfluities. I only know that that was my terror; and it was real.

After a long, long while the game stopped, and the door banged. I slept because I was dead tired. Otherwise I should have preferred to have kept awake. Not for everything in Asia would I have dropped the door-bar and peered into the dark of the next room.

When the morning came, I considered that I had done well and wisely, and inquired for the means of departure.

"By the way, khansamah," I said, "what were those three doolies doing in my compound in the night?"

"There were no doolies," said the khansamah.

I went into the next room and the daylight streamed through the open door. I was immensely brave. I would, at that hour, have played Black Pool with the owner of the big Black Pool down below.

"Has this place always been a dâk-bungalow?" I asked.

"No," said the khansamah. "Ten or twenty years ago, I have forgotten how long, it was a billiard room."

"A how much?"

"A billiard room for the Sahibs who built the Railway. I was khansamah then in the big house where all the Railway–Sahibs lived, and I used to come across with brandy-shrab. These three rooms were all one, and they held a big table on which the Sahibs played every evening. But the Sahibs are all dead now, and the Railway runs, you say, nearly to Kabul."

"Do you remember anything about the Sahibs?"

"It is long ago, but I remember that one Sahib, a fat man and always angry, was playing here one night, and he said to me:—'Mangal Khan, brandy-pani do,' and I filled the glass, and he bent over the table to strike, and his head fell lower and lower till it hit the table, and his spectacles came off, and when we — the Sahibs and I myself — ran to lift him. He was dead. I helped to carry him out. Aha, he was a strong Sahib! But he is dead and I, old Mangal Khan, am still living, by your favor."

That was more than enough! I had my ghost — a firsthand, authenticated article. I would write to the Society for Psychical Research — I would paralyze the Empire with the news! But I would, first of all, put eighty miles of assessed crop land between myself and that dâk-bungalow before nightfall. The Society might send their regular agent to investigate later on.

I went into my own room and prepared to pack after noting down the facts of the case. As I smoked I heard the game begin again — with a miss in balk this time, for the whir was a short one.

The door was open and I could see into the room. Click — click! That was a cannon. I entered the room without fear, for there was sunlight within and a fresh breeze without. The unseen game was going on at a tremendous rate. And well it might, when a restless little rat was running to and fro inside the dingy ceiling-cloth, and a piece of loose window-sash was making fifty breaks off the window-bolt as it shook in the breeze!

Impossible to mistake the sound of billiard balls! Impossible to mistake the whir of a ball over the slate! But I was to be excused. Even when I shut my enlightened eyes the sound was marvelously like that of a fast game.

Entered angrily the faithful partner of my sorrows, Kadir Baksh.

"This bungalow is very bad and low-caste! No wonder the Presence was disturbed and is speckled. Three sets of doolie-bearers came to the bungalow late last night when I was sleeping outside, and said that it was their custom to rest in the rooms set apart for the English people! What honor has the khansamah? They tried to enter, but I told them to go. No wonder, if these Oorias have been here, that the Presence is sorely spotted. It is shame, and the work of a dirty man!"

Kadir Baksh did not say that he had taken from each gang two annas for rent in advance, and then, beyond my earshot, had beaten them with the big green umbrella whose use I could never before divine. But Kadir Baksh has no notions of morality.

There was an interview with the khansamah, but as he promptly lost his head, wrath gave place to pity, and pity led to a long conversation, in the course of which he put the fat Engineer–Sahib's tragic death in three separate stations – two of them fifty miles away. The third shift was to Calcutta, and there the Sahib died while driving a dogcart.

If I had encouraged him the khansamah would have wandered all through Bengal with his corpse.

I did not go away as soon as I intended. I stayed for the night, while the wind and the rat and the sash and the window-bolt played a ding-dong "hundred and fifty up." Then the wind ran out and the billiards stopped, and I felt that I had ruined my one genuine, hall-marked ghost story.

Had I only stopped at the proper time, I could have made anything out of it.

That was the bitterest thought of all!

# My Sunday at Home

***Rudyard Kipling***

It was the unreproducible slid r, as he said this was his 'fy-ist' visit to England, that told me he was a New Yorker from New York; and when, in the course of our long, lazy journey westward from Waterloo, he enlarged upon the beauties of his city, I, professing ignorance, said no word. He had, amazed and delighted at the man's civility, given the London porter a shilling for carrying his bag nearly fifty yards; he had thoroughly investigated the first-class lavatory compartment, which the London and South-Western sometimes supply without extra charge; and now, half awed, half contemptuous, but wholly interested, he looked out upon the ordered English landscape wrapped in its Sunday peace, while I watched the wonder grow upon his face. Why were the cars so short and stilted? Why had every other freight-car a tarpaulin drawn over it? What wages would an engineer get now? Where was the swarming population of England he had read so much about. What was the rank of all those men on tricycles along the roads? When were we due at Plymouth?

I told him all I knew, and very much that I did not. He was going to Plymouth to assist in a consultation upon a fellow-countryman who had retired to a place called The Hoe – was that up town or down town? – to recover from nervous dyspepsia. Yes, he himself was a doctor by profession, and how any one in England could retain any nervous disorder passed his comprehension. Never had he dreamed of an atmosphere so soothing. Even the deep rumble of London traffic was monastical by comparison with some cities he could name; and the country – why, it was Paradise. A continuance of it, he confessed, would drive him mad; but for a few months it was the most sumptuous rest cure in his knowledge.

'I'll come over every year after this,' he said, in a burst of delight, as we ran between two ten foot hedges of pink and white may. 'It's seeing all the things I've ever read about. Of course it doesn't strike you that way. I presume you belong here? What a finished land it is! It's arrived. Must have been born this way. Now, where I used to live — Hello I what's up'?

The train stopped in a blaze of sunshine at Framlynghame Admiral, which is made up entirely of the nameboard, two platforms, and an overhead bridge, without even the usual siding. I had never known the slowest of locals stop here before; but on Sunday all things are possible to the London and South-Western. One could hear the drone of conversation along the carriages, and, scarcely less loud, the drone of the bumblebees in the wallflowers up the bank. My companion thrust his head through the window and sniffed luxuriously.

'Where are we now?' said he.

'In Wiltshire,' said I.

'Ah! A man ought to be able to write novels with his left hand in a country like this. Well, well! And so this is about Tess's country, ain't it? I feel just as if I were in a book. Say, the conduc — the guard has something on his mind. What's he getting at? '

The splendid badged and belted guard was striding up the platform at the regulation official pace, and in the regulation official voice was saying at each door —

'Has any gentleman here a bottle of medicine? A gentleman. has taken a bottle of poison (laudanum) by mistake.'

Between each five paces he looked at an official telegram in his hand, refreshed his memory, and said his say. The dreamy look on my companion's face — he had gone far away with Tess — passed with the speed of a snap -shutter. After the manner of his countrymen, he had risen to the situation, jerked his bag down from the overhead rack, opened it, and I heard the click of bottles. 'Find out where the man is,' he said briefly. 'I've got something here that will fix him — if he can swallow still.'

Swiftly I fled up the line of carriages in the wake of the guard. There was clamour in a rear compartment — the voice of one bellowing to be let out, and the feet of one who kicked. With the tail of my eye I saw the New York doctor hastening thither, bearing in his hand a blue and brimming glass from the lavatory compartment. The guard I found scratching his head unofficially, by the engine, and murmuring: 'Well, I put a bottle of medicine off at Andover, I'm sure I did.'

'Better say it again, any'ow,' said the driver. 'Orders is orders. Say it again.'

Once more the guard paced back, I, anxious to attract his attention, trotting at his heels.

'In a minute – in a minute, sir,' he said, waving an arm capable of starting all, the traffic on the London and South-Western Railway at a wave. 'Has any gentleman here got a bottle of medicine? A gentleman has taken a bottle of poison (laudanum) by mistake.'

'Where's the man?' I gasped.

'Woking. 'Ere's my orders.' He showed me the telegram, on which were the words to be said. ''E must have left 'is bottle in the train, an' took another by mistake. 'E's been wirin' from Woking awful, an', now I come to think of it, I'm nearly sure I put a bottle of medicine off at Andover.'

'Then the man that took the poison isn't on the train?'

'Lord, no, sir. No one didn't take poison that way. 'E took it away with 'im, in 'is 'ands. 'E's wirin' from Wokin'. My orders was to ask everybody on the train, and I 'ave, an' we're four minutes late now. Are you comin' on, sir? No? Right be'ind!'

There is nothing, unless, perhaps, the English language, more terrible than the workings of an English railway line. An instant before it seemed as though we were going to spend all eternity at Framlynghame Admiral, and now I was watching the tail of the train disappear round the curve of the cutting.

But I was not alone. On the one bench of the down platform sat the largest navvy I have ever seen in my life, softened and made affable (for he smiled generously) with liquor. In his huge hands he nursed an empty tumbler marked 'L.S.W.R.'– marked also, internally, with streaks of blue-gray sediment. Before him, a hand on his shoulder, stood the doctor, and as I came within earshot this is what I heard him say: 'Just you hold on to your patience for a minute or two longer, and you'll be as right as ever you were in your life. I'll stay with you till you're better.'

'Lord! I'm comfortable enough,' said the navvy. 'Never felt

better in my life.'

Turning to me, the doctor lowered his voice. 'He might have died while that fool conduct — guard was saying his piece. I've fixed him, though. The stuff's due in about five minutes, but there's a heap to him. I don't see how we can make him take exercise.'

For the moment I felt as though seven pounds of crushed ice had been neatly applied in the form of a compress to my lower stomach.

'How — how did you manage it?' I gasped.

'I asked him if he'd have a drink. He was knocking spots out of the car — strength of his constitution, I suppose. He said he'd go 'most anywhere for a drink, so I lured him on to the platform, and loaded him up. Cold-blooded people you Britishers are. That train's gone, and no one seemed to care a cent.'

'We've missed it,' I said.

He looked at me curiously.

'We'll get another before sundown, if that's your only trouble. Say, porter, when's the next train down?'

'Seven forty-five,' said the one porter, and passed out through the wicket-gate into the landscape. It was then three-twenty of a hot and sleepy afternoon. The station was absolutely deserted. The navvy had closed his eyes, and now nodded.

'That's bad,' said the doctor. 'The man, I mean, not the train. We must make him walk somehow — walk up and down:'

Swiftly as might be, I explained the delicacy of the situation, and the doctor from New York turned a full bronze-green. Then he swore comprehensively at the entire fabric of our glorious Constitution, cursing the English language, root, branch, and paradigm, through its most obscure derivatives. His coat and bag lay on the bench next to the sleeper. Thither he edged cautiously, and I saw treachery in his eye.

What devil of delay possessed him to slip on his spring overcoat, I cannot tell. They say a slight noise arouses a sleeper more surely than a heavy one, and scarcely had the doctor settled himself in his sleeves when the giant waked and seized that silkfaced collar in a hot right hand. There was rage in his face — rage and the realisation of new emotions.

'I'm — I'm not so comfortable as I were,' he said from the deeps of his interior. 'You'll wait along o' me, you will.' He breathed heavily through shut lips.

Now, if there was one thing more than another upon which the doctor had dwelt in his conversation with me, it was upon the essential law-abidingness, not to say gentleness, of his much-misrepresented country. And yet (truly, it may have been no more than a button that irked him) I saw his hand travel backwards to his right hip, clutch at something, and come away empty.

'He won't kill you,' I said. 'He'll probably sue you in court, if I know my own people. Better give him some money from time to time.'

'If he keeps quiet till the stuff gets in its work,' the doctor answered, 'I'm all right. If he doesn't . . . my name is Emory — Julian B. Emory — 193 'Steenth Street, corner of Madison and — —'

'I feel worse than I've ever felt,' said the navvy, with suddenness. 'What — did — you — give — me — the — drink — for?'

The matter seemed to be so purely personal that I withdrew to a strategic position on the overhead bridge, and, abiding in the exact centre, looked on from afar.

I could see the white road that ran across the shoulder of Salisbury Plain, unshaded for mile after mile, and a dot in the middle distance, the back of the one porter returning to Framlynghame Admiral, if such a place existed, till seven forty-five. The bell of a church invisible clanked softly. There was a rustle in the horse-chestnuts to the left of the line, and the sound of sheep cropping close.

The peace of Nirvana lay upon the land, and, brooding in it, my elbow on the warm iron girder of the footbridge (it is a forty-shilling fine to cross by any other means), I perceived, as never before, how the consequences of our acts run eternal through time and through space. If we impinge never so slightly upon the life of a fellow-mortal, the touch of our personality, like the ripple of a stone cast into a pond, widens and widens in unending circles across the aeons, till the far-off gods themselves cannot say where action ceases. Also, it was I who had silently set before the doctor the tumbler of the first-class lavatory compartment now speeding Plymouthward. Yet I was, in spirit at least, a million leagues removed from that unhappy man of another nationality, who had chosen to thrust an inexpert finger into the workings of an alien life. The machinery was dragging him up and down the sunlit platform. The two men seemed to be learning polkamazurkas together, and the burden of their song, borne by one deep voice, was: 'What did you give me the drink for? '

I saw the flash of silver in the doctor's hand. The navvy took it and pocketed it with his left; but never for an instant did his strong right leave the doctor's coat-collar, and as the crisis approached louder and louder rose his bull-like roar: 'What did you give me the drink for?'

They drifted under the great twelve-inch pinned timbers of the footbridge towards the bench, and, I gathered, the time was very near at hand. The stuff was getting in its work. Blue, white, and blue again, rolled over the navvy's face in waves, till all settled to one rich clay-bank yellow and — that fell which fell.

I thought of the blowing-up of Hell Gate; of the geysers in the Yellowstone Park; of Jonah and his whale; but the lively original, as I watched it foreshortened from above, exceeded all these things. He staggered to the bench, the heavy wooden seat cramped with iron cramps into the enduring stone, and clung there with his left hand. It quivered and shook, as a breakwater-pile quivers to the rush of landward-racing seas; nor was there lacking when he caught his breath, the 'scream of a maddened beach dragged down by the wave.' His right hand was upon the doctor's collar, so that the two shook to one paroxysm, pendulums vibrating together, while I, apart, shook with them.

It was colossal — immense; but of certain manifestations the English language stops short. French only, the caryatid French of Victor Hugo, would have described it; so I mourned while I laughed, hastily shuffling and discarding inadequate adjectives. The vehemence of the shock spent itself, and the sufferer half fell, half knelt, across the bench. He was calling now upon God and his wife, huskily, as the wounded bull calls upon the unscathed herd to stay. Curiously enough, he used no bad language: that had gone from him with the rest. The doctor exhibited gold. It was taken, and retained. So, too, was the grip on the coat-collar.

'If I could stand,' boomed the giant despairingly, 'I'd smash you — you an' your drinks. I'm dyin'— dyin'— dyin'!'

'That's what you think,' said the doctor. 'You'll find it will do you a lot of good'; and, making a virtue of a somewhat imperative necessity, he added: 'I'll stay by you. If you'd let go of me a minute I'd give you something that would settle you.'

'You've settled me now, you damned anarchist. Takin' the bread out of the mouth of an English workin' man! But I'll keep 'old of you till I'm well or dead. I never did you no harm. S'pose I were a little full? They pumped me out once at Guy's with a stummick-pump. I could see that, but I can't see this 'ere, an' it's killin' of me by slow degrees.'

'You'll be all right in half an hour. What do you suppose I'd want to kill you for?' said the doctor, who came of a logical breed.

''Ow do I know? Tell 'em in court. You'll get seven years for this, you body-snatcher. That's what you are — a bloomin' body-snatcher. There's justice, I tell you, in England; and my Union'll prosecute, too. We don't stand no tricks with people's insides 'ere. They gave a woman ten years for a sight less than this. An' you'll 'ave to pay 'undreds an' 'undreds o' pounds, besides a pension to the missus. You'll see, you physickin' furriner. Where's your licence to do such? You'll catch it, I tell you!'

Then I observed, what I had frequently observed before, that a man who is but reasonably afraid of an altercation with an alien has a most poignant dread of the operations of foreign law. The doctor's voice was flute-like in its exquisite politeness, as he answered:

'But I've given you a very great deal of money — fif — three pounds, I think.'

'An' what's three pounds for poisonin' the likes o' me? They told me at Guy's I'd fetch twenty — cold — on the slates. Ouh! It's comin' again.'

A second time he was cut down by the foot, as it were, and the straining bench rocked to and fro as I averted my eyes.

It was the very point of perfection in the heart of an English May-day. The unseen tides of the air had turned, and all nature was setting its face with the shadows of the horse-chestnuts towards the peace of the coming night. But there were hours yet, I knew — long, long hours of the eternal English twilight — to the ending of the day. I was well content to be alive — to abandon myself to the drift of Time and Fate; to absorb great peace through my skin, and to love my country with the devotion that three thousand miles of intervening sea bring to fullest flower. And what a garden of Eden it was, this fatted, clipped, and washen land! A man could camp in any open field with more sense of home and security than the stateliest buildings of foreign cities could afford. And the joy was that it was all mine inalienably — groomed hedgerow, spotless road, decent greystone cottage, serried spinney, tasselled copse, apple-bellied hawthorn, and well-grown tree. A light puff of wind — it scattered flakes of may over the gleaming rails — gave me a faint whiff as it might have been of fresh coconut, and I knew that the golden gorse was in bloom somewhere out of sight. Linnæus had thanked God on his bended knees. when he first saw a field of it; and, by the way, the navvy was on his knees too. But he was by no means praying. He was purely disgustful.

The doctor was compelled to bend over him, his face towards the back of the seat, and from what I had seen I supposed the navvy was now dead. If that were the case it would be time for me to go; but I knew that so long as a man trusts himself to the current of Circumstance, reaching out for and rejecting nothing that comes his way, no harm can overtake him. It is the contriver, the schemer, who is caught by the law, and never the philosopher. I knew that when the play was played, Destiny herself would move me on from the corpse; and I felt very sorry for the doctor.

In the-far distance, presumably upon the road that led to Framlynghame Admiral, there appeared a vehicle and a horse — the one ancient fly that almost every village can produce at need. This thing was advancing, unpaid by me, towards the station; would have to pass along the deep-cut lane, below the railway-bridge, and come out on the doctor's side. I was in the centre of things, so all sides were alike to me. Here, then, was my machine from the machine. When it arrived, something would happen, or something else. For the rest, I owned my deeply interested soul.

The doctor, by the seat, turned so far as his cramped position allowed, his head over his left shoulder, and laid his right hand upon his lips. I threw back my hat and elevated my eyebrows in the form of a question. The doctor shut his eyes and nodded his head slowly twice or thrice, beckoning me to come. I descended cautiously, and it was as the signs had told. The navvy was asleep, empty to the lowest notch; yet his hand clutched still the doctor's collar, and at the lightest movement (the doctor was really very cramped) tightened mechanically, as the hand of a sick woman tightens on that of the watcher. He had dropped, squatting almost upon his heels, and, falling lower, had dragged the doctor over to the left.

The doctor thrust his right hand, which was free, into his pocket, drew forth some keys, and shook his head. The navvy gurgled in his sleep. Silently I dived into my pocket, took out one sovereign, and held it up between finger and thumb Again the doctor shook his head. Money was not what was lacking to his peace. His bag had fallen from the' seat to the ground. He looked towards it, and opened his mouth — O-shape. The catch was not a difficult one, and when I had mastered it, the doctor's right forefinger was sawing the air. With an immense caution, I extracted from the bag such a knife as they use for cutting collops off legs. The doctor frowned, and with his first and second fingers imitated the action of scissors. Again I searched, and found a most diabolical pair of cocknosed shears, capable of vandyking the interiors of elephants. The doctor then slowly lowered his left shoulder till the navvy's right wrist was supported by the bench, pausing a moment as the spent volcano rumbled anew. Lower and lower the doctor sank, kneeling now by the navvy's side, till his head was on a level with, and just in front of, the great hairy fist, and — there was no tension on the coat-collar. Then light dawned on me.

Beginning a little to the right of the spinal column, I cut a huge demilune out of his new spring overcoat, bringing it round as far under his left side (which was the right side of the navvy) as I dared. Passing thence swiftly to the back of the seat, and reaching between the splines, I sawed through the silk-faced front on the left-hand side of the coat till the two cuts joined.

Cautiously as the box-turtle of his native heath, the doctor drew away sideways and to the right, with the air of a frustrated burglar coming out from under a bed, and stood up free, one black diagonal shoulder projecting through the gray of his ruined overcoat. I returned the scissors to the bag, snapped the catch, and held all out to him as the wheels of the fly rang hollow under the railway arch.

It came at a foot-pace past the wicket-gate of the station, and the doctor stopped it with a whisper. It was going some five miles across country to bring home from church some one — I could not catch the name — because his own carriage-horses were lame. Its destination happened to be the one place in all the world that the doctor was most burningly anxious to visit, and he promised the driver untold gold to drive to some ancient flame of his — Helen Blazes, she was called.

'Aren't you coming, too?' he said, bundling his overcoat into his bag.

Now the fly had been so obviously sent to the doctor, and to no one else, that I had no concern with it. Our roads, I saw, divided, and there was, further, a need upon me to laugh.

'I shall stay here,' I said. 'It's a very pretty country.'

'My God!' he murmured, as softly as he shut the door, and I felt that it was a prayer.

Then he went out of my life, and I shaped my course for the railway-bridge. It was necessary to pass by the bench once more, but the wicket was between us. The departure of the fly had waked the navvy. He crawled on to the seat, and with malignant eyes watched the driver flog down the road.

'The man inside o' that,' he called, ''as poisoned me. 'E's a body-snatcher. 'E's comin' back again when I'm cold. 'Ere's my evidence!'

He waved his share of the overcoat, and I went my way, because I was hungry. Framlynghame Admiral village is a good two miles from the station, and I waked the holy calm of the evening every step of that way with shouts and yells, casting myself down in the flank of the good green hedge when I was too weak to stand. There was an inn — a blessed inn with a thatched roof, and peonies in the garden — and I ordered myself an upper chamber in which the Foresters held their courts, for the laughter was not all out of me. A bewildered woman brought me ham and eggs, and I leaned out of the mullioned window, and laughed between mouthfuls. I sat long above the beer and the perfect smoke that followed, till the light changed in the quiet street, and I began to think of the seven forty-five down, and all that world of the Arabian Nights I had quitted.

Descending, I passed a giant in moleskins who filled the low-ceiled tap-room. Many empty plates stood before him, and beyond them a fringe of the Framlynghame Admiralty, to whom he was unfolding a wondrous tale of anarchy, of body-snatching, of bribery, and the Valley of the Shadow from the which he was but newly risen. And as he talked he ate, and as he ate he drank, for there was much room in him; and anon he paid royally, speaking of justice and the law, before whom all Englishmen are equal, and all foreigners and anarchists vermin and slime.

On my way to the station he passed me with great strides, his head high among the low-flying bats, his feet firm on the packed road metal, his fists clenched, and his breath coming sharply. There was a beautiful smell in the air — the smell of white dust, bruised nettles, and smoke, that brings tears to the throat of a man who sees his country but seldom — a smell like the echoes of the lost talk of lovers; the infinitely suggestive odour of an immemorial civilisation. It was a perfect walk; and, lingering on every step, I came to the station just as the one porter lighted the last of a truck-load of lamps, and set them back in the lamp-room, while he dealt tickets to four or five of the population, who, not contented with their own peace, thought fit to travel. It was no ticket that the navvy seemed to need. He was sitting on a bench wrathfully grinding a tumbler into fragments with his heel. I abode in obscurity at the end of the platform, interested as ever, thank heaven, in my surroundings. There was a jar of wheels on the road. The navvy rose as they approached, strode through the wicket, and laid a hand upon a horse's bridle that brought the beast up on his hireling hind-legs. It was the providential fly coming back, and for a moment

I wondered whether the doctor had been mad enough to revisit his practice.

'Get away; you're drunk,' said the driver.

'I'm not,' said the navvy. 'I've been waitin' 'ere hours and hours. Come out, you beggar inside there.'

'Go on, driver,' said a voice I did not know — a crisp, clear, English voice.

'All right,' said the navvy. 'You wouldn't 'ear me when I was polite. Now will you come?'

There was a chasm in the side of the fly, for he had wrenched the door bodily off its hinges, and was feeling within purposefully. A well-booted leg rewarded him, and there came out, not with delight, hopping on one foot, a round and grayhaired Englishman, from whose armpits dropped hymn-books, but from his mouth an altogether different service of song.

'Come on, you bloomin' body-snatcher! You thought I was dead, did you?' roared the navvy. And the respectable gentleman came accordingly, inarticulate with rage.

''Ere's a man murderin' the Squire,' the driver shouted, and fell from his box upon the navvy's neck.

To do them justice, the people of Framlynghame Admiral, so many as were on the platform, rallied to the call in the best spirit of feudalism. It was the one porter who beat the navvy on the nose with a ticket-punch, but it was the three third-class tickets who attached themselves to his legs and freed the captive.

'Send for a constable! lock him up!' said that man, adjusting his collar; and unitedly they cast him into the lamp-room, and turned the key, while the driver mourned over the wrecked fly.

Till then the navvy, whose only desire was justice, had kept his temper nobly. Then he went Berserk before our amazed eyes. The door of the lamp-room was generously constructed, and would not give an inch, but the window he tore from its fastenings and hurled outwards. The one porter counted the damage in a loud voice, and the others, arming themselves with agricultural implements from the station garden, kept up a ceaseless winnowing before the window, themselves backed close to the wall, and bade the prisoner think of the gaol. He answered little to the point, so far as they could understand; but seeing that his exit was impeded, he took a lamp and hurled it through the wrecked sash. It fell on the metals and went out. With inconceivable velocity, the others, fifteen in all, followed looking like rockets in the gloom, and with the last (he could have had no plan) the Berserk rage left him as the doctor's deadly brewage waked up, under the stimulus of violent exercise and a very full meal, to one last cataclysmal exhibition, and – we heard the whistle of the seven forty-five down.

They were all acutely interested in as much of the wreck as they could see, for the station smelt to heaven of oil, and the engine skittered over broken glass like a terrier in a cucumber-frame. The guard had to hear of it, and the Squire had his version of the brutal assault, and heads were out all along the carriages as I found me a seat.

'What is the row?' said a young man, as I entered. 'Man drunk?'

'Well, the symptoms, so far as my observation has gone, more resemble those of Asiatic cholera than anything else,' I answered, slowly and judicially, that every word might carry weight in the appointed scheme of things. Till then, you will observe, I had taken no part in that war.

He was an Englishman, but he collected his belongings as swiftly as had the American, ages before, and leaped upon the platform, crying, 'Can I be of any service? I'm a doctor.'

From the lamp-room I heard a wearied voice wailing: 'Another bloomin' doctor!'

And the seven forty-five carried me on, a step nearer to Eternity, by the road that is worn and seamed and channelled with the passions, and weaknesses, and warring interests of man who is immortal and master of his fate.

1/15/19
jaipur airport to GOA
bought this book w/ Ruben